DANDY DICK

OR

THE KING'S HIGHWAY

A Romance of Heath and Highway, Court
and Cottage, Prince and Peasant.
(1900–1901)

The Spring-Heeled Jack Library: Volume 5

Ned Neolan

and

Ben Brightly

EDITED WITH A NEW INTRODUCTION BY

J.S. Mackley

The Spring-Heeled Jack Library

Spring Heel'd Jack: The Terror of London (1863)*

Spring Heeled Jack: The Terror of London (2 vols.) (1886)

Spring-Heeled Jack: Articles and Short fiction (1838–1897)
The Resident of Peckham letter (1838)
The Spring Jack (1838)
Springheel Jack: The Terror of London (The Origin Story) (1878)
From *Chums* by Harleigh Severne (1878)
Spring-Heeled Jack, from *All the Year Round* (9 August 1884)
Spring Heel Jack, *or* the Masked Mystery of the Tower (1885)
Spring-Heeled Jack (The Dialect Story) (1888)
The Mystery of Spring Heel Jack, *or* The Haunted Grange (1897)

Spring-Heeled Jack: The Human Bat
The Human Bat (1899–1901)
The Black Phantom (1901)

Dandy Dick, *or* The King's Highway**
Dandy Dick (1900)
Dandy Dick's Double (1900-1901)

Spring-Heeled Jack: Man or Fiend (1904)*

The Winged Man; *or* 'Twixt Midnight and Dawn (1913)***

* Complete for the first time
** A story featuring Spring-Heeled Jack as an ancillary character
*** A story influenced by The Human Bat series

First published in Great Britain in 2021

New Edition 2024 Published by Isengrin Publishing
ISBN: 978-1-917130-05-9

www.jonmackley.com

For Tony Klinger

Contents

INTRODUCTION

This is the fifth volume in the Spring-Heeled Jack library, a project that aims to make accessible all the texts featuring this strange figure who first appeared in London in the 1830s. This volume collects the issues of a serial entitled *Dandy Dick, or The King's Highway*, which first appeared in *The Halfpenny Marvel* in April 1900. Unlike the other serials, Spring-Heeled Jack is not the focus of the narrative; instead, he is an ancillary figure and the main characters are dashing and gallant highwaymen, led by Dandy Dick and supported by a cast of colourful characters including Colonel Blood and Dick Turpin. The story is set in the wilderness of Finchlet Common and the labyrinthine streets of London in the early eighteenth century as the outlaws are hunted down by the notorious theif-taker, Jonathan Wild.

Spring-Heeled Jack Serial Stories and the Fin de siècle
The first of the Spring-Heeled Jack reports were circulated in January 1838. The initial reports were exaggerated and sensationalised; Spring-Heeled Jack's appearances are described in terms of an "Urban Ghost", whose antics were calculated to terrify the populace, so that women and children were scared to leave their homes after dark and men carried weapons. Initially the sightings were reported as an aristocratic prank to scare his victims, but in early 1838 Jack committed violent assaults on women which were investigated by the police at the time. Despite numerous apparent sightings and a series of attacks in quick succession, the perpetrator was never unmasked. These attacks stopped but there were those who copied Jack's antics and at other times the name was applied to someone who managed to evade the law. Yet, while Londoners claimed to be terrorised by Spring-Heeled Jack, there was also a fascination with him, and he became the subject of numerous stage performances as well as serial stories which simultaneously horrified and thrilled its audience. The Penny Dreadful stories were read by a newly-literate population of working class men. Because of these, Jack remained

in the public consciousness and stories of his infamy circulated long after the initial terror spread by the historical Jack's assaults. However, decades after the first attacks, there were further reports of incidents traditionally attributed to Jack: a ghostly presence that alarmed sentries at Aldershot and Colchester Barracks in 1877 and 1878; he is described as leaping Newport Arch in Lincoln, also in 1877. His final sightings were in Liverpool in 1904. Each of these instances is covered in detail in the introductions to the other volumes. On all these occasions, his actions may have been exaggerated, sensationalised, misinterpreted, or perhaps simply fabricated, but, in each case something noteworthy did happen, and the stories not only captured the imaginations of the population; they also reminded everyone of those times when Jack terrorised London.

The last two decades of the nineteenth century saw an unprecedented change in English society, both on a social and an industrial scale. Science was replacing faith, and at the end of the nineteenth century, Britain was engaged in the Second Boer War (1899–1902). In addition, the mantle of the "Terror of London" had been taken by another Jack—the Ripper—from the end of the 1880s. Thus, the new stories recast Spring-Heeled Jack as an enemy of England and her Empire or as a terrifying friend and protector of outlaws. Two serials appeared at the end of the nineteenth and the beginning of the twentieth century. Published in *The Funny Wonder* between May 1898 and December 1901, the focus of *The Human Bat* is on the courage and loyalty of the characters as representatives of the Empire who are praised for their "Englishness", while facing an adversary who rejects British laws and institutions: the identity of the Human Bat's *alter ego* is revealed as a character who had infiltrated the highest echelons of respectable British society. This is not a degeneration to man's primitive state as seen in *Dr Jekyll and Mr Hyde*; instead the characters face an intelligent and dangerous adversary who represents the corruption at the heart of 'respectable' English society which must ultimately be exposed and, where possible, defeated. This serial is published as volume 4 of the Spring-Heeled Jack Library.

Although beginning some two years after *The Human Bat*, *Dandy Dick* was, for a time, published concurrently, although, as noted above the themes of *Dandy Dick* are very different to the other Spring-Heeled Jack stories as the story is set against the backdrop of England in the early eighteenth century (around 1725–28), with the action taking place against a romanticised and glamourised backdrop of highwaymen and outlaws. and Jack himself is a minor character.

The truth of the Highwayman's life was, of course, very different: the Highwayman Act of 1692 offered a £40 reward—a substantial sum—for the capture of a highwayman, and death by hanging was punishment for much lesser crimes. The almost idyllic representation of the life of the highwayman is informed by novels such as Edward Bulwer-Lytton's novel, *Paul Clifford* (1830) and, more notably, William Harrison Ainsworth's novels, particularly *Rookwood* (1834) and *Jack Sheppard* (1839). Consequently, the outlaws are seen as chivalric, well-dressed, gallant knights of the road, rather than as desperate men living in squalid conditions, hunted, persecuted and ruthlessly resorting to extreme violence in order to survive.

Dandy Dick stands apart from the other stories included in the Spring-Heeled Jack library in that Jack's inclusion is almost *incidental* to the narrative, and it is this difference that makes it of interest and worth including in this series. In other stories published in the Spring-Heeled Jack Library, Jack is the focus of the story, either the viewpoint character as seen in the 1863 version, or the mysterious crusader who strives to restore the honourable name (as seen in the 1886 and 1904 versions) or an adversary who must be overcome (as seen in *The Masked Mystery of the Tower* (1885) and *The Human Bat*. In *Dandy Dick*, Spring-Heeled Jack is a mysterious ancillary figure.

Dandy Dick, or The King's Highway

Published over 42 weekly issues between April 1900 and February 1901, Dandy Dick was written by two staff writers at *The Halfpenny Marvel*, Ned Neolan and Ben Brightly, and it is collected here for its first publication in a single volume. The narrative is divided into two parts: *Dandy Dick, or, The King's Highway* and *Dandy Dick's Double, or, The Outlaws of Old London* which runs from issues 34 to its conclusion in issue 42. Aside from the title banners, there is only one illustration of the spectral rider, which is published on the opening page of the serial, even though the incident does not appear until the second issue.

The narrative focuses on Dandy Dick, a noble who has fled his affluent life after being accused of forgery, a crime which carries the death penalty. Dick protests he had nothing to do with this, claiming he is "charged with a crime of which I am perfectly innocent" (7). Even so, he holds a position of respect amongst the outlaws who reside at their stronghold (and he is occasionally referred to as the outlaws' leader), the Haunted Manor at Finchley. Historically, Finchley Common, situated on the Great North Road from London, was a prime location for all manner of outlaws. An ancient oak tree which stood on the common (opposite the St Pancras and Islington cemeteries) until 1952 was known as the Turpin Oak; according to legend, this was a place where Dick Turpin sheltered (despite there being no evidence to connect him with Finchley until later as the mythology surrounding him developed). Historically, it is also on Finchley Common where Jack Sheppard was arrested. Both characters feature in this story (Harper 245–6).

At this time, Jonathan Wild is known as the notorious "Thief-taker General". Wild attempts to infiltrate the outlaws' stronghold and to claim the reward, while Dick and his faithful companions attempt to attack Wild's house in Newgate.

Although living the life of an outlaw and being leader of the company at the Haunted Manor at Finchley, Dick's criminal behaviour is kept to a minimum. He is only seen to hold up one carriage. This happens to be occupied by Dick's relatives: his uncle, Sir Edgar Mortimer; Dick's fiancée, Maude Mortimer; and her cousin, Raymond Raithwood. This encounter establishes Dick's characteristics and reveals why he has been forced to assume the life of an outlaw. It also reveals the temperament of the other characters who are integral to the plot. When Dick realises whose carriage they have stopped, he refuses to take their valuables. Maude is described in terms of a romance heroine—like "a young fawn", or a "clinging maiden" with "milky white skin" and a voice "lingering and sighing"—and absolutely devoted to Dick. Raymond Raithwood's villany is shown as he attempts to murder both Dick and Maude in cold blood. Finally, Dick's companion, Colonel Blood, demonstrates his loyalty to Dick and his quick thinking, by foiling Raithwood's murderous plans.

Dick Turpin's Oak on Finchley Common (*c.* 1880s)

The narrative of Dandy Dick demonstrates a continuity of the story as it plays out over ten months. Although many of the instalments begin with a short summary of what has gone before, the narrative is written in such a way that it has occasional reminders as to who the characters are for the benefit of the reader who follows the story over the ten months of its serialisation. The authors are also aware that they are writing about an era that will be unfamiliar to their readers and sometimes include a brief definition of unfamiliar words and occasionally a footnote. These footnotes have been marked with a symbol—in this volume I have used the ° symbol to identify the start of each new issue while editorial footnotes have a numerical signifier.

Highwaymen and the Nineteenth Century Novel

From the third issue onwards, there is a short recap of the plot so far and a list of "characters already introduced" before the story starts. Many of the fictional characters integral to the plot are introduced when Dick holds up Sir Edgar Mortiemor's carriage. Of the others, some are based on historical characters, for example, Colonel Blood, who is introduced in the same chapter as Dick himself. These historical characters would have been known by reputation, and thus it was a method of introducing the supporting cast in as economic way as possible as many of the audience would have been familiar with the historical names. These characters include Dick Turpin, Joseph "Blueskin" Blake and Jack Sheppard. The cast of historical characters is completed with their nemesis, the notorious thief-taker, Jonathan Wild.

While some of these characters are less likely to be known by a modern audience, they were all historical characters. Their reputations were the subjects of historical fiction, romanticising the outlaws' lives, and well known to the contemporary audience: Joseph Blake, for example, is mentioned in the 1904 serial of Spring-Heeled Jack. As noted above, this romanticised attitude towards highwaymen is, in particular, one that was perpetuated by William Harrington Ainsworth in his novel *Rookwood* which features Dick Turpin, and in *Jack Sheppard* which chronicles the life and death of the boy prison breaker, and his accomplice Joseph Blake. Both men are hunted by Jonathan Wild, the eponymous anti-hero of Henry Fielding's satirical novel (1734), although as with Ainsworth's romances, as Claude Rawson explains, there is some distance between the historical Jonathan Wild and the character who appears in the novel, as Fielding had not intended to write a history (Fielding xvi).

In *Rookwood*, the narrator glamorises the life of Dick Turpin describing him as

> the *ultimus Romanorum*, the last of a race, which—we were almost about to say we regret—is now altogether extinct. Several successors he had, it is true, but no name worthy to be recorded after his own. With him expired the chivalrous spirit which animated successively the bosoms of so many knights of the road; with him died away that passionate love of enterprise, that high spirit of devotion to the fair sex, which was first breathed upon the highway by the gay, gallant Claude Du-Val, the Bayard of the road—Le filou sans peur et sans reproche—but which was extinguished at last by the cord that tied the heroic Turpin to the remorseless tree. (Vol II, 163–4)

Elsewhere, Dick Turpin Jack Sheppard and Joseph Blake appear in their own serial stories: Turpin appeared in *Black Bess, or, The Knight of the Road*, written by Edward Viles and published over 254 issues beginning in 1863, and a second series *The Black Highwayman* which ran for 86 issues, beginning in 1866. Montague Summers also attributes authorship of *Blueskin: A Romance* to Viles which was also published in 1866 and ran for 158 issues Summers notes that Jack Sheppard is the hero of this story (247). Consequently, it is noteworthy that the final scene has Sheppard and Blake witnessing Jonathan Wild's execution, when, historically, both highwaymen were executed before the thief-taker. Dick Turpin's popularity was further attested with the publication of *The Dick Turpin Library* by Stephen H Agnew which ran to 181 issues, published by the Aldine Company in 1902–1903. The Aldine Company also published the 1904 serial of *Spring-Heeled Jack* (Volume 6 in the Spring-Heeled Jack Library) and in the same year published a serial called *Jack Sheppard*, although this only ran to 26 issues (Medcraft 3-4). The exploits of Jack Sheppard and Joe Blueskin were indeed popular at the time featuring in another "Penny Dreadful" serial, *Jack Sheppard; or London in the Last Century* (1847). The character of Captain Macheath in *The Beggar's* Opera is based on Sheppard, who the character of Peachum is based on Jonathan Wild.

The Characters

While the readers of *Dandy Dick* may have identified with these characters, a difficulty arises from their inclusion of these historical characters: the plot becomes anachronistic. Colonel Blood had died in 1680, three years before Jonathan Wild was born in 1683, for example. It cannot be ascertained for certain whether the authors did not know this, or whether they (along with their readers) lacked the resources to check the dates. What is more likely, however, is that the authors knew of the reputations of these characters and then included them as a means of attracting an audience.

At the time that *Dandy Dick* was published, **Colonel Thomas Blood** (1616–1680) would likely have been the most well-known of Dandy Dick's companions, although his exploits are perhaps less well-known to the modern reader. Blood is most famous for his attempt at stealing the Crown Jewels around 1670. The historical Blood, according to Whittlebury Kaye, had been concerned that King Charles I planned to sell the precious stones to pay for the 'lavish expenditure' of the Court (220).

Furthermore, as a Protestant, Blood was determined that the crown should not 'rest upon the head of a Roman Catholic King' (220). Blood's religious beliefs and audacious activities have no bearing on the story—his attempt at stealing the Crown Jewels is mentioned only when he is first introduced and then at the very end as the characters take their leave—so his character has been included to demonstrate his daring demeanour. *Dandy Dick* describes Blood as being around 30 years old when the story takes place, although that date is at odds with the characters from the rest of the narrative. Blood died before any of the other characters were born, and while the other characters are near contemporaries, only a few of them had dealings with each other. Thus Blood's inclusion, in particular, is on account of his reputation.

Jonathan Wild (*c.* 1683–1725) also known as the Thief-Taker General, a government agent who also operated on both sides of the law, organising criminal gangs for profit and informing on the when they ceased to be useful to him. His gangs stole property which Wild took from them and then sold back to the original owners for a "finder's fee". His position meant that if any of his thieves were taken, he could arrange bribes or fabricate evidence to ensure their release or to ensure that another party was convicted and sentenced for the crime. However, this arrangement only lasted as long as the criminals complied with Wild's demands, otherwise Wild would inform on his associates, ensuring that they themselves were arrested and hanged.

Ticket for Jonathan Wild's Hanging

Wild's actions meant he had very little competition. However, the great number of thieves that he saw tried and executed meant that he was considered to be performing an excellent service in suppressing criminal activities. Section 2 of the Warrant of Detainer presented for Wild's trial neatly summarises this aspect of his misdemeanours as thief-gatherer and thief-taker:

> "That he had formed a kind of corporation of thieves, of which he was the head or director, and that notwithstanding his pretended services, in detecting and prosecuting offenders, he procured such only to be hanged as concealed their booty, or refused to share it with him. (cited in Skirboll 213)

Ordinary Purney of Newgate gives an account of injuries sustained by Jonathan Wild in his lifetime, describing, amongst others, "two fractures in his Skull … tho' cover'd with silver Plates" (cited in Skirboll, 218). This detail is included in the narrative, and it is Will Wiffles who claims to have given Wild these fractures and wanting to give another "forget-me-not silver plate being fixed at the top of his evil-plotting sconce" (54). When Wild was hanged in 1725 tickets were told for the best seats to view the execution. Reportedly Wild tried to cling on to one of the other prisoners hanged with him to avoid being strangled himself. Wild's skeleton remains on display in the Hunterian Museum in the Royal College of Surgeons of England.

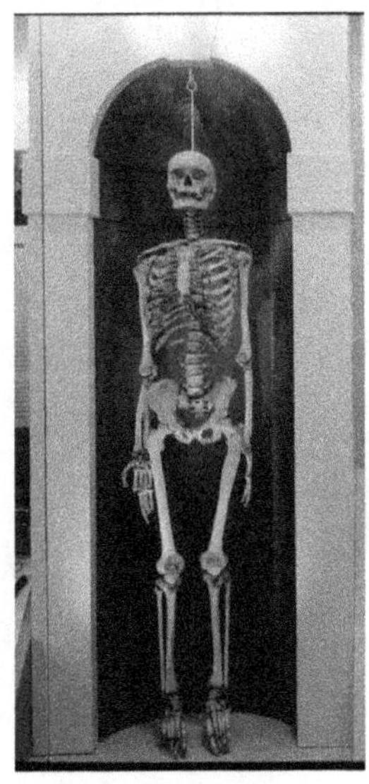

JONATHAN WILD'S SKELETON.

Two other characters who accompany Dandy Dick are the notorious **Dick Turpin** (1705–1739) and his lesser-known accomplice, **Tom King** (*c.* 1712–1737). The character of Dick Turpin is arguably the most well-known of the companions and needs little introduction. He is presented as a Robin Hood-like character, stealing from the rich and championing the poor; a highwayman who kissed young women before making his daring escapes. His famous horse was called Black Bess and one of his most famous escapades was his 200-mile ride to York in fifteen hours, which is referenced in the narrative "he of the ever-famous Ride to York" (89). The ride was to give himself an alibi after he shot and killed Thomas Morris, the servant of one of the keepers of Epping Forest, who had recognised him and tried to arrest him. Such stories are the material of legend, rather than history, as Turpin's reputation was embroidered by William Harrington Ainsworth in his 1835 novel, *Rookwood*, published almost a century after Turpin's death, and further embellished by the popularity of the Penny Dreadful series about him. For example, Turpin did indeed leave the south and move to Yorkshire, but the fabled ride to York is a physical impossibility and this part of his reputation is drawn from the exploits of John "Swift Nick" Nevison.[1]

The name **Tom King** is a mistake, the historical character's name was *Matthew* King (Barlow 262). However, this error is made in some of the earliest accounts of a failed robbery targeting Richard Bayes in which King was accidentally shot by Turpin, and the authors are simply repeating the facts as they saw them. The shooting of Tom King is mentioned in *Dandy Dick* when it is explained that King was "fated to end his career by a bullet aimed inadvertently by his dearest friend" (89).

Two other characters in the Dandy Dick narrative feature in another of Ainsworth's novels, *Jack Sheppard*: these are **Joseph Blake and Jack Sheppard** who, historically, were associated with Jonathan Wild. Joe Blueskin (1700-1724) is never named as Blake in the story: he is always given the name of "Jolly Nose", "Joe Blueskin" or a variation of these

---

[1] Viewers of the London Weekend Television series *Dick Turpin* starring Richard O'Sullivan (1979–1982) will have seen that his companion was called Nick Swift and was given the nickname of "Swiftnick" played by Michael Deeks.

when addressed by Jack Sheppard. Blake was one of Jonathan Wild's professional thieves, who was arrested with some of his associates in 1722. Blake turned King's evidence against his associates who were executed on the strength of his testimony, and while Blake was spared, he remained confined to prison facing a sentence of deportation. He was eventually released in 1724 when he worked with Jack Sheppard for a short time. In October, Blake was arrested by Wild: Blake had hoped Wild would present a favourable testimony, but when Wild failed to do this, Blake slashed his throat with a concealed pocket knife, which nearly succeeded in killing Wild. This attack inspired "Newgate's Garland", a ballad by John Gay written shortly after the event. However, in this account, Wild is killed by Blueskin's knife: the deed is described as "Jonathan's throat was cut ear to ear" which "made a sad widow of Jonathan's wife" (ll. 6, 16). Arguably, Wild's period of convalescence is one of the reasons Wild began to lose control of his criminal gangs.

The more famous of the pair was Jack Sheppard (1702–24); throughout *Dandy Dick*, Jack is described as the 'boy prison-breaker' even though he is 22. In the story, he is always seen in the company of Blueskin, and despite Jack's character comes across as significantly younger than Blueskin, their relationship could be considered as child and adult or Apprentice and Master, but there are only two years between them. Like Turpin, Jack is depicted as a charismatic folk hero—part of his story is of a boy who cannot suppress his kleptomania urges, but he is also a boy who wants to visit his mother.[2] He was also the inspiration for the Artful Dodger in Charles Dickens's *Oliver Twist*.

Historically, Jack was the son of a carpenter. His father died when Jack was still young, forcing him to the workhouse where he encountered thieves and other criminals. He partnered with his brother Tom for a while, although shortly after his arrest, Tom, fearing execution, informed on Jack. Jonathan Wild became aware of Jack's skill as a thief and wanted Jack to turn over the "spoils" of his thieving for Wild to a fence. When Sheppard refused, Wild attempted to arrest Sheppard in order to

---

[2] Jack's charisma is particularly noteworthy in the 1969 film *Where's Jack?* with Tommy Steele cast in the title role.

maintain control of the criminal gangs in London. Jack then partnered with Blueskin and, even though Jack was arrested, he escaped from prisons including Newgate and St Giles's Roundhouse (which feature in this story). His audacious escapes were sensationalised in the papers. He was finally arrested and hanged on 16 November 1724 aged 22. The "autobiography" of Jack Sheppard, which was circulated at his execution, was likely written by Daniel Defoe.

Image of Jack Sheppard in Newgate Prison
attributed to James Thornhill (1723)

The inclusion of Jack Sheppard and Blueskin in *Dandy Dick* is unusual. Sheppard was clearly meant to be an integral part of the story, but they do not really contribute to advancing the plot. His mother is mentioned on the first page of the narrative, and Jack is mentioned amid a group of others (90) but he does not appear himself until issue 18 (159). Jack and Blueskin are described as being at the outlaws' stronghold in Finchley, but they have no interaction with Dandy Dick or, more crucially, on storming Jonathan Wild's stronghold. However, towards the end of the story, Jonathan Wild's focus appears to be on capturing Jack above all the other outlaws, both heading into the Rookery of St Giles and the area inhabited by criminals and the destitute. Given the popularity of Sheppard and Blake in highwayman romances, it may be suggested that these characters were included as some comic relief from the darker plot strands, but also included to leave Dandy Dick and his companions at a cliff hanger mid chapter and not return to their dangerous predicament until the next issue.

King George. King George is mentioned throughout the story and he appears on a couple of occasions. He is named "George of Hanover" (suggesting George I), or "the tyrant" and "Good King George" and is described as "portly" and "grave-faced" (184) and from the depictions in royal portraits, this would suggest George III. Only at the end of the novel is it expressly said that the monarch is "George the Second" (reigned 1727–1760). George did not become king until 1727, two years after Wild's death. However, some of the characters see an image from the Beggars' Opera in the Rookery of St Giles which was first performed on 29 January 1728 - a date that would be in keeping with the reign of George II, but after some of the historical characters had died.

In the text, a Jacobite conspirator attempts to assassinate King George while he is out riding. Such an event never took place, although the incident may have been inspired by a real-life assassination attempt in December 1716 while George was still Prince of Wales, when George was watching a theatrical performance at the Drury Lane theatre. Joe Blueskin often refers to "spade guineas", the spade referring to the obverse image of the shield containing the royal Coat of Arms, but these were struck during the reign of George III between 1787 and 1799. However, just as with the anachronisms of the characters, the authors were interested in spinning a compelling yarn, and would not have expected their readers to have either the resources or the inclination to check every minute detail of their story.

A number of other (fictional) characters play major parts in the story. **Will Wiffles** is the only major player among Dandy Dick's close companions who is not based on an historical personage; he provides comic relief with his constant witticisms, but who also proves himself to be loyal and courageous when necessary. At the other end of the scale is the Bow Street Runner, **Officer Eustis Bilberry**, who is the comical antithesis of Jonathan Wild: where Wild is merciless and cruel, Bilberry is a cowardly, incompetent bully, but whose authority is constantly mocked. Other characters include **Ralph Drake** and his wife, **Meg**, proprietors of the Hole-in-the-Wall Inn near Hatton Garden, who are threatened by Bilberry whose accusations that they are sheltering the outlaws may well have some foundation, but in fact, Bilberry uses it as a means to avoid paying his bar tab!

One of the fictional characters who is worth considering in more detail is **Will the Witless** who is introduced on the first page along with Jonathan Wild. Will is described as "feeble minded", and "idiot boy" and a "friendless lad". He carries a long pole which he uses to cover great distances at speed and to evade capture, particularly when fleeing from the Bow Street runners. It is also a valuable weapon when required.

Will the Witless is introduced in the first chapter, and a watchman describes him as "Spring-Heeled Jack, the powerful London terror, himself" (4). The third instalment of the story begins with a list of "Characters already introduced" and in this list (up to and including issue 7, Will the Witless is described as being "known as Spring-Heeled Jack"

CHARACTERS ALREADY INTRODUCED.
COLONEL BLOOD, the man who stole the Crown jewels.
JONATHAN WILD, the notorious thief-taker.
DADDY DELPH and NAT FLINT, the gibbet-robbers.
WILL THE WITLESS, known as Spring-Heel Jack.
RAYMOND RAITHWOOD, the man who ruined Dandy Dick.
DICK THE DANDY, outlaw and the King's friend in one.

Dramatis Personae Issues 339–343 (parts 3–7)

Strangely, however, in the eighth instalment, the information about Will changes and he becomes known as "a friendless lad".

CHARACTERS ALREADY INTRODUCED.
COLONEL BLOOD, the man who stole the Crown jewels.
JONATHAN WILD, the notorious thief-taker.
DADDY DELPH and NAT FLINT, the gibbet-robbers.
WILL THE WITLESS, a friendless lad.
RAYMOND RAITHWOOD, the man who ruined Dandy Dick.
DICK THE DANDY, outlaw and the King's friend in one.
WIFFLES, the witty outlaw.
BILBERRY, the Bow Street runner.

Dramatis Personae Issues 344 onwards

It is unclear whether this was initially an early revelation of Spring-Heeled Jack's identity and was corrected in later issues to avoid further spoiling the surprise, or whether the authors changed their mind as to who would take the role of Spring-Heeled Jack. However, there is no overt revelation as to which character has Spring-Heeled Jack as his alter ego. It does not say that Will the Witless *is* Spring-Heeled Jack; nor does it say that he *isn't*.

Will is far from "friendless" in the story: Jonathan Wild refers to the "witless brat" and his ramblings, but the outlaws and their helpers treat him with kindness—Will makes a friend of "Handsome Richard" the name he calls Dandy Dick, and there are touching scenes between Will and Meg Drake, the landlady of the Hole-in-the-Wall inn. However, Will rejects any kindness that would change his circumstances from being barefoot and ragged. Will performs some important acts through the narrative. Whilst communing with the "good fairies" in the snowflakes, he often receives information about Jonathan Wild's subordinates, referring to them as "bad fairies" and warning the outlaws of their presence. His ability to know future events is almost uncanny. Dick observes "There is generally some truth in the seeming ramblings of the witless boy," he added. "I have frequently proved it" (40). In turn, Will confounds the Bow Street Runners by pouring bags of soot over them—his attacks are not malicious or physical, but simply a means of inconveniencing the authorities while the outlaws escape.

The naming of Will as Spring-Heeled Jack creates a question for the story: it is true that Will the Witless and Spring-Heeled Jack do not appear in the same scenes, but the violence of Jack's appearance is completely at odds with Will the Witless's gentle demeanour. Was Will's name in the list of characters a mistake, revealing a plot twist too early? Or, having used the name for Will, did the authors think it would be a good idea to have Spring-Heeled Jack appear in his demonic form later? I shall discuss the possible identity of Spring-Heeled Jack later.

Will the Witless leaves the story about three quarters of the way through the narrative (part 29 out of 42). He tells Jack Sheppard how to find his mother and warns him of the impending arrival of Bow Street Runners (292). There are areas of his character that could have been explored in more detail, and his role in the overall narrative more explicitly described. It does feel as though Will's role (along with several others) has been forgotten as the plot becomes too big to handle and only the major storylines are followed.

The Outlaws' life

Dandy Dick is a romanticised account of the outlaws' life, a folk hero who, despite the turn in his fortunes, he remains handsome, brave and noble— a quintessential Englishman despite being hunted for a crime of which he claims he is innocent. His outlaw companions describe him as an "idol of all that was brave, handsome, and manly" (223). This is a common representation of characters when portrayed on film and television, such as Dick Turpin and Robin Hood, where the outlaw is a dashing character with a perfectly laundered (and often impractical) costume, and their thievery is not out of desperation but often for a more noble cause, including their opposition to the tyranny of the ruling classes. Turpin himself is described as being "marked with the small pox", as he is described, for example, in the *Derby Mercury* (30 June 1737). The change in his reputation as a dashing Knight of the Road is owed to William Harrington Ainsworth's 1834 novel, *Rookwood*. Here, much of the historical evidence surrounding the highwayman is rejected in favour of this new, gallant hero. In the first volume, "Jack Palmer" notes that it is "necessary for a man to be a gentleman before he can be a highwayman" (221) listing the distinguishing characteristics as "perfect knowledge of the world—perfect independence of character—notoriety—command of cash—and inordinate success with the women" (221). He further asserts that "the gentlemen I speak of never maltreated any one, except in self defence" (228). This is very much the case in *Dandy Dick* who laments the death of one of their adversaries "We have taken human life, comrades …The evil was done in the preservation of our own, which alone can justify it. Yet, for all that, my conscience reproves me for the shedding of a fellow-creature's blood!" However, Colonel Blood justifies the action: "we provoked no attack, and, had we remained passive, I shudder to think of what would have happened to us all!" (360)

Despite Dick and his comrades living as outlaws and thieves, the authors go to a great effort to ensure that these characters are not seen as anything other than a force for good. Adhering to the proverb that "cleanliness is next to godliness", Dandy Dick lives up to his name by being "morbidly sensitive upon the state of his appearance" and always wearing fine clothing—a physical impossibility when living the life of an outlaw. Indeed, after rescuing Maude from a burning building almost at the cost of his own life, Dick is described as feeling "secretly chafed at the knowledge that he never before appeared to such disadvantage in the eyes of the girl he so ardently and hopelessly loved" (178). As noted earlier, Dick is only seen to commit one robbery, the coach containing his relatives, which acts a device to explain the plot. On other occasions, Dick and his comrades respond to calls for help, even though their actions may endanger them: "A female cry for help, Wiffles! Outlawed, despised, hunted as we are, we can never turn a deaf ear to such a plea of distress, come what may as the result!" (74). Yet, despite being outlaws, there are limits to what they will steal: "robbers, law-breakers, outcasts as we are, we must not still further defile ourselves by taking so much as a penny's-worth of the property of that hell-spawn, Jonathan Wild. The plunder would be thrice accursed—carry with it the blackest of evil luck!" (253).

Although they are all thieves, the outlaws are all depicted as brave and sensitive. The world they inhabit is sanitised for their contemporary reader, so they can be portrayed as the heroes of the story, and indeed they are. While the outlaws oppose authority, it is the corrupt authority of Jonathan Wild and the false accusations against Dandy Dick that they oppose. Dick himself is loyal to the king and to the noble aristocrats and it is this that sets him apart from those whose authority he resists. Dick may be an "honest thief", but he is held in higher esteem than the dishonest law-giver.

When is it set?

The characters and the textual evidence contradict each other. Jonathan Wild was born around 1682 or 1683, two or three years after the death of Colonel Blood, and all the other historical characters were born after Wild. Joseph Blake and Jack Sheppard were executed in November 1724 and Jonathan Wild in May 1725. Tom King would have been 13 at the time of Wild's death. King George is named at the end of the narrative as "George the Second" who ruled from 1727–60, although Horace Walpole was indeed Prime Minister during the reign of George II. However, Walpole would have found it difficult to "order any kind of punishment" on Colonel Blood, considering the Colonel had been dead for almost fifty years by the time Walpole took office. Wild sees an image of the Beggar's Opera in the Rookery of St Giles: this was first performed in January 1728. Officer Bilberry was a Bow Street Runner, however this force was founded by novelist and magistrate Henry Fielding in 1749 by which time all the historical characters featuring in the serial save King George had died.

Consequently, it is impossible to fix an *accurate* date on the events of the story. A generic time of "around the end of the first quarter of the eighteenth century" will have to suffice, However, we can also infer that the authors were not interested in historical accuracy. They wanted to create the romance of the life of the gallant knights of the road which had been employed successfully in Ainsworth's novels and in the Penny Dreadful serials featuring Dick Turpin and Jack Sheppard. They wanted to recreate the reign of terror of Jonathan Wild's London, where the inhabitants were executed for quite petty crimes, and this form of hanging was not the merciful drop and the breaking of the neck, but a slow strangulation where the condemned could take agonising minutes to die.

Each of the historical characters has a reputation of which the readers may already have been aware, and their inclusion gives authority to the text. Furthermore, it is a shorthand means of establishing the characters: the handsome and gallant highwayman, the daring attempt to steal the Crown Jewels, the cunning boy prison-breaker and the notorious thief-taker; against this backdrop is the noble aristocrat who has fallen from grace and been forced into the life of the outlaw until he can prove his innocence and take back his place in the nobility. However, he can only achieve this with the aid of his unusual friends and perhaps even a powerful supernatural entity that some say is in league with the devil himself, Spring-Heeled Jack.

Who is Spring-heeled Jack?

Unlike the other stories in the Spring-Heeled Jack Library, in *Dandy Dick* Jack is *such* a minor character that he barely features in the story and it is this difference that makes this serial interesting for inclusion. However, as noted above, Spring-Heeled Jack—or at least his reputation—is significant to the story as his name appears in the first chapter. The Irish watchman, seeing Will the Witless using his wooden pole to cover great distances at speed, declares: "if that isn't Spring-Heeled Jack, the powerful London terror, himself!" (4). As noted above, the list of characters suggests that Will the Witless is knows as Spring-Heeled Jack, although this changes as the story progresses. Whatever the reason for including him, Spring-Heeled Jack's appearance in *Dandy Dick* places him in a context a century before the historical "Terror of London" existed.

However, the watchman simply equates Will the Witless with Spring-Heeled Jack. The "terror of London" himself puts in a physical appearance later in the story. When the outlaws respond to a cry for help, they find themselves surrounded by Mohawks—gangs of aristocratic youths who engaged in unruly, and sometimes violent behaviour, assaulting citizens and vandalising property (see, for example, Guthrie 33–56). They hear a sound that is "scarcely human … but something between the cry of a man and the snarl of a wild beast". Jack is described as a "weirdly, horrible object possessed horns upon its head, great eyeballs of brilliant red, in a mask of the most repulsive shape; the thing had either long, black, limp wings, or a flying cloak … The clenched fist of the mysterious Spring-Heeled Jack was armed with steel spikes". The Mohawks recognise Jack as "the great terror of London" (76). His appearance causes the Mohawks to flee, and then he vanishes "as quickly as he had come".

Spring-Heeled Jack appears again when the outlaws attempt to escape from a burning mansion and are once again surrounded and outnumbered by Mohawks. On this occasion he is described as an "apparition" with

> A hideous head, with horns and long red, matted locks. The head, face, and whole of the body and limbs resembled brightly-reflecting, burnished metal of a bronze-red tint. So luminous was this, in the reflected glow of the burning mansion, that the effect resembled that of a human form carved out of a solid mass of live cold, or molten metal … A black cloak, with a deep hood attached, folded and unfolded its long flowing drapery now and again, at times partly rendering the mysterious wearer as a fire when closed up from view. (154)

Later, one of the Mohawks accuses a mysterious character known as the Necromancer "of being in league "Both fight by the same awful means! There is more than human agency in their deeds! They hold counsel with the Prince of Darkness himself!" (171)

It is notable that the appearances of Spring-Heeled Jack only occur when the outlaws are facing the Mohawks. On the other hand, Will the Witless—first identified as Spring-Heel Jack in the list of characters—

has limited contact with the Mohawks, whereas he recognises the Bow Street runners as "bad fairies" and is seen to thwart their progress. The apparently demonic powers of Spring-Heeled Jack are not required to defeat them.

However, there is a curious scene towards the end of the serial. Officer Bilberry is practically unconscious following excessive drinking and an assault by the Mohawks; so he does not witness the appearance of a "startling apparition" who defends him. This apparition is not named as Spring-Heeled Jack and is described in demonic terms. It appears therefore, that Spring-Heeled Jack is morally ambiguous and will defend anyone from the violent attacks by the Mohawks, even if they are inebriated, ill-mannered and foul-mouthed bullies like Bow Street runner Bilberry.

Each time Spring-Heeled Jack is described in bestial or demonic terms. All the characters who confront Jack refer to him as "The Terror of London" or the "Mystic Terror". The authors clearly wanted to convey the idea that Spring-Heeled Jack's reputation was well-established in the early eighteenth century, and sought to weave his story into a romance about highwaymen as they both existed on the fringes of society. This marginalisation is also demonstrated by other characters; Will the Witless, for example, is presented as feeble-minded, but has flashes of insight that saves the outlaws. It is also demonstrated by Daddy Delph who has a device to save condemned men from the hangman's noose and a tonic to bring hanged men back to life, and by the innkeepers, Ralph and Med Drake whose establishment is literally a liminal point between the wilds of the Great North Road and urban civilisation.

As the focus of the story is on Dandy Dick restoring his good name, the exploits of Spring-Heeled Jack fall by the wayside and there is no overt confirmation as to Jack's identity. Despite the description of Will the Witless in the names of characters, it is unlikely that he is Jack's *alter ego* simply because he is no friend to the "red robins". Instead, in the closing chapter the identity of the mysterious Necromancer is revealed, and given that Spring-Heeled Jack appears as the Necromancer supports the outlaws, I suggest that Jack could be the Necromancer's associate.

Dandy Dick's Double and the End of the Story

At the end of issue 33, a note appears at the end of the instalment announcing that the "grand story" would be "concluded" in the next issue (323). Instead, the title of the serial changes mid chapter in the issue dated 8 December 1900 (issue 34 out of 42), the Christmas issue, beginning with a new banner naming the story *Dandy Dick's Double, or, The Outlaws of Old London*, which is marketed in the front cover as a "new serial".

The change of title is also seen in *The Human Bat*, the Spring-Heeled Jack story being published at the same time as *Dandy Dick*. A new title, *The Black Phantom*, follows *The Human Bat*, although on that occasion, it is to indicate the passing of time, and also to change the focus of the characters that the story follows, as well as continuing the narrative in a much darker tone. However, in *Dandy Dick* this follows on, *literally* mid scene.

Throughout its serialisation, almost all of the new issues of *Dandy Dick* start with a fresh chapter, although there are a few occasions where part of the chapter description from the previous issue is repeated at the beginning of the new issue. However, the opening line of *Dandy Dick's Double* is "'Down! down!" he thundered'." Rather than being a new serial, the reader has no idea of who is speaking without referring to the previous issue. Presumably the reason the narrative continued for a further nine issues (although these instalments were considerably shorter than at the beginning of the narrative) was because the authors realised there were still too many principal plot strands that needed to be explored before coming to a satisfactory conclusion. In addition, the editors no doubt found it easy to suggest that readers were joining a new serial at the start, rather than a story which had already run three quarters of its length. Notably, however, there is no list of characters or summary of the plot at the beginning of any of the *Dandy Dick's Double* issues.

Without wishing to reveal too much, the story comes to a logical conclusion; as Oscar Wilde describes fiction, "The good ended happily, and the bad unhappily". The concluding episodes feel "rushed" and there are plenty of plot strands which have not been followed through. The disclosure of Dandy Dick's "double"—the title of the second part of the serial—is covered in just a few paragraphs and without reasonable explanation.

The conclusion is satisfactory in terms of Dandy Dick's fortunes and his relationship with both the outlaws and Maude Mortiemor and the reader would assume a showdown between him, and the "double" who is masquerading as Dick. They would also expect a final confrontation with Raymond Raithwood and perhaps Jonathan Wild as well. One would have thought that, considering how much time had been spent on Officer Bilberry, he would have had a pivotal place in denouement of the story and there would be more significance attached to Ralph and Meg Drake's visit to the Pig and Pink Cushion. Daddy Delph's device that saves a felon from the gallows is never employed; Jack Sheppard's visit to his mother; Jonathan Wild is identified as Squire Brancome's murderer but what happens next? At one point, one of the characters sustains serious injuries and one would have thought that these might have impacted on the group's ability or inability to achieve something (perhaps lacking the strength to save the group when finding themselves in a precarious situation). The dual identity of one of the characters is revealed without pomp, almost lost amid a list of other character names. There are additional plot strands of the highwayman with close links to the Hole-in-the-Wall Inn, the travels of Blueskin and Jack Sheppard, the role of Will the Witless … the conclusion comes round quickly and not all the characters' situations are resolved for them to earn their places in the story.

That said, each of these subplots creates suspense as they mean that the readers are unable to continually follow Dandy Dick and his band especially when they are left in a precarious situation. They also serve to provide a wider picture of this romanticised time of the eighteenth century, showing, in addition to the idealised depictions of the outlaw lifestyle, some of the wider life: the town crier, the public pillory, the Mohawks, the life of a publican as well as the dangers they faced. We get a view of London, too. For the modern reader, more so than for the contemporary reader at the turn of the twentieth century, we see how London was made up of villages, the roads that had to be travelled, and some of the dangers the characters face.

On the other hand, the narrative does contain some flash-forwards as to the fates of the historical characters. It is revealed that Colonel Blood will eventually attempt to steal the Crown Jewels, and that the King decrees that the Prime Minister is forbidden from ordering any punishment on Blood and the grisly ends of other characters are mentioned—these would have been details that the readers already knew and served simply to wrap up their fates. The historical fates of Jack Sheppard and Jonathan Wild are explained in a single sentence each.

As previously argued in relation to another Spring-Heeled Jack serial, *The Human Bat*, it is unlikely that the authors expected their works to be read more than a century after their composition, and certainly not subjected to a critical analysis of incomplete plot strands and historical inaccuracies. These stories were composed to thrill and to entertain their readers. Looking at a story like *Dandy Dick* gives us an insight into how writers were composing their serial stories and how their audience were reading them. It also demonstrates to us the development of the folk heroes such as Colonel Blood, Dick Turpin and Jack Sheppard and how more contemporary legends are woven into historical stories.

It is disappointing that the *alter ego* of Spring-Heeled Jack is not explicitly revealed although there are some clues as to his character and it is interesting to see how this further depiction of Jack has been included in this serial novel. Ultimately, Jack is not the focus of the story; nor is it about the historical characters, although there are snippets of their lives in the narrative. Instead it is about Dandy Dick taking the role of folk-hero and re-establishing his honour. But, as for Spring-Heeled Jack? He remains a mystery. Or perhaps he had simply gone into hiding until he could reappear in his next incarnation.

Bibliography

Ainsworth, William Harrington. *Rookwood*. London: Richard Bentley, 1835.

Ainsworth, William Harrington. *Jack Sheppard: A Romance*. London: Richard Bentley, 1839.

Barlow, Derek. *Dick Turpin and the Gregory Gang*. London and Chichester: Phillimore, 1973.

Bayes, Richard. *The Genuine History of the Life of Richard Turpin*. London: J. Standen, 1739.

Bulwer-Lytton, Edward. *Paul Clifford*. London: Henry Colburn and Richard Bentley, 1830.

Defoe, Daniel. *The History of the Remarkable Life of John Sheppard*. 3rd Edition. London: John Applebee, 1724.

Fielding, Henry. *Jonathan Wild*. Oxford; Oxford World's Classics, 2008

Gay, John. "Newgate's Garland" in *The Poetical Works of John Gay. Including his Fables. In three volumes. With the life of the author. From the royal quarto edition of 1720*. Vol. 2. Edinburgh: Apollo Press, by the Martins, 1784. 118–120.

Guthrie, Neil. "'No Truth or very little in the whole Story'? A Reassessment of the Mohock Scare of 1712". *Eighteenth-Century Life* 20. 1996. 33–56.

Harper, Charles George. *Half-hours with the Highwaymen: picturesque biographies and traditions of the "Knights of the Road"*. London: Chapman & Hall, 1908.

Linnane, Fergus. *London's Underworld*. London: Robson Books Ltd, 2003.

Medcraft, J. "The Aldine Publishing Company" in Collector's Miscellany. Fourth Series, no. 6. July 1943. 2–6.

Rawson, Claude, "Introduction" in *Jonathan Wild*. Oxford; Oxford World's Classics, 2008

Sharpe, James. *Dick Turpin: The Myth of the English Highwayman*. London: Profile Books, 2004.

Skirboll, Aaron. *The Thief-Taker Hangings*. Guilford, CT: Lyons Press, 2014.

Summers, Montague. *A Gothic Bibliography*. London: The Fortune Press, 1940.

Viles, Edward. *Blueskin: A Romance*. London: E. Harrison, 1867–8.

DANDY DICK

OR

THE KING'S HIGHWAY

A Romance of Heath and Highway, Court and Cottage, Prince and Peasant.

°THE EXPEDITION OF THE THIEF-TAKER—WILL THE WITLESS—THE ATTEMPTED VENGEANCE OF A HEARTBROKEN MOTHER—THE MYSTERIOUS WOULD-BE ASSASSIN—THE POLE-LEAPER—MERRIE ISLINGTON IN THE OLDEN TIME—HANDSOME RICHARD AND THE WITLESS BOY.

"The Haunted Manor at Finchley!" The man shuddered with superstitious fear.

"The Haunted Manor at Finchley! Thunders! I'm better employed than acting as my own echo for the edification of an addle-pated minion. I said the Haunted Manor, sirrah, an', if I'm again to compelled to impress the intended destination on your dull brain, you'll get it through a crack in the top of your thick sconce at the brass end of my official cudgel!"

The last speaker was a stunted, thick-set man, of middle age, and of the most villainous aspect possible to imagine. He was dressed as a somewhat better-class Bow Street runner, and was on the point of springing into the saddle of his sturdy cob as he uttered his rageful words. A number of black-cloaked and three-cornered head-geared horsemen were stationed at hand.

"I won't put you to the trouble of breaking my skull, Mr. Wild, thank you. Your orders shall be most scrupulously carried out."

A bitter oath followed, but it was stopped on the safe side of the teeth.

It was a dark, dismal winter night. Much snow had fallen, and was still falling, in unusually large flakes. Ye Chepe and Newgate Street formed most quaint pictures, with the houses of overlapping fronts, pointed gables, and crossed pieces of timbers. There was no moon, and the effect of the white snow against the dark vapour of midnight was both weird and striking.

Facing grim old Newgate, with its great circular, iron-barred gates, and dangling chains over the arch above, stood the box of a night-watchman. The watchman, or "Charley,"[1] crouched over his brightly-glowing charcoal fire, endeavouring to chill the frozen blood in his aged frame.

Suddenly a prod, prod, prod, caught his ears, and he glanced up. The road was up, for there was to be a hanging performance on the forthcoming day, quite a theatrical show in its way, and to witness which people crowded in their thousands, and paid enormous sums for good seats. The prodding sound made from the end of a long, straight pole, held by an uncouth, ragged, pale-faced lad. He was barefooted, and came along with astounding agility, bounding lightly over the thick snow by the aid of his long, slender cudgel. The great,

---

° Part 1. Vol. XIII.—No. 337. 18 April 1900. The dates here are the dates that the British Museum has stamped on each of the issues to show when they have been received.
[1] So called because Charles II established a force of paid watchmen to patrol the streets in 1663.

wide gap in the road was reached, and pole-end prodded firmly, then the little, slight-made figure was seen to gracefully bound into the air, and quite easily clear the opening of many yards in extent.

"Be the misfortunate piper, that blew himself inside out, if that isn't Spring-Heeled Jack, the powerful London terror, himself!" muttered the old Irish watchman. "But it's in the inds of the pole—fer he uses both ive 'em—that he carries the springs ive his heels. Oh, the Lud save an' protect us!"

"That witless brat again!" growled the man-tamer, Mr. Wild, as he saw the flying lad, with the pole, shooting towards the party of horsemen. A blow of the whip was aimed at the careering lad; but, with a wild, defiant burst of laughter, he bounded far out of reach.

Huddled up in a recess facing a house in Newgate Street was a black form, that of a woman, deathly pale, and emaciated, yet still bearing the traces of great beauty.

"Oh, the iniquity of man!" the creature moaned. "But a brief while back my darling boy—my Jack—was an honest, upright lad, learning a trade, and in training to become a good, dutiful son, a commendable citizen; then that monster in the form of man, Jonathan Wild, threw out his cunningly-woven snares. My poor boy fell. He is now the notorious felon, prison-breaker, a wretch hunted from pillar to post, and with a price upon his youthful head. The traitor who brought the ruin—Jonathan Wild—will hand over to the hangman the felon he himself has trained, that the blood-money may be claimed!"

The trembling of hooves started the woman from her reverie of fierce despair. She sprang up, and, firmly clutching something hidden under her long, black, faded cloak, darted over the thick white snow, keeping well within the shadows of the overhanging eaves of the buildings, until she had noiselessly neared the crowd of horsemen now moving off towards Smithfield. A pistol exploded; the man termed Wild reeled in his saddle from the shock, for the weapon appeared quite near his head, the leaden ball actually grazing his cheek. A furious oath burst from his lips as he attempted to steady his affrighted horse. A shrill, maniacal burst of laughter struck upon the cursing man's ears, as he turned, only in time to see the swiftly-disappearing garments of a woman.

"Jack Sheppard's demented mother!" he savagely muttered. "And within an ace[2] of terminating the career of Jonathan Wild in the very zenith of his fame!"

He was still tugging furiously at the bit of his prancing steed, when he became dimly aware of some object dancing over the snow-covered roadway towards him.

"Jonathan Wild!" hissed a voice, trembling and guttural with concentrated fury. "Thief-maker!—thief-betrayer!—Government spy!—father of the gallows!" With each epithet a terrific blow was aimed at the broad breast of the

---

[2] An ace – almost achieving something.

rider. He must have been instantly mortally pierced to the heart but for the vest of finely-woven chain mail secretly worn under his garments.

Finding an impediment to his steel, the mysterious assailant madly sprang at the throat of the horseman, and tore him from the saddle. The two crashed in a heap to the snow-covered earth.

Jonathan Wild yelled lustily for assistance; his men were following at the rear, and urged on their horses. But the unknown assailant fought like a fury. The knife slashed repeatedly at the face of Wild, who was now under most, and half-strangled by the pressures of the vice-like clutch at his throat.

It was a marvel how Jonathan Wild (long credited with possessing the advantage of a charmed life) succeeded in jerking his visage out of the way of the downward darting steel thrusts; but this he contrived to do until he reached one of the fire-locks, placed in a breast-pocket. This looked into the fierce, vengeful face over him, then the flint and steel loudly snapped. When the crowd of riders galloped up, their leader was standing by the side of his animal with a corpse lying prone at his feet, and the face of which had been shot away.

"Curmudgeons! You take your ease while your master's life is in peril!" growled Wild to his followers.

The night-watchmen came running up, attracted by the firing of the pistol.

"An officer of the Crown, on an expedition concerning the safety of the King's subjects, to be threatened twice with assassination, in about the same number of minutes, and with an escort of great, hulking fellows at one's heels— a pretty state of affairs, truly!"

"Who is the man?" asked the watchman, shrinking from the appalling spectacle.

"Take his carcase to the mortuary. I will explain the matter to the chief sheriff in the morning," was all the explanation Jonathan Wild deigned to offer to the night-guardians of the peace. Then he and his men resumed their way, as if nothing unusual had occurred.

"Men, we go to night—or, this morning, for the night is actually passed—to net a very choice collection of gaolbirds, every one of which will command a fine sum in the felon's market of the Old Bailey. The birds meet at the Haunted Manor at Finchley, as I have already explained to Crofton. Each of you will have leave to idly strut it about the time for months to come, with your pockets running over with King George's[3] gold medals—that is to say, if you work with a will. In which case we shall bag the whole brood of nighthawks."

Murmurs of approval greeted these words; then the party pushed on at a swift pace.

The watchmen, between them, bore away the unsightly remains of the unknown.

---

[3] It is later explained that this is George II (reigned 1727–60)..

"I tell you, friends," remarked one, "the popular feeling is running very high against the greatest ruffian on earth. These endless hangings, the unsightly disfiguring of our common-lands with bodies of executed malefactors—many of them known to have been perfectly innocent men. Who is responsible for the most of this?" indignantly asked the speaker, supplying his own answer. "Why, this bloodthirsty renegade, who is the secret leader of the greatest of the criminal classes, and Government agent, spy, informer, and thief-taker all in one—the infamous Jonathan Wild!"

Will the Witless, unseen by Jonathan Wild, had contrived to overhear most of this personage's words uttered to his followers.

The boy, using his pole—at times one end after the other—covered the ground in leaps and bounds. Hedgerows, turnpike gates, anything chancing to come in his way, he vaulted with most consummate grace and ease, nor halted until he had entered the vicinity of Merrie Islington. In the avenue of trees leading towards the Highbury Fields a horseman suddenly confronted the leaper.

"Ah, there you are, handsome Richard!" gleefully greeted the witless boy, labouring hard for his breath.

"Yes, my poor Will," replied the horsemen in keen accents of pity, "and I have not forgotten to bring you a nice hot supper, lad; and a whole silver crown-piece, too!"

The lad stood for some moments in the thick gloom of the night, contemplating his outstretched palm, into which the snowflakes thickly fell.

"My pretty friends, the fairies, are sending me their beautiful messages again. See!" he added, "no one can read them but poor Will the Witless. Ah, what loving words they send me to-night!" Then the lad reverently kissed the white, fleecy substance, afterwards gently blowing it upwards. "My answer," he said, with a sweet smile and glistening eyes.

The cloaked and masked horseman gave vent to a deep sigh of pity.

"You must get yourself boots, socks, and a suit of warm clothing, Will, lad," he said. "I have given you money enough. Why haven't you done as I wished?"

"Mrs Sheppard is very poor, an' called witless, too, like poor me, and I gave her the money. My pole always keeps me warm. Ah, Handsome Richard, Will the Witless wouldn't exchange his wooden steed for the wonderful Black Bess of Dick Turpin, nor your own beautiful mare, Jess! My faithful horse eats nothing, will lie down anywhere, never complains, no matter how hard he's worked, or how rough the weather. So long as he can be of use to his master, and rest by his side when he rests, then he is perfectly contented."

"Tell me the news, Will lad," asked the horseman anxiously.

"Ah, I was nearly forgetting it, Handsome Richard!" cried the boy. Then, in fragments, the words and an account of the movements of the great thief-taker were extracted from the lad's feeble mind.

A parcel, still steaming, was handed to the delighted boy, a few words of farewell uttered, then the mounted man sped on his way rapidly, shaping his course for the Finchley wilds.

The boy of feeble intellect sat by the hedgerow and unfastened the parcel, to find a temptingly hot steak-pudding, vegetables, and a tart there in. His delight was unbounded. Thus, but half-clad, and seated at the lonely and gloomy roadside, the homeless waif consumed his meal, chatting alternately with the good fairies, and his faithful wooden steed, and, mayhap, as happy, that cruel winter night, as was even the mighty Monarch who then ruled this great land.

THE MIDNIGHT TEMPEST ON HOUNSLOW HEATH—THE COFFIN-SHAPED CART—DADDY DELPH AND NAT FLINT, THE MYSTERIOUS VISITORS TO THE GIBBET OF THE HEATH—SCOURGES OF THE SEA, THEIR LODGMENT[4] ON THE HOUNSLOW WILDS—THE MIDNIGHT ROBBERS AND THEIR GRUESOME WORK—THE DEAD YOUTH IN THE CAGE.

"Ho! ho! ho! What a glorious night for our pretty work, Nat Flint! What brave, bonny weather for our merry, merry men—The Birds o' the Iron Cages of Death! He! he! he! Hew! hew! hew! Keep that blessed glim[5] alight, if you can, Nat Flint; but look to your hat, an' the head inside it, you'll need 'em both! Whe-w-w, the lamp's out, confound it! We'll have no end of the job to light the tinder in this driving rain an' powerful wind—or, would you call it a hurricane? Ho! Ho! Ho! Hark to the devil's music that's roaring out over this pretty Heath o' Hounslow! Hear the shriek o' the startled owl, an' the rest o' the greedy carrion creatures. We have disturbed 'em from their midnight feast an' revels; but their suppers won't run away. Ha! Ha! Hear the creaking an' groaning o' the felon-dead in their dainty, upright beds o' teeth-edge-grating, rusty iron. Ho! ho! ho! But even they are better off than them that are left clean out in the cold, with nothing in the way o' bedclothes—no warm bands o' iron blankets, nothing to keep 'em snug an' cosy, except the nice soft steel cravat, by which the Heath-lodgers are so thoughtfully left hanging by their stiff, cold necks.

"W-h-e-w-w, now you've let the lantern slip—you, Nat Flint! Look, there it goes, flying away like mad, as if scared out o' its wits—if a lantern can be supposed to possess wits! How did you contrive to let the thing be blown out of your hand, Nat Flint?"

"I was suddenly scared by the sight o' that thing there. Ough, it almost touched my face! Swayed this way by the strength of the storm-demon!"

"That thing there" was something that had once been human—a something created in the divine image of its Maker. Alas! now a felon corpse, a spectacle

---

[4] Hiding place.

[5] Candle or lantern.

too fearful to contemplate, for the body was hanging from a gibbet, without even the elongated framework of iron hoops to partly cover-up the hideous aspect of decaying mortality—the remains of a common malefactor, condemned to the cruel death and outrageous sentence of hanging in chains in a public place, after execution in the ordinary way.

A long-bodied, black-painted cart had suddenly pulled up in the pitchy darkness enveloping the wilderness known as Hounslow Heath. A man had leapt down from the seat formed at the back of the long, almost coffin-shaped vehicle, and flew after the large lantern, now swiftly bowled away by the fiercely-the howling wind. The man went sprawling more than once before he succeeded in catching up with the temporarily-stopped lantern, and pouncing upon the thing before it had recommenced its seeming frolic.

The driver on the front seat had pulled up his horse, and patiently awaited the return of his companion.

The face of the before-mentioned man was muffled up to the eyes in the huge folds of a black cravat, his three-cornered hat almost joined the top edge of the muffler, and when he spoke his voice came from behind the thick mouth-covering. One hand held reins and whip, the other was busily employed keeping the hat from following the example set it by the lantern.

"I've got the foolish thing Daddy Delph!" breathlessly cried the lantern-catcher, carrying up breathlessly to the stationary cart's side.

"A foolish thing to you, Nat Flint!" growled the driver. "You of all men, too—Nat Flint, my famous protégé—to be startled by the corpse of a hanged man, when—"

"Hush! Merciful heavens, the storm-fiends have ears. The frightened birds o' the night—nay, these awful, dangling remains of poor humanity even—did they hear our secret—the secret to the key of life and death—might whisper it, in the ghostly moanings, to the midnight winds, thence to be carried to the ears of men!"

The tones of this speaker, as he stood peering up through the blackness at the sable patch betokening his friend's presence, were pregnant with utmost fear, a most deadly dread.

The muffled-up man on the driver's box gave out a shriek of grotesque laughter—the laughter of surprised incredulity.

"Why, man!" he gasped, from behind his muffler-shawl, "even so. Let the Government actually learn our glorious secret, and arrest Nat Flint. What then? Why, they could only hang Nat Flint; and he wouldn't mind that, seeing that Nat Flint has been hanged before—and more than once!"

"Delph," shrieked the other interruptingly, "are you drunk, or mad, or both combined? Will you cease babbling like an idiot? Leave the mention of our mysterious compact and deeds for more secret places!"

"Ha! ha! ha!" responded the other. "Call the next executed felon for witness, please. Tell the obliging skeleton not to rattle up his poor old bones too dismally before the judge and jury, and perhaps the witness may be permitted not to bring his death-caged into court with him. Ho! Ho! ho!" The speaker fairly shook with merriment at the mental view of the picture he had conjured up.

"All this may appear mere laughing matter to you, Delph," solemnly chided the man with the lantern; "but," he went on, "for all the jest you find in my fear—presentiment, I term it—I tell you that, before long, I—Nat Flint—shall take up my place here, shall rank as one of these horrors, the sight of which should surely make heaven's angels weep. 'Felon scarecrows,' as heartless, pitiless men term them. Yet we know Daddy Delph—you and I—that more than one of these so-called felon scarecrows were innocent as babe unborn of the crimes for which they suffered, that their seemingly degraded remains are really those of unsullied martyrs, whose cries for justice must pierce even the very ears of the Supreme One above."

The driver of the strange vehicle peered down at the man standing below. The laugh had died out, the eyes looking like fire-glints from the deep shadow between hat and muffler.

"Nat, you know, when we wish it—Daddy Delph and Nat Flint—we can, and do, defy the gallows, and all the rest of its cursed family connections, such as the things that flourish here!" The man's voice was almost swallowed up in the din of the storm raging over the Heath, yet, nevertheless, his hearer was evidently suffering much from fearsome apprehension lest the words should be overheard by some unsuspected listener. "Tell me, Nat, what is the cause of this new condition of yours? Where is your old courage? Where your former nerves of steel?"

"Gone for ever, I think," was the quivering reply; the speaker adding: "I have seen the ghostly rider—the Phantom Horsemen. You know what that means. That dim, vapoury spectre, it is well known, always appears to one of us—one of the secret lawless class—to give warning of the near approach of the hangman's noose."

The driver quickly got down from his seat.

"Nerves, Nat Flint—nerves!" he muttered. And as he spoke a flask appeared in his hand. "Take a stiff pull, Nat" he continued, thrusting the little article forward. His companion took a long draught, and returned the vessel. The other followed the example, giving a long, approving smack with his lips immediately afterwards. "There, death—everlasting death—to the blue-devils,[6] I say; as I know of no more powerful poison to instantly kill off the infernal imps than a mouthful of white satin—commonly termed gin. W-h-e-w-w-w, the deuce take this tornado of tornadoes!"

---

[6] Alcohol.

The driver had mounted again, Nat Flint had climbed up behind, and the cart went slowly forward again. The driver was now without a light, and needed the utmost caution to avoid wide, gaping ruts, large stones, and even open trenches, lurking before him, but hidden in the black pall of midnight.

Again the driver abruptly drew rein. "I should know this spot, methinks," he muttered. "The four crossroads of the Heath! Yes; there looms the great white stake—'the "crowner's"[7] steak,' as the beastly thing is called. A poor wretch kills himself of poverty—kills himself because he cannot keep himself alive, forsooth; but there's a fine convincing logic in that! Then the good, prime, overfed crowner sits himself upon the body of the poor, lean suicide, and finds that the dead man hath committed self-murder: that he was an necessory, before and after the fact, to his own killing and slaying—to wit, that he did lay violent hands upon himself to the extent of mortal injury, of malice aforethought, predisposed. I'faith, but 'tis a sweet, beautiful jargon these legal scribes employ!

"'This sadly-misguided wretch, having died of nothing to eat,' in effect, says Mr. Crowner, 'my sentence is that the poor mortal's remains be taken and buried in a public spot where for crossroads to meet. Then, that he may hang there hereafter filled, a stake shall be passed into his body—as a goodly stake of some twelve feet long.' Ah, Mr Crowner, but 'tis a sorry joke—sorry joke! For a steak of but a few inches—given in time—would have saved the necessity of the stake of some twelve feet. Moreover, no suicide ever lived that could digest the latter stake—a grave mistake indeed—and a sorry joke, Mr Crowner—a sorry joke!"

Again the cart stayed its dismal progress. This time the poor brute of a steed drew back, rearing almost on its haunches, and snorting in great terror. The driver sprang down and did his utmost to lull the terror of the animal. Right in their path loomed up for great beams, weather-blackened and worm-eaten. The crossing timbers above could not be defined in the darkness, but the bloodcurdling shapes—jerking fitfully in the raging storm—could be seen only too plainly.

The man termed Daddy Delph pointed his whip-handle towards the heart-sickening sights.

"The nine pirates!" he cried. "Once the terrors of the seas. They put to cold steel hundreds of their fellow-creatures, massacred ship's captain and crew time after time, and spared not women nor children. Yet they most cravenly went through their final exits—pleaded, prayed, and cried. Were hanged outside grim old Newgate, and then promoted to their comfortable posts here. Paugh! Where is now their swagger, their dash, their desperation? Why, the whole nine of 'em combined haven't enough manhood left to enable 'em to keep off the beaks of the carrion birds. Scurvy knaves, keep from the path of your betters!"

---

[7] Coroner.

Daddy Delph gave a swift crack of his whip. The sudden flapping of wings and startled cries of winged creatures broke out, then a number of black hued denizens of the air flew shriekingly away.

The storm increased its fury. The long, leafless branches of tall and gaunt-looking trees violently trembled and soughed[8] in the howling tempest, like long skeleton arms and fingers the tree limbs and twigs appeared. The thick gloom of the night vapour seemed filled with horribly grotesque forms—a weird, fantastic, trooping of unearthly creatures grinning in impish glee, rage, and fiercest mockery. Their arms, hands, and fingers threateningly swaying up and down, backwards and forwards, but ever pointing towards the grim spectacles of the remains of the bloodthirsty sea-monsters.

"Hereabouts must we locate our man, friend Nat," now cheerily sang out Daddy Delph, apparently in nowise affected by his fearsome surroundings.

"The sooner our nocturnal business is over the better!" grumbled Nat Flint. "'Tis a night fit only for murder, murderers, gibbets, cages of death—"

"And deeds of reviving. That's so, of the truth, comrade," interruptingly remarked Daddy Delph. "I like the surroundings to fit in with the incidents, friend mine, therefore 'tis a right merry night for a right merry deed. Lud, there swings our lad!"

The two men had led their animal forward. They now halted again, and before them could faintly be made out the outline of a single gibbet, consisting of one upright beam, and a short arm-like piece at right angles. This stood by the road or cutting passing over the wild, barren heath. From the top beam ominously creaked and swayed an iron cage. This was without sign of rust or weather-stain—in fact it was perfectly clean and new.

The two men paused to listen. No human sound came to them, nothing but the cries of the owl, hawk, crow, and other birds, the rattling of the many gibbets—placed at various spots about the extensive wilds—and the furious shriekings of the angry elements.

The lighting of the tinder, by means of sparks struck from a piece of steel and flint, was a most tedious affair, but it was accomplished at last, and a fresh piece of candle fixed and ignited and closed in the lantern. Then two short ladders were drawn from the cart, the steed of which had been tethered to a tree. The two pieces of ladder were telescoped into one, and this placed against the upright beam of the gibbet.

Daddy Delph mounted the ladder and bent over the top beam; Nat Flint carefully held up the lantern, screening it from the strong wind, and directing its rays where most required.

The outline of a man—or youth—could be discerned within the death-cage when the rays of the light fell thereon. The form appeared to be that of a perfectly dead person, and was held in position alone by the close contact of

---

[8] A whispering sound.

the iron hoops. "Throw your light on the lad's face. Lud! Nat Flint, a half day and a long night in this charming retreat has about filled up the poor boy's book, not to mention his light fantastic cellarflap jig[9]—minus cellarflap— outside the old capstone jug!"[10]

The speaker was busy, while speaking, in the operation of forcing a liquid from a small phial between the teeth of the hanged being.

"Cursed iron hoops! They are so closely formed about the head that I can't get my hand near enough to the clenched teeth to force 'em apart."

Between the storm gusts Nat Flint caught the words, and hastily replied: "Try the padlock! If you can pick that it'll make the job easy enough!"

"He's colder than death itself. I wish I could get this into his mouth first. I know what these padlocks are like. There, I've started a few precious life-drops on their way. Now for the lock!"

But the lock on the gibbet-cage was a cleverly-constructed one, and defied all attempts to pick it, notwithstanding the exceeding cleverness of Daddy Delph.

"The big file, Nat. It's a long job filing through the strong, thick hoop of the padlock; but there's no help for it, Nat Flint, my comrade, so get the tool, and sharp's the dodge, both to you and the file!"

THE MEETING OF DICK THE DANDY AND COLONEL BLOOD—A GREAT JOKE—THE OLD COACH NEAR THE HORNSEY FOREST—A STARTLING GREETING FOR THE RAIDERS OF THE ROAD—A NARROW ESCAPE FROM DEATH.

The masked and cloaked horseman—so much as the riding-cloak did not hide—bore unmistakable proof of great splendour of dress, and the equipment of his thoroughbred mare was in keeping with his own. A great and densely gloomy avenue of elms, facing the Holloway Wastes, was reached and entered without the solitary traveller meeting a living being after leaving Will the Witless. Half-way through the thick and silent sheltered way the rider was suddenly made aware that he was not alone.

"Halt, or I instantly fire!" cried a stern voice, as an unseen steed plunged forward.

"Halt, you, or I'll blaze away! I can just locate that portion of your face under your mask!" returned the first mounted man. Two lines of light revealed the barrels of the long flint-lock pistol of the period.

The men mutually simultaneously reined up.

"That's a game two can play at, my fine fellow!" fearlessly replied the other; adding, "I must request you to hand over everything of value you have about you, your arms included. Hesitate a moment and you're a dead man!"

---

[9] The death jerking movements made by a hanging man, once the cart on which they were standing has been ridden away.

[10] Also referred to as the Stone Jug, the condemns' cell at Newgate Prison.

"And I must request you first pay toll to me! Hesitate the smallest fraction of a second and I'll lay you out for good!" thundered the friend of Will the Witless.

"Dick the Dandy!" suddenly cried out the stranger, bursting into a wild peal of laughter.

"Colonel Blood!" shouted the other, perfectly yelling with surprised merriment.

The two horsemen firmly gripped palms.

"My dear pal Dick, to think that we—the firmest of felon comrades—should seek prey upon one another—even unknowingly! What is human nature going to?"

"My dear chum," returned Dick the Dandy, still shaking with laughter, "it's the finest joke I've ever fell across—two knights of the road attempting to levy toll upon each other!"

The two so strangely met led their animals through the grove into the open, where the outstretched sheets of snow made the night comparatively light. Dick the Dandy, in a few words, informed his comrade of the news conveyed to him by Will the Witless.

The colonel, a strikingly handsome man of thirty, bore evidence of having served in the Army, and his mien was most remarkable for its air of extreme recklessness.

"Dick, dear pal, we are both on the same journey, and all the imps of the lower regions combined shall not keep us from meeting our many friends at the Haunted Manor to-night—or, rather, morning. There we shall revel in festivity and good-fellowship. Hunted felons as we are, the hand of every man raised against us, we shall there unbend[11] for once. Shake off, and forget, our degradation for a few all too brief hours. The daring Dick Turpin, his firm friend Tom King, Jack Rann, also Sixteen-String Jack, the whole world-famous boy prison-breaker, Jack Sheppard, and how many more of the midnight toll-collectors, keepers of the King's Highway, gentlemen of the Heath, &c., &c. Then last, but by no means least, the Necromancer—that man of amazing mysteries, and the firm friend of the persecuted outlaw!"

"You may well say 'persecuted outlaw'!" moodily commented Dick the Dandy. "Here I am," he went on, "charged with a crime of which I am perfectly innocent! If I am arrested, that fiend in human shape, Jonathan Wild, will take care that my bones shall bleach on one of our gibbet-decorated commons. My heritage is the prize in view. I am an outcast, with a price upon my head, and these hands—which would willingly slave until they dropped from my wrists to secure an honest crust—are left no alternative but to rob for sustenance, or take their possessor's wretched and cruelly chequered life!"

---

[11] Unwind, relax.

"Come, come, Dick, dear old pal!" cheerily cried Colonel Blood. "You have suddenly become somewhat depressed since meeting your old chum"—a backhanded compliment to the latter. "Put spurs to your steed, and will together do a long, wild canter over Nature's lovely, spotless carpet of fleecy snow."

No sooner said than done. And the highwaymen might have been many thousands of miles away from old England, and yet never have found a more wild or unfrequented locality than that in which they then were. Their spirits rose as their beautiful and marvellously fleet of foot animals swiftly yet lightly careered over the thick white covering, the landscape made unspeakably lovely in its stainless ropes, and flying like an endless panorama past the riders.

By the old Hornsey Forest a great, lumbering old coach was slowly moving on its way, its occupants, no doubt, returning from some fashionable gathering. Colonel Blood urged Dick the Dandy to join him in stopping the vehicle and demanding booty.

The daring colonel road up to the driver and fired, but wide of the man's head. It was enough; the fellow uttered a most fearful series of groans, although untouched, fell from the box into a deep rut of snow, and there remained as if stone dead. Colonel Blood urged his horse at a smart pace and reached the coach-window instantly after discharging his piece. His first act was to snatch off his hat—to which the black crape mask was attached—and placed them partly in view before the closed window, which was instantly let down, and this was followed by a most terrific explosion.

°A perfect deluge of grape-shot, iron nails, and flint pebbles tore their way through the frosty air. The smoke from the explosion took the form of a thick, black, rolling cloud.

Quick as thought, Colonel Blood—before the dense volume of vapour could clear—thrust his head into the open window, withdrawing himself instantly after, and holding in one hand an enormous blunderbuss.

"A pretty article of defence, Dick!" grimly muttered the colonel, holding the half-musket, half-speaking-trumpet-looking article toward his chum. "It would have been an easy matter to have read a newspaper through either of our bodies after, if we'd been in the line of fire of the cartload of murder-missiles with which this was located. "I've no ambition to become a mere sieve or sheet of gauze netting just yet. Get round to the other window, Dick; but look out for squalls!"[12]

Dick the Dandy drove round by the back of the coach and smashed in the side windows with the butt-end of one of his pistols. Screams from feminine throats followed. Dick placed his masked face at the opening. A flint shot out

---

° Part 2. Vol. XIII.—No. 338. 2 May 1900.
[12] A brief commotion, i.e. "watch out for trouble".

its sparks close to his cheek; the weapon had flashed in the pan,[13] or the dandy highwayman would have had face or head battered to the night winds.

Colonel Blood's eyes of reckless daring glared through his mask in at the opposite coach-window.

"Thank your lucky star that he failed in hitting my friend, young man!" he thundered; "for, by all that's sacred, you would have followed him to the land of shadows the instant after!"

An elderly gentleman in full, flowing white wig, a youth of evil glance, but most exquisitely dressed, a middle-aged lady, and a young girl—the latter lovely as a poet's dream—comprised the occupants of the stately-looking old vehicle. It was from the elderly man's hand the blunderbuss had been seized, the youth's pistol that had missed fire.

The barrels of the highwaymen's weapons covered the male inmates as the loud, ringing, fierce voice of Colonel Blood rang out with the words:

"Your jewels, cash, and other valuables—or your lives!"

FILING THE PADLOCK OF THE GIBBET-CAGE—THE EXCHANGE OF LODGMENT—THE FURY OF THE TEMPEST—STARTLING APPEARANCE OF THE SPECTRAL HORSEMAN—THE BINDING ELECTRICAL FLASH—THE ONCOMING RIDERS—THE SPECTRE OF THE HEATH.

Before commencing the filing in real earnest, Daddy Delph succeeded in forcing a few more drops between the teeth of the apparently dead inmate of the cage; the man then commenced briskly working with his long file. The weird creaking of the surrounding gibbets and the hissing and shrieking of the rageful elements mingled with the grating noise of the tool. The ladder's position had been altered, Daddy Delph now taking his place under the top beam of the gibbet and Nat Flint holding the lantern with one hand, and keeping the movable cage steady with the other.

Daddy Delph, as if to set at defiance his fear-creating surroundings, commenced to sing in a voice that, for rasping quality, quite outdid the noise created by the file, yet, for that very reason, was the better suited to the words of the song—a most popular one among the lawless classes of the period of which we write. The composition was entitled "The Hangman's Chorus."

The effect of the singing in the midst of such a combination of horrors was worthy of a place in Dante's Inferno. The song was frequently interrupted by interpolated remarks concerning the progress of the filing through of the lock loop, and commenced thusly:

"Creak, creak, creak—ever creak!

---

[13] Misfired.

An oath—a groan—a shriek!
—Use your wisdom-teeth, pretty file—use your wisdom teeth! —
Lurking, purse-cutting lads,
Moody midnight footpads.
—This iron's the toughest my honest file has met with for many a day! —
They are still at their games,
Within sound of my chains—
Creak, creak, creak—ever creak!
—Confound the cunning pate[14] that invented this padlock!—
An oath—a groan—a shriek!
—May it be used solely to lock up the fellow's inventive genius in the future,
say I. An oath—a groan—a shriek! Bravely done, good file! —
They are still at their games,
Within sound of my chains—
—How beautifully the iron sparks fly—like the moon's silvery sheen!—
Oh, my skeleton pains!
—Oh, the pains of my poor wrist! Never say die, file!—
As I rattle my bones,
I can still hear the groans!
—Good! Why, Nat Flint, I've cut the gap half-way through!—
In my poor fleshless rage,
Within my rust-red cage;
—On, on, my trusty file! Bite, bite at it; tooth and nail!—
Creak, creak, creak—ever creak!
An oath—groan—a shriek!
—Hooroar! —through! All the wealth of the East Indees to a bad farthing
that I've done it, Nat Flint! An' don't you take that bet, or you will bitterly regret
it! An oath—a groan——. Closer up, Nat, my midnight cherub. There—steady!
Take care that the poor, stone-cold ladder don't slip through your arms! Steady!
Steady!"

The iron cage of death heard divided in two, uprightwards. There was very
great difficulty in preventing its contents from swinging out, what with the still-
increased fierceness of the tempest, and the awkwardness of reaching from the
ladder. But the body was at last safe in the arms of the two gibbet-robbers. They
lost not a moment in bearing the burden through the darkness and shrieking
elements to the elongated, sable-hued conveyance, the end of which was let
down, the body carefully forced into the space, and the tail board then replaced.

"Birds of prey know their business, Nat Flint—that is to say, they know the
instinct given them, and never attack until there is sure signs of decay—which
is proof of death. In a few hours the eye-peckers would have spoilt our little

---

[14] Head.

job, Nat o' the Hard-Stone."

"That's so, Daddy," replied Flint; "but the hempen noose may have forestalled the eye-peckers," he added.

"We've no time to lose, comrade mine," returned Daddy Delph. "Follow me. We go to pay our humble respects to the nine scourges of the sea!"

A terrific crash of thunder followed the words; then came a blinding flash of lightning. The Heath became as light as day. Every gibbet-frame, and its burden or burdens, and the surrounding naked trees and bushes and pathways came into view with the most weird and shuddering vividness; then followed the dense darkness, and the wind, rain, or hail and sleet, came tearing down like a very deluge.

The candle enclosed in the lantern was safe from the wind, but raindrops fell through the holes in its top and caused the flame to splutter, and occasionally threatened to go out. The lantern was wedged between a heap of stones under the centre of the beams bearing the bodies of the executed pirates.

Daddy Delph took not the slightest notice of the contact of the storm-swaying objects of terror and disgust, but ended their midst with his ladder, and actually gave out snatches of his favourite song. The chief gibbet-robber looked up at the figure dangling from the centre of the nine.

"You, sirrah, will be least likely to be missed!" he cried; "your amiable cronies so considerably screen you from the gaze of the vulgar passer-by."

Delph placed his ladder against a beam, reached one of the top pieces of the frame, and soon crawled to the screw-bolt directly over the head of the centre body, and on the upper side of the timber. A screw-wrench came from the man's pocket; a few powerful efforts were made, then a dull thud below sounded amidst the storm tumult.

Nat Flint shuddered more than once as he and his companion bore the remains of the wholesale butcherer to the empty and open iron frame. After great exertions and extreme difficulty, the pirate's body had taken the place of the executed lad; a padlock—brought from the cart—was placed with the first one had been, and the swinging cage again contained a ghastly inmate.

"Jonathan Wild, or a Bow Street Red Robin[15] or two, may turn up here to look for traces of our merry work, Nat Flint!" chuckled Daddy Delph; "but no one will be likely to again call the muster-roll for the pirate crew; and, even if the one sea dog should be missed, it won't be suspected that he has taken huff, and simply changed his quarters. Ha! ha! He! he! he!"

The two proceeded to where the steed stood tethered, taking lanterns and ladder with them. The wet ran from the men's garments as from water-spouts.

"Take of your soaked hat an' coat, leave 'em to me, an' creep in beside the body. Put the hot-water metal cases to its feet, well wrap the rugs about the poor boy, and get as much as possible of this—my prime, secret elixir—down

---

[15] Bow Street Horse Patrol, rather that the Runners, so named because of their red uniforms.

his throat. You can leave the task o' getting home to Daddy Delph, Nat Flint, secret partner mine."

Nat Flint needed no second bidding. If the felon scarecrows of Hounslow Heath had their terrors for him, the one in the cart was quite an exception, for its blue-white face was yet handsome—nay, beautiful as the visage of an angel.

Flint crept into the opening, then the tailboard of the large, coffin-like conveyance was chained up, and the driver detached the animal, took a deep pull of his pocket-flask, and then turned, with the intention of securing the ladder and lantern. These he meant to fix under the cart, but at the moment of nearing them a mighty roar and rush of wind took them up and carried them swiftly away.

The cart was now moving forward, its driver trusting to his knowledge of the locality to lead him aright. He crushed his triangular-formed hat down until its back inside edge was in the nape of his neck, then he slashed spitefully at the poor, terrified beast, and roundly cursed both it and the tempest—for the latter was now furious enough to rouse the ire of a saint, and Daddy Delph was very far from being one. There was a small square flap in the top of the cart.

"Daddy Delph—Delph!" shouted Flint's voice from beneath.

"Well, comrade?" sang out the driver excitedly, and pulling up, as if to hear the better.

"There's a slight change," replied Flint; "just a few degrees of cold the less!"

"Hooroar!" responded Delph, becoming madlike with glee, and, in his heart, lashing at the poor brute unmercifully. "Ho! Ho!" he burst out, losing all discretion in his overpowering joy of triumph—"Ho! ho! We laugh at the cruel gallows! Ho! ho! We defy the very elementals! We defy even death itself!"

The mocking sounds had scarcely left his lips before a deafening crash of thunder responded to them. The heavens appeared to burst, revealing a throbbing sea of liquid fire beyond, and from which darted down sheets and sheets of blinding electricity. Then the tempest leapt and roared like an army of demons suddenly loosened for work of devastation and terror. The animal plunged forward, snorting in the very madness of fear. The reins started from the driver's hold, then his hat and whip flew off with the shrieking winds.

"Ho! ho!" The echo of his own laughter—but in perfectly blood-freezing tones—came to the ears of Daddy Delph. "We laugh at the cruel gallows! Ho! ho! We defy the very elements! We defy even death itself!"

"The Spectre of the Heath!—the Phantom Horseman!" gasped Delph, in a voice dry and hoarse with supernatural horror. Then his tongue forgot its use, the short-cropped hair of the man's head rose up straight, his eyeballs seemed about to burst, and his jaw dropped. There, by his side—as a blue mist or light—moved the apparition of a rider and steed—moved, or floated, for the hooves of the ghostly animal gave out no sound. The horseman was hatless, and about his neck depended a hangman's rope. On his breast were vivid stains of red, as if from mortal wound. The garb of rider and trappings of horse were of the day, and, except in colours, were of most exquisite form. The expression on the visage of the spectre was that of utter, hopeless woe; and the lips moved, as if eager to mutter words that were forbidden its utterances.

The driver felt his conveyance flying on the wind as the affrighted steed madly tore on, yet the Spectral Horseman still kept abreast. Then came still more terrible roaring of thunder and flashes of the broad electrical darts. The whole landscape was revealed again, even the eyes of the startled, careering night birds could be distinctly seen.

On the path ahead, but fifty paces off, a troop of mounted men came thundering on. In a few moments they must collide with the vehicle bearing the stolen body, and come face-to-face with Daddy Delph, the chief gibbet-robber.

The Spectre of Hounslow Heath had vanished.

Then there burst overhead a still more appalling crash of thunder, accompanied with still more blinding flashes of lightning; a rending hissing followed the mightier sounds. A great oak fell clear across the pathway, its timbers riven by the dazzling fluid, and set ablaze. The fiery barrier interposed between the onrushing horsemen and the gibbet-robber. Suddenly the pale-blue spectral rider and steed reappeared, this time in the very centre of the flaming, fallen giant oak.

"Ho! ho! We laugh at the cruel gallows! We defy the very elements!" cried the deep, sepulchral tones. "We defy even death itself!"

The pale-blue spectral rider reappeared to Daddy Delph, this time in the centre of the flaming oak. (See next week's number.)

A STARTLING SURPRISE—THE BROAD ROAD THAT LEADS TO RUIN—THE LOVE OF A TRUE-HEARTED MAIDEN—"MY POOR, PERSECUTED DARLING!"—THE CHALLENGE—THE MIDNIGHT DUEL IN THE SNOW—A DOUBLE CRIME NEAR ACCOMPLISHMENT—FOILED!—THE HIGHWAYMEN AND THE COACH ROBBERY THAT WAS NO ROBBERY AFTER ALL.

On hearing the shrieks, and seeing the fair throats from which they came, the first instinct of Dick the Dandy was to tilt his hat—his mask was attached to this—fact he had overlooked—and consequently his face became fully revealed to the occupants of the coach. The elderly lady, on catching a full view of the youthful highwayman's visage, uttered a still more piercing cry of horror, and then instantly fell into a deep swoon.

"Dick!" gasped the elderly gentleman, his florid complexion changing to that of the hue of death, "has it really come to this, lad? I had learned the painful fact that you had entered on the broad road that leads to ruin; but, merciful heavens! you should have checked the pace before descending to the wretched level of a common robber!" And there were distinct signs of tears in the old man's eyes as he uttered the latter words.

"Dick! Dick! my poor, persecuted darling! I will never—never believe that you forged the name of my dear dad to those papers! You could not have done that base thing—"

"Silence, Maude! Not a word more! I forbid it!" sternly admonished the old gentleman, whose emotion was now most painful to witness. The young girl was his only child, and once the promised wife of the youth now actually discovered enacting the part of an outlaw—a thief on the King's Highway! Maude Mortiemor was of the dainty age of "sweet seventeen," fair as a lily, perfect of mould, and of that grace and charm of mind which is infinitely rarer than external beauty, and far more to be valued.

"Dick," continued the old man solemnly, "you well know the law of the land as applied to the crime of forgery. It is the death penalty—no matter the gain, be it a million or even so low as a farthing—the degrading death of the public gallows!"

"Sir Edgar Mortiemor—Miss Mortiemor—uncle—Maude," commenced Dick the Dandy, in a perfect frenzy of grief, "I swear to you both that I never—"

"No more of this, Sir Cutpurse!" thundered the younger male inmate of the vehicle. "Animals, we know, are always innocent—poor, persecuted doves! You are no forger. Of course not. You and your fellow-outlaws are not actually desperate, bloodthirsty ruffians! And this is simply a pleasant piece of masquerading, especially got up for our amusement! Ha, ha, ha!"

Colonel Blood exchanged his firearm for rapier, and the latter's point rattled against the clenched teeth of the last speaker. "Cease the insulting waggings of that glib tongue, or I'll split into ribbons!" he hissed, and his face looks fully backed up his words.

"I'm no coward! There are two of you—my uncle is past fighting; but, give me fair play, and I'll measure blades with either of you, though I demean myself by condescending to treat mere footpaths as gentlemen!" was the retort to Colonel Blood's threat.

"It is to that reptile that I owe all my misfortune!" cried Dick the Dandy, springing from the saddle. "Let me try my cause at the steel's point. I will confess myself a degraded cur if my fine gentleman of a cousin can prove me one!"

"Dick, for my sake, refrain! Is it not enough that I am not against you?" hysterically cried the lovely girl—Maude Mortiemor—frantically wringing her hands, and turning her expressive orbs beseechingly towards the window near which Dick the Dandy still stood. Sir Edgar Mortiemor was applying smelling-salts to the nostrils of his insensible wife, and before he could utter a protest his male companion had flung open the coach-door and sprang out.

At this moment Colonel Blood detected the coach-driver in the act of making off. The former secured the latter in half a dozen swift bounds, and then proceeded to firmly bind him with the long reins to a front wheel.

Dick the Dandy had replaced his pistol in its holster by the saddle before dismounting. He now drew his elegantly bejewelled-hilted rapier, and placed himself on guard as his cousin sprang to the attack.

"Contemptible schemer, liar, rogue, and perjurer!" muttered the youthful outlaw. "If Justice slept less, we should have changed places ere this!"

"This to thy heart, felon!" savagely snarled the other, making a most impetuous lunge full at the breast of Dick the Dandy.

The highwayman was a past-master at the art of fencing. He nimbly stepped aside, and then crashed his flashing blade against the other with terrific force, and sped it down until both hilts struck. This trick was so cleverly executed, and so utterly unprepared for on the part of the highwayman's adversary, that his rapier was instantly shot from his clutch and sent flying with a loud metallic ring some yards away.

"Strike. I am at your mercy!" cried the defeated man, throwing down the pistol he had snatched from his pocket, the flint being absent from the lock.

"Raymond Raithwood, traitor as you are, I yet grant you another chance for my life!" replied Dick the Dandy, refraining from running the other through the body as the laws of duelling permitted him to do. Venting most bitter, if subdued, curses, the young man flew after his snow-embedded steel.

A slight, graceful form, clad in pale-pink satin, and with a natural mantle of streaming, golden, fleece-like locks down its back, flew from the open door of the coach, darted lightly as a young fawn over the crystallised snow, and then threw tender, love-clinging arms about the neck of Dick the Dandy.

"Raymond dare not harm you, love!" cried a voice of most thrilling music, as an exquisitely angelic face looked up into his own.

"Leave him to me, Maude dearest," replied her outlaw lover. "I have no fear on his account!"

"Dick, my darling, I will shield you from all peril with my devotion—my life!"

"Nay, nay—though it breaks my heart, dearest Maude, to say the words—we must be but as strangers until I prove that I am not the ingrate that Raymond Raithwood pictures me to be!" mournfully replied the youth.

"Come back to us, love! Trust to our power and wealth to establish your innocence!"

The highwayman gently released himself from the sweet contact of the pure maiden devotion. Enthralling though this meeting was, his heart told him that it was not rightly for such as he—an outcast, a proscribed[16] felon with a price upon his head, the hangman's rope awaiting his neck!

The sinister Raymond Raithwood had snatched up his rapier and dashed back to his former position, madly eager to claim another opportunity to pierce the heart of his rival in the affection of the being whom he loved far beyond all creatures on earth. When he beheld the exquisite form of Maude Mortiemor locked in the arms of Dick the Dandy, her small, shapely head, with its wealth of golden curls, billowed upon the broad breast of the handsome highwayman, the thick-skinned-sinister, looking youth foamed at the lips with utmost spleen, and the audible gnashing of his long, white, gleaming teeth grated harshly upon the midnight, wintry air. The richly-dressed but uncomely youth glared like a panther held at bay as he silently stood and contemplated that embrace, so eloquent of fond, truthful, womanly love.

"Divinely beautiful but foolish jade![17] Of what avail my ceaseless plottings? The more her lover is persecuted, the firmer she will cling to him. My jealous anger chokes me! Curse them! If I cannot hope to gain her love, I can at least gratify my hate!"

With such passion-impelling thoughts firing his evil mind, Raymond Raithwood madly clutched his steel, levelled its sharp, glinting point full for the spot in the slender back where he knew it would find the life-throbbing heart of the young girl, and, piercing that, enter the one so closely beating in perfect loving union with it. A frightful cry of pent-up rage burst through his clenched, grating teeth, then he frantically thrust his weapon, as he hoped, fatally home.

Colonel Blood had no sooner secured the coach-driver to the wheel that his thoughts and activities were for his friend. The whole of the critical situation was instantly grasped, the colonel's rapier out, its blade grasped, and hilt

---

[16] Outlaw.

[17] A disreputable woman or a flirtatious girl.

brought down with terrific force full upon the knuckles clutching the murderous weapon. A howl of defeated malice and extreme agony escaped the lips of the would-be double murderer.

"Look more carefully to your lives—your own and that fair young maiden's— in future, when this crawling snake in the grass is near!" rang out the powerful tones of Colonel Blood. "A footpad's honour may not be over much to boast of," he added; "but I count mine superior to thine, or I would honour thee with a blood-letting from my own trusty point!"

This was to Raymond Raithwood, who was, however, to busily employed in nursing his greatly-damaged fingers to frame any other reply than half-formed oaths and inarticulate threats. At this juncture, Sir Edgar Mortiemor came from the coach. No one but Colonel Blood and Raithwood had known of the monstrous design on two youthful lives attempted by the latter; and an evil fate prevented the meditated crime from being fully exposed at the critical moment.

"Lady Mortiemor is in a dead faint, and I cannot revive her!" wailed Sir Edgar, ingrate perturbation. "These," he continued, "are all the valuables I have about me, and a good sum of money included. My diamond snuffbox is a much-esteemed heirloom; but I suppose it might be given up! What Raithwood possesses I don't know; and I sincerely trust that you will refrain from robbing the ladies!" The old gentleman had placed all his available property inside his hat, and held this forward.

"Sir Edgar Mortiemor, we had no idea 'twas your coach we were stopping," humbly said Dick the Dandy, adding: "And, for my part, I would prefer to drop dead of want than rob a Mortiemor!"

THE PARTING OF THE OUTLAW AND THE GIRL OF HIS HEART—DICK THE DANDY FILLED WITH GLOOMY FOREBODINGS ON THE BEHALF OF MAUDE MORTIEMOR— HIGHWAYMAN AGAINST HIGHWAYMAN—WIFFLES DEMANDS THE HALF OF NOTHING—THE HAG'S PROPHECY—THE SPECTRE HORSEMEN APPEARS TO DICK THE DANDY.

"Sir Edgar Mortiemor," chimed in Dick's companion, "we crave your pardon for our error—or, I should say, my error, since the whole blames rests with me—and we, in consequence of our blunder, refrain from taking a single article from you, or those with you; and, moreover, I most heartily wish you well rid of this evil-visaged and black-hearted poltroon[18] of a nephew!"

Raymond Raithwood had crept into the conveyance, and now silently glared at the highwaymen. Sir Edgar Mortiemor had seized his daughter, and caused her to re-enter the vehicle. The two latter again attempted the revival of the

---

[18] Coward..

elder female, and Sir Edgar Mortiemor was evidently so utterly annoyed by the startling refusal of the highwaymen to profit by their opportunity of gaining a rich harvest that he had, for the time being, quite lost the power of speech.

Colonel Blood released the driver, and ordered him to climb to his box and drive off. At this point the distant sound of approaching hoofs warned the outlaws that they had better be going.

"We must mount and away, comrade!" he whispered. "Methinks the frosty air now reeks of the near scent of the famishing wolves who hunt men in the name of the law, and his favourite meat is the heart of a felon!"

Dick the Dandy leapt into the saddle, rode up to the coach-window, and, humbly lifting his hat to Sir Edgar and his sobbing daughter, then put spurs to his animal, and rode away by the side of his firm friend, Colonel Blood.

When the latter had fully made known to his young friend the intended murder of himself and Maude Mortiemor by the one thrust of a sword-blade, Dick the Dandy was overwhelmed with rage and alarm. His previously-excited condition had prevented him giving full heed to the warning words uttered by the colonel, and now that their full import had come to him his mind was filled with deepest concern for the gentle, trusting Maude, whom he felt convinced would now be daily persecuted, threatened, and plotted against by the gentlemanly scoundrel, Raymond Raithwood. As for the great service he had rendered by his timely intervention, Colonel Blood made light of the matter, and jestingly turned it off in a manner common to him.

"I am extremely loath to leave the dear girl thus, and would have preferred to have secretly followed until she had reached her destination!" moodily remarked Dick, as he swiftly rode on by the colonel's side. His companion made no answer, some dim object ahead, in the moonless gloom, having suddenly arrested his attention.

"Hoof sounds in another direction, and evidently coming this way. We must be keen on guard!" he murmured.

The words had scarcely left his lips before a mounted man smartly rode forward. He was masked, enveloped in a long black cloak, and held a pistol presented at them, the weapon being at full cock.

"Hang you, there! Pull up! Don't you attempt to touch your pop guns, or I'll riddle the pair o' you!" hailed a shrill, piping voice. "What do yer mean by a-taking the bread out o' me mouth—as the oven sed to the baker?"

"That voice!" laughingly shouted Colonel Blood; "why, I should know it if I were in my grave! It's you, Wiffles!"

"Yus, me's me, right 'nuff!" was the reply. "But who the blazes is you—as the sweep sed when 'e fell down the flue on to the fire?"

"Colonel Blood!" retorted the person known by that title, unmasking, his companion instantly following the example.

"Oh, oh, I twigs the mugs o' the pair o' ye! an' I'm special glad to see yer—special glad—as the blind man pointedly remarked to the doctor what restored 'is eyesight! But I say, Curnill Bleed—hexcuse me, but bleed is the much more politer vord for blood—I say, vhat was you an' 'Andsome Dick a-doing with that four-wheel crawler? I was jist on the wery point of 'tacking it meself, ter see if it contain'd anything waluable, when up comes two wery keen-nosed foxes an' a-nobbles me pretty bit o' game, vich the sed keen-nosed-'uns is yer respect'd selves. It's really too bad, as the old gent observ'd vhen he was compall'd ter run all over the floor with a spoon ter match every mite o' 'is penn'orth o' cheeses!" The speaker had at once put his pistol in its holster on recognising the unmasked faces, and his mood had become a very merry one.

"So, friend Wiffles, you intended holding up that coach, did you?" banteringly said Colonel Blood, winking at Dick.

"'Olding it up?" repeated Wiffles. "Well, rather!" he continued dryly. "I do assure you, pals, as I meant a-'olding it up as 'igh as whatsomever possibill—as was the misfortunate cat's intenshun whin she'd been an' gorn an' set 'er tail on fire!"

"I'm not sorry that we upset your plan, Wiffles, as that conveyance happened to contain personal friends of mine!" remarked Dick the Dandy, greatly rejoiced that their blunder had providentially been the means of averting a serious experience for the girl he loved.

"Ho, ho! he, he! 'Andsome Dick must 'ave 'is little joke, in course. All the same, me nobbly midnight toll-collectors, you vill respect our rules, one o' vich is that them as takes a job out o' another 'onest pal's 'ands dubs down 'alf o' the booty!"

"Quite correct. We took nothing at all. You are justly entitled to the half of that. How will you take it—in notes, gold, or kind?" jestingly said the colonel.

"I won't take it in chaff, 'cause that's a unkind kind of kind!" paradoxically replied Wiffles, who, however, was quite satisfied when an outline of the truth of the coach incident was given him. "In course," he finally agreed, "it 'ud be a sert o' goin' agin one's own family connections, as ther night-watchman argued privately vhen 'e thort o' taking 'is own self ter the lock-up for a-being in a bad state o' too much licker."

Dick the Dandy was in no mood for laughter, or he would have joined Colonel Blood in his outburst occasioned by the quaint sayings of the ever-amusing Wiffles.

"What caused you to take this direction to-night, Wiffles?" asked Dick of the latter.

"Same reason as is a-causing us all night-birds to flock to one spot—the 'Aunted Manor o' Finchley!" promptly answered the young wag.

"We have a great object in view, comrades," said the colonel. "I think there ever was, and ever will be, a reason for a word or two on behalf of the lawbreaker. It is possible to go too far even in dealing with the outcasts of society. There is no known crime that our chief persecutor, Jonathan Wild, has not committed. It is well-known, even to the creatures of King George's Government, who employ Jonathan Wild, that the great Government spy is himself the very king of criminals. The wretch's system is to manufacture crimes and criminals that he may lay claim to having discovered the first, and afterwards punished the latter. On the immoral principle of set a thief to catch a thief, Wild's infamies are always winked at. Posing as chief secret crime-investigator of the London authorities, he holds full licence to plan and carry out his devilish work almost openly. Our meeting together at our secret retreat is for the object of forming a combined attack against Jonathan Wild and the whole of his forces, the latter, be it known, being the very sweepings of the lowest dregs of criminality. The grim gallows yawns for every one of them, and the mere lifting of the finger of their tyrant would consign each of his followers to the most awful form of capital punishment—that of hanging, dragging at the cart's tail, and the quartering of the body in the felon shambles of Smithfield!"[19]

"Death to my arch-enemy Jonathan Wild!" cried Dick the Dandy, his eyes flashing.

A weird, gaunt, black-draped figure silently darted from the surrounding gloom. It was that of an aged and wrinkled woman. Fiercely brandishing a stick, she cried in shrill, piercing tones: "Who speaks of death and Jonathan Wild? Death is an angel of pity! Wild is the ravening wolf, whose heart is of stone! List to the prophecy:

"Should one the dreaded Spectre Horsemen see,

When he hath appear'd of times three and three,

Your doom you shall meet on gallows tree!

"Ha, ha, ha!" the old hag shrieked, as if in very fiendish glee, "ask Jonathan Wild how oft hath the pale spectral vision warned him of his fitting end?" With these strange words the midnight witch disappeared as suddenly as she had came.

"See—colonel—friend—look at that unearthful thing! Merciful Father in Heaven, 'tis the Spectre Rider and his ghostly steed!" Dick the Dandy was pointing towards a blacker patch in the sable landscape, his eyes were distended and fixed, and his whole manner exhibiting the effects of superstitious horror.

"Mortal or demon, here's at thee!" shouted Colonel Blood, drawing his rapier, sticking his spurs deep into his trembling steed's flanks, and plunging forward towards the awful apparition.

---

[19] The Elms at Smithfield was London's oldest execution site. Situated just outside the city walls, criminals were beheaded, hanged or burned at the stake. Notable executions include William Wallace of Scotland. In addition, some 300 Protestants were executed for their faith during the reign of Mary I between 1555 and 1558.

°THE FAMOUS HOLE IN THE WALL OF HIGHWAYMEN REPUTE—RALPH DRAKE AND HIS BEAUTIFUL WIFE—THE FIRE-EATING BOW STREET RUNNER, OFFICER BILBERRY—IN SEARCH OF DICK THE DANDY.

"ONE HUNDRED POUNDS REWARD!

"By Royal Proclamation of King George of England!

"This is to give notice that the above reward will be granted for the capture, dead or alive, of the notorious footpad known as Dick the Dandy, the said outlawed mail-coach robber and depredator in general having perpetrated many felonious acts at divers times and places. The sum of One Hundred Pounds will be paid by his Most Gracious Majesty's Government to any person, or persons, who may give information leading to the arrest, dead or alive, of the before-mentioned highwayman, Dick the Dandy. And a free pardon will be granted to an accomplice on the said accomplice turning King's evidence and finishing particulars leading to the capture, dead or alive, of the afore-mentioned outlaw.

"Information should be lodged with the Chief Commissioner of Police at Bow Street.

"GOD SAVE THE KING!"

The document containing this legend was fixed on the wall of the bar-parlour of the Hole in the Wall, the well-known hostelry situated near the famous Hatton House of Hatton Gardens.

These two buildings are still in existence, although they have been, time after time, much renovated. In the days of the Georges the Gardens of Hatton consisted of a very limited space of farmlands in the centre of perfectly wild, uncultivated, and practically uninhabited tracts of country.

"E'cod! Man Alive! Blood an' hounds! S'death!" muttered the voice of a man who stood reading the particulars of the "Hue-and-Cry" sheet.

A square-shouldered, broad-made, round-stomached figure was that of this personage, and his dress that of a Bow Street runner—three-cornered hat, long, red waistcoat, wide-skirted coat, close-fitting nankeens,[20] or smalls, and high jack-boots, with heavy, sharp spurs attached. The red waistcoat and facings of the same colour of the coat were the origin of the terms commonly applied to these men—namely, Robin-redbreasts and Scarlet-runners, or, rather, two of the general terms, for these were almost endless in variety.

"Stew me down to a mere jelly! Flame me alive! So my neat and nimble high-toby,[21] filch-purse, rood-rake, Toll-taker an' all the rest of it, our worthy King means nabbing your highwaymanship at last. And pretty nearly time, too, my

---

° Part 3. Vol. XIV.—No. 339. 2 May 1900.

[20] Yellow cotton cloth, normally used for trousers.

[21] Toby man – highwayman.

gallant Dick the Dandy, when our nobility, gentry, or even commercials dare not venture beyond their doors after dark—nay, in open daylight, forsooth; or at all, in fact—for fear of your Dicks the Dandies in general, an' this prime Dandy in particular. A nice state of affairs truly. May I be pounded into mincemeat. A most delightful condition of things. London at the present time is simply divided into three parties—honest folk, robbers, and Bow Street runners."

"I'm pleased to hear that you don't include the Bow Street Robins in the same category as honest folk," put in a voice from behind the bar.

The officer turned from the contemplation of the Royal proclamation, his face thus becoming visible. This was by no means the good letter of recommendation a fine countenance is said always to be. Officer Bilberry's visage was full, fat, and of the rich colour and varnished-like gloss of a freshly dressed German sausage, and its hue became even more flaring under the anger aroused by the caustic remarks applied to him.

"Look ye, Ralph Drake," jerked the officer, "if your punch was not so choice of brew, and the comely hostess, your wife, so extremely charming and attentive, may I be hanged, drawn at a cart's tail, and then quartered—as most likely will be Dick the Dandy after he is nabbed—if I would ever enter your confounded dram-shop again, there!"

"And a vast deal we should lose by your non-patronage. Why, the Hole in the Wall would be gallons to the good, and its proprietor pounds in pocket, Officer Bilberry, if you had never honoured us with your presence, for you never pay for anything, and would go on in the same way until you'd consumed all on the premises, if I or my wife would continue to serve you!" savagely retorted the proprietor.

"Tush! tush, man! us Bow Street runners are all famous swash-bucklers, an' have the privilege of quartering ourselves upon innkeepers when we are on thief-catching intent!" was the impudent reply of the swaggering official.

"You runners levy toll on us poor public caterers instead of the stranger on the highway. Is that all the difference between thief and thief-catcher? Is it scratch a Bow Street officer and find a highwayman?" sneeringly asked Ralph Drake.

"May I be devoured by performing street-bears, sir, if this isn't getting beyond a joke!" blurted out Officer Bilberry, swelling out with such excessive rage and indignation that his waistcoat buttons commenced to shoot off with the sudden strain put upon them.

"Then suppose you end the matter by paying the reckoning like a man, Bilberry," coolly suggested the innkeeper.

"You can crane your neck over the bar there, looking out for settlement, until it is as long as—" blustered out the officer, when the other interrupted him with:

"Your confounded bill! No, thank you, Mr. Bilberry. No doubt I shall see your red, fat neck lengthened on the hangman's cart in front of Old Newgate before the score you have stuck up here gets shortened!"

"What—by the—of all that—by the infernal furies, Drake, I—"

At this moment the door opened, and a most singularly-beautiful and matchlessly-formed young woman entered the bar space. Her eyes were full, roguish, and black as sloes, and thick masses of jet-black ringlets fell about her shoulders. Like magic the manner of the Bow Street officer instantly changed as the female greeted him with a most bewitching smile, and in which act she displayed two rows of most pearly-white, perfect teeth.

"E'cod! Gad's hooks an' zounds! Concentrated essence of sweetness! It is warm sunshine after death-freezing ice; sweetest honey after bitterest of bitter sloes! Your surly bear of a husband and I, dear Madam, were on the very point of demanding ample samples of each other's gore. Ah! but your bewitching presence appeared in the very nick of time, mayhap to prevent much fearful carnage. Your fascinating smile, madam, would calm the most tempestuous storm that ever raged; subdue the fiercest of raging lions, in fact!"—bowing to the floor as he spoke.

"Do anything under the sun except induce you to pay your score!" put in Ralph Drake. "Your flattering words may find favour in a young woman's ears, Bilberry; but men heed fair words less than fair actions," he added, for the innkeeper was not apt to relish too marked expressions of admiration for his attractive spouse.

"See here, my most amiable madam!" the officer cried as he took out a well-filled, not-worked purse of the period and held it up—! "See here, now! I will give your husband the lie to the teeth, for I will do far more than pay my score; I will even make the fortune of the most beautiful and agreeable creature on earth, and her sour-tempered and churlish husband, if you will—and I know he can—give me information enabling me to nab the fellow Dick the Dandy—there, madam!"

A most silvery peal of laughter came from the cherry-red lips of the hostess, and her great, dark eyes brightened up, as if suddenly charged with electricity, while her thick, long, raven tresses shook with her keen fit of merriment.

"I tell you, Officer Bilberry, that I will see you hanged first!" cried Ralph Drake, in great heat; adding: "I am an honest man, not a Government spy and informer!"

"But, Ralph dear, I tell you that asked good friend here shall have his wish granted him," chimed the rich, musical voice of the innkeeper's wife. "It is not often that I go against your wishes, husband," she smilingly continued; "but, as our good friend here has so set his heart upon the capture of this terrible highwayman, why should we not do all we can to aid him in his good intent?"

"Hush! You must be mad!" cried the host, turning pale as death, and looking into his wife's face with strangely scared and apprehensive glances.

"Ralph fears the law concerning harbouring and abetting," calmly explained Mrs. Drake. "Suppose now that we induced this notorious character, called Dick the Dandy, to visit this inn while you are concealed on the premises?"

"There is no harbouring or abetting if the ruffian is induced to come to this place so that the law may take its course, my most charming, lovely, and sprightly Mrs. Drake!" responded the Bow Street runner.

"What do you offer if my husband succeeds in bringing this highwayman and the brave and gallant officer face-to-face?"

"Half the reward, my sweetly-divine creature!" eagerly responded Bilberry; adding: "Of course, I mean after I have duly received the same."

Still Ralph Drake protested that the thing should not—could not be done.

"Excuse us leaving you for a few moments," smilingly begged the wife, gently forcing her husband into the room beyond the bar.

In a few moments the host returned, looking greatly concerned.

"Lucy insists on my going to a certain place where she thinks it is likely I may learn of this Dick the Dandy's whereabouts," he explained. "But, understand this, I must not be spied on," he continued. "Will you consent to be locked in the little smoking-room at the back of the premises? On such condition only when I go. You can be released when I return, which will not be later than half an hour from this."

"I see no harm in that arrangement," eagerly assented Bilberry; adding: "You will, of course, not refuse me a bowl of hot punch to keep me company during your absence?"

This was agreed to. In ten minutes a steaming vessel of the liquid was taken in by Drake himself, who opened the window of the room as the day was warm; then he loudly turned the key in the lock on the outside, was next heard explaining to his wife the moment he expected to return, then his footsteps could be heard as he departed on his mission.

The Bow Street officer was fully under the impression that Drake and his wife had been induced to attempt the betrayal of the notorious outlaw by a promise of half the reward, which he would take good care they should never get. He laughed softly to himself, until his fat body shook like a huge jelly. He had taken them in so cleverly, he fondly concluded. The fools could obtain the whole sum offered simply by giving the information at Bow Street.

The crafty officer took out his two great flint-lock horse pistols, saw to their primings, and then placed them on the deal table[22] by the punch bowl; then he tried his hanger, or cutlass, to make sure that it did not catch in the sheath.

The old-fashioned clock standing in a tall case in a corner of this little chamber kicked off the first ten minutes. The bloated, pimply, boiled-lobster-hued visage was buried deep in the punch basin, when the laugh of anticipated triumph again suddenly took Bilberry.

As he put down the vessel, he was fairly choking with glee and punch. The latter had gone down the wrong way; the former was about to quickly follow suit.

A deep shadow came between the daylight streaming in at the open window within two feet of the Bow Street officer, and the latter suspiciously glanced up.

---

[22] A table made of deal, a type of wood.

A Mysterious Dick the Dandy—Are there Two?— Bilberry Cleared Out—The Terrible Tail Told by the Bow Street Runner—The Stranger with the "Churchwarden"—The Question-Officer Bilberry Meets with an Amazing Surprise.

A flashing pair of dark eyes looking through a mask contemplated him. At the open window, and, as it were, framed in its space, where the head and shoulders of a young fellow wearing a roguish-looking hat, the same being ornamented with much gold lace, and feather-edged; full flowing auburn curls came down each side of the long crape mask, and that portion of the face that could be seen betokened an unusual clearness of skin and refined formation of features. As elegantly-chased pistol-but was held in a gloved hand, this barrel levelled straight at and within a few inches of Bilberry's temples.

"Dick the Dandy pays his most polite respects to the great fire-eater of Bow Street, and begs, as a return honour, that Officer Bilberry will at once and without palaver hand up whatever valuables he happens to have stowed among his many capacious pockets!"

Thus was the dumbfounded officer cheerily greeted by the personage standing beyond the open window, the self-declared Dick the Dandy, the terrible highwayman and footpad, for whom King George's ministers were willing— nay, eager, to pay down the sum of one hundred pounds!

"Man alive! Blue blazes! Blood an'—" commenced the Bow Street officer.

"Cease, you windbag! vainglorious braggart! animated bladder of swipes! Hand up the swag, or I'll scatter your much bemuddled brains upon the wall beyond you!" There could be no mistaking the determined tones, or the deadly aim of that steady tube; but, as a mere make-believe, the officer placed his hand upon one of his firearms.

"Drop your ugly-looking barker, or I'll instantly drop its owner!"

The blustering, swaggering bully was a great coward at heart, as all bullies are. He instantly withdrew his hand from the weapon, then a blue tinge crept over into his over ripe complexion, his jaw dropped, and huge frame trembled like a leaf.

"N-a-m-e—w-h-a-t—y-o-u—w-w-w-an-t?" he spluttered despairingly.

"Your watch and chain, purse, snuffbox, rings of your pork-sausage fingers, pistols, hanger, official staff, and all other articles about you worth my acceptance!" was the pitiless reply. The click of the trigger of the levelled tube warned Officer Bilberry that his life probably depended on his promptly complying with the daring freebooter's demands. Ralph Drake had not returned from his supposed quest after this very outlaw. To call Mrs. Drake would be worse than useless, and the chance of visitors to the inn was a remote one. The state of terror of the bullying Bow Street officer became complete. His watch and chain, rings, then purse were shakily handed up and placed upon the broad window-sill. Next Bilberry moved a trembling hand towards one of his pistols.

"One treacherous move and it shall be your last on this side of the grave!" hissed the voice at the window. "Remember," it went on, "I well know how you hunger after the price set upon my head. A touch of my willing finger, and there will be one bloodhound the less on my track in the future!"

"May I burn in Smithfield for a heretic if I ever seek you again after this most agreeable m-meeting!" chattered the officer. "My dear friend, pray take all—all I possessed in the world, but leave, oh, l-e-a-v-e me m-my poor life!"

"Poor, indeed! Take the flints from the pistol-locks, thus. Now place all your arms on this sill. Quick, man!" cried the robber in utmost fierceness and impatience. "Now turn out every pocket, you perambulating brewery!"

Instantly Bilberry did as ordered, with the result that a handful of silver and a dagger-knife came into view. His remorseless assailant then took each article from the window-sill with his left hand, never once moving his blazing orbs or lowering the levelled weapon until the exchange of property was completed.

"'Sdeath! blue blazes! blood an' hounds! gad's hooks[23] an' zounds, sirrah, if you dare venture your ugly head out of this window, one of my comrades here concealed shall without compunction blow your soft and worthless skull to the four winds!"

These were the desperate outlaw's last words before he vanished.

Utterly collapsed by fear-panic, the "toll-payer to a footpad" remained for some minutes, his most ample double chin burried in his would-be foppish, cravat frills, a prey to the most brain-distracting perplexity and doom.

He had seen the young, and popularly held, romantic-looking, and exceedingly handsome Dandy foot pad, highwayman, and recklessly daring adventurer all in one. Officer Bilberry had freely openly boasted of what he would do once he dropped eyes on Dick the Dandy. Alas! it is the unexpected that mostly happens.

"Actually repeated my own favourite, high-class society elegant oaths, too!" dismally moaned the completely skinned-out officer. "Cursed me in my own fine-sounding terms, in addition to sneaking all my valuable belongings!"

Then he reflected deeply for some moments more. Suddenly he struck his fist down upon the table. "Ecod! man alive! Blood an' hounds! 'Sdeath May I be flogged while tied up to a tree, an' then left there until stung to death by wasps, if I haven't seen those eyes, those teeth before, and heard those tones, too! Dick the Dandy I have never met in my life! Whom then is this cool, daring, masked devil that has so cleverly nobbled me?" An echo answered "Whom?"

The key turned in the door, it was opened, and Mrs. Drake stepped inside. "Ralph has not yet returned. I'm afraid he has failed in gleaning any information of this Dick the Dandy," she remarked. "I'm sure you will be terribly disappointed if you miss the opportunity of arresting that monster of wickedness!"

---

[23] Possible derived from "God's hooks" referring to the nails of the crucifixion.

Bilberry looked up. A stranger, holding a pipe and earthenware mug, stood behind the hostess. "Is there any objection to my entering the smoke-room, marm?" the latter asked.

The Bow Street officer took upon himself to reply. "Come inside, man. Drink your beer, and smoke a pipe in peace, you're welcome."

"Thanks, good sir." The new-comer presented somewhat the appearance of a farm-labourer. He wore a slouched hat, the lower part of his face was muffled up, and a great overcoat covered his form, being fully buttoned up, and reaching quite to his heels.

Bilberry's close examination of the stranger was satisfactory to himself, and thereupon loosened his tongue, the former quietly and gravely smoking his long "churchwarden clay,"[24] and occasionally taking refreshing draughts of the contents of the large mug.

"Monster of wickedness! Multiply that sum total by millions, and then add up with unlimited quantities of brimstone! By the—I beg your pardon, my lovely siren, but surely it is not possible that you don't know?"

"Pray, what has happened, my dear, good Mr. Bilberry? For that something unusual has happened your expressive countenance assures me beyond a doubt!" burst forth Mrs. Drake.

"Where have you been during the whole time of your husband's absence, madam?" asked the officer.

"I was over at the brew-shed across the fields. No one was in the bar, and I was anxious that the brewing should not go wrong during Ralph's absence," was the instant and apparently honest reply.

"Then, of course, you would not observe anyone enter the place, nor would you hear voices, however loud?"

"No, indeed, good sir; but I had no fear of unwelcome intruders, well-knowing the great courage and gallantry of Officer Bilberry, although in very truth he did happen to be locked in a room. Said I to myself, the doughty representative of the law, the fearless Bow Street officer, will start up as a roaring lion should any dishonest churl dare venture into the place for if love laughs at locksmiths, how much more so will laugh that terribly-courageous enemy of all those of evil intent!"

Officer Bilberry rose from his seat, and, placing his broad red paw upon the region where he imagined his heart to be, bowed so lowly that there was some fear of his bottle-shaped nose losing itself in the sawdust spread on the floor.

"Incomparable woman," he commenced; "your words go home to my heart of hearts. But how little were you aware of my fearful peril while you were all soul intent on more brewing!"

---

[24] A smoking pipe with a long stem.

"Lud, lud, sir, whatever could have happened? Pray explain, my dear Mr. Bilberry!" flutteringly implored the beautiful hostess, unconsciously creating fearful havoc upon the susceptible feelings of the Bow Street runner by the expressive glances of deep concern in her lovely eyes.

"I will explain, divinest of thy sex!" commenced Bilberry, assuming an expression and posture of heroic fearlessness. "Ralph Drake had not left his premises five minutes before I was suddenly assailed by a great band of ferocious marauders. The varlets must have lain in concealment until seeing both host and hostess depart, then entered the coach-gates, and crept down the side passage leading to this window here, madam. That is to say, some twenty odd took up a position outside that window, while a matter of thirty or more suddenly unlocked the door of this apartment and flew to the attack, levelling their loaded pieces at my head, and aiming their wholesale-assassination-knives at my breast!"

"Oh, this is too terrible! What a providential thing that you still live to tell the harrowing story!" wailed Mrs. Drake, her eyes running in tears. "But what have you done with the slain? and where placed your prisoners?" she added, "for I can well imagine the fiercely impetuous onslaught you made upon them, undismayed as you would be by mere numbers!"

"Sweet lady," answered Bilberry, "before I could do more than lay open most of the varlets' jowls with my trusty hanger, I was seized, overpowered, and stripped of every article of value about me! E'cod! man alive! blood an' hounds! S'death! stew me into a jelly! but what would I not have given to have had a man-to-man, toe-to-toe, face-to-face encounter with that cowardly, pettilogging,[25] tuppenny-'apenny[26] fop styled Dick the Dandy! He, forsooth! the Terror of the Heath! The King of Highwayment! the Monarch of the Moonlighters! the Fearless Footpad! For, hark ye, madam, these are a few of the pretty terms commonly given to the beardless boy, Dick the Fop!"

"Excuse me, sir," said the stranger, slowly laying down his "churchwarden," and looking into his mug as if to make sure none of its choice contents remained. "Did I understand you to say that Dick the Dandy was one of the number of those attacking you in this very room but a brief while since?"

"May I be poisoned by toadstools if I see that the question greatly concerns thee, youkel, clodpole[27] an' commonest of swipe consumers!" growled the Bow Street runner, seeing as he fondly believed a fine opportunity for the full display of his usual very cheap bravado.

The stranger slowly rose up, and his actions, then became quicker than thought. The overcoat was off, next the muffler, the slouched hat also, then

---

[25] Trivial.
[26] Cheap.
[27] A clumsy or awkward person.

thickly-clustering, nut-brown ringlets fell beside the half-unmasked face of a youth of most graceful and striking personality. A bejewelled-hilted rapier hung at his side, and to exquisitely-formed firearms were seen thrust in his belt. The underdress of this personage now appeared rich and costly in the extreme. A light, defiant smile lit up his handsome face as his fearless tones rang out with the startling words: "I am Dick the Dandy! Take me if you dare!"

°THE BLACK BARNS AT FINCHLEY—DADDY DELPH AND NAT FLINT—"THE EVIL OLD MAN OF BLACK"—THE WEIRD AND HORRIBLE INTERIOR OF THE HOME OF DADDY DELPH—THE GIBBET ROBBERS AND THEIR DREAD SECRET.

It is now necessary that we go back a brief period—namely, to the evening following the incidents enacted on Hounslow Heath on the night of the great tempest.

Standing alone, in the wild and deserted wastelands of Finchley, was a tumbledown-looking building of very great age and most peculiar shape. It was completely formed of wood, and more resembled a collection of great old sheds than a house, and had many most quaint-looking frontages and gables. Carelessly grouped, and almost surrounding the whole building or buildings, were a number of slabs of stone in various stages of formation, and each intended to join that ever increasing and gruesome army of "the white and silent sentinels that ever guard the dead." The whole of the direction had been painted the one depressing the colour of black.

Weird, blood-curdling, unearthly shrieks and ghostlike moaning were heard, and spectral forms and uncanny lights seen many a time at midnight by belated wayfarers.

Daddy Delph was the owner of the Black Barns, as the shed-like buildings were termed. Delph gave himself out to be the Sexton to Finchley Church, and local undertaker.

The ignorant and superstitious peasantry of the surrounding country held the strange old man in utmost dread. He lived, ate, and slept continually surrounded by horrid, unearthly, ghoulish companions, and it was firmly believed that he held incantations (charms) of supernatural powers, and was actually in league with the Prince of Evil himself.

Daddy Delph had frequently been openly accused of witchcraft, or sorcery, the accuser is complaining of blight in their crops and pestilence among their cattle, all due to "the evil old man of the Black Barns." Those making such charges were invariably so terribly afflicted in endless mysterious ways afterwards that they in very dread soon ceased to complain, or openly hint at the bewitchery; and thus, if the charges grew less frequent, the evil reputation greatly increased.

° Part 4. Vol. XIV.—No. 340. 15 May 1900.

The scene is that of the interior of Delph's office, his one solitary companion is Nat Flint, and the strange old man is conversing with the former in his usual bantering and ironical vein.

"Ho, ho! He, he! Nat Flint, I shall, forsooth, be compelled to alter thy name. Nat Sponge, Nat o' the White Feather, or e'en Nat the Little Chick! Ho, ho! body o' man, no man so little cause to fear the scaffold, yet no man so dreading it! Spectre Horsemen—Witch's Soothsaying—what of these? The Ghost-rider who scared among the ever-amiable Jonathan Wild and his gentle, dove-like crew, at the critical moment when our gibbet-filching was a-going most beautifully wrong and charmingly awry. And thus, Nat o' the Sponge, where we enabled to make clear off."

"Daddy Delph, to finally reach his lively retreat—here amidst the pleasant dead and there interesting remains—defined inside his hearse-cart two deadly dead things: one that we had snatched from the ever-greedy, red-rust maw of the gibbet; the other, one of the actual gibbet-robbers himself. Both in a faint nigh under death itself, if not actually sleeping the long, long sleep. Ecod, but the work I had!

"But at last my new gallows-chicken has cracked its shell of death, and is now hatched into life for the second time. The poor lad's end is duly recorded in that fine fat 'Black Book of Crime' in Newgate. 'Hanged by the neck until dead'—so reads the pretty legend, and the aforesaid hanged-by-the-neck-until-dead is at this present moment peacefully sleeping in a cosy bed in 'Daddy Delph's Black Barns.'

"Ho, ho! Gibbet, I defy ye! The hangman's noose is but the most comfortable of neck cravats to Daddy Delph's clients." Here the old man turns his glance more directly toward Nat Flint. "Ah, Nat, my gentle friend o' the fluttering heart, an' quick-silvernesses, and how many times, O comrade o' mine, hast thou been hanged? He, he, he!" The speaker briskly rubs one hand over the other, and chuckles as if at the telling of a wonderful joke.

"Hist, you cussed fool! You prate like a gossiping old hag! Why continually mouth at nothing, like an infant just learning to wag its tongue? You forget that walls have ears!" Thus remonstrated Nat Flint, the ever-ghastly, white, half-dead, fear-chilled-looking young man. "That which you should keep silent as the grave itself," he went on. "You rave out as if anxious for all the world to know—a secret the public knowledge of which would cost us both our lives. In Mercy's name put a bridal upon your well-oiled tongue, or—"

"Tush, tush! Man, I love our glorious secret!" replied the old man, elated beyond measure. "It is life-giving to me!" he continued, "as it is life-giving to others in a more perfect sense. It is the mystic key that unstocks the grave! The elixir that restores the dead to life!"

*

A spectacle once seen never likely to be forgotten. The interior of a long, lofty, and wide timber-built a chamber painted black, both walls and ceiling. Ranging upon shelves are great collections of grinning skulls, and numbers of complete, upright skeleton forms are to be detected grouped against the walls where there are spaces to be seen between the central stacks of coffins in various stages towards completion. At one end of this horribly gruesome chamber stands a scaffold, its size and shape exactly representing the structure generally used in the public places of execution facing the Newgate, or Newgate Gaol.

There are the three beams, two upright, and the top one at right angles to these, and joining the support to the steel ring from which hangs the hangman's noose. A horse and cart, also exactly as used at a public execution, are standing motionless near the instrument of doom. The great elongated shed is lighted up by spluttering torches, which are fixed in iron rings projecting from the walls, and cast deep, black, dancing shadows that appear like evil spirits slinking in the corners amidst the grim, ghostly-looking skeleton forms.

There are present three persons—namely, the strange old man Daddy Delph, Dick the Dandy, and Nat Flint, the latter trying in vain to stop the violent trembling of his limbs and audible chattering of his teeth. The strikingly-handsome face of the highwayman is now fully revealed.

Its expression is that of pained concern, every vestige of colour has gone, the fair skin looking like white marble. Daddy Delph is engaged in the task of explaining a-something in which all three men are evidently most profoundly interested.

"The secret neck-guard is flesh-coloured, formed of stout leather and attached to a hidden shoulder-straps, and these again to chest-bands worn next the skin. A silver tube is unseen passed down the windpipe at the last moment before the culprit emerges upon the outside stage, which runs up to the side of the executioner's cart. The unyielding neck-stock can be completely hidden by wearing a white cravat three-fold, according to the prevailing fashion. The concealed tube and neck-protector prevent strangulation. The dislocation of the spinal cord, the actual cause of death, can alone be avoided by the most careful attention to my details."

"Ah, a man may actually die, then, even when you have sworn to save him and taken his gold?" cried Dick, with keenest disappointment.

"Ecod! but I cannot prevent a fool, a-going a-fooling! When Daddy Delph has e'n done his part perfectly—brain sharp as needlepoint—the condemned man may yet bungle. Ah, but 'tis a sweet comfort to know that my client cannot complain, or come to me for a return of his money. 'Tis kill or cure. No cure, yet you pay all the same. Ho, ho, ho! He, he!" Thus responded the strange old man in ironical glee.

"I can place down the enormous sum you demand," replied the highwayman, not heeding the latter caustic comments of Delph, "to seal our secret compact that you most solemnly undertake to provide that my life pay not for the forfeit of hanging on the scaffold in the event of my capture and condemnation. But first I must have most convincing proof that you can work this miracle."

The small, round eyes of Delph brightened up with the fire of greed, and he chuckled inwardly, and rubbed his knuckles so smartly that the fingers cracked like the snapping of dry bones. "You shall have the proof, my most royal master—ho, ho! Come, come, my ever-merry an' fearless Nat Flint," he continued, turning to the latter; "come, you hang-dog rogue! out with our pretty festive car, an' place around thy charmed neck the magic comforter. I'faith, but no man ever yet died of chill, cold, or colic after one good, strong dose of hangman-hemp (hempen rope). Ho, ho! He, he! Haw, haw, haw!" The sexton, undertaker, and gibbet-robber continued to chuckle in his strangely-weird croaking tones until tears ran down his fat cheeks.

In the strongest contrast to the old man's gruesome jesting was the overpowering fear of Nat Flint, who threw himself down upon his knees in extreme terror. "Don't put me to the awful torture to-night! Spare me the death-agony this once!" he piteously pleaded, clinging to the limbs of the sturdily-built man Delph. "I am not yet over that blood-freezing fright—the appearance of the Spectre Horsemen! You know well that I shall rehearse the frightful set once too often, that the ghastly sham will one of these times become the awful reality!"

Dick the Dandy was greatly moved at witnessing the abject terror of the gibbet-robber, and at the mention of the Spectre Rider he gave a sudden start. If indeed they were any faith to be attached to the witch's weird legend, then he himself had partly received warning of his terrible doom.

The manner of Delph suddenly underwent a complete change, his face assumed an expression of rage and fierce determination. "Curse ye for a shilly-shally ape! I may whisper the word that will quickly bring you the reality, an' that without the aid of Daddy Delph!" he lowly hissed into the ear of the kneeling man while appearing to help him to arise.

COLONEL BLOOD AND THE APPARITION OF THE SPECTRE HORSEMAN OF THE HEATH STRICKEN DOWN AS IF BY DEATH—STARTLING APPEARANCE OF WILL THE WITLESS—THE SURPRISE AND ATTACK—OUTNUMBERED—THE THIEF-TAKER COMES TO GRIEF—THREATENING DOOM.

A mingled cry of alarm, terror, and restraint burst from the lips of both Dick the Dandy and Wiffles as Colonel Blood struck spurs into the side of his proudly-prancing steed and plunged forward, flushing rapier in hand, to encounter the blue-white, mystic haze termed the Spectre Horsemen. The blood of the two spectators turned icy cold, a thrill as of death itself pieced them to the very marrow. The utterly fearless colonel was seen to pass clean through the awful apparition—that of a man with the hangman's noose about his neck, most vivid mortal stain upon his pale-blue breast, and visage wearing a look of unutterable woe, yet a face that in life must have been most refined and handsome.

Colonel Blood furiously thrust his rapier swiftly in all directions, only to run its slender, glinting point into the air, or the black bushes against which the ghosts of rider and steed had appeared to have stood.

A cry—half defiant, half pain—then the colonel was seen to fall from his saddle as if suddenly stricken dead. The two highwaymen sprang from the horses and flew to the side of the prone form. Each was well supplied with brandy. Dick the Dandy forced the neck of his flask between the clenched teeth of his friend, and succeeded in getting a little of the liquid into his mouth.

In a few moments the mysterious attack had passed. Colonel Blood had sustained no injury by his fall, but he had evidently received a great mental shock.

"Heaven be thanked that I live!" he fervently muttered on rising. "And may He forgive me for my impious act! There are profound mysteries connected with that state which hovered between life and eternity, and no man hath lawful right to seek to draw aside the curtain it has pleased his Maker to close about His holy secrets!"

Truly remarkable words these for an outlaw. The most notorious man the history of the whole world has ever revealed came not before this Colonel Blood for perfect daring and unlimited audacity, the actual stealing of the Crown jewels from the Tower of London being but one of his many amazingly rash exploits; but in due course his unparalleled career will fully appear in the progress of these historical records.

Dick the Dandy and Wiffles were deeply impressed by the effect the strange attack had made upon the hitherto untameable spirit of their comrade, who maintained a complete silence as to the sensations he experienced on being struck down by an invisible and unearthly agency.

Without warning, the three animals started wildly plunging, almost to the extent of unseating the three riders—for Colonel Blood had remounted—and the horsemen were not a little scared, if momentary, by the strange sight of a small figure apparently flying over the black hedgerow and lightly landing at the very feet of the affrighted animals.

"Will the Witless an' his brave steed well know the voices of Handsome Richard, the Night Hawk. Will the Witless an' his beautiful horse could leap over the moon if their good friend needed warning of coming danger!" sang out a plaintive, boyish voice.

"'Tis the poor lad of afflicted mind," whispered Dick to his companions; adding: "It is truly wonderful how that poor boy can, with the aid of his leaping pole, cover miles and miles of most wild and roadless wastes in incredible quickness and without hurt!"

"Angels of mercy! The unfortunate child is half naked! On such a night, too!" cried the colonel, in deep commiseration.

"I have repeatedly given him money to obtain good and warm clothing, but his heart is too big for a being of this world; the first object of pity he meets with takes his all," sadly explained Dick.

"No 'at, no boots, an' not too much toggery[28] to make a winter overcoat for a small-sized ant, if 'is suit was all stitched in one. It's much too bad, as the man sed when 'e broke 'is last remaining tooth in testing a bad crown-piece." Wiffles thus expressed his pity.

"No hat? No boots? Not enough clothing?" wonderingly repeated the boy, smiling sweetly, and showing most beautiful teeth. "Bonny Night Hawks, you are got all good an' kind to poor Will the Witless; but you don't know my friends the good fairies, or you would not be so blind. Will the Witless is clothed more beautifully and warmly than even my good, handsome Richard there," he continued; adding: "But all the things made by fairy hands are not to be seen by mortal eyes."

Then the boy's mood instantly changed. Even while speaking he had been most eagerly catching the snowflakes, now falling less faster and in smaller particles.

"Hear what the fairies tell me!" he cried, his eyes fixed and sparkling, as the fleecy particles fell into his outstretched hand and assumed fantastic shapes. "The hungry wolves are now within scent of their prey. If the Night Birds are not quickly on the wing the prowling wolves will rend them with a cruel fire and sword—devour them!"

At the actual moment of pronouncing the warning words the hurried clatter of a great number of steeds' hooves could be heard, and growing more distinct each instant, the hard, frosty earth echoing the din with a metallic-like ring.

"Jonathan Wild and his janissaries!*" cried Dick the Dandy. "There is generally some truth in the seeming ramblings of the witless boy," he added. "I have frequently proved it."

"The chief of the Newgate gang has doubtless learned of the secret meeting of all known members of our class at the Haunted Manor of Finchley, and intends attempting to surprise and capture, or kill, a goodly number of us there," commented Colonel Blood.

"Curse him! My life-stream seethes at the very mention of Wild's name! We must combine our forces, and meet the bloodstained monster of iniquity steel to steel!"

---

[28] Clothes.

* The term "janissary" really implied a Turkish foot guard. The word was held in great odium on account of the unpopularity of the Turkish Army in England at the period of which we write. The great ferocity of Jonathan Wild's followers caused them to be known by the hated title of janissaries.—ED.

returned Dick, trembling with rage at the thought of facing the chief cause of his ruined career, and clashing blades within reach of that wretch's body.

"The black old rat! If I gets a" 'old of 'im 'e'll 'ave to order another silver plate ter fit in 'is thick pate along o' the three or four as 'e's got there already!" said Wiffles, in deadly hatred.

"To the main-road, comrades. We must reach the Manor before Wild can surprise our friends already there."

The suggestion was no sooner made by the colonel than the three horsemen caused their animals to face the lofty hedgerow and take the leap, which each did, with graceful, bird-like bound. But the three highwaymen had actually leapt into a trap. A great body of horsemen were seen swiftly careering towards them, within but a few yards, as coming from both sides.

The releaping of either hedgerow was now out of the question, the roadway being too narrow; and their foes were upon them before the outlaws could turn their steeds even to attempt the jump.

Jonathan Wild's short, thick-set figure and face, unmatched for its extreme repulsiveness, at once marked him out from his followers, evil indeed as they appeared.

With all the great thief-taker's notorious vices, that of cowardice could not be included, for the man's extreme ferocity was a by-word.

Colonel Blood's military experiences frequently stood him in good stead; they did so now. A few whispered words were rapidly exchanged by the highwaymen. The attackers would be unable to use their firearms for fear of killing those of their own party. The cutlass, worn by all legal officials in those days, was more than a fair match for the more fashionable rapier usually carried by highwaymen, most of whom affected extremely fashionable display both of costume and steed appointments.

Jonathan Wild led the party of horsemen interposing between the outlaws and their intended destination. Colonel Blood alone faced this force. Dick the Dandy and Wiffles confronted the enemy coming from the other side. Thus the three attacked formed up, horses' flanks together, the three riders to sustain the charge of fearful odds. The dauntless courage and impetuous spirit of the knights of the road were now to be put to the test to the uttermost.

"Remember, my men, there is a fine price upon the head of each of those notorious scamps—for I know them in spite of their thick crape masks—Dick the Dandy, Colonel Blood, and the fellow Wiffles!" Wild was distinctly heard to say.

"Then, by all that's unmanly, we've a traitor among our number!" murmured Colonel Blood to his comrades.

"Death to him, whoever he may be!" whispered Dick in reply.

"Ah! a quick an' terrible end to the same!" lowly returned Wiffles.

Then came the supreme moment. The tactics of the road-raiders were at once seen. The lightning-like blade wielded by the ex-soldier fatally pierced the breasts of the two foremost animals, and the poor brutes went down instantly, their riders shooting over their steeds' heads and coming fearful croppers.

Dick and Wiffles had as quickly unhorsed four of the foe in the same manner, much as they regretted that method of warfare; but the desperately-placed highwaymen well knew that neither mercy nor quarter would be shown them. Their decapitated heads were eagerly in demand, to add to the ever soul-shuddering spectacle of the array of malefactors' heads crowning some portion of the Tower's ramparts, and thickly clustered on the spikes bristling from the top of the arch of the Gate of ye Temple, afterwards known as Temple Bar.

The thief-takers were thrown into instant confusion, the horses of those to the rear stumbling over their fellow-animals slain by rapier-thrusts.

"Close on them!" yelled Wild, regaining his feet. "I promise you double rewards in each case! Cut them down, men! Remember it's dead or alive! Cut them to pieces, if needs be! A pile of gold's on each head!"

"There'll be a bit more silver on your devil's brain-pan, pretty mug!" shouted a voice over the head of the infuriated Jonathan Wild, who swiftly turned to make a murderous slash at the speaker with his raised cutlass.

But Wiffles was far too nimble for him; the hilt of his rapier crashed down upon the now hatless and wigless head, upon which three inlain silver plates could, in consequence, be plainly seen. The fierce blow gave out a sickening sound, and its receiver fell with a broken skull, and deluged with his blood.

The three highwaymen, as prearranged, now madly plunged their steeds into the thick of their fiercely-swaying and yelling foes. Using their steels and firearms alternately, the desperate adventurers fired point-blank, wielded the butts of their flint-locks as clubs, or furiously thrust, at the mob encircling them, with their slender and finely-tempered blades.

Many of the thief-catchers fell from the effects of the terrific onslaught made upon them; but the great superiority of numbers soon told, and the doom of the three highwaymen seemed but the work of a few moments. Then came the swift clatterings of other horsemen.

The Newgate mercenaries gave utterance to one combined shout of savage glee and triumph. The approaching horsemen were evidently a great reinforcement of their fellow-officers, and the result foretold certain capture, or death, to the outlaws!

°THE CHAWBACON[29] AND THE BOW STREET RUNNERS—A TWEAK O' THE NOSE—THE INTENDED ARREST AND HOW IT ENDED—THE TOLLPIKE-KEEPER AND HIS BLUNDERBUSS—BILBERRY, THE RED ROBIN, HAS A BAD TIME—THE HOLE-IN-THE-WALL SECRET PASSAGES.

"Very suspicious-looking! A clodhopper[30] like that mounted on an animal of such perfect points!"

"You don't often see a mere chawbacon wearing spurs, either!"

Two Bow Street runners in the vicinity of the old Hornsey Woods. They were on foot, and their remarks were called forth by suddenly finding themselves almost face-to-face with a rider and steed of unusual character—that is to say, the horseman looked more fitting for the tail of a plough, and the animal for a gallant of great distinction. The time was early morning, and proceeding certain incidents already related.

"Our instructions are to seek tidings of certain famous, or infamous criminal, an' we have warranty to arrest any suspicious character, according to our discretion," added one of the runners.

There was no further time for talk, the rider having now come within earshot. The bridle-path which ran side-by-side with a very deep cutting formed a water-conduit. The current raced at an enormous swiftness, and towards an underground tunnel, which extended for at least fifty yards, and then again became an open water course.

"Halt, lout! What do ye with that beast?" demanded the foremost runner.

"My master's; an' I be'st taakin' it on ter London Town!" was the straightforward reply.

"Dismount, clown! You must be search'd. There are horse thieves in plenty in these parts. We must take you to the nearest watch-house, pending inquiries!" roughly continued the speaker.

Instantly the yeoman dismounted. "W'ere be'st tha' warrant for my arrest?" he asked.

"Churl, I'll tweak thee by the nose for thy insolence to a King's officer! Come quietly, or my pistol shall let daylight into thy darkened brain!"

The Bow Street officer dived his hand into the skirt-pocket of his coat with the intention of producing a firearm; but before he could succeed a tremendous right-hander struck him full upon the bridge of the nose.

"First tweak!" cried the suspected man, throwing out his foot immediately after, and sending the dazed and staggering officer headfirst into the watercourse.

° Part 5. Vol. XIV.—No. 341. 29 April 1900.

[29] A rustic or uncultured person.

[30] A foolish or awkward person.

The remaining officer drew out and levelled a flint-lock tube, his finger was upon the trigger; but the yeoman was far too rapid in his movements, and crashed in a swift and most scientifically-delivered thud upon the fellow's jowl. The pistol exploded, and the ball went wide of its mark.

Then the dismayed man was snatched up and fiercely hurled after his comrade, the strength of the current quickly dragging the two frantically-splashing and half-suffocating men under the arched tunnel, full ten minutes expiring before daylight greeted them at the black passage-way's further end, and then their intended captive was beyond the range of their water-dimmed vision. The latter, with the gayest of laughter, had remounted and galloped off at breakneck speed towards London.

Soon the first turnpike-gate came in sight. Seeing the apparent farm-hireling (labourer) mounted upon a most superb animal, and racing as if for dear life, the tollkeeper, instantly suspecting something wrong, quickly flung-to the larger gate, that shutting off all progress by means of the wider path.

"My good, bonny, brave Jess!" cheerily murmured the forward fleeing horseman. "Take the gate, my beauty! Up—so. Now, good friend!"

A light touch of the whip, lighter touch still of the spurs, given her head, and like some swift, graceful bird, the beautiful thoroughbred shot over. Five-barred, and sharp-spiked topped, too, as was the great barrier, the game Jess had cleanly cleared the dangerous obstacle, and again sped onwards.

The toll keeper had darted into his little roundhouse, snatched up his great blunderbuss, flown out again, and discharged the cannon-like arm at the fleeing rider and steed. The explosion was ear-splitting, the gun burst at its breach, the gatekeeper shooting backwards into the gatehouse, amidst the terrified screams of a few bystanders and his wife, of ample proportions, and a troop of scared little ones.

Gaily laughing, the disguised highwayman, Dick the Dandy—the reader has already guessed the identity—swiftly sped on his way towards the city. In less than an hour, and in the same disguise, he had reached and entered the famous hostelry, the Hole-in-the-Wall.[31]

We already know of the second startling surprise received by the Bow Street officer Bilberry.

Two persons had now faced that official, one close upon the heels of the other, and each declaring himself to be Dick the Dandy.

"I am Dick the Dandy. Take me if you dare!"

On seeing the handsome, graceful, and richly-costumed form of the youth, after his disguise had been thrown aside, and the levelled weapons of faultless

---

[31] In *Rookwood* by William Harrington Ainsworth, "Jack Palmer" notes that the highwayman Claude Duval "was seized at the Hole-in-the Wall" in Chandos Street (Rookwood 225). As this seems a location popular with outlaws, it maybe the location that the authprs intended.

make and exquisite chasing, Bilberry uttered a feeble groan, and flopped into his seat about as graceful as would a gigantic and half-melted bladder of lard.

"By all the—" The feeble oath died a natural death in the parched-up officer's throat before it could attain to full utterance, and the extremely red, setting sunlike face became pale and wan-looking as a moon just risen from a bed of sickness.

A look of startled fear crept into the blue-black eyes of the beautiful Mrs. Drake as she stood in the open doorway, a fear that was also half remorse.

"You do not appear over eager to claim the reward offered for my head? Forsooth, the price I demand for the proud privilege of making Dick the Dandy captive is that of a whole brace of heads, sufficient in number to make a goodly show upon the ramparts of London's historic tower of ye Temple gate!"

"Say, daring minion of the law, shall I rank your fine, thick skull as the first?" The stentorian tones of the highwayman filled the chamber with its rich volume.

Officer Bilberry sank from his seat to the saw-dusted floor in most abject fear, for the brightly-flashing eyes, seen through the half mask of crimson silk, looked extremely deadly, while the two accurately-presented steel barrels appeared, if possible, even more deadly still.

"You claim to have already met one Dick the Dandy before my appearance! You lie!" thundered the young outlaw.

"The other robber—I should say, gallant!" stammered Bilberry, with a great attempt at some show of composure—"the other jesting gentleman assur'd me that he—"

"You were attacked and robbed of everything you possessed by a number of footpaths, you know, Mr. Bilberry!" cried Mrs. Drake, now somewhat recovering her composure.

"Ah—er—quite so—quite so—er—most divine creature of thy sex. I had really—er—quite—er—forgotten for the moment. Exactly fifty in number. The cold-blooded ruffians! I should say, right royal and pleasant knights of the moonlit glen—lonely lane—deserted hostelry. Ha, ha, most amiable company, I dare be sworn! Exactly fifteen, as I have already just remarked. The whole five of them attacked me at once, and—and—"

"Did each style himself Dick the Dandy?" interrupted the highwayman.

"May I be hanged on the horns of a dilemma if each of the thirty-five e'n didst flatly and soundly call upon the most solemn saints in all the calendar to prove it, goodly sir!" was the barefaced reply, the speaker still abjectly keeping upon his knees.

"You bloated, ill-shaped lump of shameless deceit! Fifty, fifteen, five, thirty-five! It is said that liars require most excellent memories, so 'tis proved in thy case, thou punch-barrel upon legs!" cried Dick the Dandy, assuming great indignation and rage, but actually having very great difficulty in preventing himself from bursting into laughter.

At this juncture the host, Ralph Drake, hastily entered the bar. His wife closed the door of the smoking-parlour, and ran to her husband, whispered something in his ear, and then returned to the presence of the highwayman, whose attention was instantly arrested by the peculiar expression upon the archly-pretty face.

"For the moment I leave you to your reflections, windbag, empty braggart; and beware of any attempt at escape!" So saying, Dick the Dandy left the room, locking the door after him.

Ralph Drake advanced and met the highwayman in the passage leading to the front bar-parlour.

"To put the fellow in there off the scent," he commenced, "I went out on the false pretext of learning your probable whereabouts. Instead, I have discovered that your presence in my inn is suspected, and the place already surrounded!"

"Then I am undone!" gasped Dick the Dandy, fiercely drawing his weapons, resolving to die gamely fighting to the last gasp rather than be taken.

"Nay, Ralph, my husband, can save you!" excitedly whispered the hostess.

"Aha, an' wilt, too!" muttered the host. "Quick! Follow me!"

He then opened a little door, and darted down steep steps hidden in gloom, the highwayman unhesitatingly following. This historic hostelry was a long-favoured resort for highwaymen, and those of outcast society in general. Dick Turpin, and his wonderfully game and intelligent mare, "Bonnie Black Bess," were frequent sojourners at the inn, and it was due to the existence of wonderfully constructed subterranean cellars and passages that Richard Turpin and his highwayman comrade, Tom King, were enabled for years to set at defiance every effort made for their capture. These long-existing and deeply secret ways were quite unknown to Dick the Dandy until the day of which we write.

Drake seized Dick by the hand and led him forward. Presently the two pulled up at the face of what appeared to be a solid wall. The host let go of the hand of his companion. The striking of the flint and steel followed, then a pine-torch was lighted by means of the flame shooting up from the tinder, as this became ignited by the falling sparks struck by concussion of flint stone and steel-bar.

Ralph Drake smiled up at his companion as he stooped and took up a long pole. "You are now to be introduced to the actual 'Hole-in-the-Wall,' an' not the inn of that name," he said.

Then he fixed the sharp-pointed end of the wedge into a small crevasse in the apparently compact surface of earth, a few jerks followed, then a round-shaped mass rolled backwards, leaving a space large enough for a man to enter. Drake led the way, the outlaw silently following.

The flaming brand revealed a roomy passage, narrowing up to the hole in which the boll of earth—one side of which alone was flat, was usually fixed. In replacing this from the farther side, Dick the Dandy's guide explained that all that was necessary to most perfectly hide the rugged gap left round the huge block of earth was the careful use of the trowel on the side nearest the cellar is usually used for storing beer-barrels, &c. The passage was mildewy, stifling, and of a most twisting and lengthened course; but at length the two finally halted before rudely-formed steps in the earth.

The amazement of the young highwayman was indeed great, when, on reaching daylight, the first object to gladden his sight was his own beautiful thoroughbred mare, Jess!

"This timber building is our brew-house," explained Drake; adding: "I contrived to bring your mare into this place soon after I caught sight of the animal fastened to a post near our inn. I feared that Bilberry might have had his suspicions aroused by the unusual and well-known fineness of Jess," explained Ralph Drake.

"You have now done me a service of great value. You are in difficulties, and could easily have betrayed me, and claimed the Government reward," remarked Dick.

"I should be poorer than the meanest wretch padlocked in the public stocks for stealing a loaf, and then such a thought would never enter my mind!" blurted out Drake hotly.

The handsome, young, proscribed felon smiled.

"Your sterling character is too well known to need backing up by your words!" he said. "I will make it my duty that you shall ultimately gain more than the Government reward by your manliness; but I must needs not tarry. Urgent matters call me hence. Is the course now clear, think you, of my foes?"

"I have brought you through one only of our hidden passages. The back-door of this barn opens direct into the lane leading to the Clerk-in-the-Well Fields.[32] By passing down the lane the high hedgerows will well screen you from chance observation if you do not mount; but, firstly let me look out to see if the road mentioned is quite clear."

Ralph Drake had spoken in an undertone. He now crept softly to the back of the old brew-house, and peeped through a crevasse between the two timbers. A view of the whole length of the straight and narrow hedgerowed path was before his eyes, and no living thing could be detected.

A brief, whispered conversation then took place. Then the two parted, the host being most anxious to return and confront the Bow Street officers.

---

[32] Now Clerkenwell.

WILL THE WITLESS—BILBERRY THE BLUSTERER AND HIS FAIRY-TALE—A MOST CRITICAL CONFLICT—DEAD OR ALIVE! —THE WITLESS BOY PROVES A MATCH FOR THREE BOW STREET OFFICERS—THE BLACKAMORES.

But a few moments before Ralph Drake had applied his eyes to the opening between the boards of his shed, another pair of eyes had been removed from the same small chink on its other side.

The highwayman cautiously opened the back-door. At the very moment of his doing so a terrific confusion of savage voices rose up.

They appeared to come from the very centre of a great and impenetrable cloud of inky blackness, now completely filling up the pathway before him.

Without a second thought as to the meaning of this, Dick stole out by the front-door of the barn. He had proceeded some fifty yards, and then sprang into the saddle, when the oncoming of horses' hoofs quickly put him on the alert.

"Surrender, Dick the Dandy!" shouted voices, as two mounted officers impetuously charged at him.

"Never—with life!" was the undaunted retort.

"Then we'll take your body! The warrant reads, 'Dead or alive!'"

The words were followed by the quick discharge of weapons. A ball shot away a portion of the feather edging of the outlaw's hat. His rapier darted from its scabbard, and plunged almost up to the hilt through the side of the nearest officer, narrowly missing his heart.

"I'm picked!" groaned the man, reeling from the saddle, his horse taking fright and bolting off.

Another shot rang out from the second piece of the remaining officer, who then dropped the weapon—seeing that his shot had not told—snatched out his cutlass, and again bravely charged the highwayman.

The slighter blade of the rapier was tested to its utmost in warding off the terrible downward slash, made with the deliberate intention of cleaving in twain the felon's head. The finely-tempered steel assumed a half-circle from the effects of the clash. Thus the outlaw's life was saved; and, before the officer could recover his guard, the thin line of steel was half-way through his own full-fleshed neck.

Dick the Dandy held his own life cheaply. No more brilliant fencer or swordsman lived; but he aimed not to kill his fellow-creatures, but simply to save his own life.

The two officers were seriously wounded, but not fatally. Loud yells quickly warned the highwayman that other foes were advancing to the attack, and in a trice he had dashed off, and quickly got beyond fear of pursuit.

*

Mr. Drake was not over-much astonished to find that the Bow Street runner had made his departure by means of the open window, which led into the inn yard.

The officer must have had great difficulty in forcing his over-fat corporation through the small window. It had been a distinct case of a "round man" in a "square place"—an expression intended to convey the very reverse of comfort.

Bilberry had experienced very considerable agony, being literally in a very tight place. His chance of actually bursting became a very near thing. Also he had torn the skin off the back of one hand, producing much display of blood; and the rotund figure had received such a squashing that for a time it retained the squareness of the aperture through which it had passed.

After the manner of a long-and-tightly-packed aldermanic sardine, the officer waddled from the inn yard out at the open gates, and then, eagerly glanced about him in search of aid, for he was perfectly convinced that the highwayman intended, on his return, to put an end to his—Bilberry's—career.

A peculiar whistle caught the ear of the officer. He started off in the direction from whence the sound had come. A number of mounted officers were stationed behind a wall, forming a portion of the ruins of a partly-demolished building.

The exertion of reaching the horsemen had restored Bilberry's face to its usual rich purple tone; his hat was missing, every pocket in his clothing turned outwards, and the blood from the cut hand had been purposely be smeared over his cravat, shirt-front, and face; the short and bristly hair on his head stood upright like those of a badly-conditioned brush.

"E'cod! Man alive! Stew me into a jelly! Blood an' hounds! S'death! You set of craven-hearted, white-livered, addle-sculled sons of a cursed banshee! I—"

Here Officer Bilberry stopped dead for sheer want of mind.

"Hush! Hush!" cautioned one of the horsemen. "Dick the Dandy has been positively seen to enter the inn there! Your bellowing will—"

"Hush, you, thou son of a mermaid, with your hush, hush, like a child on seashore trying to catch roar of sea in cockle-shell! Pussh! Twice this morning have I, single-handed, nearly captured the infamous Dick the Dandy! Twice, I tell you!" continued Bilberry, his excitement visibly increasing with his words. "And each time I had nabbed the terrible wretch, and given him most unmerciful trounsings with the flat of my hanger-blade, then what should happen? Why, his lusty cries for mercy brought about my ears a perfect multitude of other slice-wizen ruffians. Ten times, I tell you, I beat them off, until their number grew most prodigious, and I fainted from very loss of blood!"

At this moment another horseman joined those hiding behind the wall. This latter had charge of the others, and knew well how to value the words of the loud-mouthed boaster.

"Reserve thy report for our chief!" dryly commanded he.

Then an order was given for three of the mounted officers to make a cautious detour, reach the lane leading to the Clerk-in-the-Well Fields, and then conceal themselves, and to secure the highwayman should he ventured that way.

Bilberry, in the presence of his superior, had become meek as a lamb. The flintlocks and cutlass he had reported as lost in his frightful encounters were supplied him, and, excepting that, he was again ready for further emergency.

Feeling firmly convinced that the highwayman would certainly not travel the way suspected, Officer Bilberry earnestly entreated to be included with those to be stationed in the place mentioned, and his request was granted.

The three officers cunningly took a circuitous route, entered the lane by a narrow footpath, and then drew up behind a high stack of faggots, on the top of which were a few bags, evidently containing chimney sweepings for use as manure, some of which was already to be seen littered about.

Electing himself as superior in command of his two companions, Bilberry made much display of his usual bombast and most florid oaths.

The eyes that had peered into the brew-barn were those of a lad whose face and hands were jet-black with soot. This boy had been engaged placing the soot-dust manure upon the earth, and then damping the same to prevent its being blown away.

Will the Witless—for he it was—had obtained a day's employment, for which he would be rewarded by a few pence. The beautiful form of the mare Jess had caught the lad's eye, and he well knew that "handsome Richard," his good friend, could not be far away from the graceful Jess.

The feeble mind of the poor lad grew darkly and deeply troubled when he saw the cautious approach of three mounted Bow Street officers and observed then pull up by the side of the heaped-up tree-loppings.

Witless as he was, the lad instantly concluded that this meant danger to his ever-generous friend, "handsome Richard."

Knowing nothing of his patron's visit to the inn or the underground passages, and having seen the steed alone in the shed, for some moments Will the Witless paused irresolute; then suddenly there flashed into his poor, enraged brain an idea—an idea such as could only occur to one of weak intellect.

It should be borne in mind that up to this point Dick the Dandy and Ralph Drake had not yet reached the brewing-barn.

Making no sound, Will the Witless snatched up his leaping-pole and crept along under cover of the hedgerow, until he reached the reverse side of the high-stacked faggots. To leap to their top by the aid of his "jumping steed," as he termed his pole, was a simple enough matter; then he crouched down, and made no sound.

"Blood an' hounds, man! that dancing brute o' thine means bringing those tied-up, prickly bunches down about our heads! Man alive, keeping the infernal bag o' bones still! A plague on thee for a nursery horse rider!" muttered Bilberry, thinking that the noise made by Will the Witless was really due to the backing of one of the horses.

A moment after, the latter officer's fierce eye caught sight of the shouldered blade of the other rider. Its point was touching one of the overhanging soot-bags.

"Gad, zooks an' zounds, Jobson!" he raved, "pierce that black sack, if you desire to blind an' transform us all into blackmores! By the God of Mars, what flaming idiots some creatures are!"

"Liar to you! and bursting windbag, too!" impatiently retorted Officer Jobson.

The words were scarcely uttered before a great mass of soot, resembling a great, thick, falling cloud of ebony dust, thickly enveloped the three men and their steeds.

Bilberry and the other, believing that Jobson had intentionally served them the blinding and choking trick, struck out with their already drawn swords, keeping their eyes firmly closed the while.

In a moment after, copious sousings[33] of water fell over the curtain, contesting, and bewildered men. In their blind confusion and rage they were slashing out madly, but, fortunately, hitting the wind only.

Then was heard a voice shouting in mocking tones.

"Pretty Robin redbreasts are not birds of evil omen! The black bird—carrion crow—those are fittest for the servants of the gibbet! Ha, ha! Won't the good fairies laugh at ye! Those whose minds and hearts are filled with blackness should fittingly be also outwardly decked as now are ye! Ha, ha, ha!"

The growling, spluttering, sneezing, and choking Bilberry slowly and carefully blinked open one orb just sufficiently to enable him to obtain a momentary glimpse of a little black figure careering away at wonderful speed in great bounds taken by the aid of a long pole.

°WIFFLES ON THE KING'S HIGHWAY—A FATEFUL MEETING—A ROBBER WITH A CONSCIENCE—SQUIRE BRANCOME CONFRONTED BY A HIGHWAYMAN—MIDNIGHT TOLL-COLLECTING—A PIECE OF SUGAR.

"This snow, cold, frost, an' the keen, nipping winds included, make late toll-pike collecting 'just the reverse o' nice'—as the little boy sed to himself when 'e found that 'e 'ad chew'd up a bitter almond in mistake for a sweet one!"

Wiffles, the highwayman, had mounted his bonny mare and ridden out alone. The night was a typical winter's night, thick snowflakes falling, dense black clouds drifting overhead, and sparkling hoarfrost encrusting the earth, leafless trees, and

---

[33] Drenching.
° Part 6. Vol. XIV.—No. 342. 29 May 1900.

bushes. The locality was that of the Finchley Common. The time, near midnight. The solitary horsemen might have been thousands of miles away from the haunts of mortals, for not the slightest sight of habitation or sound of human voice came to him, nothing but the occasional cry of a night bird and the clatter of his steed's hooves breaking the depressing silences reigning in that barren district.

"This lan'scape of glass-like frost, falling snow, trees all dress'd in light garments, an' with ditto gloves on their many long, thin-pointed fingers, would make a very nice picture if fram'd an' 'ung over a cosy fire; but as it is—ough!— a drop o' 'ot punch a-falling within, sez I, to every flake o' snow a-falling without, an' then there'd be 'little falling out within'—as the poor hare sadly demurred as it was being skinned for the pot!"

On the night following the morning of the escape of Dick the Dandy, a great fall of snow enveloped all London in its beautiful mantle of spotless white fleece. We have already followed the adventures of the dashing young highwayman up to the supremely critical point when he, Colonel Blood, and Wiffles were thrown into a condition of extreme despair by seeing, as they imagined, bodies of reinforcements of Jonathan Wild's janizaries,[34] or guards, coming to overwhelm them. The unbounded joy of the three intrepid adventurers can be better imagined than described on finding the onrushing horsemen to consist of their own fellow-outlaws, these—as before hinted—having met at the Haunted Manor of Finchley for a secret purpose, of which we shall presently relate.

The colonel, Dick, and Wiffles—thanks to the darkness, and the confusion caused by the foeman attacking them from all points—escaped with but a few trifling flesh wounds and bruises. Wild and those of his men injured—and there were many—were rapidly carried off, the three outlaws being borne away in triumph by their exultant friends.

Dick the Dandy soon after left his comrades for a brief while, and made his way to the abode of Daddy Delph, in the immediate neighbourhood. Wiffles also pleaded to be excused for a brief time, promising to reach the Manor later on. There are circumstances in life that, at the time of their taking place, may be set down as the most trivial, yet which afterwards proved to have been most weighty. The visiting of Daddy Delph by the youthful outlaw, and the actions of Wiffles in delaying his visit to the Haunted Manor—these circumstances combined afterwards proved of the most stupendous import in both their lives, as will duly be seen.

For a weary hour or more had Wiffles impatiently written backwards and forwards over a limited stretch of the white-carpeted country before any sight or sound of traveller greeted his eagerly-listening ear. At length there came the loud, crisp ringing of iron-shod hooves; then the forms of a male rider and

---

[34] Alternate spelling of 'Janissaries' see original editor's note above, p. **.

horse gradually shaped themselves from out the surrounding darkness. The gloomy shadows cast by a thick clump of trees standing by the side of the one beaten track across the common were selected by Wiffles as an ambush in which to conceal himself until his intended victim came near, for the masked and cloaked highwayman was upon an act of highway robbery intent.

The oncoming rider was mounted upon a sturdy-looking chestnut cop, and was eagerly examining every shadow-filled spot as he rode past, evidently most anxious and fearful, and with reason, for the lonely common he was passing over was a notoriously dangerous place—one much infested, both with mounted and unmounted robbers.

As the horseman came near, Wiffles struck his spurs sharply into the flanks of his animal. The creature gave a sudden bound, and instantly blocked up the track and faced the stranger's startled animal, which at once reared in fright, and then hastily backed some yards. Its rider muttered an oath, regained his control over the cob, and fiercely urged it forward. The highwayman's quick eyes noted the pistols in their holsters on the saddle, and the blade in its sheath at the rider's side.

"Haul up slick!—as the cat cried to the man at the rope when she tumbled down the well and scrambled into the bucket—don't attempt to lay a finger on your weapons, an' keep back, man, if you don't want to travel without yer 'ead!" fiercely commanded Wiffles, his eyes glinting dangerously through his black crape mask, and an enormous flint-lock pistol—almost the size of a carbine[35]— raised and at the full cock.

"Ah!—I was warned—Dick the Dandy—the notorious night-hawk! Well, are you going to murder me in cold blood?" gasped the stranger, instantly reining up.

"I'm Dick the Dandy, am I? That's a prime lie! An' who warn'd you? Answer, quick!"

The terrible-looking weapon was levelled dead at the cob-rider's head. He saw that trifling would be most risky, and replied, in a fear-quivering voice:

"Jonathan Wild! He had learned that I to-night must cross this common, and considerately cautioned me that the scoundrel called Dick the Dandy frequently committed his dastardly deeds upon undefended wayfarers in these parts. I am not personally acquainted with my informant, he sent to me by special messenger."

"What's your name?" asked Wiffles, keeping his eyes keenly on the alert and pistol well aimed.

"I'm Squire Brancome, and have most important business at Barnet this night," was the candid reply.

"When next you meet Jonathan Wild, friend Brancome, give 'im the compliments of Master Wiffles, 'ighwayman by special command o' King George to all 'is most smug, rich, an' musty-fusty subjects, and tell old Jonathan

---

[35] A long-barreled firearm.

from me that I'm awful sorry that I damag'd the stock o' one o' my best pistols in clubbing 'is dirty old iron pate, an' that the next time I meet 'im I'll present him with another excuse for a forget-me-not silver plate being fixed at the top of his evil-plotting sconce; but I won't spoil a valuable article over the job, the 'eel of my boot will be used instead. Also kindly ask 'im to oblige me by sending 'is exact dimensions to me, as I'm a-going to prepare a nice, bran new black wooden suit for 'im, beautifully ornamented with brass nails, an' ditto plate. 'E'll want that very costume soon, an' it'll accommodate 'im so nicely that 'e'll never ask for another," banteringly went on Wiffles.

"That's but a roundabout way of threatening to murder the great thief-taker!" replied the squire, his fears vastly increasing.

"I didn't say it wasn't!" shortly replied Wiffles; adding, "but Dick the Dandy is no murderer; and not one of us outlaws, for the matter of that, ever needlessly shed blood. The only cattle we night-'awks show no mercy to is Jonathan o' the black, evil chops 'imself, an' the scurvy, an' blotchy-faced roisting members of 'is gang—pretty Red Robbins o' Bow Street an' the like. An' remember that a little blood-letting to sich as them is a kindness, an' saves 'em from now an' again visiting the leach,[36] to get rid of a few ounces o' the contents o' their over-charged veins, the fluid of which is really not blood at all, but a rank, black, thick fluid made up mostly of strong gin-punch."

"If what you state be true respecting the unwillingness to take life shown by all you robbers, you will surely let me pass uninjured on my journey if I give up a part of my property?" implored the squire, a white-wig, stout, and middle-aged man of superior appearance.

"You've got to pay the toll o' Finchley Common, an' we collectors charges extras, according to the lateness o' the 'our an' the degree of persuasion required. Now, I've jawed a 'eap, so if you don't settle up sharp, in the next ten minutes the tariff will 'ave gone up alarming!" coolly replied Wiffles, still covering the other.

The squire was silent for a few seconds; then he looked at the outlaw full in the face, and, in a tone of unmistakable candour, said:

"I have with me ten golden guineas and five hundred crown pieces. I am going to a very dear old friend who circumstances are indeed desperate. To-morrow he will be a ruined man if I fail in delivering to him the help I have promised. Can you not be satisfied with my pledge of honour to bring you a sum—say, this night week?"

The highwayman laughed softly, then lightly hummed a few words of a then popular ballad:

---

[36] The "leech" of olden times was commonly a barber also, and "cupping," or bleeding, was the usual remedy for almost every form of disease or "distemper."

"'Twas a pert, a pretty, and a dainty young miss,
An' the gallant demanded a free-given kiss
'O prithee, sir, in my eye much green do you see?
Sir Drawl, don't you wish you may get it!' cried she."

"My word's my bond!" protested the squire indignantly; "and if you plunder me, the death of a good, true man will then lie at your door, for I feel sure my friend will commit suicide rather than face his degradation. Where is your boasted concern for the sacredness of life?"

"Ten golden guineas an' five hundred crown pieces! The grapes are ov'r ripe, an' ready to fall into my mouth, an'—but you well know the rest, Sir Squire. Consider me the hungry fox o' the fable, an' remember that 'e didn't wait to ask but thoughtfully 'elped 'imself."

The squire looked beseechingly at the unrelenting eyes, and then at the murderous-looking instrument still levelled at his head, and with a finger pressed on the trigger.

"The ten guineas at most can I offer you. In mercy's name take that and let me resume my journey!"

There were tears now swimming in the pleader's eyes and, in spite of himself, Wiffles was touched although he felt it beneath the dignity of a man-hunted outlaw to let the fact appear too plainly.

"You've taken your physic like a good boy—no wry faces—an' I really must give you a piece o' sugar to take the nasty taste out of your mouth," he responded. "The piece of sugar represents five golden pieces, or five of King George's spade guineas[37]—a sweet piece of sugar you will admit, Sir Squire. So just hand over the other five, there's a nice, good lad!" Wiffles was now more like his usual cheery self.

"Do I hear you are right?" Squire Brancome was thunder-struck, nervously drew out a long purse, and, with trembling hand, took out five golden pieces, and then handed them over. "Friend, I give these ungrudgingly, if you are indeed in earnest with me!" he cried.

"Never more in earnest in all me life," replied Wiffles—"as the 'addock sed, after it was cut open an' dried." He then took the coins and carelessly dropped them one by one into a pocket of his long waistcoat. "You 'ave paid toll for the whole of your journey, Sir Squire—both ways—an' by the rules of us Road Rakers, you've no right to be molested again for some time considerable—as the cat remarked to the rat's tail, after she'd devoured the body. The words 'Midnight toll paid' will save you any further trouble, if any other gentleman of

---

[37] The guinea was one pound of gold in weight, or twenty shillings, and named after the Guinea region in Africa, where the gold for the gold was sourced. The Spade refers to the spade-shaped royal coat of arms on the reverse of the coin.

the road politely asks you to settle the same reckoning." The speaker dropped his pistol into its lethern case, and then gracefully raised his hat.

"A robber with a conscience?—A robber? A man worthy of an honourable station in life? By all that I deem sacred I swear that I never will make public plaint of our meeting, good Sir Knight of the Road, but ever cherish it as a right, good, merry, gentlemanly, roguish jest! Good-night Sir Robber—good-night!" The squire's voice rang out quite pleasantly, as he lightly gave the spurs to his animal.

The chestnut cob snorted gleefully as it galloped off, and the rider actually returned a wave of his hat to that of the mounted rubber before disappearing from view round a great ridge of elevated ground.

"The wintry lan'scape's no more, an' this is a noonday in bright, warm July. Everything 'as taken on a lovely golden tinge since the rising of them five bright an' jingling sovrays[38] through the chilly, gloomy clouds o' black, frowning poverty. Heigho! Wealth is life; poverty but death!" Thus reflected Wiffles when again alone; then he softly murmured a few words of a refrain bearing upon the theme of the "Gallants o' the Heath." Correcting the highwayman's vernacular, the ditty commenced thusly:

"Hurrah! and hurrah! for the golden chink.
That e'er lines the well-filled purse!
Hurrah! and hurrah! for the rich red wine,
The troubled heart's best nurse.
For golden coin and red wine, I opine,
Will e'er defy the blues an' pauper hearse!"

"Now, my beauty," added the highwayman, softly patting the satin-like coats of his well-fed and groomed animal, "let us direct our steps away from this silent common, 'an' put the best leg foremost,' as remarked to himself the gallant, who 'ad to wooden-legs, as 'e was a-starting off to the village dance!"

The beautiful mare briskly responded to the words of her master by galloping off at a smart pace, the direction taken being directly opposite to that made for by Squire Brancomb.

SQUIRE BRANCOMB WAYLAID FOR THE SECOND TIME—THE IMPERSONATOR OF DICK THE DANDY—A GALLANT STAND—THE BLACK DEED ON THE LONELY BRIDAL ROAD—JONATHAN WILD REVEALED IN DEEPER TINTS OF CRIME.

Squire Brancomb greatly congratulated himself upon his cheap escape from a masked, mounted, cool-nerved, and daring road-gallant. The good man was more than delighted at the knowledge that he should still be able to keep his word with his friend, at that moment doubtless anxiously awaiting his advent

---

[38] Sovereign.

with the money. The squire had reached the roughest and wildest portion of his route, a rugged stretch of open country on the outskirts of Barnet.

Suddenly a second horse and rider came within view. The squire felt some alarm, but hoped that the horsemen might turn out to be nothing worse than a fellow-traveller, or night patrol. Should he, however, chance to prove another daring outlaw, there were the secret passwords which the former robber had assured him would preserve the utterer thereof from further molestation, for the time, at least.

The two horsemen could not well avoid meeting without exciting mutual suspicion, for the horse road was some feet below the usual level.

"'Tis a bleak night an' a late hour to journey in these lonely parts, good master!" greeted a harsh, evil-jarring voice, as Squire Brancomb neared the other.

"Indeed, 'tis e'en as you state, good stranger; "but I rejoice to say that I am near the haven I seek," pleasantly responded the squire.

Then the horsemen came clearly into view, one to the other. The square instantly felt a strong revulsion of feeling.

Never had he witnessed a more repulsive-looking creature than that of the being now facing him. The latter was masked, and had his three-cornered hat tilted over his eyes, and a black muffler covering the lower part of his face. The eyes gleamed through the holes in the black mask with an expression of such concentrated malevolence as to make the beholder shudder; and there was that in the lines of the short, steadily-built form, and its every motion, which suggested more the nature of a panther—cruel, stealthily, and utterly remorseless—than man.

"A masked horsemen in these parts! 'Tis a suspicious mode of appearing abroad—" began the squire, when the other blurted out savagely:

"There need be no beating about the bush! You are Squire Brancomb, and have a large sum of money with you! I am Dick the Dandy, the terror of London's city and England generally! Your property or your life!"

The belated wayfarer, for the second time within that same hour, faced the threatening metal tube of a flint-lock.

"'Midnight toll paid!'" he cried, repeating the words Wiffles had assured him would guarantee him protection against other highwaymen.

"What cursed jargon are you using, knave?" impatiently and ragefully demanded the masked man, clicking the hammer of the pistol-lock ominously.

"I have already been waylaid but now by a mounted outlaw, and he assured me that the words I have used would ensure me a safe passage from all desperate characters I might further meet!" tremblingly explained the squire to the masked man.

"Varlet!" furiously cried the other, "that is but a scurvy trick—an invention on my own part; an' I'll slit by foolish crown in twain if thou traced any such further poltroonry on with Dick the Dandy!"

The threatened man gazed earnestly at the other. The skull was devoid of natural hair or wig, and was swathed in a white bandage, as if the man had recently been injured in the head. The whole aspect of the disguised being could not possibly have looked more repellent.

"You Dick the Dandy?" contemptuously commented the other horseman— "the youthful, gay, and handsome adventurer, whose person is so full of charm, and manners so extremely captivating that our highest born dames are all most eager to be robbed by him, and deem the same the highest mark of prevailing mode, while good King George himself—if rumour speaks true—is half a mind to grant the youth a free pardon, in consequence of certain of his most loyal and astounding daring exploits, the which have recently reached his Majesty's notice? You crook'd backed, impish-looking ruffian, thou liest!"

Squire Brancomb's ire had driven away his fears, and his right hand went to one of his horse-pistols. The other's quick eyes saw the movement, and pulled his trigger. The flint and steel gave out a few sparks, but no explosion followed. The baffled ruffian levelled another pistol with his left hand, while with the right he tugged at the hilt of his hanger, its sheath momentarily holding tight the blade.

Brancomb rapidly drew his pistol and fired point-blank. The ball passed within an inch of the bandaged temples. Another explosion instantly followed. Squire Brancomb knew that he was hit, but now fully resolved to sell his life dearly; and while yet having strength, he drew his side-arm and aimed a most terrific cut at his attacker.

By the merest chance in the world the hanger missed the man's head. The impetus of the stroke caused the squire to lurch forward and his steel to fly downwards. The other then saw his opportunity, and fiendishly seized it. His blade now flashed from its covering, made one furious swell, and then pierced the traveller through the breast.

The brave man lifted up his steel, and attempted to slash it downwards at his foeman's temple; then the life-stream suddenly gushed from his mouth and the gaping wound in his breast, as, with inarticulate but piteous cries, he reeled from the saddle, and then, with sickening thud, crashed down upon the frost and snow-covered earth.

Uttering a cry, resembling that of some wild beast springing upon its prey, the masked man leapt from his steed, and then commenced a furious stabbing at the already lifeless body, hacking it in a most heartless manner with his cutlass.

"Aha, my plans were most craftily-concocted and as craftily carried out!" thought the blood-guilty wretch, while continuing his awful work until the same was completed to his satisfaction. "Firstly, I warned this trusting fool against a probable meeting with the notorious highwayman, Dick the Dandy. This—my message—was no doubt repeated, and the excellent and zealous Mr. Wild got the credit for the very best of intentions in cautioning a wealthy citizen of the Chepe to be prepared against desperate robbers on making a journey into the lawless wilds of Finchley and Barnet, the whole details of which this addle pate gave out one night at the Blue Boar hostelry in Holborn, and little dreaming that one of my keenest spies mingled with the merry company then present.

"Then I took precious good care that the only available serving-man of this Squire Brancomb should be suddenly taken ill at the last moment of starting, and thus the rash citizen resolved that he could not delay his journey, and therefore started without escort. Ha, ha, ha!" softly the ruffian chuckled, as he now gave his close attention to the dead man's property.

It was the notorious Jonathan Wild in his secret character of robber on the King's highway, and most cold-blooded ruffian included. The great thief-taker, thief-maker, and murder-factor knew no limits to his debased passion when his ambitious views rendered crime necessary.

The mutated remains of the unfortunate Squire Brancomb presented a most awful spectacle, stretched out upon the crimson-stained snow and frost-covered earth, the eyes open, glazed in death, and looking as if in mute appeal to the great Judgement Seat for swift retribution upon the callous assassin!

"Thus I repay old scores, my defeat of the other night included, my gallant Dick the Dandy!" continued to cogitate Jonathan Wild. "In my possession is a pistol—a most elegant article—the property of the Great Lady-Killer. Ha, ha! Wait! wait! This weapon I shall swear I myself found by the side of the plundered and murdered good citizen of ye Chepe, the body being most terribly stabbed and most cruelly mutilated—evidently wantonly after death—by the most foul desperado, cutthroat, filch-purse highway terror, footpad, and most barbarous ruffian unhanged! The reward for my fine gallow's bird will be at least doubled. His exploits and fine gallantry will no longer be 'A la Mode,' as the mincing, snuff taking, diamond high for buckled exquisites at Court and at the Mall of St. James's term it. And the King will no longer harbour thought of clemency towards felons who happen to be of romantic exterior, and apt to acts of great bravery and gallantry."

The chestnut cob had remained passive after the falling of its master. The animal stretched out its neck, and, with nervously-twitching limbs and nostrils, sniffed at the mute, blue-white visage of its master, as the murderer examined the saddle-bags for the money he knew must be somewhere hidden. Presently a leather pouch or case was found. This contained a great sum in crown pieces. Gold and small coins had already been found in a purse and in the pockets of the clothing of the dead man.

The money thus netted by Jonathan Wild, at the cost of a human life, represented a small fortune in those days when an ordinary guinea meant at least four times its value of to-day. A valuable snuffbox, studded with gems, as was then the fashion, was also found; some rings, a watch and chain and seals, and lastly the horse-pistols and dress-sword.

These the murderer and pillager of the dead took possession of, and, as a supposed conclusive proof that the appalling crime was that of an ordinary outlaw-malefactor, he placed his own mask under the body, to be discovered there by a chance pedestrian, or even the persons the deep-dyed villain Jonathan wild intended to send for the object of removing the corpse to the nearest convenient place for its reception.

Carefully rearranging every detail of the discovery to meet his intended wicked plot, the kneeling wretch failed to observe the silent approach of the weird, gaunt object. An ear-piercing shriek rang out with standing suddenness upon the previously silent midnight air.

Jonathan Wild sprang up, every nerve and fibre of his being thrilled as with the result of a powerful shock of electricity. Discovery of his most foul crime meant instant and utter ruin to his most ambitious prospects, and the ending of his life on his own pet instrument—the scaffold!

°WE RETURN TO BOW STREET RUNNER BILBERRY AND HIS TORTURERS—A SOOTY YET UNSUITABLE SUITOR—THE ARDOUR OF THE BRAVE MADE SOFTER—THE FINDING OF A MARE'S NEST UNDER A BED—A BOOTLESS CAPTURE.

The utmost the Bow Street officer Bilberry could venture to do was to open one eye very slightly, the thickly-coated soot clinging to him—rendered as it was into a paste by the water that had been freely thrown over him—stuck like pitch, and caused a most painful smarting in his eyes, and the flying particles had entered his nostrils also.

Now it takes much to cause a well-seasoned snuff-taker to start on a course of long lusty sneezing; but soot-dust makes a most powerful nose-tickler, and Bilberry commenced to sneeze so loudly and violently as to make it appear that his head had determined to rid itself of its great bottle-like front protuberances by shaking it completely off for good and all.

The blustering, bullying, cowardly officer had caught sight of the soot-covered little form of Will the Witless, as the latter made off with the aid of his long leaping-pole, after casting down the contents of the manure-bags from the top of the piled up faggots, and following this up by flinging pailfuls of water over the hedgerow to "damp down" the soot-manured "Red Robins."

° Part 7. Vol. XIV.—No. 343. 13 June 1900.

Bilberry now formed an inkling of the trick played on him and his two fellow-officers, and an inkling also of its object; but it suited his then state of chagrin to attach all the blame to someone on whom he could there and then fully vent his spleen.

"Man Alive! Blood an' hounds! May I be—Echew! eschew! eschew! Of all the infernal—Echew! eschew! 'Sdeath and —Echew! Stew me into a jelly! Echew! eschew! eschew! Ew-ew-eschew-w-w! May I be hanged upon the horns of the moon! Echew! A plague take them—echew!—you wooden-headed—echew! son of wooden-doll parents—eschew!—this is your—eschew-er!—doing! You stuck the—echew!—point of your—echew!–cutlass into the–echew-er!—bag of chimney sweep's dust—echew-er!"

"You're a—hisschew!—liar—hisschew!" replied the Bow Street runner accused, and who had now also caught the sneezing infection.

"A-tissue! a-tissuer! a-tissham! You faint-hearted—er-tissue!—Weak-kneed—eschew!—over-grown, long-nosed—a-tissing!—stork! I saw you deliberately do this—a-tissue!—trick!" resumed Bilberry, at the same time roundly indulging in an under-current of cursing against the irrepressible sneezing fit. "I saw you bring down that pestiferous cloud of devil's dust expressly to—a-a-tiss-hew!—to hide up your most villainous and craven—a-chew-w!—person, so that Dandy Dick, the highwayman, might not catch sight of you and—a-cheew-ass!—let daylight into your dull, dark brain by means of a piece of lead from one of his dainty barkers!"

"You loud-sounding—urr-shi-ssush-ew!—jester's wind-bladder!" cried the insulted runner. "That trick would be more in your way!"

These words were followed up by a stinging blow, which fell full upon the large black sneezing organ owned by Officer Bilberry. The claret was instantly tapped, the sneezing as instantly stopped. It's an ill-blow (wind) that does no one any good!

Bilberry was a full-blooded person, and bled like some huge whale, spouting a red-black stream. The sight of his own gore terrified the blustering coward, and his fat face went white under its coat of black, the ashen hue being easily seen in patches where the sooty crust was thinnest.

"Ha, ha, ha!—ha—thisue!" laughed and sneezed the third runner, the sight of Bilberry, the blackened and bleeding porpoise-like creature, being so extremely funny—not to say shrieking the comic—that the man for the moment forgot his own discomfort to give vent to a most hearty burst of merriment.

The loudly-sounding laughter was taken up now by the man who had struck Bilberry. The latter was most tenderly caressing the fat end of his damaged nose, the said end now being much flattened.

Speeches not improved by receiving a serious thump on the proboscis, and speech is even still less improved by holding the end of the injured member wrapped in linen in between the fingers.

"Ban alive! Phud dan hounds! Blew be indoo a-stelling! Bay di pe dauged ubon de born sob de ob de boon!" yelled Bilberry, his favourite oaths mingling with the shrieks of laughter of the others.

"What the—Who—When the—of all the most confounded—The voices are those of three of my men! The voices have been stolen—all the three are most clever mimics—by three unknown blackamores. No, by all things wonderful, my unfortunate men have suddenly been seized by the black plague!—got the awful visitation in its most advanced stage, too!" Thus exclaimed the superior officer of the three new Black Robbins.

Then it dawned upon the mind of the former that the terrible disease— common enough in London in the days of which we write—was seldom met with in the depth of winter. Closer examination, and a few words sufficed to open the eyes of the officer to something nearer the actual facts. A clever trick had been played upon three of his men—by whom was not clear—but its probable object could be guessed at—namely, the escape of Dandy Dick!

In spite of his dignity and annoyance, the officer in charge of the party of Bow Street runners could not now refrain from giving vent to repeated bursts of laughter. Never in all his life had he seen three more woeful—comically woeful—looking objects, and of which Bilberry himself—with his mixture of red and black disfigurement—was certainly the chief knockout!

"Get ye to the Hole-in-the-Wall hostelry, ye wretched brace of black-jacks! There's nothing for it but to give you all a good sousing of water until the blackness is completely removed!" shouted their leader.

Mrs. Drake and her husband were attracted to the door of their inn by the outer unusual and mixed din of laughter, lamentation, cursing, sneezing, &c.

"Most adorable—fairest—at chew! My sweet Mrs. Drake, pray—atch-chiew! Infernal fiends seize this sneezing; it's come on again! Pray have compassion on my state!" Officer Bilberry had placed one black fat paw upon his breast, and was bowing with all the attempted grace of a fine gallant.

The archly-pretty hostess, on catching sight of Bilberry and his fellow-imps, stood motionless for a few seconds to recover her breath; and then she burst out into one long, musical ripple, and her fit of cachinnation[39] appeared as if it would never end, and excepting for the purpose of recovering her breath so that she could increase the intensity and length of her wild outburst; and, in spite of his secret worries, Ralph Drake could not refrain from adding a few startling guffaws.

---

[39] Loud laughter.

In the meantime the remainder of the runners, as instructed, seized the pails standing by the horse-trough, filled them, and commenced most lustily drenching of their unfortunate comrades with crystal-like showers of freezing-cold liquid.

Poor Bilberry's teeth set up an active dance, his enormous bulk shook like a great jelly, as he occasionally groaned most dismally. When the soot and bloodstains were at length sufficiently removed, he made a waddling rush for the interior of the inn, and, before either the host or hostess could prevent him, he had darted upstairs to the bedrooms.

Looks of apprehensive terror were exchanged between Mr. and Mrs. Drake; then the officer was seen quickly descending the stairs, and frantically indulging in much grotesque dumb show.

"He's gone mad!—lost his wits! They're been roused out clean of his ugly pate!" impatiently cried Bilberry's superior.

"Man alive, I am sound-minded as ever!" excitedly whispered Bilberry; adding: "I've lost nothing—found much! There's a highwayman concealed in one of the bedrooms above!"

"We're ruined, lass!" muttered Ralph Drake aside to his wife, who now looked as if upon the point of falling into a dead faint.

The Bow Street runners rudely thrust aside the host and his wife, and in a body crowded up the old broken stairway.

Officer Bilberry, almost frozen to death with his drenching, and shaking like an aspen-leaf, fell back upon his almost unlimited stock of highly-spiced oaths, and thickly rolled them out in the hope of putting some fire in his veins. Some of his most pet "swear words" were hot enough to roast chestnuts.

Cleverly continuing not to keep in the front, Bilberry, with shaking hand, pointed out to his officer a bedroom, at the same time hastily asserting, in an undertone, that on entering, he had distinctly seen a pair of jack-boots, of most superior make (and having silver spurs), slightly protruding from under the bed hangings. There were the brightly-polished leg-boots, plain enough; and for once Bilberry, it appeared, had actually spoken the truth. But he soon put his foot into—not the boots, but the story thereof.

"I saw the fellow dash under the bed on the instant he caught sight of me—a most ferocious-looking villain, and armed to the teeth! I would have hurled myself upon him had I even had my hanger in its sheath!" explained the now comparatively brave Bilberry, surrounded as he was by a crowd of well-armed comrades.

"In the King's name, I call upon you to come out of your hiding-place!" thundered out the brassy tones of the chief of the Bow Street runners; "and speedily, too," he added, "or we shall fire upon you!"

A MURDERER CAUGHT RED-HANDED AT HIS FOUL WORK—THE HAG OF THE HEATH—THE SPECTRAL HORSEMAN—A SUPERNATURAL INTERVENTION—WIFFLES, THE COMIC OUTLAW, AND HIS WHEEZES—THE MOHAWKS, THE TERRORS OF OLD LONDON, AND THEIR DOINGS.

"Aha! vile carrion bird! Off, vulture! Away! Away!"

This was the startling cry that pierced the ears, and, for the moment, paralysed the limbs of Jonathan Wild, while in the act of bending over the body of the ill-starred Squire Brancome, the man the thief-taker had waylaid in the desolate wilderness, known as Finchley Common, and on a weirdly dark and bleak winter's night, with snow, frost, and but the moanings of the far-spreading frost and snow fleece-laden winds to bestow their cold kisses upon the even still colder, silent, and dead marble that was so recently warm, pulsating gladsome life!

"Away! away! human vulture! Who says that the pure snow falls? The heavens rain the blood of earthly creatures; and men—sinful men—live in its depths! Away, wretch, away! Aha! I know thee, Jonathan Wild! Vampire! Ha, ha, ha! Beware the vampire's doom!"

The detected, cold-blooded murderer threw an upward glance, and, standing near him, a weird, haggard, and gaunt-looking aged crone, her long-flowing, black garments blown flapping lay upon the midnight wind as she fantastically waved aloft her withered arms, one hand of which held a long staff. The hag was in a frenzy of fearless horror and loathing.

"Away! Take thy perfidious hand from the sacred dead! Double-dyed fiend—tremble, Jonathan Wild, for I predict for thee a swift and awful retribution!"

Seeing that but a weak and withered dame had detected him in his secret crime, Jonathan Wild sprang erect, and quickly drew an undischarged pistol from his coat-skirt-pocket.

"You have seen too much for my safety, prowling hag!" he savagely hissed. Levelling the weapon, he snapped the lock. The explosion rang out, strangely contrasting with the weird silence of the wild locality, the ball tore its way through the tattered, flowing garments of the old crone, as she darted off, shrieking shrilly, in taunting indignation and newly-awakened fear.

His intended victim appeared uninjured. Jonathan Wild swished his cutlass from its leathern sheath and then bounded after the woman, determined to mercilessly cut her down, his own safety demanding it. The fleeing form stumbled and fell, a few more strides and the murderous Wild overtook the gaunt form as it regained its feet.

"Meddling lunatic, thus I deal with my enemies!" he snarled furiously, cleaving downwards at the back of the grey-haired, moving head. Another instant would have made the wretch a double murderer within the space of a few minutes, but an amazing intervention stayed the remorseless blow.

No clash, or slightest sound of the meeting of metals, a perfect silence, yet the keen cutlass-edge was held back by an unseen and irresistible agency; then, before the wildly-staring orbs of the bewildered and now fear-awed Jonathan Wild a bluish-white film floated and gradually took shape.

The misty presentment of a gallant forming itself from nothingness, the face that of a deeply woe-stricken yet handsome man, with long, curling locks and beautiful vestments; but around the neck was a hangman's noose, its end dangling down. Over the breast is a vividly outstanding blood-red patch, or else of but the one ghostly hue, and beneath the spectral form shapes a horse, but less distinct than even the floating, haze-like man.

A great, superstitious terror seized the thief taker; he tried to shriek out, but his tongue could not obey his will power; his limbs violently trembled, then an electrical, burning sensation flew through his frame, commencing at the hand clutching his upraised sword, and the ruffian fell to the earth uttering a feeble moan—fell, stricken by a mysterious supernatural power.

How long Jonathan Wild remained senseless and inert he knew not, but when he recovered the use of his faculties he was icily cold and strangely stiff. Most painful were the efforts to rise and walk, but eventually he succeeded in tottering to the spot where his steed had patiently awaited him; then he mounted, taking with him all the plunder obtained from the murdered man.

The roundhouse of Ye Saint John of Jerusalem—situated within a stone's throw of the latter famous hostelry, which is still in existence—has but been demolished within the last two score or so years. The roundhouse was used as a place of justice and lock-up, and it was here that the thief-taker betook himself to lay information of the murder—which he himself had committed—on the King's highway, and of which he was prepared to swear that he had discovered most incontestable proof that the foul act was alone due to the handsome, dashing, youthful highwayman, Dandy Dick.

Life is filled with the most remarkable coincidences, and coincidences fraught with the most momentous importance. Thus Dandy Dick—for a time at least—chanced to unconsciously avert his ignominious death upon the scaffold by the very act of secretly becoming initiated into the alleged methods of undergoing strangulation by the neck in a public place. In other words, the youthful outlaw's actual presence in the Black Barns, together with the knowledge of Wiffles, most firmly, and beyond the shadow of a doubt, proved that Dandy Dick would not possibly have committed the robbery and murder on Finchley Common, his presence long before and after the time of the crime being engaged with Daddy Delph and Nat Flint—still on Finchley, but at a very great distance from the scene of the deed.

On the event of Dandy Dick's visit to the Back Barns, Nat Flint had successfully passed through the ordeal of hanging, and revived from his death-like fate, but the horrible nature of the process was not to be mistaken. In the words of Nat Flint: "It was a thousand times more terrible than actual death itself," which, in most cases was instantaneous. The torture inflicted by the use of the silver tube fixed in the throat could not be described. Partial suffocation, long continued, being but a part of it; then the agonising strain upon the muscles of the neck, not to mention the mental state of the victim, who could never be sure that the spinal column would resist the act of the drawing away of the hangman's cart.

"What if the hangman should detect your secret methods previous to placing of his grim noose about the doomed one's throat?" anxiously asked Dandy Dick of Daddy Delph.

"Ho! ho! Ho! Body o' me!" cried Daddy Delph. "E'cod, but that would prove a jarring discord in the harmony of our most sweet music! He! he! he! Teach Daddy Delph to brew a bowl o' punch an' then consume the brew! My noble master, Dandy Dick, pray who told you that the public executioner was an enemy an' not a most special crony of Daddy Delph's? He! he! he!"

The strange words of the still stranger old man through a stronger light into the mind of the highwayman, now—in spite of himself—vastly impressed with a sense of the mysterious powers the old man controlled.

"Still, even assuming that the executioner connived at your doings, there are others connected with Newgate who might—"

"Daddy Delph knows his business, good Sir Gallant of the Starlight Heath," laughingly interrupted the former; adding: "should the safer, easier means fail, there still remains my secret elixir of life. The condemned is by law entitled to claim a passing drink from the hand of a friend—the cup handed him may contain the life-drops themselves. In a chamber of this building," excitedly continued Daddy Delph, "now sleeps the being who is living proof of my words. My pretty gallows-bird's wings are not clipped, his song not yet hushed, yet, within the past two weeks he was publicly hanged before Newgate, and afterwards taken to Hounslow Heath, there hanged in chains—in a dangling felon-cage—exposed to the cruel elements in a death-like condition until midnight, when Nat Flint and Daddy Delph visited the pretty bird and snatched it from its uncomfortable cage. Ho! ho! ho! We laugh at grim old death! Ha! ha! ha! We cheat the gallows of its victim! Ha! ha! ha!"

With these words of the gruesome old sexton still ringing in his ears, Dandy Dick left the Black Barns of Finchley. During the whole of the most trying ordeal through which he had just passed, one thought had remained uppermost in his mind, and his heart had been torn in twain as the result. That agonising thought was of the beautiful, stately, high-born maiden, Maude Mortiemor. Severed as they were for ever, they still passionately loved, and was still eternally devoted one to the other.

The queenly-looking, yet most tender, Maude, was now in the power of one of the most consummate villains alive—Raymond Raithwood. Already had he aimed at her life—attempted the double assassination of her and her outlawed lover. Dandy Dick was filled with a presentment of evil on the behalf of Maude Mortiemer, and, unreasonable as was the hour, he was resolved to ride over to Sir Edgar Mortiemer's mansion—situated at Highbury, and but a mile or two outwards of Finchley—and make what chance investigations fortune might permit him. With this determination he was about to encourage his beautiful mare, Jess, with a few cheery words, and to give her her head, when a secret signal cry restrained him. A moment after, Wiffles rode into view.

"Comrade, I wishes yer a much better night ter foller this 'un!" cried he. "It's impossible ter offer yer a warm welcome, 'cos why—the words, as they comes from me mouth, is each frozen inter icicles. Listen! you can 'ear 'em droppin'— like pebbles—inter the road."

"Never mind, good old friend," cheerfully replied Dandy Dick. "I'm grateful to you for remembering to meet me here."

"Cut that gratertude in 'alf, Dick. I ain't all 'ere!" retorted the whimsical Wiffles quaintly. "There's a part o' me still a-'anging on ter the sunbeams o' last summer!" Then he commenced softly humming:

> "Oh, me 'eart is in the 'eeland
> An' it cannot be 'ere;
> It's chasing throu' ther woods,
> A-following ther deer.

"Leastways," he laughingly added, "ther dear as I may chases 'as got two legs only!" Then he sang a few more words as follows:

> "Oh, 'er eyes they are darker than the darkest o' skies,
> An' tip-tilted is 'er dainty-'ued nose;
> 'Er mouth 'tis a rosebud fill'd up wi' pearls
> An' 'ead a garden o' brownest o' curls."

°**THE MOHAWKS AND THEIR DOINGS** *(continued).*

The high spirits of Wiffles were really but assumed, and for the object of dispelling the gloom from which he well knew his friend had long suffered. But Wiffles' good intentions bore no fruit, for if lovely Maude Mortiemor could not boast a "tip-tilted nose," the lines—"Her mouth 'tis a rosebud fill'd up with petals, and head a garden of brownest curls," exactly fitted in with the exquisite charms of the fashionable belle, now day by day drifting further from the heart of her handsome and young, but, alas! notorious, lover.

"Cheer up, Dick, old comrade!" brightly advised Wiffles. "In this here dreary world it's always best ter look on the bright side o' things. Remember what the

---

° Part 8. Vol. XIV.—No. 344. 13 June 1900.

toad sed ter 'is old pal the frog, when 'e was a-looking most awful down in ther mouth, 'cos 'e'd swallow'd 'is little brother, under the impression 'as the little 'un was a stranger ter ther family. 'Look 'ere, old 'un,' sed the toad, 'you mighth 'a' swallow'd yer father, or mother, or ther whole biling family, which 'ud been more awfuller awful still; an' what's more, you now 'ave ther comfort o' knowing as the poor, dear little 'un is now for ever more out o' snares o' this wicked world."

In spite of his dejection, Dandy Dick could not restrain a smile on hearing Wiffles' fable of a frog.

Suddenly a great clattering of horses' hooves, mingling with most boisterous shouts from many throats, startled the highwaymen as they were upon the point of riding from the spot. The great commotion was evidently nearing Dandy Dick and Wiffles.

"Them's the Mo'awks,[40] an' they're out for devil's mischief, as usual," said Wiffles. "We'd better show 'em a wide berth—as ther stickle brat remarked when he saw ther whale floating towards 'un."

"The lawless licence of the young bloods of our aristocracy frequently put to shame the worst acts of our class, yet the ruffians are seldom, if ever, punished. We'll remain and face them, friend Wiffles. I'm in a more than usual reckless mood to-night!" cried Dandy Dick, his jaw set, a fiercely defiant glitter in his deep-blue eyes.

"There is numbers of 'em, Dick; an' they stick at nothink," warned Wiffles.

"Then we may read them a lesson, if needed, Wiffles—a lesson on gentlemanly deportment."

"The lesson may cost a life ter read," seriously commented Dandy Dick's comrade.

"A life is well lost, if sacrificed in doing a good deed," returned Dandy Dick.

With a thundering din and noise the horsemen came on. Above the mixed thunderings of many throats arose—with ear-piercing intensity—the cry of a female—a cry in the most heartrending tones of terror and despair.

MORE OF OFFICER BILBERRY'S FAIRY TALES—THE KING'S OFFICERS ARE CLEVERLY DUPED—THE MIMIC AND VENTRILOQUIST—BILBERRY LAID UP IN SNUG QUARTERS—THE PLOT—THE INVALIDS—BILBERRY HOLDS FORTH ON THE CURING OF COLD AND COLIC.

"The game's up, Dandy Dick, or whoever you may be! Rat, come out of thine hole, or, by all that's commendable, I'll spit thee upon my cutlass-point! Out of it!" This was Bilberry's voice, and he tried vainly to hide the shaky note in it.

The boots never once moved. Two of the nearest officers stooped, and then seized them, then each officer threw himself backwards with all his strength.

---

40 Mohawks – a group of aristocratic thugs and street-bullies who caused mayhem with their drunken, anti-social and violent crimes.

The legs of a man might have been almost jerked off his body, so sudden and powerful were the wrenches; but, as there were no limbs in the leather articles, the Bow Street officers sprawled backwards with enormous force, striking the floor with the backs of their heads, the hardness of their sconces making the boards creak as if with pain. For a few moments the runners remained at full length, then both sat upright and commenced rubbing the backs of their skulls and swearing most lustily, the room and all in it swimming swiftly round them in the giddiness resulting from their unexpected backward crash.

"The villainous robber's pulled his feet out!" shouted Bilberry. "I swear that I saw him but a few instants back! 'Sdeath! Blood an' hounds! Why not blow the wretch into mincemeat?"

Two of the Bow Street officers sprang forward and fiercely prodded with their hangers at the dark space revealed by the drawing aside of the lower bed drapery. The points of their sword struck against atmosphere. No cry came to prove that a wound had been inflicted on any living thing. The leader of the Bow Street officers crouched down, holding his pistol at full-cock, and then crept into the black void. In an instant he returned, dragging out several articles of apparel—those were of a distinctly rich and dandyish class—and with them were a hat and mask such as a highwayman or footpad might use.

"If there were a man there, he has mysteriously slipped us. These things are most suspicious proofs of the presence of an outlaw in this inn, and it is my duty to see farther into the matter!" sternly muttered the chief of the runners, closely examining the things he had found so carelessly bestowed.

"'Sdeath! I shall die if I remain longer in my water-drenched clothing! By the memory of my departed sire, I feel as wretched as a frog frozen within a square mile block of ice, with a distant fire to be seen through its transparency, but which he can never possibly hope to get near," chatted Officer Bilberry, the water still running from his garments like rain.

"Are you convinced that you saw a man slip under this bed?" demanded Bilberry's superior, in doubting tones, and not heeding the former's reference to his condition.

"Blood an' hounds! Man Alive! As convinced as I am at this present moment that I am a human water-butt, and dripping my very life-fluid away at every pore o' me body," dismally groaned Bilberry, shivering like a huge jelly in a sudden gale of wind.

"Lud! lud! lud! Bow Street bully-boys,[41] what mean ye by all this confounded confusion, riot, and unearthly contentions? Lud! lud! But I'll petition his Most Gracious Majesty King George himself concerning this same outrage; and you, my good host, Ralph Drake, shall bear me witness!"

---

[41] Although the verb "to bully" (used elsewhere in the text) refers to aggressive behaviour, a "bully boy" is defined as "a fine person.

A stranger stood at the open door of the bedroom in which were crowded the officers. The stranger was of youthful age, and but partly dressed, as if just disturbed in the process of his toilet. He wore a full-bottomed wig of light-brown hair, one eye was covered with a green shade, and the face distorted by an affection of wrinkles. There were also a number of patches of black plaster on each cheek—such as were sometimes worn in the days of the Georges, either to denote political inclinations, or simply for the purpose of foppery alone.

Drake, the proprietor of the Hole-in-the-Wall Inn, stood at the back of the youthful stranger, and looked exceedingly pale and scared.

The chief of the Bow Street runners stepped forward.

"We are seeking the capture of a most notorious highwayman, and have found garments in this room such as might be worn by a so-called 'Gallant of the Heath.' I don't know you, sir; and you will do well not to interfere with officers of the law in the execution of their duty." This was said with much overdone importance by the leader of the runners.

"Lud! lud! 'Pon honour! I laugh, sirrah! I laugh!" The stranger spoke in a highly-pitched, cracked kind of voice. "You've entered my bedroom—rumpussed[42] an' rioted like so many street-performing surly, snarling, mangy bears! Lud! lud! You've tumbled over my masquerading costume—in the which I went as 'Dandy Dick' to the Vauxhall Gardens last night! Lud! lud! My Bow Street Bully-boys, you'd better arrest me. He! he! he! Confusion overtake me, but I must laugh! Ho! Ho! He! he! he!" The old inn echoed and re-echoed with the shrill falsetto laughter of the youthful stranger.

"You claim occupancy of this room, and the suspicious-looking articles?" demanded Officer Bolton, the chief of the officers.

"Lud! Yes, friend Bully-boy. My room—my costume! Is that so, friend Drake, mine host?"

Ralph Drake corroborated the former's statement with most emphatic manner.

"I'd like to question the hostess, too. I'm bound to report this matter," added Bolton, with lingering doubts.

The guest of the inn went quietly to the landing, and called to the upper regions for Mrs. Drake, whose voice was heard faintly in reply.

"I must beg to be excused, good sir, I'm changing my dress for afternoon wear," came her reply, apparently from a top-most apartment.

"Gentlemen, I'm sorry for this unpleasant circumstance," put in Ralph Drake. "I will prevail upon my good patron here to let the matter blow over, if our worthy friend, Officer Bolton, will, on his part, also ignore the thing; and I will also ask the favour of each gentleman of Bow Street to partake of a special brew of punch at my own expense."

---

42 Caused a disturbance.

The word punch acted like magic—as the pouring of oil upon troubled waters. But bowl after bowl of the special brew were demanded, and with each further demand the face of Ralph Drake grew longer. The strange guest betook himself to his dressing chamber—which was situated next that in which the scene just related had occurred—and sent down by Drake firm, yet polite, refusals to all Officer Bolton's requests to come down and join the company in their potations.

It was night. The secretly-hated and despised Bow Street runners had departed, with the exception of Officer Bilberry and the two others, whom, in consequence of their wet plight, had remained and been accommodated with beds in a large three-bedded room.

Ralph Drake and his beautiful, dark-eyed wife were seated in the little bar-parlour. The roguishly charming face of Mrs. Drake wore an anxious expression. That of her husband looked still more distressed. The two were conversing in low tones. No guests occupied the lower portion of the inn, and but few the upper.

"You could make a fine fortune on the stage, lass," Drake was saying. "Your notion and wonderful mimicking powers has saved us from ruin. Egad! wench, I could almost die o' laughter—spite of our dreadful shift for money—when I picture you as that young gallant, with his 'Lud! lud! lud!' false wig on, and all that. Then, when you went to the staircase an' called for yourself, an' then made your own voice answer you away at the top o' the house—why, it was as smart an' daring as assuming the character, voice, an' manner—to the very life—of Dandy Dick, an' terrifying the life out o' that old bladder o' wind, Officer Bilberry, an' compelling him to hand over something towards what he honestly owed us for his unlimited drinking-bouts."

"I've always been considered clever, both as an actress and a ventriloquist, even from a child. It was no vanity, or want of honesty that caused me to figure as Dandy Dick, you know, Ralph. This part Court-gallant, part ruffian, part bully and coward, yet wholly baboon—if I may speak in such contrary terms— Bilberry, and his fellow Robins, are quickly sending us to the public pillory as defrauders. The wretches hold us in fear of the charge of harbouring outlaws, and make this the excuse for eating and drinking here as often as they choose, and never settling the score."

"I never thought that your successfully masquerading at a bal-masque as a highwayman would lead to your playing the part in real earnest, wench; and I must open my mind to Dandy Dick, our good friend, on this subject, and crave pardon for your deception, wife," thoughtfully and anxiously remarked Drake to his wife.

"The three human sponges upstairs will make their mishap an excuse for remaining here for days and eating and drinking as out-of-home free of cost, unless we can contrive to get rid of them. And I've an idea, husband—I've an idea!"

The hostess and host of Ye Hole-in-ye-Wall of Ye Gardens of Hatton continued their converse in hushed conclave, and when darkness came they put into execution their well-devised plot.

"Blood an' hounds! Bully-boys, did ye ever hear such an infernal clattering of steed-hooves? May I be stung to death by myriads of wasps, if all London isn't a-mount an' putting up at this particular inn!"

Bilberry's head was thrust as far as it could go into a worsted[43] nightcap, no end of blankets and rugs were heaped upon his bed, and his nose was fairly aglow—like a beacon at sea on a dark and stormy night—with a comforting sense of warmth. The three-bedded room contained his two fellow-sufferers of soot-dust and after cleansing dousings of freezing water. A limber-log was blazing merrily on the hearth, and the large chamber was warm as an oven.

"I don't like the cursed din, brother officer," replied one of Bilberry's companions. "I had fully made up my mind for a week's resting, feasting, and punch-swilling; this rush of patronage will cause us three invalids to be neglected like worn-out cast-off garments."

"Gazooks an' zounds! Fish-bones in the throats of those that dare to neglect a King's officer lain up through zealous discharge o' his duty!" fiercely replied Bilberry. "A murrain[44] on me," he continued, "if I shift from these cosy quarters for the next month or two! By my wisdom-teeth—long since lost—the liquors of this goodly inn shall have run parched dry, and its larder bare enough to give a small mouse fits before Officer Bilberry finally shows the front door to this hostelry his back. Ho! ho! Ho! But I'll make that three-weeks'-long visage of Drake's still longer—in proportion with my score—an' I'll also drive the snivelling idiot quite rampasterously stark, staring mad with jealousy, such incessant court will I pay to the sweetest creature alive—namely, the amiable wife of the sour, crossgrained[45] villain who owns this house."

"We'll certainly die of cold and colic unless we lay up snug for a time," chimed in the third invalid. "I'm told much hot grog will drive out a cold."

"Man alive, fill yourself up with goodly liquor until there is no room left for the cold! For my part, if I developed a cold, as of course I must, I'll drink in hot punch till I burst back what that cold shall shift. As to colic—I'm told this particular disease comes o' certain germs a-getting into one's blood. Well, friends, how to cure colic? Why, of course, germs are only humans of smaller growth—i'faith, I don't know but that there are actually men-germs!—an' all humans being fond of good liquors, it follows that if you treat these inner germs liberally, they'll either get too drunken to be able to work any infernal mischief—or, better still, they'll all turn up their toes and die off of delirium tremens."[46]

---

[43] A high quality wool yarn.
[44] An infectious disease or a plague; as an oath it means 'death'.
[45] Someone who is difficult to deal with.
[46] Symptoms experienced by withdrawal from alcohol.

THE HIGHWAYMAN ATTACKED BY A RIOTOUS GANG OF "YOUNG BLOODS"—THE ABDUCTORS AND THEIR VICTIMS—RAYMOND RAITHWOOD—A FIERCE BATTLE AGAINST MANY ODDS—SPRING-HEELED JACK TO THE RESCUE—THE PANIC STRICKEN HORSEMEN RETREAT.

"A he-lopement an' a she-lopement!" cried Wiffles, "you may depend, comrade Dick. Which means that a young dame is a-being carried off by 'er lover be force—of her own free will!—ter the well-known Gretna Green, where there matter-o'-money-all-knot can be tied for poor old crusty, fuming, storming, an' non-consenting Daddy can overtake 'em! Steaming steeds, mud-smothered postill'ns, an' rambling, groaning old coach includ'd!" Then Wiffles warbled the words of a popular song:

> "A daring young blade as didn't oughter,
> Fly off with an old man's daughter—
>> Now wither away? and so rashly, I mean!
> Villain, oh, villain, you didn't ought,
> You go to that goal—rash lover's resort,
>> Where they'll join yer hinstanter—at Gretna Green!"

However imminent the danger, the high animal spirits of Wiffles could never be completely dampened. His cheery humour was so much a part of himself that nothing short of death itself would ever finally check it. Wiffles saw everything through the same quizzical, or comical, mental glasses.

The impetuous onrush of a troop of wild, drunken, dissolute—if wellborn and of high station—ruffians, with a shrieking female in their midst, therefore, at first blush, presented its amusing side to the youthful wag; and we by no means desire the reader to believe that this amusing personage, Wiffles, was wanting in sympathy with distressed humanity, as that would be very far from the truth.

"A female cry for help, Wiffles! Outlawed, despised, hunted as we are, we can never turn a deaf ear to such a plea of distress, come what may as the result!" cried Dandy Dick, hastily seeing that his weapons were in full readiness for any emergency. Flint and steel in proper position to ensure ignition in the powder-holes of his firearms, rapier unlikely to drag or catch in its scabbard.

"There's another shriek, Dick!" answered Wiffles, also anxiously seeing to his arms. "'I like not the prospect!' as the captive rat remarked, when it saw a crowd of snarling cats around a trap, an' a man about ter open the wire door. Oh, that our good pal, Cornal Gore, was beside us, Richard!" Wiffles added, now venting a sigh of anxiety.

"There is evidently a considerable crowd of Mohawks—for such they must be, judging by their unlicensed clamour—, and the fact of their possessing an unwilling female captive—but we must trust to the fortune of war and our valour to pull us through. With you, comrade, I regret that our brave friend, Colonel Blood, is not with us."

Like the sudden bursting of a tornado came on the body of horsemen and they dashed into the country lane in which stood Dandy Dick and the faithful Wiffles. Ear-splitting shouts, oaths, laughter, and cries of contemptuous scorn and derision greeted the two highwaymen as they coolly rode into the centre of the narrow lane and called upon the "young bloods" to halt.

"Upstarts! Marsports![47] Teach them to show respect to their betters! Spit them upon thy rapier blades! Slit their ears for their insolence! Sweep them like dirt from our path!"

Such were the threats shrieked out by the wine-maddened creatures, and in an instant blades were out, and in circling the two intrepid highwaymen like thickly-darting flashes of forked lightning.

"Hold!" thundered Dandy Dick, his quick eye making out the senseless form of a young girl held before one of the horsemen, and who appeared most anxious to keep himself hidden in the rear. "Hold, I say!" the youthful highwayman again cried in clarion-like tones. "Are ye English gentlemen that ye make this vile clamour in the early hours of the morning, and bear with ye a hapless female, or are ye wine-soaked poltroons and unmanly curs?"

"'Tis a fine bantam cock, truly; but he crows betimes, an' forsooth his comb must be cut!" retorted one of the horsemen, leaping his steed forward, and making a flying downward curve with his glinting blade at Dandy Dick's head. The latter had sighted danger in another direction, and must have been cut down but for the keen eye and swift action of Wiffles.

"Cutting combs is good, me bully blade!" cried the latter. "We'll make a note on't!" Wiffles, with his gloved hand, had seized his rapier by its steel end, and then ruthlessly crashed its steel cased handle down upon the head of the drink-maddened young aristocrat, the latter instantly falling from his saddle, his blood streaming from his temples and staining his dainty silk bow-tied cravat and exquisite blue velvet waistcoat, with its facings of gold lace.

"Have at them! Blood for blood! Show them no mercy; Lord Percy lies bathed in his gore! Revenge on the audacious strangers!" Yelling thus, the utterly furious crowd of horsemen closely surrounded the two highwaymen, who found themselves the centre of a circle of quivering, sparkling ribbons of steel.

"Have at thee, coward!" hissed Dick, furiously beating down the guard of the rider nearest him, and instantly driving his blade-point into the fellow's cheek. Then the withdrawn steel described a circle of lightning-like swiftness, leaving a blood-red gash upon many cheeks. The movement had been far too quick for eye to follow, and the sight of the disfiguring wounds dismayed and temporarily checked the attackers, numbering at least twelve to one.

"'Blood-letting for feaver-'eated brain pans! Steel-pointed pills, red draught ter foller!' sez Mr. Leech. 'Carn't 'ave too much o' a good thing,' as ther milkman sed when 'e drowned a cat in a pail o' milk. Come on, Dick; 'ave at 'em!"

---

[47] Spoilsports.

Wiffles had warmed to the work, and before the madlike roisterers had recovered their brief panic he had left the ugly trace of his blade on more than one. But the odds were too great to permit of anything but defeat for the two outlaws, whose true identity did not appear to be suspected as yet. Gaily dressed and masked men were too common in London thoroughfares to call for any particular comment, especially at night, or early morning, when the bal-masque was a chief feature of amusement.

The wild rabble—commonly termed "Young Bloods"—once recovered from the electrical onslaught made upon them by the solitary two, furiously sought the lives of the brave and cool adventurers, who, up to this point, had avoided the inflicting of a mortal wound.

With most frenzied cries they threw themselves upon Dandy Dick and Wiffles. The latter's skull had received a fracture at the back from which blood trickled. Dick's left shoulder-blade had received the shock of a steel point, and he was already faint with loss of blood; but an overwhelming heat of fury had entered heart and brain, and now, utterly regardless of the darting flashing points with which the air seemed filled, he leapt his noble mare from point to point, mercilessly thrusting, parrying, and clearing. Then Wiffles' steed received a thrust in the throat, and, rearing up, snorting in fright and agony, threw its rider.

Dandy Dick stood alone, gritting his teeth, and, firmly fixed in his saddle, he mentally resolved to send one or two of his cowardly foes to their final reckoning before his own death-plunge came.

With a deafening halloa of triumphant glee, forward sprang the infuriated mob of riders. Then came a sound, such as could scarcely be described as human, but a something between the cry of a man and the snarl of wild beast. A body had shot up high into the air, clearing the tall hedgerows, and falling clean into the midst of the horsemen. This weirdly, horrible object possessed horns upon its head, great eyeballs of brilliant red, in a mask of the most repulsive shape; the thing had either long, black, limp wings, or a flying cloak.

A combined shriek of horror and extreme fear came from the Young Bloods. "'Tis the fearsome Spring-Heel'd Jack! The great terror of London!" gasped they.

Springing with utmost care upon it a curiously high heels, the so-called Spring-Heeled Jack sprang like a tiger upon one horseman after another. It uttered a low growling, or snarling sound, and struck at each rider swiftly and furiously. The clenched fist of the mysterious Spring-Heeled Jack was armed with steel spikes. Those struck by these cruelly lacerating points fell disfigured and shrieking in exquisite agony.

The whole incident was over quick as thought, and the startling being had fled as quickly as he had come.

The—in many instances frightfully maimed—Mohawks now turned and took to flight. The eagle glance of Dandy Dick again fell upon the horsemen, bearing before him upon his saddle the unconscious form of a female.

"Merciful heavens!" groaned the highwayman. "Raymond Raithwood, and by all that's sacred the creature in his clutches is none other than Maude Mortiemor!"

Raymond Raithwood—if he it was—had turned his steed's head and plunged forward towards the far end of the lane. As this movement took place, to the still further amazement of Dick and his comrades, another mounted man was revealed, also having before him a senseless or gagged maiden.

Another second would have seen the escape of the two riders; but a third horseman dashed into the lane, meeting face-to-face the former two.

"What ho, there, Dandy Dick! What's the danger, Dick, comrade?"

"Stop those ruffians!"

The new arrival was the intrepid Colonel Blood. His cry had no sooner been answered by Dandy Dick than a flint-lock, presented at the heads of both the advancing horsemen, caused them to pull up in utmost terror. Then Dandy Dick rode forward.

"Raymond Raithwood, villain! You shall answer to me for this!" fiercely cried Dick, springing from his mare, and taking the graceful form from the abductor's saddle.

"An' someone'll answer ter Wiffles, too, an' with a broken pate as won't be easily cobbl'd up again! What's this 'ere pretty parcel o' daintiness, if it ain't my pretty, dark-eyed Dolly Tripitt, I'd like 'ter know?"

Wiffles had detected his sweetheart in the person of the second captive girl. His astonishment and rage were great indeed. This female was cruelly gagged, and not insensible. Her lover took her from the horsemen—evidently a menial—and held her gently by one arm, while he unfastened the stifling gag.

Dandy Dick had moistened the ashen lips of his lovely burden with a few spots from a spirit-flask handed to him by Colonel Blood. The lovers were too intently engaged with the rescued captives to prevent the flight of the evil-visaged Raymond Raithwood and his companion. They urged the steeds to the gallop, and flew on, making after their retreating associates.

The watchful Colonel had seen the intention of the two abductors. The heavy hilt of his rapier made one rapid swoop, and then another. The extent of the punishment inflicted could be judged by the loudness of sound caused by the crashing of the sword-handle upon the sconces of Raithwood and his confederate in an unlawful act.

"A foretaste of something to come when we next meet, coward and abductor!" cried Colonel Blood.

The fleeing Raymond Raithwood—when at a safe distance—drew a pistol from its holster before the saddle, and fired a parting shot at the colonel, who hailed the same with a scornful shout of laughter as the pellet flew wide of its mark.

The riotous band of horsemen had scarcely made good their departure by one end of the country lane before another party of mounted men appeared at the other end.

"Hurrah! hurrah!" gleefully cried out Colonel Blood. "You have been tardy in joining your faithful comrades, Dandy Dick, and therefore the guests of the Haunted Manor of Finchley are here to speed your coming!"

°THE THREE BOW STREET RUNNERS MAKE UP THEIR MINDS TO REST, AND DRINK AT THE HOLE-IN-THE-WALL ON THE CHEAP—BILBERRY, THE CHAMPION LIAR, IN HIS GLORY—DREAMS OF BLISS DISPELLED—DANDY DICK, THE TERROR—THE PLUNGE BATH.

After a pause, Officer Bilberry, from between the sheets, again held forth. "Chew me into little bits an' blow me to the four winds if I like this unexpected influx of visitors to this our most favourite resort! Here have I spread myself out for something like a month's rest, swilling, swiping, drinking, feeding, cramming, stuffing, nursing, coddling, an' all the rest of it. I didn't intend to budge until that miserable apology for a man, Ralph Drake, had come to me tearfully announcing the fact that there wasn't enough moisture remaining in the inn for a very small and most temperate fly to get even skittish on, let alone drunk, or food enough to supply a meal to a wandering tramp of a bluebottle. Then I intended to threaten the host that I would lay information against him for harbouring outlaws if he dared present his bill. In the meantime, I had calculated that, by making red-hot love to the bewitchingly beautiful and merry-eyed hostess for that space of time, she would then be so fatally impressed that I could straight elope with her, if I had not in the meanwhile killed her weak-kneed, white-livered, and tearful spouse, in which event I should, of course, then marry both the widow and the inn, and thus become the full-fledged proprietor of the Hole-in-the-Wall!"

"Do you think, Bilberry, that we may be neglected for the later patrons?" asked another of the invalid officers anxiously.

"Neglected! Blood, battles, an' endless carnage! Neglected, forsooth!" gasped the purple-visaged, indignant Bilberry. "Lives there man, woman, child, cat, or dog that dares even wink when I cry steady eye there? But the more the new guests stuff an' swill, the less the stuffing an' swilling they will remain for us, seeing that in this world there is a limit to most joys, an' I count eating an' drinking an' love-making the three primary joys on earth!"

"But the host may come an' ask us to shift into less snug quarters. We have the very best chamber," ventured to remark the aforesaid officer.

° Part 9. Vol. XIV.—No. 345. (British Library date stamp 13 June 1900.

"Let that lantern-jawed son of a melancholy mermaid dare even to hint at our moving from this until we please! Red fire an' earthquakes, I'll flay him alive, an' his fascinating dame shall weardeep-black crape for him a week after he opens his ugly mouth for the purport of 'requesting us to move'!"

"Suppose, brother-officer, that some of those deadly meddlesome road-rakers put in their noses among the fresh visitors here?" ventured to ask the remaining Bow Street runner, the tip of his proboscis alone could be seen between sheets, blankets, and fully-drawn-down nightcap.

"Blood an' hounds! Man alive! Concentrated thunder and essence of lightning! Do you wish to swim in seas of gore, man? If so, call up your highway outlaws, for, spite of cold an' colic, I have a great lust for slaying upon me this night! That prince of iniquity, Dandy Dick, hath so stirred up my bile that I shall never know rest again until I have captured him single-handed, or sliced off his highly-priced head with one mighty slash of my hanger-blade!"

While the boastful bombastic thus exercised his lungs, the host and hostess of the Hole-in-the-Wall were working out a plot, which had for its object the immediate getting rid of the three loafing Bow Street runners.

Ralph Drake had taken a horse from the stables, muffled its hooves, let it out into the open for some distance, then uncovered the steed's feet, mounted, and then ridden, with all the clatter possible, back to the inn door. This move Drake repeated many times, taking care that it could not be detected from a window of the chamber in which the officers were. Not a single guest was really in the inn; but Ralph Drake and his extremely-clever wife set up such a din below that the place seemed to the officers above to be crowded. It was this piece of deception that had set Officer Bilberry's tongue so valiantly wagging.

"Fiery meteors an' devastations without end! Officer Blowers, you are nearest the fire. Get out, man alive, an' keep up the crackling, crisping logs! Pull at that bell savagely. Daggers an' poison drugs, but I mean to swim in boiling-hot punch, an' eat of steaming venison-pie until I can neither take a drop or crumb more for fear of bursting!"

Officer Blowers, growling like a bear with a sore head, slipped from his warm bed, and heaped up closer the glowing logs, retreating to the sheets after a mighty pulling of the attendant's bell-ropes. No notice whatever was taken of the violent jerkings of the bell.

"I'm a-thinking what would happen to those lain-up officers if Dandy Dick, with a band of his felon-crew, returned an' found 'em here?" muttered Bow Street Runner Blowers, apparently speaking to the oaken rafters above his head.

"Mortal wounds, compound fractures, an' no quarter, an' the most powerful magnifying-glass that was ever made to look for Dick the Dandy's remains before I could claim the Government reward! These are a few trifling items of what will take place. Take note, Bully-boys all, for Bilberry's sworn to the deed!"

The ever-blustering officer had scarcely ceased uttering his last threat before the men between the sheets were startled by a thundering of heavy feet up the stairs.

The alarming sounds proceeded from the room next that in which were the Bow Street runners. Then a voice was heard, pitched in a loud key of ungovernable fury. Ralph Drake could also be heard as if endeavouring to calm some person or persons.

"I'll have his wretched life, I tell you!" yelled the voice of fury. "I've fifty of my most daring, slit-wizzen rogues below, an' they show up an' hack that punch-filled, hideous mountain flesh into nothingness! Where is that human wine-tub? He solemnly took oath never to molest me—Dandy Dick—again if I spared his life! Where is the living soap-bubble?"

"By all that's awful, friends, 'tis he!—that bloodthirsty terror, Dandy Dick!" gasped Bilberry in a fear-filled whisper, and springing from his bed. "We must fly, boys, fly!" he added. "If we remain a moment longer we're dead men—dead as mincemeat!"

Had the beds been discharged pistols, and the runners the bullets therein, they could not have shot out quicker; then helter-skelter away they flew from the room and down the stairs. The panic-stricken runners (now fully justifying their claim to this term) intended to secure their garments drying by the kitchen fire, and their arms, which Drake had also taken charge of; but such a wild rushing of feet came after them from above that the gasping, windblown, and almost fainting Bilberry, in nightcap and shirt alone, frantically darted out of the inn's front door into the dark, snow-laden freezing cold night.

Bilberry's fellow-knights of ye cap and ye shirt madly pelted after their snorting and puffing leader. The former outdid himself in the number and selection of his oaths as he floundered on, furious and frost-bitten by turns.

"Wicked, evil-tongued men! You'll drive away my pretty friends, the Snow Fairies!" A long pole struck against Bilberry's active, naked feet; and he fell forward, sprawling full length.

His two companions were too close behind him to pull up in time, and consequently shot over his rotund form. The noses of the three officers sharply struck against the hard, frost-covered earth, and for a space of time all three saw more stars than the vast mantle of night ever held.

Over the echoing hoarfrost came the metallic ring of steeds' hooves, and the hoarse, rageful shouts of voices.

"Curse ye, cowards, with hearts no bigger than a gnat's! If ye had not bolted first—stood by me like men—I'd have faced that rabble of fiends!"

Officer Bilberry had regained his feet, and was fleeing faster than ever as he gasped out his false and vainglorious boast. Then his glance took in the little ragged form of Will the Witless and the boy's leaping-pole. In a flash, Bilberry saw the combined cause of his sooty misadventure and later star-gazing.

"That imp of blackness! The young ruffian who poured the contents of the black manure bags over us!" panted he. Adding: "An', by all that is mysterious, 'twas his long staff that sent us snow-raking with our smellers! I'll make him swallow every inch of that infernal staff when I lay my hands on him!"

In the moonless blackness of the night the fleeing officers could not make out the forms of those chasing them with such wildly-rageful threats; but, nevertheless, the shivering men did their utmost to widen the distance between them and their mysterious pursuers.

Will the Witless, like a will-o'-the-wisp of the night, danced on ahead, taunting his followers with his merry laughter. To keep whatever distance he liked in advance was the easiest of tasks to him, so amazing were his leaps by the aid of his long and strong staff.

Bilberry was bent upon recking dire vengeance upon the idiot lad, providing the act did not delay his own escape. But, before being aware of the fact, the officers were lured by the boy upon an extensive snow and ice-covered pond. This was on a level with the surrounding land, and the thick, white-fleecing covering had completely hidden the ice.

Will the Witless, with his puny weight, had safely sped over the dangerous spot. The exhausted, breathless, and chilled-to-the-very-marrow leading officer, Bilberry, had reached the centre of the frozen surface before becoming fully alive to the peril. His companions were close at his heels. Seeing that the mocking, tormenting boy had reached the further edge in safety, the Bow Street agents, as if one, madly dashed forward after Will the Witless.

A streak of disdain came from the boy. "Foul men an' foul words go together!" he cried. "We'll wash the foulness away, then they may mix with the Snow Fairies. Those who meet my snow friends must have clean hearts and clean words!"

"Blood an' hounds! We're done for!" gasped Bilberry in extreme terror.

He became incapable of further movement when he saw the idiot boy's act. The heavy pole was crashing down swiftly upon the surface at the further edge of the pond. Suddenly the ice creaked with the loudness of a pistol-shot, the fragments split in all directions; then followed a hissing of waters, ear-splitting yells of terror, and frantic cries for aid, the moment after the three all but naked forms had disappeared from view.

Mrs. Drake—mounted, costumed, masked and armed—in her imitation get-up as Dandy Dick the Highwayman, and using her undoubted gifts of mimicry and ventriloquism, in conjunction with her husband, had created the impression of a great number of loud-mouthed persons following in those of the scantily-clothed, supposed invalided Bow Street officers.

The host and hostess had witnessed the cold plunge bath prepared for the officers by the chance whim of an imbecile.

"Go back, dismount, an' then change that dress, lass, and leave the rest o' this adventure to me!" hurriedly whispered Ralph Drake to his wife. The latter could ill repress a titter as she instantly turned her steed and obeyed her husband.

"Go! hide thee in my house, Will laddie, or 'twill fair ill with thee. Thou mayest have made three o' the Government men witless as thyself, if that has not e'en converted them into drowned Robins!" cried Drake, seizing the pole from the boy and instantly prodding it into the depths of the water. Will the Witless silently followed the sham highwayman to the inn.

Fortunately the depth of the pond was not great. In a few seconds Drake tugged at his staff, and the great round form of Bilberry, spluttering and frantically struggling for breath, came up; then the other two night-capped and beshirted figures appeared. The partly nude and desperately-discomfited men were madly locked together in a great human knot that looked like a confusion of heads, arms, and legs.

"Splutter! Piff!—ploff!—phe-w-w-w!" gasped Bilberry when on his feet again. "Where—piff!!—is that—p-l-o-ff!—boy? The imp of Satan! he's murdered me in cold blood!"

"In cold water, you mean!" Ralph Drake retorted, adding in a whisper of apparently great alarm: "You must fly, friend! Dandy Dick, an' a mighty band of outlaws, are scouring these parts. They'll rend thee in ribbons if once they overtake thee!"

"Spoff! Dear friend Drake—piff!—p-l-o-ff you well—path—know that I have ever ploffed-loved thee!" cantingly moaned the shivering, shaking and wind-wanting Bilberry. "In mercy's name, friend, f-f-e-t-c-h m-m-me m-m-m-my g-g-g-a-a-rments! Oh, I'm dead cold, an' cold dead!"

"A pretty pickle o' fish!" groaned another of the sufferers. "By the lud, there is a conspiracy afoot to freeze three Government officers to death!"

"Anyway, if we survive this, they'll be a pretty roasting awaiting us at headquarters when we report that a mere idiot brat has come a-nigh drowning the batch of us!" chimed in the third shivering and teeth-chattering involuntary bather.

Keeping up the terror inspired by the supposed close proximity of vast numbers of footpads and highwayman Ralph Drake hurried the officers towards his outstanding brewhouse, promising to return to them with their clothing and arms. In a few moments he had returned to them, and was harrowing up their feelings with further reports of the searchings of their "intending murderers."

The ill-fated Officer Bilberry succeeded in getting one of his enormous legs into a sleeve of his coat, his hat over his dripping nightcap, one top-boot on, and—in his bluest of blue funks[48]—both arms were thrust into the legs of his nankeens, or smalls—i.e., knee-breeches. Ralph Drake placed the strap holding his cutlass round Bilberry's neck, and pistols in the vacant boot.

---

[48] Ill-humour.

The three Bow Street Bully-boys, all more or less but partly dressed, then, with utmost terror lending speed to their heels, scampered off for a good half-hour's run before they could reach their destination, at the Bow Street Government Offices.

Ralph Drake and his beautiful and gifted wife sat facing each other in the bar-parlour of the Hole-in-the-Wall; the two were each in such a fit of uncontrollable laughter that tears were streaming down their cheeks.

"The confounded sponges would not have left us until they had sucked our cellars parched dry. Cormorants, too, I term them," Ralph Drake added, "for they would also have cleared out our larder until it looked as clean as a new coin; and the scurvy knaves never mean to pay up!"

°JONATHAN WILD AND HIS FOLLOWERS ARRIVE AT THE HAUNTED MANOR AT FINCHLEY—THOUGH DEATH-TRAPS—INHUMAN TREACHERY—THE HAUNT OF THE HIGHWAYMAN—THE SECRET VAULT—OUTLAW SPIES—THE HOUR OF VENGEANCE.

"Sponges, indeed!" And Mrs. Drake's silvery ripple started off again. "The sponges must have sucked up water enough to last them a lifetime. They will require no end of squeezing, I'm thinking, before they are properly dry again."

"Don't believe that, lass," replied Drake, solemnly shaking his head. "A sight, or sniff of our special brew of punch would make the wettest of Red Robins as dry as the inside of a flaming volcano."

"Flaming volcano?" repeated Will the Witless, looking up from his corner by the brightly-burning faggots, where the kind hostess had placed for him a dainty supper. "Some men have burning volcanoes for hearts," he went on, "an' their thoughts flame an' burn, their words scorch an' blister, and the evil deeds of such creatures lay waste and consume all the good of this fair earth. Ice an' cold water are good for human volcanoes."

"Poor, dear, afflicted boy!" sighed Mrs. Drake. "Though but a child in most things, yet at times his words are gems of wisdom."

At this moment the explosions of firearms, savage voices in altercation, clashings of steel blades, and the loudly-ringing thuds of horses' hooves, in one great tumult, came with amazing suddenness to the ears of the three persons in the bar-parlour of the Hole in-the-Wall.

*

"Well, of all the unearthly regions ever heard of this is the worst! Surely 'tis the house of all uncanny kin—of the supernatural fiends escaped for a brief spell from the domains of Satan?"

° Part 10, Vol. XIV.—No. 346. 26 June 1900.

It is the third night following the incidents last related. Jonathan Wild, like a cat, was credited with the possession of nine lives, and that which would have proved fatal to most men he was able to disregard, or shake off with but a few days' rest. The serious wound inflicted on his head by Wiffles, and the nerve-rending shock received by his after-contact with the supernatural visitant—the Spectral Horsemen—these combined effects had apparently gone, and the great criminal-hunter was already at his all-engrossing work again—on the scent of human blood; tracking down to the most degrading form of death his fellow-man.

"I never witnessed the like before! I could well imagine myself in the lower world of darkness. This place looks too fearsome to be part of this earth!"

"You've a finer imagination than courage, sirrah! Curse you, Craften, your visage is white as that of the country bumpkin when mistaking a white-daubed finger post for a ghost!" It was Jonathan Wild who muttered the latter during words to his Lieutenant, Craften; it was also the thief-taker who had used the terms commencing this chapter, which proves that his surroundings were not without their effect upon him, although he was undoubtedly the last man in the world to admit the same. And what were the surroundings?

The Haunted Manor of Finchley, and the wild, weird, howling wilderness forming its immediate vicinity, and no more dreadful, soul-affrighting spot ever existed on the wide world's surface than this, the last desperate resort of outlawed men, the lair of the hunted wretch when rendered remorseless and ferocious as a tiger driven to bay by its destroying intent hunter.

"The great Crown official of Newgate," as this prince of ruffians, Jonathan Wild, was officially termed, had profited by the many lessons he had already received at the hands of the outlaw bands, and had now obtained from Bow Street a great number of mounted patrols. These, in addition to the band of janissaries—or guards—at his own command, made up quite an army, all well-horsed, armed, and chiefly picked men, of well-proved pluck and hardihood. The Bow Street patrol carried, beside his flintlock pistols in the holsters of his saddle, and his cutlass, or hanger, a firearm much like a carbine, but smaller. This was termed a petronel, and, when loaded with small shot, was capable of great destructive powers, if fired at close range.

The night specially selected by Jonathan Wild for his second attempt to secure a great haul of wanted men—gathered from all parts of the kingdom for some secret purpose—was a dark and stormy one. The snow had vanished, and a heavy downpour of rain had descended for most of the day. The wily, cruel, bloodthirsty monster frequently fell a victim to his insatiable and impatient taste for human life, and, in this instance, he could not have selected a less-favourable time for his object.

The horsemen commanded by Wild were drawn up within the black recesses of a small forest facing the manor's front gates, and some ten hundred yards away.

Wild rode forward alone to reconnoitre. He found that the building itself was square built, and of enormous strength, if somewhat in ruins, and there was a vast wall composed of rough blocks of granite, completely surrounding the erection except where pierced for enormous iron gates, so that the Haunted Manor was really practically a fortress, and capable of sustaining a long siege, if held by a number of brave and determined men.

Jonathan Wild, after his inspection, rode back and selected three of the Bow Street patrols to accompany him, and then, leaving Craften in charge of the remainder of his followers, for the thief-taker again cautiously rode forward, the patrols following. The gloom was almost impenetrable, not a yard could the horsemen see in front of them; the persistent downpour had covered the earth with pools of water, some of which were of very wide extent.

"What is that light ahead there? It dances, flips, appears, and disappears like a cursed will-o'-the-wisp! Make for it, but take care, men, there are pitfalls, quagmires, an' bogs, curse them, in plenty thereabouts!"

The harsh, hoarse whispers of Wild continually cautioned the three horsemen now moving ahead of him.

"Back—back, lads!" suddenly rang out the voice of the foremost rider. He was completely lost in the darkness and sharp downpour, and it was evident that the man was most frantically tugging at the reins in vain endeavours to turn back his steed. A most horrible imprecation burst from the fellow's lips as his animal's struggles increased.

"Where is the danger?" savagely demanded Wild, instantly pulling up.

"Will you leave me to perish in this horrible fashion? I'm quickly sinking into a bottomless bed of mire!" despairingly cried the foremost man. The merest fraction of time elapsed, and then silence followed.

"Quick there! Flint an' tinder! A light! a light!" gutturally yelled the second horsemen in advance. The steed he bestrode could be heard now plunging madly, and snorting with the instinct of terror. The rider furiously strove, might and main, to stop the progress of his animal, but the poor beast continued sliding onward and downward, and nothing could stay its course.

"In Heaven's name, a light!" again came the man's tones. This time they were further away, and appeared to proceed from the earth's level.

Both the thief-taker and the third mounted man were doing their utmost to strike a light, but the rain put the tinder out every time a spark fell upon it; each man uttered oaths of impotent rage on finding the task impossible. The third rider now sprung from his steed, and then cautiously crept forward.

"Keep up a stout heart, mate!" he cried encouragingly, while, with his left hand, he seized hold of an overhanging tree branch, and, with his right, extended his sheath hanger in the direction from which he had last heard the voice. "Grasp my cutlass if you can, man, I can then drag you to dryer land," he continued, at the same time vainly endeavouring to pierce the thick, black atmosphere before him.

"This way! Merciful powers, I can't see your hanger, friend! Nearer, nearer! There, my poor animal's head is under—sucked down by this treacherous mire! In Heaven's name, save me—save me!" the terror-stricken man piteously pleaded. Then the patrol extending the cutlass succeeded in touching the sinking horseman's upraised hand, but the latter failed at the supreme moment in clutching the weapon, and an instant after, with a mingled shriek of intense horror and despair, the doomed creature's cries and struggles ceased to be heard.

The snap of a branch then followed. The remaining Bow Street patrol had missed his footing, and the slimy quagmire had seized a third victim within the depths of its foul bosom. In falling, the officer twisted his body, threw out his hand and thus contrived to catch a firm hold of the top of Wild's high Jack-boot. The former's legs were soon sinking, and nothing saved him from instantly sharing the fate of the other engulfed beings but his hold upon the leader. The latter's steed reared up, then swayed sideways, as the result of the sudden jerk and fear combined. The hind legs of Jonathan Wild's steed at once began perceptibly to sink down. To call for help was out of the question. Even if his voice could be heard, long before the most venturesome of his followers could possibly find his whereabouts in the inky blackness of the treacherous morass paths, Wild well knew it would be too late.

"Put spurs to the plunging brute, or we both lost!" yelled the sinking man.

The weight of the latter increased the steed's panic. Its rider's mind was swiftly made up.

"Let go, Fenton, man!" he hissed between his grating teeth—"let go, curse you!"

The clinging man was on the right of the horsemen, the thief-taker snatched one of his pistols from its holster and rained an electrical shower of blows down upon the knuckles of the hand, never ceasing until the hold was relaxed, which took place as a result of the patrol fainting from agony. Then the senseless man sank down, without groan or cry, to his dreadful grave in the pitch black and horridly-licking and laping morass.[49]

By a supreme effort the steed, in its final plungings, succeeded in landing all its limbs upon firm ground again. Jonathan Wild was saved! Using extreme caution—having dismounted and leading his animal step-by-step—the leader of the Government agents made his way back to the forest-path sheltering his men. The bulldog courage and tenacity of purpose of this great ruffian could not possibly be over-rated.

Before rejoining his men he had determined that the deaths of their three comrades should not be made known to them—for the present, at least—and,

---

[49] Part 10, Vol. XIV.—No. 346. 26 June 1900, p 14. Col 1.

in the very teeth of his frightfully narrow escape, he was still eagerly resolved to continue his efforts to overwhelm, and capture or destroy, the great criminal nest and its numerous and desperate brood.

*

Within the stronghold all was life and activity, yet without not a light could be seen within the building, nor sound preceding therefrom.

The outlaw spies were far from idle.

A topmost secret chamber of the Manor tower was well and comfortably furnished, a cheerful fire blazed upon the hearth, and candles burned in large bronze holders upon the old, worm-eaten, and fantastically-carved oaken mantelpiece. Pensively reclining upon a divan was a most graceful female form—that of the stately and most beautiful Maude Mortiemor.

Dandy Dick, looking supremely happy, was seated upon a chair at the couch-head, and held one of the young girl's long, slender, lily-white hand in his own.

"Darling Maude," he was saying, in love-thrilling tones, "I brought you here on the night I so providentially rescued you from that contemptible snake-in-the-grass, Raymond Raithwood, in the belief that you could find no safer asylum—at least, until I could seek your father and fully expose the doubly cunning act of Raithwood in seeking to carry you off, and force you into wedlock with him, so that Sir Edgar could not avoid making him his heir in spite of what he already knows of Raymond Raithwood's baseness."

"But for you, Richard dear, I shudder at the thought of my fate," softly and blushingly replied the queenlike creature. "Raithwood's is but a vile, coarse, brutal nature, in the outward semblance of that of a gentleman's. He must have known of my presence at a Court ball—although I thought I had disguised the fact of my going from him—and watched his opportunity. My tire woman[50] and myself were just in the act of stepping into my sedan-chair, when a crowd of young gallants suddenly surrounded us, cloaks were thrown over our heads, and I immediately lost consciousness. Where my abductors intended taking me, I could form no idea; but that it was my evil cousin's intention to force me into an immediate marriage with him I am firmly convinced, as the result of the many dark hints he has insolently thrown out to me of late."

At this moment a sound was heard outside the chamber door; this sound was remarkably like that of a good, lusty kiss. A gentle rap followed, the door opened, and Dolly Trippitt—all blushes and dimples—entered; a dark shadow loomed beyond the girl, and this bore a strong resemblance to Wiffles.

"One of my comrades, and, alas! an outcast like myself," whispered Dandy Dick into the small pink, sea-shell-like ear of Maude Mortiemor. The latter instantly rose up.

---

[50] Lady's maid.

"I shall be guilty of the term ingrate if I ever forgot what I owe to your brave, self-sacrificing friends, Richard!" warmly said the young lady, advancing and offering her hand to Wiffles. "Pray accept my most heartfelt thanks for your joint aid in the hour of my need!" she smilingly added.

"Sweet lady, my 'umble thanks is doo to you. I carn't tell yer 'ow pleased I was ter no as my Polly 'ad got inter your service; an' I 'opes as she won't now feel 'erself too much stuck-hup, as that plain yeller moth did when 'e found 'isself, wive a pin through 'im, hin a case filled wive a crowd o' werry wastly superior decorated butterflies!"

Maude Mortiemor gave a low ripple of musical laughter, instantly detecting the oddity of the comical outlaw's character.

"I've only been in her ladyship's employ a few weeks," blushingly and shyly blurted out the very pretty and dark-eyed Dolly Trippit; "but I'm sure that I have learned to love her as if I'd served her for years!"

"Dear child," cried Maude Mortiemor, impulsively imprinting a sisterly kiss upon the soft, rosy, and plump cheek, "soon, perhaps, your devotion may be rewarded!"

Wiffles had unseen made a sign to Dandy Dick; the two comrades then took hasty leave of their lady-loves, promising to pay them a brief visit a little later on.

Dandy Dick and his companion descended the stone steps of the old tower in silence. Every window in the great old pile was closed up with iron-plated shutters and thick draperies, hung over the former so that neither light nor sound could well find its way without.

When the two were highwayman had reached the termination of the narrow winding stone stairway, they stood in the centre of the great Hall; a lighted lantern alone illuminated the place, and this stood in a corner upon the flagstones. The topmost chamber in the tower could be reached only by those possessing a knowledge of the secret stairway leading thereto.

Maude Mortiemor and Dolly Trippit had been lodged in the tower, the better to keep them from hearing any sounds of merriment or conflict, as the case might be, taking place below. Wiffles stooped down, and, with the butt of one of his pistols, struck a most peculiar tattoo upon a stone flag; a few moments of silence followed, then a strange tapping came from below the stone. Wiffles recommenced his rappings. These were of too complicated a nature for any but those thoroughly initiated to imitate.

Soon after the termination of the exchange of secret signals, the slab of stone moved up as if by a spring, a great flood of light shot up, accompanied by a glow of warmth and the loud bars of many voices.

Dandy Dick and his friend descended by means of rudely-constructed stone steps, and in a few seconds were standing in an enormous underground vault of most peculiar formation. The great stone columns supporting its roof gave the place much the aspect of an underground church or chapel, but many of its other features quite altered this character. Gruesome-looking stacks of coffins were to be seen here and there, a great collection of skeleton forms, and rows upon rows of skulls crowded upon shelves. There were also endless samples of weapons of defence, and peculiar garments, masks, cloaks, sedan-chairs, top-boots, wigs upon blocks, and side-tables littered with powders, puffs, and endless articles evidently intended chiefly for the primary object of disguising the person.

Long timber tables filled the centre of the secret retreat of the lawless. These tables were most plentifully littered with the good things needful to the sustenance of man, and wines there were of the choicest vintage and an abundance.

A right merry, extremely excited, and loudly-talking assemblage was there, and a wild ovation greeted the appearance of Dandy Dick in the midst of the revellers.

"Hurray! hurray! Dandy Dick, King of Highwayman! Prince of Footpads! Best of the best fellows!" rang out many voices. Hands were extended, glasses chinked and uplifted, and the keenest of good feeling displayed all round.

"I have been with thee until this the third night, fellow Gallants of the Heath. Night-Riders of the Moonlit Glenn, Gentlemen Toll-Collectors on the King's Highway, and yet still my welcome loses nothing of its warmth. Fellow-fugitives, proscribed men, persecuted brethren, may our love for our friends ever prove as sweet as the hatred of our enemy is bitter!"

Dandy Dick had seized a bumper of wine,[51] and as he concluded his words the dashing young highwayman drained the glass to its dregs. A still more enthusiastic note of regard and admiration was struck in response to this toast.

A crowd gathered round Dandy Dick, each of its members eager to exchange a few words. Conspicuous among the gathering, the handsome, sturdily-formed, bold-eyed Dick Turpin, he of the ever-famous Ride to York. At the side of the latter stood the tall, manly-looking, fair-haired Tom King, ever-devoted comrade of Dick Turpin, yet fated to end his career by a bullet aimed inadvertently by his dearest friend; Jolly Blueskin, so named as the result of the marks left by the powder from an exploded pistol fired in his face; Jack Rann, the daring Knight of the Road; and Sixteen-string Jack, who owed his strange name to his habit of wearing that number of slight, narrow ribbons, or tapes, as decorations or fastenings at his breeches knees.[52] Not the least notable outlaw present was the famous boy prison-breaker, Jack Sheppard, a victim whose most deplorable training, career, and ignominious end upon the scaffold, the world has long since learned to have been solely due to the wretch, Jonathan Wild. This unparalleled plot to ruin the future of a mere boy was said to have

---

[51] Glass filled to the brim.
[52] Actually, Jack Rann is the same person as Sixteen-string Jack. Check this***

owed its origin to the passion of jealousy. Jonathan Wild loved and was rejected by the woman who afterwards became Mrs. Sheppard, and whose only son—left to support her in her early widowhood—was the amiable and promising apprentice to Mr. Wood, of Ye Chepe, or Cheapside, in the City of London.

Mention must also be made of the strangest and most mysterious personage of this, or any other period of our English history, the Necromancer, so-called. This being chose to link himself with the felon-classes of the period of which we write, and his life, as well as all others now mentioned, will be duly dealt with in these veritable historical chronicles.

Colonel Blood was suddenly seen to make his way towards the great group formed round Dandy Dick.

"Comrades in misfortune," rang out the clear notes of the gallant Colonel's voice, "we are met here for two great objects, one, the interchanging of friendly sentiments, and a few hours' seemly enjoyment; the other, and far more important of the two, the discussing and arranging of a supreme and combined assault upon our arch-enemy, Jonathan Wild, and the whole of his gang of bloodthirsty janissaries.

"The first part of our scheme," Colonel Blood continued, "our pleasure-making, is practically terminated; the next proportion remains. We have not discussed this in detail; but are, I assume, all agreed to it on its broad lines."

"Ah, ah!" sang out many voices in savage assent. Then the speaker continued:

"Well, fellow-outcasts—hunted men!—the fiend incarnate and his gallows satellites, Jonathan Wild and his gang of debased, blood-seeking mercenaries, are now ambushed within a short distance of us. Their object is to destroy—blast us from the face of this fair earth!"

A mighty roar of rage—seething, merciless in its intensity—rose up from many throats. "Death! Utter annihilation to Jonathan Wild and his carrion crew!"

An underground, subdued rumbling, as of the furious growlings of many savage beasts suddenly aroused, came to the ears of Wild and his crowd of horsemen now cautiously advancing. The men looked into each other's faces, something warning them that a terrible storm of human hatred was about to burst in overwhelming powers about them.

°BILBERRY HAS THE BILE—THE TOWN-CRIER—THE PILLORY—HIGHWAYMEN DISPENSE JUSTICE—THE PLOT OF THE GREAT THIEF-TAKER—THE "HUE AND CRY" SHEET—HIGHWAY ROBBERY AND MURDER.

"Blue blazes! Blood an' hounds! Man Alive! Here am I, a duly-appointed member of the Bow Street officers of the peace—most exalted agents of the Royal crown—sturdy, loyal pillars o' the State, an' I, too, forsooth, sworn by

---

° Part 11. Vol. XIV.—No. 347. 10 July 1900.

solemn book-oath to capture that plague of all plagues, Dandy Dick! Ah, to capture the gory-minded, purse-cutting, coach-halting, woman an' child scaring rogue of all rogues single-handed, dead or alive! For, by all my hopes of near promotion, if that highwayman will not tamely surrender to me alive an' whole when next we meet, then will I bring along—after our encounter—all the trifling particles that shall remain of his vile carcass in a little satchel, as boys carry their marbles! For I swear, by the bones of the first Bilberry, that no one of another name shall ever obtain the reward for the arresting of an outlaw I—Bilberry—have already lain by the heels a score of times, an'—"

"A truce to thy tongue, man! Why all this windy rigmarole?"

"Windy to me! Rigmarole to Officer Bilberry! May I be—"

"Silence, you blithering idiot!"

Officer Bilberry, and his two fellow-loafing comrades, on reaching headquarters after their flight from the Hole-in-the-Wall had given in their report. This was concocted by the vividly-imaginative Bilberry, and was a very fine piece of fiction in its way, for most of that gifted author's lies were tall enough to lose their heads in the clouds. The three fabricators were not believed. Bilberry's yarns were, however, secretly a source of much amusement to those in authority at Bow Street.

The Champion Yarn-Spinner had now presented himself before a superior on the afternoon of the formation of a great band of Wild's followers and Bow Street patrols, the horsemen then being on their way towards Finchley.

Officer Bilberry was privately greatly elated at the fact of his not having received orders to join the expedition; and he had given the latter ample time to get on its way before presenting himself at headquarters, apparently greatly hurt and indignant at the fact of his not being included in the party, whose mission was looked upon as a very hazardous one indeed.

"Look ye, my terrible fire-eater, if Dandy Dick hath none but thee to fear, an' will never be arrested until Bow Street Bilberry claps a hand upon his shoulder, zounds, man, he'll die with a whole skin, and of extreme old age, an' in a featherbed!" commented Bilberry's chief after a pause.

Bilberry silently contemplated his superior as the latter uttered his jeering words. The great round, full moon-like face of the officer grew a long dated, the vivid blotch of vermilion, so bounteously spread over the end of his nose, changed to a deep purple—a sure sign that its owner was mentally greatly disturbed—and the except extensive padding, forming the fine, full chest Bilberry ever sported, became agitated as a threatening earthquake.

"The lie to my teeth! Tweak me by the nose! Nail me by the ear to door-post, as baker detected in the giving a short weight, an' has it come to this? O ye gods, what's the next affront?" gasped Bilberry tearfully.

"The next affront will be my boot behind! Get out, you old tinkling cymbal!"

The great Bow Street official fiercely rose up, then one of his great jack-boots shot forward, its toe sharply striking Bilberry in a very soft part of his anatomy, with the immediate result that the great mass of flesh passed through the open exit into the courtyard like a ball sped from a powerful bat.

After this gentle, backward hint, Bilberry at once commenced his process of gently simmering down. When Bilberry found that the "Raging Lion" mood was a failure with anyone he desired to impress, he generally tried next the "Bleating Lamb" aspect; this could also be replaced by the "Cooing, Dove-like" manner, if necessary, as a last resource.

Officer Bilberry, if mostly fool, yet possessed some degree of worldly shrewdness. The knowledge of the moods conditioned prove this. To brow-beat the timid or retiring, the "Raging Lion" mood is worth a gold-mine. When bent on the borrowing of money, or asking favours generally, the "Bleating Lamb" aspect is a very sure card to play. The "Cooing Dove" demeanour is most attractive at select tea-parties. Human nature was and always will be the same as in the time of Bow Street Officer Bilberry, as to-day, and as it will be in countless centuries hence!

A few moments after his discomfiture, Bilberry was accosted by a messenger. "You are to take this parcel of bills, a bell, paste-brush and paste. Town-cry the text of the bills, and afix them on all public places retained specially for that purpose."

"By whose orders?" meekly asked Bilberry in the Bleating Lamb key.

"Our chief has just sent me out to you with that commission."

"Tell our honoured chief that Officer Bilberry's life is ever at his command!" added the latter, now assuming the Cooing Dove style. But no sooner was Bilberry alone and say from eyes or ears, then he instantly dashed into a fuller, deeper octave. "'Sdeath! Rattlesnakes! Scorpions! To put this indignity upon a Bow Street agent of such great distinction! I am to enact the part of town-crier! By all that's—"

"Are you prepared to start?" The great chief had suddenly turned an angle of the building, and was sternly confronted the rage-inflamed Bilberry, whose gills at that moment resembled those of a turkey-cock after a mighty battle with a rival bird. Bowing lowly to the earth, as if attempting to put an extra polish to his boots with the bristling, coarse foretuft of his hair, the officer replied:

"Honoured chief, I am overwhelmed with my sense of gratitude for the important duty you have relegated to my humble hands!"

Swallowing his indignation, Bilberry finally strode forth with the "Hue and Cry" sheet. Perched upon his prize-piglike head, he wore the gold-lace-trimmed, parish beadle[53] hat, sometimes to be seen in these days. A long, wide,

---

[53] A minor parish official.

dark blue skirted coat, red waistcoat, red britches, and stockings of the same hue, and shoes with broad brass buckles, made up the costume of the town-cry out. A large, brightly-polished brass bell, pastecan, brush, and slung canvas-bag of printed sheets, formed the articles necessary to the duties of the public-crier.

"O yea! O yea! Harken, all ye whom it may concern!" commenced Bilberry, as town-crier. He taken a bill at random from the slung bag that he carried, and yelled out its contents bit by bit as he walked on, occasionally pausing, laying down the printed sheet, and then with both hands giving a number of deafening claps with the bell's tongue.

"O yea! O yea! Harken, good citizens! This day, an' for the next five, exposed in the public pillory, one Ruben Simon, for that he did to Mariam Jeggs and diverse others sell loafs of bread previously short of weight, against and contrary to legal statute! O yea! O yea! an' the aforesaid Ruben Simon, Baker, of Pipe Lane, Eastcheape, shall also pay a fine-forfeit of twenty-five crowns. O yea! O yea—"

"Hee-haw! Hee-haw! H-e-e! h-a-w!"

It was most unfortunate for the due impressiveness of the items of legal pains and penalties cried out by Bilberry that a misguided ass, at grass in a neighbouring meadow, should certainly take it into its head that it could give out quite as lusty and intelligible notes as the properly-elected officer himself, and so delighted with its success appeared this same misguided quadruped that each time Bilberry "O yea'd!" the other donkey "Hee-hawed!"

Bilberry was in the vicinity of the Cross at Charing (now Charing Cross), a rural spot, with but a house dotted here and there, and a public pillory and public stocks erected by the side of the old stone Cross.[54]

The officer, with "his lungs of brass," in the form of bell, and his own mighty human organ, not to mention his imposing bulk and gaudy garb of office, had begun to get quite reconciled to his new line of duty.

"O yea! O yea! All ye—"

"Hee-haw! H-e! h-a-w! A-w y-e-e!"

"May the earth open an' completely swallow up that long-eared fiend!" mentally cursed the disgusted crier, trying to awe into silence that donkey by a long and piercing glare of his distended eyes. But the fearless animal gave a most contemptuous squish with its tail, and then shrieked out again at its top and most rasping pitch, as if in utter defiance of all town-criers in general and this one in particular.

"Thesir bee two asses for sure an' sarten; but it's main eeasy to judge which o' thim is the biggest!"

---

[54] The Eleanor crosses were series of monuments built by Edward I in memory of his wife Eleanor in the twelve locations where a procession carrying her body travelled from Lincoln to Westminster Abbey. The cross at Charing, the most ornate of the twelve, fell into disrepair and was demolished in 1647. The statue of Charles I now marks the site of the cross (and would have done so at the time this serial is set).

Two simple-looking farm-labourers stood grinning like mad by the roadside, and the few very small boys that had hitherto followed Bilberry now gleefully took up the chorus of derision.

A town-crier carried no arms. Bilberry bitterly regretted this. The ass in the meadow, two vacant-looking "farm-hands," and a group of pipe-shanked-legged brats were actually making chafing and game of a Bow Street runner!

"O yea! O yea!" Bilberry had determined to treat the scoffers with most caustic and lofty disdain, and had taken out another "Hue and Cry" sheet, and was about to bellow forth its particulars in most pompous manner.

"Huwa! huwa! huwa!" chorused the pipe-shanks. "Hawh! hawh! hawh!" laughed the farm-bumpkins. "Hee-haw! Hee-haw!" mimicked the moke[55] in the meadow.

"Blood an' hounds! Man Alive! 'Sdeath! Stew me into senseless pap for chicken-food if blood an' bone can tolerate this!" So saying, Bilberry seized his pastebrush, and, after carefully selecting out the smallest and most weak-looking boy, made a dash after him; but with the magic of boyhood's movements, each lad was hopelessly beyond reach before the puffing-like porpoise form could take his second step forward.

"Those well-known, highly-spiced, swashbuckler oaths! Surely 'tis that perpetual punch-parish and tavern-keeper's terror, Bow Street Runner Bilberry?" muttered one of the seeming farm-workers in the ear of the other.

"Champion tippler, unmatched liar, most arrant knave, bully, and coward! I owe the contemptible creature a well-merited and long overdue grudge, Tom!" was the reply.

"Settle up now, an' don't forget full honest interest!" was the ironical reply.

"Ho, there, right worthy! O yea! O yea! Hands off the stripling! Do battle with men!" boldly cried one of the seeming labourers.

Bilberry paused in sudden awakened terror. "That voice!" he hoarsely muttered.

"Dick Turpin, at thy service! Ah, friend scarlet-runner, we meet again!" calmly retorted the disguised man.

"And your companion?" falteringly asked the now visibly quaking Bilberry.

"The renowned Tom King!" added the same speaker with fearlessness and pride.

"Then I have but been crying at my own funeral, for I'm as good—nay, better, than dead an' buried!" Bilberry commenced to blubber like a hungry babe. "I did ye a scurvy trick once, Dick, I'll own; but you High Toby men[56] are generous. Have pity, I'm unarmed!"

"You shall not remain unharmed for long, my o'erripe Bilberry!" went on his

---

[55] Donkey.

[56] Highwaymen.

tormentor, producing a firearm from under his smockfrock[57] and coolly adjusting the flint in the pan.

Although broad daylight, Charing was a most deserted locality, and no pedestrians were within sight but Bilberry, the group of boys, and the self-proclaimed robbers.

"Get thee to that pillory, varlet!" sternly commanded one of the disguised robbers, pointing to the timber stand by the stone cross.

Trembling as if with a fit of ague, the officer silently shambled off as directed. The troup of boys, scenting the development of something novel, kept in view. The pillory stand reached, one of the highwayman sprang upon the raised platform, and in a moment after the lock was picked.

Then Bilberry was compelled to mount, and, in spite of his frantic pleas, his great neck was fixed within the circle formed by the two grooves in the top beams when joined together. The great red hands were next placed in the holes, pierced for that purpose in the under joining beam; wrists fixed in the steel rings by a steel snap, ankles secured by iron rings and chains, the unfastening and fastening up of the pillory accessories appearing but as a mere child's play to those so employed.

In those days printing was something of a rarity. To indict public notice of the offence of a culprit, doing penance in the stocks or pillory, a large blackboard was commonly used, the details being written in chalk upon a weather-begrimed surface. A piece of chalk attached to a slight chain depended from this square of timber. Fixed upon a stake driven into the earth, the noticeboard was on a level with the top beams of the pillory, the better that it could be seen.

Mounting up beside Bilberry, Dick Turpin seized the soft white substance, and wrote upon the black ground as follows:

> "O yea! O yea! O yea!
> 'Tis a fine donkey bray!
> Attention pay, all ye who may,
> As by this spot ye chance to pass,
> Behold in bonds and empty ass!
> A Guy Faux rig an' o'ermuch noise,
> Will make fine fun for little boys.
> Alas! to make a real good Crier,
> Needs evil-minded, famous liar!
> For if the truth could but be known
> All the crimes he cries are his own!"

"I'faith, the lines are not bad, Dick!" remarked Tom King laughing heartily.

---

[57] Garment worn by rural workers.

Dick Turpin leapt down to his comrade's side.

"Dog-grel[58] rhyme to fit a cur such as he!" replied Turpin, a roguish twinkle sparkling in his fine, full, brown eyes.

The pastecan and bills were upon the ground. Bilberry commenced groaning, pleading to be released, and groaning again by turns. Tom King had picked up the "Hue and Cry" bills.

"Aha! What is this?" He had unrolled a fresh sheet, and then commenced to read out the first lines:

"'Highway robbery and murder on Finchley Common. The ill-fated victim, one Squire Brancome; the perpetrator is known to be the notorious Dandy Dick, the highwayman!'"

THE FUGITIVES FROM JUSTICE IN THEIR SECRET RETREAT— THE GIBBET CHEATED—DADDY DELPH, THE MYSTERIOUS— BACK FROM DEATH—THE NECROMANCER—THE DOOM OF A TRAITOR—THE SKELETON HEADS IN THE QUAGMIRES— FIGHTING THE UNSEEN.

"Dandy Dick and I take command in our combined attack upon Jonathan Wild and his forces—is that agreed, comrades?"

The clarion tones of Colonel Blood put this question to the great assemblage of outlaws swarming the secret underground vault of the Haunted Manor of Finchley, on the tempestuous night selected by Wild for a combined attack upon the stronghold, long since selected as the lair of the persecuted outcasts of society. The reply given to Blood's request was most flattering.

Daddy Delph suddenly stood before Dandy Dick. "You here, friend—you honour us!" cried Dick, extending his hand and smiling a welcome.

"Body o' me! Ecod! There are a few men the Newgate Crow—Jonathan Wild—loves less than old Daddy Delph! How many feasts of blood have I juggled out of the claws of the black vampire, think ye? But hist! hist!" The strange old man came nearer, so that none but Dandy Dick and Colonel Blood heard his concluding words. "Step aside with me, bonny gallants, step aside— so, softly—so!"

Delph had passed over to a dark corner of the vault, and then drawn thick black hangings aside. Dick and Colonel Blood, in spite of their nerves of steel, were strangely-awed by the manner of the mysterious old sexton. The thickly-drooped drapery fell again, and the three men stood in a small cell-like place, brilliantly-lighted, most sumptuously furnished, and agreeably warm.

"Ho! ho! ho!" This laugh was but softly uttered. Delph's usually yellow, parchment-like, and deeply-wrinkled visage was aglow, his eyes like stars, a bony finger pointed to a couch. "My gibbet babe!" he triumphantly hissed. "My

---

[58] Irregular or badly written verse, often for comic effect.

gibbet babe! He! he! he! Hanged before Newgate! Dangled in gibbet-cage for one fateful day and night. Born again the next day! He! he! he!" The old man could scarce restrain his triumphant joy, and rubbed his bony knuckles until they cracked again and again.

Dandy Dick and his friend had of one accord silently moved over to the couch-side, upon which they had immediately on entering seen a sleeping form, that of a youth of extreme beauty. The face resembled white marble, and was surrounded by beautiful tresses of a rich nut-brown, the features were most perfect, the sleeper gently breathed, and was evidently in most profound slumber.

Bending over the youth's reclining form, Daddy Delph, with the tenderness of a mother with her sick infant, unfastened the lace cravat. When the cream-white neck was bed, a great livid indentation could be seen. Dandy Dick and Colonel Blood drew back in horror from the sight. Delph readjusted the lace-frills hiding up the wound. The next moment the three men had left this chamber and rejoined their comrades in the larger vault.

"Well?" mysteriously asked Daddy Delph, glaring straight into the eyes of Dandy Dick, then into those of Colonel Blood. "Well, Knights o' the Lonely Lane an' Midnight Heath, what makest thou of my pretty prize?"

"'Tis a handsome youth, an' on more fitting occasion I should like to hear further of this history," replied Colonel Blood.

"Upon more beautiful face mortal eyes never rested! Body o' me, is't not so?" meaningly continued Delph, chuckling inwardly, and still busily cracking his knuckle-bones.

"Sweet face, indeed! I should delight to call its owner a dear comrade!" enthusiastically added Dandy Dick.

"Hist! hist! Bend thine ear closer! closer!" Daddy Delph placed his mouth to the ear of Dick, then to that of the Colonel. The two latter drew back in blank and speechless amazement.

"Anon ye shall know more!" The instant after Daddy Delph had returned to the inner vault.

"Wonder of wonders!" was all Dick could remark to the colonel before the attentions of both were claimed by more vital matters. A weirdly-startling being had suddenly entered the great underground chamber, and a profound silence had instantly fallen where previously all had been excited tumult.

"The necromancer! The necromancer!" These words went from mouth to mouth in hushed whispers, heads were quickly uncovered, backs lowly bent as if in homage to a king.

An unusually tall, stately, suavely-complexioned personage majestically strode forward, graciously bending his head in response to greetings from every quarter. The necromancer once seen could never after be forgotten.

Black-bearded—at a time when beards were seldom seen—eyes that flamed like burning coal, orbs that held one spell-bound at will. A cone-shaped hat covered with strange hieroglyphics covered his head, straight long strands of raven-black hair descending therefrom quite to the girdle of a fantastically-shaped and decorated robe, amber-coloured, and figured with black dragons, serpents, lizards, and many other most hideous creeping things. Reposefully coiled round the waist of the tall, slender, graceful form was a glistening moving snake, and one of the deadliest of the species, the cobra di capello. This sinuous, gliding reptile's head moved slowly about the necromancer's neck, sometimes burying its head and gleaming, gold, bead-like eyes under the thick, flowing beard, the forked tongue darting restlessly the while. The reptile was continually caressed by its owner as a pet.

No less strange and impressing was the deep, musical voice of this being, who professed a knowledge of the supernatural or black art.

"We are to be driven forth from this our refuge, friends," he cried. "Let the evil man who leads the bloodhounds to our asylum beware the dread powers of the necromancer."

As he uttered these words, the right hand of the speaker quickly drew from some unseen pocket a black, writhing, hissing adder. He held the horrid thing aloft full within the sight of all assembled there.

"Behold!" he continued, in ringing tones, "I hold the mystic power thus to utterly blast, or blot, from out the page of life mine enemy, thus!" The held-up hand, firmly clutching the black, deadly reptile, made a forward swoop as if it cast the snake down upon the floor, when the living thing completely vanished into air!

A great cheer of wondering admiration greeted this unaccountable feat, every being present feeling that he had indeed a powerful friend in such a man.

Disdainfully disregarding his act, the strange creature now turned his remarkable orbs as if in search of a particular visage. "Stand forth, traitor!" rang out his startling tones. Then, as if irresistibly impelled by some unseen power, a trembling, ashen, and evil-visaged man came slowly into the centre of the dumb-stricken outlaws. "You have undertaken to secretly lead the bloodthirsty ruffians now surrounding us into our stronghold by our secret underground passages when a favourable opportunity presents itself? Speak!" thundered the awful tones.

"I am a guilty wretch! Wild tempted me with promises of free pardon and a large sum of gold! I cannot hope to hide my guilt from the necromancer! Have mercy! Have mercy!" The self-confessed traitor fell upon his knees, and imploringly threw up his clasped hands; the foam of mortal fear babbled upon his bloodless lips.

"Comrades! Fellow-fugitives!" rang out the rage-trembling notes of Colonel Blood's voice, "we favour not the needless taking of human life; but in the case of such black-hearted treachery as this now revealed, there can be but one course."

"Death! Death! Death! Death!" The word of doom hoarsely, fiercely hissed from every throat of the desperate men now surrounding the traitor. A billowy sea of steel surrounded the craven, shrieking wretch.

"Death be it!" answered the unpitying tones of Dandy Dick and Colonel Blood.

Dartings, as of the flashings of forked lightning, a mingled storm of vengeful oaths, then the body of the traitor outlaw fell, pierced through and through, covered in gore, and writhing in its final throes.

The ghastly spectacle was swiftly removed. Then Dandy Dick and Colonel Blood prepared their friends for the coming contest.

Out in the black, tempest-throbbing night, Jonathan Wild had heard from time to time booms of seeming underground thunder. The great thief-taker felt that he had work of deadly enormity before him, or the choice of retreat. His iron will, dauntless courage, personal ferocity, all forbade the latter. Craften, his lieutenant, was by his side.

"Take your selected horsemen to the rear of the building. Our object must be first to surround the place, to capture it, kill all who fall in our way, and starve out those that remain!"

"There is another mysterious light flitting about in the quagmires ahead. These treacherous marsh-graves surround the whole place, curse them!" growled Craften.

Wild made no reply; but, levelling his flintlock, fired at the light. Instantly after another appeared, or the former one had changed its position.

Jonathan Wild had so far craftily kept back from his men the knowledge of the deaths of the three of their number in the marsh-mire; but, for all that, a wholesome terror of the place already possessed them all. Mysterious glimmerings now began to be seen in all directions where it was believed that no mortal foot dared venture.

°THE SKELETON HEADS—FIGHTING THE UNSEEN (CONTINUED).

Wild had previously sent spies to examine the locality in broad daylight. These had returned with the information that dangerous marshlands, thickly intersected with trees, completely surrounded the Haunted Manor; but the outlaw hunter had concluded that there must be certain safe roads or paths, although as yet he had quite failed to trace them. Suddenly he and his horsemen began to ask themselves if they were awake or dreaming.

In the very centre of the dreaded quagmires there appeared the most startling apparitions. The fleshless heads of skeletons, and from the eyes of which darted brilliant shafts of blood-red fire, the effect of the horrid things was vividly terrible. The grinning, fleshless ovals, with their glaring orbs, appeared to move through

---

° Part 12. Vol. XIV.—No. 348. 10 August 1900.

the inky blackness at will, and as if really flying through the murky atmosphere.

"Mere juggler tricks to frighten us, men!" muttered Wild. Then whispered orders went about to concentrate their aim, and send a volley from their flintlocks into the ghostly-looking objects.

The roar of the combined fire rang out; the vermilion ribbons of light perfectly located each horsemen. An answering volley came from the blackness, and wrought most frightful havoc among Wild's horsemen. Amidst their shrieks of mortal agony up rose the voice of their leader, ordering his men to present another weapon, and fire again. For the skeleton heads had appeared in other spots, and were silently defying storms of bullets.

Mingled curses, oaths, and yells of execrations rose up from the Newgate agents; then there spared a second volley from the pistols, the flash again exposing each horsemen. Instantly, and before the deafening din of their own discharge could leave their ears, came another from the mysterious black void.

A mound of human beings and steeds, dead, dying, maimed, groaning, had grown up around the rage-maddened, utterly-mystified Jonathan Wild. His bursts of execration were terrible; he appeared frenzied with passion.

All at once Wild saw one of the skulls with flaming orbs coming silently, as if floating in midair, direct towards him. Silently the leader of the Newgate mercenaries reloaded a pistol, and carefully adjusted flint and lock. The mystic object became stationary at about ten paces direct in front; no sound came from its direction. Then something cut through the air hissingly, a steel blade struck Wild full in the breast.

No earthly power could have saved the thief-taker but for his secretly-worn shirt of steel mail. The force of the thrust lifted him clear of the saddle; he fell amidst the human mound, his steed plunged forward in a sudden panic of fear, instantly to be swallowed up by the unseen foul quagmire.

Thinking that their chief had fallen mortally wounded, Wild's followers set up the most terrific yells, calling each other to retreat to the forest, where lighted torches had been placed to mark its locality. The savagely-thundered out commands of Wild to his troops, ordering them to keep their ground, were completely drowned in the yelling tones of his men. The horsemen, in one dense, confused mass raced towards the forest, the flaming brands lighting up their path with broad patches of vivid red and yellow. As the foremost horsemen neared the outer fringe of trees, plunging into the brilliantly-lighted radius, a most withering volley of fire leapt out to greet them, followed by its startling detonation.

Jonathan Wild, foaming with chagrin and disappointed venom, sprang up, drew his hanger, and flew on foot after his retreating men. It was well that the terrible clatter of the racing steeds silenced the torrent of threats he hurled after his followers. In the madness of their defeat his life might have paid for his insane reproaches and taunts.

The closely-clustering, frantically-contending horsemen were within but a few yards of their intended shelter, when the earth opened in their very midst to belch forth fire and instant destruction. Wild felt himself torn from his feet and dashed headlong through space!

THE CHAMPION LIAR COMPELLED TO SWALLOW AND DIGEST HIS OWN LIES—OFFICER BILBERRY, AS TOWN-CRIER, DOES A LITTLE CRYING STRICTLY ON HIS OWN BEHALF—THE PELTINGS AT THE PRISONER OF THE PUBLIC PILLORY—DICK TURPIN AND TOM KING PLAY THE PARTS OF PRACTICAL JOKERS—BOW STREET MOUNTED OFFICERS ON THE TRACK OF DICK TURPIN AND TOM KING.

"'Highway robbery and murder, on Finchley Common, by the most notorious desperado, Dandy Dick!'; 'Tis a lie!—a foul plot! Highwayman and footpad, Dandy Dick may be; but deliberate, cold-blooded murderer, never!"

Dick Turpin's voice grew thick with rage, his brows black with fierce indignation! "Knave, have you dared to make this lying charge public?" he demanded, glancing up at Bow Street Officer Bilberry, fixed in the timber-stand of the public pillory, stationed by the white stone cross at Charing, and which, in process of time, became known as Charing Cross.

"Most noble, worthy, brave, knight-gallant Richard Turpin, an's vow, equally illustrious knight-gallant Thomas King, believe me when I do assure thee that I had not even seen, let alone read, that printed proclamation! It was rolled up with others, and I had not yet unfolded it."

Inveterate liars, even when they speak the truth, are seldom believed. Bilberry, for once in his life, told the actual truth, and was adjudged to have told a still greater lie than ever!"

"Villain! boiled lobster-complexioned renegade! you have mouthed aloud this cowardly, black calumny.[59] We must avenge our wronged friend, Dandy Dick. Scurrilous mountebank, thou shalt take back the lies to the teeth—swallow thine infamous lampoon!" So saying, Dick Turpin savagely pressed the false proclamation-sheet into a compact ball, dipped it into the liquid in the paste-can, and then, springing upon the platform of the pillory-stand, roughly forced the material into the mouth of the greatly-alarmed officer.

"You'll not find that mouthful over toothsome, Sir Robin; but if it's not on its way down your gullet before I can count three, I'll give you a leaden pill just to aid the process of digestion!"

Turpin had leapt down from the pillory-frame as he addressed his victim; and

---

[59] Slander.

then, coolly presenting a pistol fully cocked, commenced to count.

"One!" he cried, in a fiercely determined tone.

Tom King next drew a flint-lock from his belt. "Another leaden pill," laughingly said he, "just to keep the first one company, as it might feel lonesome in such a wilderness of blubber as our most cheerful crier's carcass presents!"

Bilberry's fat face changed to every hue of the rainbow. The grey light of a winter's day sparkled along the tubes of the firearms.

"Two!" rang out the voice of Dick Turpin.

The efforts of the discomfited Bilberry were redoubled. The task of swallowing the hard, round mass of paper was a most trying one. He gulped and gulped, after the manner of a gluttonous dog trying to bolt a long bone broadside. The tears spurted from his goggle eyes like a heap of white gooseberries running a race. Then, with a loud pop, the giant paper-pill shot into the broad, red neck. For a few moments Bilberry's windpipe indulged in spasmodic jerkiness, like unto that of a small duckling's after picking up a large, hard white pebble in mistake for a nice soft new potato; then the imitation snowball progressed well on its way to the interior works at the moment of Turpin giving out the word "Three!"

"The evil old ostrich! He now looks as grave of visage as a boiled owl, and is flabby about the gills as a codfish badly crossed in love!" commented Turpin, laughing merrily and long in chorus with his companion.

"Or as dismally depressed as an old hen on suddenly finding the supposed egg, upon which she has closely sat for a month, nothing more than a chinaware imitation!" smilingly put in Tom King.

"Gallant blades, noble freelancers, I am a doomed man!" sadly moaned Officer Bilberry. "This indignity ye have put upon me—the clapping of a most distinguished Bow Street officer into a public pillory—will set the whole City o' London agog!" Then he added: "Ye have furthermore also poisoned me, for I shall certainly die of the deadly acids in printer's ink!"

"Nay, nay! Sir Robin Bilberry, Knight o' the Pillory, you have long thrived right well upon lies, though others have found your fairy romances hard of digestion. If the printed fabrications you have swallowed failed to digest, reverse the order of things and—gest die!" banteringly retorted Dick Turpin.

The group of urchins, previously scenting fun in the distance, had now formed round the pillory-frame, a few farm labourers had also added to the crowd; and vast indeed was the delight occasioned by the practical joke played upon a Bow Street runner, for the latter class were not by any means popular with the masses.

Dick Turpin and Tom King were duly cautious of their true identity becoming known. Bilberry will knew this; but to open his mouth too soon would be fatal to him, and he, therefore, bided his time. Turpin had examined all the "Hue and Cry" documents, but failed in finding any concerning Tom King or himself.

King had, meanwhile, added to Officer Bilberry's tortures by taking up the paste-can and brush, mounting the raised platform of the torture structure, streaming the thick liquid over the officer's head and face, placing the tin vessel helmet-like upon Bilberry's head, and forcing the brush-handle between his teeth, compelling the pillory prisoner to hold it first, as if in the act of smoking a remarkably large and strangely-shaped pipe.

Not one of the onlooking, grinning, shouting, and gleefully dancing boys but had more than once suffered unjustly at the hands of a "A Scarlet Runner," "Red Robin," or "Bow Street Bully Boy," to quote three of the most popular terms then applied to the officials of the second important court of justice for London.

"Hurra! hurra! hurra! O yea! O yea! O yea! Old fat, red-gelled Bilberry's calf's head's in the pillory! Hurra! O yea! Hurra! O yea! O yea! He'll wear a wooden collar for a month an' a day, the Government penance to pay, O yea! O yea! O yea!"

Thus the elfin-like little fellows yelled as they joined hands and, in a ring, madlike whirled around the penance cross.

"Bow Street bully of the chicken heart an' braggart-tongue; toll-collector on poor innkeeper's larder an' wine-cellar; robber, not on the King's highway, but of venison-pie an', unlimited punch; thirsty sponge, that never yet was known to be filled or pay; we leave thee to hue-and-cry thine own offences, an' mayest they'll never cease thy blubberings till every drain of unpaid for liquor in thy hogshead carcass have drivelled down thy Dutch-cheese-like cheeks!"

Dick Turpin, after his final fling of irony at the ill-starred officer, took Tom King by the arm, and together they left the spot, the two laughing most boisterously.

The departure of the highwaymen was the signal for further suffering on the part of the victim of the timber cross. A lad came in sight, carrying a basket loaded with eggs and rolls of butter. The crowd collected whatever pence they possessed, and purchased all the eggs and butter the money permitted.

A few moments after the black-painted top beam of the pillory cross presented a startling sight. The great round visage of the moaning and snivelling Bilberry had presented a fine study in purple on a background; but all this was changed in the twinkling of an eye. Clods of yellow, white, orange, and orange-red plops all over the purple patch with dull thuddings, intermingled with oaths, moans, gasps, pleading, protests, and direst threats as to what would overtake his tormentors when the victim of their practical jokes should again recover his liberty.

"Flayings alive! decapitations! hangings an' quarterings! these will be but merest trifles to what ye all shall suffer! Imps of Satan—good lads!—Will ye desist?" Thus threatened and pleaded in the one breath they utterly-wretched Bilberry.

"Blood an' hounds!" he continued. "Man alive! How many times do you intend to put to death a defenceless man? Carn't ye see that I'm more than dead ten times over already? Sweet youths, in pity sake! Thrice accursed, degraded, low-born brats! Dear, gentle lads, hold my hands! May I be—con—stew—thun—"

A most accurately aimed bullet of butter had suddenly shot into the widely-opened mouth of Bilberry, and stifled his words. It is a common saying that "butter cannot melt in the mouth" of a person remarkable for certain mental qualities. The reader by this time has a pretty fair estimate of what the mental qualities of Officer Bilberry, and it but rests with the faithful chronicler of that person's career to state that the compound in question did melt in the latter's central face orifice, or division, for the opening extended to the ears.

The melting process was a very rapid one, too, the heat of the Bilberry-brand swearword being equal, in its full sulphury vapour strength, to the melting of one solid ton of hard, cold butter per minute. But this is by the way.

The mingled din occasioned by Bilberry, his tormentors, and the before-mentioned donkey of the finely-developed imitative faculty—it continued to bray in the meadow like a mad ass—and the frequent shrieks of laughter from passing pedestrians, had the effect of finally attracting to the spot two of his Bow Street brethren, chancing to be in the vicinity-of Bilberry, the muchly be-buttered and be-egged martyr.

No sooner did the choice study in white, yellow, orange, and purple catch sight of the Bow Street gentry than he set up a terrific cry of "Rescue! Rescue!"

The crowd of practical jokers instantly dispersed as if by magic. Then dashed up the strangers.

For fully five minutes the new arrivals could do nothing beyond relieving themselves of the most hearty outbursts of amazed laughter.

"Did you ever see such a side-splitting sight, Mark?" gasped one of the new-comers, when at length he could recover breath sufficient to enable speech.

"Side-splitting ain't the word, Gregory!" laughed the other, the tears streaming down his face, as he added: "Why, a far less comical sight nor that 'ud cause a brass monkey to laugh, that it 'ud" Ho! ho! ho! ho!" And the man pummelled his sides with his fists to induce his breath to return.

Then Bilberry commenced one of his exceedingly-entertaining yarns, and, sandwiched between his thick, crusty, full-flavoured oaths, the story surpassed any one included in the "Arabian Nights' Entertainment." He had tracked down Dick Turpin and Tom King, he roundly swore; compelled the two highwaymen to surrender to him, unarmed as he was; and when on the return journey to Bow Street, with his fierce, cutthroat captives, he had been surprised, attacked by a great gang of footpads, beaten within an inch of his life, and then locked in the pillory-frame by the vast numbers, so that they could make good their escape.

The release of the prisoner of the penance-frame could not take place until proper keys were obtained from headquarters—Bow Street runners not usually carrying skeleton keys with them. But the cleaning of his face and livery of office went on apace, richly flavoured by the unmerciful chaff of one officer, while the other went off to obtain the instruments necessary to unlock the timber joints and iron rings.

Officer Bilberry's assumption of the character of town-choir, as it is put in the stage lingo of to-day, had turned out "a most deadly, diabolical frost!"

We must now follow the fortunes of our new characters, Dick Turpin and Tom King. The two had left the Haunted Manor at Finchley at early morning, and were now contemplating their return thither. Within twenty minutes after their leaving Bilberry, the Government officers at Bow Street were astir with extreme excitement, the cause of which was the receipt of information proving that two of the most dreaded highwayman and footpads known were at large, and had already made their presence felt by committing a most daring and unlawful act connected with an officer of the Crown, named Bilberry. The statements of this officer were usually taken with a very large grain of salt; but, nevertheless, a party of well-armed mounted patrols was quickly sent out in search of the notoriously-desperate outlaws.

The Swan was a small and seldom frequented hostelry at Charing, and here it was that the disguised robbers had put up their steeds, and, after partaking of a hearty meal, wandered forth, with the result of their meeting with the new town-crier, the result of which we already know. A practical joke that was destined soon to bear most tragic consequences.

CHASED BY BOW STREET PATROLS—A BRILLIANTLY-DARING TRICK—THE STRONGHOLD OF THE OUTLAWS—THE MYSTERIOUS MINE EXPLOSION—FOILED—TRAGEDIES OF THE DARKNESS—JONATHAN WILD AT BAY—DEAD OR ALIVE.

Ill-patronised innkeepers sometimes found the lawless classes their chief supporters in the days of which we write, and the secret help of the host of the wayside hostelry had much to do with the daring defiance of all laws commonly shown by law-breakers.

The two highwaymen passed a most pleasant time in snug quarters at the Swan until nightfall, when they paid their reckoning and then departed. They had ridden away but a few yards, when a sudden rattling of hooves and uproar of voices told an alarming tale.

"The hares are scented, the hounds in full chase!" muttered Dick Turpin, instantly looking to the condition of his firearms.

Tom King gave a reckless laugh. "My blood is sluggish, Dick; a good canter this frosty night, or a crossing o' blades, will put some manly fire into me!" he cried.

"Mayhap there will be a leaden pill or two included in the fire, Tom!"

remarked Turpin.

A moment passed, the chase had begun in earnest. The wonderful lightning-like speed of Black Bess ever betrayed her identity. Turpin could have ridden out of sight of their pack of pursuers in a few moments; but Tom King's animal, although a sturdy one, gradually fell behind, and Turpin was not the man to desert a friend in need.

A gallop of ten minutes brought the robbers to the stable doors of the Hole-in-the-Wall hostelry in the gardens of Hatton.

Amidst a most furious climber the posse of Bow Street horsemen dashed up, sparks flying from the iron-shod hoofs of their foaming horses.

"Surrender!" the officers lustily yelled. "Surrender, or we'll cut you down!" they added.

"Two can play at the cutting-down business. You forget that Dick Turpin was once a butcher!" jeeringly answered the latter, at once following up his boast by slashing open the cheek of the nearest officer. A tremendous tumult ensued, the savage shouts and loud clashing of steel reaching the ears of the host and hostess of the inn.

Turpin and King swirled their steeds round, and for a time made a most gallant stand against overwhelming odds. The doors of the stable of the inn suddenly opened, and then as swiftly closed, but not before the two highwaymen had plunged their steeds into the black void within.

This act was favoured by the obscurity of a moonless night, and greatly surprised and confused the mounted officers. Three of their number had tasted the severe quality of the highwaymen's blades, and were thus rendered harmless for the time. A dozen men leapt from their saddles and rushed into the inn by the usual door.

"Your pardon, good sirs!" cried the voice of Drake, who had again thrown open the gates of the stable. Most of the officers instantly took advantage of this, trooping into the place, uttering yells of rage and dire threatenings. The stable stalls were all found to be perfectly empty.

"Confusion! We should have arrested two notorious free-booters but for your act, fellow!" thundered the leader of the party, looking much inclined to cut down Ralph Drake with his cutlass-blade.

"I thought I saw two simple farmers set upon by robbers—in my confusion an' the darkness I did not note the red facing of your coats, gentlemen. When the two horsemen I thought to rescue drove out the rear door of the courtyard I saw my error, and then instantly admitted you." This explanation was given in the manner of a man of most torpid brain, Drake appeared to require five minutes thinking between each word.

Nothing but the cursing of Officer Bilberry could be at all compared to the heated words that came in swift currents from the lips of the enraged Bow Street men. If ill words could injure Ralph Drake would have not only there and then expired, but his body would have resolved itself into mere nothingness on the spot.

The deeply-chagrined horsemen sullenly rode out by the back entrance to the inn's courtyard and soon disappeared in the outer darkness of night.

As the tall, wide, stout staple gates were opened and pushed back to each side wall, a couple of staples held them thus. Between each inner surface of the gates and wall to which each was secured an angle was formed, quite commodious enough to contain a mounted man and his horse.

If the officers had created less noise, and remained near the gates or insisted on the closing of them, Dick Turpin and Tom King would have at once found themselves in a seething hot corner. But Dame Luck dearly loves the daring, they are her most cherished favourites.

"The hares cleverly doubled that time, Tom. The hounds will now trail their noses along the earth in vain, the scent is hopelessly broken. Ha! ha! ha!" Dick Turpin laughed with the glee of a schoolboy, not as a man a moment before face to face with death, or capture, with a degrading doom at its termination.

The princely generosity of Dick Turpin was a by-word. His constant boast that he "took from the rich to give to the poor."[60]

Ralph Drake and his beautiful wife found themselves more than amply repaid for the act of the former. An hour after the departure of the disappointed Bow Street patrols, Dick Turpin and his ever-constant comrades were wending their way by a devious, cross-country route to the secret retreat of London's hunted felon-bands—the Haunted Manor in the wilds of Finchley.

We must now precede them on their way.

Jonathan Wild was dashed to the earth with enormous force, and for some time found himself dazed and aching in every limb, but the man's strength of will did not leave him. His eyes and mouth were filled with particles of earth. Painfully rising to his feet, he brushed the clammy dew of fear from his brow, and strove to peer through the dense blackness of the stormy night.

The thief-taker knew that his horse had perished in the deadly embrace of the black ooze of the bogs existing between the scattered trees surrounding the whole extent of the grim-looking old manor. His pistols were useless, but he unsheathed his hanger and steadily crept forward. That a most terrible upheaval— underground explosion—had taken place, he knew. No signs of the precise spot could now be detected; but the heaped-up mounds of earth, loosened masses of rock, and fallen timbers were all mutely eloquent of the terrific destruction wrought.

Stumbling forward in his onward progress through the thick veil-like vapour of

---

[60] This attitude is normally attributed to Robin Hood; the historical Turpin does not have this moral characteristic.

the night, his hands had alighted upon the still warm bodies of men; then upon a rider and steed, both prone in death. In every case he—after some difficulty—identified the dead as of his own followers. Such a crushing defeat maddened him to a degree no pen could adequately describe. The loss of men and animals he counted no more than the loss of so many pins. But to be outmatched, completely beaten by an unseen enemy, this was worse than the bitterness of oblivion itself.

°Jonathan Wild ground his teeth, tore at his head, shrieked out his fury at the inky atmosphere, and struck at it in the very excess of his impotent spleen.

The flaming torches fixed to the tree-trunks in the belt of forest arranged as a retreat in need for his party guided him on his way.

Suddenly a black, moving object loomed up before him. Snapping his teeth viciously, Wild crouched down in the darkness and held his breath.

A second indistinct object came after the first; both appeared to be examining the earth.

"Waste no more time. If he's dead, so much the better!" whispered a guttural voice.

"Wait, comrades; I'd give ten years of my life to gaze upon the corpse of Jonathan Wild!"

The tones were mere whispers, and the pattering fall of rain rendered them still more indistinct. But no doubt existed in the mind of the hearer that two of the desperate outlaws were within his reach.

Like some huge, black, ungainly reptile, Wild silently crept along. A few wriggling movements more, then he knew that he was within reach. He could have shrieked aloud in fiendish joy. "Dead or alive!" The words rang in his rage-heated brain over and over again. Dead or alive, each of the felons represented a fine sum of glittering gold!

The nearest object of blurred outline turned breastwards towards the crouching Jonathan Wild.

A hiss, a dim flash, a piercing shriek; then a dull thud to the earth, and silence—the silence of death!

"Merciful heavens, comrades, what ails thee?"

The second unknown black figure came forward, breast exposed to the unsuspected glittering steel. Then followed another hissing through the air, a dull glinting, a fearful cry of mortal anguish, then a fall, a quivering moan, and the lapsing stillness that means eternity.

"Ha! ha! ha!" It might have been the yell of the demon. "Dead or alive! Ha! ha! ha!" Jonathan Wild sprang up and raced onwards. Regardless of frequent falls, he reached the nearest tree to which a lighted torch was attached. Snatching this, the

---

° Part 13. Vol. XIV.—No. 349. 14 July 1900.

thief-taker turned and retraced his steps to the place of the enacting of this inhuman deed.

"Ha! ha!" Not all the defeat should be upon his head. "Dead or alive! He! he! he!" The carcase of an outlaw represented gold. With a kick he turned first one body over, then the other, both face uppermost; then he lowered the flaming brand, to permit its dancing gleams to fall upon the visages of the murdered men. Open, fixed, staring, the dead eyes looked up heavenwards, as if appealing for vengeance.

Jonathan Wild recoiled, his jaw dropped, the impious curses died prematurely deep down in his throat, the flaring brand fell from his nerveless grasp—he had slain two of his own men!

After a brief pause this monster of iniquity was himself again.

"Traitors!" he hissed between his set teeth. "They took their food from my hand, I saved them from the doom of felons, yet they secretly longed to gaze upon my corpse. My error is but their just merits." The callous-hearted ruffian spurned the bodies with brutal kicks, and then went in search of those that remained of his own followers, whom he expected to find awaiting him in the prearranged place of concealment.

Concealed by rushes, tangled undergrowth, and the thickly-spread, leafless trees of the marsh pools, were long, flat-bottomed, square boats, or punts, firmly grappled end to end. These formed hidden bridges over the quagmires in many directions, but always ended ten yards or more from any possible outer landing-place. Fixed upon long, thin, black rods, invisible at night, were imitation skulls made of transparent material, having gleaming red eyes, and slow-burning tinder flame inside.

Dandy Dick and his two devoted comrades securely lashed cutlass-blades upon the ends of other long and sable-painted rods, and also taking as many carefully-primed firearms as each could conveniently carry, the three intrepid adventurers had silently stolen out from their retreat. The hidden punts were cautiously gained, each skull-bearer carrying the same high above his head. The back of each of the ghastly-looking objects was of opaque black material, and by nimbly turning the unseen supporting rod, the gleaming, ghostly-looking thing instantly appeared to completely vanish in the murky gloom of night.

Jonathan Wild and his men spent their fury and their bullets utterly in vain. Their leaden hail, directed at the skeleton heads, passed harmlessly over the holders of the same, who were crouching low down amidst the reeds and brambles in the very centre of the deadly marshes. The discharge of a volley clearly located the position of Jonathan Wild's forces. Dandy Dick, Colonel Blood, and Wiffles separately sent their pellets darting through the darkness like fireflies at every opportunity. Then the three unseen denizens of the dreaded swamps would steal forward over the punts and swiftly and noiselessly plunge their long lances deep into breast of horse or rider of a foe.

Thus it was that Wild himself nearly lost his life from a furious thrust made by Dandy Dick.

All through this desperate attack Wild and his followers utterly failed to discern one of their foes, although the galling fire kept up from the supposed impenetrable recesses of the quagmires before them was more than proof enough of the enemies' presence and powers. Another most dismaying feature of the contest was now noted by Wild. His men became convinced that they were attacked by supernatural beings, a panic seized them, and it was at this point that their leader gave out the command to retreat; then, but a moment after, the appalling explosion took place.

Dandy Dick, Colonel Blood, and Wiffles at once, on hearing the appalling detonation, exchanged signals, and then made for land. They met outside the walls of their garrison.

"Our secret underground powder-stores have exploded! What can that mean if not further treachery in our midst?" asked Dandy Dick of his companions; adding: "The dying shrieks and groans and the momentary flashing up of the mangled remains told of wholesale carnage of men and horses. One half of Jonathan Wild's bloodthirsty minions must have perished."

"By no command of ours was that mine fired. There is another traitor in our midst!" sternly commented Colonel Blood.

"The vampire has taken flight! Friends, follow our arch-enemy and make complete his crushing defeat!"

The three highwaymen turned. The mysterious being termed the necromancer stood facing them in the gloom.

"What think you, comrades, of the cause of the firing of our powder-stores?" asked the colonel eagerly; and Dick and Wiffles as anxiously awaited the reply.

"Seek the cause outside our ranks, friend. We have no further spy or inform up with us. I have proved this by my mystic tests."

Without a word further the outlaws prepared to return to the vaults. The illuminated skulls now served as lanterns. The necromancer silently led the way. Presently the party halted before a small, low-down, window-like arched way, protected by a strong network of iron bars. The necromancer stopped, touched a secret spring, and the crossed ironwork opened as a door. All crept into the opening. In a few minutes the great vault was gained.

The crowds of outlaws eagerly gathered round Dandy Dick, Colonel Blood, and Wiffles, and wildly demonstrated their joy as the news furnished them, but at the same time regret was expressed by all those not having the privilege of taking part in the contest. Observing this, Colonel Blood raised his powerful voice.

"Comrades in misfortune," commenced he, "we are soon to set out for

London's City, and there—in Newgate Street—attack the retreat of that prince of informers and receivers of blood-money, our common enemy. We shall make a combined assault upon his stone fortress, which is a portion of the vile stone cage, Newgate itself. Each and all of ye shall have a hand in this. Death to the gallows carrion-crow, Jonathan Wild!" The notes of Blood's voice rang out like those of a bugle. The secret lair of the proscribed bands of London town were filled with a thousand dying-away echoes:

"Death to Jonathan Wild! Death to the prince of informers! Death to the receiver of blood-money! Death! Death! Death!"

These terrible echoes had not ceased before another fearful note was added to their din, mingled also with the sound of a great contending of savage men.

"Behold the wretch who fired the mine!"

A crowd of men emerged from one of the many passages leading into the larger vault. Between them was the form of a struggling, ghastly, blood-stained creature, his clothing torn to utter shreds, himself frightfully injured.

The captive spy in the power of the outlaws—Back from the grave—Daddy Delph and Nat Flint fear for their great secret—A meeting of old friends—Evil tidings—The daring resolve.

"The spy and craven ruffian who fired our secret underground magazine!"

The deathly-white, blood and earth stained, struggling, panting, clothes-riven creature was savagely thrust forward by his enraged captors, the din of fierce blows, kicks, taunts, and threats mingling with his abject pleas for mercy.

"Hold!" The clear, fearless, musical tones of Dandy Dick filled the main vault of the Haunted Manor as the dashing, handsome young highwayman stepped forward. "Comrades," he continued, "if we are creatures of outlawry we can still act as men, and treat with justice a pleading enemy!"

"Hurrah for Dandy Dick! Hurrah for the King of the Highway! Dandy Dick never forgets that he is a gentleman!"

The few well-chosen words uttered by their favourite had acted like a charm, and the thickly-packed crowd, formed of felons of every grade, was at once quelled. The captive had fallen to the stone-flags of the vault, overcome with extreme terror and exhaustion. He resembled more a hunted and torn wolf at bay than a human being.

"What are your injuries?" asked Dandy Dick, stooping over the crouching captive.

"Greatly shaken, and many flesh wounds!" came the hoarsely-muttered reply. "Give me water! Let me quench this burning thirst at least before you kill me!" continued the prone man, evidently suffering extremely from mental fright and bodily hurts.

"Your name?" demanded Dandy Dick, it being impossible to distinguish the features under the grime of blood and dust.

There was a lingering pause before the reply came, then it was uttered in the tone of one pronouncing his own death-sentence.

"My name is—Craften."

"Craften? Jonathan Wild's cruel bloodthirsty lieutenant?" incredulously repeated Dandy Dick, receding in amazement and loathing.

"Yes, Craften, lieutenant to Jonathan Wild!" admitted the kneeling and fear-frenzied man, shaking and clasping his hands pleadingly, his eyes starting from their sockets, white foam covering his ashen lips.

The mention of this name was as the exploding of a bomb in the very midst of the outlaws, each became as if possessed of the very demon of fury. No more heated term could have entered their ears, excepting that of the name of Wild himself!

The fiercest howls of excretion rose up like the deep, ominous roaring of lions. A very arsenal of knives, pistols, and cutlasses menaced the captive; another moment and he would have been cut to shreds. Colonel Blood, Dandy Dick, and Wiffles sprang forward together and surrounded the intended victim of the general wrath.

"Friends, if ye value our comradeship, leave this prisoner of war to our discretion!" cried Dandy Dick. "Remember, we are victors, and therefore can afford to be merciful!" he added.

"Neither Jonathan Wild nor Craften ever heeded the call of mercy! We shall be fools if we hearken to it now!" shouted many voices in unison.

"Shall we degrade ourselves to the level of either this spy or his master?" indignantly asked Colonel Blood. Adding: "Moreover, this Craften must be closely questioned. Our lives may depend upon it!"

This consideration told with all those assembled. The outlaws became calmer, and silently permitted Dick the Dandy and Colonel Blood to act as they would. The prisoner, in answer to questions put, stated that he had repeatedly secretly examined the surrounding locality, and had eventually discovered the mouth of an underground tunnel, which he had concluded led to the interior of their stronghold.

Jonathan Wild had given him—Craften—orders to explore this passage, and find out its termination. This, the spy stated, he was in the act of doing, while his leader and fellow-members of the thief-taker's forces were continuing their attempted assault upon their mysterious and unseen foes, who were evidently in some marvellous way able to glide about unseen and in safety in the very pits of death itself—the swamps that encompassed the old manor.

Craften declared that he was alone exploring the secret tunnel, carrying with him a lighted torch. In his hurry and excitement, he stumbled and fell, the sparks of the pitch brand scattering in a shower, a terrific explosion instantly following.

How the spy escaped instant destruction simply baffles explanation. Not one of the outlaws was missing. A few of those attacking Wild and his gang is in the darkness had received serious wounds; but the whole destructive powers of the exploded mine had been fully limited to the killing and maiming of the great thief-taker's followers. This fact told well for the spy.

"I am in your power, and you will doubtless kill me!" he said. "I can ask no mercy from those who, when captured themselves, receive none at our hands; but, before I fall a sacrifice to your vengeance, I will say this—that I am grown heart-sick of the business of man-hunting, and I hate and despise my chief from the lowest depths of my soul!"

Craften had already struggled to his feet, and now looked somewhat calmer.

"Our prisoner shall receive humane treatment," cried Dandy Dick, "and, when perfectly restored to health, must stand before our tribunal and take just trial on the charges so many of us can bring against him! Say, comrades, is that wish unanimous?"

A mighty roar of approval greeted this suggestion. A gleam of hope came into the bloodshot orbs of the spy, then his look again changed, and his whole aspect suddenly became of the most startling and horror-stricken nature. He threw out his hands, as if to ward off some indefinable horror; his protruding eyeballs appeared almost bursting from their sockets, and Craften's frame shook like a frail reed in a tempest.

"Take thy glance from me!" he piercingly shrieked. "Merciful Providence, protect me from those reproachful eyes, or I shall go mad—mad! It was I who betrayed thee, boy! I who cunningly prepared the way to the gallows for thy young neck! And now thou hast come back from the grave to mock me in this the hour of my deadly peril!"

Every eye was at once directed to the spot at which the palsied-like fingers of the shrieking, terror-filled spy pointed.

In a darkened recess, forming the entrance to a smaller chamber, black hangings had been moved aside, and a face of exquisite form, yet most deathly-white, was protruded. This countenance reflected the amazed horror seen upon the visage of the spy. A still more alarming cry of extreme terror escaped the lips of Craften, then his body crashed down facewards upon the stone flags, the limbs convulsed in the throes of a fit of terror.

The angelic face and head instantly withdrew from view. Two figures sprang towards the prostrate spy.

"Delph! Delph! Our secret is discovered!" This was the voice of Nat Flint. He threw up a brightly-flashing dagger-blade. "It is his life or ours, Delph! Our secret! Our secret!"

"Friends, hearken!" The passion-quivering lips of Daddy Delph were moving, but his guttural words could scarcely gain articulate form. "The spy has wormed out our secret—the secret of the grave! I can never more hope to serve ye, my persecuted brethren, unless by this wretch's instant death!"

Delph had snatched out a knife, jerked open its blade, and in a moment after two murderous steels would have plunged downwards into the back of the insensible Craften; but Dandy Dick and Colonel Blood had exchanged glances, and then sprang forward in time to prevent the intended crime.

"Your secret must be safeguarded, but not at the price of a human life!"

Dick had seized Daddy Delph's wrist, and wrenched the knife from his hand; while Nat Flint found himself jerked away from his intended victim by a powerful hand at the back of his coat-collar.

The insensible body of the spy was then carried to a small stone cell, in which it was intended to keep him close prisoner for the present.

The capture of Craften in the tunnel—where he had been found in a senseless condition immediately after the firing of the magazine—had rendered it advisable to postpone the intended assault upon the residence of Jonathan Wild until after putting his lieutenant through a severe cross-examination, with the view of learning the weak points of the thief-taker's stone retreat in Newgate Street. This questioning could not well take place until the captured spy's condition had improved.

It was the evening following the night of the crushing defeat of Wild and his gang.

Dandy Dick, Colonel Blood, and Wiffles took a temporary leave of their fellow-outlaws, the former promising to rejoin the latter before midnight. Although safeguarded by the watchful devotion of their lovers, Maude Mortiemor and Dolly Trippit were greatly rejoiced when Dick and Wiffles presented themselves in the elevated apartments of the old manor's tower, and announced their intention of taking the ladies to their former quarters, Sir Mortiemor's mansion at Holloway.

Great care was taken in keeping the ladies from contact of the rougher class felons. The two maidens were conducted down a secret flight of winding stone steps, which terminated at the entrance of an underground passage, apparently of endless twisting is and length; but in reality this underground cutting travelled to and terminated at the Black Barns, owned by the strange old man, Daddy Delph. Dick, Blood, and Wiffles each carried lighted pitch brands. The tunnel was wide and lofty, and owed its origin, with the others connected with the Haunted Manor, to the turbulent times of Oliver Cromwell.

"Body o' me! Sweet visions o' the night, indeed!" greeted the rasping tones of

Daddy Delph, awaiting his guests at a flight of steps which led up to his back chamber of the Black Barns.

"'O the lightsome an' the lovely Fairy Queen,
    Guided her stately train down the silvery sheen.'

"Ho! ho! He! He! The silvery sheen o' the moon is not to be found in our most convenient if foul-smelling an' ever dismally dark passages, sweet young dames; but the lightsome an' the lovely Fairy Queen an' her attendants, prim, pert little damsel, lend a charm an' grace to these surroundings never before seen, I'll warrant me, since the days of the Court of the luckless King Charles, when, mayhap, some of the Royalist dames may have used this very same mole-like burrow for the object of fleeing from Cromwell's Roundheads! Ha! ha! ha!"

The maidens smiled sweetly at the grim old sexton, if they inwardly shuddered at his gruesome and grotesque exterior.

Daddy Delph conducted the ladies to a chamber he had specially prepared for them, and where a dainty meal awaited them. The old sexton drew Dandy Dick aside and whispered in his ear; the latter then begged Maude Mortiemor to excuse his temporary absence, and then withdrew. Without a word further, Delph conducted the three highwaymen by means of a secret door out into the outer darkness, littered with grave belongings.

"Friends!" cried Daddy Delph. An instant after two horsemen shaped out of the surrounding black vapour.

"Dick Turpin! Tom King! Thrice welcome, comrades!" The voices of Dandy Dick, Colonel Blood, and Wiffles mingled in expressions of delight at the unexpected meeting of those they had not seen for many a day.

"Alas! I come with the bad news," sadly said Dick Turpin, after a while. Then was related the meeting with Bilberry and the details of the latest crime charged against Dandy Dick, as read by Turpin and King in the "Hue and Cry" document.

"Body o' me! The lying sheet is worthy of Father Satan himself!" muttered Daddy Delph, "for at the hour an' date mentioned Dandy Dick was here, an' remained, too, the best part o' the night!"

"I claimed toll o' Squire Brancombe on that night an' in the 'our named, an' when 'e left me 'e was as well an' 'earty as a fightin' cock a moment afore entering the cock-pit!" gasped Wiffles.

"Dick, dear friend," cried Colonel Blood, trembling with the fervour of a desperate resolve, and taking his loved comrade's hand in firmest grip, "we will face Jonathan Wild in his own den, and force confession of this calumny from his vile throat, or die in the attempt!"

A returning pressure was all that Dandy Dick could do, for his heart was too heavily burdened with grief at the learning of this bitter blow.

After arranging to meet again in a few hours at their return, Dandy Dick, Colonel

Blood, and Wiffles took leave of Dick Turpin and Tom King, the latter two at once riding off for the Haunted Manor, and the others returning to the Black Barns.

OLD BILBERRY HAS A VERY BAD TIME—WHAT THE SNOW FAIRIES DID—DOLLY TRIPPIT'S NOTIONS OF HIGH BREEDING—WIFFLES' JOKES AT NAT FLINT'S EXPENSE—A COMPACT BETWEEN TWO VILLAINS—JONATHAN WILD NARROWLY ESCAPES A WOMAN'S FRIGHTFUL VENGEANCE.

We left Officer Bilberry in the public pillory, a brother officer engaged in the unpleasant task of cleaning the nasty and squashed mixture of eggs and butter so freely spread over the purple face and shock head of the torture-frame's captive.

The remaining Bow Street Runner had grown tired of waiting for the return of his mate with the keys to release the trapped Bilberry. Promising to return in a few minutes, the officer stated his intention to walk over to the Swan Inn for a tankard of foaming ale. Bilberry's tongue instantly protruded from his mouth, and he commenced to pant like a dog with a parched throat—the sufferer's gullet was on fire. But his departing brother-officer did not take the hint. Not many of his fellow-creatures loved Bilberry.

No sooner was the pilloried man alone, and his mate out of sight and hearing, than the former was startled by a well-known sound—the plod! plod! plot! of a pole-end. Seeing the little form of Will the Witless suddenly appear before him, the rage of the officer almost choked him. The puny figure never came but to bring disaster to the old Bow Street bully. A fearful torrent of abuse greeted the boy.

Will the Witless brought the end of his staff down upon the new town-crier's sconce with loud-sounding result.

"My Snow Fairies have not come down to speak to me for the whole of to-day, your foul words anger them!" Again and again the heavy staff welted the crown of the captive, until his oaths ceased, and he blathered for mercy. By a strange coincidence a few large snowflakes now fluttered down from the dull grey, leaden winter sky. The idiot boy most gleefully shouted his greetings to his imaginary friends, caught a few in his extended hand, and then gazed most intently at them for some moments. The white, pinched little face and unnaturally large eyes became troubled-looking. The boy turned and addressed Bilberry:

"List to the commands of the White Fairies!" he cried. "You, who are ever eager to cause others to end their lives upon the gallows, must yourself now also be hanged."

"Sweet child, desist. Play no more pranks upon a helpless man. I will give thee money, clothing, food, when I get free. Desist, pretty boy—desist!" The officer's alarm was indeed great on seeing the boy's movements.

"Foolish old man!" contemptuously replied Will the Witless. "The Snow

Fairies dress the idiot boy in warm, beautiful ermine and ruby velvet, give him to eat of honey, grapes, and whatever he asks; and as for money—Will the Witless is master of all the wealth of the world! The good and beautiful Snow Fairies always do their kind acts unseen of man, and so they clothe and feed and bestow riches upon me only when I sleep."

As he thus rambled on, the mad boy had taken a strong cord from a pocket, one end of which he deftly formed into a noose with a slip-knot, and the other tied firmly round one end of his leaping-pole, a notch in the same keeping the cord in position.

Bilberry's brows exuded beads of sweat. Vaguely the lad's intention it came into the officer's brain, and he desperately pleaded for mercy. The pole-end went up, and the nurse slipped around the victim's neck, then an upward jerk tightened the cord almost to strangulation point. Bilberry in vain attempted to yell for help; his eyes and tongue protruded, and his face changed to a dark-blue purple tint that grew blacker each moment.

The struggling man's desperate efforts to use his hands—locked fast in the tight-fitting holes of the under top cross-beam of the pillory—most vastly amused Will the Witless, who screamed with insane joy, until tears streamed down his cheeks.

The feet of the officer swiftly danced, as far as their manacles would permit, and his huge body frantically twisted from side to side. The victim fully realised the awful fact that the imbecile was scarcely responsible for and unable to estimate the enormity of his act. The whole of Bilberry's past life passed before his mental vision, with its every wrongdoing brought into startling prominence; then he despairingly commenced a silent prayer, his last moments seemed at hand.

A larger fleecy particle of snow now drifted downward, and was caught in an open palm, as Will the Witless still held taut the cord by elevating the long staff high above his victim's head. With a side glance the boy closely contemplated the snowflake.

"A reprieve! a reprieve!" suddenly rang out his shrill, childlike tones.

The pole was lowered, the deadly strain relazed, and with repeated appeals of maniacal laughter, Will the Witless placed his "wooden horse" in position and commenced a series of his amazing flying leaps, in a few moments becoming lost to view.

When his fellow-officer at length returned, he found Bilberry in a death-like faint.

*

We again take up the fortunes of Dandy Dick and his friends.

No time was lost in removing Maude Mortiemor and Dolly Trippit from the Black Barns and their awful contents and outer horrors. But Daddy Delph had contrived well in this, and the ladies were consequently prevented from seeing much that would have chilled their gentle blood with feminine terrors. Some little distance from the Black Barns five saddled steeds were in readiness for the party. Nat Flint was in charge of these.

A depressing gloom hung over Dandy Dick and his friends. Wiffles was a most strange human compound, and, although his heart ached for the great grief of his comrades Dandy Dick, yet his mercurial temperament asserted itself as buoyantly as ever.

Nat Flint led the animals intended for Wiffles and Dolly Trippit over to them; these latter three were thus beyond hearing or notice of their other friends for the time being, and Wiffles seized the opportunity for a little chafing at Nat Flint's expense.

"Ho, there, friend Rock!" hailed Wiffles, pointing to Dolly, who hung lovingly upon his arm, "now, if you 'ad a nice, soft piece o' tender like this"—touching his sweetheart under the chin—"Flint and tender," he rattled on, " 'ud make the sparks fly, an' then ye'd make a nice bright match."

"Comrade Wiffles," replied Nat Flint, with a long-drawn sigh, "I've often wondered what on earth a youth like you could ever find to joke about. Soon you may be hanged, and there'd be no joke in that; and if you're never hanged that will be even a still more serious matter; and, again, if you die naturally of extreme old age, why, then there'd be no excuse for a laugh to come in, even at the finish."

"You're quite mistaken, Brother Rock," laughed Wiffles, "for in life the joke comes in pretty often."

"Tell me when," asked Nat Flint curiously, "because I can never see it," he added.

"No, you wouldn't!" retorted Wiffles roguishly, "because the joke mostly comes in when you go out!"

Nat Flint scratched his head ruefully and made no reply, but went over to the others of the party.

Dandy Dick had assisted Maude Mortiemor to the side-saddle of her steed, and then mounted his own, and the lovers were side-by-side. The lilywhite, silk-soft hand of the blushing maiden rested upon one of her lover's, her sweet, low, musical tones vibrated in his ear, now quite close to her cupid bow-shaped, ruby lips.

"Dick, darling," came the thrilling whisper, "for my sake endeavour to keep out of peril."

"I will, my sweet, gentle, queenly Maude," came his passionate murmured reply, although he fiercely despised himself the next moment for his fervour. He, a wretched, proscribed, hunted felon, to dare breathe tender, love-like words into the ear of one so good, so pure, so noble as the girl by his side. His heart filled with the bitterness of despair at this reflection.

Wiffles had lightly thrown Dolly Trippit into her side-saddle.

"Well, I'm sure!" ejaculated that young personage, turning her pretty little nose towards the night sky—"well, I'm sure!" repeated the little maiden, as if vastly affronted and hurt.

"That's just what the Winkle remarked when a hextree large pin was stuck inter him, as a perlite request ter wacate 'is shell!" cheerily remarked Wiffles. He had sprung into his saddle; his lips were now dangerously near those of Dolly, and the night was most favourably dark. "Well, you're sure o' what, Dolly?" asked he.

"I've always understood that a true knight-gallant invariably—ahem—kissed his sweetheart before assisting her into a saddle."

Wiffles carefully wiped his lips with his sleeve. "Accordin' ter strict court eat-a-cat—"

"Etiquette, booby!" interrupted Dolly, correcting her lover's English.

"Eat-a-key? That's a flam,[61] Dolly—a flam! No one in this world ever eat a key. But as I was a-sayin, according ter strict eat-a-cat, a knight-gallant, be rights, kisses 'is bit o' sweetstuff twice afore 'e assists 'er into a saddle." No sooner said than done, and Miss Dolly Trippit affected to be so shocked by the receipt of the double salute that Wiffles uttered a threat to the effect that "she could 'ave both busters back agen if she was a mind to."

Dandy Dick and Colonel Blood rode first, the females next, and Wiffles taking up the rear. All that now remained was the leave-taking with Daddy Delph and Nat Flint; that over, the three highwaymen and the two maidens started on their journey—one to be fraught with most momentous consequences.

[°]A COMPACT BETWEEN TWO VILLAINS—JONATHAN WILD NARROWLY ESCAPES A WOMAN'S FEARFUL VENGEANCE *(continued).*

Great indeed and widespread was the excitement aroused by the temporary defeat of the chief limb of the law of the City of London and his vast number of followers by the criminals collected in the ruins known as the Haunted Manor, and situated in the desolate wastelands of Finchley. The Government and their sanguinary agent, Jonathan Wild, were at their wits' end.

On the evening following this disastrous affair the ever-restless and bold Jonathan Wild was seated in the stately library of the London abode of Raymond Raithwood. The latter faced the thief-taker.

"This is the proposed compact," Wild was saying: "The death or arrest of Dandy Dick, and, in either event, his body to be handed over to me. I am to have full credit of the affair and the whole of the reward, now doubled, as the

---

[61] Nonsense.

[°] Part 14. Vol. XIV.—No. 350. 24 July 1900.

result of his last crime—the robbery and murder of one Squire Brancome, on the night of the fifteenth of November, at Finchley Common."

"I, as leader of the London bloods, or Mohawks, and to incite all our young gallants to combine, and direct their efforts to this one object. In place of our unusual midnight pranks—some term them 'orgies'—we are to hunt down, and take the body of the fashionable outlaw you name. Dandy Dick is to be handed over to you. What consideration comes to me?"

Two pairs of the most evil eyes ever formed by Nature glare fixedly into each other.

The thief-taker is dressed in his usual careless way—a suit of faded black; his bullet-head is wigless, and wrapped in bandages, complexion yellow, prominent cheekbones, green-grey eyes, deep-set, round, and piercing, wrinkled jaws, blue-black for want of shaving. Raymond Raithwood is an exquisite of the period (fashionable swell is the term to-day), whose jewels, plum-coloured, gold-laced velvet coat, vest, diamond-buckled shoes, &c., represented in value a very large sum. No greater outward contrast could be found than these two, yet their hearts were very similar, and black with infamy.

After a long pause, Wild answered:

"You want to brush this viper from your pathway that you may secure the girl who loves him, and, in securing her, the moneybags of her father at his death. If you aid me you also aid yourself. Still, I will deal generously with you, and refrain from arresting you for more than one deed that would cause you to make your final earthly exit before Newgate!"

A swift, double movement, Raithwood was upon his feet, his rapier-point within an inch of Wild's throat—the latter had covered the dude[62] with a pistol.

"Ha! ha! my peacock of the Mall, put down thy courtly toy blade!" rasped out the harsh, sinister tones of Wild. "We are useful to each other. Do as I wish, and you shall be free to abduct all the beautiful dames of England, one after another. The price of my non-interference is the body of your rival."

A green tinge crept into the cheeks of Raymond Raithwood. It was the very pall of madness to find himself completely in the toils of this prince of ruffians; but Raymond smiled a ghastly smile, and the fiendish plot was then determined upon, and the plotters parted.

Jonathan Wild was inwardly chuckling with a sense of supreme triumph as he left the mansion in St. James's wherein resided, when in town, Raymond Raithwood.

"Hee! hee! hee! my charming Adonis, my bold, bonny night-gallant, Dandy Dick, by this cunning move of mine to-night I enlist every one of the drink-inflamed, reckless rakes[63] that make mad riot through our town and outer districts

---

62 Someone from the city who dresses in a stylish way.
63 A man in a high social position who lives in an immoral way.

o' nights. A thousand blades will soon thirst for thy life's blood, Dandy Dick. Ho! ho!"

Thus reflecting, Jonathan Wild strode through the deserted spot now known as St. James's Park towards the hostelry where he had left his steed. A shuffling sound from behind caught his ear. The streets of London, and more especially the semi-rural quarters, were all more or less infested by dangerous characters at night, the danger was still greater to the universally excreted Jonathan Wild. He quickly covered his face with a black mask, and then thrust a hand into each pocket of his coat-skirts to grasp in readiness a firearm.

A stray dog had taken a fancy to follow at Wild's heels. The shuffling noise was again heard. The thief-taker paused, then turned quickly; a horrid imprecation darted from his lips. The demented Mrs. Sheppard was rushing towards him.

"Jack, my ruined boy, I will most terribly avenge thee!" the mad creature was muttering. Then the dying form stood within a few feet of the cursing man. A shower of liquid streamed full over him. An instinct had caused him to turn his head. An ear-splitting shriek of maniacal hate followed, then the woman darted off. Most piteous yelps from the dog behind him at once made Wild aware of what had happened.

"Vitriol!"[64] The evil ruffian recoiled in shuddering horror. The cries of the dog became heartrending. The burning fluid had drenched the animal. Drawing out both weapons, the infuriated man discharged first one, then the other, aiming as best he could through the gloom of the winter's night. The fleeing female disappeared round a corner. A night watchman, with the lantern, came into view, the second bullet struck him, and with a feeble moan, the man fell.

Filling the air with foul curses, Jonathan Wild darted from the spot.

Raymond Raithwood, within an hour of his parting with Jonathan Wild, had ridden to Holloway and gained the presence of Sir Edgar Mortiemor. The latter was foaming with utmost fury. Snatching out his dress rapier he rushed upon Raymond Raithwood with the words: "You villain! how dare you face me?

RAYMOND RAITHWOOD CONFOUNDED—"TAKE BACK THAT LIE!"—THE BLOW—THE DUEL IN THE SNOW—DANDY DICK IN PERIL—A STARTLING NIGHT CRY—THE YOUNG BLOODS— THAT WARNING: "FLY! FLY!"

"Treacherous, smooth-tongued wretch!" raved Sir Edgar Mortiemor, "you forcibly took away my child! You, a honoured kinsman, to so basely use those who trusted you!"

The handsome old aristocrat was in a fit of ungovernable anger and indignation, and would have plunged his drawn rapier into the breast of the fop, Raymond

---

[64] Sulphuric acid.

Raithwood; but the latter drew his own sword with great agility, and warded off the advancing point.

"Calm yourself, sir. I am a better swordsman than you, and have no desire to harm you!" warned Raithwood, his eyes lighting up with fire, and yellow face turning to an ashen hue.

"You utterly base villain! The sheep's clothing hath been torn from thee, and the ravening wolf now stands revealed in all his evil nakedness! You would have pierced the hearts of Richard, your cousin, and my daughter Maude; but your assassin's steel was stayed! Not content with this horrible impulse, you next surprised my child and forcibly abducted her!"

"Stay, Sir Mortiemor!" replied his nephew, with a sinister sneer curling his lip. "Lies uttered by crime-stained men are beneath my notice. My accusers are highwayman and footpads—yet, alas! your friends."

Sir Edgar Mortiemor's rage was not abated by Raithwood's insolence.

"Do you deny taking Maude off by force?" demanded he.

"I do!" was the cool reply. "Her outlaw lover was the treacherous and cowardly abductor!"

"Raymond Raithwood, take back that lie!"

A startling, clear, ringing voice filled the great chamber. The voice was that of Dandy Dick. Colonel Blood and the former came from a draped alcove and stood forward, fierce rage and pride gleaming in their glances.

"So, contemptible cur and traitor, we meet again!" continued the imperious tones of Dandy Dick, as his handsome, graceful, and exquisitely-garbed form interposed between Sir Edgar Mortiemor and Raithwood. "Do you dare deny," he added, "that my friends and self rescued from you and your companions the fair Maude Mortiemor and her attendant maid?"

"Yes, I dare deny the charge!" insolently retorted the livid, snarling Raymond Raithwood.

The word was no sooner uttered than a loudly sounding, back-handed blow left the lividly crimson impress of five fingers upon the left yellow cheek of the electrified, aristocratic young gallant. The swift clashings of steels and scabbards instantly followed, as brightly flashing rapier blades darted into view.

"Your life alone can wipe out the dishonour of that blow!" hissed Raithwood, facing Dandy Dick in seething hot hatred, and displaying his teeth, bared like those of a snarling tiger.

"Your life it shall be, poltroon!" contemptuously retorted the young highwayman, firmly gripping his rapier's hilt, and preparing for an onslaught.

The rapier blades met in an impetuous clash, sparks flying from the flashing, twisting points.

"Hold!" shouted the tones of Colonel Blood, his own blade meeting the others. "'Tis not seemly that a duel should take place here. You must seek a convenient spot without."

"The ladies of the house will overhear and become most grievously terrified," added Sir Edgar Mortiemor to Dandy Dick. "If you must fight, let it be as your friend advises."

At the back of Raymond Raithwood was an enormous mirror set in the beautifully green and gold decorated library wall. The three men with crossed blades—the onlooker, Sir Edgar Mortiemor—were all vividly reflected in the glass.

Suddenly Raymond Raithwood lowered his rapier. "I will not cross swords with you!" he fiercely muttered, glaring maliciously at Dandy Dick. "Seemly, indeed! It is not seemly that a true gentleman should condescend to measure swords with a dishonoured man!"

"I am outlawed—have a price upon my head, 'tis true, but were I ten thousand times deeper steeped in degradation, I should still have more just claim to honour than thee, Raymond Raithwood!" bitterly retorted Danby Dick, his eyes filled with fiercest glitter.

"A forger!—a robber!—a cold-blooded murderer! Ha! ha! an' yet he dares prate of honour?"

As the words were scornfully flung at the young highwayman, a hot oath jerked from the lips of Colonel Blood.

For an instant Dandy Dick's visage became colourless as white marble; his eyes shot out steel-like flashes, breath came short and quick, then the tempest of his pent-up wrath suddenly broke its bonds.

"With the forging of Sir Mortiemor's name, I tax thee, Raymond Raithwood; and the robbery of the proceeds of the forged bonds; and, as to cold-blooded murder, you would have slain my fair cousin and myself but for my friend's keen eyes and active wrist!"

The thus accused man briefly appeared confounded; his looks most eloquent of guilt. From one to another he widely, defiantly glared; then he gave utterances to a loud burst of reckless laughter.

"Liars! Liars! Traducers! Felons! Who will credit thy words? Who but the simple Sir Edgar Mortiemor? Ho! ho! Ho!"

Three swift, forward strides, a tremendous battering ram-like a blow from the right, the loud crashing of glass, and oath, cries of alarm, terror, and torment. Then it was seen that Raymond Raithwood's head had dashed into the mirror, smashing it into a thousand star-like atoms, and seriously cutting the back of the scalp of Dandy Dick's bitter foe. He sank down, madly gritting his teeth, and breathing most horrible anathemas.

"If you refuse to fight me point-to-point, I will whip you hence as the meanest-spirited cur cumbering the face of the earth!"

Dandy Dick had sheathed his steel, snatched from the library wall a heavy hunting-whip, and now held it aloft over the head of the crouching, cursing, writhing, and blood-stained Raithwood.

"So be it! We will wage the contest until one or other is slain! I swear it!" replied Raymond Raithwood, rising to his feet.

A light of most crafty meaning had crept into the eyes of rat-like cunning of the last speaker; but this was not missed by the keen vision of Colonel Blood.

Sir Edgar Mortiemor, being anxious that the affair should not be suspected by those of his household, cautiously crept to the door, opened it, and listened. This chamber was situated in a comparatively disused wing of the mansion, and far removed from the rooms of the general inmates, with the result that the stormy words of the contending men had not been overheard beyond the library's limits.

A moon of silvery sheen looked down upon a beautiful winter-night landscape, frost, snow, black, grey, drifting clouds, leafless trees, shrubs, and silence—a silence filled with poetic charm, but soon to be broken by the clamour of fiercely raging and contending men.

Far to the rear of his mansion, Sir Mortiemor brought his companions, selecting a wild, deserted spot in his vast acres for the coming duel. Disdaining the usual custom of selecting seconds, the intending combatants silently prepared the encounter. When divested of their coats and vests, the white shirts of the duellists vied with the surrounding snow, thick up tree, bush, and earth, with here and there a patch of green verdure affording most harmonious contrast to the predominating whiteness. A gentle snow had commenced, thus completing the romantic and weird aspect of the surroundings of a weird and romantic incident.

Sir Edgar Mortiemor and Colonel Blood stood some a few yards away as Dandy Dick and Raymond Raithwood impetuously coiled their steels together. Each foe fixed the other with unflinching glance, their faces contorted with deadliest hatred, breath coming in excited gasps, and their movements agile with the fascinating grace of tigers.

"But for the gallant acts of yourself and that ill-fated boy, my dear child would yet be in Raithwood's clutches, and I tremble at the thought of what would have been the end of that outrageous plot. If it were not for the scandal that would follow, I should not grieve to see the abductor mortally disposed of!" said Sir Mortiemor in a low tone to the colonel, who stood by his side.

Dick's faithful comrade bowed. "We need no mention of the service done to you and your daughter," replied he, adding: "As to that cunning villain, the sooner his career is somewhat checked—if not fatally—the better, for my comrade in particular and the world in general!"

The eyes of the onlookers were now intently fixed upon the two swordsmen. Dandy Dick was a most consummate master of the rapier, alert of eye, swift of movement, and with wrist of steel. Raithwood well knew his own inferiority, but trusted to his innate craftiness. His feints were clever enough to have fatally trapped a less wary or accomplished fencer; but Dandy Dick laughed them to scorn, and had already inflicted two slight wounds, one upon each arm, the smarting of which goaded Raithwood to the very verge of madness. Suddenly, by a most daring mode of attack, the latter beat down the guard of his adversary, and made a terrible lurch direct for the heart.

Colonel Blood and Sir Mortiemor caught their breath with quick gasps. Dandy Dick's doom appeared certain; but at the supreme moment the agile young highwayman sprang aside. Then there was a flash as of the darting of a ribbon of forked lightning, then up to its hilt the highwayman's rapier had passed through an upper muscle of his foe's sword arm. A fountain of crimson blood spurted out, dyeing the turned-up shirtsleeves and staining, in a circular clot, the snow-covered earth.

Raymond Raithwood stood, tottered giddily for the moment, then furiously sprang forward, again aiming for the other's heart, utterly reckless of the guard stroke aimed to meet it. The wounded man's point was again diverted, and for the second time the steel pierced the sword arm, the defeated Raithwood now dropping his rapier, and instantly after sinking to the earth, faint with loss of blood and the agony of his wounds.

At this moment a peculiar sound rang out upon the far-off night air. Then came another, equally distant, but in an opposite direction. There was followed by a vast number of exactly the same orders, and apparently coming from all points of the compass.

A most exultant, cruelly grating laugh burst from the pale lips of the prone Raymond Raithwood, whose eyes gleamed snake-like from their deep, shadowy hollows under his contracted black eyebrows. Then, at the utmost of his lung-power, he threw out the same strange, piercing cry.

"The signal call of the Mohawks!" cried Colonel Blood, casting a swift, warning glance at Dandy Dick. The shouts came nearer, and the trampling of many feet added to the highwayman's alarm.

"I have faced the coward in fair fight, and he now seeks to betray me!"

Dandy Dick levelled one of his elegantly-formed pistols at the head of Raymond Raithwood.

"Your fellow-rioters—prank-players upon women and the poor and defenceless generally—shall find your dead body!"

Dandy Dick, maddened with the sense of his cousin's baseness, pressed the trigger; his fire case, for a marvel, flashed in the pan!

A tall, graceful form down darted from out the gloom, and with a great sob of despair a female threw her shapely arms about the neck of Dandy Dick. It was the beautiful, stately maiden, Sir Edgar Mortiemor's daughter.

"Fly, dearest! Fly, Dick, while there is yet time! Oh, heavens, another moment must bring with it either your arrest or death!"

THE COUNTRY FARMER AND THE HIGHWAYMAN—A NOVEL PURSE—THE UNSEEN ROBBERS—RALPH DRAKE'S TERROR— VISITORS TO THE HOLE-IN-THE-WALL—WIFFLES A WELCOME VISITOR—BILBERRY HAS A FRIGHT.

"Hee! hee! Haw! haw! Oi beest told that Lundun footpards an' oighwaymon beest moighty smart an' fierce, beest that true, zur?"

"Ha! ha! sure enough, my fine fellow. I hope you don't carry anything of value about with you? It's a true saying that 'to rob an empty pocket means twice the work, and for no pay.' You see, the robber must first fill the pockets before he can empty it; and then he makes nothing out of the job. Robbing one's self is a fool's pastime!"

"Thun all my pockets beest empty, an' oighwaymon or footpard thut tries to rob Oi 'll play at fooul's parstime, eh. mister?"

"Certainly; the more especially if the trick amuses you!"

A tollgate on the London Road which cut through the London Fields, and one end of which directed it way towards north London. Time—night in winter. A country farmer, evidently, by the cut of his garments, was in bantering converse with an old toll-keeper on the road mentioned, and the mounted bucolic appeared highly pleased, with a sense of his own great sagacity.

Paying the toll-collector's fee, and obtaining directions as to his intended course, the farmer rode off. The shaggy dirty-white coat of the rickety old cob he rode might—like its master's rig—have been also fitted by a very bad tailor, and made of the shoddiest material, if appearance counts for anything.

The long, thin-jawed, grizzled old toll-keeper stood for a few moments softly chuckling, dangling his great lantern, and peering after the vanishing horseman. Then he darted into his little, round, wooden hut. A young, graceful, richly-dressed, and masked man, with much profusion of dark, curling locks about his shoulders, eagerly rose up to meet the toll-keeper.

"You heard? The wayfarer carries nothing about with him but emptiness!" muttered the latter, a merry twinkle in his eyes.

"So far as his head is concerned that statement is no doubt strictly true; but the chawbacon found you the toll demanded?" This was said in a cheery, musical voice.

"Ha! Ha! Yes; an' didn't appear to quite leave himself penniless."

"Then bring me my steed, friend Morgan. Lundun oighwaymon beest moighty smart an' fierce, they beest, so doin't keep Oi waiting, mon!" These words were given in such perfect imitation of the farmer's, that the old toll-keeper for a moment paused in open-mouthed wonder, and then burst into a hearty roar of laughter, and ran off towards an obscure spot, where stood tethered to a tree a noble-looking chestnut mare. This animal was trotted back to the toll-lodge, and there held in readiness. Quickly the slight, graceful, lithe form was seated in the saddle, a long black cloak assumed, and then, a few hurriedly-whispered words, the rider urged on his steed to a smart pace, and followed the direction taken by the countryman.

"Pull up, fellow; and keep your hands clear of those holsters, or I'll blow the top of your head off!"

The traveller hastily drew rein. Before him in the darkness was a masked and cloaked horseman. The bright tube of a pistol flashed within a few inches of the chopfallen[65] rascal's head. The eyes, staring through the apertures in the black mask, flashed like burnished steel in the sunlight. The robber and his animal had made so little sound in their approach that the provincial might well be excused for, at first glance, taking them for supernatural creatures.

"Put a bullet through his wizzen! No favour, comrade, kill your man as we do all others! A leaden pellet will do the trick! When he's reduced to cold, motionless clay the pillaging will be easy!" From the rear of the masked robber, somewhere from the impenetrable gloom came three other voices. Evidently, concluded the attacked man, the tones of companion-ruffians of the one facing him. The country-bred victim had little knowledge of the art of ventriloquism, or he might have detected the slight motion of the lips of the desperado while the supposed other predators were speaking.

"Quick, Sir Knight of the Order of the Turnip, I demand toll! You must pay a fee for the freedom of the highway, the amount of said fee being exactly the sum total of all you possess!" It was a voice of stern command, the clicking of the trigger of the flint-lock keeping time with the words.

"Thou beest a Lundun oighwayman, and thy mates beest Lundun oighwaymen too?" muttered the wayfarer in trembling awe; adding: "An' Oi've yeard that Lundun oighwaymen an' Lundun footpards beest moighty smart an' fierce, they beest!"

"Beast?—not so much of the beast! The creature somewhat jars upon my nerves, as I'm not quite dying to hear what you have 'yeard,' Sir Gallant of the streaky bacon and plum-pudding persuasion, so quickly turn out all the specimens of King George's currency, with all other valuables you have in your possession. Hand over promptly, or your life will not be worth a pin's purchase if my friends in ambush near by determine to join in this affair."

"Thou'lt but play at fooul's parstoime. I've nout o' valley wi' me."

"Villain, I crave not for valley, neither pine I for meadows green, bubbling

---

[65] Dejected; literally, the lower jaw hanging loosely.

brooks, smiling hills and dales, and sunny meads. Golden guineas are the boiled-down essence of all those and every other desirable joy of life. So come, Sir Guinea-pig, hand over the guineas, an' I'll not claim the pig!"

Under the robber's assumption of great sternness was a faint suspicion of roguish mirth. Without appearing to observe this, the countryman nevertheless secretly took some comfort from it.

The victim turned out the linings of all his pockets—a goodly number—promptly took of his riding-boots, inverted and shook them, then lifted his hat, and finally opened his mouth to most alarming dimensions. As the hat was held aloft the startling explosion of a pistol rang out. The head covering fell heavily to the ground, a jingling sound mingling with the thud.

"A novel purse! A man who carries his bank upon his head must needs be greatly oppressed by the burden of his riches. I will relieve thee of much mental and moral worry, Sir Cabbage. Come, the hat, sirrah!"

With a fine, flowery, bucolic oath, the farmer dismounted, picked up his head-gear, and then handed it to the robber.

The turned-up flap of the three-cornered hat had all been carefully stitched to the sides of the crown, but the crips within had betrayed their presence by their tuneful jinglings. A knife-blade ripped open one sewn flap, and a stream of gold and silver money pieces showered down into the frosted, snow-covered road ruts.

"Ha! ha! taake that, thee blarm'ed rogue!"

A bullet whistled past the mask-covered temples, the startling explosion of a pistol following. The shot was repeated by the highwayman's weapon.

"Very pleasant exchange of friendly compliments, eh, Sir Hedgehog!" smilingly remarked the robber.

The dismounted man had taken advantage of the diverted glance of the other, snatched a loaded weapon from one of his holsters, and fired point-blank, but, nevertheless, missed his intended mark. The return shot cut an ugly grove in one of the red, fat cheeks of the rustic.

"Ha! ha! Oi beest told, money's the time, that Lundun oiwaymen an' Lundun footpards beest moighty smart an' fierce, an' now Oi know as that beest true, for certin sure!" most dismally wailed the wounded man, tenderly placing a handkerchief round his face, although the flow of blood was but slight and the farmer more frightened than injured.

"Gather up those coins, Squire Broccoli-sprouts, and transfer them to this bank."

The highwayman held forth his own hat, its cavity uppermost. The pieces were tremblingly collected and placed where requested.

"Your watch and other articles of value you have yet hidden about you. I will waive my claim to those if you at once make a graceful and rapid exit. If my comrades dart from their concealment and attack you, they will show no such clemency."

The victim needed no second bidding. He hastily mounted, and, putting spurs to his cob, galloped away into the darkness ahead, the voices of the unseen robbers each yelling after him, as if in utmost rage at his departure.

*

Ralph Drake sat with his head clasped between his hands, and elbows upon his knees, in the little bar-parlour of the Hole-in-the-Wall Inn. "My poor, loving, but strong-headed lass, where will thy rashness lead thee to?" His usually pale and grave visage was paler and graver than ever, and his breast rent with deep-drawn sighs.

Will the Witless crouched by the blazing logs upon the hearth. The demented boy was excitedly examining a number of small articles he had ranged about the floor. "Good Fairies! Bad Fairies!" the lad was softly repeating to himself as he changed the position of his playthings.

The galloping of a steed suddenly broke upon the ears of Drake and Will the Witless. The hoof-sounds could be heard coming towards the inn.

"Get thee to thy hiding-place, Will. Quick, boy!" cried Ralph Drake, rising and entering the bar. Through the unlocked gates and into the stables went the hoof-clatterings; then all became still again. The innkeeper wearily returned to the bar-parlour and resumed his seat, and dejected posture.

Some time passed, then a light footfall came near, a pair of warm, shapely arms were thrown round the neck of Drake, and his wife's sobs was sounding in his ear. The hostess was dressed in her usual neat and attractive manner.

"This will kill me, Meg, lass why did you venture the deadly business again?" muttered Drake; but more in sorrow than anger.

"I was heartbroken to witness your despair, Ralph dear. I dressed in my male attire, took mask and arms, saddled the mare, and secretly rode out, while you were away in the brewhouse. I left but an hour back, and, with the aid of our true friend, Morgan, have now the means of staving off the ruin threatening us. Our creditors will not wait an hour longer than to-morrow at the midday hour! Never mind the dangers of my adventure, I'll not talk of them!"

"But the sin, the infamy!" moaned the innkeeper. "An' exposure means death to both of us, wife—death!" Ralph Drake distractedly strode the floor, and hopelessly wrung his hands.

"What's there! The ever-melancholy Drake wiv the ever-saucy goose to mate! Goosey, goosey, gander, where shall I wander? I'm a livin', parched-up desert, a burnin' for ther sweet, dewy nectar what never, never comes its way. Now, dear, tender, tough old Drake, be kind ernuff ter put both legs foremost at one time, an' let me 'ave moisture, moisture, moisture!"

Ralph Drake and his wife gave a shout of astonishment, in which was mingled a note of pleasure, for the irresistibly droll and mirthful face of Wiffles was glowing upon them from the outer bar.

The host and hostess instantly lost their grieved aspect, and sprang forward, and the youth warmly grasped their extended palms.

"We are alone, friend; but 'twere safer not to remain in the public-bar," cautioned the innkeeper. And Wiffles at once followed Mrs. Drake into their own private parlour, where the host soon followed, bearing a bright tankard of ale, the head of which resembled a prize-winning cauliflower.

"I 'ave soaked so little of late that me windpipe is choked up wiv spider webs," said Wiffles, at one draught consuming the ale, prize cauliflower included. The host quickly refilled the measure.

"How fairs our gallant Dandy Dick? I had hoped to have seen him before this," remarked Ralph Drake.

"That most forcibly reminds me—as ther man remarked when the brick struck 'im on the 'ead," smilingly replied the facetious highwayman. A hand was then dived into an inside pocket, then a sealed paper packet placed into Ralph Drake's hands. On opening this a large sum, in solid bullion, met the amazed eyes of the host and hostess.

"What means this?" asked Drake, in a dazed, husky tone.

"That Dandy Dick is allus as good as 'is word—as ther deaf-an'-dumb feller sed when 'e kicked ther rude little boy, after 'earing 'im a-callin' 'im most insultin' terms."

Grateful tears filled the eyes of Drake and his wife.

"How strange it is that from the hand of the outcast comes such sweet charity, Meg, lass!" murmured the former, adding: "the so-called felon sets an example of loving kindness that we do honour to the best citizen of all London!"

"Good an' bad fairies—all the world is peopled with good an' bad fairies. I heard someone speak of handsome Richard—he is a good fairy!" Will the Witless had crept from his hiding-place, and he again entered the presence of his friends and recommenced his strange pastime by the hearth.

Wiffles affectionately stroked the head of the idiot-lad. The highwayman had dismounted and left his horse by Ralph Drake's brew-house. Wiffles was on the point of leaving the inn to bring the animal to the stable, when a steed rattled up to the inn-door. Like a flash the witless boy had vanished. Mrs. Drake threw open a door hidden behind falling drapery, and Wiffles also passed out of sight a moment before the loud, blustering, coarse notes of Officer Bilberry filled the in with its ringing echoes.

"Earthquakes! roaring cataracts! tornadoes! fiery cloud meteors, playing a game o' ninepins! am I to be done to death with each breath of life I draw?"

Thus commenced the Bow Street bully-boy, his face, as he entered the inn door, glowing like the setting sun.

"Curse ye! Ever as unwelcome as a counterfeit coin!" growled Ralph Drake under his breath, and savagely glaring upon the portly form.

"So you're there, coffin-visage, melancholy mute? Why don't ye die an' leave the most beautiful an' charmin' of all earthly creatures to wed more fitting mate?"

"I will die of joy the day after you are hanged!" thundered Ralph Drake, stung to the quick, and forgetful of the danger of insulting the Bow Street bully.

"Good an' evil fairies, Officer Bilberry is an evil fairy!" A distant, smothered-up voice gave out these words.

Bilberry started back in rageful surprise. "That imp of Satan! You have here somewhere concealed that supposed imbecile, Will the Witless, so-called. But, if his mind is crazed, it is with a lust for blood!"

"Who says that the poor afflicted lad is hidden here? And where is the evil if he is?"

Mrs. Drake had stepped forward, her fine eyes fired with indignation, cheeks glow, and bosom pulsating with rageful scorn.

Officer Bilberry, on catching sight of the graceful, comely dame, instantly changed his demeanour. Bowing to the floor, turning up his codfish-like eyes, and sighing like a blacksmith's bellows, he said, in his softest possible notes:

"Most beauteous, amiable, witty, gifted, fascinating of mortals, Bilberry, thine ever-devoted slave, fears not death, let him even come arrayed in his grimmest terrors! Thrice three times, an' thrice, an' thrice three times again hath that most foul imp—I should say, poor afflicted boy—nearly lain me out for good—I beg pardon—I should say for bad, for it will be bad business indeed for Officer Bilberry when he is finally lain out!"

"'Yus, but gran' business fer everyone else,' as ther tiger observed when 'e scrunched up a tax-collector!" muttered a second muffled voice.

"Ah, who spoke?" It was hard to judge where the insulting tones came from, but the roaming eyes of the suspicious Bow Street agent fixed themselves upon the hanging drapery screening the door of the closet in which Wiffles was hidden.

Bilberry made a fierce rattling of hanger-blade and sheath. "In the name of the King, I call upon you, Ralph Drake, to aid me in investigating this matter!" he pompously shouted, drawing his cutlass and pointing towards the hangings.

"Matter? What matter?" asked Drake, trying to appear calm, but sadly failing.

"What matter? Why the matter o' 'is own fat-'ead!" again cried the mysterious voice.

°RALPH DRAKE AND HIS SPOUSE HAVE A TRYING TIME—OFFICER BILBERRY BEWITCHED—WIFFLES CONSUMED WITH A THIRST—THE BITER BIT—RALPH DRAKE ACCUSED OF POISONING OFFICER BILBERRY ALL—BILBERRY PICKLED.

"Blue blazes an' epileptic fits! This surpasses high treason!" Bilberry gasped; and then made for the hanging.

"Ho! Ho! Ho! Bilberry, the waddling wine-bibber! Champion punch consumer! Coward! liar! ass!" This time the galling words were spoken apparently from behind a door at the back of the officer. He instantly turned, sprang to this door, and kicked it open. The place proved to be an ante-room, and was perfectly empty.

"Ha! ha! Try again, swaggering gas-bag!" But that he was looking upon the very spot, the dazed officer could have taken oath that this last insult was uttered in the very centre of the empty ante-room.

Again had Mrs. Drake's gifts saved herself and husband from danger. The idiot boy and the irrepressible Wiffles had both, within a hair's breath, betrayed their presence before the hostess had tried her ventriloquial powers as a means of confounding the Bow Street officer.

The latter now turned to the hostess, and saw an expression upon her face of deep alarm, mingled with pity.

"Queen of beauty, empress of all graces, tell me I am bewitched, or—or am I going mad?" asked Officer Bilberry, greatly agitated by vague terrors.

"Ask thyself, dear Mr. Bilberry!" replied Mrs. Drake in most sympathetic tone. "You hear imaginary voices, and find as owners for them persons you know; then you insist on searching an empty room, and almost appear to persuade yourself that a voice addresses you from empty space!"

"Persuade? What? Do you tell me that I alone have heard the words of most insulting taunts, applied to me, a most important official of the Government services?" shrieked Bilberry, in utmost confusion and consternation.

"Have you heard any voices save those of us present?" asked the hostess, turning to her husband.

"Why ask such a foolish question?" growled Drake, in well-acted contempt.

Officer Bilberry suddenly seized his left wrist in the fingers of the right hand. "I must be bled!" he cried in quaking terror. "I must to the leech! The loss of a little blood may put me right. My pulse is kicking like a horse put for the first time in harness! Pray, sweet Mistress Drake, what think ye ails me?"

"If I dared believe in such things, I should certainly say that thou art cast under the spell of some evil-spited witch. But most like 'tis the form of mind-disease, termed delusions!" As she replied thusly, Mrs. Drake looked the very picture of pity.

° Part 15. Vol. XIV.—No. 351. 8 August 1900.

"Delusions!" wailed Bilberry, now in most abject terror. "I know! I know!" he continued. "Dandy Dick, Dick Turpin, Tom King, Will the Witless, the imp of Satan—all these are responsible for my undoing! I have gone off my feed! gone off my drink!—oh, Lord, an' now I've gone off me head!"

Ralph Drake and his wife were upon thorns.[66] The daring of Wiffles was not to be checked, and Will the Witless was scarcely to be held responsible for his actions. Should either of them make their presence known to Officer Bilberry, the consequences would be very serious to the host and hostess, the more especially after Mrs. Drake's clever voice-deception tricks.

"If that merry rogue Wiffles, and the crazed creature little Will, keep silent for a while, we may be able to induce this monster jelly-fish to float off to other latitudes," Mrs. Drake continued to whisper in her husband's ear.

"Heaven grant that we are not discovered in our deception, Meg lass!" anxiously muttered Drake in reply. This converse would not have been easy but for the fact that the officer was now in a too distracted state to observe it.

"Spells o' witchery! Charms o' sorcery! Incantations! Midnight callings up of the Prince o' Darkness! The hind leg of an aged toad! A hair from the head of the damsel that died o' fright. The tooth of a man-eating shark! A piece o' the coat-cloth worn by the last murderer hanged! Mingle all these in vinegar, boil them on top o' a grave in the church yard until they have bubbled for one hour! The church clock must chime of the midnight hour, then commence the awful devilry thus:

"Pains an' torments, torments an' pains! May needle-points pierce the brain an' heart, day an' night, night an' day! Gall, bitter aloes, thorns, stinging nettles, nightmares, ghosts an' goblins! May all these, an' still more evil things, afflict the accursed man Bilberry! Ha! ha! I well know the vile methods of those foul-minded, hideously-wrinkled, dried up, parchment-skinned she-devils that fly the moors on broomsticks o' nights! Aha! See there! See there! What face—what form is that that has drawn aside the hangings there, and now leers at me like the foul fiend himself?"

Bilberry now threw himself full length upon his broad back, kicked up his legs, squirmed, groaned, chatted his teeth, wildly threw his arms about, and finally wound up his highly artistic and sensational performance by most piteously pleading for "A sup o' brandy, wine, or draught o' punch! In mercy's name, quick, or I die!" he feebly groaned.

Now, Wiffles had waxed impatient of his long confinement in a close, stuffy little room, and, stifling for a breath of fresh air, had silently opened the door and thrust his head out of the division of the tapestry hanging before it. Then, seeing Bilberry looking direct towards him, Wiffles instantly contorted his face to such a terribly diabolical degree that a demon pantomime mask would have looked quite

---

[66] Anxious.

lovely by contrast. Officer Bilberry no longer doubted that the fabric of his mind had really, temporary at least, given way; and, like all drink-soakers when in an extremity, his first great craving and demand was for his tipple!

"Poor dear, dear friend!" gushingly murmured Mrs. Drake, darting forward with a soft cushion, and placing the same under the officer's head. Ralph Drake had carefully selected a fiery spirit of the most inferior brand in his house, and, stooping down, poured at least half a bottle of the fluid into the open mouth, Drake, in his spleen, secretly hoping that the liquor would at once terminate Bilberry's career in a fit of suffocation, induced by his reclining posture. But the inn-keeper could as easily have carried water in a sieve, or a live eel upon a small spoon, as to choke Bilberry with anything in the way of tipple. The reclining man gave one soft gurgle of satisfaction, and then thrust out his tongue as a sign that the damping process could go on.

In the meantime, Drake's spouse had contrived to steal to the hiding places of Wiffles and Will the Witless, and by dumb motion impress them with some sense of the importance of still keeping themselves concealed and silent.

Mine host of the Hole-in-the-Wall had seen the disposal of two bottles of his deadliest "fire-water," and Bilberry continued to pile up the agony in proportion to the supply of suction forthcoming. Mrs. Drake also piled up the agony, but in quite another direction. The devoted wife, in her anxiety to keep in the good graces of the troublesome Bow Street officer, had become far too tender in her expressions of concern on his behalf to please her somewhat jealous husband.

"Poor, ill-fated, badly-used soul!" sweetly cooed the hostess, bathing with vinegar the broad expanse of florid flesh representing Bilberry's countenance. "Do, pray, calm thyself! The attack may soon pass away, poor, dear creature!"

"Pour an' dear! I may continue to pour until the crack o' doom, an' it's a dear pour, an' a pour dear, too! An' another thing's certain, an' that is, if the attack upon my liquors don't soon pass away, it's mighty certain that the spirits will, for I've little more left—three bottles at the utmost!" bitterly and tearfully remarked the innkeeper.

"My ever good, true friend Drake, have I not always loved thee an' thy sweetly amiable wife—I should say, loved thee, an' esteemed thy sweetly amiable wife? Stand by me, Ralph! The remaining bottles may save me, if I am not already a dead egg!"

"Stand by thee!" indignantly snapped Drake. "While I do, I stand by a cesspool that ever consumes my drinkables, and returns me nothing in exchange. To stand by thee is to fall to my own ruin!"

"Less power to thy churlish tongue! Am I not going to make thy fortune?—swell thee out with riches until thou shalt swagger about for all the world like a huge human money bag? I have promised thee half the reward—an', mark me, 'tis doubled now—when I capture that infernal chief of all depredators, Dandy Dick!"

The innkeeper's liquors had certainly produced an effect, for the Bow Street runner was now somewhat more himself. Every moment Drake and his mate feared exposure. At the boast, concerning the arrest of Dandy Dick, something very much like a partially smothered-up fit of laughter came from Wiffles's hiding-place, and indications were not wanting to prove that the imbecile boy had become restless on hearing mention of Dandy Dick's name.

"Let me prevail upon thee, gentle friend, to retire to an upper room for a while. The hour is late, the night more than usually severe. A special brew of punch, for which this inn is so justly famous, may greatly improve thy state." Thus pleaded the hostess, but her husband frowned darkly upon her.

The prospect of Bilberry remaining was too terrible. A meaning look was given to Drake by his wife, and the former became somewhat reassured.

"Punch! Special brew! Man Alive, but I'm vastly better even by the mention of the words! Angelic, adorable, lovely being. I thank thee! Drake, friend nearest me heart, do help me to an upper chamber, e'en as thy paragon of spouses so thoughtfully suggests." Thus saying, the Bow Street bully assumed a sitting position.

Ralph Drake was ready enough to comply with the request, yet he soon found the task much like attempting to dance a quadrille with a dead elephant as partner.

The ever cheery Wiffles no sooner found himself consigned to close quarters in the semi-dark and stifling interior of a closet than he commenced an inspection.

The place was used as a storeroom. On a shelf was a number of bottles of a kind usually used for wine or spirits, and having the labels upon them. A prisoner, in an almost atmosphereless space, and in some natural alarm at the near proximity of a professional felon-hunter, it is not to be wondered at that a prize-winning thirst claimed the highwayman as its "very own."

The removing of the cork was simple enough, as it had previously been drawn and then lightly replaced. Wiffles had taken a very stiff pull at the neck of bottle number one, he had well thrown his head back, expanded his chest, and otherwise carefully poised his body so that the liquid should have every opportunity of thoroughly lubricating the inner man. Fi-s-s-u-s-s-h!

"Oh, shades o' all ther mother-in-laws as was ever an' ever will be if the stuff ain't winegar, an' ther strongest an' sourest winegar, too! Oh, crimiky, I shall never live ter get ther taste out ev me poor mouth!"

Wiffles's face was a study for the wrinkles of extreme old age, as he continued to spit out the taste, for the fluid itself had shot out of his throat like quicksilver from a furnace.

Further samplings proved that the spirit-bottles had all been used for the same purpose, that of containing the bitter, sour liquid of which Wiffles had already had more than enough. It was at this point that the pleadings of the funk-stricken officer for the remaining three bottles of liquids caught the ear of the concealed robber. He cautiously opened the closet door, and peered through the opening in the hanging drapery.

Ralph Drake and his wife were bending over the outstretched form of Bilberry. The backs of host and hostess were towards Wiffles, the officer's head hidden by Mrs. Drake. The spirit bottles were at the rear of the innkeeper and his wife, and within three feet of the youthful highwayman's hiding-place. Three silent steps upon tip-toe and the glass vessels were exchanged. Wiffles had regained the interior of his prison-place, and then, somewhere deep down in his inner anatomy there were fiercely fermenting an endless number of savage swear words, for, alas! Wiffles could discover no corkscrew. The corks could not be drawn, and to knock off the neck of a bottle would make too much noise.

"Never mind," philosophically reflected Wiffles, "old Bilberry'll get the winegar if 'e's lucky! 'Sweets ter the sweet,' as ther bachelor whispered ter the old maid when 'e offered 'er a sour crabapple."

Officer Bilberry, groaning most dolefully, and bitterly bewailing the calamitous results of his visits to the Hole-in-the-Wall, was at length disrobed and assisted into a bed in the chamber he had once before occupied.

No sooner had Ralph Drake partly mounted the stairs with the officer than Mrs. Drake opened the door and beckoned Wiffles from his hiding-place.

"I'm so sorry for your plight, my dear friend Wiffles!" softly murmured she, adding: "pray, how do you find yourself?"

"Pickled, Mrs. Drake, pickled!" he most dolefully replied, pulling a fearfully wry face. "But, my good dame," Wiffles continued, "'tis sed that out o' much sufferin' an' triberlashun ye shall find wisdum; and that's true, for I've found out a secret that 'asn't been knowed for thousands o' ye'rs!"

"Bless me, how wonderful! Do tell me, my dear Wiffles!"

"The secret o' the embalmin' o' them Egyptian mummers, Mrs. Drake!" replied Wiffles in most solemn strain. "I'll swear be the Book," he continued, "as they was pickled in your winegar! Nothin' else in the world 'ud do it, dame, an' a dose o' the same 'as already conwerted me into a livin', movin', pickled Wiffles!"

The dark-eyed, attractive hostess smiled. "You're a whimsical Wiffles, at any rate," she said. "Where is the vinegar you speak of?"

Before the former could reply, a most terrific spluttering, roaring, and fuming came from above.

"Man Alive! Blood an' hounds! Drake, you fiend incarnate!" roared the well-known tones of the Bow Street Bilberry. "What in thunder have you given me? The foul fluid is sharper than a knife, an' bitterer than death itself!"

"That dear old, lamb-like, pertic'ler friend o' yourn up above 'as got your above-proof, knock-me-down-strength winegar, Mrs. Drake!" now answered the cool

Wiffles, adding: "Old Bilberry fresh wasn't too over tasty; but old Bilberry preserved in winegar 'ull be too cross-grained, tough, an' indegestuble for anythin'!"

LOVE'S ALARMS—"MY PLACE IS BY THE SIDE OF THE MAN I LOVE!"—COMRADES, BRAVE, CONSTANT, AND TRUE—THE MIDNIGHT MOHAWK BANDS—THE ATTACK UPON SIR EDGAR MORTIEMOR'S ABODE—FIENDISH WARFARE.

"Fly! The mansion is surrounded by an excited rabble, composed chiefly of those reckless, heartless creatures termed young bloods. They are clamouring for Dandy Dick, and declaring that you have been seen to enter this residence!"

The high-born, exquisitely-robed, lovely, and stately Maude Mortiemor had locked her bare, shapely arms about the youthful highwayman's neck. The maiden was in low-necked eveningwear, and, all unmindful of the freezing winter night, her alabaster bosom palpitated excitedly against the breast of her lover.

"Sir Edgar, I beseech thee, convey thy fair, fragile Maude within doors. Exposure to this chill night must needs be dangerous to one of such delicate nature." Dandy Dick thus addressed the sweet girl's sire, and already the latter had entwined her momentarily-forgotten cloak and hood about her and was attempting to lead her away.

"My place is by the side of the man I love in the moment of his peril, father!" frantically pleaded the girl. "Has he not saved me from worse than death itself? And would you counsel me to repay such devotion by meaner service?" she added.

"Nay, child; my arm, my house, my fortune are now at thy unfortunate cousin's command. The Mortiemors are not unmindful of those that so devotedly serve them; but the youth must seek safety within. To remain here is to court capture or death."

Maude Mortiemor instantly saw the wisdom of her father's words.

"You will not leave me, dearest? My love, my life, come to the security of our roof. Who knows, my father hath great power with the King, and may yet obtain your pardon!" the loving Maude breathed into her lover's ear.

"Hush, hush, sweetest! Ye know not the impossibility of thy words!" was all Dandy Dick could reply before Sir Edgar Mortiemor had led his child away, hastening towards the house.

Dandy Dick turned to Colonel Blood.

"What think ye, comrades mine?" he asked, with reckless mein, the cries of the young bloods growing louder and fiercer.

"That black-visaged, craven cur Raymond Raithwood slunk off on seeing your attention engaged with his fair cousin. I had not the heart to stay his progress. That wretch is badly wounded, and see, he hath left a trail of blood in his wake," replied Colonel Blood, adding, as to the Mohawks, "Let them come on!"

The glistening hoarfrost and snow vividly revealed the course taken by Raithwood, the crimson clots here and there hurriedly disfiguring the pure whiteness of the earth's mantle.

The arch-plotter Raymond Raithwood had arranged his plans well and swiftly. Before starting on his journey to Sir Edgar Mortiemor's mansion, he had sent special messages in all directions to secure a gathering of the young bloods, or Mohawks. These latter were to remain in ambush near the mansion at Holloway, and await the signal of their leader, but certain suspicious circumstances had induced them to give out the first secret signals. These suspicious circumstances were in the form of mysterious horsemen arriving upon the scene and then stationing themselves in an obscure spot and remaining there, as if for some sinister object.

The double cunning of Raithwood had enabled him to conclude that Dandy Dick, his persecuted and proscribed kinsman, would lose little time in restoring Maude Mortiemor to her father. As a matter of fact, Dandy Dick had secretly sent to Sir Edgar Mortiemor and informed him of the recovery of his child, and his intention of conveying her to her sire's mansion. Thus, expecting the probability of exposure and its consequences, Raithwood had resolved to have help at hand.

Indistinct forms could be made out swarming into the grounds at the rear of the mansion, and exchanging signal-calls.

Dandy Dick paused as he wiped his rapier-blade upon his cambric[67] handkerchief.

"We have the choice of seeking safety in the house, or attempting to reach our steeds," said the colonel to his companion.

°THE ATTACK UPON SIR EDGAR MORTIEMOR'S ABODE—FIENDISH WARFARE (*continued*)

"We are evidently surrounded by great numbers, yet I am most loth to bring trouble and disgrace upon Sir Mortiemor," said Dandy Dick, in a perplexed tone.

"May not this gathering of well-born and wealthy desperados mean a second attempt to secure by force the person of Maude Mortiemor?" asked Colonel Blood.

Dandy Dick uttered a furious oath.

"I am dull-pated indeed, comrades, that I did not suspect this!" he cried; adding: "But I will defeat any such outrage or sacrifice my life, even if I face singly a whole legion of these midnight, roistering ruffians!"

"Before you face them alone, Dick, the craven crew will have torn your friend limb from limb. Ah, and his limbs into shreds! Forsooth, Dick lad, an inch or

---

[67] A white, plain-weave linen.
° Part 16. Vol. XIV.—No. 352. 8 August 1900.

an ounce of living flesh of thy good comrades counts equal to any one whole wine-filled, woman and aged man-attacking Mohawk! Let's at them, boy! I love carnage when ravening wolves oppose the good and true."

"Bless you, devoted friend!" was all Dandy Dick could trust himself to utter, for their foes were gathering closely, and the black, looming pile, Sir Edgar Mortiemor's abode, had yet to be reached.

Colonel Blood and Dandy Dick were now silently fleeing towards the black expanse denoting the mansion's whereabouts. The early dawn was near, but as yet the atmosphere was as a black pall.

"Night-birds on the wing!" A low, hushed voice gave this signal, as dim, moving shadows sprang up before Dandy Dick and his companion.

"Their feathers should be clipped!" The answering signal was whispered by Colonel Blood. A moment after five black outlines of men were eagerly exchanging hand-clasps.

"Dick Turpin, Tom King, Wiffles!" gleefully muttered Dandy Dick, in unbounded delight.

"Yes, Dick," whispered Turpin and King in a breath. "We were not deaf or blind, and didn't intend being far away when our friend was rushing into peril!"

Dandy Dick expressed heartfelt thanks for proofs of his friends' devotion.

Wiffles had been requested by Dandy Dick to take a certain package to Ralph Drake, and to await the former outside the mansion at Holloway. While on his return journey Turpin and King had unexpectedly joined him. Seeing the collecting of a great concourse of horsemen near Sir Mortiemor's mansion, the three friends had dismounted, left their animals in a secure spot, and then stole to the rear of the Baronet's abode on exploring intent, and with the result already made known.

No time was now lost by the outlaws in seeking shelter. The old aristocrat came from the rear of his mansion, and in a few words was made aware of the arrival of friends. He asked no questions, but was more than rejoiced, as he had but two male retainers, and secretly feared the result of the visit of the Mohawks.

The party of highwaymen entered by the rear entrance. The door was then locked and bolted, the two serving-men being placed there on guard.

"My daughter, and Lady Mortiemor, with all the female domestics, are already in a secret hiding-place. In the event of the young bloods daring to attack my dwelling I think we muster strong enough to hold our own until morning. These roaming bands of midnight adventurers are a scandal to the exalted society of which they are all members," said Sir Edgar Mortiemor. Then he at once went to the balcony before the windows of the first floor chambers of this building.

Wiffles now addressed his friends, finding they were alone:

"Turpin, King, an' yer 'umble obedient ever ter command," he commenced, "is all armed ter the eyebrows. I've got six pistols, two daggers, an' me us usual 'anger—extreme keen-edged, an' warranted ter split a 'air at sight. Turpin an' King are also likewise plentifully supplied wiv tools. There's nothin' like prowidin' fer a rainy day, as ther gallant remarked when 'e'd pawned 'is fiftieth umbreller."

Stealing to the hall, the friends were enabled to hear the words of Sir Edgar Mortiemor, addressed in a loud, fierce tone to the crowd menacing his residence.

"Known to be the sons of honourable sires and dames, yet ye are not ashamed to infest the streets o' nights to make riot as thine evil wills dictate. Nor consider ye wives, daughters, aged men, or even tender children, when either are so unfortunate as to fall within thy debased clutches. Your features hidden under masks, it is almost impossible to trace the identity of any of your number. In your lawless acts ye prove yourselves far more debased than any highwaymen or footpads, for neither their temptations, unfortunate circumstances, or poverty can any of you claim as excuse for your infamous doings!"

Hideous howls, threats, and a confusion of oaths answered the bold words of the aged, white-haired, handsome man.

"Admit us, Sir Edgar Mortiemor!" cried out one of the Mohawks, in a rageful shriek. "We seek your kinsman outlaw, whom you unlawfully shelter. If you refuse to deliver him up to us we will pull down your habitation about your ears—brick by brick!"

"Most promising members of our future nobility!" sneeringly shouted back the baronet. "Aristocratic thief-takers, forsooth! Were I unwise enough to open my doors, mayhap my child would be included as an item of your demands!"

Furious retorts and the discharging of a firearm were the instant replies to Sir Edgar Mortiemor's defiant words.

Then a stifled cry from the brave old man told that he was hit. Dandy Dick sprang up the stairs and out upon the iron balcony, barely in time to catch the falling man.

"Dick, boy, if I die, defend my wife and child!" despairingly pleaded Sir Edgar Mortiemor, and then fainted. There was a ghastly wound upon his temple. Dandy Dick bore his burden to a couch and tenderly placed it thereon.

Colonel Blood, Dick Turpin, Tom King, and Wiffles now streamed into the chamber.

"That cowardly deed must be avenged!" hissed Colonel Blood, fearlessly stepping out upon the balcony. The lighted chamber threw his form out in sharp relief. The howling multitude below was but a black, indistinct mass. "The shooting down of an old man we expect from such carrion as ye! I would give five years of my life to find myself face to face with the coward who aimed that shot!"

"Raymond Raithwood himself!" mentally concluded Colonel Blood; but the wounded nephew of Sir Edgar Mortiemor had been previously taken away to the nearest leech, or surgeon.

A perfect hail of bullets pattered about the tall form of Colonel Blood, and he was thus compelled to withdraw from his dangerous position—a storm of savage snarls, resembling the terrible groundlings of famished wolves when suddenly baulked of an assured victim, coming up from the young bloods.

Dandy Dick had meanwhile convinced himself that Sir Edgar Mortiemor's wound, although a serious one, was not likely to prove fatal with proper care. The young highwayman therefore deemed it wise to at once call up two of the serving-men and instruct them to carry their master to the secret retreat of the ladies and female domestics. This was done. One of the retainers brought back a joint message from Lady Mortiemor and her daughter—an agonised request that Dandy Dick and his friends would defend the place to their uttermost, and not desert those now surely relying upon them for their lives. To this Dick returned a reassuring reply. Then he and Colonel Blood held a hurried consultation as to the best manner of holding the building against the great number of attackers. Chance decided their plan of repulse.

One of the retainers guarding the door at the rear dashed into the presence of Dandy Dick and Colonel Blood with the information that an effort was being made to enter by a window at the back.

All the lower windows—both back and front—were protected by strong iron bars, save one, that being a small window, some ten feet from the ground, and over the stout, oaken back-door.

The whole party immediately darted to the spot, but using the utmost caution. There came to the acute ears of the highwaymen the low mutterings of many men.

"They are intent on defending the front of the place an' forgetful of its rear," a voice was whispering. "You, Brunton, brought down the old dotard Mortiemor, an' to you, therefore, rightly belongs the distinction of first entering the defended building."

"Ah, indeed, an' I brought down the bravely crowing old cock neatly, for I warrant he'll crow again no more!"

Dandy Dick and Colonel Blood gave lowly muttering instructions to their three friends, with the result that Turpin, King, and Wiffles rushed up to the front chamber on the balcony of which the head of the household had received his wound. Without needlessly exposing their bodies, the three outlaws commenced to rain a brisk discharge of bullets into the madly-excited, black, surging mass before the building.

Colonel Blood posted himself in a shadowy corner by the little window through which they would-be murderer of the baronet was about to enter. Dandy Dick remained with the two men stationed on guard on the inner side of the back door. To reach the one window unprotected by bars, the Mohawk Brunton had clambered up to the shoulders of a companion, his head and neck then being above the window-sill.

The window opened sideways, and was easily unfastened. The assaulter held firmly to the framework by his hands, sprang up from the supporting shoulders of his companion, had one knee the upon the sill, and the next moment would have succeeded in entering the mansion.

Colonel Blood had waited for this. Emerging from his hiding-place, he hissed between his clenched teeth: "So, craven cur, you boasted that you had brought down the bravely crowing old cock neatly, an' you'll warrant he'll crow no more; but you recked little on a younger brood that might seek retaliation!" These words were followed up by a terrific blow delivered upon the head with the butt-end of the colonel's pistols. The Mohawk seized his assailant by the arm, and attempted to draw himself within. Colonel Blood then dropped his weapon, closed his fists, and struck out right and left, the Mohawk's head rebounding by the force of the blows.

A shout from the colonel was the prearranged signal for Dandy Dick. Aiming at the thick oaken beams of the back door, the latter sent a bullet crashing through. No cry followed the shot. Then Dick drew his rapier, and thrust his blade into the jagged hole left by the leaden pellet. A second swift thrust. The keen point had pierced a yielding substance. There were cries of terror and agony intermingled. A crashing right-hander full between the eyes, which caused the clinging climber to at last released his hold of the window frame and sink down, the man supporting him at the same moment falling to earth, uttering terrible oaths and groans of anguish.

Dick Turpin now quickly sought Colonel Blood. Wiffles flew down to Dandy Dick. The alarming fact that the strongly bolted and chained front door was yielding could not be disputed. A long, compact stream of Mohawks formed a human battering-ram. Each worked as one. A great shout would go up, then the crowd withdraw from the entrance by a few feet. Another shout, and the dense formation of bodies would strike at the door. The force was simply irresistible and eminently hazardous, as those in front must have been crushed to death if the oaken entrance had not yielded to each blow, and finally utterly collapsed.

Frenzied with their success, the young bloods streamed into the spacious and stately hall, uttering deafening demands for the surrender of Dandy Dick, the highwayman. The assaulters had no suspicion that a whole party of proscribed men were opposed to them, and determined to defend the mansion if needs be, even at the cost of their lives.

Dandy Dick, the two lusty retainers, and Wiffles had joined Colonel Blood, Turpin, and King in the upper floor rooms. On the suggestion of the colonel, every movable article of furniture was taken from this chamber and hurled down the broad stairway. The richly-beautiful contents of a back chamber on the same floor then followed. A great barricade had been thus formed as if by magic. The young bloods found their progress up the broad stairway almost an impossibility.

Several of the most daring, uttering defiant shouts, clambered over the heaped-up goods. One by one these were deliberately felled by shots fired by the highwaymen, who were themselves safely screened behind the piled-up confusion of goods.

Firing from both parties took place at intervals. The rear door had now also yielded, giving admittance to another stream of Mohawks. Colonel Blood and Dandy Dick had at their disposal all the pistols carried by the party. Wiffles rapidly primed and adjusted the flint-locks, while King and Turpin went up to another floor in search of articles, and continually added to the strength and completeness of the novel and impregnable barricade.

Suddenly the Mohawks gave vent to most exultant yells. Those of them congregated in the hall below danced, shrieked, and otherwise conducted themselves more like demons than men. A dense, black, blinding and suffocating volume of smoke came, swiftly curling its way through the space between the top of the heaped-up furniture and the staircase ceiling. Then followed great dazzling tongues of darting, lapping flames. The fiendish young bloods had fired the articles in the hall and crowding the hall flight of stairs.

OFFICER BILBERRY IN A BAD WAY—WILL THE WITLESS AND HIS FRIENDS THE FAIRIES—GRATITUDE TO DANDY DICK—WITCHCRAFT—"DELUSIONS" WITH SHARP POINTS—GOOD AND EVIL FAIRIES.

"Mercy o' me! However did it happen? And what ever will be the result of that unfortunate man Bilberry swallowing my extra strong pickling vinegar?" Mrs. Drake looked the picture of consternation.

"You see, dame, in this 'ere wale o' tears we all is supposed ter take the sweets wi' the bitters; but some o' the double extree kind an' charetable folks, they manage ter nobble all ther sweets themselves, an' most thortfully palms off all ther bitters ter their neighbours an' poor relations. The ever good, kind, truthful and 'onest Bilberry is one o' that sort, an' in concequince was most perticcler anxious ter perish all ther bottled sweets as you'd get in tow, an' a-leavin' poor me ter expire o' mortification in me loneliness, a-tearfully comtemplatin' three bottles o' sour goods. So what should I do but play old windbag ther neighbourly trick, an' exchange them corked-up juices. An' that reminds me as I must be flittin', as ther small fly on that web thoughtfully resolved when 'e saw ther great spider about ter spring on 'im. But fust, Mrs. Drake, I'll thank you for a corkscrew, an' then drink long life ter yerself an' yer good man!" concluded Wiffles, deliberately winking the off eye.

The hostess could not forbear a smile in spite of her anxiety. The corkscrew was found, and eatables placed before the hungry and thirsty, whimsical outlaw.

"You must not think of departing before Ralph and myself have framed a fitting message of thanks to send to our good friend Dandy Dick; and pray keep on the alert, in case that pestering Bilberry takes it into his obstinate head to come down here before your departure."

With this Mrs. Drake left the whimsical Wiffles and flew upstairs, taking with her two of the exchanged bottles.

"What ever means this, my good friend Officer Bilberry? I was under the impression that your condition was mending," said the hostess. Drake gave his wife a meaning glance, at the same time secretly handing her the vessels containing the vinegar, and taking those holding the spirits.

"The symptoms are becoming still more alarming, Meg lass!" gravely answered Drake. "Utter collapse must soon take place!" he continued, as if in great grief. "And our poor old friend has now lost both the senses of taste an' smell!"

"What! By this an' by that you're a most florid liar, Drake!" madly shrieked Bilberry from the blankets, his nose still as usual, resembling a freshly-worked ripe radish; but a greenish tinge had crept into his flabby cheeks.

"May I for ever more be impaled upon darning needles, or, like friar of old, compelled to trudge to distant holy shrine with hard peas in my sandals, if you, Ralph Drake, have not attempted to poison me with some decoction[68] that could only have been mixed by the foul fiend himself!" the alarmed man added.

The bottles were exactly alike in every detail, the once spirit-containers having been used for the keeping of pickling liquid. The hostess took up one of the original samples, afterwards exchanged by Wiffles. Its cork was drawn, and its neck placed to the dainty lips of the hostess.

Bilberry, having no suspicion of the exchange, eagerly watched the tasting operation.

A cleverly-assumed expression of pained alarm and pity came over the pretty face. The eyes he so vastly admired filled with tears. With all his vagaries, the Bow Street runner had a most sincere regard for the beautiful hostess, and a blind faith in her truthfulness and honesty.

"Come, my goddess of feminine loveliness," cried he, "are you now convinced that thy sour-visaged, cramped, jaundiced, madly jealous mate there stands confounded as my would-be assassin?"

"Alas! my poor, dear, most unfortunate friend!" sighed the dame. "This is indeed a good, true, wholesome liquor enough; and if you have judged it to be otherwise, I must fear me that your attack of delusions has fatally increased!"

"Bloods an' hounds! Thunderclaps an' squeaking pigs! If I've indeed lost sense o' taste, an' sense o' smell, when good liquor's to the fore, then I must be deader than the deadliest doornail! I, Bilberry, about whom it hath so truly been said

---

[68] A concentrated liquor often prepared as a medicine.

'that the flavour of a properly brewed bowl o' punch would cause his spirit to revisit earth at any time within, say, a thousand years after his death'—I, lost to the taste an' smell of the divine nectar—punch? Then carry me hence! Bury me, in all due pomp an' solemnity, place an empty punch bowl an' silver ladle upon me grave, an' then let chaos come!"

Ralph Drake's teeth set firmly. "Addlepate!"[69] he hissed, under his breath. "This jargon is the very essence of brain-tottering drivel!" Then he abruptly went from the chamber.

"Sweet dame," softly cooed the officer, turning up the whites of his goggle eyes like a dying duck in a storm, "thy presence gives me hope! Hast thou some preparation known to have power to remove the curse o' witchcraft?"

"Aha, that have I!" responded Mrs. Drake, adding: "And who knows but that the same may restore they lost taste and smell? I will return with the precious charm mixture in a trice!"

On rejoining her husband, the hostess entreated Wiffles to depart, both for the sake of his safety and their own. He had vastly enjoyed his supper, the close proximity of a Bow Street officer not having affected his appetite in the least. The message of grateful words to Dandy Dick was framed. Wiffles had gone, to rejoin his comrades at the mansion of Sir Edgar Mortiemor, as we have already seen.

The gratitude of Ralph Drake and his wife knew no bounds, more especially as Wiffles had convinced them that the money sent was not dishonestly obtained.

Officer Bilberry could now sponge upon them for a time if he chose, for their extreme poverty was now a thing of the past. While Mrs. Drake hurriedly whispered with her husband, and at the same time concocted a harmless mixture to give to Bilberry, as a mystical charm to remove the evils of witchcraft. Will the Witless had again noiselessly joined them and became busy with his tiny toys on the floor near the hearth.

"Good an' evil fairies!" softly muttered the idiot boy, "good an' evil!"

Ralph Drake stooped down and picked up two of the articles.

"Poor Will," he muttered, "these things are but farm nails, some straight, others with their points turned down or battered!"

Will the Witless rose to his feet. "Good fairies can walk on air—tread in safety a thread light as gossamer wing!" he smilingly said. "But evil fairies, or spirits," he continued, his tones becoming grave, "are borne down by the weight of their wicked deeds. My good fairies make merry sport, leaping from one nail point to another. The evil fairies cannot do this—they are too heavy, and pierce their feet or bend the iron points."

The hostess stooped, and tenderly kissed the pale, pinched face, and smoothed the wild, elfin locks. "Go to thy hiding-place, and to bed, poor lad!" soothingly murmured she.

---

[69] Fool, literally "confused head".

"Aha, I must see to my beautiful, noble, faithful steed first!" he answered, clapping his little hands in glee. "Then," he went on, "I must guard against the wicked fairy upstairs coming down on us to work evil spells in the night!"

"What does the poor, afflicted one mean, Ralph?" asked Mrs. Drake, after the boy had most affectionately kissed them and then stolen away.

"The presence of that brawling, empty-pated ass Bilberry always throws the boy's wits into more than their usually confused state! The one gleam of intelligence in the darkened brain tells the lad that the Bow Street swashbuckler rogue is an enemy to all Will's friends and himself!" was Ralph Drake's reply.

Officer Bilberry, on the instant of the hostess leaving him, noiselessly stepped from his bed, and was greatly elated to find himself much improved. With this improvement returned his usual crafty, suspicious traits.

The sound of hushed voices then the hearing of heavy footsteps, followed soon after by the receding sounds of clattering hooves. What could these mean?

The Bow Street agent's boots were off. In stockinged feet, he crept to the top of the stairs, and then cautiously commenced to descend.

"A melancholic, plague-pinched, fretful toad! mangy, grip-twisted, whining, wandering mongrel! That Drake's preventing his spouse bringing me the charm, an', mayhap, brooding o'er another device to murder me!" Thus thought the officer, silently creeping down the stairs.

"Good an' evil fairies!" In a hushed tone these words were wafted up to the runner's ears.

"Oh! Ough! Murder! Blood an'—W-h-w-o-g-h!" The harsh, powerful notes of Bilberry's lungs filled the inn with bewildering, ear-piercing echoes.

Ralph Drake and his wife excitedly flew from their private parlour. The sixteen-stone or so of flesh representing Bilberry was seen midway down the lower flight of stairs. He was but partly dressed, and without his boots. The large, splay feet were moving as if in imitation of an active bear dance. The oaths the dancer was scattering were awful enough in their profanity to turn a black man white.

"What the—Well, of all—Do ye want to bring the old inn down about our ears, or is it more delusions?" yelled Drake.

"Ough! Wh-h-w-o-o-g-h! Curse you for a living delusion!" shrieked back Bilberry, choked with rage. "Delusions, forsooth!" he raved on. "Fine delusions—at least two inches long, and with points like daggers!"

He was nursing one foot now as he sat upon the stairs, his stockings covered with small discs of blood, as he, yelling lustily, drew long, pointed nails from the soles of his fat broad feet.

Flinging these one after another at the head of Drake, Bilberry went through the whole of the most extensive list of his choicest oaths, until he was fairly forced into silence for want of words and wind.

Groaning most dismally, the runner painfully hobbled up the stairs, and presently reappeared fully dressed.

"Bewitched! Poisoned! Maimed! My life isn't safe in thine accursed place, Ralph Drake!" he furiously growled, shaking his brass-headed staff of office at the innkeeper. "Now I know where my delusions come from! Evil eye! Sorcery! Witchery! Plagues an' pestilences! All these can I plainly trace in thy door-knocker face! May I be flogged to death with stinging nettles this next summer, if I have not thee dragged through a mill-stream as a man-witch, possessor of an evil eye, necromancer, an' the conjurer up o' the prince o' Satan himself!"

896, rec 17

°**"NO MERCY! NO QUARTER! NO SURRENDER!—THE BLAZING BARRICADE—WIFFLES UNDERTAKES A DESPERATE TASK—THE BLACK SEDAN CHAIR-BEARER—THE NECROMANCER, HIS PROMISE AND ITS FULFILMENT—THE STARTLING APPARITION—DISMAY—PANIC—DEFEAT.**

"The Mo'awks men ter smoke-dry us—conwert us into 'ams, an' we'll be in luck, too, if we save our bacon!"

Thus muttered the youthful highwayman Wiffles on seeing the thick, black, quickly curling volume of smoke coming towards them. There were bright, crimson patches in the on-rushing, writhing black cloud, and the loud crackings and hissings also plainly made known the dismaying fact that the barricade of household goods had been fired.

"Dick," said Colonel Blood, "this is ominous indeed. We may be driven out by the flames, and then caught upon the sword points of the young bloods!"

"If we could but find means to subdue the flames all might yet be well," was the reply of Dick the Dandy. He then hurriedly questioned the menservants as to the possibility of obtaining water; and found that this was hopeless, the supply being entirely from a well in the outer grounds.

The tumult caused by the incendiaries was now most deafening. The slight glimpses now and then to be obtained revealed them most eagerly plying their fell purpose. They resembled demon Salamanders in revelry.

"I have not yet ventured to visit the desperately wounded Sir Edgar," Dandy Dick whispered to Colonel Blood; "but we must soon cast aside all reserve, comrades. The women and the injured must be our chief care, next to defending the place while that remains possible."

"Suppose we drop all those Mohawk fiends within range? We may thus check their fun!" chimed in Dick Turpin, holding the ends of his cravat over his mouth. The smoke threatened to stifle them.

° Part 17. Vol. XIV.—No. 353. 8 August 1900.

"No mercy! No quarter! No surrender!" cried the colonel. "This is barbaric fighting. We must use their own methods!"

The one advantage the defenders had was that they could not be near so easily seen as the attackers. The flames threw into strong relief those crowded into the spacious old hall. Dandy Dick, Colonel Blood, Dick Turpin, Tom King, and the two robust retainers kept up a brisk fire, Wiffles priming the weapons and handing them back.

Every now and again a Mohawk shrieked out a piercing note of agony and crashed down, a few of the most daring falling into the flames, their companions falling beside them when in the act of attempting to snatch the former from the ceiling, leaping, lapping, destroying element.

The band of devoted defenders were as black men, their eyes reflecting crimson, their mouths covered with their cravats and handkerchiefs.

Dandy Dick held a few whispered words with his faithful henchmen Wiffles.

"Yus, it can be done, wive a little risk," replied the latter; "an' by your leave, I'm ther party as can do it."

"I would insist on taking that risk myself, for I have led my brave comrades into a fearful trap; but I dare not leave the place, at least, until I see the females in safety!" returned Dick the Dandy, firmly gripping a smoke and powder-blackened hand of Wiffles.

Not another word was said, Dandy Dick joining the colonel, and the four remaining outlaws, venturing near as the flames and heat would permit, to continue discharging their pieces at the incendiaries whenever a chance presented itself.

Wiffles had stepped aside with one of Sir Edgar Mortiemor's retainers.

"White wig? Yes, sir, an' livery. Come this way, sir!"

In an ante-room on an upper floor the articles were found. The face of Wiffles was grime-blackened, the white wig rendered his skin black-looking as a negro's by contrast. In a few moments he had put on a most gorgeous livery, and resembled a negro Sedan chair-bearer to the life.

Then the retainer conducted Wiffles, by means of a secret stairway, to the coach house and stables. The fire had not yet reached this part of the back of the mansion. The intention of the fearless Wiffles was to make his way to the grounds, mingle with those besieging the mansion, and then make his way to the Haunted Manor, obtain a party of mounted outlaws, and return with utmost haste to the aid of those defending the fired building. A silent, hearty hand-grip was all the parting the devoted fellow Wiffles had taken with each of his brother outcasts; but men who are daily—hourly—facing death make little display of emotion when about to confront the devastating monster, and no living creature held death in more contempt than the young highwayman, whose delight it was to make merry jest even in the moments of supremest peril.

"Yus," mentally mused Wiffles, "the job can be done wive a little risk, as ther frog decide afore turning 'isself inside out for ther purpose o' giving 'is stone-cold innards a nice warmin' in ther sun!"

A side door in the extreme end of the coach building opened upon the extensive ornamental grounds. Caution and silence did the rest. Wiffles stood in the black shadows cast by the fire-glow at the rear lower windows. Within a few yards of him was a great crowd of Mohawks. They were dancing, shouting, and gesticulating like demented creatures; firing their flint-locks whenever a figure was seen at a window, and working destruction on every hand. In the dense, winter gloom, the young bloods looked like men of ebony, streaked with vivid, glaring patches of yellow and vermillion.

"'I'm out o' the fryin'-pan inter the fire!' as ther small boy-truant cried w'en 'e 'ad scrambled out o' the thorn bush ter flop down upon a 'ornet's nest!'" was the reflection of Wiffles on contemplating the fearful surroundings.

The livery of the flunky did not properly permit the wearing of the cutlass; but the thoughtful Wiffles had well provided himself with pistols, loaded and concealed in his larger coat-pockets.

The confusion of shouts were most bewildering. By cunning contrivance the disguised robber had mingled with the rabble, and worked his way beyond their outer flank. It was not possible to reach the concealed steeds, these being tethered in an outhouse with a crowd of Mohawks grouped before it.

On the fringe of the gathering Wiffles observed an old gentleman mounted upon a sturdy cop—the rider was simply a spectator. The ready-witted highwayman, unobserved, crept behind a tree-trunk close to the horsemen, snapped off a long twig, and with the point silently and secretly goaded the animal in the flank. The cob instantly grew restless, and finally plunged forward.

"Have a care! Pull in that brute, or I'll put a leaden reminder in the pair of ye!" threatened a young blood.

The spur-like point of the twig again pricked the animal, and the beast again almost dashed into the thickly-packed throng before it.

Wiffles sprang to the cob's head. The old gent quickly dismounted.

"Thanks—thanks, my man! Whose Sedan chair-bearer are ye?" he asked.

"Sir Edgar Mortiemor's, good sir, let me take charge o' this 'ere brute," said Wiffles.

"An infamous preceding this attack, young man—infamous; but my life would pay forfeit if I uttered protest to this madly-excited, lawless crew!" whispered the cob owner, readily permitting the young outlaw to lead his animal away, under the impression that Sir Edgar Mortiemor's Sedan chair-bearer would remain with it at a safer spot until it was again required. The old gentleman remained at the same spot, sadly contemplating the shameful proceedings of the Mohawks.

Leading the cob to a spot where he would no longer be observed, the disguised highwayman quickly sprang into the saddle and rode off. Wiffles, on reaching the highroad, stuck his spurs into the steed, and made for the Haunted Manor.

The last verse of the most appropriate words of a song of the day entered his head and refused to be ignored, spite of the imminent danger threatening those dear to him:

> "They hanged him up high, so roomy and dry,
>> That black-arrayed crows at his grave might attend.
> Alas! and alack, this world's without hope:
>> Whose true human sympathy? Honest friend?
> A poor man hanged for merely stealing a rope—
>> Though there chanced to be a horse at one end!"

Then Wiffles gave a growl of impatience.

"Well, I wouldn't keep this 'ere useless consumer at no price. I've of'en 'eard that snails pride theirselves on their slowness. The snail what takes ther longest time ter travel over two inches o' space is made chief o' their kingdom; but ther slowest snail as ever was, if he once caught sight o' this article's deadly crawl, 'ud instantly die o' envy!" Thus spitefully ruminated the outlaw as time flew on.

It was in vain that the highwayman piled his sharp spurs. The cob had for years been accustomed to one even drowsy order of progress, and it could not be induced, either by spur-point, threat, or kind word to move the slightest degree faster. The thought of the frightful fate of his friends, in the event of his task taking too long to be of avail, made Wiffles furious with impatience.

He had reached the commencement of the high road to Finchley, when the unexpected appearance of a mounted horseman momentarily startled him. The next thought took the form of a possible exchange of animals.

"Stay, man, a word with you!"

The highwayman thus challenged drew rein, eagerly handling a pistol in his pocket.

"Stranger, my time's much shorter even than a young pig's tail. Make your tale still short, or I won't—"

"That's my young friend Wiffles!"

To his astonishment and delight Wiffles heard the well-known tones of the necromancer, whose mask and black cloak had effectually hidden his identity.

In a few hurried words this mysterious personage was made aware of the desperate condition of those defending the mansion at Holloway, and the errand of their comrade. The necromancer became plunged into deep thought for some moments, and when he again looked up his eyes were gleaming like those of a tiger at bay.

"Think ye that I will suffer this?" he sternly asked. "When my brethren are in danger let them call for the aid of my mystic prowess, and, though they are at the furthermost extremity of the earth, I shall hear and quickly respond!"

The youthful robber was dumb-stricken by the sudden change in the being before him. An indefinable awe crept into the highwayman's mind. "This strange being must be something more than human!" was his conviction.

"Return to your friends! Even before you reach them there will be a most powerful, terrible ally there, who will strike utmost terror into the fiendish hearts and craven souls of their foes! Meanwhile, I will fly to our stronghold and despatch hither our brethren. Will you trust to my word?"

"You are our firm friend!" gladly responded Wiffles. "We trust our lives to you!"

"Then, hastened back, brother. Take thy stand by the side of thy friends. Leave the rest to me."

Not a word more was spoken. Each horseman gave rein, darted spurs into his animal, and rode off in opposite directions.

Wiffles, when near the place of action, dismounted, and tied the cob to a tree-branch where it could easily be found by its owner.

But a brief period of time had elapsed since his leaving his fellow-outlaws, but Wiffles was dismayed to witness the astounding progress the fire-demon had made in so short a time.

Most dwellings were of timber, or mainly so, at the time of which we write. Sir Edgar Mortiemor's mansion was a most elegant and substantially-built edifice, but unfortunately mostly of wood. The coachhouse was now a mass of flame. To return to those he had left was thus an impossibility. Wiffles bit his tongue, clenched his fists, and danced with excess of rage.

How fared it with the small band so gallantly defending the doomed building? The hall, lower floors, and hall staircase had completely caught. The articles of household goods crowded into the hall, and packed up to the ceiling as a barricade, were now a complete network of dazzling yellow and red fire that scorched the eyes when looked at.

Beaten back by the advancing volume of fire, Dandy Dick and Colonel Blood—both blackened and their garments singed—had thrown together another barricade at the head of the second flight of stairs, Dick Turpin and Tom King flinging articles down from still higher floors.

The black, swiftly-curling, up-rushing smoke, blinding and suffocating in its density, was everywhere.

With the exception of blistered flesh, Dandy Dick and Colonel Blood were unharmed. Dick Turpin and Tom King were equally fortunate; but one of Sir Edgar Mortiemor's retainers had been shot, and now lay stark dead on an upper floor, with the red and yellow fire-glow flitting over his face, mocking with its brilliant tints the sickly power of grim and silent death. The fellow-retainer had received a bullet in his lungs, and was piteously moaning away his last moments on this side of eternity.

Wiffles, finding himself totally unable to reach his friends, appeared to suddenly loose all self-control. He fought his way to the front of the red-glowing a building. The multitude of Mohawks, now feeling quite sure of their triumphs, acted as wildly-elated conquerors, giving way to their unlicensed passions.

The fury-choked Wiffles strode into the open, levelled two pistols, and shot down that number of revellers; then he deliberately commenced to re-prime his weapons. Another moment would have seen him cut to pieces by the completely infuriated young bloods; but a something stayed their purpose. A most amazing sight had presented itself.

"Ho! ho! Merry sport, my masters—merry sport!"

A voice of sardonic, shrill laughter, rising clear above the general din.

A weird, startling, fearful form had suddenly appeared, from whence no one could tell. The apparition, if such it were, was of most extraordinary aspect. A hideous head, with horns and long red, matted locks. The head, face, and whole of the body and limbs resembled brightly-reflecting, burnished metal of a bronze-red tint. So luminous was this, in the reflected glow of the burning mansion, that the effect resembled that of a human form carved out of a solid mass of live coal, or molten metal.

A black cloak, with a deep hood attached, folded and unfolded its long flowing drapery now and again, at times partly rendering the mysterious wearer as a fire when closed up from view. Then the creature's movements could scarcely be followed, and when the hood was drawn over face, head, and horns, it was as the flitting away of a man-will-o'-the-wisp!

The Mohawks was stricken as if dumb and motionless. The laughter of the unexplainable form was of such a perfectly fiendish nature that its heroes were appalled by the sound, their hearts feeling as if turned to ice.

In perfectly incredible leaps and bounds the thing neared the outer ranks. Its unearthly shrieks grew still more appalling as it came on. Then, with a more terrific bound than ever, it shot upward like a fiery meteor, and landed safely upon the iron balcony facing the windows of the room in which Sir Edgar Mortiemor had received a bullet wound.

"Ho! ho! Merry sport, my masters—merry sport!" again shrieked out the unearthly awful tones. A most peculiarly-horrible thing then followed.

Luminous twisting objects, taken from some place of concealment carried by the visitant, commenced to shower down. Small, glowing, living things they were, their tiny bodies apparently like the showers of burnished red metal. Some mysterious chemical covering had produced this effect, for when they struck the upturned, scared-looking faces the touch was icily cold and clammy, save when the objects gave out a horrid hiss and darted their heads into the flesh. Then there followed a swift burning sensation, resembling a stab from a red-hot needle-point.

Like an electric flash the impression spread among the petrified young bloods that numbers of foreign-imported, deadly, venomous, if extremely small, reptiles were being scattered in their midst. Many of the most daring of the Mohawks fired up at the brilliant form. Its hideous laughter grew still more startling and awe-inspiring.

Then burst out the cries and lamentations of those bitten. They threw themselves to the earth, making the night ring with their awful shrieks.

An indescribable panic then seized every member of the attackers. The fear-inspiring cry had gone up of "Spring-Heeled Jack, the Mystic Terror!"—The unknown, unfathomably mysterious being, whom neither steel nor bullet could ever touch, whose speed of progress the fleetest steed could not match, and whose true nature—neither spirits nor mortal—or identity, if the latter, never up to this day has ever been known or even suspected.

The party of defenders in a front chamber of a second floor of the mansion had fallen back, and remained perfectly passive while this astounding incident was enacted. No sooner was the rout of the young bloods in full force than, with another series of its blood-curdling shrieks of laughter, the mysterious form took a flying down with swoop, and scattered the gallants in the most astounding manner.

Dagger-like spikes bristled from the backs of both clenched fists, which shot out with merciless swiftness and force, not one of the Mohawks making the slightest attempt at resistance, but fleeing in terror-panic headlong in any direction, impelled only with the one object of escape.

In a few moments what a change had taken place! The mansion flamed still more fiercely. The whole of the building must soon be enveloped, and those remaining therein fall victims to a frightful fate.

Springing to a window—a dazzling reflected mixture of white, yellow, pink, orange, and fiery red—Dandy Dick and Colonel Blood anxiously peered downwards into the outer night.

But one solitary spectator could they see remaining. This was the negro in most gorgeous livery—the supposed Sedan-chair bearer—actually the disguised Wiffles!

A ringing shout came up from their comrade, and an answering echo went back to him. Then Dick turned to his companion. There was a grim, set look of resolve upon his face. "I have set myself the task of saving those I love!" he said. "If I fail my charred remains shall bear testimony to the same!"

THE OUTLAWS HEMMED IN BY FIRE—DRIVEN TO THE BELFRY TOWER—WIFFLES DRIVEN TO DESPAIR—LOVE AND DEVOTION—IN DEADLIEST PERIL—LIVES HANGING UPON MOMENTS—DEADLY DANGER OF DANDY DICK—HEROISM OF COLONEL BLOOD—SPARTAN-LIKE EFFORTS FAIL—THEIR LAST HOPE.

"We must now, indeed, attend to the inmates of this mansion!" anxiously muttered Dandy Dick.

"I am with thee there, Dick!" readily agreed Colonel Blood. "It was impossible even to give a thought to the rescue of those we were defending while the enemy surrounded us. The mystic being, known as 'Spring-Heeled Jack'—for the want of a more clearer knowledge of his true identity—hath worked us most royal service, this being the second time that the man, or monster, hath interposed between us and the cowardly and unlicensed miscreants, commonly termed Mohawks!"

"The actual individuality of Spring-Heeled Jack is a thing no man can even so much as guess at. Many insist that he is not mortal, and there are those who actually believe him to be Satan himself!" mused Dandy Dick.

"That cannot be, or he would assuredly assist, not defeat, his own chosen imps—the young bloods!" answered his comrade.

The dawn, like a great steel, grey veil, was creeping over the heavens; there were streaks of deep-red on the horizon line, looking as if they were vivid smears of blood drawn by giant fingers; and the warm glow reflecting upon myriads of snow-covered tree branches, and the pure, sparkling hoarfrost, and virgin snow that enwrapped everything, gave a most charming effect to an otherwise most bleak and depressing-looking landscape.

The crackling, hissing, dancing, darting, great tongues of fire were gradually nearing the highwaymen now, driven up to the third floor. The four—Dandy Dick, Blood, Turpin, and King—were unrecognisable, each being black as negroes, their flesh blistered, hair singed, clothing clinging to them in charred rags.

The lower stairs were consumed; the third flight was gradually igniting. To convince themselves that the besiegers had indeed retreated and not returned, Dandy Dick and the colonel cautiously approached one of the windows and surveyed the outer extensive tracts of open country.

A black man, dressed in a most gorgeous livery of blue and gold, and wearing a white wig, stood without. He was fixedly-staring up at the windows, and making wild gestures.

"The fellow's a Sedan-chair bearer, judging by his fine array. What can the idiot mean by his erratic actions? A dancing doll at a fair is a thing of grace and beauty by comparison!" commented Colonel Blood.

"He wears the livery of Sir Edgar Mortiemor!" cried Dick, throwing the French window open and stepping out upon the balcony.

"They're all gorn, an' ain't left not the ghost o' a shadder behind 'em, as ther wale smilingly remarked ven 'e'd took in a soft-'eaded an' ditter roed shoal o' 'errings!"

"No one but Wiffles could be merry under such grim conditions as these. He must have jested the moment he was born, and will do the same with his last breath. Road Rakers abroad!" Dandy Dick sang out the last words.

"Seek their lair at dawn!" shouted the Sedan-chair bearer in return.

"Our last secret password! 'Tis the rogue Wiffles himself!" agreed the colonel.

Dandy Dick motioned to their cleverly-disguised friend to remain where he stood and keep a keen look-out. Then the four comrades ascended to the topmost floor.

In the belfry tower of the mansion were crowded together the ladies, the wounded Sir Mortiemor, and the domestics. The heat and smoke had all but stifled them, and all but the gallant old aristocrat, his peerless daughter, and Lady Mortiemor, were frantic with grief and terror. Sir Mortiemor was conscious, but otherwise in a desperate condition. Lady Mortiemor rang her hands in silent despair. The sight of the highwaymen gave those in the belfry tower a great shock; but the perfect calmness exhibited by the gallant defenders soon took away the alarming fears caused by their disfigured appearances.

The deep, rich, musical tones of Dandy Dick alone made his presence known to Maude Mortiemor. The creamy-white, exquisitely-shaped, bare arms of the tall, queenly creature, impulsively locked themselves round her young outlaw lover's neck. "Dick, dearest, tell me the worst!" she softly breathed into his ear. "My poor, injured father!—distracted mother; but for their peril, Dick, I could be content! Content, love, e'en to perish, if only thy strong, loving arms were about me!—thy brave, true heart, sweetest, beating next mine own!"

"Raymond Raithwood and his followers are defeated and gone. We have but the flames now to face, far less cruel than pitiless man! Courage, sweet cousin—courage, and all may yet be well!"

Thus murmured Dandy Dick, eager to give hope, but secretly filled with great dread, if not despair.

It had been thought wise to leave the dead servitor and his companion—who was quite beyond hope of recovery—in a lower chamber until the fire rendered it absolutely necessary that they should be brought into the belfry tower, the last refuge of the flame-threatened party.

Sir Edgar Mortiemor beckoned the highwaymen to approach his couch. His state was too desperate to permit of speech, but in dumb motion he made it clear to them that they were to pay no heed to himself, but to do their utmost to rescue all others. The old man then took one of Dick's grime-covered hands, tenderly kissed it, then let it fall as he sank into a death-like swoon.

No further time could be lost. Lives hung upon moments. Dandy Dick, keeping up outward aspect of perfect calm, took a whispered conference with the intrepid Colonel Blood, whom the most critical moments of danger always found, if greatly defiant, completely unmoved.

"The bedrooms are all completely enveloped in the destructive element, or we could have turned the bedclothing into ropes. If we could but find a rope of sufficient length the rest would be easy," muttered the colonel.

There was the alarm-bell, high up amid stout, oaken beams. Dick hastily moved to where the bell pull end was twined round a staple in the wall. The line proved, not only far too short to be of any use for their purpose, but was also too frail and rotten to bear a human being.

Dolly Trippit and the other female domestics were frantic and fainting, as the joint results of blinding smoke, the heat, and the advancing flames.

The four outlaws descended to the lower floor. They gazed blankly into each other's faces. "What is to be done, comrade?" their looks implied, but not one of them could answer. Dandy Dick dashed blindly through the thick, black smoke— it scorched his flesh like a heat-cloud—reached a window, opened it, and attempted to gaze down. The curling vapour, and long, writhing ribbons of fire drove him back. A snapping, crackling, then a roar. The very mouth of Hades itself appeared to open to engulf him! The floor upon which he stood gave way with snapping splinterings, and then fell with a final loud crash. A sheet of flame leapt up, like a wave of blinding, liquid gold. But for a stout, oaken beam that still withstood the raging fire-tongues, Dandy Dick must have fallen into the awful cauldron of white-heat, molten fire below.

A dizziness seized him; he madly clutched the window-frame to prevent himself from falling. The wood was blistered and burning hot, his hand relaxed its hold, and nothing could have saved him from reeling into the consuming void but for the devoted action of the gallant Colonel Blood, who, seeing Dick's fearful plight, instantly sped over the blazing beam, seized his friend in his powerful arms, and then stepped back over the narrow bridge that now alone spanned the raging pit.

Turpin and King gave a shout of admiration, forced from them by the splendid daring and unselfish heroism thus displayed. Then a side window was thrown open, the inrush of cold air at once revived Dandy Dick. Instantly he again became fully alive to a full sense of the surrounding peril.

"Never say 'die,' Dick, old comrade! We four are yet worth a million of dead men!" grimly shouted the colonel.

"Deepest curses upon these fire fiends!" cried Dick Turpin. Adding: "But for the poor souls above, I would throw myself from this window. There is a tree some ten feet or so away. I would risk my chance of reaching it. As well be dashed to pieces below as to end one's career with a fine roasting in the hell-like regions beneath us!"

"Never fear!" bravely chimed in Tom King. "Those born to be hanged, such as you and I, Dick, can neither drown nor burn!"

"Thank you for less than nothing!" growled Turpin. "I'll never grumble at the hanging after this, only let me escape becoming a man of charcoal!"

"Friends," said Dandy Dick, facing his fellow-outlaws, "I fear not death, come in what form it will! But," he solemnly added, "there is one thing we all must dread!"

"What is that?" they all demanded, as if in one breath.

"The stigma of cowardice! We must save those in our sacred charge. There is but one way—that of ringing the alarm-bell. The saving of the lives of those we have thus far defended will mean our own arrests and consequent deaths!"

"The belfry tower is as yet intact, but in less than half an hour the whole of this building will be utterly destroyed. The position of this mansion is too isolated for help to reach us in time." Thus replied Colonel Blood. There was no denying his contention.

The four friends now neared the open side-window. The rush of cold air somewhat drove back the terrible heat. A great shouting came to their ears. On looking out, Dandy Dick saw the tree already mentioned by Dick Turpin. Wiffles had climbed into its topmost branches. His white wig was off, and he was yelling and tearing his hair like a demented creature. The piercing shrieks of Dolly Tripitt could now be heard, the girl having caught sight of her lover. From a window in the belfry the frantic girl implored Wiffles to save her and those with her. The helplessness of her outlaw lover threatened to result in turning his brain.

Colonel Blood had examined the four rooms upon the floor below the belfry. He rushed into the presence of his friends. He held an iron bar in one hand, the perspiration running from him at every pore.

"This way!—this way!" the colonel exhaustedly shouted. "Courage, comrades!"

The three followed him. They entered an old lumbar room, partly ablaze. A hole could be seen in the flooring through which the flames emerged. The researchings of the colonel had resulted in his finding a stout iron bar. With this he had already prized up a long oaken plank of the partly-consumed flooring of the lumbar-room. Without wasting time in questionings, the others lent their aid in the wrenching up of other timbers, until four planks were loosened. Then the colonel's intention became clear, as he carried one of the pieces of oak to the side window and thrust it out. The planks were about eight feet in length, and of great thickness and strength. It required the help of Dandy Dick before the weighty article could be well advanced. The window, pierced in the side of the building on this the third story of the mansion, was placed low. Colonel

Blood's intention was to rest the further end of the plank upon a top branch of the tree, which reached to some three feet below the level of this window-sill, and was about ten feet distant.

At least three feet more of plank length was required. With all possible speed the timber was drawn in. Colonel Blood requested his companions to take off their waist-belts. This was done, and the leathern articles firmly lashed round two ends of planking. Great care was required in making the joint firm and secure. This done, the four highwaymen needed their utmost strength to push out into space the enormous weight of timber. Their strength was soon exhausted; but by frantic efforts the further end was at last within a few inches of the extended hand of Wiffles, as he climbed to the highest possible bearing power of a top limb of the great old tree.

Before the outer highwayman could reach the end of the timber nearest him, the strength of those clinging to the first at the upper window suddenly failed them. The load shot from their grasp, and fell to the great depth below, both planks smashing into fragments. Cries of dismay escaped the outlaws. The flames without and within shot up with redoubled fury, hissed, roared, danced, and greedily lapped up everything within reach with their consuming tongues. Shrieks of terror and despair were heard to proceed from the belfry window, where a few of the females had stood and witnessed the failure of their defenders to make good their intended plan of escape. It seemed, indeed, that the last earthly hope had gone!

°JACK SHEPPARD AND JOLLY NOSE, OR BLUESKIN—JACK'S LOVE OF FUN AND FROLIC—THE SUPPOSED WATCHMAN—A FOP OF THE DAYS OF KING GEORGE—PRACTICAL JOKING—JACK SHEPPARD AND BLUESKIN IN A TIGHT PLACE—ARREST—THE ROUNDHOUSE—TO THE RESCUE—THE ESCAPE.

"Jolly Nose, I've a fit o' the dare-devil comin' on, an' there's no cure for that but a desperate scrape."

"T'faith, Master Jack, but I'll beg, borrow, or steal a nice piece o' rusty old iron an' scrape ye until there's nothing remaining, and how will ye feel then?"

"An all-gone sort o' feeling, I ween,[70] Jolly Nose; an' if ye scrape me all away, that remaining will be nothing to nobody, will it? By me gizzard, but I should be delighted to examine the size, shape, colour, an' weight o' nothing, and also shake hands with his twin-brother Master Nobody!"

"Ho! ho! ho! ho! You're a droll beggar, Jack—a droll beggar! Shiver me sides if I ever saw a droller! He! he! he!"

° Part 18. Vol. XIV.—No. 354. 15 August 1900.

[70] Suppose.

"You might easily see a droller he-he-haw, if you could venture to gaze into a looking-glass without the fear of the fire of your face-handle splintering the glass into fragments before you could detect what a fine overgrown donkey there was returning your glance!"

"Ha! ha! ha! Keep thy chaff, Jack—keep thy chaff! Cut it, boy—cut it!"

"Keep my chaff an' cut it? Chaff must be cut before it becomes chaff. There's a fine Irish bull for you. And imagine a donkey refusing chaff. Let him loose in a meadow to browse on thistles, thorns, an' weeds. If he gets nettles—I mean nettled—'twill serve him right."

It was but a few hours previous to the incidents related in the preceding chapter. Two persons, a man and a boy, were leisurely sauntering together in the vicinity of Islington. The man was an enormous fellow, and with a great red nose. This was Jolly Nose, or Blueskin. He carried a stout, heavy cudgel, his clothes was somewhat slovenly worn, and he smoked a long churchwarden with great gusto and dignity.

As for the youth, how shall we properly describe him? A boy who stood alone—the only one—in all the world's history for unique ingenuity and perfect daring. This was Jack Sheppard, the most unfortunate victim to man's utter heartless cunning ever heard tell of. Sturdily built, and tall and manly-looking for his age—but sixteen; a round, smooth, pale face; black hair, and cut so close to the head that his skull resembled a cannon-ball; wonderful eyes, black as sloes, and filled with the fires of firmness of resolution and reckless courage that were never quenched but by the dull film of death itself. Perhaps not the least remarkable trait in the lad's extraordinary nature was that his love of fun and frolic, in the shape of practical joking.

As we have stated, it was but a few hours previous to the enacting of the thrilling events at Sir Mortiemor's manor at Holloway, and the time was that of night.

"Ten o'clock an' all's well!" The loud, harsh voice of a night-watchman going his rounds, and calling the hour, as was then the custom.

When the "Charley" came into view, it could be seen that he was extremely old and of enormous bulk.

"Past ten o'clock and all's well!"

"How do you know that all's well? All may be ill, lain upon a bed o' sickness, for what you can tell!" most impudently called out Jack Sheppard.

"Get thee gone home to thy mother, stripling!" indignantly retorted the old guardian, holding up his great lantern that its square, tiny glass windows might show their yellow light upon the speaker and his companion.

"Never had a mother, friend chanticleer. I was won in a sixpenny lottery!" leeringly remarked Jack.

"By all that's good an' true, then, the person that paid an honest sixpence for ye was clean jilted out o' fivepence an' three farthings!" surlily growled the old night-watchman.

"A farthing! You're but a far-thing when seen at a distance. An' pray are ye not afeared that your wife, if ye have one, 'll be taken up for big-amy?" saucily went on the vastly-amused lad.

"Big-gamy or little-gamy, what do ye mean?" impatiently snarled the rotund mass.

"Big-game, eh? or little-game, eh? Why, Charley, thou art a punster! An' ye know the true saying: 'A man that can make a pun can pick a pocket.' A-pun-my-word, you deserve to be pun-ished! What do I mean by saying that your wife hath committed bigamy? Why, that you are two or three men rolled into one, consequently the woman that married ye all was guilty of large-amy—I should say bigamy." Thus rattled on Jack, Blueskin laughing uproariously at the lad's word-twisting.

"By me tooth, the jade that'll wed thee will be a she-baboon!" grunted the watchman savagely.

"Why so, my three-in-one friend?" asked Sheppard archly.

"Because a she-baboon will wed but one o' her own species, clown!" was the smart answer.

But Jack Sheppard had got a Roland for the last Oliver.[71]

"Bad old man," he commenced, in mock gravity, "now I see your crafty desire. It is that ye marry one of thine own daughters to me, under false pretences. Shame upon thee, great chief of the whole of the monkey tribes!"

"Ho! ho! ho! But you're a terrible rogue, Jack lad!" gasped Blueskin in jerks between his bursts of laughter. "We'll cry mercy, good old man," he continued, placing a crown-piece in the broad, fat palm of the astonished watchman. "Get thee, an' pour goodly balm upon thy innards."

"Can I believe mine eyes?" ejaculated the delighted old fellow.

"Alas! no, unless they are more truthful than thy tongue," remarked Jack, under his breath.

The night-guardian bowed to the earth.

"I crave thee pardon, my good masters, for now are my eyes gladdened by the sight of two of the noblest gallants possible to find in the whole confines of this merrie England."

"And my lamps are gladdened by the vision of one of the most elegant, youthful, an' sprightly blades that ever killed fair maiden dead upon the spot by the brilliant beams shot from his glorious orbs. Thus ye see, oh, Charlies three, Jack's as tall a liar as thee!"

But the man sagely shook his head, his age-dim eyes brightening up with pleasure as he hobbled off to Ye Boar and Spear Inn by the wayside.

---

[71] A reference to the 11th century epic poem *Le Chanson de Roland*, meaning to give as good as one gets.

"He would melt part o' the silver crown-piece in a tankard o' foaming ale," he mumbled, begging Blueskin to take charge of his lantern the while, so that none might know of his disregard for the rule forbidding a night-custodian to enter hostelries or to take strong drinks.

"No sooner had the portly form squeezed itself into the inn door than a diminutive-looking fop came gingerly ambling along. The very tall heels then worn caused a gallant to trip upon his toes in those days much in the style of the stilt-heeled young lady of this period.

"Bistrew thee, thou scurvy-pated knave!" shouted he to Blueskin, whom he took for a watchman, on seeing the great lamp in one of the former's hands, and cudgel in another.

At a nudge from Jack Sheppard, Blueskin instantly took the hint, and became watchman pro tem.

"I cry thee mercy, fair gallant. What service can I render thee?" hailed Jolly Nose.

"I'll cry thee mercy at my rapier-point, thou lazy, lurching lout! Thou seest a gallant who hath lost his way, and without link-boy[72] or Sedan-chair. Foul night that it is, I shall ruin my crimson heels, tarnish my buckles, bespatter my silken hose. Curse thee! a link-boy and Sedan-chair, e'en if ye kidnap the one and steal the other!"

Truly a fine gentleman this. Peacock-blue satin three-cornered hat, richly ornamented with white feathering and gold lace; one corner of the hat almost rests upon his nose; a white wig puffed out at the sides, blue ribbons decorating its tail; peacock-blue satin cut-away coat faced with much gold lace; a billowy cravat, with three blue ribbon bows setting it off; waistcoat one mass of gold lace, and costly gems set in the place of buttons; the nankeens were of black satin, gold lace at their outer sides, and diamonds at the knee in place of buttons; pale-blue silken hose, ornamented with gold clocks, otherwise scroll-work, from the outside ankles upwards; the shoes were of dark-blue leather, having very high heels of bright crimson; a pale-blue silk scarf passing over the right shoulder to the left side, at which end hung a rapier in a sheaf of dark-blue satin; and the hilt of the sword was ablaze with gems.

The indulgent reader has now before him, or her, a fashionable gentleman of the days of the Georges, and the "get-up" of such creatures often represented a sum amounting to a fortune. Gallant, exquisite, dandy, were then terms of the same meaning as those of dude, fop, swell, or toff of to-day.

It was the common custom of the wealthy classes to treat with the utmost disdain the lower orders, in language, and every way using them in great contempt.

Blueskin and Jack Sheppard budged not an inch, but set up loud, laughing tones of ridicule.

---

[72] A boy carrying a flaming torch who guides pedestrians through the streets when dark or foggy.

"By the lud, but I'll have at thee, thou mangy dogs!" The gallant slashed out his blade, ran forward upon his toes, and attempted to strike Blueskin across the cheek with the side of the narrow steel.

The great, strong fellow easily seized the circling blade in his horny palms, jerked it from the dainty little gallant's grasp, snapped it across one knee, threw the jewelled hilt, with half the blade, to the owner's feet, and then, with perfect an air of unconcern, made as if using the point of the broken blade as a toothpick.

"Furies! Varlet, I'll report ye! My rapier cost me fifty golden guineas!"

"An' if it cost thee a million, I'd serve it the same, thou gilded sparrow. Take thy fine feathers from thee an' thou art no better man than the blackamoor doll hanging as a sign outside the shop of the dealer in cast-off garments!" jokingly laughed Jolly Nose, still keeping busy with the toothpick.

The gallant waxed too wrathful for words. A bejewelled, toy-like firelock pistol was snatched from one of his coat-pockets, but before it could be presented a skilful kick by Jack Sheppard sent the weapon flying yards away into the surrounding darkness. But the miniature exquisite was game, and another fire lock displayed itself. Jack Sheppard, however, saw it, and threw his foot behind the gallant, a shove at the same time in front defeated the object of the latter; he fell backwards, but discharged the weapon.

The startling explosion instantly brought a posse of night-guardians to the spot. Seeing help at hand, the gallant set up a most terrific yelling of: "Murder! Footpads! Cutthroats! Purse-filchers," &c., &c.

"We are in for it now, Jack! We've a merry scramble before us. I hope you'll get all the scrapping you require!" laughed Blueskin, laying about him with his cudgel with lusty enjoyment.

"This will do me the world of good!" gleefully replied Jack Sheppard, using his fists only, and battering the not over-active night-guardians till they more than ached again.

"I was getting rusty, mildewed, cobwebby, cramped!" Jack was calling down to his comrade, when a brass official bludgeon struck him down.

Seven or eight watchmen hung on to Blueskin like grim death. The old fellow came from the inn, saw the conflict, rubbed his eyes, and then added to the general din by bawling with all his might for further assistance, although at least a dozen of the watch were attacking one man and a stripling.

Jack Sheppard was down. The gallant saw this, and stooped, with the intention of braining the lad with the butt of one of his recovered pistols. By a mighty effort Blueskin—dragging those clinging to him along with him—got near, shot forward one of his jack-booted feet, and caught the fop a kick in the ribs that he never forgot until his dying day. He fell in a heap, like a wet rag.

"I'm safe for the Big Drum,[*] or Stone Jug[†], Jolly Nose; but the cage isn't built yet that can keep this bird captive!" cheerfully sang out the dauntless lad, now firmly secured. "Get away, comrade, an' take the latest court news to our pals!" he added.

Blueskin's cudgel had marked every one of his attackers, each had a cracked pate. The powerful fellow threw his foes about like a set of skittles placed upon an uneven floor. Sheppard begged his devoted companion to make off, knowing that, under the circumstances, this was the wisest thing to do.

Jolly Nose made a complete "floorer" of the human skittles, and then bolted off, getting away under the cover of the darkness, Jack Sheppard being conducted to the Roundhouse of St. John's, near by.

Blueskin hung about for hours. Concealed in the black shadows of the hedgerow he took off his wig and bound up his broken head as best he could. His cravat was used for this purpose, and his wig then forced over the bandage to hide it as much as possible. At about the hour of one he was silently contemplating the roundhouse near the Templars of St. John's gates.[73] From the outer gloom Jolly Nose could plainly see into the well-lighted space beyond the open door of the lock-up. A guard of two men were seated at a table. They were drinking and playing cards.

Creeping away some distance, the highwayman suddenly set up a cry for help, rendering his voice feeble as that of a very old man. The ruse succeeded, as he had hoped. But one of the men came from the lock-up and quickly ran towards the concealed robber. In an instant the guard was fixed by the throat in the powerful grip of Jolly Nose.

"Make so much noise as would wake a sleeping fly an' you'll be badly wanting half a head!" hissed the latter, clapping a cold pistol-rim against his captive's forehead.

Two minutes sufficed to enable the highwayman to most securely gag, and tie arms and legs of the roundhouse keeper. Then a feeble cry for help went up from another spot. The second guard walked into the snare prepared for him as quickly as did his mate, and to meet with exactly the same treatment, his own cravat and handkerchief being used for gag and binding, as in the former case.

Blueskin then coolly walked into the lock-up, took up one of the two bottles of ale standing upon a deal table, and straightway emptied one at a draught.

"Egad, but the cudgelling o' heads, an' the getting cudgelled o' one's own head, may be fine enough sport for roistering rogues, but for a quiet, peaceful citizen like myself 'tis but dry work," he reflectively cogitated.

A slight scraping sound now caught the ears of Blueskin. "Where are the cell-keys kept?" he muttered, looking for them in vain. He was on the point of

---

[*] A round house, termed a "Big Drum" in consequence of its shape.
[†] The "Stone Jug" was the name by which Newgate Gaol was generally known among the criminal classes.
[73] St. John's Gate, Clerkenwell.

returning to the guards to search them when the peculiar sound again came to him. It was so faint that two persons laughing and talking would have failed to hear it.

Noiselessly, and fully on the alert against possible surprise, Blueskin crept on tiptoe to the outside of the Roundhouse. A head protruded from the cone-shaped roof.

"Hist! Is that you, Jack?" whispered Blueskin anxiously.

"Hurrah, old pal!" softly replied Jack Sheppard. "What have you done with the dragons that guard this ogre castle?" he asked eagerly.

"They're just now employed in the study of the stars, Jack. That's a most interesting science when a man's gagged, on his back in the open, unable to move, an' can't find anything to do but to look out for the unlucky planet under which he was born, so that he can quietly give it a piece of his mind—a very hot piece."

Jack chuckled gleefully. "They most thoughtfully provided me with a fire," he explained. "The poker enabled me to break this pie crust. The inside is not at all to my taste—sour, stale, musty. The fruit of the lock-up-pudding is in the getting out of it—to somewhat alter an old saying."

"Down, down, Jack!" suddenly cautioned Blueskin, darting into the deepest shadows. Approaching sounds were heard, the outlaws were upon the sharp thorns of an anxious suspense.

THE TERRIBLE THREAT UTTERED BY THE MYSTIC NECRO-MANCER—FUGITIVES FROM JUSTICE AT THE HAUNTED MANOR—THE CHARGE TO THEM—WHAT THE MAGIC CRYSTAL GLOBE REVEALED—OUTLAWS SWARM AS LOCUSTS IN THE PATH OF VENGEANCE—DANDY DICK AND HIS COMRADES IN DEADLY PERIL OF THEIR LIVES.

We must take the reader back to the moment of Wiffles leaving the necromancer—for my no other name was this most mysterious being known. The latter horseman pulled up soon after the young outlaw's departure. The solitary rider turned his steed until its head faced the City of London, whose chief inhabitants were still buried in silent repose, for the hour was about that of the third of a new-born day.

"Thrice accursed hive of infamy! Thou great nest of all evil! Sleep—sleep on! Men-scorpions! Human adders! Sleep on! An' thou spirit of slumber—twin sister of the angel of death—why permittest thou yonder hosts of men-vipers ever to again awaken to renew their demon-like courses? Those whose eyes dart out consuming fires. Whose breath is as poison and pestilence. Whose deeds are so shameless that their master—Satan himself—must needs blush deepest red at the knowledge thereof. Little wonder that our once fair England is now but a most corrupt blot—foul, festering, hideous blotch—upon the sweet face of Dame

Nature. Little wonder that our people are steeped in crime, and continue to wallow in their vicious ways. Honest men dare not venture beyond their doors. Virtuous women lose their precious reputations even by showing their faces in the streets.

"Armed ruffians, day and night, leer from every nook and corner. Outrage, rapine,[74] murder, robbery, lying, fraud, injustice. These hell-spawn batten, and shamelessly blink their eyes in God's own pure light o' day. The example set by the head of a nation is most sure to be followed by the masses. Corrupt rule begets corruption in those so ruled. O, but thou hotbed of all vices, thou art doomed! The necromancer shall quickly mature his great and devastating plans, an' then to apply a torch that will burn, and burn, until the great, hideous, leprous-like, ever-spreading canker of all combined vices shall be utterly purged, its rottenness completely consumed in a fire so great that it shall, by contrast, rendered dim and small even the ever-flaming kingdom of Hades itself!"

The demeanour of the necromancer grew most terrible to behold as he uttered his strange and frenzied threats. His great eyes filled with fire, his face grew crimson, his teeth gnashed savagely, and his right hand extended heavenwards, as if in the act of invoking the aid of the Deity in the furtherance of the dread desires of the mystic doomster.

This pause was but for a moment. The necromancer again turned his animal's head towards Finchley, and urged on his beast to its utmost. Not ten minutes sufficed to enable the rider to reach the vicinity of the Haunted Manor. But, strange to relate, the horseman rode past the outlaw stronghold for something like a quarter of a mile. Then the main road gradually sank until there was a great steep sand-hill on each of its sides.

Not a soul appeared in sight. The masked and black-cloaked rider rode up to the left perpendicular natural wall. The covering of frost, snow, and ice displayed no indication of an opening in the earth's surface; but a few powerful kicks resulted in forcing a door, the outer side of which was most cunningly covered with a coating of earth, clay, and sand. No one but a person with a knowledge of the fact would have believed the contrivance a possibility. Dismounting, the horseman led his steed into a great, square-shaped tunnel, forced the door again into its place, remounted, struck steel and flint, and then, by the assistance of a coil of flaming tinder, rode on through a spacious and lofty cutting, originally delved by Royalists, in the time of Cromwell, with the object of secretly escaping from their abode in the event of a raid by the Dictator's troops.

Many of the outlaws were feasting and making merry at the moment of their mysterious friend, the necromancer, presenting himself. The manner of the latter was far more excited than was usual with him.

"Brother outcasts," he hurriedly cried, "our comrades, Dandy Dick, Colonel Blood, Dick Turpin, Tom King, and Wiffles are in extreme peril! Aid, in one

---

[74] Abduction.

form, has been given them! It may be needful that a strong body of their friends also join them! To horse, men—as many of ye that have animals! While ye prepare, I will consult my magic mirror and crystal globe. I shall thus learn the extent of the danger threatening our comrades."

Like magic the outlaws uprose from their seats, and dashed for the caves in which were tabled their steeds. The necromancer had entered the doors of his own private vault. An astounding chamber was this. Literally alive with snakes, lizards, and thousands of other creeping things. A most beautiful specimen of an Indian tiger crouched in a large iron cage. Small alligators frisked about in an enclosed tank. Birds, beasts, and reptiles were the ever constant companions of the man of mystery known as the necromancer.

In the centre of this great vault stood a huge globe of glass. In a trice a strange vapour of pale-blue cast filled the place. A copper vessel of Egyptian design stood on the floor under the supporting-rods of the great transparent hall. Flame and smoke came from the brazen urn. The glass globe suddenly changed colour. Like the hues of a rainbow became the surface of the mystic crystal. The beautiful tints came crowding over one another, like the changing clouds of a most glorious sunset. Suddenly the hues formed into shape. A most brilliant, startling, and clearly-defined picture was suddenly fixed, as it were, in the very centre of the crystal. Then the wonderful view as swiftly vanished. The beholder displayed the utmost alarm. Bursting into the presence of the outlaws, now, with their steeds, crowding the central vault, he excitedly addressed them:

"A building almost consumed by fire! Our dear comrades calmly facing the oncoming death that will seize those most dear to their beloved leader and brother, Dandy Dick, as well as themselves. Not an instant's delay, lads—up-saddle! One of ye come with me. The others await our return!"

In two seconds the necromancer and the felon accompanying him had returned. Each carried a slight-made but very strong ladder of iron. The outlaw flew off to bring more of the frames, while the man of mystery quickly made known to the onlooking robbers the means of so joining the sections that a ladder of almost any length could be instantly formed.

Those of the fugitives from justice having sought their beds were aroused by the noise made by the clattering of iron-shod hooves upon stone flags. There was an enormous number of outlaws collected at the Haunted Manor. In but a few brief moments of the necromancer's return a great body of fierce men, armed to the teeth, defiled into the Finchley high-road by means of one of the many secret exits of the hunted felons' retreat.

Each mounted man carried a length of the iron ladder. Off the horsemen sped. Topmost speed was gained, those having sections of the iron contrivance keeping together. A great crowd of robbers on foot followed those mounted.

It was as if Mother Earth had suddenly and instantaneously created an endless length of men and horses, and belched them forth. A swarm of men, furious, and intent on savage doings.

Not one of the denizens of the Haunted Manor but burned with utmost resentment, hottest hatred, against the masses of respectability. So fiendish were the judges of the period in inflicting punishment for even the most trivial offences; so degraded, besotted, and utterly corrupt all police-officials, that the unfortunate creature guilty of the slightest lapse from the lawful path, literally, instantly after, found every man's hand against him, his life not worth a pin's purchase. Such a creature as the infamous Judge Jefferies[75]—who has left an undying stigma upon his honourable profession—made more criminals by his most monstrous severity, than were ever formed by any other means. Next, as a creator of terror-panic, came the wretch Jonathan Wild.

The multitude of law-breakers, literally swarmed like locusts. Many of them brandished naked cutlass-blades, daggers, and knives. Many were armed with long-handled axes—sharp, bright choppers. Not a few brandished reaping-hooks fastened upon the ends of long, stout sticks.

As this desperate body of society-hounded creatures swarmed into the open wilderness facing the manor, wild the shouts of dismay rose up from their throats. Sir Edgar Mortiemor's dwelling was as a house formed by fire—one whole compact edifice of bright, blinding flame.

"To the rear of the building!" shouted out the powerful tones of a voice. And, to the utter amazement of all, the form of the necromancer was seen, mounted upon his superb steed, and evidently intending himself to lead the rescuing-party. With a most thunderous roar of eager response, the outlaws flocked to the other side of the building.

A mighty uproar instantly followed. The Mohawks had returned! They had conveyed away Raymond Raithwood and all others, either killed or wounded, of their number, and now returned. To gloat in fiendish triumph over their cruel work was the return of the young bloods now due. Little calculated they upon meeting such an opposing force. On the instant of the outlaws bursting into view, the Mohawks saw the intention of the rescuing-party. And those mounted, with one ear-splitting, combined yell of defiance, formed up at the only spot where rescue could be attempted. This move caused the eyes of every friend of those in the burning building to be upraised.

As the smoke and flames were wind-drifted for a moment, smoke-blackened and frenzied-looking female faces were detected at the belfry windows.

---

[75] Judge George Jefferys (1654–89) also known as the 'Hanging Judge' after the 'Bloody Assizes; on Taunton in 1685 when up to 700 individuals were executed for treason following the West Country Rebellion which attempted to overthrow King James II.

"We may yet be in time! Cut down your foes, lads, as mere grass before the sickle! Lay down thy lives, gallant lads, if needs be, for those who would do the same for thee!" Thus yelled the necromancer. Those surrounding him stayed for no second bidding.

Like hate-demented creatures they flew upon the young bloods. The outlaws on foot had seized the ladder sections and secured them together. A most strong and ample means of escape stood against the tree. To the unspeakable delight of the felons the iron frame was suddenly seen to sway to the walls of the mansion. A form was then observed climbing like a cat up the topmost rungs. The climber had been concealed in the higher branches of the giant tree—had sprung with it therefrom to the flame-covered back wall of the building. The man's face and neck and hands were like those of a negro. The slender rungs and outer portions of the ladder were here and there hidden in dancing tongues of flame, here and there completely lost in black, spiral-climbing clouds. The man was apparently swiftly flying upwards without means. A black fire-imp, or salamander.

A mighty cheer of admiration, delight, madlike joy. Be he whom he might, no brave deed was ever attempted by human being.

The Mohawks had thrown themselves upon the rescue-party in utmost vigour and rage.

"Down with them, lads! Strike to kill!" Thus savagely thundered the necromancer, leaping his steed forward into the very thickest of the fight. He had drawn a rapier of finest Indian steel. The thing flew about him as if endowed with life.

The necromancer literally cut his way to the ladder end. The young bloods had seized it and were attempting to drag it away. An irresistible rush of unmounted outlaws gained this position. The leader was in their midst most furiously fighting. He stooped and whispered a few swift words. His men fell back from guarding the iron frame. Quicker than eye could follow the necromancer had wound a something round each ladder side—a coil connected with a small black box. The latter he had placed on the earth. A coil in circling each iron support; a small, square case at the foot of each upright iron.

The leader of the criminal band next directed all his powers of the beating-off of the young bloods from the vicinity of the ladder. A number of them succeeded in fighting their way through. These, uttering yells of triumph, as one man, seized the iron frame—the gallant climate was now within two feet of the belfry window. Then up froze the most awful cries of agony. Next, every man touching the metal was seen to fall to the earth, an inert mass—struck down by some mysterious agency secretly transmitted to the metal contrivance by the necromancer.

"Touch, who dare!" exultantly cried the defiant felon leader to the ever-swelling numbers of the cowardly gallants. But not one accepted the challenge. They shrank back in awe.

A wildly-cursing, mounted Mohawk carefully took aim with his flint-lock, intending to bring down the form reaching the ladder's top. Unseen, the necromancer reached the side of the heartless coward. What next happened no one could tell. The pistol was still held poised upwards, the finger on the trigger; the sinister grin still overspread the evil face. But the trigger remained motionless. The Mohawk and his animal had become motionless as statues. They were apparently pulseless, lifeless, turned to stone.

"Ho! ho! ho! Who dares the powers of the necromancer? Behold, I render mine enemies dumb, motionless! Those who arouse the demon within me I slay, even with a glance! I solemnly swear, here in the presence of ye all, that, as I have smitten this inhuman thing, so will I smite every one of ye! Craven-minded, black-hearted, soulless wretches!"

The necromancer, as he ceased, threw over each shoulder the end of his long, black cloak. A moving, blood-red eyed cobra-di-capello of great size was then revealed. The darting forked tongue of the gliding reptile repeatedly struck each cheek of the man. The crimson poison-fangs passed harmlessly over neck and face and hands, when the latter caressingly came near.

The Mohawks were dismayed—awed with terror. The man appeared endowed with superhuman powers.

An unmounted young blood near, and less impressed than his fellows, had primed his flint-lock and fired point-blank at the breast of the necromancer. The next moment the Mohawk was seen frantically writhing upon the snow-mantled earth, with the snake-coils quickly gliding round his neck.

The serpent had been thrown, lasso-like, about the shoulders of the gallant. The necromancer appeared unhurt and smiling.

The deadly reptile angrily raised its head and drew it back twice. The third time it would strike, after the manner of its species. But the mysterious being had sprung from his horse and seized the snake in time to prevent its fatal intention.

The young gallant had already fainted as the result of fear.

The enormous gathering of aristocratic night-brawlers commenced to waver.

"The man is in league with Spring-Heeled Jack, London's terror!" they shouted. "Both fight by the same awful means! There is more than human agency in their deeds! They hold counsil with the Prince of Darkness himself!"

"At them, my friends! The well-born, wealthy, but, for all that, worse than the commonest bully-cutthroats! Read them a lesson, lads—a lesson at the steel's point! The music of your firearms in their ears. The hail of your bullets as aids to their memories, if their brains remain their own!"

Meanwhile Dandy Dick, Colonel Blood, Dick Turpin, and Tom King had all carefully and deliberately calculated their chances of life or death.

The firm, devoted friends grimly faced each other.

"But for the women-folk," commenced Turpin, when Dandy Dick interrupted him. A ring of anguish was in his voice, but it was the calm anguish of one completely resigned to his horrible fate.

"The flames are kinder than would be the wretches below, if they once regained possession of Maude and the other women," he said. "This I well know they also fully believe, otherwise the brave creatures would not have so well retained their presence of mind."

"Heavens!" cried Turpin, "there is a ladder! See, it is falling this way! Now it reaches the wall! We are saved—comrades, we are saved!" The speaker's voice trembled with deep emotion.

"Ah!" gasped Dandy Dick, becoming wild with joy, "the good, brave, loyal Wiffles is coming up to us! Of what can the ladder be formed to thus withstand the fiery elements—and whence came it?"

The moment after Wiffles had reached the window. Eager hands clutched the daring, devoted friend. He stood within the oven-like mansion.

"The Mohawks—keep 'em clear o' the ladder—get down safe ernuff!" gasped Wiffles, as he desperately laboured to recover his breath.

The highwaymen were in a delirium of joy. Each in turn hugged the scorched, blistered, black-visaged Wiffles. The strong, self-reliant, courageous men wept, as sometimes weep gentle women and tender babes.

"The vile Mohawks flee! They are put to the road by our friends! See, there rides the necromancer, gallantly urging our comrades to follow up their victory, and cut down the panic-stricken wretches so eager for our destruction!" Thus excitedly declaimed Dandy Dick.

The colonel reminded his companions that moments were most precious, and the oncoming flames within scorching distance.

Dandy Dick turned to his friends, tears coursing down his smoke-grimed cheeks.

"Come, dear comrades," he said, in hoarse, trembling tones, "we go to save the helpless—those whose lives are in our keeping!"

°THE BOY PRISON-BREAKER AND THE ROUNDHOUSE LOCK-UP—A HUGE PIE—JOE BLUESKIN, OR "JOLLY-NOSE"—THE RECKLESS DARING OF THE PRISON-BREAKER—WILL THE WITLESS AGAIN—THE CHASE—THE SCENT—OFFICER BILBERY.

On the highwaymen entering the belfry tower Sir Edgar Mortiemor was found to be in an insensible condition. The women were, from the lowest depths of despair, lifted into the highest transports of delight at the assurance of rescue. Yet one and all calmly requested that the wounded Sir Edgar should be the first

---

° Part 19. Vol. XIV.—No. 355. 28 August 1900.

rescued. Not a fraction of time was to be lost. Dandy Dick and Colonel Blood bore the aged aristocrat down to the next floor. The task before them was a most critical one. The weight of the insensible man seemed enormous. The window over the ladder-end was reached. A great tongue of flame leapt in as the casement was opened.

"Merciful Father in Heaven, now have pity on our lot!" suddenly gasped Colonel Blood, in utmost despair. "We cannot leave by any other window, the fire is too close upon us from below. The ladder cannot reach the belfry-window."

"But we are going to creep out of this casement," answered Dandy Dick cheerily.

"Impossible, Dick," was the disheartening reply, "Sir Edgar Mortiemor's bulky form can never be passed through that narrow opening."

*

Jack Sheppard crouched flat upon the roof of the roundhouse and listened intently. Blueskin hid himself well within the night shadows, and tried to make out the cause of the sounds approaching them. It was not in the nature of the boy prison-breaker to keep his tongue still, even when his listeners were no more than the stone walls of a captive place.

"Bluemug!" he called in a hoarse undertone to his friend below, "are you down there?"

"Yes, Jack, very much so. Are you up there?"

"I'm very much up; and I'm very much down, too—down in the dumps—Bluechops, old 'un," Jack replied in a cautious undertone; adding: "And jolly good—no, I mean jolly bad—reason to. Here I am, a free lad—free as the air—down to me waist only; the rest of me's in custody—'cribb'd, cabin'd an' confin'd'. I can't budge an inch further either way. I'm stuck fast, like the ankle of a poacher caught in the teeth of a mantrap!"

"It's a pity your tongue isn't stuck fast in a mantrap!" growlingly whispered Blueskin. "You will be overheard by whoever's coming this way."

"What worse mantrap than another man's tongue, pray? More men and women have been trapped—taken in—by other tongues than—"

"Stow it! Hist!" came up a whispered caution from the concealed Blueskin.

Plod—plod—plop—plod—plod! came the peculiar sounds.

"Tell you what, Joe; but some unfortunate fellow that's got odd legs. When Dame Nature was serving out the lower limbs, his trunk arrived at her warehouse over-late. 'Serve yer right!' sez the dame. 'I've only got two more legs on hand now. One of 'em was intended to glue on to the body of a giant, the other made for a three-year-old an' stunted child. In the hurry of business,' sez she, 'all through over-covetousness, some human bodies have sneaked wrong legs instead of the ones intended for 'em, so now you must travel through life the best way you can, either as a person with odd lower limbs, or on no legs at all!'"

Blueskin was gazing intently into the outer darkness of the pitch-dark night, and towards the road in the direction of the approaching noise.

"Lord save us!" he presently piously ejaculated. "I have heard that there are weird, uncanny objects that at times made night terrible with their presence. but this oncoming object is surely the most extraordinary night-goblin man ever heard tell of. A thing flying along—a sort of long, white pole, with a heap o' rags hanging at one end. I can't see clear enough to tell which is responsible for the quick motion; perhaps both together form some unearthly visitant from the shades."

"A leech's or barber's pole, an' the clothes of a victim he has bled to death—in two ways, over-cupping-(blood-letting), an' over-charging—that's the ghost. An' it's come to warn me not to patronise the same gentle an' considerate bleeder, unless we want likewise to be turned into ghosts resembling barber's poles, with bunches of rags clinging at the ends."

This was Jack Sheppard's whispered version of the strange object. The moment after the suppose it unearthly apparition was within a few feet of the lock-up.

"May my nose turn a sickly-looking white for ever more, and my friend never pay me the compliment of terming me 'Jolly Nose,' if the flying rags don't hold a boy within 'em—an' such a boy, too!"

"Tush! don't try and be funny, Bluegills; 'tain't in your line a bit. A boy, two—that's three boys, an'—"

"Ho! ho! ho! He! he! So there's the pretty cage in which ye would chain up poor Will the Witless—make the idiot-boy a captive for ever more? Poor Will would never never again see his dear friends the Snow Fairies! Hee! hee! But the Red Robbins have yet to catch the boy-bird an' clip his wings—clip his wings! Ho! ho! ho!" And plod—plop—plod again went the boy and the pole.

"Jack, Jack! did ye hear that? The poor lad calls himself witless—idiot-boy!"

"There's not a few others that I know pluming themselves upon their great wisdom, who, if they were honest an' truthful, would also call themselves witless and idiots. But hark, Blueskin; horsemen follow on. They are hunting down that poor little two-pennorth o' humanity stuck on the end of a pole—hunting him down!"

"That must be it, Jack! For mercy's sake make another effort to force yourself through that roof!" anxiously pleaded the gaol-breaker's companion, now fully alive to the danger of their position.

"Throw me thy cudgel then, Joe, deary. I haven't a fork to break in this pie crust—toad-in-the-hole pie? No, boy-in-the-hole pie—that's its correct label."

A few well-directed poundings at the roof-slabs had the result desired. Jack Sheppard was now enabled to completely emerge from the "gaol pie-crust," as he had wittily termed it, for a roundhouse lock-up, with its conical-shaped roof, was really more like a huge pie than a house, and the red tiles gave even greater semblance to the former article. The red-brown roof suggesting that the cook's primitive architecture had got somewhat over-baked.

The blows of the stout staff had also a result not desired—the loud, hollow sounds threw their echoes upon the night winds. There were ears to hear!

"Now, dear old dyed dial, will you kindly step up an' join me at supper?" lovingly said Jack, dangling his freed legs. "There is no one in the old drum, I really feel peckish, and I think I could very well made a meal off the crust of this famous boy-in-the-hole pie. Ah, la! as the dandies say in the Mall."

"Curse you for a jaw-me-dead! Ah, they're here! Red Robbins, as I live!"

In a twinkling Jack Sheppard dropped from the roof and crouched in the deep, black shadows by the side of his companion.

"'Ecod! Man alive!" yelled loud, coarse tones. "'Sdeath! Blood an' hounds! Blue blazes! Gad zooks an' zounds! Concentrated essence of mania! Thunderstorms an' sour vinegar! Did I, or did I not, most narrowly escape sanguinary death times out of count—by the skin of my teeth, so to speak—at the doing of that foul fiend of a boy—that Will the Witless? Will the Witless, forsooth. By the most sacred bones of the first Bilberry—who lived in the far remote fossil age—but that so-called witless brat hath more cunning hidden away in his tomtit-like sconce than all the combined monkey tribes in the vast Indies!"

"Is that thing wound up to go for very much longer, Joe Spoiltface? Because if it is I shall be compelled to throw its inner cog-wheels out of gear!" lowly muttered Jack into his friend's ear.

"Jack, lad, it gives me the creeps to hear a man murder the King's English in that way. I should have a deadly attack of lockjaw if I went in for a blank quarter of that lusty cursing. The thing's alive, depend upon it," replied Blueskin.

"Why didn't the indefinite article live in the far remote fossil age itself? Fossils might have been able to calmly tolerate it, whatever it is. Don't you think, now, if a man were to tie a brick to its neck an' drop it into the Fleet Ditch, that the public would afterwards eagerly plank down piles of money to erect a statue to the second Saint George of England?"

"There's little doubt about it, Jack boy. I'll subscribe the brick, if you will carry out the mere minor detail of drowning."

"On second thoughts, what has the poor, useful Fleet Ditch done to deserve such awful contamination? Why, if the sewer-rats were only to hear those most shocking oaths the little fellows would all turn grey in a night, or become bald-headed on the tips of their tails, as I understand the members of their tribe are apt to do, as the result of either over-study in cat and dog dodging tactics, or extreme old age."

"The pole-and-rags something has given the runner the dodge. The fellows have dismounted. The smell a rat!" hissed Blueskin.

"One of the sewer-creepers I've been talking about, you may depend upon it, Joe."

"You've aroused suspicion by your thundering thumps up there, Jack. The Bow Street bully boys are scenting around."

"I won't budge till I twig their little lay.[76] The swearing machine don't alarm me too much. I can dimly make out its shape. It's just like a big pumpkin, with a turnip—painted red, and with an extra daub where the nose should be—stuck on top, and just two jackboots supporting the pumpkin. A thump of my head in about the region of the second waist-coat-button of the aforesaid pumpkin would bust up the works. Then it would be a case of a second deluge. Extra big pumpkins, you know, are mostly all water."

"There's something stronger than water in that great flesh-ball, Jack."

"The thing-a-me-jig," went on Jack Sheppard—"you can't call it a human form divine—the what-you-may-call-it is in training for a human balloon. That's it! Now I've hit it I'm happy!"

"Well, don't hit it too hard; were not provided with boats."

"By the thunders, but there's something amiss here!" yelled the voice of Officer Bilberry—for he it was.

"By the thunders, but there's something a-boy here!" softly mimicked Jack.

"Hist! hist! Keep still thy perpetual tongue!" muttered Blueskin. "The officers have scented our game. Now we must watch an opportunity to bolt it!"

"I'm not a-going to bolt any game; might stick in—" Blueskin had clapped his hand firmly over the boy prison-breaker's mouth. He kept it there. The dismounted Bow Street officers were now cautiously peering into the shadows of the place of concealment of Joe Blueskin and Jack Sheppard.

CONFRONTED BY A TERRIBLE DOOM—THE BRAVEST OF THE BRAVE—THE NARROW WINDOW—THE NECROMANCER—MAUDE MORTIEMOR AND WIFFLES—RESCUED AT LAST—PARTING OF LOVERS—THE MALL OF ST. JAMES'S—A LADY-KILLER—THE UNKNOWN SEDAN-CHAIR—HIGH-WAY ROBBERY IN BROAD DAYLIGHT.

"We are all doomed to perish!"

"And by the most frightful of deaths!"

"Blackest curses fall upon and wither up those craven wretches, the Mohawks!"

"Ter be roasted like tramp-sneaked taters in a lime-kiln!"

---

[76] Understand their position.

"We'll end it gamely, comrades—defy this cursed fire-fiend e'en to the last gasp!"

Dandy Dick, Dick Turpin, Tom King, Wiffles, and Colonel Blood respectively thus grimly expressed themselves. The five fearless friends looked into each other's blackened, sweat-wreaking faces. The fire glow daubed each visage with brilliant touches of yellow and crimson, making striking contrast with the sable grime. Each highwayman now wore thick leathern gloves to protect his blistered hands. Smoke-blackened and scorched cravats covered the men's mouths. Their rich costumes and had, in places, been reduced to rags and tinder. The lavish display of pure gold lace facings of Dandy Dick's once gorgeous plum-coloured velvet coat and waistcoat were tarnished even to blackness. His thoughts, concerning the females crowded in terror panic in the belfry tower, were like dagger thrusts piercing his burning, madly-throbbing brain.

In this terrible situation Colonel Blood yet remained apparently outwardly calm. Death at their feet, and completely surrounding them; the air they breathed a red-hot vapour that scorched their lips and throats like a firebrand. The startling confusion of crackling noises. Frenzied shrieks and despairing pleas of helpless women. Sight of the insensible, blood-disfigured and bandaged Sir Edgar Mortiemor. These were enough to appal the hearts of lions; to fill with hopeless dread the bravest creature the world ever knew.

The long, narrow window—the chief cause of the despair of the rescuing-party—was now closely examined by the keen eyes of the Colonel. A great cry issued from his lips. There was hope in his tone. A moment after he was working with might and main. The iron bar, with which Dandy Dick had prized up the floor timbers, was held in the grip of the powerful Colonel, and he was swiftly pounding its end against the wide wooden window frame, sunk into a deep recess, as was the fashion in old English dwellings.

The anguish-filled orbs of the highwaymen brightened as the frame gave way. It was about to fall, when a strong hand seized it. The face—red with the fire-glow and heat—of the Necromancer looked in upon the highwaymen.

"For heaven's sake, tarry no longer! Are you mad? See ye not that the building may collapse any moment?" he shouted. Then the bulky form of Sir Edgar Mortiemor caught his glance. The delay was thus explained.

Almost mad with dread, Wiffles had flown up to the belfry tower. His voice made known his identity. Maude Mortiemor sprang forward, and seized one of his blackened hands in her own of dainty, creamy white.

"Dear friend, my poor father! Is there any hope? Are we all doomed to perish? Oh, if even my poor, aged parents, and—and my darling Dick, if those could be saved, I might then meet my fate with resignation, terrible as indeed it is!"

A shower of glistening, pearl-like drops came from the lovely eyes of the aristocratic maiden. Dolly Tripitt and the other female domestics had seized

Wiffles, whose deep emotion had rendered him speechless. Suddenly a great coil of strong-looking rope, lying in a corner of the tower, caught his view. With a glad shout he pointed it out. It was brought him. Then Wiffles almost rudely tore himself from the frantic women, and dashed down to his friends with his precious prize.

"Providence befriends those that are patient and brave in the presence of adversity!" cried the colonel, seizing the rope.

Two loops were quickly formed. One passed under the arm-pits, and the other round the waist of Sir Edgar Mortiemor. The loops were connected with the main length of rope. The body then gently passed out of the window, now at least two feet wider as the result of the absence of the deep timber frame.

The Necromancer uttered many heartfelt expressions of pious thankfulness as he now saw hope of rescue. There was scant time for words. The great length of the joined iron ladder caused it to dangerously cave in towards the building. Ascending flames and dense volumes of spiral smoke here and there covered it. The man of mystery had gallantly climbed up through perils of fire and suffocation. Feet foremost came the body of the old baronet. The rope slowly lowered it. Four strong men firmly held the coils. Watching his opportunities, occasioned by the wind-drifted flame, the Necromancer shouted out to those paying out the rope, and thus the burden soon reached the eager hands of outlaws clustering up the iron framework as far as they dared venture their united weight.

The greatest of their task was over. The females were each separately secured by a loop under the arms; then induced to climb through the window space and descend the ladder, those below crying out to a frantically-clinging creature when the drifted flames and vapour enabled a safer descent.

The last of the women, Lady Mortiemor, had been safely rescued. The highwaymen closely followed. The iron frame shook violently under their united weight. The brave men laughed gleefully as merry schoolboys. When the last to leave the flaming volcano-like mansion had placed his feet upon the earth at the ladder's foot, a mighty roar of admiration, unbounded delight, and thanksgiving went from his fellow outlaws, each of whom would have deemed it an honour to have lain down his life for the comrades now so mercifully restored to them.

Three of Sir Edgar Mortiemor's own Sedan-chairs were obtained from an outhouse near the stables. The latter were almost consumed by the fire. The outhouse in question had not been injured. It was, perhaps, a most merciful circumstance that Sir Edgar's insensibility continued. The peril of the fire and agony of his wounds alike remained unknown to him.

To a near neighbour and friend of the Mortiemors were the Sedan-chairs all carried. The outlaws were simply taken to be an ordinary crowd of willing rescuers, such as a fire usually caused to be collected.

Dandy Dick was, perhaps, never before so anxious to leave the beautiful, tender, clinging Maude. He was usually morbidly sensitive upon the state of his appearance. The handsome and gallant young highwayman now secretly chafed at the knowledge that he never before appeared to such disadvantage in the eyes of the girl he so ardently and hopelessly loved. But in the estimation of Maude Mortiemor he looked every inch a hero. Grime, burns, blisters, rags—these were all proofs of his unselfish devotion, chivalry, and daring. But not one whit less were these shared by his chief comrades.

"Thy poor sire is grievously hurt, Maude, fair coz. A physician should attend him instantly and examine his injuries. Farewell, sweet girl, I must away. Bright day is here, an' the hunted hare must seek his dark earth caves!"

"Fairly well, Dick dearest!" lingeringly sighed the clinging maiden. "May just Heaven guard thee an' they brave friends, and restore to me a deeply-beloved father! He will bless thee for the remainder of his life should he recover, and thine and the welfare of thy comrades will henceforth be his special task!"

"Alas! sweet love, peerless queen of beauty, thou knowest not how grievously beset is thine outlawed kinsman. Another barbarous deed is set down to his doing. Those able to prove my innocence of this last false charge must not speak. Outlawed like myself, their evidence would be deemed tainted, and would not be heard in a court of justice."

"There is a Judge above. I will never cease to pray to him, Dick. I have faith in the Supreme. He hath led us safely through all our earthly snares so far, and will continue to do so."

"Amen to thy sacred hope, sweetest maid!" A long passionate kiss, and the high-born maiden and her proscribed lover again reluctantly tear themselves from their impassioned embraces.

*

The Mall, St. James's Park. A bright, crisp, winter day. One of those far too rare winter days, when old King Sol rises from a long sleep to yawn, stretch his lazy limbs, and do a little make-believe work just as a relief from that hardest work of all—the labour of doing nothing!

The unexpected brightness of the weather filled the Mall and the park walks with gay, dazzling crowds. The din of loud chatter, banter, merry jest, boisterous laughter filled the air. High-born dames of all ages were there in more or less extended crinolines and heaped-up coiffure. The most brilliant colours were displayed in dress. The male dandy vied his gems and rich brocades with the most gaudily-apparelled lady.

If the interchange of greetings, compliments, and other specimens of small talk were in a merry key, they were also mostly marked with a degree of vulgarity and coarseness—not to use a stronger term—that would to-day shock the ears of even the lowest street rough. In the days when the Georges reigned, the respectable and virtuous had no safeguard save in their own homes.

A Sedan-chair, remarkable for its design and stylish getup, had been seen darting about in all directions. The bearers appeared to be negroes. Their uniforms of pale-blue satin and gold facings contrasted well with their rich point lace, black skins, and powdered wigs. The blinds of each window were drawn. The fops in this fashionable resort of the day were mad with curiosity. It was considered a sure thing that some rare, coy beauty occupied the chair.

The drawn blinds, grand attendants, and gaily-decorated chair were responsible for this belief.

"Observing without being observed! It was too bad! The lovely crewtcher wearly must be revealed!" A dude of dudes had chased the chair in all directions. He was dressed within an inch of his life, and carried in his hands a snuffbox completely formed of gems. When the winter sun caught it, the costly bauble became painful to one's eyesight.

"All ther diamuns in ther Ingees wouldn't change a pig inter a porkeypine, or a porkeypine inter a pig! An' that ere noodle thinks as 'e's a-passin' for a wery fine court gallant. Vhy, anyone could see wive the millionth part o' 'is off-side optic, as that thing was sent inter the vorld wholly an' solely ter be stuck outside a tailor's shop as a dummy! An' not a fust-clarss dummy at that!"

The front Sedan-chair bearer was at the side of the conveyance. A splash of mud on its side appeared to be entirely engaging his attention. His words, however, found their way beyond the closed curtains. A reply came:

"Are you quite positive that the fellow was one of the Mohawk gang that fired Sir Mortiemor's manor?

"Ven yer vants ter reckeneyes a feller ther next time as yer focusses yer 'ead lights on 'im, jist gently compliment 'im vive a black optic. I should know ther Wiffles's black-eye-brand a mile off. That finnikin dummy's been a-doin' 'is level best ter spoil the beauty-spot I gave 'im on the night o' the flare-up; but ernuff of its beauty remains fer me ter swear by, as ther cannibulls sed ter each other as they sadly gazed on ther 'eel o' the boot o' the missunairy, vhot vas all as remained o' their toothsome snack!"

A few hurriedly whispered words came from beyond the drawn curtains; then Wiffles, for he it was, as the reader has already seen, entered the space between the front poles, picked them up at the same instant as the rear bearer, and moved off.

The persistent fop quickly followed on foot. A dainty cambric handkerchief fluttered to the ground. The dandy had seen it leave the interior of the chair. He was quite positive now that a lovely damsel was inside. She had given him the signal that his attentions were agreeable to her. He would follow to the death.

The negro attendants darted off with their burden, and never paused until a remote, unfrequented part of the park was reached. The chair was then set down. As the eager lady-killer mincingly came up, a form left the chair by the further door, and was consequently unseen by the swagger gallant. The Sedan-chair contained no bewitching fair one, but a masked man of fierce aspect!

"Sir Cad! Incendiary! Fighter of aged men! Terrifier and abductor of innocent maidens!" The tones were terrible to hear in their intensity of mingled contempt, scorn, and rage.

"Lud! lud! A footpad, as I live!" The startled creature turned to flee. The Sedan-chair-bearers each presented a fire-lock, their barrels sparkling like burnished gold in the sunlight.

"Three footpads, my gallant peacock!" cried one of the seeming negroes.

Closer scrutiny convinced the victim that their African origin was of burnt cork and lampblack only.

"Sir Knight of the Mohawks, pray permit me to introduce my esteemed friends, Colonel Blood and Will Wiffles. As for myself, I am known as Dandy Dick. This is a return visit!"

In the last speaker the waylaid gallant saw a tall, graceful youth. He wore a black mask, and had a profusion of natural curls reaching his shoulders. But his clothing was tarnished, greatly singed with fire, and in rags. Even his jack boots were brown, blistered, and cracked. He held his long and exquisitely-chased weapon at full cock, and within a few inches of the fop's temples.

A RECKONING DEMANDED—A MOHAWK AT BAY— AMBUSHED ASSASSINS—TIMELY AID—KING GEORGE AND THE HIGHWAYMEN—A CHANGE OF NATIONALITY— SURROUNDING FOES—THE GREAT THIEF-TAKER AND DANDY DICK.

"Some thousands of pounds' loss to Sir Edgar Mortiemor; two serving-men killed; almost the deaths by fright of several females; the more than probable death of the good old baronet. These are but a few of the items of the bill ye dogs of Mohawks will have to face. But, firstly—since it is the most pressing need—I call upon ye, knave, to replace my fire-destroyed wardrobe. Your costume is the most dainty raree show I have yet seen in the Mall. Come, we will exchange!"

"I commend thy taste, Dick!" cried Colonel Blood. "Altogether there are no less than five damaged suits to be exchanged. That delightful gem-studied snuffbox may go some way towards finding the means to remove the parched thirst a long roasting hath afflicted a number of us gallants with." So saying the colonel snatched the box, and coolly put it in one of his waistcoat pockets.

"Friends, I 'umbly perpose as we slit the throat o' thus 'ere mongrel disguised as a thoro'breed, melt 'is diamuns an' pearls in wine, an' then drink long life an' 'ealth ter 'im, arter we've buried 'is body. 'E is far too pretty ter live—as ther fox thort, whin 'e'd made up 'is mind ter wring ther neck o' a bantam cock, an' then make a supper on 'im."

"Sirrahs, I'll shout for aid! Ye'll all be arrested, and then end the final chapters of your lives by gracefully dangling from Tyburn Tree!"[77]

Thus threatened the greatly affrighted fop, his affected drawl quite gone. Fear had improved his speech, if not his tranquillity.

"Contemptible worm!" sternly thundered Dandy Dick. "Raise thy voice, and it shall end in thy death-cry! What think ye withholds my finger? No consideration for a Mohawk. Where highwayman or footpad—nay, even hired assassin—would pause, and withdraw in compunction, a Mohawk but marks the first grade of his infamous courses. Liked I not bloodshed less, thy debased brains would before this have ceased to be of further use to thee!"

"I am no Mohawk! Ye are mistaken! I tell ye—"

"Thou liest!" hissed Wiffles. "For yer still sports ther pretty forget-me-not I gave thee on thy left 'ead-lamp on ther night as they ugly crew tried ter conwert a few o' us road-rakers inter nice roasted meat!"

"Strip—peel off, scurvy varlet!" The colonel's pistol-tube left an indented ring upon the fop's pale, sweat-bedewed forehead. Two other black rings hovered close to his eyes. The agitated, violently-trembling Mohawk commenced to disrobe. Dandy Dick had set the example. An exchange of each article of wearing apparel then took place. The fop was permitted to alone retain his white wig. Dress, rapier, cravat, gems, diamond buckles, &c., represented a sum of enormous proportions. By leaving coat and waistcoat unfastened at the chest, Dandy Dick made them fit him fairly well. He looked indeed a picture—every inch a man. As for the effeminate fop, dressed as he now was, in the fire-destroyed suit, a self-respecting the scarecrow would have been put to the blush on finding itself looking so ungainly. The gem-decked cane, valuable bangles, and money of the latter were also seized. Then the punished Mohawk was ordered to depart.

"Tell all your cowardly fellow young bloods that each shall, one by one, be served as we have thee this day. Ye have had fine sport—as such vermin as ye term thy cowardly work. The piper must now be paid for furnishing the music."

The crestfallen, silent young blood was eager enough to get away with a whole skin. Dandy Dick, Colonel Blood, and Wiffles we are alone.

"We have made a blunder in letting him go, for in a few moments every blade carried by gallant fop now strutting the Mall will be eagerly seeking our hearts, Dick. We had better be nimble and get off!" remarked Colonel Blood.

"'Nimble ain't the proper vord,' as ther snail sadly remarked, when it tried in wain ter outrace ther streak o' lightnin' an' found itself suddenly conwerted inter a charcoal creeper. Ply is the term, comrades," put in Wiffles quietly.

---

[77] The Tyburn gallows was an execution site located near present-day Marble Arch in London.

"You an' I, Wiffles, will come for our exchange garments another day," said the colonel. "In the meantime I agree with the that we fly forthwith."

"We'll leave our Sedan-chair here, and make our way from this by unfrequented parts," advised Dandy Dick.

"Aha! the young bloods are already aflame with the result of the news of our presence in their fashionable resort!" cried the colonel. A mighty uproar of rageful triumph now came upon the breeze as if in answer to their words.

The three highwaymen crept into the dense undergrowth and the heart of the forest belting the south-west corner of the park, and were cautiously speeding away. Suddenly Dandy Dick, who was some yards in advance, pulled up and held up a hand warningly to those following.

Some hundred paces in front of him was an ambushed party of mounted men. The outlaws noiselessly sank to the earth, and then cautiously crept forward. Dick in a few moments had stolen up to within hearing distance.

"This is the spot, captain. The King' Walk it is called, in consequence of its having been the favourite promenade of Charles the First." These words came to the acutely-listening ears of the concealed highwaymen.

What could be their meaning?

"Hist! Ready! He approaches!" the same voice added.

"Treachery afoot!" muttered Dandy Dick.

The yells of the Mohawks came nearer and nearer.

Dandy Dick raised his head until it was above the bush of tangled briars before him. In a flash he had taken in the scene, and the meaning of the words of the concealed horseman.

The portly, grandly-robed, and decorated person of the King of England, mounted upon a magnificent white charger, came into view. The Monarch was quite alone, and leisurely riding into the very centre of the unsuspected ambush.

Dick, the colonel, and Wiffles, of one accord, silently drew their firearms and saw to their priming, carefully adjusting flint and steel.

A rider now quickly urged his steed into the path, faced the King, and, presenting a large horse-pistol, savagely hissed:

"Thus I exterminate a tyrant ruler!"

Before his finger could press the trigger another firearm exploded, the horsemen furiously yelled to his companions to shoot down the King, then fell bathed in his blood. The remainder of the hidden riders rode from cover, to instantly see two of their numbers lurch forward and shoot over their steeds' necks, in response to two more explosions of flint-locks. A moment more, and the conspirators had swiftly galloped off, imagining they were attacked by a stronger force, for they had utterly failed to discover from whence came the bullets.

The King, overcome with fear and agitation, remained gazing down at the two men brought to earth. Presently he recovered the use of his tongue.

"By my troth," he cried, "but this fair England would have been monarchless anew, but for some right royal and brave-hearted subject! What ho! Come, reveal thyself! Whosoever thou art I swear, by my Royal sceptre, thou art King George's friend—or, if there be more than one, thou art all the King's friends!"

Dandy Dick, in his borrowed plumage, suddenly revealed himself. The highwayman took off his hat and made a graceful, sweeping bow. The colonel and Wiffles silently strode to his side.

"By my faith," cried King George, "a handsome deliverer, and a person of consequence, or he would not have such gay attendants! Come, tell me, why didst thou and thy serving-men save thy King's life? and thy name?" asked King George.

"Sire, we have saved thy life in return for thine act of signing away our own. My life is preserved by men whose heads thou art so eager to see fixed upon the grim spikes of Temple Gate, or those of the Tower's ramparts. We are the subjects of cruel outlawry. Our names are inscribed upon the criminal records in the black book of Newgate!"

The King was then left to his own astounding reflections. With his last word, Dandy Dick had given the sign to his companions, and the three had vanished.

The devoted comrades swiftly pushed their way through the dense wilderness of tangled bush and leafless timbers. In a few moments they had, unperceived, reached the spot where the palanquin (Sedan-chair) had been left.

"George of Hanover was too much amazed to note the direction we took, and even if he had it would be impossible to follow us, unless he dismounted. The fellows we brought down were but insensible from loss of blood, I think. I did not aim to kill, although it would have been a small matter to brain such cowardly renegades," said Colonel Blood.

"I winged the intending assassin in the shoulder-blade; he will recover that an' get right enough to face a charge of treason, at the end of which he'll be just a head shorter," replied Dandy Dick.

"I jist tickled my beauty in ther full part of the thigh—a leaden wisiter in that region o' man's anaturme usually kicks up dust considerable," remarked Wiffles knowingly.

The yells of the gallants of the Mall could be heard proceeding from all directions.

The concealed highwaymen must soon be run to earth.

Wiffles at once became busy. There was much display of gold scroll ornament covering the blue exterior of the palanquin. In a few seconds the point of a knife caused every particle of this to fall off. The black canvas of the dome-shaped roof was also easily removed. The top surface of the chair was now a bright yellow. Next, the former red window-curtains were replaced with black ones. In the meantime the colonel had taken a bundle from under the seat of the conveyance. A large towel was in his hands. By dint of much rubbing he had removed the lampblack and grease of the blackamoor and became a white man.

Wiffles brought about the same change of nationality in his own case. But he remained distinctly of African origin about the ears, eyes, and portions of the neck, until the colonel took upon himself to wipe the negro Wiffles clean out of existence. In a trice the removed gold decorations and towels were concealed in the brushwood.

The colonel and Wiffles next frisked their blue satin, gold-laced coats and waistcoats off, turned them inside out, and frisked them on again. Coat and vest, in each case, were now yellow, with broad black stripes. The colonel had taken off his white wig, and put on a green shade over one eye. Wiffles also now appeared in his natural hair, and had damped and then stuck various patches of black court-plaster[78] over his face, and suddenly became so bandy in the pins that to stop a runaway pig in a passage would be an impossibility.

All of this was but the work of a few moments. Every article of former disguise was hidden. Dandy Dick had entered the conveyance, drawn the blind, and closed the doors. The colonel and Wiffles snatched up the poles and hurried off, taking no heed of their direction. Two seconds sufficed to find them completely surrounded by a madly-excited, furiously-yelling, and gesticulating throng. Their cries were deafening; rapier-blades cleaved the air in brilliant flashes.

"An attempt has been made upon the life of the King! An outrage committed upon Sir Eveland Chiveral!—Robbed and stripped of his apparel! These deeds are due to Dandy Dick and his fellow-robbers! Let no person—male or female—pass without examination!"

The loud, savage, harsh, and guttural tones with those of London's greatest police-agent—Jonathan Wild!

°KING GEORGE OF ENGLAND AND JONATHAN WILD—THE FOPS OF ST. JAMES'S—JONATHAN WILD—THE YOUNG BLOODS AND THE OUTLAWS—THIRTY AGAINST THREE—A DEADLY AND DESPAIRING STRUGGLE.

"Assassins are abroad! The King's life hath been attempted! Sir Eveland Chiveral attacked, robbed, and his clothes exchanged! Dandy Dick and his fellow-outlaws are responsible for these heinous crimes. The notorious highwayman and his fellow-robbers are now present here in the Mall. There is an enormous sum offered for the capture of Dandy Dick, or any of his gang. Gentlemen, loyal gallants, I appeal to ye every one and to aid me in the capture of these terrible desperados!"

---

[78] Adhesive fabric made of cotton or silk and used for both medical and cosmetic purposes.
° Part 20. Vol. XIV.—No. 356. 7 September 1900.

Thus yelled Jonathan Wild at the uttermost of his lung-power. The Newgate agent had but a bodyguard of four of his own men, and now looked to the fashionable fops office and. James's, and such of the Mohawks as chanced to be present, to aid him in his object.

"Not so fast, friend—not so fast! No one but myself saw those who attacked me, an' would have claimed my poor life, therefore I am best judge of the identity of the disloyal villains. They were traitors of quite another order. I know a political spy from an ordinary malefactor! Moreover, the bloodthirsty rogues were mounted, and are miles away by this. Marry, but it would be passing strange if my brave rescuers should prove to be this purse-filching felon Dandy Dick and his desperate fellows!"

It was King George himself who thus addressed the thief-taker.

The portly, grave-faced King had ridden up in time to hear Jonathan Wild's harangue, and a look of deep annoyance had settled upon his face on hearing the conclusion expressed in the latter's words.

The wily criminal-hunter instantly threw himself down upon one knee before the King. "Sire," cried he, "I humbly crave pardon for my error! Let the robbers be captured and brought before thee!"

"Good! But methinks thou art counting thy chickens before they are hatched! First catch the hare, an' then skin it. Ye know the cookery-book maxim?"

Good King George was smiling, spite of his recent narrow escape. The Newgate felon-Hunter rose up. He bit his lip in vexation, and turned to renew his instructions to the gathering crowd. Again he roared out:

"Treason! Treason! The King's life hath been attempted! Sir Eveland Chiveral attacked by footpads and robbed! I, Jonathan Wild, representative of the Crown officials of Newgate, call upon all loyal gallants to assist me in detaining every unknown person present in the Mall. All Sedan-chairs should be stopped and examined. His Majesty believes that those who attempted his life have already escaped. Yet there may be some not yet got away; and, moreover, the footpads may have had a hand in the far greater crime, and have intended to have lain their impious hands upon the sacred person of their King!"

The presence of his Majesty in their midst created the utmost excitement. The gay throngs crowded to the spot, and were far more intent on viewing their ruler than attending to Wild's request.

"Our arch-enemy! We must look to our lives!" muttered Dandy Dick, cautiously thrusting his head out of one of the palanquin windows and addressing his friends.

"Jonathan Wild! What cursed ill-luck!" savagely gasped Colonel Blood.

"Old, bald bullet-pate! Well, we are nicely spotted now, as ther plain-duff sed when some plums was stuck in it!" gloomily chimed in Wiffles, whose mind had far from recovered its terrible shock of the fire at Sir Mortiemor's manor.

Colonel Blood carried the Sedan-chair by its front handles. Wiffles held the hind supports. Dandy Dick, it will be remembered, was garbed in the fine plumes he had taken from the Mohawk fop in exchange for his clothes destroyed in the flaming building at Holloway.

The colonel's face was now of its usual colour. Wiffles had also wiped out the negro tint. The two were in the livery of Sir Mortiemor, but trusted to the green shade in the first case, and the imitation brandy-legs in the second. Still, there was risk of the livery being recognised. The Sedan-chair had had its appearance greatly changed, as the reader doubtless remembers.

A number of the male frequenters now became most extreme to distinguish themselves in the eyes of royalty. Their rapiers drawn, the gallants spread themselves out in the shape of a wide circle. Then the mass of frequenters, in chairs or on foot, were by threats and even blows forced into a compact mass, huddled together like sheep. Then Wild's rasping, high-pitched voice was again heard. This time ordering all the chair-bearers to come forward and collect their burdens in a row before him.

Countless eyes watched the movements of every Sedan bearer. Dandy Dick and the colonel looked upon capture as a certainty. Wiffles and the colonel, in their characters of attendants, wore their side-arms, and had each a little arsenal of fire-locks secreted in their garments. But it would mean three against as many thousands.

Dandy Dick, still seated in the Sedan-chair, carefully looked to his pistols, and make sure that his blade would not stick in its sheath in the moment of danger. The chair had now stopped dead. The three highwaymen were completely hemmed in, and surrounded by thousands of their foes, any one of whom would count it a very great honour to kill either or all of the outlaws whose many deeds of daring were the continual talk of all England!

"Look to the occupier of every hand-carriage, gentlemen!" shouted the voice of the thief-taker. At the same moment Dandy Dick was startled by a sudden rending sound at his back. He quickly turned. A knife-blade had pierced the canvas back of the chair, and rent it open from above the seat to the roof. For a brief second Wiffles's face was partly to be seen.

"Force yerself out backwards, yer won't be twigged; but yer must be as quick as a streak o' lightning in fits!"

The words were barely uttered before Dandy Dick had shot himself through feet first. The thief-taker's eyes had examined the inside of the conveyance a fraction of time after.

Unseen, Jonathan Wild was covered by two firelocks. Had a word of suspicion escaped him, the two weapons within two feet of the body would have belched forth their forerunners of grim death! The breeze blew about the light material of the curtains, thus hiding the gap in the chair back. For the moment, Dandy Dick had escaped. The colonel and Wiffles were not recognised. The madly-excited, thickly-packed, swaying crowd immediately surrounding the outlaws failed to observe the movements of Dandy Dick.

"Empty hand-carriages, pass on!" bellowed forth Wild. Dick shot himself into the palanquin again with the speed of thought, Wiffles keeping close behind Dick, and thus hiding the act.

The colonel and Wiffles snatched up the handles and trotted forward. The drawn curtains hit the occupant. In two seconds the carriage was fifty yards beyond the fringe of the turbulent throng. Another few moments and they would be beyond danger. It was not to be! A form, dressed in a fire-damaged suit, and heading a body of Mohawks, emerged from a pathway hidden by trees and bushes. The blue and gold livery of Sir Edgar Mortiemor's retainers was at once recognised by the gallant with whom Dandy Dick had exchanged suits.

"We've ran them to earth! Cut them down, Mohawks! Dead or alive, we'll secure their bodies!" The voice was a shrieking treble—that of Sir Eveland Chiveral. He came flying to the attack.

Colonel Blood greeted the attackers with a furious oath. Wiffles and he put down the chair. Dandy Dick sprang out from the further side. Sir Eveland Chiveral thrust his head into the near window. Colonel Blood and Wiffles, acting as one, seized the fop by the legs and lurched him forward. Head now resting upon the bottom, feet kicking in all directions, the hand-carriage darted off.

The party of young bloods following the discomfited fop stood spellbound. What was to happen next? their expressions appeared to ask. A few strides, and the flying dandy-chair bearers had reached a wide and deep pool, in which gold and silver fish distorted themselves. The carriers were seen to withdraw themselves from the handles, face the body of the upright box-like article, and then, after giving it a few swings, flung it into the air, whence it fell, with a terrific splash, into the centre of the deep, ornamental pond.

A few mighty bounds, and the colonel at his companion rejoined their comrade.

A howl of guttural, choking fury, and the band of young bloods threw themselves upon the three highwaymen.

"Ten to one!" hissed Dandy Dick. "Friends," he added, "remember our roasting at the hands of these white-livered incendiaries!"

"Short reckonings make long friends!" sang out Colonel Blood. His brilliant upguard turned aside a down-coming cutlass-blade with which one of the attacking party was armed. The weightier metal would have broken the colonel's lighter steel had he not caught it close to the hilt of his own. Then best part of his ribbon-like blade was to be seen dripping blood, and protruding from the back of the neck of his adversary. The man fell, uttering oaths and feeble moans.

The three outlaws arranged themselves so that their blades describe the circle—a circle as of living lines of dazzling quicksilver. The eye failed to follow the efforts of the perfect swordmanship the outlaws displayed. In a few moments there was a ring of writhing, groaning, cursing, and pain-moaning beings upon the earth, the running streams of red telling of the marvellous science, dash, and daring of three against thirty or more!

"Give 'em good honest weight, comrades, an' a bit over ter send ther scale down wive a merry fop!" shouted Wiffles, slashing about him with utmost fury. Howver cheery his words, Wiffles's blood was up. The thought of Dolly Trippitt and her sufferings nerved his arm with the strength of a giant. Never before had the usually light-hearted Wiffles displayed such a savage demeanour.

As for Colonel Blood, he fought like a very god of war. With every thrust he did more or less terrible execution. His impetuosity carried everything before him.

"That, you dog, for the poor old man Sir Mortiemor!" he hissed, as his darting rapier cut a red groove the whole length of a snarling visage before him. A fraction of time after the gory steel had shot through his fingers, to be grasped a few inches from its point, the hilt then crashing down upon a hatless skull, to send the receiver groaning to grass.

"On behalf of the fair Maude!" added Dandy Dick, not to be behindhand in the settling of old scores. His blade had lost half its length in the side of a mohawk. Before he could withdraw, a steel's snake-like, trembling point was within three inches of his heart; but a swift whizz cleared the air in time. The hand aiming the fatal thrust fell, a broad, red-dripping bracelet running round its wrist.

"That pretty stroke was but just in time, Dick!" cried Colonel Blood, still busily showering lightning-like strokes.

"Thanks, dear comrade!" gasped Dandy Dick, with a smile, although still terribly hard pressed.

At this crisis the main body of young bloods had taken in the scene of conflict between a party of their friends and three highwaymen. This battle against long odds had taken but a few moments, despite the damage wrought.

A terrific onrush, accompanied by a din ear-splitting and dismaying to the stoutest-hearted. The Mowhawks, with Jonathan Wild at their head, came on. A black cloud of infuriated men, like famished wolves, madly furious to strike, rend, devour.

The Newgate agent was the first to reach the still cool, dauntless three. In his impetuosity to cut down Dandy Dick—whose features he knew far better than of the Colonel or Wiffles—he shot past Colonel Blood. The latter did not miss this opportunity. The butts of his heaviest firelock flew up, and then curved down with a sickening thud, and fell upon the bared temples of the hatless, flying Wild. Instantly he tumbled to the dust, and then, in senseless condition, rolled under a moving palanquin.

Dandy Dick and his two intrepid comrades grimly prepared themselves for the irresistible, oncoming, devastating wave of foes—defiant, if hopeless.

Then it was suddenly seen a completely black Sedan-chair borne by two fierce-looking negroes. This came with incredible speed towards the three outlaws.

"Ho, there! Rescue! Rescue!" came a voice in peals of thunder from within the sable-painted, wheelless conveyance.

JACK SHEPPARD AND JOE BLUESKIN CONTINUE THEIR ADVENTURES—ANOTHER MISHAP TO OFFICER BILBERRY—THE WAYSIDE SHELTER—GAME FILCHERS—THE GRUESOME OLD FARMER—THE DISGUISED PRINCES FROM A FOREIGN COUNTRY—THE CHAMPION KNOCKOUT SPREAD—DANGER!

"Ho, there! Imps of darkness come forth!"

Two dismounted Bow Street runners had stealthily crept to the spot where Joe Blueskin and Jack Sheppard were crouched and concealed, deep down in the black shadows at the back of the roundhouse, or St. John's lock-up.

Officer Bilberry was one of these officers, loud and terrible in windy words, as usual. His attempt to play the part of town crier—like most of his efforts—had ended in a very tame fizzle, as the letting off of a fatally damp farthing squib[79] on a bright day. Bilberry was now back in his old form of Bow Street bully-boy—"Looking large as life, an' twice as natural," as the penny showman of the country fair so elegantly phrases it, when describing a human attraction.

Blueskin lay nearest, Jack Sheppard behind him. Officer Bilberry's oaths were now in proportion to his degree of funk. Urging his fellow-officer forward, Bilberry took up the rear, peering over the other's shoulders.

"Blood an' saltpetre! Carnage! Mountains o' slain, an' no time to give 'em decent interment! Ho, there! Imps o' darkness come forth!" Terrible as Bilberry tried to make his voice ring out, there was a trembling squeak of fear in it.

Blueskin silently raised his cudgel. The broad end of it shot forward, and then buried itself in the fullest part of the nearest red waistcoat. A something resembling the bursting of a water-pipe, the roar of a bull, and the squeak of a pig combined, followed. The receiver of the cudgel-thrust writhed in torments until his wind returned. To give it a fair chance he had thrown himself flat upon his back; his head had struck Bilberry in the mouth, cutting into one of his choicest samples of swear words, and sending a number of his false teeth down his throat. The daring officers now sprawled upon their backs, and the sulphury nature of the invectives issuing from their mouths caused the insects of the air to drop in a condition of deadly stupor for a wide radius round the venters of the shocking samples of the Saxon tongue.

---

[79] An explosive device consisting of a parchment tube filled with gunpowder.

"Come forth is it?" disdainfully sang out Blueskin, pulling his big frame upon its feet—"come forth? I usually come first, and the small fry—known as Scarlet runners—mostly come last!"

"I don't know, Joe; if you're of first rank, so am I, and I find that the bully-boys mostly come after me—unpleasantly close after me, to—that makes 'em second rank!"

The two were pelting away like mad as they thus commented. The officers were cursing loud and exhaustive enough to supply a whole army in red-hot anathemas for a twelvemonth. But, like the overturned turtle, they appeared unable to regain their legs—at least, until the unknown lurkers in the shadows had put a long distance between them and the said police-agents.

Blueskin now suddenly paused, and then threw himself down full-length upon a patch of grass that had bravely withstood the rude assaults of winter, and valiantly stuck to its colours. Like Hamlet, Blueskin was "fat, and scant of breath,"[80] and very little running went a very long way with him.

"We've given the bully-boys the slips," he said. "After all, Jack lad," Jolly Nose continued, in a reflective vein, "in the garden of life a Bow Street officer figures as but a very small potato—an' a sorry an' blighted spud at that!"

Jack Sheppard had spread himself out beside his friend.

"One of the murphies was a pretty large very small potato, I think," he replied with a merry chuckle; "and the fellow more represents a living Mount Aetna than a spud, if judging only by the white-heat-lava curses he belched forth. Any one of those original oaths of his was worthy of being placed in a gilt frame with a glass before it."

"If it were hung up on a wall it 'ud set fire to the house, Jack lad," remarked Blueskin.

The early dawn was breaking. The cold was intense. Snow and ice still covered the earth in scattered patches. The vicinity in which the two chums were was wild and deserted. An isolated shed loomed before them. Blueskin and Sheppard found the door open and plenty of straw within. In a few moments after they were in as sound a sleep as if resting in a bed of swansdown.

A fresh, bright, wintry morning smiled upon the two outlaws—for the elements show not one whit of distinction in their treatment of mortals—on Blueskin and Jack Sheppard opening their wondering eyes in the cold and draughty timber shelter.

"Zounds! I'm that famished I could eat my own head off, Jack lad!" growled Joe Blueskin, vigorously rubbing his limbs to drive away the cold and stiffness.

"I'm surprised at your bad taste, Joe. The flavour of the chops would give ye the blues; and if your top end didn't disagree with you, it would be the first time it ever

---

[80] Hamlet, Act 2, Scene 5.

coincided—I should say go-inside it—with anyone else," jokingly responded Jack.

"Jack lad, you've been well educated, but learning's thrown away upon ye. A silken purse can't be made out of a sow's ear!"

"Have you tried the experiment on one of your own, then? In that case you'd be a he-sow, though!"

"Jack lad, observe how shallow ye are, with all your fine education. How could my head—a part of myself—disagree with myself?"

"Why, you would be beside yourself before you could do it!"

The door of the timber outhouse crashed in with a loud swing.

"Aha! I thought so! Farmyard poachers! My geese an' ducks, my fowls and ducklings an' little chicks have long been killed an' stolen, an' now I behold the poaching varlets!"

The form of a man darkened the doorway of the shed—a lean, grizzled, exceedingly sour-visaged man. He carried a stout staff.

Blueskin leisurely arose. Jack followed his example.

"A right good-day to thee, good master!" presently replied Blueskin.

"An' a merry one to boot!" added Jack Sheppard, noting the vinegarish scowl upon the old man's visage.

"Thy livestock killed an' stolen, sayest thou? A foul deed indeed!" went on Blueskin, with comic affectation of concern.

"Murder most foul,[81] as in the best it is, but this most foul and—"

But Jack was rudely interrupted in his quotation from Shakespeare.

"Thieving knaves! Barn-breaking rogues! Game pilfers—"

"Stay!" commanded Blueskin, whose voice could be fierce enough when he chose. "We know nothing of thy dead livestock; but I can show thee a choice killing stock—the stock of my merry barker!"

The old man fell back in consternation.

"A pistol-stock! See the joke? Oh, you don't; well, I'm not surprised at that, for the joke within this barker mostly kills a man before he can see it. An' that's not much of a joke, is it?" The speaker made the trigger click.

"I cry thee mercy, good gentlemen! I'm an old man!" stammered the visitor.

"Come! good gentlemen is a great improvement on your previous highly, complementary terms. We can't help you being an old man. You are old enough to know better than to have entered the world so long ago," remarked Jack solemnly.

It will be observed that the lad Sheppard's wisdom was a bit mixed. But this is frequently the case with far more aged wiseacres.[82]

---

[81] Hamlet, Act 1, Scene 5.
[82] A know-all, scorned by those with whomn he shares his knowledge.

"I beseech thee, noble gallants—I am a lonely man—spare my poor life!" The terrified pleader sank to his knees and clasped his upraised hands.

"My most trusted and reliable friend here will decide what shall be done," firmly replied Blueskin, pointing to his shooter. Then he placed the stock to his ear and affected to listen most attentively for a few seconds. "Not only can this living thing of metal spit fire, bark, bite, and kill, but it can also speak, and possesseth abundance of wisdom. Its decree is that ye, in penance for thy false charges, provideth thy illustrious guests with a most substantial breakfast."

"That will I most gladly do if, in return—"

"No ifs!" chimed in Jack Sheppard; adding: "Thy face is grief-stricken enough to kill a dead man for the second time; thy tongue sharp enough to skin a flint stone; an' eyes so cruel in their glances as to cause the marble image of man to faint dead away at the sight of them. Get thee hence, an' lead us to the goodly fare, wherever it may be!"

The dejected-looking old fellow, occasionally casting terrified glances at Blueskin's weapon—still held close to the former's temples—led the way. A farmstead was now seen at a short distance. A blue-white volume of smoke curled upwards from a red-brick chimney.

"Acres of bacon rashes—gammon rashes, an' no gammon as to size; fried eggs in countless number, floating in vast seas of bubbling, boiling fat!" Thus proceeded Jack Sheppard, as if thinking aloud, smacking his lips now and then like the loud slash of the whip.

"Hark at the lad! Why, Jack boy, I really believe you're peckish!" laughed Jack Sheppard's comrade.

"Peckish? You toast an' butter a stone doorstep, an' just to see if I don't eat it! Peckish! Offer a donkey strawberries an' note if he'll refuse 'em!" remarked the lad, in what he intended to be a sarcastic vein.

"I'm sorry they're not in season, an' that I've got none about me, or I would try you, Jack!" retorted Blueskin.

"One to you, coloured parchment," replied the boy prison-breaker.

The house was now reached. A snug cottage indeed it turned out to be.

"Rose! Rose, wench!" cried out the old man of the cottage.

"Call a rose by any other name 'twill smell as wheat," murmured Blueskin, sotto voce. The great fellow was well pleased with himself at the prospect of a meal.

"Call a rose by any other name 'twill smell as wheat, bacon, eggs, an' other delicacies too numerous to mention, Joe of the moonlight complexion," saucily remarked Jack Sheppard.

A red-cheeked, bouncing, buxom young maid suddenly appeared in the doorway. Her round face was looking as solemn as that of an undertaker at a wedding until she caught sight of the strangers, when she at once gave them a smile of welcome, accompanied by the old-time bobbing up-and-down curtsy.

"That's a sweet smile," quietly remarked Jack, in a whisper, to Blueskin, "if it is somewhat on an extensive scale—"

"Extensive countenance," corrected Jolly Nose, also in an undertone.

"It's a sweet smile, I was saying—if over-large," Jack added. "When old Dame Nature was serving out smiles you may depend upon it her shears slipped when it came to this poor sufferer's turn, and her grimaces were snipped off miles and miles too large—why, one of 'em's wide enough to go the rounds of a good-sized family, an' then leave enough to put by for chance visitors."

"Rose, wench, these gallants are my very good friends; place a right good, ample meal before my guests, an' not forgetting a flagon o' foaming ale."

This order pleased Blueskin hugely. He became one broad grin—the grin commenced at the crown of his head, and extended to the broader toes of his shoes. Jolly Nose drew the old farmer aside confidentially.

"Friend," whispered he, placing his great nose in the listener's ear. "This is a great secret. Myself and the lad yonder are Royal princes in our own right, but we are travelling England in 'guise (disguise) to learn its language an' customs. There is a spade guinea for thee, friend of the most jovial visage. I pray thee entertain us as befitting he becomes our exalted rank."

"'Egad! By my old bones, but I will!" replied the old man, trying to smile—the first time for many years. "But, sir," he suspiciously added, "do they speak English where ye come from? For ye each have the uncommon gift of a fine tongue?"

"English tutors, do ye see," added Jolly Nose gravely. "Here is a specimen of our own native tongue: If—ro, I find—yoo, up to any tricks—roo, hang me—carroo, but—o, I'll—moo, twist—mooi, your, scragg—weei, confounded—scruff—old neck—yiffoo!"

"A very pretty tongue, too—very pretty!" delightedly remarked the woebegone, grizzled-visaged old man, all the while his eyes glued to the golden piece resting in the wrinkled and dirty palm of his hand.

Stating that he was most anxious to examine the evil done his livestock by the usual mysterious midnight poachers, the farmer retraced his steps. Jolly Nose and his comrades then entered the farmstead.

The buxom, bonny, smiling wench in no time had covered a great mahogany table with a snow-white cloth and eatables enough to satisfy a dozen Robinson Crusoes after living a year on periwinkle-shells and hope, neither of which articles is said to be over-filling. Joe Blueskin had contrived to acquaint Jack of his double deception played off upon the owner of the wayside cottage. This consisted in Jolly Nose assuring the host that his barn-looting guests were foreign princes, and giving him a spurious golden coin, representing a spade guinea.

"If the old churchyard goblin plays us false, he may keep the base coin as his due reward; but if he turns out loyal, I've as good a golden coin to give him as King George himself ever handled!" concluded Joe Blueskin.

Jack Sheppard commenced to do the gracious and gallant towards the waiting-maid.

"Do you know, sweetheart, that you bear a most remarkable resemblance to our sister, the Royal Princess Toe-ragi? She is the most lovely creature to be found in all our far away native country, which is called Gutter-heep-ao."

"Lor' a-mussy me! You don't say no sich thing!" giggled the maiden, blushing like a freshly-boiled lobster—two freshly-boiled lobsters, in fact—one for each cheek. Then the gal placed on a dish, on which was a large ox-tongue, before Jack.

"Thanks, I've enough of my own!" he frankly confessed. "In the land of Gutter-heep-ao the nobility are remarkable for their blueblood and high caste!" the roguish lad went on. "The mothers never give their infants any other food but on occasional suck at a thing exactly like what you term in England a blue-bag, and used for the purpose of giving a nice tint to freshly-watered linen. That's how we get the blue-blooded mobility of Gutter-heep-ao. You observe, my friend here is all blueblood, except in the nose. The blue fluid, you see, got benighted, and lost its way before it reached that point. Further proof of his high caste is to be found in what in your language is termed 'a squint.' Eye-cast, we term it. Pronounced in our tongue, boss-oo optic-muchoo."

"Lawks a mussy, but you never say so? You've got naught but red in my cheeks!" said the maid, much perplexed.

Blueskin now saw his chance. "Do ye see, the Queen Draggle-tail-mi, my friend's royal mother, unfortunately suffered from colour blindness; and, in consequence, by mistake, frequently gave her infant the red ochre bag to suck, with which we of our country red-raddle the brick floors of our habitations with. Consequently, my poor friend possesses in his veins the commonest blood imaginable—a fluid, in fact, that you Britons would scarcely condescend to use in painting a pigsty!"

"Here, you're dabbing it on too thick, Joe!" cried Jack, flinging a bare hambone at Blueskin's head.

"The pigsty will stand it!" lovingly retorted Jolly Nose.

The maid had gone to fill Blueskin's ale-jug for the tenth time, and so missed the latter remarks.

"Jack lad, I've not faced a square meal equal to this since my boyhood days, sometime before the flood! It would be a sin an' a shame an' a-tempting Providence like to leave any o' these good things behind. Pass over to me that suckling pig, poor little fellow! He looks lonesome an' preoccupied like. Evidently got something on his mind!"

"Yes," reflectively answered Jack. "Tell me, Joe," he went on, "why this little porker may be supposed to be sick and an object of pity?"

"I'm no hand at riddles. Past his pigship this way!"

"The answer is because he's a pork retcher—pork creature—poor creature! See now?"

°THE GLUTTONS AND THEIR KNOCK-OUT TUCK IN—THE FOREIGN PRINCES AND THEIR REMARKABLE LINGO—BLUESKIN AND JACK SHEPPARD WRECK THEIR HOST'S BREAKFAST-ROOM—A DESPERATE DASH—INTO THE EMBRACE OF THE ENEMY—ARRESTED!—"FIRE, JOE! DON'T LET ME BE TAKEN! SHOOT!"

For answer Jolly Nose savagely threw a German sausage at Jack's head, which the latter ducked in time to permit the article to continue to sail gaily on its way, and this led through one of the panes of glass in the cottage window.

"Say, Joe, old chum," asked Sheppard, after a pause, "what's wrong with thy voice? Can scarcely hear ye speak."

Joe Blueskin gave a sigh. "The good things I have stowed away, Jack lad. I'm so full that to use my voice is like trying to force a large elephant through a hole in a sieve!"

"So I per-sieve!" cunningly remarked Jack.

Blueskin was now making a sad havoc of the infant porker. The girl had returned with the last relay of ale, and was speechless and like one petrified now that for the first time she saw the terrible slaughter that had overtaken her master's stock of eatables, mostly set out for a make-believe generous display than for wholesale consumption.

Jack Sheppard was teaching a fat and tender young fowl how to do the vanishing trick most beautifully. A wing-bone had gone the wrong way of his throat, just as his eyes caught sight of something through the window.

"Costumphpthnomsay!" he gasped, turning his eyes upon Blueskin.

"What—you—mutsh—how—if—when—of course!" gurgled Jolly Nose, a huge slice of the porker, a cold potato, and a pint of ale fiercely contending for first dive down his windpipe.

At this a crowd streamed into the cottage interior.

"Seize the poachers!" rasped out a rageful voice. "Look at the horrible marauders! Game alive, game cooked—it's all the same to 'em! Lud! Lud! They'll create a famine in the land, and then they'll give us a false golden guinea in payment!"

"Look at the wreck o' me larder, friends! That soft-headed, soppy house wench has put the week's store o' eatables on't table at oust; and them there two gormed gluttons have been an' gorn and devoured ther whole biling lot! They'd create a famine in the land, I tell you, friends, an' then pay fer the mischief done wiv a base spade guinea o' no value!"

The old farmer of the sour visage now shook with excessive rage, like a tree tossed about in a gale. He had been most cruelly robbed of his live stock, and

---

° Part 21. Vol. XIV.—No. 357. 7 September 1900.

now his dead stock had followed suit, until, in fact, all his stock had left him, excepting his stock of ire, and that it appeared likely to remain long enough to choke him, and to thus throw himself as dead stock upon his own hands.

"You confounded old villain!" ejaculated Blueskin, in finely affected indignation. "Get your face straight while it's yet morn, or it will break. He pressed my friend, his Imperial Highness, of the Empire Mudsquash, an' myself, to partake of thine hospitality. You then passed a false guinea upon me, under the plea that you required silver money an' had none in the house. You entreated us to enter here an' eat our fill, saying that your neighbours were all so mean that they would live on the skins of flint-stones, an' if any called here for a meal you wished 'em to be received by an empty larder!"

"What! Do I hear right, or am I the victim o' nightmare?" squealed the old farmer.

"I never wish to shake hands with a more frightful-looking nightmare than thyself!" snapped Blueskin.

The irate old yeoman had discovered the spurious nature of the gold piece given him by the romancing Blueskin. He had then quickly collected a great number of his agricultural neighbour; informed them that the midnight poachers—whose depredations had almost beggared many of them—were then at his house, and induced a crowd to arm themselves, and with himself attempt the capture of the ruffians.

Jolly Nose and Jack Sheppard saw the place surrounded by a great number of smock-flocked yokels, armed with every available kind of article likely to maim or kill. The two friends exchanged glances which spoke volumes.

Blueskin saw that his wits would require their keenest edge if they were to be of any service in the present pickle.

"Neighbours," shrieked the old man, "I trapped them two sneaking, crawling rogues in my barn! A dozen more fowl had gone o' the night! Them there poachers then, bold as brass, ups an' tells me that they be o' Royal blood—princes—o' summut like! I tell thee, friends, them's the game filchers! Ter the lock-up wi' 'em!—ter the lock-up!" The old man was armed with a great reaping-blade, and looked like the twin brother of Old Father Time. "Thee be'st liars, robbers, coining rogues, an' desperate poachers!" added he, eager to excite his followers to the attack.

The two Royal princes, travelling in disguise to observe the manners and customs of the English, commenced to converse in their own tongue.

"Jack-moke-oh," said the big prince, winking the off eye, "the fat's in the fire-vo! But I'll solo to these chawbacons—comi in the devil's own tune—some. Just ye twig—moko!"

"Joe-ass-much," gravely replied the little prince, "we'd better not use—como our spitfires—amo. The barking might—a few bring the pretty Robins—some about our ears—lugo!"

"Did mortal ears ever listen to such infernal gibberish before?" muttered Old Father Time's double, adding: "Varlets, are we to bring every brick an' timber o' my old house about yer ears, or will ye give in an' come quietly to the lock-up?"

"Look here, old skull an' crossbones, keep a civil tongue within thy chops, or we'll make you wish ye was never born!" boldly threatened Jack Sheppard, producing and coolly cocking a fire lock, but which he had no intention of using.

"Born!" contemptuously repeated Blueskin. "That curiosity born? Never! It was won in a sixpenny lottery, an' the winner straightway committed suicide when he found out what he was burdened with!"

The crowd of bucolics backed up their hesitating leader facing the homestead door. They also glared in at the one low, wide window of tiny panes of glass, which contained bosses in their centres, looking like the bottoms of bottles that had thoughtlessly strayed from their proper locations just for the fun of the thing.

"I'll tell thee one thing, knaves," leeringly added the leader of the would-be arresters, "I sent along to the roundhouse for officers to come an' seize two desperate fowl-robbers! Will ye come out?"

The maid had fled by an inner door on the first approach of her master and the crowd following him. Blueskin and Jack Sheppard held possession of the breakfast-room. The table and dressers were filled with dishes, plates, and earthen-ware jugs, and other like articles. Jolly Nose had placed no less than two pairs of huge-looking pistols upon a side-table near him, and beside them his cudgel. The besieged reflected that to attempt retreat by the front of the house would be useless.

"Friend," coolly said Blueskin, "ye are far from sparing in your insults an' threats. You an' your company will deport, an' leave myself an' brother prince a clear path. There is thy base guinea!" The speaker took from his pocket a counterfeit gold piece, and sent it spinning among the outsiders. "We know nothing of your poaching charge," he continued. "As for the meal we have had—like our wretched host—it already disagrees with us. Your ham, sucking-pig, veal, lamb, pigeon-pie an' giblets were all most distinctly off, an' now we're also most distinctly off! So clear the path, boiled face!" Blueskin snapped up a pistol and his cudgel with a fine affectation of great fury.

"Yes, cheerful, wet-Friday afternoon mug, stand aside, an' make way for Royalty!" added Jack, levelling his two loaded firelocks, and attempting a look of most blood-curdling demeanour.

"We'll bring the building down about yer ears if ye don't surrender peaceably!" answered the leading farmer most fiercely, flourishing his awful-looking weapon.

"Very good, my most cheerful, hoary-headed, old fire-eater, that vote's carried unanimously! This choice abode of thine's got to come down!"

A further secret wink was given by Blueskin to his companion. Then the former and Jack Sheppard, with sudden and astonishing activity, snatched up article after article from the well-stocked table and dresser, and in utmost apparent rage hurled them towards the open door. These were so aimed that they all struck the door posts or lintel. In a few seconds of thousands of particles of broken earthenware had flown out into the faces of the astounded yokels, while the floor became heaped up with the jagged fragments.

Three great dishes crashed through the one window of the room, completely wrecking it. The elder of the robbers paused.

"Come, no skulking!" cheerfully sang out he to those outside. "This work must be got through quick!" he continued. "Lend a willing hand. The prince and myself will require another meal and unlimited ale. The task is fatiguing and dry!"

There was a confused parlay now going on outside. The would-be rescuers had retired some yards, and were evidently greatly dismayed.

"This game is getting stale, flat an' unprofitable, Jack!" reflectively remarked Jolly Nose, pausing in the work of destruction.

"The flavour of the police is on the wane, and there'll be no fun at all in it if the red waistcoats visit us!" remarked the boy prison-breaker.

"Let's make a dash for it, lad. The invitation to remain is pressing, I'll own; but with other fish to fry," advised Blueskin.

"Yes; let's stand not upon the order of going, but instantly chivvy!" agreed Sheppard.

No sooner said than done. There pistols were pocketed. Blueskin seized his great cudgel; then, taking the lead, and roaring like a bull as he went, the great, powerful fellow shot out of the door. He disdained striking the old farmer, but dashed full butt against him, sending the astonished and dismayed man flying, a dozen others in his wake scattering like a "floorer" at the game of ninepins.

Sheppard sprang after his comrade. An open-mouthed farm-labourer savagely thrust out a stable-fork. The lad ducked, struck his hapless, bullet-shaped head full in the stomach of the former, and sent him flying backwards, but not before Jack had grasped possession of the iron-pronged weapon.

Blueskin and Sheppard then ran amock amidst cleaving hooks, sythes, bill hooks, choppers, flying spades, stable-forks, and such like crude but deadly weapons. More than once the legs of the flying two were struck at by long circular mowing blades. But for quick eyes and great agility on the part of both, they would have been most desperately maimed. Twice a timely jump saved the lower limbs of Jack Sheppard; the second time the sharp prongs of his fork jabbed into the face of his murderous assailant, and the fellow fell back howling most dismally, his face streaming with blood.

The fugitives refrained from using their pistols, but Blueskin made most telling use of his weighty bludgeon. Each blow he gave struck a head with sickening force. Then the two cleared the fringe of their assaulters. As ill-luck would have it, Jack Sheppard now rushed clean into the extended arms of one of two Bow Street runners. He was instantly secured.

"Fire, Joe! Fire! Don't let me be taken, comrade! Shoot! Shoot!"

The lad was in despair. He saw the gallows looming over him in his mind's eye. His dread of Jonathan Wild was overwhelming.

"What have ye to charge the lad with?" hoarsely demanded Jack's companion, quite spent with his exertions.

"Poaching, on the information of the old man yonder!" was the curt reply.

The loaded firearm of Blueskin moved from one officer to the other.

"I've four barkers on me!" he said, his brows black as thunder. "By heavens, I'll shoot if ye don't release the boy! The charge is a lying one!"

"Draw your shooter, mate. I can't get at mine. Make short shrift of the big fellow!" Thus shouted the officer clinging on to young Sheppard, whose eyes were filled with despair, and cast appealingly towards his friend.

"Short shrift to you!" yelled Blueskin, blasting away at the man's legs; then, quick as thought, drawing another pistol and aiming at the other runner's lower limbs.

The onrushing mob now halted. The bullets were whistling a threatening tune. The two officers threw themselves to the earth, nursing their injured limbs, and shrieking shrilly for aid.

The lad no sooner found himself at liberty then he drew a pistol and fired full at the wavering crowd in the background. This was the signal for an instant stampede on their part.

The cries of the wounded officers were redoubled.

"Leg bail, Jack lad!" shouted Blueskin, catching the glint of more red-coat facings and waistcoats coming from the direction of the Roundhouse of St. John's. Off like the wind sped the two. They were desperately done up, but the fear of capture lent them swift wings.

A solitary wayfarer saw the two fleeting forms approaching. The man sprang into the road and threw out his arms.

"Stand aside an' let your betters pass!" commanded the elder robber, pulling up and panting like a ball.

"You're footpads, that's the ticket! Ye sha'n't pass!" the man replied, with the utmost boldness. Yet he was small and meagre of stature.

"You're a brave little grasshopper! I don't want to harm ye! Stand clear!" warned Blueskin.

But the stranger stood his ground. Then the burly and powerful Blueskin shot forward, and caught the little man under the armpits as his arms was still held wildly apart. The latter felt himself lifted from the earth, carried quickly to the nearest hedgerow, and then lightly thrown over. Unknown to Blueskin, there was a wide and deep ditch on the further side of the hedgerow. The victim splashed into the green-covered, slimy liquid with a great noise, and commenced to laboriously fight his way out. But the fugitives were soon far away.

"Jack," puffed his comrade, when at length the two were beyond fear of pursuit, "I don't think there was too much frolic in our pranks after all!"

"No, indeed; and they came near enough to end seriously, didn't they?" was the answer. "How can I thank you, dear old Joe, for helping me out of my plight?" added Sheppard.

"By doing a similar turn when necessary, Jack lad. Stay, what's this?" The latter had placed his hand to the back of his neck. A tiny stream of blood was trickling down the nape of his neck, and there was a great gash in between his hair; the latter was clammy and matted. The brave Blueskin made very light of his wound, although it pained him exceedingly, and the blood flowed copiously. They were in a deserted, wild locality. The elder robber threw himself down by the road. His companion took off his cravat and bound up the other's head, using his pocket-handkerchief to remove the flown blood.

As for Jack Sheppard himself, he was all aches and bruises, as the result of unlimited kicks and cuffs received in running the great gauntlet of savage and armed men.

But they were delighted to find themselves perfectly free, and able to secure a much-needed rest, and to refill their exhausted lungs.

"I regret much being driven to the extremity of allowing my merry barkers the privilege of impressing their ugly trademarks upon the shanks[83] of those two pretty robins, Jack lad," thoughtfully remarked Blueskin.

"Aha Dame Providence played me a shabby trick in bundling me clean into that runner's clutches. Had it been at my sweetheart, I could not have flown and embraced her more eagerly an' lovingly," said Jack, laughing now until the tears ran down his cheeks. Thus a thing of great evil becomes the matter of jest—when averted—in the estimation of youthhood.

"A pair of addle-pated codfish are we. At our secret stronghold there is food, choice wines, an' the merriest of merry company, yet we must needs—like children—play with double-edged tools to fully enjoy ourselves," thoughtfully observed Blueskin.

"Well, you've got cut for your pains, an' I'm as full of bruises as a careful housewife's cushion is stocked with pins an' needles," replied the lad.

"The tiny earthquake I've got in my thick upper-crust will do me a power o' good, Jack lad—let some of the wildcat blood out of my knowledge works." And to show his utter contempt for the wound the elder robber commenced to softly sing his favourite song. "Jolly Nose," was its title, a term long applied to the singer himself, in consequence of the great size and bright colour of his own facial adornment.

---

[83] Legs.

"A beacon-fire that ever glows,
    Or—object rare—a human rose;
    Is full ripe end of red, red nose—
        Jolly nose! Jolly nose! Jolly nose!

A welcome warm to friend,
The cheery, glowing end
Of goodly red, red bend—
        Jolly nose! Jolly nose! Jolly nose!

An anger-sign of red,
A fearsome object dread,
Or warming-pan to bed—
        Jolly nose! Jolly nose! Jolly nose!

"A goodly ballad that, Joe; an' the poet who wrote it must have dearly loved his tipple," archly remarked Jack Sheppard.

"The greatest of the earth are also the most famous swashbucklers, Jack lad. Look at me, for instance!" Jolly Nose was swollen out with pride.

"Well, I must confess that you have a wonderful talent for emptying full measures—if there's anything in that," agreed the lad.

"Alas! no, Jack lad, there's nothing whatever in an empty measure," deeply sighed the other, adding: "An' that reminds me that I've again got a terrible thirst on me. We've created a famine in the land, according to old death's-head, of the missing game, an' it would be my fault if there comes a drought o' the land if I can but find a hostelry where the milk o' human-kindness flows freely, in response to the invite of King George's profile in silver."

"But to return to your song. I have a suspicion it's of your own composing?" said the lad.

"Your suspicion's justified," replied the other, suddenly commencing to wildly roll his eyes, under the impression that that was the proper thing to do as a poet, as he replied: "I wrote those verses on my own nose."

"Really? I thought I detected an ugly squint in them. A man who writes upon his face-handle can't be expected to see straight enough to correctly scan his verses; and I suppose you composed the music on your head?"

"Ough! W-h-o-o-u-g-h!" squealed Blueskin, putting his hand up to his bandage. "Speaking of my roof, you remind me that the draught's coming in through the hole in the rafters. O-u-g-h! The fellow who marked that base cleft in the musical score of my knowledge-box was but a poor composer, an' if I don't look to it his composing may soon commence to de-compose."

Jack Sheppard and Blueskin were both without hats. The latter robber was bloodstained and pale, in spite of his apparent excellent spirits. Keeping to the by-lanes, and concealing themselves whenever a wayfarer came in view, the two now made their way towards Finchley.

THE MOHAWKS CONFRONTED WITH A STARTLING RESISTANCE—THE BLACK SEDAN-CHAIR—THE MASKED HEAD—A POISON CLOUD—A TERRIBLE PANIC—VANISHED—JONATHAN WILD AND THE SECRETS OF HIS ABODE—A SUPERNATURAL WARNING.

"Rescue! rescue! The startling cry filled the hearts of the three highwaymen with sudden hope. Their position was indeed a desperate one. Jonathan Wild had not been seen since his falling under a Sedan-carriage, but the great gathering of inflamed Mohawks, and their friends of the Mall, were, as one man, coming to the assault. There rapier-blades were out, and flashing like streaks of flying quicksilver. Another moment would have seen the three devoted comrades swept away by the impetus of the onrushing mass, against whose numbers it would be sheer madness to contend.

The sable-coloured Sedan-chair, borne by its black-visaged bearers, was swiftly carried to within a few yards of Dandy Dick, Colonel Blood, and their companion Wiffles, and then set down, as if its attendants were fully bent upon its and their own destruction.

The use of blackamoor serving-men was much in vogue in the days of the Georges, but a perfectly black, funereal-looking palanquin was the thing to excite wonderment and remark.

The onrushing, charging men sent a great white cloud of dust whirling up before them. They were within but ten yards of the outlaws, the Sedan-chair, and its bearers. At this critical moment the head of a man protruded from the black conveyance. The face was completely covered by a full, black mask, and a hand was next seen in the act of repeatedly hurling a number of small circular objects. Startling detonations burst out, then blinding flame followed, and instantly ceased, to be followed by a dense volume of jet-black vapour. This most quickly spread—fan-like—along the whole front of the attackers. The Mohawks and their co-attackers instantly found themselves completely enveloped in a blinding mist, and which was filled with so strange and powerful an odour that the breathing of it was as death itself. The Mohawks were brought to a halt; then all became utmost confusion and panic. Each man looked upon himself as lost, and fell shrieking to the earth, then to madly struggle, fight, or crawl in endeavours to escape the foul pestilence-laden, thick, black, clinging smoke.

When their appalling panic had somewhat abated, as the result of the vapour clearing away, the staggering, half-poisoned crowds found to their utmost astonishment and fury that the sable Sedan, its bearers, and the three intended victims, had all vanished, as if into thin air.

*

A month or so had passed since the last incidents narrated. Jonathan Wild had not made any further important attempt upon the Haunted Manor, or strenuous effort to capture Dandy Dick, or other of his associates. The wily Newgate agent had more than one motive for his seeming to recognise and accept defeat at the hands of the combined outlaw gangs of London and the provinces. Time would lull the felons into a false sense of security, he believed, and also enable him to perfect a great scheme he had in mind for the object of rooting out all law-defying creatures coming within his reach. Could he but succeed in this, his most ambitious plan, there would then remain no bar to his future greatness.

We find the great criminal-hunter in his own study on a certain night in October of the winter in which our chronicles commenced. The watch had just passed, and wailed out his doleful cry: "Twelve o' the clock, an' all's well!" The monotonous repetition of the words could be heard as the crier moved on his way, along Newgate Street towards Ye Chepe, now known as Cheapside.

An attendant stood facing Wild, as villainous-looking a ruffian as his vile master.

"Murdoch, bring Baithman from his prison-cell. Keep your flint-lock presented at the hound's head. Bind him in that chair at the further end of the chamber—the chair with the strap attached thereto—and whatever happens, remember, you are to be ever after blind, deaf, and dumb concerning the name."

"You can trust me, I hope, sir," replied the man, in an injured tone.

"I'll hand ye over to the gallows the day I have reason to doubt ye! Go!"

The thief-taker's voice resembled that of a snarling bulldog. An imperious movement of the hand, holding a pen, accompanied his last word. He then commenced to mutter savage oaths, as his goose-quill scratched over the sheet of paper on the desk before him, snarling vicious anathemas, for a very volcano of fiercest passion ever seethed in the black heart of this most repulsive and depraved of mortals.

Presently the door was thrown open and two men entered. The foremost looked wild-eyed, ghastly, and despairing. A strong rope noose was round his neck; the man Murdoch held its other end, a pistol in his hand, and held close at the back of his captive's head.

The brutal-looking capitor growling he directed his charge to the chair with straps; then, placing his firearm aside, forced Baithman down, and then strapped him securely, by the arms and feet, upon the seat. This process completed, Jonathan Wild impatiently threw his pen down and motioned Murdoch to leave the room.

"Remain on guard outside the door. On no account permit anyone to enter until I give you leave." An emperor dictating to a slave could not have spoken in more haughty disdain and contempt than did Wild when addressing his creatures, most of whom were criminals of the most loathsome type, and could readily be doomed to death by hanging on his but speaking the word.

Murdoch cringingly backed from the chamber, keeping his firearm still in his right hand. Thus armed, he took up his position outside the closed door.

The prisoner was of a superior class to the usual brood surrounding the great thief-taker, and was most evidently in a state of extreme fear and apprehension. Jonathan Wild, when enraged, had the savage habit of grinding his teeth together with a most horrible jarring sound. Contemplating the helpless man before him for some seconds, he now freely indulged in this startling trick. At length he spoke.

"Hugh Baithman," he commenced, in guttural, venom-filled tones, "I shall waste few words on thee. When that renegade Criss Crafton deserted me, and threw in his lot with the outlaws of the Haunted Manor—as I have now every reason to believe he did, on the night I was rebuffed by the proscribed gangs, then secure in their stronghold—what did I for thee? The much-envied post of Jonathan Wild's lieutenant was granted thee, and its many profits. No sooner done than, like the ingrate Crafton, thou didst flout me to my face, and even refused to fulfil my decrees, and—"

"You need to waste even less words than you promised," interrupted the captive. "I faithfully served you until one of your commands shaped itself into that of my murdering a fellow-creature. God knows I am vile enough, but not yet so utterly lost as to stoop to the act of a common assassin!"

"Scum of the earth!" furiously retorted the thief-taker, rising from his seat, the red lust of blood in his wolf-like eyes. "I, who hold in my hand the lives of such vermin as thee, to brook refusal of my mandate! Curse by imbecile fears! Implicit obedience, unquestioning loyalty—these I want, and will have, from my creatures! Agree to these terms, an' I will reinstate thee in office; refuse them, and you well know the penalty!"

Hugh Baithman cast his bloodshot, anguish-filled orbs upon the person of the man towering in pitiless rage before him, then looked helplessly around.

Jonathan Wild was clad in his suit of depressing black, and hatless and wigless. A tigerish grin of conscious triumph convulsed his most repulsive and inhumanely cruel countenance. The chamber in which the two were was of stone, the walls of which were hung with many strange chains and gyves and instruments of torture, occasionally resorted to by Jonathan Wild in his private capacity. The great criminal-hunter's abode was really a portion of grim old Newgate itself, and quite as much a gaol—nay, possessing secret terrors of its own not to be met with anywhere else in all England, but of which more anon.

A pine torch, stuck into an iron staple fixed in the wall, illuminated the dungeon-like chamber. Yellow and red ribbons of glare danced upon the thief-taker and the helpless victim.

"In mercy's name, think well before you act, man! I've a wife an' little children. Would ye make a widow o' the one an' orphans of the helpless bairns?" most piteously pleaded Baithman.

"Bah! You waste words. Implicit, blind obedience to my orders! Do you consent?"

"I cannot stain my soul with blood—the blood of the innocent!"

"Then by all the furies of the lower regions ye shall go to Tyburn Tree! Take thy journey seated upon thy coffin in the cart o' straw, the hangman thy companion!"

"My life would pay forfeit for a theft of but two shillings. The populace should first hear some horrible things I wot of concerning thee, Jonathan Wild!"

The desperate captive had thrown out this hint as a last hope. If he could but inspire the bowelless wretch before him with the fear of public exposure, the monster might relent. So thought the doomed man; but little recked he of the true nature of the worse than savage being in whose complete power he was.

Jonathan Wild gave out a cry, part rage, part surprise, part triumph.

"Blind, babbling idiot!" he hissed. "Hast heard o' the slimy, poison-filled Fleet Ditch? Its teeming millions o' famished rats, that, for want o' food, tear and devour each other? Hugh Baithman, thou hast let loose a word too many! Wilt never more see wife or children! My secret well yawns beneath thee. At its bottom of inky blackness ever madly swirls an' rages and inklike cesspool o' the Fleet torrent, an' that alive with stirring waves of war-waging, black-coated vermin!"

The monster, as he thus shrieked, had seized an iron bar projecting from a shadow-filled nook in the wall, and given it a swift downward plunge.

A terrible cry, pitiful pleading, anguish, despair, accompanied by the harsh and loud-turning sound of rusty cog-wheels. Hugh Baithman, chair, and a great stone slab included, had sank down out of sight, leaving a gaping black void; then the open cavity again closed, with a sound like thunder. And a rising up of a cloud of dust. The stone slab had turned completely over before resuming its former position!

Like an exultant demon stood the wretch Wild, gloating over his terrible deed. Suddenly his attention was arrested by the loud spluttering of the one torch lighting up the place.

"The fools have given me a damp pitch-brand!" thought Wild.

"Past midnight, an' all's well!" came the doleful, muffled-up cry of the watch from without. The flaming brand burned low down, so low that it appeared almost on the point of flickering out. Its flame became of a pale-blue, like the sheen of moonlight. The great awe of a nameless horror suddenly took possession of the man. The dungeon-like chamber became aglow with the mysterious blue gleam.

In the midst of this, shaping itself out of the vapour-like light, appeared a misty figure, the face that of a young and handsome man or youth, with long, curling locks, beautiful vestments, and about its neck a hangman's nose, the rope's end dangling down; and over the breast was a blood-red patch, otherwise all else of the form was of the same ghostly hue as the dim light flooding the place.

A low, hollow, wailing sound, scarcely a voice, issued from the weird spectre:

"How long, O Lord, how long, shall tarry this iniquitous mortal? Hath he not yet reached the furthermost limit of his fell work? Woe! woe! woe! to thee and thine, Jonathan Wild! For ever more accursed be thee and thine! For ever more—for ever more!"

The wailing then died away like the moaning of midnight wintry wind stealing through the branches of leafless trees upon some barren waste. The spectre slowly faded—vanished, its misty finger lingeringly pointing at the being before it.

A frantic, pent-up cry of supernatural horror burst from Jonathan Wild.

The thief-taker had fallen in a dead faintness upon the very spot a few seconds before occupied by the chair and the bound and doomed Hugh Baithman.

The door was now flung open; Murdoch and others dashed into the place.

"Master! master!" Murdoch was yelling while entering the doorway. "Your house is surrounded! An army, formed of fierce outlaws, armed to the teeth, an' all mounted, besiege the place! They are commanded by the notorious Dandy Dick and Colonel Blood. Their yells for vengeance are fearful to hear. They cry 'Death to the black rat Jonathan Wild! Death to the gallows crow!'" Then Murdoch ceased.

His eyes had rested upon the outstretched, motionless form of the thief-taker, as there came booming from without thunder-like groans, welling up from many hearts aflame with a great and implacable hatred!

FURTHER ADVENTURES OF JOLLY NOSE AND THE BOY PRISON-BREAKER—THEIR SARCASTIC AND QUAINT EXCHANGES—THE STRANGE NIGHTINGALE—THE GENIE OF PLENTY—BLUESKIN'S BLUFF—A SLEEP AND ITS RUDE AWAKENING—A CONFLICT OF DEADLY DANGER.

The early morning was bright, frosty, and excessively cold. Joe Blueskin, otherwise Jolly Nose, and his young companion, Jack Sheppard, or more commonly known as the Boy Prison-breaker, were on the outskirts of the Hornsey Woods, some little distance north-east of which stood the picturesque old Sluice House. Suddenly Jack pulled up some yards in front of his friend. The lad cocked his head on one side, and assumed an expression of comic gravity that would have well beffited a thick-headed old judge who wanted badly to impress onlookers with a great sense of his supposed wisdom.

"Prince Mudanslush, is it measles, whooping-cough, or a wisdom-tooth? I'm told either of those delights make the infantine frontispiece straighten itself out, smooth and creaseless, as if newly-starched an' laundry-ironed."

"Jolly Nose, drop the Prince. I've given up Royalty. As a Royal personage I got more kicks an' cuffs than kisses. I'm plain Jack Sheppard in future. No, sir," continued the lad solemnly. "What troubled me was the contemplation of the sadly-battered old hulk—cast high an' dry on the lee shore, as the song says—of what was once the gay an' festive Joe Blueskin. Why, Jolly Nose, if your poor old mother could see you now she would never forgive herself for ever having had a son."

"Oh, in that case we should be even then; for the son has ever forgiven himself for ever having had a mother. I have long felt convinced that if I had never been born I should have got along much better in life, an' made a far better man than I am now," thoughtfully replied Blueskin, tightening up the bloodstained bandage round his wounded head. Perhaps his temples were getting somewhat swollen as the result of the amazingly clever remarks he had uttered.

"But—but——Joe—Joe——" perplexingly commenced Jack.

"Now, don't butter me and Joe me in the singular, Jack lad. I'm a singular Joe, don't you know—and that's rhyme!" Blueskin laughed.

"But how could—" Jack was renewing the attack, but was again driven off.

"Now, Jack lad, little boys should never ask big questions. Upset their digestive organs, you know. Speaking of organs, Jack lad. I'd dearlt like to wet my whistle an' also give those organs a right good go to the tune of, say, 'The Lord Mayor's Banquet.'"

"I could now well take my share of a banquet. The morning's over-raw," remarked the lad.

"Yes, the morning's extremely raw, Jack. Now, if it could be placed upon a grill, over a slow, clear fire, nicely done through, ye know, an' then served up with mushrooms, fried an' buttered, the morning 'ud be a deal more palatable, don't ye think?" Jolly Nose was taking his turn now at the game of poking fun at a friend.

"I'd make a pal-at-table before that prime steak, an' there'd be no mis-steak, if I had a cut at it," put in Jack Sheppard, not to be done in the way of quaint remarks. Then he added: "Speaking of 'The Lord Mayor's Banquet,' here's a wet-bank—bank-wet let's seat ourselves by that—see the joke?"

"Your pun on the word banquet is the reverse of a dry joke," commented the lad's chum, elongating his cheeks. The two then threw themselves down by the roadside. Each laughed, mainly because there was nothing to laugh at.

"Bestrew me, for an honest rogue, but old coffin-chops gave us a goodly meal; but the choice an' merry little diversion he put upon us after made me dry as a red-hot cinder, an' empty as a poor widow's purse. There should be a goodly, thriving inn hereabouts; but, curse my shoe-buckles, it wouldn't be either safe or wise for either of us to enter, hatless and betussled as we now are!" thoughtfully observed Blueskin, gently caressing the linen covering his aching wound.

"No, indeed. We have had a few narrow escapes, Joe Blue-complexion, an', for my part, I'm for halting nowhere until we reach the retreat. It's a stiffish hop, step, an' a jump yet, though," wilfully replied Jack Sheppard.

Blueskin commenced to hum, in a reckless vein:

"For his Lordship, he could write well swill,
        An' right well, too, his Lordship could stuff;
But yet oh never had he his fill,
        Or of goodly wine quite near enough.
        The mayor he stuffed,
                The mayor he swilled,
        Till his cheeks out puffed,
                An' grew purple-gilled."

"Hist! Shut up your feeding-trap, Joe, old 'un. I can hear a voice an' footsteps in the distance." Thus cautioned the lad to his elder comrade. A moment after they had crept through a gap in the hedge-row and were hidden from the view of any wayfarer traversing the main road.

"A songster, too, Jack lad," said Jolly Nose, as the voice came nearer. "Did ever mortal ear listen to such a voice before?" he continued. "A sack, filled with old, rusty files, an' savagely shook up would produce sweetest harmony in comparison."

"I confess," agreed Jack, "that I would much prefer to hear the efforts of a donkey suffering from a very bad cold in his head, a sore throat, and a severe attack of the gripe, attempting to imitate the song of a lark or linnet. A creature with a voice like that would tempt a thunderbolt to come out of its way to bowl him over, or an earthquake to wake up and swallow him."

"I loves me pipe, an' I loves me glarss—.
        Ah, I'm mighty fond o' me beer!
Or lover's walk wi' a pretty larss
Oh, it's my delight o' a shining night,
        O' the season o' the yeear!"

"Jack! Jack!" excitedly whispered Blueskin, cautiously glancing along the roadway, his head through the gap in the hedgebush—"Jack lad, there's corn in Egypt; an', what's more to the purpose, there's malt in England!"

"Lor' now, you don't say so? Did you know that the great Julius Caesar was dead? It's a fact! Teach your grandmother to twirl her thumbs! Malt in England! Well, I shouldn't have thought it now!" Jack Sheppard could be terribly sarcastic, in his own way, when he felt like it, even if others didn't always see its razor-like edge.

The elder footpad had crawled through the bush-opening, and took up a position in the centre of the road. Jack saw his pal take one of his flintlocks from a pocket of his wide-skirted coat, and coolly hide the weapon at his back. His great sides were trembling as a result of inner laughter. A moment more and another object came within the radius of Jack's view. A great, stout, awkward, overgrown, rural-looking youth. He carried in each hand a long, shelf-like arrangement fixed to a pole, and in which were placed a number of earthenware jugs of a row, and with white, crested heads. The broom-handle-like pole acted as a holdfast for the hand. In addition to the filled-up jugs there were plates containing most tempting supplies of bread and cheese, and a number of long pipes and supplies of tobacco.

"So, my rustic nightingale, you've arrived at last. I'faith bestrew me for an honest fool, I had like to have died of parched thirst, my tongue lolling out o' my mouth by the yard, an' fallen dead of hunger for what ye'd have cut short thy sweet tune an' bestirred thee."

"Be thou o' the wool-staplers, o' the building yonder?" sang out the bearer of the horns of plenty, adding: "an', if so be, what might be thy name?"

"Alas! magic genii of peace, plenty, an' pipes an' bacon included, I know not what my name might be. One never knows what the future hath in store for one. I might even in time be known as Joe Blueskin, the highwayman, footpad an' what's not," solemnly replied the cool and humorous robber.

"I've no tiome fer foolin'!" grumbled the man. "I've got breakfasts for they wood-staplers!"

"Good, foaming ale, crusty bread, goodly-flavoured cheese, an' pipes an' bacca—the best an' most fitting early meal for those that toil an' moil an' sweat o' the brow, for the want o' knowing better. Good genii, I await the reward o' my labours," answered Jolly Nose.

"Be thou Luke Jessen, the manager?" asked the porter.

"I be!" answered Blueskin, beaming delightedly at the prospect of the good things to come.

"A full measure o' ale, an' chunk o' bread an' slice o' cheese—them's Luke Jessen's." The speaker placed a mug—its head like a cauliflower—down by the roadside, a large plate of bread and cheese beside it.

Jack Sheppard had stealthily gained the side of his comrade. The possessor of the eatables and drinkables stared confusedly on seeing the latter, but made no comment.

"Next meal, please!" called out Jolly Nose, giving Jack a wink and a nudge.

"'Ther next ale an' bread an' cheese be for Meester Luke Sharp," said the inn-porter.

"For Mister Luke Sharp—correct. Hand over to my friend, mister, and look sharp, too!" cried Jolly Nose.

At this, the man grew suspicious, rightly concluding that persons who make puns are not to be trusted.

"If you two be wool-staplers, where be t'other 'uns?" he asked.

"All gone wool-gathering, my friend of the inquiring mind—all gone wool-gathering, as also, in fact, are we two, only we've found the sheep likely to give the most wool an' we're going to fleece him clean to the skin. 'Baa, baa, baa-lamb, have ye any wool? Oh, yes, mister, mugs an' mugs quite full!' Bestrew me for a right simple rogue, but the heads of your merry mugs grow the finest wool I have ever seen!"

Blueskin by this time had handed a vessel of ale and plate of bread and cheese to his chum. As he spoke, the former had a lump suddenly formed on one cheek, almost as big as one of his fists, but this alarming growth was due only to a cannon-ball of delectable flavour inside the jaw.

°**FURTHER ADVENTURES OF JOLLY NOSE AND THE BOY PRISON-BREAKER—BLUESKIN'S BLUFF—A CONFLICT OF DEADLY DANGER**—(*continued from last week's instalment, procurable at any good newsagent's*).

"L-o-v-e-l-y bre-a-d an' c-h-ee-s-e!" gasped Jack Sheppard, performing the most difficult feat of talking through a compact depth of beer and bread and cheese, his voice having to fight its way up from unknown latitudes.

"Mark Truman comes next, Simon Trout, then Caleb Lamb, and—" went on the custodian, when he was cut short by Blueskin.

"Mark me, that Truman's a false man, an' ye mustn't serve him. As for the next, let him sigh, man, an' content himself with shout. Then, for Caleb Lamb—you mean ad lib. lamb—he's got enough lamb for himself an' all the rest to make a breakfast on, therefore I claim the whole show; an' no heel-tape, mark ye!"

"There be twenty-one wool-staplers, all told. Twenty-one carn't be one, an' one carn't be twenty-an'-one, can it?" ruefully questioned the man from the inn.

Jolly Nose had before this returned his pistol to his pocket. He now produced a golden piece.

"What coin is that?" he asked, holding it up between finger and thumb.

"That be a coin o' the rell-um—a King George spade guinea, that be. I should think as any fooul could see that!" was the sneering reply.

"Well, as one fool can see it, that answers my purpose. There are twenty-one shillings represented by this piece o' metal. One is twenty-one—twenty-one are but one! I'm twenty-one wool-staplers, an' yet but myself. You had in all twenty-one measures of ale; yet the twenty-one were but one—my own jug. I'll claim what remains of it, thank ye!"

Without more ado Jolly Nose coolly walked up to the utterly bewildered fellow and took up one measure after another. He most generously left a very small portion at the bottom of each, which he handed to Jack Sheppard.

The final mugful at length demolished, Jolly Nose gave a long, drawn sigh of great satisfaction.

° Part 22. Vol. XIV.—No. 358. 12 September 1900.

"Twenty-one—more or less—goes into one. That's a feat of arithmetic that is warranted to make anyone attempting to work it out bald-headed in five minutes," concluded Blueskin.

"Who is a-going ter pay fer the twenty-one draughts?" dolefully asked the porter, still perplexedly scratching his head, and looking appealingly from the tall consumer to the little one. But the former was still equal to the occasion.

"As wooden men go, you are not an over-bad specimen," he said, with an amiable smile. He then spun the spade guinea into the air towards the questioner. "That will pay the racket, friend Gosling. Now get thee to thy master. Tell him that the trade of a wool-stapler is extremely dry work; that the wool gets into the throat, clogs it up, and takes no end o' washing down. Bring further relays for your friends the Trueman, the Finny Member, an' the Bleating Lamb. And now adieu! Ta-ta!"

"Well, thee beest a moighty one at thy suctions, thee beest; but thee beest a moighty good and Royal gallant ter settle ther score too. I'll bid thee a foine morning an' a right merry toime, too, meester!"

So saying, the man of the inn gathered up his empty vessels—for the breads and cheeses had gone the way of the ale—and then grinningly departed.

Jolly Nose and Jack Sheppard reseated themselves by the roadside.

When the man had gone from view, Blueskin at once commenced to moralise:

"Good fellow—right-down good honest fellow that, if awfully chuckle-headed! Never lowered such tasty liquid amber in all my life. Very lovely-looking, too, the frothy tops, but infernal frauds; not near a half-pint o' liquor in each measure. Life's much like a mere stoup o' ale—a great show of frothy nothingness; very little real, good, satisfying quality at bottom. Froth! Froth! Froth!"

"Friend Bluegills, that liquor's got into thine head. Strike thy flint an' steel. Light thy pipe, an' let us blow a cloud," advised Jack, assuming the gravity of a frog that had seen much of the world, and calmly filling the bowl of a pipe.

But nothing could turn Blueskin from his philosophical and moral reflections.

"My consciousness smites me right heavily, Jack lad," he recommenced. "I fear me that I gave that a sweet warbler a base guinea—'twere base indeed, if I did. I'm most wayward in my deeds, an' in my reflection gross."

"Well," cuttingly replied Jack "I carn't deny that you're now a gross fellow; but I have offen heard you state that you were once a grocer."

A mighty snore was all the response Jack Sheppard's caustic remark evoked. Overmuch ale and moralising combined had thrown the burly robber into a state of slumber as sudden as it was deep. His head had found for a pillow the twigs of the hedgerow; and the mimic chunders of his nasal breathings were creating a state of utmost panic amidst myriads of flying insects darting from the bush and buzzing over them, most awful Mount Etna mouth and fire-and-death belching nostrils.

How it happened he never knew; but, in spite of the freezing cold and the light of early morning, Jack Sheppard soon grew "top-heavy," and fell into a state resembling that of his comrade. The God of Sleep admits not Father Time to his doorless cavern in the Silent Mountains; in fact, the offspring of Sleep, Morpheus, keeps guard with a thick stick to act as "chucker-out" in the event of the old destroyer and chief enemy of man attempting to get a look in, even in the dreams of the Father of Sleep.

It appeared that but a few moments had passed, when Joe Blueskin was rudely awakened, yet he had reposed for at least an hour. Jack Sheppard was profoundly slumbering by his side. Black shadows fell across the trio. Quick as thought, Jolly Nose had shouted into the ear of the lad; then the former struggled to his feet.

Blueskin's wrists were locked together. A swift glance told him that his companion was also handcuffed. Three waist-coats and ditto coat-facings completed the story the two had been neatly secured as they slept.

"Up, Jack lad!" shouted Jolly Nose. "The sweet, pretty cock-robins have come to take care of the two lost, innocent, little sleeping babes in the wood. Only the kindly, thoughtful robins haven't covered us over with leaves; they've presented us each with gyves. That's rhyme; but the confounded tune's too much like that of the Rogue's March to please me!"

Jack Sheppard sprang to his feet.

"Blaze away, Joe! I'll be shot dead before I'm taken! Curse 'em, I'm fixed!"

For the first time the lad now realised that he and his faithful pal were wearing the Newgate bracelets. A groan of rage and despair was sent from the heart of the ill-fated boy, who knew well that his capture meant certain death.

"Stand behind me, Jack lad. I'll promise ye, boy, that these red wasps won't sting ye!" cheerfully sang out Jolly Nose.

The lightness of the coat-pockets told the two that their firearms had gone. These two-of the runners held presented at their owners' heads. The third man flourished Blueskin's cudgel.

"Robbing on the King's highway, my pretty birds, with blood-red on thy breasts, blood in thy minds, an' in thine hearts too—the blood of hunted men!"

There was merry laughter upon Blueskin's lips, but there was deadly evil in his eyes.

"You're under arrest, fellows. The Crown claims the property of felons," replied one of the Bow Street runners, with a great show of valour.

"What charge, and at whose instigation, pretty robin mine?" smilingly asked Jolly Nose.

"Farmer Grimstun's. Killing an' stealing game; rioting and damage at his homestead," was the gruff reply.

"'Umph! My compliments to complainant, an' when next we meet the Prince o' the Empire o' Mudsplash will do himself the pleasure of putting Farmer Grimstun's face to the grin-stone, or grindstone and try to make it less ugly an' thundercloud-like.'"

Blueskin was talking to gain time. His tongue wagged loosely, but his mind was busy on quite another subject.

Jack Sheppard possessed a thick wrist, and an extremely slender hand, and he had made a profound study of gaol manacles. A few frantically-severe tugs, while hidden by his chum's broad back, and one of the steel circlets was off. Both hands were now free. The officers had placed their own pistols in their coat-pockets; the butts were protruding. The active and light-fingered tricks of the lad Sheppard were a theme of wonder. Before anyone could tell what had taken place, he had snatched a flintlock from the pocket nearest and fired point-blank at the same officer. The bullet tore its way through the lobe of the runner's ear. With a terrific howl the man threw himself to the earth, quite convinced that he was mortally wounded.

Before the smoke from the tube had cleared, Jack Sheppard had pressed the clasp-lock of his friend's wristlets and set him at liberty. The latter instantly became electrical in his movements. A mighty kick in the waistcoat sent an officer toppling earthwards in a doubled-up condition. Blueskin fell upon the man, and a moment after regained his feet, holding in each hand a loaded firearm.

Two ear-splitting explosions followed. The bandage flew off Blueskin's head. He felt convinced he was hit; but the concussion caused by the powder and atmosphere alone was responsible for the shock. Jack Sheppard fared worse. A ball tore open his cheek; a great flow of blood followed; then a deadly faintness seized upon his heart, and the lad fell limp upon the outstretched arm of his companion.

A hoarse yell of triumph went up from the runners, the third of whom had regained his feet. Blueskin felt that he was now most surely confronted by immediate arrest or death.

A DESPERATE ATTACK ON JONATHAN WILD'S HOUSE IN NEWGATE STREET—CHRIS CRAFTEN SELLS HIS LATE MASTER—THE FLEET TORRENT—A STARTLING ENCOUNTER—THE BATTLE ON THE THAMES—DEADLY WORK.

On seeing the prostrate form of the dreaded tyrant and remorseless wretch Jonathan Wild, his creatures were for some moments completely helpless and speechless with amazement and consternation. Their master lay motionless, and face downwards. The ruffian who had led the capture into the thief-taker's presence, and then remained an armed sentinel on the outside of the closed-door, anxiously examined the prison-like chamber of stone.

The blood-curdling shrieks of the doomed prisoner had prepared his fellow-janissary for something very terrible. But the absence of the former was to the latter an appalling mystery. The square edges of the revolving stone trap, with its mildewed surface now uppermost—these signs told a tale. Murdoch concluded that there was a secret chamber beneath the one in which he stood, the victim probably being in the lower space. But was he alive or dead?

Fearing for his own neck, Murdoch resolved to keep his own counsel—at least, until Jonathan Wild proved to be dead. The thief-taker was lifted from the stone flags and placed upon a couch. Bathed with icily-cold water, and brandy forced down his throat, the creature soon revived.

On opening his bloodshot eyes, he threw a swift look of supernatural apprehension round the grim stone chamber. Seeing nothing to excite alarm, Jonathan Wild rose, and uttered a reckless, defiant laugh. The one pine torch burned brightly once again. A mighty effort, and the man of iron will was himself once more. In fear and trembling the creature Murdoch repeated the story he had before told to insensible ears, then stood in silent terror.

"Evil maledictions wither thee!" gasped the astounded Wild. "If this story turn out false, look to thy safety, knave!"

Then the Newgate agent suddenly became dumb: his face grew of a bluish tinge. A mighty uproar came from the streets, as if in confirmation of Murdoch's words:

"Jonathan Wild, the human devil! Out with his hated carcase that we may tear it into shreds!"

These words came distinctly to his ears, followed by the equally appalling, and evidently yelled by many throats:

"Hurray! Hurray! Dandy Dick, the avenger! Out with Wild, the human rat! Out with the devil's imp!"

The chief-officer of Newgate was as if transformed into a raging demon. He flew in all directions, hissing out hot curses, intermingled with instructions for the defence of his place, and the repelling of the rabble, composed mainly of outlaws, but also made up of hundreds of citizens. So odious had the man become, so execrated his person, that thousands of Londoners, not at all in sympathy with the felon class, were constantly clamouring for his dismissal, trial, and condign punishment for his many widely-known, execrable crimes.

Selecting a good number of the most trusted members of his guard, Wild directed them to attend to the defence of his house.

Then he called together more of his retainers, and bade them follow him, he and they previously plentifully providing themselves with arms.

In his own private study, but a few feet from the terrible stone trap through which the black-hearted wretch had hurled his victim Braithman, Jonathan Wild opened a black-painted iron door, previously looked upon by all his people as the outer side of a safe. But the black void disclosed resembled a well, and contained a very steep descent by means of stone steps.

The thief-taker and two of his followers carried flaming links. The stone steps were slime-covered, and extremely dangerous. A fearful odour arose from the impenetrable depth before them, and enormous numbers of great sewer-rats raced squeakingly down the treacherous footway before the descending party.

Jonathan Wild, after proceeding a few steps, turned and addressed his men:

"By this secret stairway we shall reach the Fleet Ditch, the fierce torrent of which takes its course beneath my house on its way direct to the Thames. This means there is practically a river. I have a boat always in readiness, and we must make our way to the Thames, and then to the Tower. The troops there will be at my disposal. We shall kill or capture a grand haul of outlaws. You, my men, may make a fine harvest in your share of the rich rewards offered."

Then the police-agent again led the way. His creatures had made no comment upon his words. "Promises are good things, but performances are better," thought they. And fine promises alone came mostly to their share.

The Fleet Ditch—as its name implied—was a most swift and dangerous torrent, that portion of the Ponder sewers lying very much lower than at any other place. All the surrounding and outlying sewer channels disgorge themselves into this great, wide, and in some parts quite open, flood. Fleet Street takes its name from the Fleet current, a part of which actually exists to this day.[84]

With great caution the party descended the secret, stone-walled, well-like way. When reaching the end the roaring of the madly-tumbling, boiling, black liquid was startling in the extreme.

Wild's men drew back in terror. Their master snarled and leered at their fears. Hanging by the damp, wreaking wall from rusting chains was an old, mildewed boat. There was enormous difficulty in unfastening the chains and then launching the old craft; greater trouble and deadly risk, too, in entering the thing, tossed up and down as it was by the boiling and hissing waters.

A stout rope attached to an iron ring in the wall now held the boat in tow. When the last man had entered, Wild—who had little charge of the line—sang out a caution, and then let the rope go.

Like a stone shot from a sling the skiff flew, madly carried away by the terrific rush of the raging course, boiling up on its way through a tunnel of inky blackness.

"Cling for your lives, men!" suddenly raved out Wild.

---

[84] Fleet Bridge crossed the river at the eastern end of Fleet Street which is now Ludgate Circus. The river is now entirely underground.

The next moment the frail boat would have been dashed to atoms against a sudden outcurve of one of the sewer walls, but that two of the men grasped their oars and stuck them against the jagged, ooze-covered, stone surface. The sculls were snapped off short, with a sound like the firing of a gun; but the boat remained intact, righted itself, and then darted out from an arched way, and some five minutes after into the gloom of the Thames stream.

There was no moon, and a thick, opaque mist hung over the water's surface. It was impossible to see more than two or three feet ahead. But two sculls remained in the boat, and with these two rowers were compelled to struggle against a full tide in their efforts to row eastwards in the direction of the Tower.

"Boat ahoy, there!" Stern, commanding tones echoed through the still night. The plashing of swift, regular oars could then be heard.

"If we are followed none but that thrice-accursed traitor Craften can have betrayed us! Fool that I was to have revealed to him my secret way of reaching the Thames side!" bitterly railed Jonathan Wild, his teeth grating horribly.

"Halt, there! Jonathan, you triple-dyed villain, you're tricked!" rang out the same powerful tones.

"Ten thousand furies! Whoever you are, your blood be upon your own head if ye attempt to stay my course!" hoarsely yelled Wild, throwing the yellow glare of his flambeau well to the stern of his craft.

But he could see nothing; but the hissing sound of a swiftly-following boat-prow, and the regular dip, dip of powerfully-handled oars, warned him of an enemy not to be despised, and swiftly gaining upon him and his crew.

Cautiously Jonathan Wild crept past his rowers, and reached the stern of his skiff; then he levelled two flintlocks direct towards the oncoming sounds, and pulled the triggers. The echoes following the explosions sounded like so many returning shots fired from ever-increasing distances.

A defiant yell responded. The unseen pursuing skiff cut its way still swifter through the boiling surf in the wake of the first boat.

Jonathan Wild spat out strings of curses. He was beside himself with intense spleen. The yellow, spluttering streams of light from the links carried by his men formed excellent guides for the bullets of the pursuing party, while the latter's boat and themselves were completely shrouded by the heavy and impenetrable mist.

To extinguish their lights would be to court almost certain destruction, for any moment might bring them into collision with a bridge-buttress or other serious obstacle, in which case the rotten old tub containing them would break up like the cracking of a nutshell.

Bullets now pattered about them like a hailstorm. Frantic yells sprang from Wild's men whenever hit. Bullies and ruffians generally are mostly wanting in the heroic quality—valiant enough when outnumbering and victorious over weaker foes, but mere infants when the prospect of a beating is facing them.

But, to do the monster Jonathan Wild justice, there was nothing of the coward in his nature. His amazing daring formed the only redeeming trait in his otherwise most depraved and hardened disposition.

Three of the thief-taker's men lay helpless, groaning, cursing, and weltering in their blood at the bottom of the small and frail craft.

With Jonathan Wild's number now reduced to but two beside himself things looked blackly desperate indeed. All but one flambeau had been extinguished. The remaining light, with the daring of madness, Jonathan Wild himself held as he stood erect in the prow of the barque, frantically directing his two remaining rowers as to their course.

He also took possession of all that remained loaded of the firearms. With these he perforce aimed at the grey wall of mist that completely hid his oncoming enemy. Once only a half-stifled cry told him that one bullet had found a billet, but all the rest of his leaden pellets failed in their destructive mission.

"Lads," hoarsely whispered the thief-taker, as a last desperate resource, "we know not whom are those now so close upon us. They may be small in number and turn tail if we properly bark and snap our teeth in their faces. Anyway, they must overtake us in a few moments more, and our only chance is to face about and fight like a cornered rats. Ten golden guineas apiece, boys, for everyone in yonder boat finally put to sleep! Twenty golden guineas, me fine fellows, if their corpses turn out to have the Government brand on them!"*

A fierce yell greeted the promise, which was so casually given as to inspire hope that it would be kept. The rowers shipped their sculls, unsheathed their cutlasses, and eagerly strained their sight to catch a glance of the onward hissing skiff-prow.

Not many seconds had they to wait before the sharp, knife-like snout of the pursuing barque shot into them with a tearing, scrunching sound.

Mingled oaths and yells of blasphemy filled the air.

"Put down thy barkers, Jonathan Wild!" cried the clarion-like tones of Dandy Dick, as he leapt to the former's side and seized him in a grip of steel by the throat. "Drop that pop-gun, you mangy dog!"

The weapon fell to the boat's timbers. The felon-hunter was already half strangled. Reversing the end of the link in his left hand, he desperately attempted to dash its flames into the half-masked face of the young highwayman.

The heavy butt of a great horse-pistol crashed down with sickening force upon Wild's temples. His eyes glazed with blood-red gleam as he saw in the aimer of the blow Criss Craften, his late lieutenant.

"Coward! renegade! I'll yet live to see the hanged!" with extreme difficulty gasped the Newgate agent, his throat slightly loosed, as he and Dandy Dick

---

* Felons. Men branded by the offering of a Government reward.

suddenly swirled the boat to one side, and then the two, with a mighty splash, fell into the sullen-looking, seething river.

"You infernal son of Old Nick! If ye have luck, ye'll yet live ter see yeself drown'd!" a voice was shouting—that of Wiffles—at the moment of the two fiercely-struggling beings shooting over the side. In a fraction of time—frantically contending while locked in each other's powerful embrace—they sank from sight.

"Quick, comrade! Reach forward! Seize Dick! Leave our arch foe to my careful attentions!"

This voice was that of Colonel Blood. He stood erect in the dangerously tossing skiff, a scull grasped in both hands and poised aloft.

In the vengeful flashings of the colonel's eyes could be read a short sentence of death for Jonathan Wild.

THE DEATH-STRUGGLE OF THE DEADLY FOES BENEATH THE THAMES SURFACE—THE HIGHWAYMAN'S TERRIBLE ERROR—DANDY DICK IN DIRE PERIL—WHAT THE OUTLAWS SAW BEYOND THE NIGHT MIST—THE WATCHMAN.

Jonathan Wild's conjecture proved correct. Criss Craften, his late lieutenant, had revealed to Dandy Dick and the latter's comrades Wild's method of secretly leaving his house in Newgate Street and reaching the Thames' side.

Colonel Blood, Dick Turpin, Tom King, Wiffles, and Criss Craften were selected by Dandy Dick to accompany him on the risky mission of reaching and taking guard of the outlet of the great sewer-tunnel.

Jack Rann, Sixteenstring Jack, and many others, whom Dandy Dick was assured he could well trust, were instructed to direct operations in the attack upon the chief Newgate official's house until Dandy Dick could rejoin them.

The capture and holding of Jonathan wild's body as hostage was the chief intention of the outlaws in their last amazingly daring scheme. The actual death of the execrated felon-hunter might even follow his seizure, this point not yet being finally determined on by the outlaw leaders.

Our last chapter terminated at the critical moment of Dandy Dick and his most bitter enemy, Jonathan Wild, falling into the River Thames.

Colonel Blood sprang to his feet—one foot planted upon the bottom of the skiff, the other upon the boat's gunwale—and held a scull poised above his head ready to batter with his utmost force the head of the common enemy when it should appear above the bleak, heaving bosom of the Thames stream.

The head did not appear. Neither could any sign be detected of their beloved comrade, Dandy Dick. Fateful moments passed. The eager, breathless watches grew sick with suspense.

Craften lent over the boat's lee side, casting the bright yellow, dancing patches of light from his pine-torch wildly over the inky waves.

Dick Turpin had received a bullet-wound in his right arm, which was now bound up. In his left he held a link; and he also vainly peered over the port side of the boat for any sign of the missing outlaw.

It should be remembered that the outlaws had carried no lights, but were guided on the course by the flambeau held by Wild when erect in the foremost barque.

On the instant of the two fiercely-struggling men falling over the foremost boat's side, Wild's torch was extinguished. The firearms then instantly exploded, bullets singing out their death-mission close by the heads of the outlaws in the rear boat.

No time was lost by those in the rear boat in igniting a particle of tinder by sparks struck by contact of flint and steel, and then setting one of the dry tortures brought with them ablaze.

The sound of the thief-taker's boat being swiftly impelled through the stream and thick veil of grey mist caught the ears of those in the other craft, and their light proved the fact of the former crew's escape, the two shots and a yell—half laughter, half anathema—coming from the wall of vapour now concealing them.

Wiffles despairingly glared in all directions. His face became haggard and ghastly-looking in the deep gloom and with its contrasting outline of flickering yellow from the torch-gleam.

"Dick! Dick!" he shrieked.

There came no response. The impulsive nature of the young outlaw could brook no further suspense. Off came his jack-boots, then his outer coat, hat, and cutlass-belt.

Before his companions could utter a word of protest—even if they had so desired—the impetuous and loyal-hearted fellow had sprung up and then taken a header.

"Our skiff is drifting away with the current! Take each an oar, friends. We must remain stationary, if possible," sang out the colonel to his comrades.

"Ay, ay!" responded Dick Turpin, bravely grasping a timber with the hand of his one uninjured arm.

Tom King followed his example, Colonel Blood and Craften carefully bending over the boat sides—lee and portwards—silently praying that the black convulsions of the Thames' bosom would cast up their immersed comrades.

Presently a round, black form dotted a lighter dip between two black waves. The object was agitated by the efforts of a desperate struggle, and inarticulate cries came from its vicinity. A few vigorous strokes of the oars brought the boat alongside.

The blue-white, chilled face and dripping-wet head were instantly recognised.

Wiffles it was, and evidently fighting like a very fury—a something clinging to him with a clutch as of death itself!

Tom King moved his oar, and it was instantly seized. Wiffles was evidently far too exhausted for words, but he madly clutched at something under the water. In a trice he was pulled aboard, the clinging object with him.

For some moments the rescued outlaw spluttered vainly. At length words shaped themselves.

"I vas as near as no matter a givin' up ther ghost!" he feebly gasped. "An' Dick 'e stuck ter me under water like werry fust-clarss glue, or a young bride to 'er 'usband ther fust 'our o' their vedding!"

A sudden indescribable roar burst from the colonel, Turpin, King, and Craften.

Their fury and disgust almost choked them. Dandy Dick was still in the river's depths. Jonathan Wild's wretched life had by mistake been saved by Wiffles!

The roar was repeated. The colonel and Craften together seized the body of the half-unconscious police-agent with the intention of hurling it back into the waves.

"Stay!" shouted Turpin, his eyes of flame. "The river may take pity upon him. If Dandy Dick is lost to us, by all that's sacred, I'll drain that monster's remains of every drop of his foul, black life-fluid!"

The mistake was scarce discovered before Wiffles, exhausted as he was, had re-entered the river.

°THE DEATH-STRUGGLE IN THE THAMES—DANDY DICK IN DIRE PERIL—THE WATCHMAN—(*Continued from last number; still on sale*).

Disdainfully the bearers threw the apparently insensible body to the boat's bottom. Without pausing to lighten his form of a single article, the colonel leapt into the depths.

Tom King then sprang over the skiff's further side, Craften at the same moment madly clinging to the wounded Turpin to prevent him following.

The boat swirled, rocked, and keeled like a cockleshell as the result of the quick movements of those plunging from her.

Craften presently prevailed upon Turpin to ply an oar with him; one hand each, the former still throwing the link's rays out upon the troubled waters in the hope of catching a sign of Dandy Dick's floating body.

A shout penetrated the thick, dark-grey vapour-cloud. Turpin and Craften cast glances in the direction of the sound.

The shout came again. The opaque cloud completely surrounded the little skiff, and shut out everything from view; but there could be no mistaking that call.

° Part 23. Vol. XIV.—No. 359. 28 September 1900.

It was the latest secret signal of the outlaws. Most lustily Turpin and Craften took up the cry. The colonel, Wiffles, and Tom King—all expert swimmers— had dived, re-dived, and struck out in all directions, but still with no result.

The endless echoes of the signal word sounding in their ears, hope flamed anew, and all swam back to their craft, the link held by Craften acting as their beacon.

The colonel was speechless and rage-consumed with his vain efforts. He was drawn into the boat. Then came Wiffles, utterly exhausted and despairing. Tom King followed, Turpin and Craften tried to buoy up the others with stronger hope. The secret signal cry must have come from their missing friend, they insisted.

The little boat was now crowded. The apparently insensible form of Jonathan Wild had remained huddled up in a pool of water on the boat's timbers.

In an impulse of ungovernable spleen, Colonel Blood gave a most savage kick at the ribs of the prone man.

Jonathan Wild must have assumed an aspect of insensibility, for he no sooner felt the impress of the colonel's boot than he sprang up direct.

Wild was instantly seized by the colonel, whose glances became most deadly-looking.

"You villain! We have you now! The hour of reckoning is come!" muttered he.

His horrible habit of grating his teeth was all the answer Wild made. He concentrated his utmost powers into one supreme effort for self-preservation.

The ruffian well realised that a most critical moment of his life had now arrived. His utmost nerve, courage, and dash were all needed in this supreme emergency.

Without the slightest warning the boat rocked leeward, then swiftly capsized. Jonathan Wild by superhuman strength had given a sudden jerk, clinging to Colonel Blood, and carrying the highwayman with him into the stream.

The overturned skiff continued to float. The colonel felt himself swiftly drawn downward, as if by a great stone. He instantly descried Wild's intention. The latter had seized him by the throat, and was driving his utmost to suffocate him, or cause him to open his mouth that the water might effect the same object.

But the colonel was a man of enormous physical powers, as well as most expert swimmer and diver. His clenched fists pounded into the other's face with such crashing effect that Colonel Blood quickly released himself of his burden and regained the surface of the river.

By great good-fortune—or luck—Craften had glided into the Thames as the boat upturned without extinguishing the brand he held. This was indeed fortunate. Each comrade counted his companions. All were clinging to the floating boat. By one accord they determined by might and main to reach the spot from whence the shouts still came.

No second thought could be given to the great enemy. Dandy Dick's safety or death was the one case now fully engaging their minds and efforts.

The boat was soon righted. Tom King and Wiffles had each seized a floating scull; then the five scrambled into the skiff and pulled away.

Jonathan Wild had vanished. A few lusty strokes through the thick mist; then the portion of a bridge-arch could be dimly made out. The outlaws were facing old London Bridge.

Leisurely seated upon a projecting stone step-like portion of a buttress was the form of a man. The flickering light of the blazing torch revealed the well-known and deeply-loved features and figure of the missing Dandy Dick.

Such shouts of unbounded delight sprang from five lusty throats that old Father Thames must have started from his couch of weeds and asked if the immediate world had gone crazy with joy. The loudly-ringing echoes raced each other until quite lost in the gloom-enveloped distance.

"What of Jonathan Wild?" was one of the first questions put to his comrades by the soaked and shivering Dandy Dick.

"What of thyself?" replied Colonel Blood, fumbling in his garments for a flask, usually carried with him, but now somewhere—floating or otherwise—in the river.

"That grandfather of Satan did his utmost to keep me below the river's surface even at the risk of his own life," explained Dandy Dick. "I think," he added, "that I shall never live to get the taste of this awful Thames soup out of my mouth."

Wiffles was crying and laughing together. His delight at seeing his idol of all that was brave, handsome, and manly was unbounded.

"Soup, it is!" he remarked, in reply to Dick's last words.

"Ve ain't any ov us missed 'aving our fill on it, niver," he continued. "Oh, it's a real turtle too, it is, an' werry nice an' filling—as ther turkey remarked, casual-like, when a-undergoin' ther operation o' stuffin' fer Christmas."

"How did you contrive to shake off Jonathan Wild, Dick?" asked Turpin.

"Ah, ah! a devilfish could have taken a lesson from the old fiend, for no cuttlefish tentacles ever stuck faster than did his claws cling to my windpipe; but I banged at his ribs so unmercifully that he quickly fell away from me. Then I reached the surface of the stream. As I did so, a skiff grazed past my shoulder. I instantly seized it. Seeing that it was Wild's boat, I let go on finding myself within a few yards of this spot of safety. The rowers were in too great a state of panic to notice me, or become sensible to the weight temporarily hanging to the stern of their barque," was Dandy Dick's reply.

All were overjoyed at the providential escape of their hero. Turpin would hear no mention of his wound, and cursed soundly that not one of them had a drop of spirits to drive the cold from their frozen bodies, and especially that of Dandy Dick's.

It was mutually decided not to seek further for Jonathan Wild at the present juncture of affairs, but to endeavour to land by old London Bridge, and then, without further delay, proceed to Newgate Street and their friends there gathered.

The arch supports of the famous old bridge enabled the outlaws to guide their boat to a landing-placed eastwards of the river.

The party on landing paid no further heed to their little vessel than to let it drift away with the tide. To reach Newgate Street was but a walk of ten minutes.

The dark-grey mist had deepened. The cold increased. Every one of the group was hatless. Tom King and Wiffles were also without their coats and boots. The night was silent and deserted.

At this spot a few houses were scattered about, but became more closely packed the nearer was approached Ye Cheape and Newgate Street.

The six comrades boldly strode forward, walking into a void resembling dirty wool. They were in a sorry plight, and three-parts dead with chill, but not one of them would admit the same; and all lightly jested, like schoolboys bent on a frolicsome errand.

Presently a vague yellow glow pierced the grey void before them; then the great, stout form of a watchman gradually came into view.

"What oh, there! Whence come thee, fellows?" the man gruffly demanded, viewing the shivering and bedraggled band with great suspicion.

Colonel Blood strode to the front. He looked perhaps a trifle less woebegone and mud stained than the others.

"Friend watch, ye see before ye a party of unfortunate gallants who have been upset by Thames pirates out upon the river. We were upset, too, and all but drowned, like so many puppies, so badly marked as not to be worthy to live. What think ye, friend o' the watch?"

"Marry, sirs!" pompously replied the old fellow. "'Tis a most foul night on which to be beset by the Thames pirates—not that 'tis fair to be beset e'n on a fair night. That ye have been near drown'd 'twould take less than a witch to tell; an' that ye are so many puppies, so badly marked as not to be worthy to live, that of a surety is not for me to deny."

The affectation of gravity and wisdom with which these words were delivered, and the quaint satire conveyed in them, caused the hearers to break out into a most uproarious shout of laughter, the colonel enjoying the thing hugely.

He continued:

"Come," cried he, "sage father o' the mist, I acknowledge thy wit. Now to put it to further test. 'Tis said that in all fair London town one would seek in vain for a watchman who cared for the flavour of punch of a goodly brew. Is that true?"

"I'faith, good gallant, the Prince of all Evil ne'er uttered a greater lie—unless he ever predicted that so fine a gentleman as thyself could ever find it in thine heart to refuse a drain o' punch to a poor old fellow like me, if he had the chance of so doing. That would be even a still greater lie!"

"Ha, ha!" The colonel laughed most heartily at this pert sally.[85] "By mine honesty, old man," he replied, "then should'st have thy fill, for the river thieves have left me one gold piece, if the goodly nectar could but be obtained."

"That such a generous intent should be foiled by a mere sleepy-headed host an' a bolted hostelry, I hereby, in the King's name, call upon ye all as good, loyal citizens to at once help me open the way for the melting of that same gold piece into its equivalent in punch!"

JOE BLUESKIN PLAYS A PRETTY GAME OF BLUFF WITH THE BOW STREET OFFICERS—GOLDEN BALM AND GOLDEN PILLS—JACK SHEPPARD PROVES HIMSELF AN ACTOR—THE OUTLAW SPY—BRIBED POLICE OFFICERS—HOODWINKED.

We left Blueskin and Jack Sheppard in the barren wilderness north of London and near Finchley, with no dwelling or wayfarer likely to be met with for miles.

"Stand off! Hold your hands, cowards! Would ye fire upon a defenceless lad?"

Blueskin's mind was almost filled with despair. He would not have much feared even a single-handed contest with three Bow Street runners in the ordinary way; but he was badly hurt in the head, and the fracture was now making itself felt in consequence of more or less exposure to the extreme cold of a winter's morning.

His trusty cudgel was lying in the road beyond his reach, his pistol discharged, and one arm encumbered by the senseless and limp form of Jack Sheppard.

The steel bracelets—sometimes presented by Dame Justice to her most especial pets—had been forced by the boy prison-breaker from his wrists, as the results of long and patient experiments when incarcerated in "The Old Stone Jug," or Newgate Gaol.

Jack Sheppard had also acquired a trick of snapping—by a peculiar twist—the locks of steel gyves this he did when they could not more readily be removed.

Those placed upon the wrists of Blueskin were of so crude a make that the lad had no difficulty in removing them, as previously described.

"You half busted me with your ball-like kick, an' that little spitfire wretch—your companion—would have thought no more of snuffing-out either of us than he would of swallowing an oyster!" savagely expostulated one of the officers.

"You'd better give the game up an' surrender quietly, or I shall be compelled to try the logic o' powder an' shot," threatened another, clicking his levelled pistol's trigger.

"Pray keep those triggers from numbing your delicate fingers, my fine bully-boys. The grandest logic in all the world is that of the yellow colour, my friends. It's never been known to fail when piled up high an' broad enough.

"Do you think now that the persuasive powers of five guineas apiece might have weight enough with ye, my noble an' o'er bold cock-Robin, to cause ye to

---

[85] Witty saying.

put aside for good those miniature field cannons?" softly argued Jolly Nose.

The Bow Street officers of old were—like the police of to-day—not paid quite princely stipends.

The three latter lowered their firearms, and glanced meaningly into each other's faces. Then, indulged in a long series of most extraordinary winks.

"Ten pieces each might have more weight," one of them ventured to observe.

"Exactly double in the scale!" explained Blueskin briefly.

"You knocked all the wind out o' me; an' I'm sore as a worm what's been trod on twice in the same place," protested the sufferer from a kick from one of Blueskin's boots, which was about equal to two kicks from a hind leg of an ordinary horse.

"My golden salve, well rubbed in," Jolly Nose went on, "would bring a dead miser back to life again. If your stomach don't quickly mend, then add a few pills to the ointment. The golden salve an' pills are exactly like spade-guineas— can't tell one from the other, in fact. And if you carry a few about in your pockets with you, there are potent enough to ward off the worst evils of all life's calamities—such as sheriffs' writs, bailiffs' documents, and one's poor relations!"

"Make the physic up to fifteen doses each," finally suggested the damaged officer; "then we might shut our eyes an' keep 'em closed for, say, ten minutes. Who knows? Before we open'd 'em again you might have slipped off with your pals! More wonderful things have happened before to-day."

"Redbreasts, our poor lives are not worth the sum you ask," touchingly replied the burly robber. "I'll purchase our joint freedom for thirty-five guineas."

This sum was finally agreed upon as the amount of the bribe for which the two fugitives were allowed to go free.

Under the assumption of perfect calmness Joe Blueskin smarted with a keen sense of injustice. The officers did not know either of the outlaws, but simply acted upon information that was not based upon fact.

The first thing, now, insisted on by the elder was that the younger prisoner should be restored to his senses. One of the officers readily brought from a pocket a flask of spirits. With a few drops of this Jack Sheppard was soon revived. Then his wounded cheek with carefully bandaged up, the police agents supplying 'kerchiefs for the purpose.

Joe Blueskin then amazed the officers by producing a glittering heap of gold pieces. The exact number of guineas were counted into the eagerly-extended palm of each man.

Blueskin still retained an ample store of the sparkling coins. Jack Sheppard, immediately on coming round, displayed the utmost disdain for his wound, and carefully noted every detail of the proceedings.

"How do you feel, Tim Hodge?" asked Jolly Nose of Jack Sheppard, thinking it wise to fit his friend with a new name to suit the present company.

"Luke Sprouts," replied Jack, continuing the rechristening, "I'm mountains better after that taste of reviver! Still, the desert of my tongue continues somewhat parched up."

"Tim," solemnly added Jolly Nose, "it's a grand thing for your friend Sprouts that he is such a small drinker, for he is now got a thirst raging within his anatomy factory that would, even in wintertime, knock down a regular tippler with an attack of sunstroke!"

"Sprouts, you are the most abstemious insect I ever met with in all the world, excepting every other living thing!" most gravely retorted the lad prison-breaker, his love of repartee getting the better of the pain of his wound.

"Gentlemen," remarked the officer who had received Blueskin's complimentary kick, but was now quite restored by the magic golden balm, "I must really admit that ye two of the most courteous, amiable, an' generous gallants it has ever been my happy fortune to have met with. The charge of stealing game, an' committing riot, damage, and murderous assaults, an' for which we sought to arrest you both, must be one of the most wicked fabrications ever heard tell of! I'm convinced of it!"

"The knave that made that charge deserves shooting!" indignantly remarked a second officer, carefully examining and counting his coins in fear of cheating.

"Shooting would be too good for him! A hangin', drawin', an' quarterin' in Smithfield, I say—an' I say it in all charity—would be but a mild punishment for the monster!" added the third Bow Street agent, while trying one of the spade guineas between his teeth, for the passing of base coins was of alarmingly extensive practice in the days of which we write.

"Bully boys, it's very good of ye to credit us—since ye've been regarding us through golden spectacles—with possessing so much virtue. But the best of virtues are somewhat dry. Have ye either one of you a small distillery or two in your pockets?" dolefully pleaded Jolly Nose.

"We possess all the virtues under the sun, an' a good many more besides. And we are so angelic that we feel it's only right that we live chiefly on suction.[86] Does anyone of ye so much carry a pint or two of rum about ye?" quite innocently remarked Jack Sheppard.

"Most worthy gallants, I think you can be somewhat obliged!" cheerily replied the kicked runner, producing a very small horn flask, with a brass stopper, from a breast-pocket. "There may not be quite enough spirit in this to create a second deluge perhaps, but," he added, "there's more than enough to whet both your whistles, if they're not too large."

Joe Blueskin eagerly snatched the vessel, unscrewed the top, and then took a long an' hearty sniff[87] at the flask's interior.

---

[86] Heavy drinking.
[87] Drink, take a draught.

"Hold!" cried the owner, in great alarm. "If ye smell like that, man, ye'll dry up the whole. I don't like to be done in generosity," he went on. "You, sir gallant, have acted like a prince, an' so will I. There's enough brandy in the bottom o' that flask for at least three smells, and then, maybe, enough'll remain ter moistened the tip o' one tongue. There's no in hereabouts for a quarter of a mile, yet I'll let ye take, for a mere paltry crownpiece, the whole of that glorious liquor!"

"I once heard tell of the highwayman who robbed a gallant on the King's highway of all he possessed, including a locked-up basket. When he opened this basket it was found to be filled with nothing else but venomous reptiles. The robber had no market for them. The address of the owner was on the basket. That road-gallant immediately repented him of his iniquity—limited to the stealing of the poisonous things—an' sent a messenger to the reptile collector, offering to return them if the owner would hand the message-bearer four times the value of the deadly creepers. Ah, but you are even more disinterested than that robber!" Having thus delivered himself, Jolly Nose searched for, and found a five-shilling piece, and gave it in exchange for the spirit, which he instantly handed to his companion.

Jack Sheppard affected to drink heartily, but the flask was quite empty! Then Sheppard's comrade made believe to take a deep pool at the supposed liquor, noisily smacked his lips, and then returned the vessel with profuse thanks.

The officers had each by this most firmly concluded that their burly victim was both an escaped lunatic, and a walking mint or gold-mine. They were each secretly thinking how the mint or gold mine could be made even more productive. The distant sounds of a heavy, lumbering vehicle now came to the ears of the party. Meaning looks was instantly exchanged between the two robbers. The lad appeared to be again taken with a faintness.

"Friends, if a chance of a lift on the journey offers itself for my companion, he must take it. The boy's state is worse!" cried the elder outlaw in well-assumed alarm.

"We are all poor men, each with a large wife an' family—I should say, a wife an' large family. We're unable to refuse your gold, an' a bargain's a bargain," replied one of the officers.

The other two made a great show of agreeing with the first, but Jolly Nose could very plainly see that the fellows were loth to let him go without his subscribing still further donations towards the fund for blind officers of the peace.

The noisily-jotting wheels were those of an old cart. The sleepy-looking horse came slowly along. A solitary driver nodded, as if in a doze, on his seat in the vehicle. The man was dressed as a usual smock-flocked rustic, and looked about as full of life as a stone statue.

"Hi! Going to Barnet, friend?" sang out Blueskin.

"That be Oi," lazily replied the yokel, eyeing in very great wonder the bound-up, hatless heads and generally dilapidated condition of the outlaws and the seemingly serious state of the lad.

"Take my friend to the old Inn at Barnet, an' the host will well repay thee. He is a firm friend of this lad, and the boy has met with a nasty mishap."

After scratching his head hesitatingly for a few moments, the driver finally gave utterance to a grunt, which might have meant anything in the world but a word in the English language, and then rose from his seat, and helped Jolly Nose to place Jack Sheppard in the straw littering the bottom of the old cart.

Joe Blueskin had at once recognised a closely-disguised spy from the Haunted Manor stronghold. On the former mounting into the vehicle, the following very low-toned and rapid conversation took place:

Blueskin (to driver): "Glad we fell in with you, comrades. Got any nice fire-spitters with you?"

Driver (to Blueskin): "Four as pretty tubes as ever coughed out fire, lead, an' smoke. I'll place 'em here in the straw. Your friends in the road don't look quite the right sort for a nice, cosy tea-party, Joe, old crony."

Jack Sheppard (to driver): "The pretty robins have given me a toothache on the wrong side o' me cheek. Old blue gizzard's bribed 'em with untold gold; but still, I think, the sweet, pretty redbreasts mean to have a playful peck at us, just as a parting joke, like."

Blueskin (to driver): "Do you think, old pal, that you could make that ancient article you imagine to be a horse attempt a gallop?"

Driver: "I wouldn't care to back him to cover a mile in less than a week, unless he knew for dead sure there was a good bust-up feed awaiting him on ending the race. Then he might possibly get over the mile in as short a time as six days an' a harf!" was the reply.

This exchange of words took but the briefest time.

Jolly Nose, after making comfortable the make-believe almost-fainting lad, leapt from the cart.

"So you've been staying at Barnet, stranger," said one of the police-offices, with newly-added suspicion.

Blueskin nodded his head.

"Only briefly," said he.

"Do you know that hereabouts is a swarm of robbers in hiding—thick as ants in an ant-nest?"

"Should I travel in open day with plenty of gold, if I knew that?" said Blueskin, putting a question for an answer.

"Well," continued the same Bow Street official, "we are really on the watch for stray members of the robber-gangs; and as we are now compelled to regard your companion and yourself with greater suspicion, we must demand at least another guinea each, or we can't allow you to go."

"Ha, ha, ha! Well, that's really too funny!" laughingly replied Jolly Nose, his great sides shaking with extreme merriment. "You'll see the point, an' almost die o' laughing yourselves, when I tell ye I've almost altered my mind—gone back on my word, the same as have ye most honourable gentleman—he, he, he! Ho, ho, ho!—an' mean to have all my rightly-shining, musically-thinking bullion-nieces returned!"

°JACK SHEPPARD PROVES HIMSELF AN ACTOR—THE OUTLAW SPY—BRIBED POLICE OFFICERS—HOODWINKED. (*continued from last number—359—still on sale*).

At the last word uttered by Jolly Nose, the Bow Street runners burst into varying expressions of bitterest rage. Unfortunately for them, their pistols were all unprimed. They fiercely drew their cutlasses. Yells of derision from three throats responded to the clatterings of the officers' steels. The runners saw the simple-looking rustic driver in the cart coolly smiling, and with one eye glancing along the beautifully-polished steel tube of a firearm that unmistakably had a level beeline for one of their heads. The grinning, daredevil face of Jack Sheppard could be seen over the cart-end with tube number two resting on the closed-up tailboard to the right of his head. The great stranger—hatless, bandage-headed, and grinning like a baboon as he stood in the roadway—had two levelled flintlocks. Where this array of firearms had suddenly sprung from, those threatened had no time to imagine.

"Out with those goodly King George's medallions! Quick's the word!"

There was a note in the great Blueskin's ringing tones and a gleam in his eyes which reminded his hearers of sudden deaths, "croner's 'quests'," and other most woeful things.

In a second the heaps of coins were disgorged.

"Hand 'em up to the cashier, pro tem.," added Jolly Nose.

One of the officers timidly approached the cart, and let the coins fall over the tail board. The three runners had emptied their pockets, and handed over the money to the one conveying it to the vehicle.

"Aha!" suddenly gasped one of the police-agents, in extremely dismal tones. "I have parted with my own money! Zounds! There was six silver shillings an' eight copper pence!"

"Pray don't apologise. I take no offence!" replied Jolly Nose, with a most roguish leer. "Indeed," he added, "I shall claim the sum as legal fee for the most excellent advice I am now to favour you with, the said advice being that you hereby,

---

° Part 24. Vol. XIV—No. 360. 28 September 1900.

forthwith, without prejudice or malice aforethought, instantly resort to legbail, which, translated into pure Saxons, means that you mount Shanks's pony,[88] otherwise skip it on your marrow-bones, or gamble ahead on your indispensable pins!"

The officers were completely checkmated. They glanced round them in every direction. In that wilderness no habitation could be found, and the chance of meeting any but those of the outlaw class was remote indeed.

Blueskin's tones again rang out.

"I'll count ten!" he cried. "If the last pair o' heels hasn't turned the bend in the road beyond ye, the owner of the same will quickly find himself the unwilling possessor of a leaden ball! Scoot!"

Knowing that to trust to their cutlasses would be more than useless, the runners made good their claim to the title by instantly bolting for dear life.

"One! two! three!" and finally "ten!"

The fatal number was no sooner called than its echoes were silenced by the mingled explosions of firearms. The weapons had been purposely aimed well skywards; but the stampeding officers, with loud shouts, frantically threw themselves to the earth.

The outlaws set up a deafening yelling, in imitation of most terrible anger, and effected to be hurriedly re-priming their shooters.

Each officer, finding that he still lived, and concluding that to rise erect meant deadly risk, swiftly crawled past the turn in the road until out of range and sight. Then each of them could be heard fleeing away at topmost speed.

Jolly Nose joined his friends in the cart. His companions were now carefully collecting the coins from the straw into which they had fallen. The driver looked not a little excited.

"Joe Blueskin, you are a masterpiece!" he cried, in great admiration. "You've honoured King George's mint with a visit, ho, ho!"

"Not so, comrade," replied the robber addressed. "These coins," he added, "were minted at a secret counterfeiting crib in the Rookery o' St. Giles.[89] They're quite as good as the real Simon Pure[90] guineas, in every respect except one—they're short in weight. They ring beautifully, will stand the teeth an' every other test, except the scales—an' they're dirt cheap!"

"I carn't agree with you there, friend blue gills," put in Jack Sheppard. "The poor wretch detected—if having a quantity in his possessions—would find them dear enough; for then there'd cost him his life."

---

[88] To travel on foot.

[89] St Giles, Patron Saint of lepers, but also considered Patron of outcasts and vagabonds. Hence, the Rookery was a place of crime and destitution as depicted in Hogarth's image "Gin Lane" and features later in this story. Now the location of New Oxford Street.

[90] Authentic, untainted. Dervived from the play *A Bold Stroke for a Wife* (1718) by Susannah Centlivre where one character is impersonated by another.

"That's true as this clear daylight, Jack lad. I cheerfully accept the correction," admitted Jolly Nose. "An' for that reason," he continued, "I never intended letting the pretty redbreasts go off with the imitation coins without first letting them know that they were in possession of most rare introductions to the hangman an' his hempen comforter."

The outlaw spy now directed his horse's head for the Haunted Manor, the outlaws' great stronghold at Finchley.

But what was the meaning of that sudden uprising triumphant din, coming from the direction the officers had taken?

Blueskin uttered his pet swear-word.

"Boys," muttered he, "the sweet, pretty redbreasts have met with a roaming band of their fellows! How true is the saying, 'Birds of a feather flock together'! Now, unless we can infuse some life into this wooden-toy horse, in a few weeks' time at most, they'll be a fine trade a-doing in printed sheets, containing a pretty view of the Newgate scaffold an' the last dying speeches an' confessions o' those merry outlaws!"

THE STRANGE OLD WATCHMAN AND HIS REMARKABLE WAY OF OBTAINING PUNCH—A FORTUNATE MEETING—TRAPPED—WIFFLES AND HIS "HOARY-HEADED INFANCY"—A STARTLING THING TO CLING TO ONE'S CONSCIENCE—THE SAVAGE RABBLE ATTACK WILD'S HOUSE—VENTURING INTO THE LION'S DEN.

Needless to state, while apparently humouring the old night guardian, the colonel had obtained exactly what he wished, and might have failed in securing by any other means.

A tumbledown, extremely ancient-looking inn stood within fifty yards of the talkative old watchman. He straightway led the strangers—his suspicions quite swept away by the colonel's words and manner—and at once commenced a most deafening tattoo at the inn door, using his cudgel in preference to the knocker.

"Fire! Fire! Fire!" he yelled, at the topmost pitch of his voice. "Fire! Ho there! Open! Fire! Fire!"

A window was soon heard to open somewhere up in the great vapour. Then a voice hailed:

"Fire! Where—where is the fire?"

Then, without waiting for a reply, the questioner closed the window with a loud bang, and a few moments after the scared face of a man, wearing a nightcap, peered out from the opened doorway.

"Heavens! Where—where is the fire?" he demanded, in the same fear-trembling tones.

"On thy hearth, thou addlepate! Where else should the fire be when belated, bedrenched, an' frozen travellers bestow their patronage upon thee, Sam Wooten, thou wooden-headed son of a mouse!" most indignantly replied the old night guard, disdainfully ignoring his grave breach of the law in crying out a false alarm in the City of London, and in the dead of night.

The half-sleeping innkeeper, however, was soon restored to a most beaming condition when he found the disreputable-looking visitors willing to pay most liberally for all their demands.

A great big fire soon blazed merrily. Food and a famous brew of punch and dry garments were all quickly forthcoming. The watchman had most exhaustively sampled the hot, spicy, pungent liquor. Then he suddenly sprang up in newly-awakened alarm.

"Zounds!" he gasped. "I had quite forgotten my errand!"

"What's wrong, oh, sage?" asked Colonel Blood, with awakened interest.

"What's wrong, friend? Why, the world's wrong! It's continually turning round an' round to find out its proper course; but, depend on't, it never will. Here have I clean neglected my duty. A great, fearful, an' bloodthirsty outlaw rabble has besieged the habitation of Jonathan Wild, the head an' chief of our police-forces. I was on my way to the Tower to give information, an' cause a body o' King George's valiant troopers to hasten to the scene, an' when there, they are to show no mercy to the varlets, but to mincemeat 'em all, the vile herds—Mincemeat 'em!"

The outlaws exchanged glances. Dick and the colonel both burst into immoderate laughter.

"We have treated you well, Father Philosopher, have we not?" asked the colonel.

"Marry, Sirs, that ye have! Ye have made me a man!"

"And in return you now transform us into mincemeat—for we are members of the varlets an' vile herds, as ye term them—to be chewed up by King George's troopers!"

"Outlaws! Then may I be hanged if—"

"You'll be duly hanged, never fear, sir, after your betters!"

"I'faith," replied the old man, "I hope you are all my betters, then; for I have no objection to see every one of ye nicely hanged! I'll most patiently await my turn until every one o' my betters is strung up, an' my inferiors can then take their turn—for I'm a devil at patience!"

In a twinkling the old watchman now found himself firmly bound to his chair. His amazement and annoyance were, however, considerably mollified on finding his right arm remained free, and that the ladle in the steaming liquor of the punch vessel was still within his reach.

The host had done a prime stroke of business, and winked at the strange doings of his most liberal patrons. The latter could not find it in their hearts to take the night guardian seriously, but laughed loudly at his quaint and caustic words.

A second brew of the tasty liquor was ordered, and duly paid for, the "Old Charley"—as all the night watchmen were then termed—roundly declaring that he should not wish to budge an inch so long as the generous tipple remained to sample. The party then departed, flinging a final jest at their victim as they left the old inn.

The outlaws were now changed men. They had dry and warm clothing, had had a hasty meal, and enjoyed a brief spell at a bright fire. Weapons were wanting; but those, they knew, would be easily obtained from their friends, whom they expected to find assembled in Newgate Street, before the thief-taker's dwelling.

"Comrades," sang out Dandy Dick, once again moving on through the night greyness, "we must displace every stone of that den of infamy and hiding-place of most awful secret crimes! Mayhap we may find Jonathan Wild—the Evil One's most favourite pupil—lurking there, by the time we reach his notorious building!"

"Aha, the iron-plated old villain! I'm almost regretting that I didn't settle his hash[91] when he was at our mercy. But the act would have seemed too much like cold-blooded murder. And, outlaws as we are, it behoves us to avoid, whenever possible, the crime and sin of shedding blood. In fair, manly contest the taking of a fellow creature's life is terrible enough, Heaven knows, and I like not such accursed deeds upon my conscience!"

Colonel Blood thus expressed himself. He was a man of many strange moods, and frequently astonished his friends by the utterance of most noble sentiments.

"Torking o' conscience reminds me," remarked Wiffles, "that I must 'a' been a most depraved an' bloodthirsty infant; fer I commenced ter prowl about ther King's 'ighway at ther 'oary-'eaded age o' two ye'rs an' one month, like a roarin' lion, a-seekin' who I c'uld dewour! I vas armed a-mpst desp'rite vive a long piece o'iron pipin' an' a small paper bag full o' 'ard peas. One o' the fust o' my misfortunate wictims vas a boy of about in me own age. One morning I clapt me lamps on 'im a-coming along the road, in a state o' perfect content an' stickiness, a-chewin' ov ther grandest nugget o' stickjaw as I'd ever then seed in all ther long two ye'rs an' one month o' my creepings up!

"'Stand, an' stop that chewin', warlet!' I thinders, in me most terrible lower chest notes. They vas like the squeakin' of a rusty gate. 'Stand, an' deliver particular quick, or you can utter a varnin' cry!' I added; 'fer I've got yer covered vive me iron pipe, an' ther deadly green pea is ready ter do its horrible vork!'

"Vat does me victim do but drops ther lovely nugget an' bolts—vich 'e supposed vas the proper style o' standin' an' deliverin', no doubt.

---

[91] Subdue or kill.

"I didn't a little bit mind ther 'alf a pound o' dry dust as the luxury took a likin' to as it lay in ther roadvay. It looked a bigger prize still, do yer see? Aha!"

Wiffles paused to utter a long-drawn sigh of fond regret.

"I ain't likely ter forget that day as long as I lives. Ther sight o' a little boy in smalls (kneebreeches) alvies brings me most painful mem'ries. No cherub vat 'ad played truant from 'eaven ever enjoyed 'isself 'alf as much as I did. It's most awful ter think on that a dark deed can sometimes give pleasure! But there I vas, a-quietly sitting be the 'edge-side, an' a-verkin' 'ard ter put meself outside o' that lovely piece o' paradise.

"Vell, ter make a long story short, that vas vhere me poor little victim's mother found me. I can see 'er now! She vas a fine, 'earty, strong voman, vive a most open count'nance when she smiled. V'en that nice person spied ther 'oary-'eaded footpad o' two ye'rs an' one month, an' ther proof o' is crime—e' vas caught red-'anded—I should say sticky-'anded—then ther quiet, motherly party suddenly became a thunderbolt! She had got a 'and made special for ther bringin' up o' children in ther vay as they should go—an' not sit down too oft'n, 'cept vhen they c'uld find somethin' verry, verry nice an' soft, as wouldn't pain 'em too much!"

"Vell, the female thunderbolt verry kindly took me on 'er knees, an' commenced most thortfully a-slappin' me. Yer see, vhen I caught sight o' her a-loomin' to'ards me, I, frog-like, svollers what remained o' the booty instant'r-like. So the good voman meant a-making me bring it up ag'in, in case the bolted goods vould upset me innards, like.

"That there female's sledge-'ammer paw kept a-playfully bangin' me like kicks from a wicious 'orse, only verry much more so. Ther awful joltings as I got so shook me that the stickjaw wandered about me innards as if it couldn't decide where ter settle down for good.

"At the finish the sweets must 'a' run agin my poor brain an' firmly clung ter it, an' it's been stuck there ever since. I shall die wive that stickjaw a-lying 'eavy on me conscience!"

Wiffles's auditors laughed immoderately over this reminiscence of their quaint and comical comrade. No one could have imagined for a moment that they were proscribed men, risking enormous danger of capture by venturing where they had, and that such apparently light-hearted creatures were bent on a mission likely to mean to one or all a sudden and violent death.

The murky midnight pall had not lifted in the slightest. The outlaws had much difficulty in picking their way, and therefore gladly welcomed the appearance of a linkboy. A circular blur of yellow, like a will-o'-the-wisp hovering over the vapour uprising from a bog, first appeared; excited exclamations followed; then the boy came dimly into view, looking like a figure in ebony splashed with liquid gold where the torchlight caught his form.

"Great rabble collected in Newgate Street! Attack on Mr. Wild's house! Fearful riot! Dreadful doings! King's sojers a-coming! Light yer on the way, me noble gentlemen?"

The colonel eagerly questioned the linkboy. His replies were alarming. A coin secured his services, and the little fellow nimbly moved on, carefully selecting the best paths for those following.

The distant sound of a great concourse of angry voices gradually came drifting on the cold night air, the frequent discharge of musketry mingling with the din.

"The King's troops have arrived!" muttered Dandy Dick. "We have tough work before us if we join our friends, and to fail them would be to proclaim ourselves the vilest of curs!"

"Those discharges of greater volume may be from petronels—the small guns carried by the Bow Street mounted officers. We must get our comrades away, in the event of the King's Guards having turned out, and reached Wild's domicile," remarked Colonel Blood.

"It is scarcely possible for the soldiers to have so soon been dispatched to the scene. We thwarted Wild's intention—the villain's corpse may now be resting in the mire of the river—and the Tower could not yet be reached even by other messengers."

Criss Craften, Jonathan Wild's late chief officer, thus expressed himself.

"But there are the Guards at Whitehall. Those may have been summoned by the Newgate authorities," said Dick Turpin.

"The King's chosen troopers would be vastly affronted if ever sent to do more police duty. The foot detachment, always retained at the Tower, would be available. No; the thief-taker's own janissaries an' Bow Street mounted patrols are those we may expect to find disputing matters with our comrades."

This was Dandy Dick's view.

"Well, well, pals," cheerily put in Tom King, "our people are mustered pretty strongly. We're going to have things in much our own way this venture."

"I thinks the old black rat o' Newgate is got 'is vhiskers werry nicely curled this time. I wote as ve now spoils 'is Newgate nest. There's nothink like a-finishin' a job out an' out, as ther man said vhen 'e'd pitched is old gal from the top-garret winder for the second time," quaintly observed Wiffles.

THE GAOL-LIKE HOUSE IN NEWGATE STREET—THE HIGHWAYMEN VENTURE INTO THE LION'S DEN—A DARING RUSE CROWNED WITH SUCCESS—CRAFTEN'S TRIUMPH—DARING EVEN TO MADNESS—HOT WORK—ESCAPED BY A MIRACLE.

The party of outlaws and Craften now reached a spot where they commanded a distant glimpse of the concourse of fighters. The heavy fog still continued. Facing the house in Newgate Street, next to the gaol, and on its east side, was a great black, ever-moving mass, its outer limits swallowed up by the gloom. The red and yellow glow of flaming torches, darting hues of crimson fire and blue-white smoke, lit up heads and passion-contorted faces. A raised cutlass, cudgel, clubbed pistol, or musket, could be seen here and there, thrown out by the red glow or white smoke, otherwise the black, billowy, crowded body of living beings might have been an agitated river of ebony.

Furious yells of rage, defiance, and groans of agony were mingled with the clashings of steel, explosions of fire-tubes, and weldings of clubs. The battle raged at its fiercest. So far as could be made out, Jonathan Wild's men were stubbornly contending against an enormous throng. The contesting masses were composed of foot and mounted men. The outlaws distinguished themselves by their furious demands for the body of the great Newgate official, while the thief-taker's followers could be known by their semi-official dresses and plain, gold lace-trimmed, three-cornered hats.

The first-floor windows were opened, and a most terrible fire now and then was rained down upon the outlaws, where they were revealed by the flickering lights of torches, either held by themselves or their enemies. To have put out the links would have resulted in the attackers mistaking their friends for their foes.

"The possession of the building would be quickly followed by the routing of our foes if, as it appears, there are on the premises liberal supplies of pistols or muskets, powder and ball," said Dandy Dick, in anxious consultation with his friends as to the best means of assisting those of their party already so hotly engaged.

"There is a most extensively-filled armoury—weapons and power and shot, enough to resist a long-sustained siege," explained Craften.

"Those fellows at the first-floor windows are making fearful havoc in the ranks of our friends, and must be driven from their position. Could we reach the rear of the house?"

Colonel Blood put this question to Jonathan Wild's late lieutenant. The latter remained in deep thought for some moments, then replied:

"If we can gain entrance to the next further building from the gaol, it might be possible to reach an upper window in Wild's dwelling. The top of the party-wall reaches to within a few feet of an unbarred side-window."

The hint was enough for the highwaymen. Wiffles went forward and passed into the gloom, and in a few moments had joined the outer fringe of the attackers. He was well known to most of those he saw, and collected all the arms, powder, and shot his friends and self would be likely to require in their attempt to enter Wild's house; but Wiffles had been cautioned against making this intention known, as its success would depend mainly on its unexpectedness, as well as extreme daring.

The building next to that owned by Jonathan Wild was the combined business firm and private abode of a merchant. The latter and all the household had been most rudely awakened by the tremendous uproar taking place, and were collected in the top rooms, and upon the roof of their abode, watching the scene of conflict, and in a state of fear panic.

The madly-excited mob extended far beyond the front of this warehouse. The highwaymen and Craften hustled their way to the door. Some of the attackers recognised Dandy Dick, Colonel Blood, and the others; but a few timely-whispered cautions prevented any noisy demonstration from resulting.

The closed shutters and door of the shop were found to be well bolted, barred, and chained. The struggling, shouting, contending rabble concealed the party of friends, the murky mist also aiding them in their designs. Dandy Dick and Colonel Blood together carefully examined the shutters, doorway, and the little window under the closed-up shutters. The latter was unprotected. A few vigorous kicks resulted in breaking the glass and window-frame, the result being a cavity large enough to enable a man's body to pass through.

Little notice was taken, no questions asked by those looking on. The ever fearless Colonel Blood lead the way. He found his feet resting upon a large table. From this he sprang to the floor, all his friends rejoining him a few moments after.

A glimmering light from above enabled the adventurers to find their way to a flight of stairs, and thence into the passageway on a level with the street. No one appeared. The comrades got their weapons in readiness for a probable surprised by foes. The noise of entering had been totally swallowed up by far greater sounds.

Craften, by mutual consent, acted as leader. The latter crept to the back door at the end of the hall. This was easily opened. A square, walled-in, paved space was seen. On the right the top of the enclosing wall reached, within a few feet, an unprotected window in the thief-taker's house, as described by Craften. A ladder rested against this wall.

The attackers saw at once that the way was clear and easy enough. They had evidently, so far, neither been seen nor heard by the inmates of the City merchant's house, the latter, as before explained, all having sought the top rooms and the roof, from whence to watch the progress of the battle, furiously raging below.

As the adventurous little band stood concealed in deep black shadows, Dandy Dick, in a low tone, addressed his friends:

"My faithful comrades, our intention was to endeavour to capture our arch-enemy, Jonathan Wild, alive, to convey him to our retreat at Finchley, and to keep the rabid dog there in our own interests. I have a privately personal details in the connection with this scheme. Roughly, it means that Jonathan Wild shall confess to his infamous plots against myself, or engage in a duel with me, which should end only by one of us falling mortally injured."

"Crime would decrease in this fair country, like snow under fiercest heat, if Jonathan Wild were deposed. It would be a good deed if the fiend were disgraced, a better if he were killed! The physic I would proscribe would take the form of a long rope and a short shrift!"[92]

This was the view expressed by Colonel Blood.

"Shrift!" remarked Wiffles, in much contempt. "I'd 'ang the black rat and naked!" he added. "A shirt, or shift, is thrown away on carrion, an' ther long rope as I'd adwise as best ter 'ang 'im wive 'ud be—so long as it vas strong enough—common an' cheap as dirt!"

Dick Turpin next commented.

"We may surprise the old devil-toad, hidden away somewhere in his own lair. In which event I would pledge myself that he will live to a green old age if once the sharpeners of my pretty barker gets full scent of the old musk-rat; for you can't imagine how unreliable my trigger-finger becomes when its owner stands behind its butt-end, and his foe before its tube!"

"Pals, I propose," put in Tom King, "that we lose no more valuable time in goose-cackle, and that we send word to our comrades without, that they follow us by this way, an' help us take possession of Wild's house, kill its owner if we find him, an' then wreck his prison-like quarters!"

"That plan would involve much bloodshed. Our deadly feud is with the thief-taker himself. Our contempt only befits his creatures," said Dandy Dick. "We must rout them," he added, "and then let our after actions be guided by events."

A ladder rested in the black shadows against a portion of the wall. This article nearly reached the twelve or fourteen feet high wall-top. It was silently placed in position. Dandy Dick first mounted. The wall-top reached, he stood erect. The window was without protecting bars, and could easily be entered. A lurid glow of light flooded the interior of the passageway, into which the masked outlaw peered.

Much caution would be needed if the defenders were to be taken by surprise. By the simple process of removing the ladder a foot or two each time one had mounted, the whole party soon gained the narrow summit of the wall. Rapier-blades were silently drawn, then forced under the bottom of the window-frame. A few moments after, the sill had been prised up. It had evidently been considered such an unlikely matter for anyone to attempt an entry by this window that no care had been taken even to keep its frame fastened, and it was more than likely that Jonathan Wild deemed that there was as much likelihood of robbers attempting to enter his house as that of the all fear-inspiring, grim old building of Newgate itself.

The ear-splitting din of frequent bursting volleys of firearms, followed by the shrieks of those struck down, told the adventurers that the battle now raged fiercer than ever. The most destructive of the fire-hail evidently rained down from the front windows.

---

[92] Time available for confession before execution (in this case, insufficient time – "short shrift").

Dandy Dick and his friends had now each climbed through the side window, and gained an entrance to the stronghold of their deadliest foe. Craften's aspect of triumph was a thing to be remembered.

"Caution!" he muttered. "I can guide ye by a side passage to the armoury. If we can gain possession of that, the battle's won! Follow me!"

"We shall not underestimate the value of your services to us in the undertaking of supreme peril, my friend!" whispered Dandy Dick as they proceeded into the ear of Wild's once chief officer.

"It is enough, an' more than enough, reward to me that I am enabled, by the aid of thyself and thy friends, to repay evil turn for evil turn. You little dream of the extent of the misery that I have endured as the result of the demon-like moods of my late tyrant!" earnestly whispered back the man Craften.

A few moments after, he paused before an open door, and then motioned to his companions to cautiously glance through.

They saw beyond a large, square, stone chamber, in which was much smoke and a red fire-glow. This light came from blazing torches, fixed in irons protruding from the walls. A deafening and confusing din of tongues mingled with rapid discharges of firearms. On the right of the concealed watchers were the attackers, crowded together by the front windows. On the left, when the smoke drifted nearer the ceiling, a glimpse of large, open doors could be obtained. Gunpowder-kegs and arms of many kind could be seen within the inner room.

To gain undisputed possession of the arms and ammunition stores, all that was necessary was to noiselessly flit over a space of flooring of a few yards. The thickly encurling clouds of blue-white powder-smoke from a volley, discharged in the midst of their friends in the street, enabled this bold move to be taken. The six daring men, unseen and unsuspected, had concealed themselves within the armoury.

"We're raking the cursed fellows merrily. If they don't soon lose heart, turn tail, an' flee, we'll each have some 'andsome sums o' reward-money to finger when the chief comes to learn of the fine work we've done!"

These words came in harsh, jeering tones from beyond the gunpowder-vapour floating by the front window. The boast had scarcely been uttered, when the words were followed by a death-shriek from the same throat. The man had been picked off by one of the rabble facing the building. He fell writhing in mortal throes.

"We'll most terribly avenge the fall o' our mate. Bring more power an' plenty o' ball, boys. We're clean out o' both. Quick, lads!" sang out the fierce, guttural voice of one evidently in command, in the absence of the great police-agent.

The sound of heavy footsteps coming towards the place of their concealment was the signal for action on the part of the surprise-party.

"Hold! Stand back! Advance an inch further, an' ye're doomed!"

Wild's retainers instantly paused. Their movements were held in check by unbounded amazement and sudden-awakened soul-chilling terror.

Presently, partly recovering from their extreme panic, the janissaries commenced to vent furious curses. They could see nothing, in consequence of the dense smoke. Little by little it cleared. Six masked faces gradually caught their view. Six levelled firelocks hovered between the masks and themselves. Wild's men could not credit their eyesight.

"If ye would spare your lives, throw down your arms!"

The tones filled the stone chamber with their startling echoes. The metallic sounds of weapons clashing to the floor at once proved that the offer was accepted.

Dandy Dick and his comrades emerged from the gloomy interior of the stores. Their beholders were still more or less dazed. The successful ruse was so supremely daring, so utterly unsuspected!

"You are outnumbered!" cried Dandy Dick, guessing that the fellows would believe the powder and arms stores to be filled with others of their foes. "You will be remorselessly slain to a man unless you instantly quit the place!"

"As well be butchered here, as instantly on appearing outside!" growled one of the threatened men, with a despairing scowl.

"Retire to the courtyard at the rear of this building, and remain in hiding until the besiegers have drawn off. This side window on your right, at the back of this building, will afford the means of exit, as it enabled us to enter. Three seconds only will be granted ye. If at the end of the third—"

Dandy Dick's further words were cut short by the sudden discharge of a firearm. A bullet struck splinters of the surface of a stone immediately behind his head. His life had been saved by a hairbreath.

A terrific howl of savage indignation burst from the lips of the young highwayman's friends. The next instant five pistols belched forth. There was a feeble cry—half-groan, half-curse—and the being guilty of the treacherous act fell limp and lifeless, five bullets lodged in his body.

Dandy Dick had refrained from lifting his flintlock, even at the man who had so nearly proved his assassin.

IN THE LION'S DEN—MIDNIGHT BATTLE—THE THAMES RIVER GIVES UP ITS IN VICTIM—SUPREME PERIL OF DANDY DICK—WILL THE WITLESS —A MONSTER THWARTED IN HIS EVIL DESIGN—BLACK DEEDS ON A BLACK NIGHT.

Colonel Blood, Dick Turpin, Tom King, Wiffles, and Craften drew their cutlass-blades and leapt forward, their eyes darting fire, and most furious threats coming from between their rage-clenched teeth. Clemency was a virtue little understood by Jonathan Wild's creatures, but the sight of flashing steel moved them exceedingly. They vied with each other in their haste to make good their retreat. They had not left the chamber before a few had been compelled to take with them a nasty reminder of the fact that a blow from the flat of a strong steel cutlass-blade is a thing that continues to loudly ring within one's pate for a very long time after its reception.

Jonathan Wild's followers were unarmed, and momentarily fearful of being ruthlessly torn to pieces if discovered by the lawless bands, infuriated beyond description now by the greatness of their number wounded, or killed outright.

Dandy Dick and his comrades, Craften excepted, together went to the windows. Each held a flaming link, so that his identity could not for an instant remain in doubt.

The swarming, yelling, madly-excited concourse—consisting of a mixed medley of citizens, outlaws, and Crown officers—had in wonderment seen the party of defenders suddenly withdraw from the lower windows of the house. One of their number had been seen to fall; but it was hardly to be expected that they would accept defeat as a result of the disabling or loss of one of their number—and the only one, so far as known. The outlaws continued their struggle with the common foe for a long time, with varying fortune, yet sanguine of a speedy triumph.

The spectacle to be seen facing Jonathan Wild's abode might well have been one transpiring in the lower world of torments. The night's black pall shut out all but those objects chancing to catch the yellow rod, and purple flashes thrown by great numbers of moving, spluttering, smoking pine brands, which sometimes appeared to shower down from out their flames brilliant nuggets of gold.

The most awful confusion reigned. Many of the Bow Street patrols had had their horses killed under them—shot or stabbed, and hacked to death. The police-agents had suffered terribly. Many had now ridden off to the Bow Street headquarters for further assistance. They were vastly outnumbered, and were momentarily threatened with complete defeat, if not destruction.

A most terrific uproar suddenly burst from countless hot, dry, hoarse throats. The combined efforts of great numbers of rage-maddened beings to express to the full their sense of triumph over the great Newgate agent was the thing no pen could adequately describe. The appearance of Dandy Dick and his most personal friends, side-by-side, coolly posing with confident, easy grace, actually within the thief-taker's house—the lion's den—was the proof of the complete triumph of the lawless classes over their powerful, bitter, and implacable enemy. So, at least, the latter, in their rage frenzy, firmly believed. But they were doomed to most speedy disappointment.

Through the thick, choking, chilling, and blinding mist a figure glided, using extreme caution, glancing apprehensively in all directions as it made towards the spot, lighted up by countless torches, and the centre of an ear-splitting babble of fiendlike disputing voices.

Mire-covered from head to foot, hatless, dripping wet, exhausted, threads of blood trickling down from under dirty bandages slovenly twisted round the temples, the harsh, horrible grating of teeth, flashing orbs, convulsive twisting of the face muscles, and claw-like workings of the strong, loose hands, these all indicated the possession of a spirit of ungovernable fury.

The bosom of the Thames river had vomited up Jonathan Wild. The creature had in some marvellous way escaped death by drowning, and was now stealing towards his house. The mist-vapour shadows enveloped him—screening from view the demon-like orbs that would have darted death-dealing glances wholesale, if in their power, and failed the writhings of the horribly sinister features as volumes of bitterest anathema seethed down the passion-trembling lips.

Darting from one spot to another in his efforts to remain concealed and yet to get a closer and better view of the scene and all its details, Jonathan Wild appeared like a crazed creature, or one possessed of an evil spirit. Presently he caught sight of a hat with a black crape mask attached, probably dropped by an outlaw in a contest with a police-officer. The thief-taker eagerly picked up the articles, and placed the hat on his head, and mask over his face. His identity was now the better concealed. His fear was that, if recognised, the enormously-increased rabble would give him little chance for his life, and most likely tear him from limb to limb.

Immediately opposite his own house there was a dark recess, leading to an entrance of a mercer's warehouse. Into this the mad and baffled Wild crept, and watched the progress of events. The clattering of steed-hooves, sudden clash of cutlass-blades, and loud altercation caused the watcher to cautiously creep from and to the entry's mouth. A number of Bow Street patrols were stoutly defending themselves against a crowd of outlaw rabble, on foot. Some few of the latter were armed with long, lance-like poles, having steel pike-heads. These were used with the utmost ferocity.

Helpless, and frantically cursing at his powerlessness, Jonathan Wild had the bitter mortification on to witness the spectacle of half a dozen officers being cut down in as few moments. The terrible pikes pierced the horsemen before their cutlass-blades could reach their mark. The fight was too closely contested, the mixture of friend and foe too intricate, to permit of anything like the free use of pistols.

"Down with Jonathan Wild and all his merciless class! Down with the King, his ministers, an' the cursed police-spies!" yelled the outlaws, as two of the patrols fell, each with a pike-head buried in his heart, their death-groans most shuddering to hear, blood gushing from their great, gaping wounds and mouths and nostrils as, in a few moments after reaching earth, they writhed out their parting breath.

A riderless horse, with blood-red, snorting nostrils, in fear panic, plunged past the very spot where the Newgate agent lingered. With the speed of thought, the animal was caught by the bridle. A terrific struggle of a moment, and the steed was subdued. Wild sprang into the saddle. Two loaded pistols were in the holsters. A snarling-like chuckle came from between the teeth of the mounted man.

Dandy Dick stood fully exposed to view. The glare of torches, held aloft and fastened to poll-ends, fell full upon his handsome, unmasked face and figure of youthful grace. He was in the act of exultantly addressing the mixed assemblage in the street below.

With the stealthy caution of a panther, the thief-taker was making deadly sure of his intent. One firelock was deliberately aimed for the breast of the figure at the window, the other clutched in readiness in the hand also holding the reins.

"Ha! ha! Little reck ye, my fine peacock outlaw," he was fiercely muttering— "little reck ye that I, Jonathan Wild, at this moment have a bullet directed dead sure for thy heart! My finger lovingly presses the trigger. A tiny second more an' the messenger of death goeth forth, and thy corpse shall proclaim my triumph an' revenge! He! he!"

The firearm was most accurately aimed, the trigger was all-but snapping, when the thief-taker became sensible of a crashing sensation on the back of the head. A blood-red flame shot before his vision. The two firearms fell into the road. At the same instant Wild realised that he had been struck a terrific blow with some blunt instrument. He half-reeled, half-sprang from the saddle the moment after to recover himself. Snatching up the pistols, he swiftly set them in order, then turned to look for his assailant.

Speeding away into the gloom was the diminutive figure of the idiot boy Will the Witless. The sight of the lad's leaping-pole was enough for the infuriated felon-hunter. Remounting, and regardless of every other consideration for the time being, he urged the steed into a gallop, and in a few bounds rode the boy down. This might not have happened, but that the boy appeared already in an exhausted state, and fell to the earth. The moment after, with the growl of a wild beast, the horsemen had leapt from the saddle, and seized the pale-faced, feeble boy by the throat.

"Curse thy dazed brain an' its infernal vagaries!" vindictively hissed Jonathan Wild, closing his grip like that of a vice round the small, thin throat.

"Caitiff,[93] keep thy fury for men!"

A powerful blow caught the thief-taker under the jawbone. The idiot was free, and speeding away like the wind. A burly fellow, with indignant rage flashing in his eyes, confronted the man he had struck.

"Scurvy hind, knowest thou whom thou hast dared to lift thine hand to?" demanded the masked Jonathan Wild.

"Not I, nor care! Come, I'll trounce thee, thou contemptible cur! Take off that

---

[93] Cowardly or contemptible.

mask, an' show the blushes of cowardice, thou valiant throttler of children!" was the jeering, defiant answer.

The man drew his cutlass, and sprang forward, evidently with the intention of snatching the mask from the other's face.

His imminent danger, in the event of identification by the outlaw concourse, madly alarmed the chief police-agent. He took two steps backwards, then levelled a pistol and fired. The oncoming outlaw was within but a few inches of the firearm's tube when its discharge rang out. The charge completely blew away a side of the ill-fated being's face. The corpse collided against Wild in tottering earthwards.

Many of the rabble had witnessed the ferocious act from but a few yards' distance. A crowd surrounded the monster holding the still-smoking weapon. Jonathan Wild instantly saw his great peril. The first man to reach him held aloft a long-handled axe, but before he could use it he was deliberately shot dead.

Then came the irresistible crash of a great body of men, but not before the fiendish Wild had batted at several heads with the butt-end of his pistol. He was borne to the earth. A dozen steel blades at once darted for his heart, but in every case their points were turned aside by his secretly-worn coat of steel mail.

Then up dashed a reinforcement of patrols. The mob was temporarily checked. The thief-taker seized his opportunity and regained his feet.

For an instant Wild found himself unmolested. He sought out for a weapon, having lost both firearms in his fall. A great cutlass, still clutched in the hand of one of the dead, caught his view. Snatching this, and now thoroughly alarmed, he turned to flee, but had again been observed by the outlaws as one of the common enemy.

With the utmost fury the thief-taker fought his way through a compact wall of surrounding foes. The cutlass he had reeked with human blood as he now tore on at topmost speed, making direct for the Tower.

°OFFICER BILBERRY SEEN IN A NEW CHARACTER—THE HOSTELRY OF YE PIG AND YE PINK CUSHION—THE CHAIRMAN OF THE SMOKING-ROOM—BILBERRY, THE FATHER OF ALL LIES—A YARN.

On the night of the most daring and determined assault upon the stone-house owned by the head police-agent of Newgate Gaol something little short of a panic reigned at the police head-quarters of Bow Street.

A mounted police-officer, desperately wounded, had ridden into the courtyard. The man had barely time to relate the startling incident taking place in Newgate Street before he relapsed into a deadly faint, as the result of his injuries.

° Part 25. Vol. XIV.—No. 361. 9 October 1900.

The chief officer on duty was thrown into a most fearful state of excitement. Few reserve men were at his command, and, in consequence, the whole neighbourhood had to be searched for all available officers off duty.

Now, it so happened that Officer Bilberry was spending a most jovial time of it at a hostelry nearby the police headquarters. The inn was known far and wide for its especial brew of punch. The name of this hostelry was the somewhat peculiar one of Ye Pig and Ye Pink Cushion.

A signboard swung from its post outside the Inn. On this board was the representation of an animal that possessed the unique advantage of resembling any and every known member of the lower animal kingdom, excepting the one for which it was intended, and is usually described by the name of pig.

The non-descript creature would have done equally well for an elephant, a mouse (except in size), a bear, a donkey, or one of the monkey species.

The little boys of the neighbourhood had shown their high appreciation for this great flight of the artistic imagination by at divers times flinging "mud-pies" at the "pig" and the broad patch of startling red upon which the non-descript sat. A black cake of hardbaked mud had fixed itself with the eye of the unnameable thing had once been.

Several other equally well-aimed blobs of nice, soft mire had in times past attached themselves to the body of the supposed squeaked.

The result of this somewhat confused state of the pictorial outer adornment of the inn resulted in the frequenters waggish the re-christening the house.

"The piebald puzzle seated on the vermilion nightmare" was the term the wags applied. But this is by the way. Officer Bilberry solemnly presided at the head of a long oaken table. He was surrounded by a number of his "very choice particulars"—men who actually looked up to the Bow Street runner "as a thing of beauty and joy for ever."

As a venter[94] of gas—otherwise lies—Bilberry stood unrivalled the world over. His ever-favourite topic was that of his own unmatched valour, and his pet grievance the shameful overlooking of his most sterling merits by the authorities.

The majority of the frequenters of the smoking-room of the inn of uncertain title swallowed the Bilberry inventions with almost as keen a relish as they lapped down their favourite tipple.

Seated round the long oaken table were some two dozen men, all old, all bald, all with rich, ripe-red, round countenances, and so shining these as to give one the notion that they had been previously polished with an oil rag.

The company all gravely sucked at a long clay-pipes, and a sky of blue-white drifting clouds hovered above their heads between them and the ceiling.

Chairman Bilberry on this particular night had varied the entertainment he usually supplied by favouring his admirers with a song. It was something in the following strain— Bilberry's grog-song:

---

[94] Inventor.

"A red, smiling moon his comely face,
Who wields the spoon with matchless grace;
Gently pauses till the ruby, boiling punch grows colder.
Hip, hip, hurrah! We'll extol the ladle-holder.
A right good fellow; so fat, red, and mellow!
A noble gallant, a cheery soul,
Is he who presides at the flowing bowl."

Smartly and loudly knocking their many pipe-bowls upon the polished top of the oak table, the company had testified their high approval of the song.

Bilberry usually sang as if his throat had been filled up with iron-rust, flint-pebbles, and cobwebs. But this was, nevertheless, supposed to be "the good old trusted sort of harmony." Mere ordinary music was voted a bore by warbler Bilberry and his many great admirers.

"A yarn, Comrade Bilberry!" eagerly invited one of the company. "Come, good old crony, a yarn! An' let it be one of thine own, Comrade Bilberry—a yarn concerning the marauding cut purse, footpad, or mounted robber o' the King's highway, who daringly cries 'Stand and deliver!' to farmer wayfarers, or demands felon-toll o' the riders in a midnight coach. Let it be of the handsome, dashing Claude Duval style.[95] Somewhat thusly: The masked robber catches sight o' a sweetly beautiful young damsel in the coach, an' cries he, 'Come, fair an' gentle ladie, grant me a trip on the green sward of this glen—a graceful whirl, a minuet—in the calm, cool moonlight; the surrounding trees an' the night winds our music; gay party of travellers—who would right gladly shoot me dead if they dared—the spectators of the merry scene. Come, sweet lass, I kiss my finger-tips to thee; but trip it with me o'er the sward on this lovely eve, an' I swear by me troth I'll ask no other toll, an' that thee an' thy friends shall unharmed pass on thy way!'"

"Blood an' hounds, Crony Swips! But one would think thee thyself a romancer o' the 'Arabian Nights' entertainment order, so glibly thou puttest thy request!" pleasantly responded Chairman Bilberry.

Then the pipe-bowls again noisily rattled upon the oaken table-top.

"Chairman Bilberry will oblige the company by the recital of one of his own thrilling experiences—breathlessly exciting episodes in connection with his official encounters with sanguinary law-breakers!"

"Nay, nay!" smilingly demurred Bilberry, almost breaking a blood-vessel in his attempt to assume a blush of modesty. "Nay, nay, esteemed gentlemen! I

---

[95] 1643–70. Duval was a French highwayman operating in England. Few historical details survive, but Duval became romanticised as a highwayman and was the subject of serial stories including one written by Charleton Lea, who also wrote the 1904 Spring-Heeled Jack serial (volume 6 of this library), both published by the Aldine Press.

love not to ever prate of the deeds it has sometimes been my happy lot to do in duty's cause. Some day—thunderclaps an' squalling brats!—I, Officer Bilberry, hope to have the honoured privilege o' laying down my life for my King an' country. But what o' that? A truly brave man rates his life at but the value o' a pin's-point!"

The churchwardens again rattled upon the table-top louder than ever, and most eager demands were again made for the recital of a personal yarn by the Bow Street runner. Finally, that personage, with a clever assumption of modest reluctance, gravely settled himself in his quaint oaken chair for the deliberate deliverance of his secretly-pleasing task.

"Most jocular, generous, and flattering of friends," commenced Bow Street Bilberry, "you all have heard of that most infamous of knaves, Dandy Dick, the list of whose crimes would take one a long month to merely count, let alone give details of; but there is one of the many adventures that I have had when the unpaced villain that, mayhap, ye may be interested in hearing on't. As for the truth o' my story—well, may every bone in my body become thin an' brittle as the pipe-stem I now hold in me hand if there will be one word of exaggeration in what I have to tell!"

Many of the company present instantly expressed their intention to fully believe the forthcoming yarn, no matter what its nature.

"There was only one more truthful man on the whole face of the earth than their esteemed chairman," a grave-looking smoker protested; adding that "that man had been, from his birth upwards, perfectly dumb!"

Thus encouraged, Bilberry went on:

"You must firstly learn, gentlemen, that the Government authorities have all got their knives an' forks in me—and deeply, too! But this is the penalty that all truly great, brave, wise, enterprising—an' not to say rash, in my own case—men have to pay to their inferiors. The thought of this makes me curse! You will excuse my sudden fit o' wrath, gentlemen; but blue blazes! concentrated essence of snake-poisons! blisterings of scorpion-stings! collected then spat out by old toads afflicted with severe attacks of cholera-morbus! This, I say, is the premier curse—scourge of all earthly scourges!—This black, blighting, blasting, withering thing called envy! But aside with the evil thing, an' to me truthful tale."

He had contrived to get a ribbon of his favourite oaths of his chest, and Bilberry consequently felt that he could now breathe with much greater freedom. He resumed:

"One night after supper I was taken with an unusually severe mood o' righteous wrath. By the bones o' me only mother's son, this shall not continue, sez I, starting up an' seizing me hat, coat, cutlass, an' to brace o' flintfires. I happened to be on patrol-duty. My steed was at bait at an inn hard by. Ten minutes after I was on the Oxford Road. The rumour was rife that the terror of all terrors, Dandy Dick, had taken up his nightly beat on the same Oxford Road. There was many a night-coach, many a noble gallant, many a belated traveller to be met with in that direction, an' the story went that this prince of all midnight, unlawful toll-collectors and road-rakers was busy with his murderous pop guns, an' that fortune after fortune was flowing into his coffers.

"Man alive! Thinks I, blood an' hounds! Thinks I, you'll have to capture alive this man scorpion, Bilberry, thinks I. You'll have to subdue and arrest this belcher of fire an' spiller of blood single-handed, yourself alone, unaided, and without assistance—to be precise and particular—thinks I. And, Bow Street Officer Bilberry, this night you'll hand yourself down to posterity. There'll be in the time to come statues in bronze, statues in marble of all shades, statues here, statues there, statues everywhere.

"There will be long leaves clustering about the majestic brows of those carved figures. The heads, visages, and graceful forms will all be the same, those images all of one man, an' that man the great Bilberry—the one an' only being daring an' capable enough to rid his country of a fearful man-devouring dragon! That ancient fellow who rode horseback naked an' without a saddle—St. George of England[96]—must then rank as a mere mythical fraud, and Bilberry as the true knight who slew the foul monster who had for so long terrorised over the land, made pillage, laid low, wasted, shed blood as rivers, an' utterly devastated this fair an' merry England!

"These were the pretty visions floating through my mind, gentlemen, as I cautiously traversed the bleak, wintry quarter of the Great Western road that ran from Holborn to Tyburn.

"The night was misty, black, depressing, chilling to the very marrow, an' made quite a proper framing to a picture of fierce robbery, horrid outrage, an' cruel carnage!

"Presently, at a most dismal, dreary, shuddering spot, I espied a tall horseman, black-masked an' cloaked, an' mounted on a grand steed, sable-black as its own master's mask an' cloak. The eye-holes in the rider's mask were as those to a furnace of living fire.

"I could detect, spite of the darkness o' the moonless night, that the man carried arms enough for nearly fifty ordinary midnight highway desperados. The horseman sat motionless, he and the horse looking as if carved out of one huge piece of black marble.

"The sum of one hundred pounds then offered for the capture, alive or dead, of the notorious Dandy Dick—the thought of this made me fingers tingle to

---

[96] Bilberry is mixing up his mythology. St. George slew the dragon; Lady Godiva rode naked through Coventry.

handle the gold, the stirrups itch to gallop to the attack. Then the horse an' rider together suddenly looked my way. Their four eyes were for all the world like the same number of lantern-bull's-eyes, but of a blood red hue.

"I never heard a sound; but the masked horseman was instantly within two yards of me, two extraordinarily long-tube pistols full-cocked and level at me head, while I could see his rapier already drawn half a foot or so out of' his scabbard.

"'So, ho, there!' I challenged. 'You're a fine fellow. An' is that the way you tell a traveller the time o' night?' You see, I was first trying the dodge of equivocation.

"'Oh, yes,' replied he, quite saucily, 'the time o' night is pea-shelling time, in readiness for my dinner to-morrow. So clean out your pods, an' right quickly, too, me dull blade an' take precious good care that peas are very plentiful this season, an' all of a distinctly golden tint!'

"'Aha!' I cries, 'that's a pretty, playful way o' putting things! But pray inform me what happens to the pods when they give forth no peas?'

"'Oh, they are just riddled until they resemble honeycomb, then are buried in the earth, for, do you see,' sez he, 'they make nice manure for growing soil—especially pods so full an' greasy as thyself,' sez he.

"'Now,' thinks I, 'blood an' hounds! I've let the villain have his joke. He goes for work—hot, strong, an' lusty. By the slave that tended the nose of the illustrious Caesar whenever the Roman Emperor had a severe cold in his head!' cries I, 'this fooling hath gone far enough! I'll have thee know, unmatched cutthroat, wholesale freebooter, an' murderer of multitudes, that before ye stands that fearless Bow Street officer named Bilberry! He was never known to quail before such toys as black masks, flint-locks, or rapier-blades, even when the same tune was a-being hammered out by as many as twenty performers!'

"The name of Bilberry was a pill that instantly stuck in his throat. The furnace fires died out quickly. The black mask itself grew quite pale. Even the ebony hue of the steel commenced to display a suspicion of white.

"Dandy Dick dropped his pop guns and commenced to tremble.

"'You forget, gallant Bow Street bully-boy,' whimpered he, 'that I have no less than a hundred an' fifty of my band concealed in that black patch o' forest just up the road to your right there.'

"'Aha!' cried I, 'let me think!'

"In a flash my mind was made up. It was clear that a hundred an' fifty-one would mean risky work, an' I had decided to capture my man by stratagem first. I had foreseen this contingency, an' was prepared with a large bag of gold.

"'See here,' sez I, producing this bag, 'peas are plentiful-enough this season, an' golden peas they are. This large sum o' money I am taking to the Round House at Tyburn. What story can I tell my chief when I return to Bow Street? You must make believe,' sez I, 'that we've had a most fearful encounter.' I took off me hat. 'Fire a bullet through that,' sez I, extending it out at arm's-length.

"With a laugh, my fine high toby man discharged one a pistol at my head covering, sending a ball through it true enough.

"'Next you must pass a ball or two through each skirt o' me coat; then another through me saddle-bag o' despatches. It will then look as though I'd made a fine stand for the bullion, an' me character won't be impeached.'

"Carefully and precisely enough this fine peacock of a road-robber did as I told him.

"'Marry!' cried he, 'if you had fifty balls sped at ye at close range you might not have had so many close shaves such a devil's night as this!' laughed he; adding: 'I've now emptied every one of me cheerful little barkers.'

"This was the moment I had waited for. I clapped my two loaded pistols within an inch of his mask.

"'Trumps!' sez I. 'You played that game with a wretched bad hand, an' ye've lost it very much. But I'm of a forgiving nature, I am. Don't even so much as attempt to take your lips apart. Draw your meat-skewer an' hand it over to me.' He silently did this. 'Now,' sez I, 'you've got a head on your shoulders at the present moment, Dandy Dick. There's also the usual small an' weak supply o' brains in it that you usually carry. But just try the slightest attempt of trickery, to give a signal to your pals up the road there, and you'll be wanting a head an' brains very badly the next moment!'

"The greatest highwayman of the age was my prisoner. 'One hundred pounds reward!' The pretty song was sung by a million voices in my head. Every way I looked I saw the tinge of gold. It was up among the night clouds, down in the black earth of the road, on the bark of a tree, and everywhere. The highwayman an' his steed were now carved in one mass of gold.

°NEWS OF DANDY DICK.

"'Man alive! blue blazes! double-distilled essences of deadliest poison! universal reprisals! endless deeds o' gore!' thundered I, putting on my most awful form; whereat Dandy Dick dropped his gills, an' started a-trembling like the aspen-tree—trembled as no man ever shook before. 'Zounds! blood an' hounds!' added I, following up my advantage, as he appeared almost on the point o' dropping to pieces.

"'Dismount, thou white-livered son of a weak-kneed tom-tit!' I raved, whipping out my blade.

"He was off his animal an' a-cringing on his knees in the road before a fly could wink twice. Then, disdaining to soil my steel on such carrion, I furiously boxed his ears till the clouts filled the night with their stunning echoes.

° Part 26. Vol. XIV.—No. 362. 31 October 1900.

"'Ecod! Grilled toadstools an' frazzled adders! Take that! an' that! an' that! Now call thy band of one hundred an' fifty dirty-visaged cutthroats, an' by my sainted mother's shoestrings I'll serve 'em, each an' every one, precisely as I am serving thee!'

"This fine terror of a dandy midnight toll-collector at once displayed such an abject terror that he, perforce, commenced to crawl at my feet an' lick the mud off my boots till I called upon him to desist:

"'Arise an' mount, sirrah, or I'll chaw thee up an' spit thee to the four winds!'

"Mermaids and Ingin squaws! You may rest assured that I hugged my prize pretty close, gentlemen, until I safely got him to Bow Street headquarters. Of course, the one hundred an' fifty of his felon associates had flown upon hearing the tones of my rageful voice. How the addlepated chiefs of Bow Street contrived to let Dandy Dick slip through their fingers an hour after he was in the lock-up is a thing I will try to explain on another evening!"

"Dear! dear! dear! You had really captured that devil incarnate, Dandy Dick!" burst in the voices of the admiring company surrounding Officer Bilberry—"really outwitted, hoodwinked the smartest highway robber known, an' arrested him single-handed? Why, we never before heard of the fellow having ever been secured by the police. He has always, so far, utterly defied all attempts at capture!"

"It's every word true for all that," unblushingly asserted the Bow Street officer, and father of all lies.

Further most awkward questions were on the point of being put, when a great commotion was suddenly heard at the door of the smoking-room.

"Any Bow Street officers present? Gentlemen, we're bringing in every officer we can find. Dandy Dick, the highwayman, an' thousands of his desperate gangs, are assembled in Newgate Street. They are seeking the great thief-taker, and solemnly vowing to have his life. Already many of our men have been cruelly butchered. Aha! I see Brother-officer Bilberry! Come, man, ye must be up an' doing!"

But Brother-officer Bilberry's deep-florid face, as he sat in the chairman's honoured seat, had turned to a light purple-bluish tinge. Brother-officer Bilberry looked like a victim to the very bluest of the blue funks.

CRAFTEN AND HIS FRIENDS UNEARTH AN APPALLING MYSTERY AND CRIME—STILL DEEPER TINTS OF EVIL—THE VANISHED VISION—A TERRIBLE SECRET CAGED FOR YEARS.

The sight of the party of highwaymen in possession of the great police-agent's house had the effect of completely dismaying every officer engaged in the sanguinary contest raging outside. Ten minutes after the Bow Street patrols and runners had drawn off, leaving the prescribed gangs masters of the situation,

Wild's men having retreated previously on concluding that their task was hopeless without the assistance of the King's Regular troops.

Dandy Dick addressed a few brief but encouraging words to the rioters; then a select number were admitted to the building. A search was next made. Every person found in the place acknowledging allegiance to the owner of the gaol-like abode was driven out at the point of sword or mouth of pistol-tube.

No sign of Jonathan Wild was discovered. His rooms were thoroughly overhauled. Many startling documents were found and examined, but those Dandy Dick most anxiously sought could not be traced.

In the lower regions the explorers paused before the closed-up entrance to a chamber or cell.

"That stone chamber holds some terrible mystery. Its black door—one solid sheet of iron—conceals some horrible secret. Of that I dare be sworn. Some ten years back, an' soon after my entering the services of Jonathan Wild, he, for a few weeks, daily visited that cell-like apartment, and on every occasion took prepared food—enough for at least two persons—with him. I had just previously seen the place untenanted. Soon his mysterious visits entirely ceased. There is an inner iron door similar to this outer one. Both doors being closed, no human cry could ever reach beyond this thick iron plate. One might batter at the inner one utterly in vain. No sound would ever penetrate beyond this entrance, the whole arrangement being evidently for such a purpose. A passage of quite ten feet separates the two doors. I have tried in vain all these intervening years to find this entrance unlocked. The dust-choked state of the keyhole plainly enough tells that the key has never been placed therein for a very long period."

"Stay, friend. Did anyone ever detect a captive or captives in that chamber?" asked Dandy Dick.

"Yes, I myself once heard a voice proceed therefrom. Wild had evidently come out for the object of returning with something he may have forgotten, and left the further door open. As I had often done before, I crept after him unobserved, and was in time to catch the hum of two voices—male and female—in the space of time taken up by him in entering this outside door. The instant he closed and locked it on the inside not the faintest further sound could I detect."

Craften paused. The highwaymen looked into each other's faces with grave, questioning glances.

"We will not so completely degrade ourselves by robbing this unparalleled wretch, our most powerful enemy; but if there be some fell, unlawful secret hidden beyond that door it were well that we knew it," Colonel Blood thus expressed himself.

"The discovery might give us a hold upon the old rat should he turn up again. Those born to be hanged cannot drown," remarked Dick Turpin.

"'Egad! There may be great treasure stowed away there; and, i'faith! I am not so squeamish but that I could permit a few precious stones, or, say, spade-guineas, to stick to my fingers, even if the property of the vile caitiff who honours us with his enmity," said Tom King.

"An' I wote as ve shouldn't leave ther dirty old black toad a single coin, if ve could 'elp it—not even so much as a farden ter take to the grave wiv im, so as 'e'll be able ter arterwards toss a feller-g'ost fer a drink o' somethink vorm on a perishin' cold night as they're a-takin' their midnight constectutionul," put in Will Wiffles.

"No, comrades; robbers, law-breakers, outcasts as we are, we must not still further defile ourselves by taking so much as a penny's-worth of the property of that hell-spawn, Jonathan Wild. The plunder would be thrice accursed—carry with it the blackest of evil luck!" firmly protested Dandy Dick.

"Dandy Dick is right," added Colonel Blood. "We shall take no booty from this house; but we may do well to investigate the mystery that lurks beyond that grim portal."

He pointed to the black sheet of iron as he spoke, and the question was at once tacitly settled.

"Aha, friends," put in Craften, "it is easy to determine, but sometimes difficult to execute! How will you force that stout door?"

"A firm determination to do means that the difficulty is already half overcome," replied Dandy Dick.

Then he strode to the door, threw it open, and called for aid. A crowd of outlaws instantly rushed into the chamber.

"Men, can ye find anything in this building likely to fulfil the use of a battering-ram?" he asked.

A few of the fellows rushed off, and in a few seconds returned, bearing between them a great length of hewn timber, evidently duly intended for sawing into fire-logs.

"The very thing!" gleefully hailed Dandy Dick.

The outlaws—two aside and two at the further end—ranged themselves in position, the great timber-length directed at the dust and rust disfigured keyhole.

By directing the full force of the blows of the ram at the lock, Dandy Dick and his companions agreed that the lock-bolt must soon give way. In this they proved correct. A dozen tremendous thuds smashed the lock-ward and jerked open the powerful iron sheet, a blinding cloud of dust following. The success was hailed with great acclamation. In fitting terms Dandy Dick requested all to leave the outer chamber with the exception of his most chosen and trusted associates, which, needless to state, was limited to those usually joining him in his most dangerous exploits.

Some time elapsed before the settling of the blinding and choking dust. Then the passageway was found to be filled with endless spider-webs, which hung in dirty, raglike festoons. These were partly cleared away by the aid of a broom found in the first chamber. Then Dandy Dick and his comrades commenced their exploration.

A torch had been ignited. The sickening odour of mildew had to be endured. Rats and countless other creeping things sped out of sight before the bright yellow light thrown about their long secret abode.

"We have overlooked the existence of this second door, Dick," said Colonel Blood, the mildewed and red-rusted surface of the same catching his glance.

Dandy Dick was in advance, with the lighted brand. Stooping to avoid contact with the dirt-filled web festoons, thicker than ever as the second door was reached, a certain object had first been seen by him—namely, an iron bolt attached to the centre of the door, and driven into a slot in the stone wall.

"No need for the battering-ram here, comrades!" cried Dandy Dick, with great difficulty shooting the bolt back.

Years of accumulated rust had fixed the thing almost as if partly cemented in the wall.

The united efforts of four of the adventurers were required to open this time-fixed entrance. Then came another darkening cloud of dust, and further sight of spider-webs, but no living thing was seen or heard.

The atmosphere was extremely chilling and damp; the stone floor covered with a thick crust of soft, down-like dust resembling chalk. This, it was seen, had been for years falling from the whitewashed ceiling.

Dandy Dick felt himself strangely agitated, and paused irresolutely on the threshold of the apartment, in which reigned a stillness so complete that those about to enter felt a great and mystic awe fall upon them. It was as if they were about to enter some solemn chamber claimed by the sacred to the dead.

"More lights, comrades," muttered Dandy Dick in a whisper so strangely charged with reverential feeling that he himself was most startled by it.

"Yes, Dick," replied Colonel Blood, in a like hushed tone. "I almost feel that I shall commit a sacrilege by entering that stone cell, and I can tell that the same influence is at work within thee, friend."

Wiffles and Tom King, being nearest the further door, went in search of further torches, and presently returned, each bearing a flaming brand. These they had taken from their holders in the walls.

Dandy Dick and Colonel Blood, their steps made perfectly noiseless by the thick carpet of dust, slowly went forward into the black void of the inner chamber or cell.

An oaken table, inches thick with the same greyish-white that covered up everything afterwards seen, then a few chairs—these were all that first claimed the attention. The place represented a large prison-cell with an arched roof. There was one strongly-barred and closed window. The odour of the cell was so extremely nauseous as to be almost unbearable.

"Your conjectures or suspicions must have been wrong, Craften," said Dandy Dick, with a temporary feeling of relief, "for no being could live in this place. It must have been hermetical or airtight when this centre door was bolted. See! the window is quite choked up with dust. Not a breath of air could ever enter by that way. There is no fireplace. A fly could scarcely exist in such a confined space without a further supply of air."

Craften's eyes were riveted upon a dim something the roaming light had just revealed.

"Now, pitying angels, protect all mortals!" he piously murmured, pointing a violently-trembling finger.

All eyes were instantly turned in the direction indicated.

Colonel Blood slowly and fearfully advanced a few steps. His hands suddenly went up and covered his eyes. The strong, brave man remained thus for a second, as if turned to stone; then his voice came—the hushed, awed whisper still more hushed, awed:

"Saints in heaven bear witness! Was ever more inhuman, saddening, heart-ringing sight seen than this?"

The face of every beholder turned a startling white, in spite of the ruddy glow of the torches reflected thereon. Each visage became drawn with the agony of deepest pity, presently to change to that of extremist indignation and a most righteous wrath.

"Behold this work!" murmured Dandy Dick, the tears now welling from his eyes, no discredit to his manly heart. "How piteous! how powerful that dumb plea to heaven for a most righteous, most awful doom of vengeance upon the devil's brain and heart of steel that planned and executed this awful deed!"

"Ah, that spectacle bears the impress of the remorseless heart, the tigerish cruelty, of Jonathan Wild! And surely it will bear damning testimony to his evil life, and work his speedy undoing!" cried Dick Turpin.

"We, as subjects of outlawry," replied Colonel Blood, "have no lawful being, voice, or right in the opinions of the judges of this land, but we can admit all the world to see this proof of Jonathan Wild's crime."

A mystery there had indeed been, and grimly caged beyond two doors for years and years. What was its nature? The fearful object—which had so overwrought its beholders that they found the tears of compassion streaming down their cheeks like rain—took this form: A low couch, with the slight, graceful, reclining figure of a female at full length. Kneeling by the couch's side the bent form and figure of a man. His face was resting upon the settee's edge, and held in both his hands were those of the female. Both their attitudes were inexpressibly touching, eloquently proclaiming the fact that their love for each other was stronger than all else, even in the cruel moments of the approach of an untimely death. Their resting-place and bodies were completely, and very thickly covered up with the same light-grey, chalk-like powder that enveloped everything else in the death-cell.

"We must have a strong current of air," said Colonel Blood.

Then, with his rapier-hilt, he smashed the glass in the one window. But this was accomplished only with the utmost force, the material being of great thickness.

"The covering hiding from view those poor devoted souls completely removed, mayhap we shall discover their mode of death," sadly remarked Tom King.

Craften and Wiffles, unable to bear the harrowing sight longer, had silently stolen on tiptoe from the vault-like place.

Dick Turpin and Tom King followed them. But the object of the two latter was to open windows and doors in the outer apartment. This done, they as noiselessly as possible—with that feeling of reluctance to noise that all feel in a death-chamber—returned.

The cold, fresh atmosphere rushed, as if moaning piteously, into the oval-roofed cell. The result was as startling as unexpected. The ashen-grey powder was blown up like flying swan-down or a whirling snow storm. [***][97] quickly that in a few moments those within it must have choked.

Turpin and King blindly stumbled on their way until each window and door had been again closed. Instantly the flake-like particles recommenced to softly settle down. The links turned the falling dust into millions of tiny golden sparks as they fell into the flaring brands, threatening to gradually extinguish them.

Colonel Blood had partly attained his object.

"Most surely a pitying angel's unseen hand hath aided our efforts, Dick," he said, his tones tremulous with grief. "See! the face and upper part of the body of the dead woman are quite uncovered."

"Ah! an' the head, shoulders, and hands of the man, an' those he still clasps!" added Dandy Dick.

"By my soul, but this [***]!" cried Dick Turpin, with deep feeling, as he and the others moved towards the couch, cravats before their mouths and nostrils to keep out the floating dust-vapour.

The face of the lady was turned towards the kneeling male figure, whose head rested lovingly near her breast.

Sweetly beautiful as the countenance of an angel's was that of the female. She appeared sleeping only, but for the pure white marble of the perfectly bloodless skin. The hair—a rich nut-brown—was massed in great profusion about the face. So much of the dress as could be seen had once been of rare texture. The hands, both of male and female, were apparently as perfectly preserved as was the lady's face. No sign of wound of any kind could be seen.

---

[97] [***] Half line illegible.

"Poisoned, perhaps," remarked Dick Turpin.

"Impossible!" replied Dandy Dick. "The positions are those of persons who have passed away in peaceful sleep, or when in a state of insensibility."

Craften and Wiffles had silently returned. The former, with ghastly visage, gazed at the lovely female face.

"It is most vital that we learn the cause, or causes of death. The state of preservation is so complete as to point to a most recent date of decease. The thick layer of dust argues a period of years," put in Turpin.

"I will say nothing yet," remarked Craften, "but I have my theory," he added.

"Heaven forgive me if I do wrong now!" said the colonel; "but I must gently remove the poor kneeling soul to examine his breast. If the female were also turned slightly, a dagger thrust may be discovered in the left side, on which she reclines."

"I have no fear of this angelic-looking clay," replied Dandy Dick solemnly. "We will together make this examination, Colonel," he continued.

Simultaneously Dandy Dick and Colonel Blood, with utmost reverence, placed their hands upon the dead. They had no sooner done so than mingled exclamations of dismay, bitterest regret, and unbounded wonderment filled the cell. Like the swiftly-disappearing sleep visions in the awakening mind, so had the apparently real and tangible forms vanished.

"Heaven help us! What—what have we done?" gasped Dandy Dick, his flesh creeping in utmost horror.

"There's some hellish witchery in this! We need Heaven's aid!" ejaculated Colonel Blood, beads of moisture glistening upon his pallid face.

"I knew it, friends," broke in Craften, "but dared not mention it before. The crime is too frightful to be human. That inner door was never shut until the fiend Wild had finally doomed his unfortunate captives to death. Once that second entrance to the tomb was finally closed, the cell became airtight. Those ill-fated creatures calmly met their awful doom in loving handclasp as we found them. Their murderer hath not opened that door since the hour of his horrid crime!"

"I see it all!" cried Colonel Blood. "In the lava-destroyed city ruins overlooking Lake Como, thousands of years after the fatal mountain eruption, perfectly preserved bodies of human beings were come across—even the colour remained in their cheeks; but, as the contact of living flesh and the atmosphere, the forms instantly crumbled into dust, bodies and raiment alike vanishing as a mere film!"

So, indeed, had those two gone, but a small mound of white ash remaining in their place.

The highwaymen were mad with spleen. This proof to the world of the secret crimes of Jonathan Wild must have brought about his speedy downfall from power. But it was not to be. The evil Fates worked on the side of their chosen instrument of wickedness.

With a sudden inspiration, Craften had taken off his hat, and was eagerly fanning the dust from the table-top. Certain forms could be traced raised beyond the proper surface—a quill-pen, and ink-horn, and, lastly, an open sheet of age-browned paper.

"Quick! bring all your links this way!" cried Dandy Dick, in keenest excitement, on Craften placing the paper, perfectly free from dust, into his hand.

The eyes of all were strained in the direction of this article.

"Writing! A date of close on ten years back! The names of Rupert Trittun and Julia Trittun!" Dandy Dick read on aloud: "'Jonathan Wild, I, Rupert Trittun, and my sweet, devoted wife, Julia Trittun, are resolved to defy ye and die together rather than sign away our possessions in your favour, in return for your restoring to us our darling—our lost little angel Julia! Inasmuch that we cannot trust ye, either in pledged word, solemn oath, or deed, we entreat ye, if there be a spark of pity existing in thine heart of stone, to terminate our sufferings with despatch.

"'(Signed)

"'RUPERT TRITTUN AND JULIA TRITTUN, the former's wife.'"

AN UNSUSPECTED AMBUSH—A DEATH-DEALING SURPRISE—CAUGHT IN A TRAP—FURTHER FEARFUL TERRORS—CRAFTEN AS ADVISER—THE ONLY HOPE—A CHOICE OF DEADLY EVILS.

"To witness two seemingly but sleeping beings vanish into actual nothingness on the instant of coming into contact with our arms is a circumstance that I shall never forget while the breath of life remains in my body. Moreover, I feel that I was guilty of the most terrible sin of sacrilege."

Shuddering at the thought expressed, thus spoke Colonel Blood.

"The two young creatures looked, indeed, as if in life," agreed Dandy Dick, adding: "Their appalling death by asphyxia, or suffocation, in an airtight cell accounts for their most amazing resemblance to actual life. The thick coat of white ash-like dust that completely covered them may have also helped to have kept them so fresh-looking as to have led us to imagine that, if they were not alive, their deaths must have been of a quite recent date. Yet, comrades," he sadly went on, "there was no impious act in our touching them; for, beyond a doubt, their bodies had long ago been turned to dust."

"That name, Trittun, sings most strangely in my ears. I could swear that I have heard it before the finding of that paper," continued the colonel, speaking in a puzzled strain, as one vainly trying to recall a lost note in his meaning.

The remainder of those present in the secret stone chamber of Jonathan Wild's house in Newgate Street also expressed the firm conviction that they had previously heard mention of the name of the mysterious dead; but they were also so deeply affected by the sight they had witnessed that it was not surprising if their memories were in a confused condition.

The dust-covered paper found, if the hand that penned its writing had perished, was yet intact, if age-discoloured, and formed most evidently a strong clue to some great mystery, which had led up to as cruelly foul a deed as ever disgraced humanity.

Dandy Dick carefully placed the document in a breast-pocket. As he did so, a violent knocking came to the ears of the adventurers.

The grim cell was instantly vacated. Loud bangings were made at the closed door of the outer apartment. A crowd of outlaws met Dandy Dick's gaze on his opening the entrance.

"A discovery! a discovery!" they cried, motioning to their leader to follow them.

Their visages were stern set and ghastly white.

Dandy Dick, Colonel Blood, and the remainder of the party instantly followed their humbler friends. Strict commands had been given that nothing should be taken in the way of loot from the premises, but it soon became evident that the crowd of felons admitted to the place had been seeking treasure.

The friends descended to a still lower region. This proved to be a collection of pitch-like dark and most noisome dungeons. The explorers carried several links, and the rays of these were all directed towards a white mass scattered over the age-blackened and mildew-covered flags.

"Our curiosity compelled us to batter in that black, frowning door. We used the same log, and as we had used it on the upper-cell door at your request," explained one of the robber gang to Dandy Dick.

"You were seeking valuables, in spite of my instructions to the contrary!" rebuked their chief.

"We found no booty, comrades," replied the man addressed; "but," he continued, "on the instant we sent in the strong iron door, we heard a strange clattering noise. Some creature of a most evil destiny had been held captive in that gloomy and most foul-smelling dungeon, no doubt for years. The doomed unfortunate must have died standing near the portal that denied him or her freedom. There lie the whitened bones of a ghastly skeleton. Look closer, friend, an' you'll see a heap of what, at first sight, might be taken for red bones mingled with those that are bleached and crumbling; but the red-like bones are the deep-rusted loops of gaol-manacles. Those cruel emblems of captivity must have left their victim only on the latter falling with the movement of the door, and becoming dismembered."

Dandy Dick fell back in shuddering disgust.

"Dante's Inferno presented no more sickening sight than those we have been compelled to gaze upon in this surely heaven-accursed den!" gasped he. "Comrades, my nerves can brook no further horrors," he added. "Let us quit this devilish lair of our implacable foe. I long for a breath of fresh air and a glance of the pure face of Nature after breathing pestilence and gazing upon soul-sickening, festering relics of monstrous crimes!"

Not even the chance of solving this last mystery could induce Dandy Dick to remain a moment longer in the gruesome dungeon regions. He hastily ascended the slimy stone steps, the colonel, Dick Turpin, Tom King, Will Wiffles, and Craften following him.

But before leaving the second underground cell in which was found the skeleton, the colonel had requested two or three of the humbler outlaws to search the interior, a task for which few could now find stomach.

The passage of the house was barely reached before a member of the felon gang rushed in by the open door with the alarming intelligence that Jonathan Wild, mounted on a trooper's charger, was furiously riding onwards, and immediately behind him a great body of the King's Guards. Some delay had stayed the progress of the soldiery in Cheapside, otherwise they would have completely taken by surprise those of the robbers in possession of the thief-taker's dwelling.

This detachment of cavalry was reported to be so exceedingly strong in numbers that the rioters could hope for nothing more than utter annihilation in opposing it. Dandy Dick therefore deemed it wise to at once pass the order for an immediate and general retreat. Not until the last of the crowd of rioters had dashed from the front entrance of Wild's house would Dandy Dick and his friends venture to seek to make good their own escape.

Arms in abundance had been found on the premises. Free use had been made of these, as the highwayman deemed this fair enough between deadly foes; but in no other respect would he permit, so far as he knew, his followers to remove Wild's ill-gotten spoils, upon which, indeed, most of the outlaws held, must hang the curse of blood-guiltiness.

Dandy Dick, Colonel Blood, Dick Turpin, Tom King, Wiffles, and Craften were now in readiness. The last remaining of the felon gangs—three in number—had but an instant before swept out into the gloom of early morning. The distant oncoming of steeds' hooves could be faintly heard, otherwise the outlook had appeared perfectly clear of the enemy.

A sudden, most startling volley from unseen and unsuspected muskets burst upon the still air. The darting serpents of fire located a suddenly-formed ambush-party concealed in a recess almost facing the front entrance to Jonathan Wild's house. With the stunning detonations came mingling the shrieks of the last three of the rabble. Each man had been riddled with bullets.

In a few moments the three fallen outlaws had groaned out their death-throes, and then lay in a ghastly heap on the broad stone steps, in what appeared by the dim lights to be pools of blackness, but which instantly showed shuddering red when the light of a pine brand fell upon them.

Dandy Dick, in suddenly awakened fury, called upon his friends to follow him to avenge the cowardly attack. He was about to spring out into the darkness when the colonel seized him, and drew him into the protecting shelter of the passage not a fraction of time too soon. Indeed, before the colonel could well withdraw both their forms behind the great, stout open door, a second volley had yelled out, this time from smaller firearms. A shower of leaden pellets whistled past the heads of the party in the passageway. The balls hissed upon their course, and harmlessly spent themselves upon stone walls. Yet it was little short of a miracle that Dandy Dick and his comrades escaped injury or death.

The moment and situation were indeed most critical. The heavy door was banged to, then locked, bolted, and its iron beam shot into place. Then broke upon the ears of the outlaws the quickly-increasing loudness of clatterings of the hooves of many steeds. Soon after, King George's Guards, on their proudly-careering chargers, thundered up to the front of the great Newgate official's residence. Before them, side-by-side with the commanding officer, rode Jonathan Wild. What with his fiendlike rage, fear of discovery of hidden secrets and vast treasure in the house, his wounds and plight occasioned by his immersion in the chilling Thames, the ruffian looked a spectacle of humanity not seldom to be met with or soon to be forgotten.

"We are now caught in a death-trap. The building by this is doubtless surrounded, every known exit guarded," gloomily observed Dandy Dick.

"We can hold it for a good time, and our friends will not fail to return if they learn of our situation," cheerfully replied Colonel Blood.

"You forget that Dick gave the order for swift and general retreat. All our supporters are by this time a hopeless distance from us, and doubtless fully cherishing the belief that we may not rejoin them until they reach the Haunted Manor."

Thus commented Dick Turpin.

Then spake up Tom King.

"This lovely fog, rich an' thick as a City banquet's real turtle-soap, sticks to us to-night—or, rather, this morning—like a true, faithful pal," said he in his usual hearty manner. "I suggest," he went on, "that we cautiously, in perfect silence, unfastened this door, and then, with our links doused, an' one by one, creep out an' rejoin at a prearranged spot near by."

"I opine that not one of us wish to add to that heap of breathless clay on the steps before the door. Your notion, if acted on, would but result in adding a few more, if not all, of us do that equally sad and horrible mound!" protested Colonel Blood.

A scattering shower of leaden hail against the door and the following deafening explosion of simultaneously-discharged firearms came as a convincing clincher to the colonel's contention.

"Your advice, Colonel, is ever cool, well-timed, and wise," said Dandy Dick. "I fear me," he added, "that I am more often rash in thought and action."

"Yours is the rashness or recklessness of headstrong youth, which acts first and thinks afterwards. My impulses are those of a riper age, Dick, my dear friend," considerately replied the gallant colonel.

"If yer don't mind, 'I'll put in another spoke,' as ther wheelwright said to ther broken wheel," said Will Wiffles. "Seems ter me, frien's," he added, "that ve're going ter sleep in a 'ouse of wipers, an' wiv a nice swarm o' singing, leaden 'ornets a-knockin' at ther door fer permissun ter come in an' sting us to death. 'I wotes as ve sneaks out o' this,' as ther vise bluebottle advised 'is feller-insects vhen they found as ther treacle wasn't thick ernuff ter safely valk on, an' too thick ter let their feet go!'"

"Wisdom in a nutshell, if not too elegantly expressed," commented Dandy Dick, smiling at Wiffles.

Then the former turned his gaze upon Craften. This person Dandy Dick found in very deep thought. The other adventurers all followed with their eyes the mute, questioning appeal made by the leader.

"You rightly judge that I, who was long in the capacity of chief officer of the wretch who owns this den, should be best able to point out a way of escape from our present seemingly hopeless peril," said Wild's late lieutenant, his face extremely grave and anxious-looking as he addressed his companions. "I was the most trusted of all of the chief officer of Newgate's followers, and knew many of his secrets. There exists another secret way by which we may venture to escape—a way that will not be suspected and guarded, for the simple reason that Wild himself firmly believes that certain death must overtake anyone venturing to leave his present abode by this secret exit."

°CRAFTEN AS ADVISER—THE ONLY HOPE—A CHOICE OF DEADLY EVILS. (*Continued from last number; still procurable.*)

"'Sdeath, the proposal is not too alluring!" jerked out the colonel. "I would prefer to end my last chapter of life gracefully and sword in hand!"

"Amen to that, Colonel!" chimed in Dandy Dick. "Death, met in manly fight, should bring down the final curtain on the termination of the play of life, amidst most lusty and universal plaudits."

"For my part, gentlemen, I'm not in too great a hurry to ring down the sable cloth that betokens my end!" cried Dick Turpin. "What is this back stairway

---

° Part 27. Vol. XIV.—No. 363. 19 October 1900.

like? An' must we wade through blood, fire, boiling oil, or what, to reach a place of safety?" he asked, turning to Craften.

At this there came once more against the door, which most fortunately was iron-plated on its inner side, a scattering volley of bullets, followed by ear-splitting explosions from flintlocks. Then immediately after a terrific metallic ringing of steel blades sounded against the oaken entrance, accompanied by a most thundering clamour of voices demanding admittance in the King's name.

"This goodly, substantial door was never designed for its present purpose," said Dick Turpin, "but was clearly intended for the object of keeping its owner's enemies outside; whereas it now haply[98] protects them, an' displays a cold shoulder to its master."

"It's a case o' turning ther tables—I mean door—with a wengeance, as ther poor spider reflected vhen 'e found 'isself stung ter death be the vasp as 'e'd caught on 'is fine, strong veb," put in Wiffles, quite unable to resist the opportunity of jerking out one of his never-ending, quaint comparisons.

"Beyond that door most certain and sudden death awaits each of us," said Colonel Blood. "Jonathan Wild will be content with nothing less after this last daring affront offered him. If there be but the faintest chance of success of our escape by the way you suggest, friend Craften, let us venture it."

"Ah! ah!" cried the remainder of the robbers. "We fully trust thee, Craften, an' will follow where thou leadest!"

"Be it so, comrades," chimed in Dandy Dick. "Our case is desperate!"

"That, I suggest, is a most desperate remedy for a most deadly disease," answered Craften.

He then strode down the passage with speedy steps.

The noise of great batterings now came against the entrance-way. Large stones could be detected, dashed with enormous force. No time could now be spared for further deliberation.

At the extreme end of the stone flags could be seen a black-painted iron trap, which took up the space of one of the floor-slabs. A movable ring was formed in a circular noose at one of its edges. Craften seized this, pulled lustily; then the trap came up, and a black, square void was revealed. There followed a mighty roar of escaping air of such a foul nature that the party fell back, temporarily overcome by the awful effects of the pestiferous gas.

"Heavens, 'tis the entrance to Hades itself!" gasped Dandy Dick.

"The long-confined air will clear in a few moments. Rest assured, my comrades, every other secret avenue—and there are many—are all most cunningly guarded by Wild's fellows. This one, being deemed almost certain death to anyone adventuring its passage, thus offers us our only hope!"

---

[98] Fortunately.

Thus excitedly declared Craften.

All instantly agreed to risk the chance of life or death.

Craften hurriedly explained that a perfectly perpendicular iron ladder-like arrangement was attached to one of the walls. To this a descender must firmly cling. The bottom level was some twenty feet, and reached a sewer-course.

The thunderings at the door had now become so powerful as to give fears of its quick destruction. Every member of the adventurers tied a kerchief over his mouth. Craften was the first to be on the way. When the last of the party had descended a few feet, the voice of Craften was heard calling up to him to pull down the trap, and then shoot a bolt, to be found on its under side, into its socket in the stone wall. But this bolt could not be moved in consequence of rust.

The utmost difficulty was experienced in descending, and yet still keeping hold of the burning brands. The party's movements were extremely slow. Any moment might prove too late.

The uprushing of poisonous gas threatened to totally overpower each of those descending, so fearful were its fumes. A great roaring and rushing of waters came to their ears. Then, with the hollow clang of the closed trap above their heads, the foul atmosphere instantly became even fouler. The links commenced to give out a bluish flame, then spluttered for a few seconds, and finally went out. They failed to burn in the foul odour.

The terrors of a darkness that almost could be felt were now added to the deathly dangers surrounding those seeking escape by an unknown way from their great enemy's dwelling.

OFFICER BILBERRY AS CHIEF OF THE PIGS AND PINK CUSHIONS—A DISCORD IN THE HARMONY—A DEADLY INSECT—BILBERRY'S BLUFF—THE PIG AND PINK CUSHIONITES ON THE WAR-PATH.

Officer Bilberry found himself the observed of all observers. He pulled himself together, and endeavoured to assume an aspect of extreme bravery, not to say ferocity.

"Three cheers for the gallant and fearless Bow Street Officer Bilberry!" shouted many of his ardent admirers. "Three times three for the faithful, zealous, and fear-nought guardian o' the peace an' terror to all evil-doers! Hurrah for the bravest of the brave!"

A deafening chorus of yells and hammerings upon the oaken table-top then followed, the vice-chairman's little mallet leading the pipe-bowls in their most feverish form of devil's tattoo.[99] A multitude of hands then offered a multitude of glasses, these mostly filled with steaming liquids more or less fiery and rich-tinted.

---

[99] Impatient drumming of the fingers against a table.

Officer Bilberry was now undoubtedly the hero of the Pink and Pink Cushion hostelry. In the ordinary way wild horses would not have forced a blush from Bilberry, otherwise than that of the boiled-beetroot tint due to excessive punch. But the present proved an extraordinary way of calling up the fuller hue of flesh tint, and Officer Bilberry really blushed.

His pickled-cabbage-like-visage-covering was the result of hearing such unscented praise for the possession of virtues he well knew he did not possess. However, there really was a unique species of daring this officer could rightly lay claim to. He could empty more filled glasses of grog, toddy, tipple, gargle, throat-tickler, or what not than any other man breathing, and yet ever retain his perpetual torrid-zone-like thirst.

Eagerly the valorous Bilberry seized offered glass after glass, and threw the contents of each down his extensive swallow, until the long table-top became an army of closed-up ranks of empty glasses, and "fire-water" soon after commenced to ooze from the old tippler's skin. A misguided fly, settling upon his polished, German sausage-like nose, caught the exuding flavour, immediately to fall off in a most deplorable state of intoxication.

The famous Bow Street bully boy now became filled with inspiration and hot and strong drinks combined, where of certain posts are made. His rich, liquid-filled veins grew heated, and the drink fumes filled the space where the brains should have been had they not long ago been dried up with overmuch punch.

"Esteemed an' thrice noble—hic!—friends!" commenced the officer, getting his bulging, water-butt-like corporation with difficulty upon his short and broad legs. "My rights—hic!—confound this windy spasm—I was about to—hic!—observe that—hic!—this night—I should—hic!—say morning—must—witness the—hic!—capture or—hic!—certain death of that great monster—hic!—excuse my excessive—hic!—emotion, my most noble patrons—must witness the capture or—hic!—death of this unmatched—hic!—villain, Dandy—hic!—Dick—hic! I, Bilberry, do now most solemnly—hic!—swear it! Swear it, I say—hic!—most solemnly—hic!—by the future—hic—names of all my forthcoming—hic!—dead an' gone illustrious—hic!—ancestors yet to come!"

The wild plaudits fortunately drowned the latter words of the gifted Bilberry's speech, which had certainly got somewhat mixed.

"Come, come brother-officer, bestir thyself! Up an' doing, man! Up an' doing!" impatiently entreated the runner, who had looked upon the company to collect any officer chancing to be present.

"Beshrew thee, man alive! Blood an' hounds! Let a thirsty soul anoint his desert-parched lungs!" indignantly declared the former, getting rid of his hiccough in his sudden rage. "If I'm in demand for wholesale carnage, limitless slaughterings, I must first moisten the inner man!"

"You've taken more than enough for twenty men at least during the time I've waited your coming! That inner Bilberry's as great a soaker as the outer Bilberry, an' the pair o' ye together would drink the whole o' creation dead!" protested the second runner in disgust.

"Order! Order! Order! S-S-S-hame on ye, s-stranger. S-S-S-uch in-s-s-sulth to the v-ery face-sh of our m-m-ost w-w-w-orthy-ish chair-sh cannot-sh be per-per-per-mitted-sh!"

The vice-chair had rose unsteadily to his legs, his face aflame with outraged feelings and the sampling of too much gargle. The sudden jerk of hastily springing to his feet proved too much for the success of his experiment of turning himself into a vat of liquors. He instantly became top-heavy, sank down like a wet rag falling from a nail, and took cover under the long oaken table. Safely there, the vice-chair sprawled forward full upon his face. A spitting platter was upon the floor near his head. In his condition of extreme drinkology, the vice-chair consoled himself with liberal potions of sawdust snuff, while he continued to growl out his indignation at the great indignity offered to the worthy chairman Bilberry.

Officer Bilberry's hint concerning "his desert-parched lungs" at once resulted in the thrusting forward of many more glasses of liquids. With the said liquids he again most neatly, and with astonishing dispatch, performed the vanishing trick, then turned his scorn-filled goggle-orbs full upon his fellow-officer, and thundered out, in his raging-lion form: "Thou miserable-minded, narrow-chested, mackerel-backed, knock-kneed descendant of a field scarecrow! Presume not to bully men, but follow the light natural beat, an' fright away little birds an' small insects!"

"What! Why you contemptible old swipe-bibber, if ye were not as drunken as a drowned puppy, by the Lord Harry[100] I'd tweak thee by the nose!" responded the former's brother officer, turning livid with annoyance.

"Aha!" Bilberry snatched at his hanger, and put on a very fine aspect of extreme rage. "Flouted to me very boots! Thou under-sized, ill-fed, rash-minded gnat! Get thee gone, thou shadow of a man an' echo of a groan! Get thee gone, or I'll split thee on the point o' my blade as ready as I'd stick a herring there to toast before the fire-logs!"

"You blithering man-frog! You make contradiction of yeself in the multiplicity of the insults applied to one person. I'm this an' that an' tother, everything an' nothing in the one breath!" retorted Bow Street runner number two, adding: "But I'll settle this dispute with thee another time. I'll report that I found ye an' an' if ye tarry in thy duty ye know the penalty!" Then the speaker abruptly left the company and the inn.

---

[100] Henry VIII. In the late eighteenth century did this expletive become "Old Harry", referring to the Devil.

Bilberry appeared to be almost on the point of bursting out with a volcano-like eruption of lava fire, so terrific seemed his fury. The old fraud was a very long way from being a bad actor. Fully assured that the runner had gone, he affected not to be aware of the fact, but lustily yelled out:

"Ho, there! Mine host! A private room! Pistols for two, an' coffee for one! Blood an' hounds, it should be a duel to the death! But one man shall leave the apartment alive! The coffee shall be his, an' if he be a true gentleman, he'll decently inter the slain, and honourably settle mine host's score!"

The Pig and Pink Cushionites threw themselves before the inn parlour door, and most strenuously struggled with the great, fat, round form of the officer to prevent him following the departed Bow Street agent. Needless to state that, although Bilberry most loudly and savagely declared his intention to overtake and hack to pieces the traducer if he did not come back to fight, he, Bilberry, really had no more fight in him than is in a dead butterfly.

The make-believe struggle over, more drinks resulted. Then, secretly growing alarmed at the consequences of his delay in returning to headquarters, Officer Bilberry again resumed his game of bluff. The Pigs and Pink Cushions, all more or less drunk, declared their firm intention of sticking by the chair. "The Noble chair," they insisted, "should not be sat upon by the notorious Dandy Dick!" Bilberry seized upon this hint, and accepted the temporary aid of his friends and supporters. The proudly-swelling chief of the Pig and Pink Cushionites led the way from the inn to the Bow Street police depot. As well try to make a parish pump drunk as to expect Officer Bilberry to become worse for drink. In fact, the drink was always much the worse for Bilberry. In the temporary dearth of runners, the Pigs and Pink Cushions were eagerly accepted as ancillary offices, supplied with cutlasses and flintlocks, and Bow Street Runner Bilberry elected as their officer.

Officer Bilberry was promoted at last! It was true his exalted position as superior officer of a band of swipe-giving volunteers was but temporary. Still, the glory of the fleeting moment was his to grasp.

The daring band sallied forth into the damp, depressing, and choking fog of early morning. Superior Officer Bilberry, with a proud, mincing step, led the way towards the Temple Bar. From thence their way would be direct down ye Street of ye Fleet, on to Snow Hill, and thence to Newgate Street.

Suddenly Bilberry halted. He had espied and inn not yet finally closed. There was no stringent law regulating the closing of a hostelry in the "good old times" of which we write.

"Brother heroes," said the leader of the Pigs and Pink Cushions, "we are about to enter into a sanguinary contest with, mayhap, legions of the degraded and desperate enemies of society. The very thought of the peril we may have shortly to encounter converts my poor tongue into a state of dryness comparable only to the condition of a rag that had aimlessly wandered into an oven and remained there secretly baking for centuries. Brother martyrs, as we are indeed destined to fall in the glorious cause o' duty, 'tis well! But 'twould, methinks, be a thankless end to die o' thirst, therefore let us procure a final bowl o' punch!"

THRILLING ADVENTURES OF THE PARTY OF OUTLAWS BENEATH WILD'S HOUSE—THE DEADLY POISON GAS—THE FEARFUL DESCENT INTO A PIT OF INKY BLACKNESS—THE ESCAPE FROM THE FOUL AIR—GREATER FEARS AND DANGERS—A TERRIBLE DOOM.

"Hold on for your very lives! Descent quickly yet cautiously! One false step on the part of either of us may cost all of us our lives!" This was the voice of Craften. It came up with a distant, dim, and hollow vibration. He had descended into the black jaws of the depths below the trap opening. The foul air rushed up through the impenetrable darkness with a threatening roar, as if most eager to destroy those it had caught in its awful embrace.

Each of the highwaymen had, as the result of the poisonous gas, all but let go his hold upon the iron frame, acting as but a very perilous means of descent at best.

The warning words of Criss Craften had the effect of inducing its hearers to use their utmost efforts of both desperation and caution. If they were to die it would not be without the fiercest of battles with the grim monster Death!

Dandy Dick descended second to Craften. These found that the over-powering effects of the pestilence-laden atmosphere decreased the lower the depths reached.

"Merciful powers!" Colonel Blood was heard to ejaculate. "I must drop! My senses are fast leaving me!"

"In Heaven's name I implore you to keep a stout heart, dear comrade!" rang out the voice of Dandy Dick. "The confined space in which we are adds to the poisonous power of this up rushing air; but a few steps will bring you out of its deadliest fumes."

"I thank all angels of mercy that thou art right, Dick," the colonel soon after was heard to fervently reply. "The poison is already less nauseous. There may yet be hope for us. Wiffles, Turpin, an' King, how fairest thou, dear lads?" he added, addressing the descenders above.

"When I tell thee that each time I open my mouth it is like swallowing a mixture of molten lead and bitter aloes, you will perhaps excuse the brevity of my remarks."

This voice was from Dick Turpin, whose hardihood of temperament and body were well known.

"T'faith, never did I expect to experience the moment when I should regard the possession of the organs of smell and taste as the very reverse of blessings!"

Thus chimed in Tom King, instantly afterwards firmly closing his mouth.

Then the voice of Wiffles was heard:

"This 'ere nice an' sweetly balmy spot 'u'd be a wery choice paradise fer wultures!" he growled out. "A dainty court scent o' this 'ere clarss, though, 'u'd be all ther better fer being nicely bottled up. Ther stopper 'u'd require some 'olding down, too. I really do think," he went on, in gasps—for he only opened his mouth at intervals—"that if I was to leave go o' this 'ere ladder as I shouldn't fall, fer this awful smell is thick ernuff ter 'old me up. Of all ther cussed cussedest cuss this 'ere is ther most cussedistist!"

Wiffles's hearers were in two great danger to pay much heed to his remarks, and it is more than probable that he did not wish them to. It was a kind of mental moral duty with Wiffles to make quaint or funny comments on every possible occasion, in season or out of season.

In their alarm and anxiety there appeared no end to their quickened movements, but this was not really the case. A shout of thankfulness now rang out from Craften. He had reached the bottom of the inky and poison-laden abyss.

"Steady! steady!" he warningly cried. "The earth is treacherously slimy! A few feet from this the Fleet roars and rages on its madlike course. Steady, friends, and caution, caution!"

Craften's words were taken up as if by many mocking demons of darkness stationed at receding points. The terrific roaring of the underground torrent mingled with the weirdly-sounding echoes as if attempting to silence them.

In the first moment of their attack of stupor from the poison fumes the outlaws let fall the torches they carried. These were two in number, and had been extinguished by the foul air. Craften's first thought was to find the pitch-soaked hempen brands. He stooped down, and groped about with his outstretched hands. The darkness was still most profound. The highwaymen each involuntarily gave an utterance to words of thankfulness on reaching the end of their descent.

One of Craften's hands had come in contact with something which he had grasped. The moment after a sharp cry of pain, followed by an oath, was heard. The thing he had clutched, under the impression that it was one of the torches, was a huge rat. The startled creature had turned, and fastened its long front fangs in the man's hand.

After this warning each outlaw joined in the search, but refrained from using a hand. Their lower limbs were protected by the jackboots, and the missing articles were searched for by moving about the feet. The pattering of many tiny feet told of the scattering of the loathsome vermin. Eventually the missing brands were recovered.

The outlaws found the air still extremely bad, but by no means dangerously so now.

Dandy Dick's voice was heard again, this time reminding his companions that the care of their weapons was of vital importance.

Criss Craften was looked to to act as pilot for the time being, no other of the party of adventurers having the faintest conception of their bearings.

The colonel had brought out his flint, steel, and tinder—articles he never failed to have in his possession—and was endeavouring to ignite a torch held by Wiffles, when a lowly-muttered caution came from Craften.

"The trap above is opened! Our retreat has been detected!" he whispered lowly.

He overlooked the fact that the voice ascends, and increases in volume when confined in a narrow space.

Bursting stars of red fire cut into the inky darkness of the deep pit's top. Then ear-splitting explosions followed. A peltering of leaden hail darted down to the very spot upon which the party of outlaws had stood but the merest fraction of time before.

Fortunately the distant, sudden glare of light had been seen by all in time. They instantly decided, and blindly plunged into the darkness. The steep, square cutting merged into an open, cave-like formation, the iron ladder's bottom end being secured by stanchions that were fixed at acute angles into the earth.

Thus the outlaws were sheltered from the bullets of those firing into the black void in the exultant hope of exterminating them.

"Keep well under cover, comrades!" lowly cautioned Colonel Blood. "Bullets are curious things—almost endowed with impish life! Some of those now coming may rebound!"

He had dimly caught a glance of forms bending down above the open trap, and rightly guessed what the intention was.

Another volley burst forth. The roar of the combined detonations sounded most terrific to the ears of those below, while the spluttering onrush of fire and led gave out a most singularly peculiar whistling sound. The echoes of the explosion flew away, apparently in all directions, to lose themselves in the end in faintest whispers in distant catacombs.

During the pause that followed, Dandy Dick silently drew one of his firearms, adjusted the flint and steel, made sure that the priming was perfect, and then carefully took aim at a dimly-seen head, framed in the square of vivid yellow light far above. He pulled the trigger. The explosion caused his comrades to jump in sudden alarm, so unexpected had been his movements.

"By all that's commendable, I thought that we had fresh foes below, and hidden somewhere near!" remarked Colonel Blood.

His words were cut short by muffled curses above. Instantly after another tongue of fire cut through the blackness below. Wiffles had as silently followed his leader's example, firing his piece at the same object.

A mingling of savage shouts now came dimly down to those in the blackness. Then, like a flash, the trapdoor appeared to close, next to partly open; then were seen glints of lights of changing shapes, a swishing, rushing noise following. Next came a sudden crash against the earth, followed by one long-drawn feeble moan.

The outlaws shrank back in horror. A dead or dying person had fallen down that steep, dark opening. What if it should be Jonathan Wild!

Fiercely exultant shouts came from the throats of the hunted men. The striking of flint and steel followed. The sparks failed to ignite the shreds of tinder, but they threw their light upon the body.

A frightful spectacle indeed met the horrified view. Blood-stained, fearfully battered, as the result of coming in contact with the iron ladder, the many jagged, projecting portions of stone, and the ending crash, the silent, motionless object was already soulless clay.

Those attempting to obtain a further view of the remains had the narrowest escape from another storm of lead, the deafening explosion following.

Dandy Dick had convinced himself that the body was not that of their arch-foe. He hastily communicated this fact to his comrades, adding:

"Wiffles, or myself, or both of us, are, I fear me, responsible for this sad affair. Had it been but the wretch whom I aimed at I should have felt far less compunction over the deed."

"Let us seek a way out of this!" cried Colonel Blood. "Those above vastly outnumber us, and any moment they may risk the descent. Our powder and lead would soon give out if we attempted to keep our ground against such odds as would be certain to come against us. Craften man, put thy wits to work! Can our escape be prevented?"

Craften's voice could be heard to reply:

"Jonathan Wild originally intended this sewer-way as one of his secret modes of escape, in the event of the rabble attacking his house for the purpose of taking long-threatened vengeance upon him. Happening to get all but suffocated on his first attempt to descend for the object of investigation, he gave up the notion of using this exit. There are said to be many sewerage tunnels branching off from this spot. But we cannot venture to seek our way without a light; one false step might mean death."

Again Colonel Blood and Will Wiffles attempted to procure a light. They groped their way into a sheltered corner, where the rushing, roaring air was less fierce, and, turning their faces to the wall, eventually succeeded in setting fire to the readily inflammable material of which the links were composed.

Thousands of sewer vermin could now be heard flying off in all directions, terrified by the powerful yellow, dancing flame and its spitting and spluttering noise. Up the black, reeking, filthy walls, into crevices between the rough stones, darted the sable-coated, squeaking rodents. Others plunged into the black, swift torrent a few yards away, and still more darted into low, circular openings, far too small for the passage of men.

A great noise was now set up at the trap opening—shouts of rageful threats.

Then something dashed downwards with a terrific noise. This crashed upon the dead body with sickening force. Another weighty body instantly followed. The dead man's form was in a few moments battered out of all semblance to humanity by many great rough stones. These were intended for the living.

Criss Craften took one of two now flaming links, and anxiously peered into the surrounding gloom. A dry cavernous opening presented itself.

"We must trust to Providence, friends!" he shouted, so that his voice could be heard above the roaring, rushing stream of water, by the side of which he was now standing. "If there should be no opening in the extremity of this—the only safe passage presenting itself—and Wild should descend with his men, our fate would indeed be a frightful one an' a speedy, for the stone-hearted monster could then exterminate us like so many rats caught in a trap!"

"We will place our trust in that good Providence that hath befriended us so oft! What sayest thou, friend Dick?" sang out the colonel.

"Go on, Craften!" firmly cried out Dandy Dick for answer. "To remain here is a certain and a speedy death, unless we elect to surrender. That we never shall do! Therefore we fare no worse if we find elsewhere awaiting us the grim old spectre that claims all men without distinction at the end!"

Craften hastily pushed forward.

Jonathan Wild and the furious multitude surrounding him composed of troopers and his own bloodthirsty guards, would have attempted to follow the escaping outlaws but for the fact that each time they attempted to stand over the opening to place a foot upon a ladder-rung the most horrible poison stench drove them back. Thus the fumes, after nearly suffocating the fugitives, now became their most powerful ally. Time after time were the rage-filled men utterly baffled.

The being whom Dandy Dick and Will Wiffles both imagined they had one or other, or both, shot had, with the rashness of a maniac, persisted in standing over the onrushing poisoned air, until a deadly faintness had seized him causing him to fall into the opening, to be dashed to pieces in his fall. The bullets sped up the opening had missed their mark.

In time the opened door enabled the long pent-up, foul air to escape. Then a descent became possible. The intrepid Jonathan Wild himself led the way.

Meanwhile, Craften darted on and on. The passage he traversed appeared comparatively dry. The outlaws followed close upon his heels. The arched covering of this tunnel was festooned with damp, dripping Thames ooze. On the upper sides were small openings, through which came dribbling water and fresher air. The party were indeed thankful that they would now breathe with comparative comfort. Suddenly a cry of dismay came from Craften.

"As I feared!" he gasped. "We are in what is termed a safety-conduct. A place of temporary rest for the sewer labourers, and wherein to keep their tools of trade. There is no outlet; it is, in fact, an underground blind-alley!"

"What is that distant booming? Surely 'tis thunder? There's a storm breaking above!" said Colonel Blood. The circular borings in the upper sides of the tunnel now instantly commenced to belch forth black streams of water, and which swiftly increased in volume.

"A storm has burst overhead! The Fleet torrent will speedily swell until even this place will become choked up with filth-laden water. We must hasten back! It is our only hope!" anxiously added Craften.

He at once strode on in advance of the others, and ran ahead. Not twenty steps had he taken before a most fiendish laugh—or, more properly described as a yell—greeted him, and abruptly stayed his progress. Innumerable echoes took up that shout and the words that followed.

The words came from the lips of Jonathan Wild. His own and a closely-packed crowd of savage faces were lit up by flaming links. The outlet was hopelessly blocked up.

"So! so! Ho! ho! Ha! ha! ha!" The aspect of triumph displayed by the thief-taker utterly baffles description. "So, my good lieutenant Craften, it is ye who invites my enemies on to attempt thy master's destruction! Ha! ha! But, as thou well knowest, friend Criss Craften, Jonathan Wild never neglects to pay a debt of vengeance!"

The discharge of a flintlock burst out. A cry of mortal anguish instantly followed. Craften was seen to drop his link, then throw up his hands, and, with a quick, convulsive movement, then fall dead!

°THE TWO TRUE CHUMS, JACK SHEPPARD AND JOE BLUESKIN, GET THE BETTER OF THEIR WOUNDS, AND VENTURE FORTH IN SEARCH OF FURTHER ADVENTURES—JACK IN A GRUMPY MOOD—SOME CURIOUS LOGIC, WRANGLING, WORD TWISTING, AND PUZZLING POSERS PASS BETWEEN THEM— JACK RELATES A RIDDLE OF A MOST PECULIAR KIND.

We must by no means overlook the claims of the ever-valorous, desperately daring, yet singularly modest and unassuming Bow Street official, commonly termed Officer Bilberry.

We left this most estimable personage in the company of a number of the distinguished members of the Piebald Pig and Pink Cushions Club, otherwise the frequenters of the smoke-room of the Pig and Pink Cushion Inn.

° Part 28. Vol. XIV.—No. 364. 31 October 1900.

Officer Bilberry was in a condition known in nautical phraseology as "three sheets in the wind," or "half seas over." Among landmen there are various terms used to express the same state—"out on the loose," "light," "boskey," "muddled," "filled up," "boozed," or "scew wiffey."

These represent a few of the favourite phrases in vogue among tipplers in the present day. At the time of which we write, the good old Saxon word, "drunken" was considered as all-sufficient to express that condition popularly denounced "as reducing oneself to the level of the brute beast."

This is an unwarrantable libel upon the lower members of the animal kingdom. They do not get drunk. The drunkard is himself the brute beast, and a self-degraded creature, walks lower than the lowest of the meanest of animals!

But to return to Officer Bilberry.

"What ho, comrades mine!" he thundered. "It must most assuredly be quite ten minutes—nay an eternity!—since moisture have I tasted. Man alive! blood an' hounds! a conglomeration of icily friendships! breathes those living friend-brother o' mine, i'faith, that will of malice aforethought, pre-meditation, and in cold blood, permit his Bilberry to fall in a dead faint at his feet as the want of o' due an' decent lubrication?"

This appeal to the piebald pigs and pink-cushionites, coming as it did from their "most esteemed and worthy chair," was at once responded to.

The brother piebald pig was surrounded by his admirers, and quickly accompanied to the inn's interior.

It was on the point of closing-time, but mine host of the inn, seeing a prospect of gain, promptly, swiftly ignored the fact of his premises being three-parts bolted up for the night. The lights were retrimmed, fresh fire-logs set ablaze, and the smoke-room placed at the disposal of Bilberry and his particularly boorish companions.

Great flagons of liquor commenced to fly about each trailing a long tail of steam in the air. Most of the contents of the said flagons finally found their way down the iron-lipped throat of that bloated human bull of swipes, Bilberry.

In ten minutes or so most of the swash-bidding crew were as drunk as boiled owls—more so, in fact. The more liquids Bilberry lowered, the more alarming became his oaths, the more deadly dire his threats against Dandy Dick.

At length most of the piebalds became fairly convinced that they were regaling two "most worthy chairs." Bilberry, the chair, also saw a duplicate of each of those ever handing him relays of the beloved, steaming toddy, punch, or what not.

Now, this gift of double-sight would have been of little moment but for the fact, when the officer of the flowing bowl saw two Bilberrys, he mostly gave the vessel to the phantom worthy chair; and when that officer saw two of precisely the same one person handing him sweet suction he mostly took the phantom drink from the phantom officer. Then many drinks got mixed—floorwards. Then the company followed suit getting even more mixed than the spilt liquids, each one being suddenly seized with the firm conviction that the man nearest him was no less a person than the very much-wanted Dandy Dick.

Officer Bilberry eagerly accepted the impression that the smoke-room was filled with Dandy Dicks. He also suddenly became convinced that the very best way to secure all the assembled highwaymen was by flopping down to the floor and grabbing everyone he could reach by the legs.

Then there followed a rapid building up of a pyramid of cursing, yelling, scratching, tearing, and kicking matches. Mixed, indeed, like the evil liquors, in which those bottom-most soaked, wallowed, or laved[101]—which ever word may express their true state best.

Mine host, as the result of the terrible, dim, and demon-like struggles and contortions of his over-late patrons, appeared to completely lose his wits.

Someone put out all the lights of the inn, and left the scene of the pandemonium in complete darkness, and then another someone locked the smoke-room door, and left the pyramid to simmer down as best it could.

In the early morning, the ill-fated proprietor was removed in a raving state to the nearest asylum for lunatics. The members of the piebald pigs and pink-cushions were all found entangled like too many eels in a too small space, but sound asleep, and mostly piled up, upon the rotund form of "the most venerated, esteemed, and worthy chair"—to use their own very flowery terms when addressing their chairman, Bilberry.

How the ever-irrepressible Bilberry managed to survive that whole night of heavy wet, heavy sleep, and heavy mangling is a mystery that may never be explained; but alas! he really did survive it. And we must here perforce leave him for a while.

There were two members of the lawless class of the community at least who were not rejoicing with unmixed delight over the subject of the recent assault upon the house of the chief of the Newgate police.

These two exceptions were Joe Blueskin and Jack Sheppard. It would not be quite fair, or true, to state that they were displeased that the affair had taken place. The actual cause of their somewhat want of triumphal full joy was that they had not had an opportunity to earn a part of the triumph themselves.

Blueskin was suffering from the effects of a cracked skull, and his constant chum, Jack Sheppard, carried about with him an ugly bullet-furrow in his cheek, the scar of which he would take with him to his grave.

Dandy Dick had flatly refused to give permission to either of them to take part in the attack upon the house of Jonathan Wild.

---

[101] Washed.

Sufficient time had now passed to enable the two to venture again into the open air. Blueskin still had his skull decorated with a fantastic design worked in slips of plaster.

The cheek of the lad had healed quicker than his friend's head, while, as to the former, a red gash was all that now indicated the result of his most narrow escape from death.

The two outlaws had secretly left the Haunted Manor at Finchley in broad daylight, most gaily attired. Neither Blueskin nor Sheppard owned a horse of their own; they were therefore on foot.

There was no lack of garments—even of the richest kind—in the stronghold of the outlaws, and there everything was practically regarded as the common property of all. Blueskin and Sheppard could have even taken a steed each without fear of denial; but this they would never think of doing unless the mission they were bent on was intended for the profit of the Felon Brotherhood, as was termed their collected classes.

The two outlaws were now in the wild wastelands known as the Finchley Fields, or Finchley Common. There was little to fear on the chance-meeting with mere private persons of prying eyes, as the two firm friends were well armed, the chief risk they ran being that of meeting with police agents happening to know them, or likely to attempt to arrest them as suspected persons.

The exceedingly swagger and rakish get up of Blueskin and Sheppard was just of that kind likely to awaken suspicion in the minds of any member of the felon-hunting order chancing to catch sight of the wearers.

This was only another proof of the complete daring of the lawless classes of the period in general, and Jolly Nose and his pal in particular.

It was a fine, crisp, frosty morning. The sun had peeped out in a half-hearted sort of way, as if afraid of running the risk of getting his nose frostbitten, and the hard frost, covering trees, hedgerows, and filling the ruts in the roadways, sparkled like scattered showers of countless diamonds.

Jack Sheppard was a lad of strange moods, of a headstrong, impetuous temperament; gentle, generous to a fault; a kind—nay, almost affectionate—friend one moment, the next taking offence, flaming up into a most towering rage, or blackly sulking with a friend, and even refusing overtures of peace as if from a most deadly foe. But no one knew the really sterling qualities otherwise possessed by that sadly wayward youth so thoroughly as did Blueskin, and he really loved the lad far too dearly ever to actually lose his temper with him, although it was common for him to affect to do so. The very worst of all God's creatures is never altogether bad. The good and evil qualities are so closely allied that it is not always easy to divide them, and no stranger or more contradictory being ever lived that he usually best known during his very brief life as the "boy prison-breaker."

Jack Sheppard, on this particular bright, health-giving morning, was in one of his most rare moods. A snappish growling, find-falting-with everyone-and-everything kind of temper. But his firm friend had no intention of trading words with him beyond those of their usual serio-comic, angry kind.

The thing most wrangling in Jack Sheppard's mind was his absence from the fierce battle of Newgate Street, as he termed it. Joe Blueskin was no less tender on the same point, if more reserved in his comments concerning the same.

"It was all your fault that we were unable to go, you old blue-parchment chops! Entirely through you!" Jack Sheppard was saying to his companion. And the lad was as puffed up as a male tom-tit on observing a bird of much larger growth attempting to make up to the Mrs. Tom-Tit of the future.

"May I be hanged for a most honest an' tender-hearted villain," blurted out Blueskin, "if I ever attempt to afford you a little pleasant an' harmless diversion again! Once or twice already have I helped you out of a roundhouse. Torn ye, piecemeal, from the stocks, an' rescued ye—ungrateful grain o' sand on the seashore as ye are!—from the tender mercies o' the sweetly pretty red robins, whose chief nest is built in Bow Street, an' those principal grubs an' crumbs o' nourishment we poor squirming things o' the felon class are!"

"An everlasting murrain on ye!" indignantly snapped out Jack Sheppard. "For every time ye've aided me in skipping out o' a lock-up or stocks, ye've gotten me again into the infernal drum (Roundhouse) or love-me-leave-me-not wooden maiden,[102] by the which I mean that, if ye have rescued me once, you've got me taken twice for the same!"

"A murrain, or cattle plague, on thee, Jack, lad! You are a donkey of donkeys, an' wherever ye go your Irish bulls are swarming all over the place like busy bluebottles on a nice meaty beefbone long left in the sun! Seeing that ye've never once been nabbed but 'old blue-gills,' as ye term him, always has turned up at the very nick o' time to help ye creep out o' yer nice an' tight-fitting stone overalls (a gaol), an' regain the blessed freedom, limited only by the four walls of the whole universe an' the star-spangled roof of heaven itself, how, in thunder, could I have gotten ye lagged twice for the every once I've helped to rescue ye, when I've aided ye to break out each an' every time?"

Joe Blueskin struck his arms akimbo, tilted his head on one side, and looked at his companion with an expression of visage which seemed to say: "There, you contemptible little speck of humanity, I've tied you up in a firm knot, get out of it if you can!"

Now, perhaps it is not quite correct to indite "seemed to say" in connection with an expression only, therefore the authors beg most respectfully to take off their hats, and meekly bow to their ever-indulgent readers, and correct that

---

[102] An ironical name given to the stocks.

sentence by placing the words "seemed to imply the following meaning," in the place of "seemed to say."

Jack Sheppard still continued in that precise state of mind that a bear with a sore head is said to be in when he is confronted with the additionally irritating cause of finding, on waking up, that his shaving hot water is not yet ready for him.

"I'm a donkey of donkeys, forsooth!" he indignantly commented. "Again, I'm a manufacturer of Irish bulls! As if donkeys an' Irish bulls were of the same breed; an', worse still, my Irish bulls swarm! Bluebottles an' their kind swarm, not balls, even if the said bulls are Irish; yet worse still follows. To give the lie to your consistency an' logic, you wind up by asking me a riddle of this kind: 'If,' sez you, 'I aided you to escape limbo every time you did escape, how many times didn't I aid you?' Now, please don't throw any more Irish bulls in my face after that prize one of your own. Another thing, dear old blue-bag breed, understand, in future, that I detest persons who ask me riddles! There was a boy I once knew was always asking them. This was one I remember he often put to me: 'If it would take three pounds of butter to well cover thirty slices of bread cut from a large-sized loaf, an' six fresh herrings thirteen minutes to get properly toasted through before a very slow fire, how long would it take a hungry fly to completely soak up one ounce of sugar, if the latter were well soaked and the fly was not disturbed?' Now," continued Jack, "I've not the least doubt that, as riddles go, that one was simple enough; but, for the life of me, I've never yet been able to find its solution, an' the thing has ever since nearly driven me mad. I have not the slightest doubt that, when my last moments come, I shall be vainly trying to work out that, no doubt, quite simple problem!"

"I've always told you, Jack lad," put in Blueskin, with make-believe very sharp-pointed sarcasm, "that you were an ass! Why, the answer to that enigma is a simple as shelling peas, and as plain as your own face! If it would take thirteen pounds of bread to cover an ounce of flies, when they were being toasted before a very slow fire, and the fire was not disturbed, how long would it take a large-sized loaf to completely soak up a fresh herring if the thirteen hungry flies were not—No, I've not got it quite right. If—oh, but any fool can see the solution to that riddle; it's the easiest I've ever heard!"

"Well, it appears that one fool can see the answer without requiring to know the riddle!" returned Jack Sheppard, with a very fine sneer curling his lip.

"Fool thyself, indeed!" curtly retorted Jolly Nose, adding: "If thou art wiser than an empty-pated gnat, answer me this: What is the difference between a man of wisdom and a fool?" Blueskin pulled himself up short by the roadside the better to await the answer. He considered that he had given his companion a most trying poser.

The usual roguish, merry sparkle now shone again in the fine, bold eyes of the youth. He directed his glance for an instant to the earth. Then he looked up again.

"I've told ye that I hate persons who put riddles to me," he said; "but," he continued, "as it will instruct ye, I'll make an exception in thy case, blue-bag blood! The difference between a very wise man and a most errant fool is, as we are at present standing, about one yard an' three-quarters, and the wise man proveth of his wisdom by telling the fool a thing that his folly would not permit him to know! Ha! ha! ha! What do ye say now, dear old beautiful summer-sky visage?"

JOE BLUESKIN AND JACK SHEPPARD CONTINUE THEIR ADVENTURES—JACK RECOVERS FROM THE "DUMPS" AND GETS A FIT OF THE "BLUES"—THE TEST OF HORSEFLESH, AND WHAT CAME OF IT.

"Ho! ho! ho! He! he! he!" Joe Blueskin laughed in unison with his chum, as the latter thought, in consequence of his smart explanation of the supposed poser put to him; but, in reality, the former laughed, and in unfeigned pleasure, as the result of seeing his dearly-esteemed pal throw off his fit of the dumps.

Joe Blueskin took the hand of Jack Sheppard. "Jack lad," he said, in a kindly tone, "had we joined our friends in the attack on Wild's den, the wet, damp, or cold, or all combined, would have found a way through the gaping chink in the roof of my thick sconce; and your double-breasted cheek-ache, left you by that leaden pill, would have been none the better for exposure during the whole of a freezing cold winter's night. There is a very pretty excuse for a visit from the undertakers—its name is erysipelas[103]—and a raw cold in contact with a bad wound will soon introduce that complaint. A man only requires a respectable dose of the article once in his lifetime to finish up his career with a black wooden suit, an' that's a garment that wooden suit this contented-with-his-lot biped just a while!"

"Yes, Joe, old pal, you're in the right; an' I hope you haven't heeded my very hasty an' unpalish words!" now meekly apologised Jack Sheppard. "But it gives me the spider-creeps," he continued, "to see the way a few of the cronies plume themselves on the strength of their deeds on that occasion; an', mind, I'm not such a mongrel cur as to think for a moment that the fellows have not a right to strut about like peacocks owning two tales apiece!"

"Don't apologise, Jack lad," smilingly answered Jolly Nose. "I wouldn't for the world have you otherwise than you are," he added. Then he suddenly thrust out his tongue as if to give it an airing.

"Are ye taken bad, Joe, old friend?" asked the lad, in serious alarm. Blueskin's talking instrument was the size of a bull's.

The red rag disappeared with the flash. "No, I'm not quite two seriously ill; but, tell me, please, if my tongue's spongy-looking, full of holes?" Again the internal terror shot out. Jack stood upon tiptoe, and, in fear and trembling, examined the thing Blueskin had the extreme hardihood to term a tongue.

---

[103] A disease caused by bacterial infection.

"It looks very mop-like an' inflamed—just like the tongue of a dog with a very bad attack of rabies, only more so!" cried Jack, in alarm.

"Then I won't answer for my life, Jack lad, unless you take me instantly to that most inviting-looking hostelry a little ahead of us, an' liberally anoint my poor, threadbare nobbler! How many holes saw ye in it?"

"Well, a good number—say, five large ones, an' about six smaller ones."

"Five pints o' ale, six half-pints, an' two or three extra measures, in case you've miscounted, Jack lad. It will take quite all that balm to heal up my poor perlaverer, an' a full pint more for every minute longer ye keep me a thirst!"

"On the strict condition that ye limit yerself to eight pint measures full, I'll take ye into the inn an' pay the score. None of your base coin tendency, please!" added Jack Sheppard gravely.

"Base, or otherwise, I'll produce no coin, Jack lad," answered Jolly Nose. "I'm at your services for today, but you'll have to find the shot. The doll won't dance until you pull the string!"

"Certainly you're wooden enough to enable ye to justly compare yourself to a timber doll!" slyly put in the lad.

"An' may I be throttled for a most honest thief an' a tender-hearted, reputed butcher of livestock, if you're not waxy enough to enable ye to justly compare yourself to a wax image!" merrily retorted Jolly Nose.

On nearing the inn, Jack and Blueskin caught sight of two nags of good form, and in very fresh condition. The animals were impatiently snapping at their bits like two old seadogs chewing tobacco.

"Just the very thing we want—a good mount!" remarked Jack Sheppard.

"The value of those creatures place them before the narrow limits of our persons, Jack lad, even if they are for sale, which I doubt; and horse-lifting is a dodge I don't approve of, it's too deadly," remarked Blueskin.[104]

"Yes," chimed in Jack, "in picking up a rope with a horse at its end you are liable to soon after hear tell of another rope with a fool at its end. Taking away a steed from its halter may lead to the placing of the neck of an ass in another halter. An', in respect to the latter halter, it recognises no halternative but that of finally altering its victim's course of life by abruptly terminating it; on the principle of that youth, who, wanting to rid himself of the nuisance of the continual barking of a dog, cut the animal's tail off very close up behind its ears."

"It's a pity, then, that the poor dog you mention couldn't have sung with equal truth with that seafaring warbler: 'My bark is on the ocean,' commented Jolly Nose, in an assumed tone of comic grief, adding: "But thereby hangs not a tail!"

The two went on a few yards in silence; then Jack all at once displayed an aspect of extreme dejection. His mood had again changed.

---

[104] It was for 'horse-lifting' that Dick Turpin was eventually arrested and hanged.

"What ails ye, Jack lad?" asked his companion in sincere alarm. "It's that wound, mayhap—cheek-ache?"

"No, Joe,"—the boy's voice was sadness itself—"it's heartache. I'm thinking of my poor mother."

"Aha!" The great rough fellow Blueskin gave out a deep sigh. There had not been wanting in the past rumours pointing to the possession of a very tender passion on his part for the singularly beautiful creature who afterwards became Mrs. Sheppard, the mother of the notorious boy prison-breaker; and, most regretfully, this poor pen must add boy heart-breaker, too, since it is a historical fact that Jack Sheppard's mother became a broken-hearted and demented woman as the result of her only son's departure from the path of rectitude.

The son himself sincerely held the cause of his mother's insanity to have been primarily due to the vile persecutions of Jonathan Wild, and doubtless there was some show of reason for this belief. But the fact must not be forgotten that Jack Sheppard was, without a doubt, a lad of shrewd sense and most remarkable gifts; and, alas! historical records, dealing most minutely with his criminal career, showed no indication on his part to have ever made any serious effort to reform.

"Jack lad, I love thee none the less for the display of an occasional glimpse of virtue. Aha!"—Another long sigh—"with such a sweet, loving, devoted soul for thy mother, boy, how camest thee to be a thief?" Great tears glistened in the eyes of the speaker. A violent outburst of grief was the only reply the boy could give, and for some moments it seemed as if his young heart would render itself with its over-charged anguish.

Joe Blueskin turned his head that he might not appear to witness the outburst, and he walked on in advance. Presently they stood before the roadside inn. Jack Sheppard nimbly caught up to his pal. There was a bright, bold smile upon the remarkable face of the lad now, but the tears—big and glistening—still hung upon his boyish cheeks, if his grief had really departed.

"The sunshine of happiness quickly follows a storm of sorrow when the heart is young," mentally remarked Jolly Nose, but his lips spoke not a word.

"I've made up my mind to visit the Rookery of St. Giles's, old pal!" hailed Jack, with sudden show of bravery and determination.

"The devil you have, Jack lad!" cried Blueskin. "In broad daylight, too? I'm with you—that goes without saying; but, remember, we're got up as two over-fine dandy gallants—Court toothpicks hanging from our shoulder sashes; much real silver-lace facings about our velvet toggery, an' hats included. We are well provided with trusty popguns, I grant ye, but we look much like persons of substance—"

"Especially yourself, below the chest!"

°Joe Blueskin and Jack Sheppard continue their adventures.

"Don't interrupt, Jack lad, please. I repeat, we look like persons of substance, an' if we venture to enter those vile, secret dens and catacombs, where mere murderers, daylight cutthroats, kidnappers, body-snatches, an' those particularly deplorable wretches, the pitch-plaster rogues, are actually regarded as the better classes of the community, what think ye will happen to us? An' what is thy motive for venturing into regions by comparison with which black Hades would appear a place of respectability and calm repose?"

"I won't ask you to take the risk, I'll go alone. My motive is to learn tidings of my poor mother. Neither Jonathan Wild nor any of his known creatures dare ever venture into the precincts of the Rookeries of St. Giles's. That plague-spot of all that's evil has, I know, before now proved a very haven of refuge to many whom that law-supported butcher of his fellow-creatures, Jonathan Wild, had marked out with his brand of blood."

"Enough, enough!" Joe Blueskin eagerly seized Jack's small, girl-like hands in his own broad and strong palms. His eye grew very moist, and there was a trembling in his voice as he added: "May I indeed be scragged for an over-honest villain if I ever hesitate to hazard my life when either Mrs. Sheppard's or her boy's welfare demands it!"

A warm pressure of the hand was all the answer Jolly Nose received, for Jack Sheppard could not trust himself to speak. The heart of this wayward lad grew tender, and his spirits gentle as those of a little child whenever thoughts of his terribly-afflicted and only remaining parent entered his mind. Omitting, perhaps, Joe Blueskin, there was not a soul on earth the boy loved but this same poor, demented creature, who not only failed to recognise her boy when he found her, but frequently repelled him as an entire stranger to her.

Joe Blueskin called for and consumed liquors at the inn-bar in a manner calculated to lead a beholder to firmly believe that he carried within his interior the blazing fire of a furnace that he was intensely anxious to put out before it completely burned him up.

There were a number of rural-looking men occupying the bar-parlour. Two of these were engaged in heated debate.

"I tell thee, Giles Screwin," one was saying, "that my mare is the fleeter o' foot nor yourn."

"An' I tell thee, Mark Muff, that my horse flesh can outrace thine—an' I'll wager thee a sum o' five shillin' on't, too!" cried the other.

"An' maybe these two stranger gallants will help us come at the real truth o' this moighty contenshun!" put in a third man.

° Part 29. Vol. XIV.—No. 365. 31 October 1900.

Jack Sheppard had again become himself—the merry word-twister, punster, and incorrigible joker.

"Gentlemen," commenced he, assuming the gravity of a man of ninety, "I understand both of ye insist your horse is swifter than the other. You will therefore permit me to state that it is not possible for two animals to each be swifter than the other. Furthermore, you may depend upon it, that if one steed can out-race the other, it is not so much the case that he be quicker as it is that the other one is slower, and I dare venture to wager that, if put to the trial, an' one wins, the true, exact and most particular reason for that will be because the other hath lost."

The company stared at the lad speechless in open-mouthed wonder. The logic was so new to them that they could not quite see the fun the impudent Jack was poking at them.

"Come—don't no—put—softs—your-ri—foot-mo—into—son—the pie— now—Jack. I've—got—fluff'em a notion—vee'm that—trick lara—may-ja— suit-com—our liffe purpose." Saying this to his companion, Joe Blueskin then turned to the company. "Excuse me, friends," he commenced, "I addressed my brother here in a foreign tongue, which he understands better than English. I was pointing out to him the fine qualities of those animals we observed by the in-door before we entered."

The owners looked exceedingly pleased.

"Worthy gallants, would ye so far condescend as to oblige us by yerselves putting our beasts to the trial of speed?" asked one of those of the dispute. "He can ride well, I'll be bound!" he added. "Such noble-looking gallants as he must needs be most famous in the saddle!"

Jack Sheppard held his tongue, but indulged in much winking, unseen by any but his companion.

"We will oblige ye with great pleasure, friends," returned Jolly Nose. "Say we race the steeds about a mile out and another back! My brother and I ride equally well. The trial will be an equally fair one in all respects," concluded Blueskin.

The assembled company thought nothing could be fairer. In a few moments Joe Blueskin and Jack Sheppard were mounted and darting away. A crowd collected outside the hostelry waving their hats and urging the riders to put forth the utmost efforts of the animals. When they had left the inn well behind, the two riders eyed each other.

"Jack lad," laughingly remarked Blueskin, "I don't think it would be quite fair not to give these fine fellows a longer spin!"

"I really shall require to go quite as far as the Rookeries of St. Giles's and back before I can properly judge of the qualities of the beast I ride," answered the lad saucily.

"That's the ticket, Jack lad; the Rookeries and back!"

Death of Criss Craften—Dandy Dick, in a fury, again handles the thief-taker's throat—Desperate men at bay—No escape—Jonathan Wild and his guards triumphant—The underground flood.

We must now return to the scene of the underground sewers near the house of Jonathan Wild.

Criss Craften slain! A man in the very prime of life ruthlessly shot down! The doomed being had not time even to draw a weapon in his own defence.

For some moments following, foes and friends alike paused. The horror of the thing held the outlaws spellbound. Jonathan Wild knew neither feeling of pity or remorse. He was simply calculating his advantages, as to which would mean the greatest honour and profit—the taking of the highwaymen alive, or the slaying of them while they were securely in his power, as he now fully deemed they were, even if they made desperate resistance for a time. Their possession of some of his terrible secrets alarmed him not a little. He therefore secretly determined on the utter destruction of Dandy Dick and his companions.

The torch held by Craften had shot forward from his hand into a pool of water, and was extinguished. The outlaws now had but one burning brand.

Dandy Dick no sooner shook himself from his trance-like terror than he uttered a shriek of ungovernable rage, and threw himself bodily upon the grinning and chuckling Jonathan Wild. The swiftness of the action took the thief-taker unawares. His throat was seized in a grip of steel. The impetuous nature of the attack bore the latter backwards. The two, locked in a deadly embrace, crashed to the earth.

Dandy Dick was now entirely at the mercy of Wild's followers. Had they but had their presence of mind, the young highwayman could have been dispatched by a cutlass-thrust through the back with impunity; but, seeing their chief thus down, and with a being over him, and fastened upon him with the very fury of raging tiger, they paused before striking a blow. To have fired at Wild's assaulter might have meant the killing of both the undermost and the uppermost man.

Colonel Blood's a quick glance took in the situation in all its grim and perilous details. The fearless outlaw flew to the aid of his rash friend. Without compunction, regarding Wild as wild beast instead of man, the colonel kicked him swiftly and mercilessly in the ribs, not ceasing until the breathless creature released his grip of Dandy Dick. At the same instant the latter was pulled away by Wiffles and Turpin.

By this the Newgate janissaries had recovered their full presence of mind. A volley, composed of twenty or thirty bullets, would have swept the little outlaw-band from off the face of the earth.

The colonel saw the death-storm threatening them. The remaining flaming brand shot through the air like a fiery meteor, striking full in the face the nearest

Newgate guard, then, in its swift and twisting course, dashing into the face of another, and spreading showers of bright, golden sparks about the heads of the crowd of mercenaries facing the tunnel in which the highwaymen stood at bay.

A softly-muttered whisper came from Colonel Blood in the very nick of time, to induce his comrades to crouch down, as a terrific volley of lead shrieked over their devoted heads.

The outlaws were now in complete darkness. The narrow dimensions of the oval-shaped passage, into which they had further retreated, would not permit of the light from the links held by the enemy entering beyond a few feet.

Tom King was hurriedly instructed to run to the furthermost extremity of the tunnel, and endeavour to, as best he could in the darkness, find for certain if the statement of their slain friend Craften was correct, and that there really existed no possibility of escape that way.

The chief of Newgate police was again up, and directing his merciless followers.

The outlaws—grim, resolute, but having little hope—intently awaited the return of Tom King. They held their firearms—those remaining loaded—in their hands. Their rapiers, too, were drawn. Each man looked the picture of a brave, defiant hero, calmly resigned to instant death if it needs must come to him.

The flambeaux darted about in all directions beyond the mouth of the cave of utter darkness in which the outlaws stood. The ever active form of the thief-taker, who appeared to regard with contempt risks of life and death, could be seen instructing and urging on his men to a more-determined mode of attack.

The numbers of the enemy seemed countless. Their blackened forms were slashed with darting gleams of yellow and crimson reflected light. Never a more hideously repulsive set of beings could anywhere be found than Jonathan Wild and his crew of human vultures.

The complete blackness perfectly had from view those the police-agents sought to capture or destroy. The former were unable to tell if any or all of the outlaws had been brought down. So vastly outnumbering the little party as they did, yet they feared to dash into the tunnel of blackness, judging that those of their intended victims still alive would make a most heroic resistance, fighting while a gasp of breath yet remained, or strength to but lift firearm or steel.

"Down, comrades, down!" suddenly muttered Dandy Dick, not a moment too soon.

A wildly-sweeping, terrific fusillade burst into the sewer-cave.

The highwaymen had thrown themselves prostrate, getting half covered with ooze now pouring still faster from the small inlets pierced in the upper parts of this tunnel.

Tom King had not yet heard the whisper of caution. A smarting, as from the stab of a red-hot knife, located in itself in his shoulder. He knew instantly that a bullet had entered there, but he heroically kept the fact secret. The streaming blood could not be observed by his friends as he staggered back to them. In hoarse tones he made them understand that Craften's statement had been correct. There was no possible means of escape for them by the further end of this boring—there was no visible outlet.

The thunder of the explosion seemed to render all in the tunnel perfectly deaf for some seconds, a most profound silence following. Then another and still more terrible volley came tearing into the blackness. Bullets fell in every direction, flattened and rebounding. A shower of spent balls fell about the men, this time all stretched full-length upon their stomachs in the foul-smelling liquid. A sudden ping and hissing, as of a snake near, told whenever a ball fell into the now shallow-running stream, covering the bottom of the tunnel.

"Comrades, a few moments more must decide our fate!" muttered Dandy Dick, springing to his feet. "Let us face our end like men. I, for one, will no more grovel here in filth—fitting place only for loathsome vermin. But, before I finally fall, my rapier shall lave in the black blood of my implacable enemy, Jonathan Wild. His bloodthirsty career terminated by my steel, my name shall go down to future ages as a benefactor of the human race!"

"You may be slain, and not even gain the distinction you covet, Dick, dear comrade," lowly answered Colonel Blood, adding, "but I am with you in a wild and sudden sortie. We might perhaps succeed in fighting our way through yonder wretches, and even reaching the place of descent by which poor Craften led us. 'Tis an improbable venture, I admit; but anything will be better than this. In a few moments more our doom may confront us!"

The determination was no sooner taken than the remainder of the party rose up. They were drenched, and, to make their positions still more dismaying, the streams of liquid, shooting from the small, circular sewer-inlets above the outlaws' heads, and on each side of the tunnel, had now increased into fiercely hissing and foaming waterspouts. The possibility of keeping the firearms and powder available for use was also becoming a most alarming matter.

"What is to be done, comrades?" lowly asked Dandy Dick, tremors of desperation and despair mingling his tones.

"Fight like fiends to the last gasp!" replied Colonel Blood, gnashing his teeth.

"I'faith, I'm for that, pals! If I can but rapier-skewer a few o' the choice gallants out there before they give me my mortal quietus,[105] I'll turn up my toes contentedly!"

Thus grimly muttered Dick Turpin, impatiently thrusting out his steel to prepare the muscles of his sword arm.

Tom King maintained silence. The agony he now endured was excruciating, and he feared that, if he ventured to speak, his voice would give an inkling of

---

[105] Final settlement; removal from activity. In this case, Death.

his sufferings. He thrust his 'kerchief up his coat-sleeve, to, if possible, prevent the flow of blood.

"Frien's," whispered Will Wiffles, "powder won't keep dry under these 'ere nice an' blood-coolin' streams o' slosh. I've got a canal as means business a-navigatin' itself beautiful a-down me spine, an' I calcerlates as in two minutes more I shall become a walkin' waterfall, wery pretty to look at—if you'd got a light turned on me—but considerable dampish to the feel. I therefore wotes as we instanter clears out our popguns—complamentary-like—in ther direction ov them there 'uman sewer rats outside!"

"The suggestion's a good one, dear friends; but, as it will mean the last shot each may fire on earth, pray let it not be wasted!" primly assented Dandy Dick.

There was evidently a most serious deliberation being carried on by the enemy. Jonathan Wild's evil and rasping voice could be distantly heard. He was endeavouring, by the making of most princely promises, to induce his men to make a sudden dash into the black opening, and to put all found still alive therein to the sword.

The outlaws prepared to fire a volley. A startling vibration followed the pulling of their triggers. Then snarling oaths, awful groanings, and fierce cursings mingled. The thickly-crowded thief-takers were hit. It was impossible to tell the full extent of the blood-letting, but the many yells of dismay pointed to the serious and extensive nature of the wounds inflicted.

This desperate blow of vengeance on the part of the fugitives had the effect that the combined threats and promises of the chief of the Newgate emissaries had so far failed in producing. The highwaymen were now to be attacked at the point of the cutlass, which really meant that they would be mowed down by overwhelming numbers, and ruthlessly hacked to pieces.

The doomed men silently exchanged firm, manly, farewell hand-grips. Their hearts were full. They dared not speak, lest the emotion of one should unman the arm of another. That hand-clasp was eloquent enough. If unspoken the words, each well knew how to translate that pressure.

"Farewell, beloved friend! If it be the decree of Fate that we fall, it will be as men! Farewell for ever, and Heaven bless thee!"

Thus read the genial leave-taking.

Then each man darkly knit his brows, firmly clenched his teeth, and fully braced up every muscle of his body for the coming crash of arms. They would not await the assault, but meet it. A ringing yell of defiance burst from their lips, then the hunted men at bay furiously hold themselves forward.

Jonathan Wild was completely astounded at the daring displayed by the hopelessly-outnumbered handful of adventurers. But for their surprise, the followers of the thief-taker could have instantly despatched their victims by a ball and blade.

There was, however, another foe to content with. The long-threatening storm above had by this time burst forth with great impetuosity. The thunder crashed with frequent and alarming force, and rain descended from the heavens in an unbroken sheet.

The safety-tunnel, in which the outlaws had taken refuge, was of higher level, and its floor gradually sloped upwards.

As Dandy Dick leapt forward, his swiftly-gyrating steel formed circles in the air above his head, as of flying ribbons of quicksilver. The enemy fell back before him.

To the rear of Wild's men a great volume of water came thundering on. The sewer-passages were over gorged, and belching forth madlike volumes of foaming, hissing, leaping streams.

The highwaymen soon found themselves wading waist-deep. They fought like maniacs. Many of the thief-taker's followers became sheaths for steel, fell back, and disappeared in the raging torrent, that swept them away with resistless force.

"Back, lads, or we shall drown!" shouted Dandy Dick, as he felt himself almost lifted from his feet.

The command was swiftly obeyed.

A party of janissaries, stationed on a dry mound, levelled their firearms, and fired at the retreating highwaymen. The latter were so closely pressed by others of the foe that the bullets intended for the outlaws brought down three of their enemies.

Quick as thought, the fugitives flew into the gloom of the tunnel. The raging mass of waters threatened to engulf the remorseless thief-taker and his savage servitors.

Now, fully expecting almost instant death, either by shot, steel, or waters, Dandy Dick and his devoted little band darted to the extreme end of the sewer causeway. Suddenly a most startling sound burst upon their ears. Totally unlike anything they had heard before in those underground regions was the unaccountable noise.

Gay birds in borrowed plumage—Jack Sheppard and Jolly Nose again on the warpath—Blueskin holds forth on certain subjects of grave import—Will the Witless—The Red Robins scent out Jack Sheppard and Blueskin.

Jack Sheppard and his chum Joe Blueskin were riding side-by-side, very leisurely trotting their steeds, so that the conversation was not only easy, but also pleasant. The two outlaws were dressed in very handsome apparel, their fine plumage having been borrowed from their friends of the Haunted Manor of Finchley. The animals the robbers rode were also not their own, but, as the reader is aware, had been entrusted to the two strange visitors to a certain inn for the purpose of testing which of the two steeds was capable of the greater speed and formed of the better metal.

The two rogues had, however, determined that they would not hurry themselves in returning the nags.

The locality they were now in was frequented by very few human creatures, and almost void of sight of any habitation.

It was a delightful winter morning, cold, yet bracing. The snow still covered the earth, and the hoar-frost and icicles clung to and hung from countless numbers of branches, twigs, and everything else possible in the landscape. The bounteous night dewdrops had become sparkling frozen diamonds, silver beads, or pearls, and all Nature seemed covered over with a lovely silver sheen, which, when the sun occasionally came out—as it did at rare intervals—was instantly transformed into a dead-gold tint, lighted up everywhere with bright dots or studs.

"Aha, Jolly Nose, it is a grand thing to be alive!" gleefully cried Jack Sheppard.

"A slight improvement on being dead, Jack lad, I admit; but only a very, very slight improvement!" growled Blueskin, in affected stumbling protest, as was his wont.

"Odds, bodkins, what a wooden-nutmeg head is that on thy shoulders, sky-tint visage! One must be either alive or dead, I take it!"

"Jack lad, ye are at perfect liberty to take it or leave it. That pimple which hath formed upon the top of thy neck—if ye have luck, it may someday come to a head!—At present it is of little value to you, and, moreover, 'tis a very sad disfigurement!

"There is, I tell thee, numbskull, a state between life and death! There is the hostelry Life; there is the hostelry Death. But there is also on the road, midway between the two, an inn, and its title is that of Sleep. That's the half-way house between Life and Death.

"You can get every luxury, joy, an' comfort in life there—and nothing to pay! You have but to dream them! As for enemies—ye can just hang them off in thy dreams. If ye are a king an' wretched, ye'll have but to dream ye are a beggar. If ye are a beggar, an' wretched still, you can then call up a vision in which you appear in Royal state!

"Ah, Jack lad, the man who invented the somnolent state was a great genius! He knew a thing or two, and I fancy he must have been a poor devil of a tramp, worn out, overheated with the raise of a powerful son, badly wanting a meal, an' with a delightful patch of green grass, just under the cool shade of a green tree, a-tempting him!

"Then the poor beggar must have hit upon the delightful idea of half dying—commonly called 'sleeping'—getting into that state wherein he could bamboozle his unhappy, worried mind into thinking itself in a condition of complete bliss!

"Heigho, if I'd known as much, when I commenced my career, as I do now, I have started a sleeping-spell that should have lasted all my lifetime. Then I'd have waked up in death, an' gone on believing that to still be life!"

"Now, Blueskin, you're getting mixed. Ye'd better drop that idiotic vein. Thy tongue we'll get tied up in a knot else, an' hard corns will soon grow on thy soft brain!"

Blueskin was about to attempt a retort, when the words were stayed upon his lips by an unusual sound.

"What's that remarkable noise?" asked Jack, pulling up, and gazing around at the barren landscape.

"What, indeed?" reiterated Blueskin, also pulling up his animal, and anxiously peering round. "Sounds like the footsteps of an enormous giant. His strides are a week long!"

All at once an object, much like a scarecrow stuck at the end of a long pole, caught the attention of Sheppard and Jolly Nose. It shot up some yards from the earth, then sank down again from their view, a hedgerow intervening between. A moment more, the dark, moving mass was seen to fly through the air, and then to land on the near side of the bushrow, a few yards from the two riders.

"That's a banshee, bog-goblin, some rare kind of waterfowl, or a scaffold-poll with a bundle of rags attached to one of its ends, that's persuaded itself that it hath a mission in life!" muttered Jolly Nose.

"Why, Joe, old chum, don't you remember? That's Plom—Plom, the what-ye-may-call-it-thing-a-may-gig that so completely scared us on the night I broke through the pie-crust-like roof of the Round House of St. John's!" excitedly explained Jack Sheppard.

The strange visitant was no less than Will the Witless. The boy barely waited to recover his breath, evidently after much exertion, before he cried out, in his thin, piping tones:

"Black, bad fairies are abroad even in this bright, beautiful daylight. They are getting ever bold. And the good fairies will send a thick, black fog, as they always do when evil spirits are roaming the earth. You see, the good fairies send the thick, blinding mist to prevent the wicked goblins from finding their prey—us mortals. And the evil shadows are eaten up—consumed by the demon Fog. Ha! ha! ha! My friends, the good fairies, love us mortals, and are ever most kind and good to us—especially to poor little Will the Witless, for they shelter him at night, and feed and clothe him always!"

"Heaven's mercy upon thee, thou poor, afflicted lad! I now remember the boy, Jack. 'Tis the idiot child I have oft heard Dandy Dick speak of."

So saying, Blueskin dismounted, and went towards Will the Witless.

"Ho! ho! ho! he! he!" laughed the little fellow. "What a fine gallants! Ah, Will the Witless knows thee, Jack Sheppard! Their mother is a good fairy, an' loves poor Will. Thou wilt find her in the Rookeries, bonnie Jack."

"He speaks of my poor mother, Joe. Here, child, get food an' make thyself contented," added Jack, throwing Will the Witless a crown-piece.

"Stay!" muttered Blueskin, catching the coin as it spun through the air. "It is a true one, I hope, Jack?"

"True is the heart of that poor child," was the reply. "Come, take the coin, little fellow. An' now get thee gone, for the pretty red robins seem to love thee not one bit more than they do less honest folk," feelingly said Blueskin, placing the silver piece in the tiny palm.

"Red robins!" suddenly repeated Will the Witless, placing a finger to his forehead, as if to bring back a lost thought. "Aha," he continued, "that was it! Will the Witless came to warn his friends. The red robins are coming after ye!"

The words were no sooner uttered than the sharp, clattering, metallic ringing of horses' hooves upon the hard, frosty-covered road came to the startled ears of the two outlaws.

Will the Witless had bounded out of sight at the actual moment of three horsemen turning from a by-lane and dashing swiftly up to Jack Sheppard and Blueskin.

The officers appeared somewhat excited and nervous-looking.

"We were watching you two fine bloods," said one, guiding his horse close up to the side of that upon which the great form of Blueskin was seated—"saw you both enter the inn, come out again, mount those nags, and start off on the animals in very fine style!"

"Emph! Did ye think it a good show, Robin dear?" sarcastically asked Jack Sheppard, his eyes flashing danger.

"A mighty brave show, Sir Gallant—mighty brave!" was the reply, with sarcasm thrown in, and with compound interest,

"Beshrew me for a fire-eating dove! I never saw one so serious over his fun in all me life before. You approve of the show, but you haven't paid for the performance!" burst out Jolly Nose in his most powerful lower-chest notes.

"No! I'faith, and the pair of you will soon go through another performance, in which the show and payment are not to be separated! You'll both perform a fine balancing-an' cut a capering, grotesque dance, on air. The only balance you will have will be a hempen noose around thy necks. Understand, I know you both—hang-gallows rogues as ye are—Joe Blueskin and Jack Sheppard; and there are warrants long out for the two of you!"

The one officer had so far acted as leader and spokesman. His two comrades appeared too startled to do anything else but look on.

The quick eyes of Blueskin had taken in everything. One of his pistols was concealed up the wide coat-sleeve of his right arm, butt-end outwards. The firearm could slip through his fingers and become a club in a twinkling.

"Thou liest!" thundered he. "Were a tadpole thy sire, sirrah, he'd blush to own thee! Dare to call two fine an' daintily-nurtured gentleman by the names of notorious outlaws, an' I'll break thy pate to mend thy manners!"

The foremost officer instantly backed a yard or two, then whipped out a flintlock.

"The blue cast of my face is the well-known badge of Joe Blueskin. And the youth. Cool disregard to all danger and fierce, black eyes of the lad there are points by which Jack Sheppard, the boy prison-breaker, cannot be mistaken. We found that those nags were entrusted to you under the impression that ye were both honest gentleman. Surrender quietly. We're well armed, an' three to two!" concluded the Bow Street runner, levelling his weapons, full cocked, at Blueskin's temples.

"Zounds, you throw the colour of my complexion in me face!" gasped Blueskin, assuming a terrific rage. "By all that's ugly," he went on, "I'll get me chops dyed a greeny saffron colour! Put me head, face upwards, under a heavy cartwheel, then sit an' jump upon it for a week or two, after which it shall go through a finishing course by being thrown to famished chickens, which shall peck at it, and toss it about through the mire! If I'm not then as like thee as two peas in a pod, well, I'll then loan out my utterly-spoiled mug to a showman who's a-building up the figure of a sea-serpent, or that of the Prince of all Darkness!"

"Flesh and blood can stand no greater insults!" hissed the foremost Bow Street officer, pressing his trigger.

The pistol, most fortunately for Blueskin, but flashed in the pan.

"Keep the head cool, an' powder dry, when ye meet with bucks as fierce as my pal an' I. There's a rhyme for thee, an' a broken sconce to the better permit the wisdom o' the maxim to reach thy poor, dull brain-works!"

Blueskin's steed had leapt forward. The butt-end of the rider's pistol had crashed down with amazing force upon the officer's three-cornered hat and the head inside it, and the man was seeking for the return of his lost faculties and a glimmering of what had really happened, beneath the shadow of his fear-trembling animal.

A MYSTERIOUS THUNDER-LIKE CLAP—ENTOMBED ALIVE— MOMENTS OF TERROR AND DESPAIR—TOM KING'S AGONY— AN AMAZING DELIVERANCE FROM A DEADLY DEATH-TRAP— FANGS, THE HUMAN RAT—THE TERRORS OF THE THAMES.

Suddenly, startling and alarming as an unexpected and deafening clap of thunder was the unaccountable noise the outlaw party had heard, and at a moment so fraught with danger to them that death by drowning seemed, in contemplation, but as a merciful deliverance.

Tom King was secretly suffering from a terrible bone fracture—the result of a pistol-shot—in the left shoulder or upper portion of the arm. The agony he endured in perfect silence, although it was excruciating enough; but the great loss of blood—it continued to trickle down his sleeve and over his hand—had made him feel so weak and faint that he could scarcely stand.

The blind-alley-like sewer tunnel in which the outlaw adventurers were was completely enveloped in darkness, and the air simply deadly, so extremely foul it had become. To make the situation of the fugitives even still worse a tremendous inrush of most horribly smelling liquid slush had rushed into their place of retreat.

Dandy Dick, Colonel Blood, Dick Turpin, and Will Wiffles were together swept off their feet like so many straws, and hurled with great force against the thick slime and ooze covered rugged stones of the extreme end of the sewer boring.

King was caught by the violent crash of his companions. His irresistible groans of pain ceased as the foul wave washed over him. The whole party were then engulfed and swiftly carried back by the force of the receding waters to the mouth of the tunnel. Dandy Dick was the first to regain his feet. His plight was fearful enough, but no worse than that of each of his comrades. The sewer liquid had suddenly become quite calm, and now reached up to the men's shoulders.

Those of their firearms not lost were rendered utterly useless by saturation in the onrush of water.

The highwaymen were drenched to the skin, and each terribly bruised and shaken. Tom King felt that he should little longer be able to keep from his friends the knowledge of his serious injury. The complete darkness had alone enabled him to do this so far, but the agony had now almost become unendurable.

"Great heavens!" cried Dandy Dick. "We surely have been washed into another cutting!"

"What do you mean, Dick?" shouted Colonel Blood. "If so," he added, "our plight is still worse than before. This foul air is choking me to death!"

A terrible groan now came from Tom King. His companions thought it due to the horrible feeling of suffocation now overpowering them all.

"Oh, for a light!" gasped Dandy Dick. "Where the mouth of this place was— or appeared to be—I find a compact stone wall. Wild and his crew have all vanished like phantoms, I can no longer hear a sound of the storm; and the water surrounding us is as placid as a mirror."

"If we were hurled into another passageway we had better lose no time in searching for the place we came through, or we shall each soon stifle, like a fox in a sealed-up warren." This voice was that of Dick Turpin. The suggestion was at once most diligently acted upon. Wiffles remarking meanwhile:

"I'll swear, be all I'm worth—which ain't over-much at the present moment, it's true—that we ain't never left ther same shelter as we fust flew into a-tryin' ter give ther go-by ter Wild an' 'is men!"

A most careful search soon convinced the outlaws of the truth of Wiffles's remarks. In some amazing way the entrance to the place had become blocked up by a wall of solid masonry. This, then, accounted for the thunder-like noise that had so amazed the outlaws. This wall so perfectly filled up the opening that the water within remained placid and undiminished in quantity.

"We are entombed! The whole thing is a profound mystery. We cannot live many moments thus hermetically shut up. The atmosphere is becoming more deadly poisonous with each moment," despairingly remarked Colonel Blood.

"A most ideal death, truly for a ferocious beast perhaps, but not for man!" chimed in Dick Turpin, almost in a tone of complete despair.

"Ve might as vell be glued tight down in a great big snuff-box, we might!" commented Wiffles disgustedly. "Ther snuff as ve're a-gettng' is strong ernuff, too, ter please ther greediest an' biggest-posed sniffer as ever snuffed; but I really can't say as its aromer or flavour is too over-choice. Ugh!"

The comrades groped their way through the inky darkness. The thought of meeting death together, firmly grasping hand to hand, was the only grain of comfort now to be found in their most terrible predicament.

Tom King, on finding his friends grouped around him, lightly—even in the face of a most hideous death—explained the fact and nature of his wound. The expressions of sympathy offered were heartfelt. He would not permit his companions to attempt to stem the flow of blood.

"Needless, dear old comrades," he protested, with a most grim and hollow mockery of laughter. "If we are all to finally snuff our glims[106] here I shall do the graceful exit first, an' so take the last mean advantage of my pals. Ha! ha!"

The attempt at hilarity was feeble and wretched enough. Was that merely an echo, or was it indeed another human laugh?

Every eye was directed to the spot from whence the slight echo-like sound had come. The pitchy blackness of the rock of the captive-place was now cut into by a dazzling slip of yellow light. This slip widened, and became a square of a warm, bright yellow hue.

"We are saved!" Every voice in the black prison-place fervently, if lowly, echoed these words.

Next faint, distant, harsh tones were heard chanting some few words of a most gruesome song, and muttering strange remarks between.

> "Oh, the rats they wade the black, black slush,
> Love to burrow the soft, clinging mire.

Oh, yes, i'faith, but the rats love other pleasures as well—

> The stranger greet with departing rush—

---

[106] Literally "put out our lights", so "Snuff out the light of our lives".

Especially if that stranger happens to be a Government officer

> To lurk in the darkness void of din,
> > Nor ask they for light, not ask they for fire
> Save the light and fire that burn within.

Ha! ha! That last line refers to a goodly hot, steaming bowl o' punch!

> A snap—before squeal—
> They'll make ye feel.
> Nor will shirk they to bite,
> But as demons will fight!

Ho! Ho! 'demons' is good—very good!

> So take heed, you good folk—get ye to bed,
> Or beware of the rats—the rats that are red!"

A rattling sound of something falling followed the peculiar words of the singer. The outlaws were enabled, by the light above, to observe a rope ladder now swaying in their midst.

°DANDY DICK AND HIS FRIENDS CONTINUE THEIR ADVENTURES.

The starting voice, and the still more remarkable words, were not without an effect of vague dread upon their hearers. But the one strong hope of life rose up above all other considerations. Each highwayman silently unsheathed his water-dripping rapier. Whatever the mystery existing above, there, in their very midst, was the most providentially sent means of escape from the awful fate threatening them where they stood. If fresh dangers were yet to face them they would at least have a chance for life.

Dandy Dick eagerly seized the swaying rope-ladder with the left hand. He held his drawn blade in readiness in the right, and was on the point of placing his foot upon the lowest rung when a shadow came into the yellow square of light above. A man was preparing to descend. The same voice was again heard, but this time it was much louder:

> "So take heed, ye good folk—get ye to bed,
> Or beware of the rates—the rats that are red!

"Ah, indeed, the human rat—the fellow who walks erect, and yet ever flatly lies as he walks erect—is much more to be feared than the little black people on all fours—commonly called sewer vermin! Ah! how many of the latter have I now caught in my grand, old-fashioned trap? I'll warrant me some fifty or more, for my trap-floor slopes upwards, and when a storm pelters down

---

° Part 30. Vol. XIV.—No. 366. 12 November 1900.

somewhat sudden, the little sewer people all fly to the dryer places, for they fear too much water. Bless 'em, they are my food and lodging, fine slate carriage an' all. But when I get the latter it's mostly to go to gaol in!"

The descending man carried a lighted lantern in one hand and a large coarse sack over one shoulder. His appearance was not yet to be judged.

"I'll dare be sworn, now, that this fine storm hath driven me near a hundred of my little patrons! Ha! ha! 'A snap before squeal—' Hallo!"

The man on the ladder felt himself suddenly seized by each wrist. He glanced round, and jerked his lamp upwards.

Five deathly-white, and hatless, and completely drenched men were fiercely glaring up at him. Four rapier blade points were fiercely sparkling in the reflected light of the lantern, were each within an inch of his breast.

"A grand catch, truly! Five of my fellow rats! Nor will shrink they to bite, but as demons will fight! My good masters, I am but a poor rat-catcher. Man-catching is Royal sport, I freely admit; but 'tis not in my poor line. Men rats—good rats, draw in those long steel teeth, or fangs. But my trap is ne'er baited for such as thee. How came ye in it?"

The stranger displayed much surprise, but little fear. This latter fact disarmed the suspicions of the outlaws. In a few words Dandy Dick related the whole truth—he thought it impossible, otherwise, to account for their presence in the place they were in.

"P-h-a-g-h! What a catch indeed!" gasped the man. "Here I am," he went on, "more than content to secure sixpence a head for every one of my little visitors I can manage to nab. When, lo! this night—or, more correctly speaking, morning—I catch but five victims, yet each will bring me, not sixpence, but one hundred pounds, at least, per head!"

"Ah, villain!" thundered Dandy Dick. "Caught in thine own vile trap! You go not from this with life!"

Four steel points already pricked the man's flesh.

"Stay! Thy long, gleaming fangs bite! Hear me, my good masters!" yelled the fellow, now displaying very considerable fear.

"Speak quickly, then, an' come to the point!" sternly put in Colonel Blood.

"Malediction! the point comes to me! I would evade the point!"

"Cease thy fooling, fellow!" impatiently cried Dick Turpin, thrusting his sword-tip slightly into the back of the rat-catcher's red neck. The man gave a fierce cry of pain, and then solemnly promised to clearly explain himself.

"Firstly," said he, "to prove mine honesty." Here he leapt from the ladder into the water, taking care that he kept his lantern dry. "One of you, my good masters, precede to the upper regions. This place is distinctly dampish. Above, it is at least dry—ah, and warm, too!"

Dandy Dick only to eagerly sprang up the ladder. Colonel Blood followed next, in case of meditated treachery. Then the rat-catcher made a third. Wiffles and Dick Turpin, between them, assisting Tom King to follow. This proved no easy task.

Dandy Dick, using extreme caution, thrust his head beyond the open space. He saw a well-lighted stone chamber, and nothing to create alarm. Dick clambered up, and in a moment Colonel Blood was beside him.

"If the stranger means fair by us, I swear that I will know no rest until he is most handsomely rewarded!" the colonel whispered in Dick's ear.

"He is a most repulsive-looking being; but, for all that, I am strongly inclined to believe that he was the instrument chosen by a most merciful Providence for our deliverance," Dandy Dick earnestly muttered in a return whisper.

The rat-catcher now came through the opening. Seeing Tom King's condition, the man humanely knelt down and assisted Turpin and Wiffles to help the wounded man up. Then the opening in the floor was closed up by a stone flag that fitted it exactly.

The alarm and concern of Tom King's friends were plainly indicated now that they could clearly see his condition. There was a rude couch in this chamber. The rat-catcher busied himself with the assistance of the others, in undressing King, placing him in the not uncomfortable bed, and then attending as best they could to the binding up of his injured arm. The hideous-looking rat-catcher reached down a bottle from a shelf. This, he explained, contained a powerful cordial and which he induced King to partake of. Five minutes after Tom King had sunk into a deep, calm sleep.

There were a few barrels, on end, in this stone cell-like chamber. Upon these the outlaws seated themselves. Great, rough logs burned in a crudely-fashioned fireplace. Stuffed rats, in glass cases, and uncovered. Rat-skins, and stuffed dogs and cats were piled up upon timber benches, evidently all the work of the rat-catcher.

The outlaws were invited to take off their sodden garments, and to dry them by means of the blazing logs. This kindness was declined, although the highwaymen gladly gathered nearer to the cheerful embers.

Dandy Dick now critically observed their strange deliverer. He was of large and powerful stature, but amazingly ugly. His face was almost as black as that of a negro, and covered with short, raven-black hair that grew even up to the small rats-like eyes. Two long, gleaming white fangs protruded from the large, coarse-looking mouth. The lower limbs were extremely bandy; the other was very muscular, long, and covered, like the face, with thick, black hair. His head was uncovered, except by the thick, short, stubbly hair that grew within an inch above the eyes. In fact, this creature was as much like a human rat as a man could well be; and perhaps this singular aspect was in some degree due to the man's life-long trade as a rat-hunter, for it is remarkable what an influence and occupation will in time bear upon the person exclusively following it.

The rat-catcher suddenly rose up and assumed a respectful attitude.

"My good masters," said he, "you must be impatient to learn the mode of your rescue. Know then," he went on, "that your good luck is mainly due to the priest-architect who designed and constructed the one and only bridge of which our River Thames can boast. His work was begun so long ago as the year 1176. It took thirty-three years to build old London Bridge, but its constructor never lived to see it finished.

"This good priest well knew that at times of great storms and floods the Thames would so overflow, in consequence of the nineteen or twenty arches of the bridge, that there would be a great fear of the whole of London at times becoming inundated. The rising floods would force their way into the sewer-cuttings, and, over-swelling these, flood the streets above. To prevent this, Father Peter caused traps, formed in solid masonry, to be constructed at various points. These traps had stone doors, worked by powerful levers; the doors to drop down at end of blind borings to shut out the water when it threatened to reach beyond a certain level. Thus the good Father Peter, centuries back, caused to be made several noble rat-traps, by the which I—'Fangs, the rat-catcher,' as I am called—now earn my bread."

"The lowering of the stone doors closed us in, and shut out those madly thirsting for our lives," replied Dandy Dick; adding: "we are all deeply indebted to you, and it will be a great pleasure to us to handsomely requite thee, friend, if we further find no treachery meditated."

Fangs replied: "I live as ye see me. I study books and rats. To my thinking, all humans are but rodents of larger growth. They love each other, yet prey one on the other. Here, below, in my world, we do the same thing. I love my little people, and yet I beguile them into my snares, and then sell them. The world itself is only a great rat-trap. Ye are caught in it when born, and ye only escape from it when dead. Ho! ho! Ho! What think ye, my good masters? He! he! he!

"Truly a most remarkable creature," thought the rat-catcher's listeners.

Dandy Dick and the colonel solemnly pledged themselves to send to an inn the rat-catcher named a very large sum. The messenger would meet the former there on a certain night, and then hand over the stipulated amount. This had the effect of greatly delighting their rescuer.

Dandy Dick, now that his excitement and anxiety were greatly allayed, gave a regretful thought to the slain Criss Craften. Jonathan Wild's late lieutenant, from the moment of his casting in his lot with the outlaws, had proved himself a most brave and faithful adherent. His end had been terrible indeed. Ruthlessly slain by the inhuman wretch, Jonathan Wild, without an instant's warning, his sins unrepented and full upon his soul. Dandy Dick expressed himself thusly to his friends.

"We owe that fiend in the form of man, the Newgate thief-taker, a debt that, for the opportunity of settling, I would willingly give ten of the best years of my life!" fiercely muttered Colonel Blood.

Fangs, the rat-catcher, gave utterance to his most peculiar laugh. He was now seated, crashing over the leaping flames from the fire-logs. The flickering light through a deep red glow into his cruel-looking eyes and upon the two long, sharp fangs, the eyes and to prominent teeth thus appearing blood red.

"Jonathan Wild!" he almost shrieked. "He! he he! That black-souled wretch, an' the captain of the Thames Pirates, the Terrors of the Thames, and the Red Rats—for they are known by all these terms—those two villains have tried their utmost to hunt me down; trace me to this, my secret underground lair; catch me—the denizen of the bowels of the earth—in a trap, that they might then draw my fangs—ha! ha!—an' kill me! Kill me, Fangs, the poot rat-catcher, who harms none but his own little pets—and these he would scorn to molest, but that he needs must live!"

The man's vindictive mood rendered him most terrible to contemplate. The highwaymen shuddered at the sight. A demon moodily crouching over eternally burning embers, weird red glow-patches flitting over the hideous face, dyeing it crimson, and the bare, hairy, long, muscular arms, and great, strong hands. An impish giant of enormous strength, and evidently swayed by most terrible powers when once aroused.

"So, mine host, of the earth's depths, our great foe, Jonathan Wild, is also thine enemy?" meaningly remarked Colonel Blood.

"Aha! What sayest ye, my good Masters? Speak but the word, and Fangs, the rat-catcher, will do thy bidding!" The man sprang up erect. His voice thrilled his hearers through and through with its tones of mingled hatred and exultation. "The great thief-catcher," he cried, "and the chief of the Thames Pirates would willingly wade knee-deep through blood to capture and kill the notorious and daring highwayman, Dandy Dick—ha! ha! ha!—but Fangs, the poor rat-catcher, will deliver unto thee both thy enemies—ho! ho! Say but the word, my good Masters, and I will trap them—the two vilest human rats inhabiting the earth— and deliver them up to thee. He! he! he!"

Jack Sheppard and his pal Blueskin on the road to the Rookeries of St Giles's—They resume their bantering, jesting, word-twisting jestings— Blueskin holds forth on the subject of Irish blunders, or Irish bulls, and relates some samples of the same.

Meanwhile, Jack Sheppard, muttering most terrible threats, had snatched his brace of pistols from his belt and discharged them, but aiming wildly. This was enough. The remaining two officers frantically dug spurs into the sides of their poor, startled animals, and drove off like mad things, Sheppard and Blueskin continuing to discharge their pieces after them for the sole purpose of increasing the fear, panic, and speed of the disappearing limbs of the law.

The two robbers then turned their steeds and galloped through a number of deserted rural lanes, and in a few moments again slackened their pace and unconcernedly recommenced their gay chatter, as if nothing out of the common had really happened.

A pause followed, Jolly Nose wanting to rake up some pert idea to amuse his companion. The latter being also influenced by much the same motive.

"A beautiful, crisp, bright morning such as this makes one feel glad one's alive," at length remarked Jack Sheppard. "After all," he added, "life's little else than a battle—and a tough one, too, to some of us—and, once we enter the strife, it behoves us to wage it bravely, and never think of throwing up the sponge till after we get the final knock-out."

"You've now got your philosophers cap on again, Jack lad," laughingly replied Joe Blueskin. "And I've noticed," he went on, "that, if the said cap generally covers a calf's head, it also frequently gives birth to a good Irish bull or two. "He! he! he!"

"He! he! he!" Jack sneeringly mimicked the loud, hearty laughter of his companion, as well as his weaker lung power would permit. "Irish Bulls, indeed!" the lad continued. "A cap to cover a calf's head, forsooth! Ye must sneak the article and put it on, when my back's turned. Yours is the only calf's head that's gone astray that I know of. A cap to give birth to a bull or two! Well, of all the Irish bull's bulls that I've ever met with, the cap that gives birth to bulls cap the champion bull o' the lot! Ho! ho! ho!"

Jack Sheppard terminated his satirical remarks with another imitation of his companion's laughter; but, as before, the music was, perforce, in a much higher octave of the scale of the human tones.

"'Never think of throwing up the sponge till after we get the final knock-out.' That was the extremely elegant and correct sentence, I think, word for word?"

There was a merry, roguish glitter in the eyes of Jolly Nose, as of one who would say: "See now my superior wisdom and your own extreme simplicity!"

"Let us examine thy clear and precise language, Jack lad, and what do we find? By 'final knock-out,' you mean death?"

"Certainly I do, old blue dial!" confidently snapped Jack Sheppard.

"Very well Sir Philosopher, observe thy word picture. A dead man thinking after his decease, and, if he decides that way, going through a pretty little gymnastic performance with a sponge! Ho! ho! ho! Irish bulls in galore!"

Jolly Nose shook his sides in his saddle.

"Chuck it, Jack lad—chuck it!" he concluded.

"Chuck it?" reiterated the lad savagely. "Irish Bulls in galore, or in England? Chuck it! If the dead man's chucked it, what need I? Chuck it thyself, thou animated bluebag! Check thy laugh, chucklehead, or ye'll scare away all the bulls my cap hath bred—an' that's rhyme for ye!"

"Ho! ho! He! he!" yelled Blueskin, the tears streaming down his cheeks, for nothing delighted him more than arousing Jack Sheppard's spitfire mood. "I meant—he! he! Chuck up thy—ho! ho!—fit o' thy would-be philosophical—ha! ha!—vein. He! he! he!"

"Look here, tinted frontispiece," spitefully retorted the lad, "one can judge a man by his laugh, as one can tell a donkey by its bray. A man who laughs overmuch proves himself a fool of fools; a donkey that brays excessively marks itself a donkey of donkeys!"

"Jack lad," answered Jolly Nose, with a sudden assumption of great gravity, "I'm not acquainted with the creatures you mention—evidently they are friends of thine!—You must honour me with an introduction!"

"They are one. Speak of them in the singular—very singular—case, Jolly Nose. And I would gladly introduce thee—if it were needed—to the fool of fools an' donkey of donkeys combination; but I don't happen to have in my possession just now the only means for the said introduction—namely a mirror."

"Now, Jack lad, I have roused up the wild-cat in thee, and I'm consequently now quite happy!" merrily laughed Jolly Nose. And the laughter became so infectious that the lad could not help joining in it with his own boyish musical ripple.

"Speaking of Irish Bulls—so called," remarked Blueskin after a thoughtful pause. "I know a few examples, and perhaps I'll tell 'em thee if thou wilt promise to keep an attentive ear an' take the edge off thy razor-tongue."

"Come, Joe, old pal, you will admit that I can sometimes say sharp an' smart things?" asked Jack Sheppard, quite delighted at the hint conveyed by his companion.

"Sharp an' smart?" repeated Jolly Nose. "Red-hot pins an' needles are as the bluntest and coldest of icicles, in comparison with some of thy flashes of sarcasm!" Blueskin was now really merely paying the lad back in his own coin—satire for satire—but so solemn and truthful appeared the face of the former that the boy quite believed him in earnest and his vanity became vastly soothed in consequence.

"Now, speaking of Irish blunders, or Irish bulls," recommenced Blueskin, "the best example of all the kind that I ever remember to have heard was this:

"A conversation had been started at a party, assembled somewhere in the Emerald Isle, of course. The subject was upon the changed appearance in the human countenance while its owner was fast asleep.

"'How will Oi look whin Oi'm fast asleep, an' wid me eyes shut close as ther toightest iv oysters?' remarked a typical Patrick. 'Faix,' he went on, 'howld yer whist! It's this blessed noight that Oi'll lay wide awake, wid me peepers staring open all ther toime, so that Oi kin thin see how Oi appear whin O'im dead aasleep, an' wid me eyes closed!'

"Here is another sweetly choice Irish blunder," continued Blueskin. "Two tramps were travelling through a wood, each doing the journey on Shank's pony. 'How miny moiles iv we ter go before we reach the next town, Mickey?' asked one of the other. 'Twinty moiles, Doolan me honey, replied the latter. 'Aha, that's good news indaad!' commenced Doolan; adding: 'We'll moighty soon slip over that bit sure! Faix, it's onlee tin moile ter each iv us!'

°JACK SHEPPARD AND HIS PAL BLUESKIN ON THE ROAD TO THE ROOKERIES OF ST GILES—(*continued*)

"Yet another, Jack lad. A broth of a boy[107] woke up one morning suffering with a very severe cold. In the course of their early meal his wife commenced to relate to him a remarkable dream she had had. 'Oi drempt,' said she, 'that you an' me, Tim darlint, was a-tossing about out on the wild, raaging seas in the dead o' noight, an' freezing cold, an' he had nothing ter yer poour back but yer night-shirt, an'—' When up jumped Tim, in a boiling rage, an', savagely thumping his fist down on the breakfast-table, he cried out: 'Arro! Begorro! Now I know where Oi got me divel's own coold from! An phwat in ther name o' suddent death dis yez mean, Bridget, ye thoughtless gossoon,[108] be a-taaking me out in that boat, in ther killing coold for, whin it's a noice warm blankit or two ye moight have thrown around me, whin ye'd made up yer simpleton moind ter expoose me in me noight-shirrt alone, avish, ter a blue, muthering thing iv a mid-noight storm at seaa?'"

"An' here is a fine, an' a concluding, example," Blueskin continued: "an Englishman, travelling in Ireland, met a son of Erin by the roadside.

"'Good-day, Paddy!' hailed the former, in greeting.

"'The tip-top iv the morning to yer honour!' was the feisty reply.

"The Englishman paused.

"'Oblige me by giving me a good definition of an Irish bull,' said he, 'and I'll give ye a crown-piece.'

"'Done, your riverence!" gleefully responded Patrick, adding, while pointing to the objects of his remarks: 'Ye see them beeasts beyont, in the field, there?'

"'Yes,' replied the traveller, observing a number of cows, feeding amidst the tall grass, in the centre of the meadow.

"'Well, they're, ivery wan iv thim, cows, sure, an' they're all a-laying down, an' all farst asleeap.'

"'That's correct,' was the answer.

"'Faix, thin, if ivery wan iv thim is a cow, an' all iv thim asleeap an' a-lying down, the wan that's wide awake an' a-staanding up must be an' Irish bull!'

° Part 31. Vol. XIV.—No. 367. 15 November 1900.

107 Sturdy youth.

108 Lad (even though it is aimed at Bridgit), it has the same root as the French *garçon*.

"That was a most witty an' perfect definition of an Irishman's blunder."

"They're not over bad examples of the usual kind of blunders that we are told Irishman frequently and innocently make in their ordinary conversations," remarked Jack Sheppard; "but," he added, "I have often met with the ever free-hearted, rollicking, fun-loving sons of Old Erin, and it's my conviction that they all have such an irresistible relish for wit, humour, and fun of every form that their so-called blunders are really deliberately intended for the express object of creating merriment."

"I think you have hit the right nail on the head, Jack lad," replied his chum. "I love the true Irish lad," he continued. "He has a jest for every friend, his heart is big as a mountain, an' his fist, in fight, heavy and hard as any milestone."

The road the two trotted over still continuing much like that of the open country, the friends still continued in their talkative frame of mind.

Suddenly Jack Sheppard gave out a long, windy sigh, and startled Blueskin by asking him if he had ever been in love.

"Beshrew me for a confoundedly honest an' amiable villain!" muttered the great fellow. "If thou wert my father confessor, an' I spake but the truth, I'd be compelled to say that I had been, say, some few hundred times in love, Jack lad. But what of it? It's as easy to get in love as it is to get into debt, and is difficult in each case to get out of it. But I think, of the two, I'd sooner be in the Fleet Prison than again in love!"

"Aha, friend Joe," sighed Jack, rolling his eyes most dismally, "you have never, never seen any being on all this earth at all comparable in beauty, grace, and charms of person to my divinely sweet, intensely loving, and—"

"Oh, yes, Jack lad! No more, thanks!" distractedly protested Jolly Nose. "I know exactly what's coming. You're evidently bitten badly. The best remedy for the care of that terrible disease, called 'love,' is to get married, and rear up, say, half a dozen—or more, or less—olive branches on a princely income of fifteen shillings per week. What will remain of your savings and love you'll then be able to carry about with you in your empty purse without knowing it!"

Jack Sheppard threw a glance of lofty disdain at the other.

"You are insensible to the tender passion," he remarked. "But I will recite to you a little poem I have learned. It exactly fits itself to the charmer with whom I'm smitten. It—Let me see. Yes, this is how it goes:

> "My love she is a modest flower;
> Yet buds and blooms with ev'ry hour;
> She's sweetest of all in Flora's bower.
> My love she is a blithesome swallow,
> Dancing, darting, skimming o'er the green."

"Hold! I faint! In Mercy, I cry thee, no more!" pleaded Jolly Nose, in mock horror, and clapping his hands to his ears.

"I thought you boasted of the possession of the poetic vein!" disgustedly muttered Jack Sheppard, high tilting in his nose in supreme contempt.

"And so I do, I wot me, an' passing well," replied Jolly Nose. "My last love, however—beshrew me for a most gentle ruffian!—was not—ahem—quite incomparable, either for her beauty, or dislike for strong tipple!"

The horsemen now dropped into silence. They were nearing the heart of London. Signs of busy life were on every hand. It now behoved the outlaws to use the utmost caution. Indeed, their venturing into town in broad day was little short of madness. Their arrests, or even deaths, would soon follow, did Jonathan Wild but suspect the fact of their near proximity. Before the two light-hearted outlaws most terrible dangers lurked, even on that bright, beautiful morn.

THE KING OF THE RAT TRIBES AND HIS ASTOUNDING PROPOSAL—VOWS OF VENGEANCE—REGRETS FOR THE FATE OF CRISS CRAFTEN—THE RAT-TAMER AND HIS ARMY— AN INCIDENT OF TERROR AND LOATHING—THE MYRMIDONS OF JONATHAN WILD, OR THE THAMES PIRATES, CAUGHT IN A DEATH-TRAP.

It was a weird and most romantic scene. The cave, or vault-like stone chamber, existing in the very bowels of the earth, and possessing no apparent entrances or exit!

The fireplace was simply the flag stones, with an opening in the stone wall, some few feet above, for the outlet of the smoke if it chanced to pass therein. This rude chimney-space sloped upwards, probably into some dry gutter. The wind roared down this, and drove the smoke from the blazing logs in thick, curling clouds about the forms of the highwaymen and their strange preserver. The heat from the bright embers was welcome enough to the outlaws, whose garments were dripping wet, and their wearers chilled to the very bone. But the black, spiral-twisting smoke was simply blinding and suffocating in its density.

Dandy Dick—ever garbed in the most costly, fashionable, and even foppish taste—now looked a splendid wreck, so far as his garments were concerned. The same may be said with equal truth of all his companions. Great—even lavish— display of dress was the custom of all, but the sewer slime and slush had completely ruined their plumage. The water was slowly dripping from theirs steaming clothes, as the adventurers were seated upon the ends of inverted casks.

Fangs sat crouching closely over the up-darting tongues of flame, evidently unaffected either by the great heat or stifling vapour.

Tom King still slept on in a deep, sound, refreshing sleep that surprised as much as it gratified his friends. The couch was a rude one; but the patient's clothing had been partly removed, his wound carefully tended, and warm, if old, rugs placed over him.

The rat-catcher presented a shuddering sight, with his two protruding upper fangs gleaming from under his thick, black moustache, his bullet-head of close-cropped, jet-black hair, deep-set and piercing eyes, repulsively course features, enormous and muscular frame, and whose long and powerful arms had no covering, from the shoulders downwards, save a thick, sable, down-like growth, extending even to the fingertips.

"You say that you could deliver up to me Jonathan Wild, the thief-taker, and the captain of the Thames Pirates. A startling offer, I must admit. I know not the Thames pirate chief, save by repute; but I have most solemnly sworn to take the life of Jonathan Wild, the man who has so utterly wrecked my career, made life a hateful blank to me!" fiercely answered Dandy Dick, addressing Fangs, the rat-catcher, the former's handsome and youthful face now distorted by the mad like rage that ever seized him at sight, or even mention of the name, of the chief criminal-hunter of Newgate.

"And I shall not die content—no matter what form my death may take—unless I have previously utterly wiped out from the slate of life the name of Jonathan Wild, the notorious criminal-maker and criminal-exterminator!" added Colonel Blood, an ugly look lurking in his fearless eyes, and his right-hand fingers nervously entwining themselves about his rapier-hilt.

"'Tis said that a cat hath nine lives. That hell-cat Jonathan must have ninety lives at least! I have known him to be killed no end o' times, or certainly to have received wounds, any one of which would have given his quietus est to an ordinary man!" put in Dick Turpin. "But, forsooth, 'tis well," he added. "I, also, am pledged to lay the black mark out—tuck him up for his final sleep. If so many are sworn to have a slice at his beef, 'tis most fortunate that the joint is of the 'cut an' come again' form!"

"For my part," chimed in Will Wiffles "I'll be content ter knock 'oles in his most nicked an' flinty cokernut till there von't remain a square inch without one ev the silver-plate patches as 'e's so wery partial to. I think as 'e's got three o' them already, one o' which is a forget-me-not kind o' present from 'yours ter command.' 'It's an ill wind as blows you no good,' is and old an' true sayin'," went on Wiffles. "Ther doctors an' ther silversmiths reaps ther advantage when old pretty ugly mug gets a smash in ther lid o' 'is knowledge-box. An' I reckons, if yer could jist lift up one o' them silver traps wivout ther black old fox a-knowing it, you'd be able ter see all as 'e was a-thinkin' about, an' hear all ev 'is horrible secrets!"

"Ho! ho! ho!" sardonically laughed Fangs, the rat-catcher. "I burrow in the bowels and the darkness of the earth, and, unseen, steal into the most secret closets of men; and I could, in this same hour, place you within striking-distance of the hearts of your deadly foes—even as they slept—unsuspecting, undefended!"

The highwaymen exchanged meaning glances. Colonel Blood instantly divined what was passing in the mind of Dandy Dick—namely, that the prospect of meeting Jonathan Wild, face-to-face, grip for grip, steel to steel, would count before all other earthly desires.—

"Dick comrade," said the colonel, "we have a desperately-wounded pal to think of, sadly in need of a day or two's rest; and, moreover, there are most important affairs awaiting our attention at our stronghold at Finchley. Anon we will avail ourselves of the advantages offered by our friend here. Meanwhile we cannot thank him to heartily nor pay him to handsomely, for the great and most opportune services he has rendered us."

"Good masters mine, you have arranged to pay me most royally. I am a very poor man, otherwise would not accept your gold. Pray say no more on the question of gratitude," put in the rat-catcher.

"Your counsel is that of wisdom, my faithful friend," replied Dandy Dick to Colonel Blood, "and it shall be followed. Why do you class the captain of the Thames Pirates—Red Rats, as ye term them—with my foes?" he asked, turning to the rat-catcher.

"The chief of the Red Rats is in secret league with the thief-taker. He is of great assistance to the head of the Newgate police in many ways. While it suits Jonathan Wise to make use of the Thames cutthroats, they will remain unmolested by him. When the time is ripe, he will hang every one of the gang. The Red Rats are so-called on account of their many ruthless acts of blood!"

This was the explanation given by Fangs, and much more to the effect.

Dick Turpin changed the conversation by reverting to the awful fate of Criss Craften

"Is there any prospect of recovering the body of our ill-starred friend?" he asked of the rat-catcher. "We should take a melancholy satisfaction in bestowing it in a fitting place of burial. The thought of the poor fellow's remains floating about in the abominable sewer-ways below is too horrible!"

"The body must have been swiftly forced along by the irresistible fury and strength of the storm, and carried out into the Thames stream a few moments after your comrade was shot down," Fangs replied. "Jonathan Wild and his men, if they did not instantly succeed in fighting their way back to their starting-point—must also have been torn from their foothold and hurled along by the suddenly-created deluge falling from the street-gutters by means of thousands of inlets, in hundreds of tons to the minute."

"The devil needs the assistance of such a vile imps as Wild hence the apparent immunity from all the dangers enjoyed by the thief-taker," put in the colonel, in a tone of caustic bitterness.

A long silence now ensued.

The rat-catcher at length shook off a fit of deep musing. He suddenly looked up and gave out his startling laugh. The flames covered his hideous face with a vermilion flash, and transformed him into a monstrous goblin of red.

"Ho! ho!" he laughed. "I know well what is now passing in all thy minds, my masters," he said. "How doth Fangs enter and leave his underground home? How also doth he live in perfect peace and security therein, defying all the combined efforts of Jonathan Wild and the Thames Terrors to unearth him?"

The man rose up from his cask by the fire, strode over to a corner of the cave, and took an article from an iron-bound black chest, after unlocking the same. The place at once became filled with a powerful and more pleasing aroma. Fangs displayed a large earthen bowl filled to the brim with something resembling a mixture of coarse meal, but evidently impregnated with something of most agreeable odour.

"Behold, my masters, my secretly prepared food! This is the greatest dainty I can possibly offer my little people. The hand that once presents this to any one of them becomes the hand of their friend. My most carefully-selected, extremely intelligent, and highly-trained little pets can, in a moment be taught to love my friends or hate my enemies. With a secret known to the thief-taker, or the captain of the Thames cutthroats, the millions of my subjects could then most easily be tempted to sell their king. Phash! Rats are much like men! In the world above ye have the Jacobites plotting to sell their lawful monarch. Here, in my domain, I, also have Jacobite plotters among my rat subjects. Above, the traitor is caught, and given over to the executioner to be dealt with. Below—here, in my kingdom—I catch the Jacobite rat, put him on his trial—his fellow rodents gravely thronging the court—condemn him, and afterwards hand him over to the executioner—a dog in the rat-pit of a show. The villain, I warrant ye, my noble masters, will be as mercifully and as neatly strangled, beheaded, and courted, as ever any slaughterer did his butchery. Ho! Ho! So, my good friend, see how much rats are like men! But the former are much the better of the two!"

Then the weird and giant-like rat-catcher placed a quantity of his secret compound into each hand of his guests.

°THE KING OF THE RATS AND HIS ARMY—THE THAMES PIRATES CAUGHT IN A DEATH-TRAP—(continued).

"When I commence to feed my pets, do thou likewise on the same instant," Fangs cautioned them. "Seek not to injure one of them, or thy lives, and even mine, will surely pay forfeit—we shall be torn to pieces, and quickly devoured!"

"Are you mad?" demanded Dandy Dick, in shuddering alarm. "you surely are jesting, and cannot seriously intend what you say?"

° Part 32. Vol. XIV —No. 368. 30 November 1900.

"My army is my sole protection!" solemnly answered Fangs; adding: "My friends, ye have to run the gauntlet of the blood-loving fiends—the Terrors of the Thames. The Red Rats fear their black brethren, and fly from them. At the most ye may be glad of the co-operation of my subjects. Keep perfectly still, and sprinkle the flags with the dainty food, and have no fear!"

The outlaws held a conference. To say that they were horrified and filled with loathing would but poorly express the full extent of their feelings. The rat-catcher, however, gave them little time for further thought. He had, with a quick movement, drawn out a loose stone from the bottom of a wall. A sibilant sound came from his lips. An instant passed, then a swiftly-moving mass of black bodies streamed into the cave. Eyes like darting beads of fire, flying, rushing, leaping, glossy sable-coated creatures swarmed into the place. The floor became one compact mass of living horrid, fear-inspiring vermin.

"The food—the food!" warningly screamed the rat-catcher. Scarcely knowing what they did, the highwaymen mechanically obeyed. The previous ferocity of the swarming creatures instantly changed as if by magic. They became tame as kittens. Climbed up the rat-catcher's body, perched themselves upon his shoulders, and in many other remarkable ways testified their fondness for him. The fear-inspiring little animals sprang upon and raced over the couch and the body of the sleeping highwayman. In their eagerness to get at the tempting food they leapt upon the knees, backs, and shoulders of the outlaws, who, in spite of their intense loathing, coolly did exactly as instructed. The last crumb of the food was no sooner consumed than Fangs flew to the hole made by the loosened stone, and gave out the peculiar sound by which he had summoned his trained creatures. Then they sprang into the black cavity with the speed of lightning, the stone was replaced, and the whole incident had changed, as if a scene in an affrighting vision.

"Famine will convert a good man into a deadly-destructive savage!" cried Fangs. "Famine will produce the same result in the lower animals. If ye would tame them, feed them—make them contented and happy. The most venomous snake that ever crawled in bracken or hid in leafy tree, most fierce tiger that ever roamed to the wilds in search of prey—these become harmless as butterflies when the fierce cravings of Nature are satisfied!"

The rat-tamer next minutely instructed his guests as to the intricacies of their way of escape. Dick Turpin expressed his desire to remain with his bosom friend Tom King; but the rat-catcher earnestly protested that the wounded man would be perfectly safe.

"There is a path before you all in which death lurks at every step," he said. "Were I to accompany ye, and unable to return, your comrade would awaken to find himself in a living tomb, and from which he would find no escape, except into the rat-infested and closed-up gallery below the flagstone trap."

"We are convinced that you have the power to protect our friend until he is fit to be removed," remarked Dandy Dick. "But," he continued, "what proof can you give us of your loyalty?"

"My good masters, before you leave me I will place before ye all such proofs of the relentless enmity of Jonathan Wild and the Thames Terrors nourished towards myself that ye must e'en become convinced that the cause of Dandy Dick, the daring, dashing highwayman, his outlaw friends, and the king of the rat tribes is one!"

The highwaymen were so struck with this speech that, in spite of the horror at the man inspired, they each silently exchanged a hand-clasp with him.

"I would that we could judge of the hour and the state of the elements," remarked Dandy Dick.

Fangs instantly rose up from his seat and strode over to an iron tube that pierced the arched roof of his strange underground abode and passed down into the stone flags of the floor. The strange being drew a slight wooden plug from the pipe. A low, hissing sound instantly followed, and a jet of water shot out some yards over the flags. The plug was replaced. Then the rat-catcher placed his ear close to the tubing and listened intently for some moments. "Ho! ho! A strange weather-test an' timepiece, my good masters!" he said uttering his remarkable laugh. "The great rush of waters down that conduit-pipe tells me that the storm still rages furiously as ever. Sound travels easily with rushing waters. Those mingling with the noisy tempest aloft are the rumblings of the big, heavy wheels of country vans laden with garden-produce for the London markets. The hour is that of four, or thereabouts, or early morning."

The outlaws looked their astonishment. The colonel had gone to the side of the couch on which Tom King lay. He remained in the same state of profound slumber as since the giving of the cordial by the rat-catcher.

"We should tarry no longer; and it is impossible to remove our injured comrade," said Dandy Dick to his friends.

"Can we indeed trust him with thee?" asked Dick Turpin of the rat-catcher.

"You can, my worshipful master; and I will answer for his safety with my life!" earnestly replied Fangs. "I obtained that wonderfully curative cordial from my great, good friend, one Daddy Delph—one of the most profoundly gifted—"

"Daddy Delph?" the outlaws all echoed in a breath. "He a friend of thine?"

"Yes, my worthy masters," was the sincere reply. "Delph is looked upon as a most mysterious old man, but I shall never ask for a truer crony."[109]

This convinced the highwaymen that Tom King might be safely trusted with the rat-catcher until such times as an arrangement could be made for the removal of the former, the method of which had already been explained to them, and of which the reader will learn later on.

---

[109] Close friend of companion.

"I will not disguise from you that you must expect to encounter most desperate danger should ye meet with the River Pirates. Their sanguinary gangs deeply infest the underground levels, and their chief lair ye must pass through before the riverside can be gained."

"By heavens," thundered Colonel Blood, "if they push us to the extremity, we will wade through their blood!"

"My good and right worthy masters must e'en be prepared for that. Fangs, the poor rat-catcher, can supply ye all with powder of the driest, and bullet of the deadliest mould—these the property of the pirates themselves, too. Ho! ho! ho! To kill a man with his own powder and shot is surely unkindest cut of all! He! he! he!"

The adventurers, thanks to their weird rescuer, were amply supplied with powder and lead, and even the loan of two brace of pistols, to replace those they had lost. The vermin-trainer again withdrew the plug from the conduit-tube. He then announced that the storm had ceased as suddenly as it had arisen. Next the hideous-looking giant was observed working with enormous vigour at a great, rusty-looking crane, not before observed. The awe-inspiring, thunder-like rumbling sound that had once before so dumbfounded them, again startled Dandy Dick and his friends.

"Good old Father Peter, the designer and constructor of old London Bridge, when he also invented these wonderful underground dams, to prevent the inundation of London by the overflowing of the Thames stream, little thought of the use of his work would be put to, e'en centuries after his time!" cried Fangs, when his task was completed. And he came forward, reeking with great sweat-drops. "The galley below us is now open, the waters will have subsided. I have other secret passages for reaching the Thames side, but the way ye entered is safest of all others for your departure," he explained.

The denizen of the earth-bowels again burst out with his horribly startling, screech-like laughter. "Ho! ho! Ho! Then his voice as suddenly sank to a significant droning-like tone:

> "Take heed, good folks, get ye to bed,
> Or beware of the rats—the rats that are red!"

The expression and gesture of Fangs most plainly indicated his meaning. The outlaws drew back as their host lifted up the stone flagged trap. It was indeed fortunate that they did so. A deafening, thunder-like mingling of explosions followed. A perfect tornado of lead burst through the trap opening.

Quick as thought, Fangs, with one great bound, leapt to the great crank. The underground thunderclap instantly followed. Then came an appalling shriek.

"Ho! ho! ho! One of the guards of Jonathan has fallen foul of the stone door of my monster trap—Wild's myrmidons or Thames Pirates, 'tis all the same!" yelled Fangs, screaming like a demon in the excitement of his fury. "I have caught them!"

So saying the giant flew to the loosened stone in the wall, removed it, and hissed out his signal to his tribes. Like a lightning flash, they flew to his call. He pointed to the dark cavity in the floor. The hurried creatures darted into it. They were met by a terrific volley of fire and lead, the bullets flattening themselves out against the arched stone roof of the cave. A heap of dead rodents now edged the trap-opening. Then a mixture of cries of indescribable terror, loathing and fear-panic came up from below.

RALPH DRAKE AND HIS WIFE ON THE TRACK OF OFFICER BILBERRY—THE STRANGERS FROM A FOREIGN CLIME—THE HARMONIC BRETHREN AND THE "CHAIR" AND "VICE-CHAIR"—A SONG THAT WAS FORGOTTEN.

On the night following the incidents of early morning related in connection with the Bow Street officer Bilberry and other frequenters of the hostelry of most puzzling name and situated near Bow Street, two persons stood on the opposite side of the road and were engaged in deep conversation.

Both were cloaked and in the middle-class garb of the sterner sex. One tall of stature and of somewhat thin and haggard countenance; the other younger, extremely handsome-looking, and with a pair of large, black, and piercing eyes, and with masses of dark, curling hair reaching to his shoulders.

"I tell thee lass," the latter was saying, "I most strongly protest against these periodical outbreaks of thine. Thanks to the princely generosity of Dandy Dick we have got over our monetary difficulties, and you have since consented to give up this deadly risky masquerading. You'll venture it once too often, Meg; and this death on the scaffold awaiting us both on discovery. Death on the scaffold! Think of it, wife—think of it!"

The voice of the next speaker was as musical as that of a singing-bird, and decidedly feminine in quality.

"When we had got over our monetary difficulties, Ralph dear, I did promise, and indeed intended never more to assume male attire; but what has happened since that promise? We are now threatened with a far greater calamity than that of poverty. We are to be tried for the crime of harbouring and abetting members of the felon class! You insist that nothing can be proven against us. Dandy Dick, Dick Turpin, and many other highwaymen and robbers of the lower grades have. at various times, frequented our inn, and these things can be proven by one person, and that is the old fossil Bilberry. If he is at the bottom of the mischief we are undone. I am determined to find that out, and—if we've really that man-frog to blame—to inflict most condign punishment upon him!"

"This hostel of the strange sign—The Pig and the Crimson Cushion," put in the other, is Bilberry's favourite resort now, an' will be until he has covered every square inch of its inside with his score—a score which he will never settle; then, when he gets the hint to take his patronage elsewhere, he'll inform against the innkeeper—guilty or no—an' the charge will be that of harbouring and abetting members of the felon-class."

"If the confounded and animated old bladder of wind is there, Ralph, he will be bound to indulge in his vainglorious romances, an' might be tempted to speak of us."

"Yes, Meg lass; but look at the risk—the risk!"

The reader has by this recognised in the strangers Mr. and Mrs. Drake of the Hole-in-the-Wall Inn.

Before venturing on this errand Ralph Drake had left a well-tried and trusted friend in charge of his house. He and his wife had also cleverly disguised themselves. A dark stain—easily removable—had been washed over their faces, necks and hands, the pair now looking like Indians of high caste. Drake had also placed a black shade over one eye. They were well-dressed, and gave the appearance of having recently arrived from some southern climate.

Anxiously cautioning his wife for the second or third time, Ralph Drake drew his cloak closely about him, crossed over the road and then entered the inn-door, with his wife following him.

The innkeeper came towards them with most mincing gait and smiling as only an innkeeper can smile when he scents rich game.

"Welcome, welcome, most noble and gallant strangers!" greeted he, bowing so lowly that he burst his apron-strings. "Any an' everything my humble hostelry can offer are at thy commands, myself and the ever-obliging hostess included!"

"Always supposing that we can pay!" curtly answered Ralph Drake. "A thick boot an' a prompt messenger for the visitor with empty pockets! Ha! ha!" Drake, although a caterer for the public himself—hated a welcome that was too much overdone, and merely a trick of the trade. He produced a long, net-work purse, and shook it, so that the glitter of its golden contents would catch the eyes of mine host. The latter's orbs sparkled like those of a hungry mouse on suddenly discovering a tempting piece of cheese and a clear coast.

"What can I place before your honours?" most obsequiously asked the host, not appearing to have heard Drake's caustic remarks.

"To be candid, friend, we were tempted to visit this resort out of curiosity!" said Mrs. Drake, now speaking up. "We have heard many reports of the goodly company and the right merry entertainment to be found here, and will pay liberally for the privilege of joining thy extremely jovial guests."

"Aha, marry come up!" responded the proprietor. "The Pig an' Crimson Cushionites are very, very exclusive!"

"Pigs usually are!" remarked Mrs Drake, sotto voce.

"And, you see, the Pig an' Crimson Cushionites—ahem"—he went on, "pay for their room exclusive like."

"Pigs would," again murmured the disguised lady, in a whisper, which her husband alone heard.

"And, what is more, the Pig an' Crimson Cushionites most strongly object to any other company than their own," continued the host.

"Again, that is most piggish-like!" softly muttered the small, shapely lips. Then, speaking aloud, Mrs Drake continued: "Come, come, Boniface, the porkers may unbend—"

"Porkers! Most worshipful sir," cried the host, in extreme horror, "I would not have our most esteemed, right noble, an' most respected chair hear that derogatory term applied to the harmonic brotherhood over which he has the exalted honour to preside—no, not for worlds, I assure you, young sir!"

"Then I must humbly apologise to the—the—er—cushion crimson pigtilites, or thing-a-may-jig—whatever you term them!" hastily added the male-robed female, seeing that she had opened her mouth too wide, and, consequently, put her foot in it.

"If a golden guinea would—" began Drake, placing a sample of the coin mentioned into the palm readily offered.

"Pray, my most worshipful master, never dream of suggesting such a thing!" disdainfully protested the caterer, nevertheless taking the coin and nimbly transferring it to a pocket in his baggy smalls.

The owner of the house of call again assumed his business smile—this time almost at the cost of slicing his head in two—and said, in a tragic stage-whisper:

"My generous and right Royal bloods, I will do my best—approach the chief of the Pig an' Crimson Cushionites, and endeavoured to induce him to for once set aside the rule against the admission of strangers." With this, and a great show of mystery and importance, the host darted down the passage, from the end of which there came a great, yet subdued, hum, as if from a considerable number of excited bluebottles engaged in a humming contest one against another. A door opened, and the buzzing waxed loudly for a second, then again simmered down until it more resembled the singing of a boiler pot that was quite contented with its lot and at peace with the world.

The two disguised visitors went to the bar and their awaited the return of the innkeeper. Presently he returned. He was flushed with victory and a deep draught of punch. Motioning the visitors to follow, he led the way into the presence of the buzzing bluebottles—or, rather, the Pig an' Crimson Cushionites.

The "Harmonic Brethren," as the pigites sometimes termed themselves, were duly assembled in all their glory. Brother Bilberry constituted the "Right Worthy Chair." In meetings of this kind—in the present day termed "smokers"—the chairman is generally looked upon by his supporters as a being next in importance to the head of the State, and the amazing deference paid the former might well excite the envy of the latter. Make-believe is a great thing in this world. If a fool can succeed in believing himself to be a wise man, he will become as vain and proud as the latter. If a pauper can but believe himself a millionaire, he will ask alms of none. But to the pigites, Brother Smugmug presided at the opposite end of the before mentioned long table as the "Vice-Chair," usually termed "Vice." The company had assembled in strong force, and, as previously described, they were nearly all of white hair, and with bald heads and pink complexions."

Brother Bilberry presented somewhat of an exception to the uncovered human pink tiles, inasmuch that he had only a bare circle at the back of his head. This open space was much used by flies as a skating-rank and general recreation-ground.

Leading the visitors forward, the smirking host performed a most abject bow to the Chair, and again broke his apron-string.

"Most revered, beloved, and right worthy brother-chief," said he, "I present to you the two strangers who have travelled from afar climes, overseas, in the desire to themselves witness an' here the most charming sights an' sounds forming the entertainments occasionally given by our most brilliantly-accomplished members of the Pig and the Crimson Cushion Harmonic Brethren."

"Merchants freshly returned from a visit to Spain, mayhap?" beamingly concluded Bilberry. "These fellows will be good for a flagon or two of the best!"

As a brother-harmonic had previously announced to oblige the company with a sample of quality, the strangers were conducted two seats at one end of the smoking-room, and to the rear of the "Vice."

"Brother Timithy Dolan! Order, gentlemen, please!" Bilberry had resumed his seat of honour, and now commenced hitting the oaken table-top in that playful manner so much in vogue with undertakers, who love to keep up a merry time with their hammers between placing and driving home of each nail.

Brother Timithy was evidently bursting with song, and commenced to yell forth in a style that might have been appreciated by those afflicted with complete deafness. His ditty was of the Emerald Isle order and commenced somewhat thusly:

> "'Twas on a could Winter's noight,
> About two in ther morning,
> In ther middle o' June,
> on a bright summer's day."

Brother Timithy had commenced on the upper C, and his voice soon tied itself up in knots. He ceased, made the excuse that he had forgotten the next words of the song, and most generously offered to sing another song. This he attempted, and also some dozen more, but always with the same result. The words would not come. Timithy touchingly pointed out to the company the difficulty of singing a song without the knowledge of the words, or the tune, and, he might have added, without the possession of a voice. But he didn't. Timithy, still eager for "deeds of daring do," next ferociously tackled the classics, in the shape of the soliloquy of the Duke of Gloucester.[110]

> "Noow is thur winthur ive our Miss Contint,
> Maade glooriouslee drunk be this son of pork;
> And all the swipeers that lowered gin in our hoase,
> In ther deeap boosum ive ther ocean buried."

The worthy and revered Chair majestically got upon its feet, and solemnly held up his hammer as a sign that the reciter temporarily ceased.

"Howevery much," commenced Bilberry," our brilliantly-gifted brother can improve upon the original text of the Classic he is honouring us by reciting, I beg leave to state that the lines should stand as originally set down. To prove that our esteemed brother has greatly beautified the lines of Shakespeare," continued the Chair, "it is only necessary to give them as they were before his marvellous imaginative powers so vastly enriched them:

> "Now is the winter of our discontent,
> Made glorious summer by this son of York,
> And all the clouds that lower'd upon our house,
> In the deep bosom of the ocean buried," &c.

Brother Bilberry had given out this fragment in the very best style of the penny wayside-barn setting, and had received thunders of applause, as he gracefully returned his seat.

Brother Timothy acknowledged the graceful compliment paid him, and regretted that he could not proceed further, as he had most unfortunately forgotten every other word of the soliloquy in question.

The Vice now rose to his feet, and gazed fondly from his end of the long table to that so grandly garnished by the esteemed Brother Bilberry.

"Gentlemen," cried the Vice, "I beg to call upon my brother-Chair, and urgently request him to favour us with another of his ever deeply entertaining reminiscences!"

The Chair tried desperately hard to assume a blush of modesty, and narrowly escaped bringing on a fit in consequence. More pressure being added, Bilberry at length consented to entertain his friends assembled with "a trifling yarn," as he put it, concerning the doings of his younger days.

"In my extreme youth, my worthy friends," Bilberry commenced, "I went in for pets an' hobbies of every kind. Perhaps the most singular an' interesting of

---

[110] Richard III.

all the pets I ever had was in the shape of one of the, so to speak, small fry of creation—a creature usually termed a whelk. I secured the unique thing of life firstly in its wild state—just as it was when it fiercely roamed the fastnesses of its native jungles in search of prey—"

"Ahem!" nervously coughed a harmonic brother, bashfully rising to his feet. "Ahem! Did I hear the most noble and deeply-venerated Chair aright? I don't profess to be an—er—an authority on shellfish, excepting, perhaps that dainty and graceful little fellow who sports a spiral tail and a miniature chest-plasterer for a month. I have studied this species very closely and deeply at times, and usually armed with a pin, in case of a sudden assault by the vicious thing. But I wanted to observe that I was always under the impression that the ordinary whelk species confined themselves to the sea and its shores."

The gimlet eye[111] of the august Chair fixed at the interrupter, and pierced him through and through.

"Blood an' poisonous compounds!" cried he, in awful wrath. "Is the veracity of the Chair to be doubted?"

"S'death, no! most indignantly responded the unanimous voice of the assembled company.

THE OLD BARNET ROAD AT MIDNIGHT—THE MOUNTED ROBBER—A MEETING AND ITS STARTLING CONSEQUENCES—JONATHAN WILD'S SPIES—JACK RANN, HIGHWAYMAN—THE CUNNING PLOT—ARRESTED—A TRAITOROUS PROPOSAL.

We are in the vicinity of Old Barnet, on the high-road. The night is a bright and clear one for winter, and the moon occasionally displays herself from behind swiftly-drifting, black crepe-like cloud-masses.

A very peculiar-looking cloaked figure, mounted on a dapple-grey, well-conditioned cop, rides leisurely down the Barnet road towards Finchley. The rider wears a great white wig, which is much becurled and fluffed out at each side, and having a pigtail with no less than three little blue silk bows, which hang down the wearer's back, and look much like the tale of a modern kite.

The reins dangle loosely about the neck of the slow-moving animal, while the rider contentedly takes huge pinches of snuff from a box of chased silver, and otherwise conducted himself as if there were no such dangers to be encountered on the lonely roads as footpads, highwaymen, and roaming cutthroat bands of gypsy robbers.

The tall trees line each side of the main road way, and are joined at their base by hedgerows, tall wooden palings, and crudely-formed bramble offences.

"Tissue! er tissue!" sneezed the snuff-taker, in most evident enjoyment of the mixture, which he continued at intervals to place in his nose in such liberal

---

[111] To stare in a piercing manner.

quantities as to convey the impression that he imagined himself to be a dustman, and his nasal organ a dustcart he was most anxious to load up.

"The—er tissue!—confounded—a-t-i-ss-u-m!—infernal feller don't—tiss-yer-r!—appear too likely to—ahem!—a powerful snuff this—ootiss——yow!—turn up. I'm almost afraid that he won't fall into our—yer—tiss-o-o-o!—trap!"

The excessive sneezing awakened many echoes along the deserted country road. These echoes suddenly appeared to take the form of the ringing hoof-clatters of a steed, and the clatters, getting the better of the other sounds, became louder and closer each moment.

"Steady steady!"

The strange and aged-looking figure snatched up the reins, and held in check his startled animal, which appeared as nervous and uneasy at its rider was confident and easy.

The long black shadows, thrown by the tall, leafless elms, obscured the roadway ahead. But suddenly from their vague darkness came a definite shape, and the shadows sent forth a moving black patch, the outline of which looked much like those of a mounted man and horse. A few minutes more, and there was no longer any doubt that the shades had vomited forth a rider and steed.

"Halt there!" cried the black patch representing the mounted man.

On closer inspection the new-comer proved to be a rider wearing a rakish-looking three-cornered hat, a long crape mask, and a voluminous riding-cloak. As the folds of the cloak flew partly open, a very fine riding-habit of vermilion and gold lace could be seen beneath, and also a belt holding a brace of pistols, while the end of a rapier-sheath saucily poked its nose from under the left side of the flying black cloak.

"Halt is it, my right worshipful stranger?" coolly asked the man on the cob, adding, as he pulled up: "And now what may thy business be, my fine fellow?"

"To demand toll of thee, my good friend. Give freely, quickly, an' with a good grace, an' I promise in return that you shall not again be robbed until you have something more to take!"

"Really, your moderation quite overpowers me!" responded the strange-looking old man on the dapple-grey cob, calmly indulging in a sly chuckle.

The highwayman's orbs darted sparks of fire through the black crape mask. With a swift motion he had whipped out a pistol from his belt, and the bright tube pointed to the space exactly between the eyes of the other.

"Put back your pop guns, young blood. You're a bold feller, no doubt; but you're nabbed!"

Thus saying, the latter gave a shrill whistle of the lips, and an instant after the onrush of many heavy footsteps broke upon the stillness of the night.

"Secure him, lads!" shrieked the old rider. "He's one o' the outlaws of the Haunted Manor. Mr. Wild will pay us handsomely for his capture. Ha, ha! ho, ho! Trapped, by Jove!"

"Confusion!" muttered the surprised robber. "But I'll take the music out of thy laugh!" he yelled, firing full at the grinning face of the old man.

The latter threw himself from his steed a fraction of a second before the trigger snapped, and thus most probably saved his life.

Every surrounding shadow suddenly seemed to become a man. A crowd closed about the highwayman, and furiously sought to unhorse him. He discharged the contents of two of his pistols into the midst of his foes. But, owing to the darkness and confusion, no harm was done. Then he was torn from his horse and felled to the earth by several powerful blow upon the back, dealt by heavy bludgeon is and pistol-butts.

Covered in blood and completely dazed, the highwayman was securely bound, and then thrown over the back of his horse, the latter led along at a smart trot until a wayside inn came into view. The hostel was closed for the night; but the man on the cob thundered at the door with the horn handle of his riding-whip until the owner was aroused.

The host, half dressed, and shuffling in slippers, made his appearance, and drowsily admitted his guests.

The captive was brought round by a strong dose of brandy. His captors were then considerate enough to clean the blood from his face and bandage up his head. Fortunately, none most of the blows had been somewhat softened by the thick felt of the hat, which he had kept on at the time of the furious exchange made upon him, otherwise his head would have been so brutallybattered that his life must have paid forfeit to the drumming.

"Well, my gay bird of beautiful plumage, we've nicely clipped your wings, and your high flying's now over the good an' all?" tauntingly sneered the leader of the highwayman's captors.

The robber had been unceremoniously thrown upon the floor of a back room of the inn.

"I'm tricked, I own!" he replied, with a defiant grin, although his face was white as that of a corpse from loss of blood. "You're of the Bow Street kidney, of course?" he asked, in a tone of supreme contempt.

"We're Mr. Wild's janissaries, my fine feller. My name's Dankly—Mark Dankly, if you please, and I'm entirely at your pleasure!"

The speaker was the old-man rider of the cob; but he had removed his disguise, and now proved to be a young, and powerful man of most ferocious aspect.

"So you're one of Jonathan's bloodsuckers, eh, Dankly? 'Dankly' will suffice at present, and I'll take the opportunity to 'Mark' you when my limbs are free!" retorted the prisoner caustically.

"Ho! ho!" laughed the guard. "You're a droll, a wit, I observe. But you'll admit," he continued mockingly, "that the bone of your very fine jest on meeting me went the wrong way of your throat. He! he! We've been roaming these dreary wastes for weeks past, in the hopes of nabbing some of you cutthroat fellows of the Haunted Manor, and I think we've got one at last, and perhaps I shouldn't be many thousands of miles away from the truth if I said that his name was Jack Rann, eh?"

Mark Dankly appeared well informed; for the handsome young fellow of most dashing aspect, and blue-eyed and flaxen-haired, was no other than the outlaw of that name.

Jack Rann for a moment turned, if possible, a shade whiter, for there was the sum of one hundred guineas offered for his arrest, with the gibbet to terminate his young career if once grim old Newgate claimed him for its own.

"Jack Rann, eh? It's more likely to be Jack Ran-away, before long! But never mind my name!" defiantly answered the bound highwayman. "You will have some trouble to prove my identity!"

"Not in the slightest, my merry wag. Why, if our master but wished it, he could prove you to be anyone or anything—from the man in the moon down to a dead stickleback buried in the bottom slime of a stagnant pool!"

"Such loathsome vermin as his janissaries and professional perjurers are capable of the vilest deeds possible. Of that I am well aware!" bitterly replied Jack Rann.

Mark Dankly rose from his seat by the fire, and gave the highway man a fierce kick on the shin of one leg.

"Keep a civil tongue, hound!" he snarled.

The latter then beckoned his followers into a further corner of the room, where they reseated themselves, took occasional sips at their potations, which had by this time been served them, and discussed together in a low undertone for some time.

At length Mark Dankly—evidently the leader of the party—rose from his seat, and strode over to the man reclining full-length by the fire. The cowardly ruffian again struck out his heavily-booted foot, kicking his victim with savage force upon the ribs.

For some moments the robber was quite unable to speak, as the result of the agony he endured. Then he glanced up at the extremely repulsive-looking being standing by and leering over him in exultant triumph. "You shall pay very dearly for such unmanly actions!" Jack Rann hissed between his clenched teeth. "I'll exact enormous interest for the gratification such cowardly conduct affords a brutish nature such as yours!"

The police agent drew his hanger and placed the gleaming steel blade to the breast of Rann. Its point pierced his clothing and drew blood.

°JACK RANN, HIGHWAYMAN—THE CUNNING PLOT—ARRESTED—A TRAITOR'S PROPOSAL—(*continued*).

"I could spit you now—as a fowl before roasting!" laughingly taunted the officer. "You are worth the same amount to us dead as alive; and if dead there would be no fear of your giving us the slip—and you outlaw rogues are like eels! One thrust, and you would groan out your last adieu to all earthly things."

"My comrades would never rest until my death were most terribly avenged," quite calmly replied Rann. "Many of you creatures have felt the teeth of our barkers and rapiers," he added. "Slay me, curse you, and take the consequences!"

"Bah!" contemptuously snapped the man-hunter, sheathing his blade with a ringing snap. "I would kill you with as little compunction as I would a dog! But I have an object in sparing thy worse than worthless life."

"Name it!" demanded Jack Rann sternly.

"I will be plain with you. We seek the means of entering your stronghold," answered Dankly. "We could then bring a large body of men and surprise and capture, or put to the sword every member of the proscribed bands we found within the walls of the Haunted Manor. Lead us to one of the secret entrances, and, in return, I will solemnly pledge myself that your free pardon shall be granted."

"You dare suggest an act of such black-hearted treachery to me?" thundered Rann, his eyes lighting up with fury, his face turning scarlet with a burning sense of indignation.

"I swear, by all the saints in the calendar, that I will dispatch you where you lay, unless ye give speedy consent!" stormed Wild's agent in fiercest wrath. "Ten minutes only will I allow you to decide; refuse at the end of that time, and, by all that's holy, you die!" uttering this threat, Mark Dankly strode from the room, his companions following him. The key was heard to turn in the lock, and Rann felt himself securely imprisoned.

Left alone, Jack Rann made most desperate efforts to burst his bonds, but soon became fully convinced of the impossibility of this. Every outlaw of those banded together under the leadership of Dandy Dick had taken oath to die, if needs be, one for the other. Rann would die ten thousand deaths, if such were possible, rather than give up his faithful comrades to the enemy. The only hope or chance remaining to him existed in the possibility of being able to hoodwink the police-agents.

"Time is up! Yes or no?" abruptly demanded Mark Dankly, on re-entering the room.

"Firstly answer me this," commenced Rann. "Dandy Dick, Colonel Blood, and some few others of our comrades are missing! are they taken?"

° Part 33. Vol. XIV.—No. 369. 30 November 1900.

"Humph!" Missing since the night of their outrageous doings in the house of my master?" muttered Dankly.

"Yes; have not been seen since their reading your employer a lesson he isn't likely to forget for some time to come," viciously put in Jack Rann.

Dankly threw a side glance of deep meaning to his fellows.

"It's no secret," he added, again turning towards his captive. "Dandy Dick and several others have been arrested, and are now safely lodged in Newgate Castle."

Jack Rann's heart fell like lead. All the fugitives in asylum at the Haunted Manor were experiencing the agonies and torments of doubt and apprehension concerning the fate of their dearly-loving leader, and all the others still missing of their number.

Mark Dankly actually knew nothing whatever concerning those mentioned, but the notion had entered his mind that it would help his plans if Jack Rann could be impressed with a due sense of the great power of Jonathan Wild.

"Now, villain, your answer! Not another moment's delay!" Dankly impatiently demanded, and sheathing his sword-blade.

"I can't faced death at my age," meekly returned Rann. "I'll do your bidding!"

Dankly chuckled like a fiend of Hades on the advent of a lost soul.

Refreshments were ordered in and placed before the captive, and his limbs untied. But the doors and windows were guarded by Dankly's men, while their leader never once took his tiger-like orbs from Rann's movements.

Each mouthful of food or liquid threatened to choke the young robber; but he was playing a part, and on the cleverness of his assumption depended not only his own life, but—infinitely dearer still! The safety of all his fellow-fugitives.

The brave and devoted young felon had firmly resolved on either escaping from the limbs of the law, or encompassing their utter destruction, even if his own life were necessarily included in the sacrifice.

His meal ended, Rann was given his hat and cloak—all his weapons had been taken at the moment he was first secured—and led from the inn. At the porch of the hostel some of Wild's myrmidons now held lighted torches, another held the head of Jack Rann's steed. The latter mounted. Mark Dankly sprang into his saddle, seized two pistols, cocked and kept them in readiness, and ordered all his followers to carry their flintlocks in their hands, and to instantly shoot down their prisoner at the slightest attempt at treachery in any form.

In this way the party made for the Finchley wilds, the animals walking briskly, those on foot trotting immediately behind. The moon had vanished. The Haunted Manor loomed, an almost white object, against a black shroud of sky. The outlaws' stronghold looked like a ghostly spectacle of a castle of the middle ages—a phantom habitation for creatures of another world. More links were set aflame, then Jack Rann was sternly ordered to dismount. A dozen steel tubes were silently presented at his temples. Twenty-four fiercely-brilliant eyes threatened death!

A STRANGE ARMY—AN APPALLING BATTLE—TERRIBLE RETRIBUTION—THE CAVE IN THE BOWELS OF THE EARTH— PLIGHT OF TOM KING—THE ATTEMPT TO REGAIN FREEDOM, AND WHAT BEFELL DANDY DICK AND HIS FRIENDS.

Dandy Dick and his friends were filled with extreme repugnance and horror at the notions of their weird deliverer, Fangs, the rat-tamer and trainer. The adventurers would have fiercely thrown themselves upon the deformed giant and stayed his horrible purpose, but the whole incident was so thrilling in its fearsomeness and loathing, and swift in the action, that, before its beholders could recover their full presence of mind the deed had progressed too far to be prevented, or aid to be of value to the men entombed in the great trap-like tunnel and attacked by the great and sweeping multitude of sewer-rats, these ferocious creatures having been trained for the express object of giving battle with the enemies of their self-styled king.

The terrible nature of the awful contest could be only too well-judged by the various sounds coming from below to the ears of all above by means of the still open trap, formed by the removing of a flagstone in the floor of the rat-catcher's underground stone cave.

On the rat-catcher admitting his army of rats in his cave, and then directing them to spring into the trap cavity, the fierce creatures were instantly met with a deadly, crashing volley of objects. The square opening was at that moment completely blocked up by a black, writhing, squealing mass. The lead tore a jagged space through the very centre of the hissing wedge, scattering the maimed, dying, and dead vermin in heaps upon the four sides of the opening in the flags of the rat-tamer's strange abode.

The check was but momentary. There appeared no end to the broad and black column darting from the cavity in the wall, flying over this intervening space, and then plunging down the dark void, to fly at those desperately contending for their lives.

The conjecture of the terrible underground giant had proved quite correct— namely, that those he had entrapped in his "great rat-trap" below his cave were members of the Thames piratical gang. These ruffians, at the period of these historical records, were notoriously the most cruel and wanton robbers and assassins known in any portion of Great Britain.

On the principle that "Dead men tell no tales" they made it an almost invariable practice to put to death all those they plundered. Either the knife or the bottom of the Thames stream did their fiendish work, according to circumstances or convenience.

A number of the cutthroat gang had penetrated into the opening by which Dandy Dick and his companions had entered the underground cul-de-sac. As we have already seen, the monster Fangs had directed his terrible army to the attack on becoming aware of the presence of his enemy below by reason of the fearful fire directed upwards.

Before this the giant rat-catcher had sprang to his great crane, or lever, and let down the wall-like mass of stone, which completely imprisoned those in the blind alley-like sewer-way under the abode of the weird, deformed, and terrible dweller in the bowels of the earth.

The Thames robbers at first thought to drive off with powder and ball the frenzied creatures springing down in one unbroken stream, until the limited and closed-in space became literally filled with them—a compact body a foot or more in-depth.

When their powder had given out, the desperate men drew their swords, belt-dirks, and knives, and defended their lives like furies.

The water in this boring had quite receded with the ceasing of the storm. The terrible rodents were cut down until they lay scattered in thickly-piled-up numbers, but quickly to be covered up by throngs of uninjured of their species, which flew to avenge the deaths of their fellows with deadly thirst for human blood.

The horrible contest was commenced, waged, and terminated in but a few seconds. Frightfully injured, weakened from loss of blood, and terror-panic, the pirates were borne to the ground by sheer weight of their countless enemies, or sank down in utter despair, eager to have their sufferings terminated.

The explosions of firearms had ceased, the clash or thud of steel could no longer be heard. Terrible imprecations, yells of rage, oaths of agony, shrieks of fear, all these were no longer to be heard; nothing but feeble groanings, or most piteous pleas to be released or shot, that their torments might sooner end.

"In Heaven's name, if it is yet possible to save their lives, spare the unfortunate wretches! They can do no harm to us if that flag is kept down!" appealed Dandy Dick to the rat-trainer.

In reply Fangs started to the opening in the wall and replaced the stone. No more rats came into the cave. Then its owner lowered the flag into the former place in the floor. The cave was now quite clear of the giant's deadly pets.

"Stay! Is not this too inhuman?" sternly demanded Colonel Blood of Fangs.

The latter confronted the colonel with extreme boldness.

"Inhuman or not, it is a stern necessity," he firmly replied. "My good master, I have saved your life and those of your friends from devouring by black rats. I would now render ye a like service in respect to the far more to be dreaded Red Rats of the river."

"You stated that you could take us from hence but with a risk of meeting the Thames robbers, therefore this monstrous act was unnecessary," gravely put in Dandy Dick.

"Aha, my most gallant friend, an' I told you so in very truth; but that was before the men-rats came below, and caused me to block up our only safe means of departure ha! ha! ha! What say my noble masters now? There are at least six less of the Thames assassins to stand between thee and thy chances of life!"

Fangs, as he uttered this, gazed upon the outlaws like some unearthly and grinning fiend.

"How know ye that it was not Wild's followers you loosed your vermin army upon?" asked Dick Turpin.

"None but the Red Rats would have the madlike courage to attempt to trap me in my secret lair!" was the answer.

"I would not for a king's ransom have unheedingly listened to the heart-piercing cries coming from that awful pit below," said Dandy Dick to the giant Fangs. "You will have a heavy load on your conscience, friend," he continued, "if that slaughter was avoidable."

"That question will be answered, my master, before you shall have escaped the monsters below—the Thames terrors," quietly rejoined the rat-catcher.

All was now silent below. The outlaws exchanged glances. In spite of all stated by the rat-catcher, they were horror-stricken and depressed, as the result of the destruction of the captives in the sewer-way.

Remarkable to relate, the badly-wounded Tom King still slept. All through the whole enacting of the horrors below the same trance-like condition had remained. The wondrous power of the cordial given him by the strange denizen of the sewer-cave was to be credited with this fortunate circumstance, since it not only saved the injured man much suffering, led to the knowledge of that which had so deeply affected all his comrades.

Final preparations were now made for the departure of the highwaymen.

When all were in readiness, Fangs pushed aside from the stone cave-side near the fire a great, heavy barrel. An opening between the stones, large enough for a man's body to easily pass through, was then revealed.

"Ho! ho! Fangs, the hunted man-rat, hath many burrows wherein to flee fox-like, and must cunningly double upon his pursuers. Ha! ha! We shall see!"

While thus exclaiming, the giant had lighted several torches by means of the flaming fire-logs. He gave one to each of the outlaws, and retained another for himself.

The rat-trainer minutely directed his guests as to their underground course, precautions, and tactics—the latter in the event of meeting with either Jonathan Wild's myrmidons or the Thames terrors.

Fangs was the first to creep into the exit now open. He proceeded head-foremost, the lighted link held well in advance of him. Those about to follow heard him savagely driving away in his trained creatures.

Shuddering in loathing, Dandy Dick next followed, Colonel Blood next. Wiffles, whose detestation of the rodents had produced a result few others could do—namely, rendered him grave and silent—crept after. Turpin remained until the last movement, silently and sorrowfully contemplating his beloved pal whom he was extremely reluctant to leave.

In a few moments the cave had been vacated of all save the sleeping Tom King. Some a few yards of crawling through a steep incline brought the rat-catcher and his party into a level gully—a circular cutting, devoid of water, but extremely foul-smelling.

All stood erect. The cutting appeared of great length.

"This I must not venture beyond this tunnel's end, my brave masters. I will not leave my charge until the day I have undertaken to bring him to our meeting-place."

These were intended to be the parting words of Fangs, but Fate willed otherwise. A scampering of tiny feet suddenly caught the ears of all.

"My scouts! They flee towards us in alarm!" The words were hurriedly whispered by the rat-catcher in mingled rage and apprehension. "Look to yourselves, my masters!" he hissed. "We are discovered!"

The words were no sooner uttered than a terrible uproar from many fierce throats broke upon the ears of all. Next a fear-imposing figure sprang from some secret hiding-place. Brandishing an enormous cutlass, the being dashed at Fangs. The latter threw his blazing link full in the face of the advancing man, and, uttering a yell of defiance, drew his long-bladed dagger.

The attacker trod upon a small fleeing body, slipped, and fell face downwards to the earth. With a bound like that of a panther, Fangs had sprung forward, and slashed at the back of the prone figure. Three murderous plunges of the glistening steel point, then the hideous giant sprang erect again—a moment only. Fangs' echoing, ringing terms warned his companions.

(This grand story will be concluded next Wednesday)

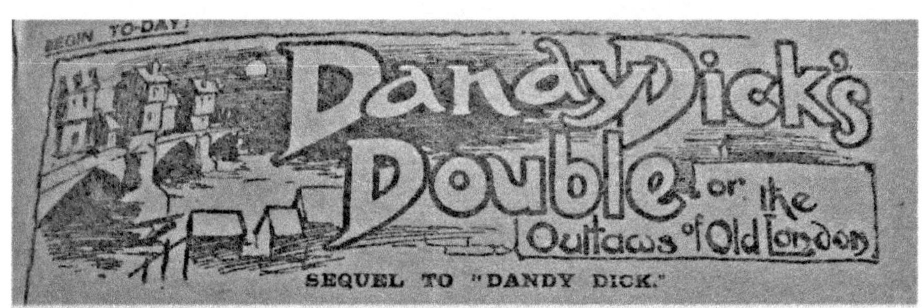

DANDY DICK'S DOUBLE,

or the Outlaws of Old London.

°A strange army—What befell Dandy Dick and his friends.

"Down! down!" he thundered, not the millionth part of a second too soon.

A terrific volley shrieked out. Bullets madly tore on their way, striking and chipping the stone walls on their course, filling the tunnel with their whistling hymn of death.

"Charge, charge, my brave masters! It is our only hope!"

Fangs dashed forward with most splendid recklessness as he uttered these words.

Two more of the enemy sprang within the yellow-glare radius of the blazing links. Murderous downward swoop of steels threatened the denizen of the cave-sewer. His movements were electrical. The great head, with its thick covering of short-cut black bristly hair, and had shot forward, striking the nearest man with irresistible force full in the stomach. The latter heavily collided with his fellow. Before either could recover balance, the yellow light-reflecting knife-blade had shot upwards and downwards again. The lifeblood of Fangs' victim dripped from his murderous blade. Three sacrifices had the fiend-like being already claimed.

Scarcely had the rat-catcher charged the latter two of the enemy than a repeat volley from the highwaymen's pistols burst forth with earsplitting effect.

The smoke was now almost blinding. The echoes, dying away in distant passages, seemed never-ending. All again became silence.

Fangs, lowering his link, went forward into the circling vapour. Presently he returned. The wildest degree of savage triumph contorted his brutal features.

"Six less Red Rats!" he gleefully whispered, adding: "But the scent of the slain will quickly bring their fellows. We must fight our way like men-rats driven at bay—tooth an' nail! Come, my steady masters, come!"

The motionless bodies of six men littered the way of the adventurers. They sped past the horrid sight of carnage and death. Their lives were in their hands, all pity and gentle feelings replaced by the gall of hatred, and no thought now but that of cruel devastation.

"Death in the most horrible form before capture by the Thames pirates—the secret, bloodthirsty allies of the wretch Jonathan Wild!"

These thoughts turned to stone the hearts of all, and nerved their wrists for remorseless deeds.

The end of the long, circular tunnel was now reached. No sight or sound of the enemy, Fangs, after further whispered cautions and directions, then left the outlaws.

Rough-hewn steps terminated the sewer-passage. The mighty rush of a fierce torrent came to the ears. There was a rough but strong timber-raft always moored at the bottom of these crude steps. The Thames pirates used this raft

---

° Part 34. Vol. XIV.—No. 370. 8 December 1900.

only upon extremely rare occasions. The outlaws were to trust themselves to the lashed timbers, cast off the moorings, and allow the floating timbers and themselves to be carried out by the swift and most powerful current into the bed of the river. Fangs had explained all these things most minutely.

The devoted comrades carefully looked to the priming of their firearms—rubbing the flints, and making sure their wads were tightly round home, the powder dry.

Dandy Dick and Colonel Blood lead the way. The glare of the brilliantly-flaring flambeaus fell upon slimy walls, green-moss-covered in places, reeking with water in others. The slippery nature of the uneven steps rendered the downward progress extremely difficult.

Like an unexpected clap of thunder burst out a multitude of yells of most awe-inspiring terror and deafening din.

The highwaymen recklessly threw themselves down the remaining steps. Dandy Dick and Colonel Blood sprang for the raft, which their links' rays instantly revealed.

"Surrender, Dandy Dick!" yelled a horridly coarse, guttural voice.

The eyes of the outlaws swiftly took in the situation. From innumerable shadowy holes and corners sprang forth fierce-eyed, brutal-visaged, full-bearded men.

The handful of highwaymen appeared to be surrounded by legions of desperate men.

"No surrender!" fiercely and defiantly yelled Dandy Dick, in reply. "Death before capture!" he added, hurling himself upon the foremost of the Thames terrors.

Dandy Dick's cries were echoed by his comrades, who gathered like Spartans around him, prepared to do or die. Swords flashed, pistols exploded, oaths were exchanged. The dancing, yellow, serpent-like torch-gleams lit up a weird and startling spectacle—a battle in the bowels of the earth, fierce outlaw against fierce outlaw, yet twenty to one against the intrepid little band owning leadership to the persecuted youth Dandy Dick.

OFFICER BILBERRY, THE CHAMPION YARN-SPINNER, AGAIN HOLDS FORTH—THE TALE OF A FIERY UNTAMED WHELK—THE TAMING THEREOF, AND WHAT FOLLOWED—THE STRANGE VISITORS TO THE HARMONIC BRETHREN—THE CHAIR IS INTERRUPTED—BILBERRY IS DISCOMFITED.

It is a very sad breach of courtesy to the Pig and Pink Cushionites that we have overlooked them for fully a week, the more especially that we have left the "deeply venerated, and noble and worthy Chair"—we have not by any means exhausted all the adjectives usually applied to the Chairman of the Pig and Pink Cushionites by his supporters and admirers—still standing on his legs.

The Chair most gracefully and urbanely bowed, resumed his seat, and proceeded with quite touching condescension to reply to the question put to him.

"The whelk," he learnedly commenced, "being amphibious in its nature and habits, roamed the forests, when in its savage and altogether unsubdued state, and—"

"Did the wild and untamed creature possess legs, most venerated, right noble, and superlatively worthy Chair?" very bashfully and timidly asked the interrupter again.

The gimlet eye of the Chair—before referred to—performed several more perforations.

"It did!" severely retorted Brother Bilberry. "Like certain of the starch-like living forms to be found in the sea depths, the untamed fiery whelk could at will leave it shall and put forth from its body limbs. Well, to proceed with my story concerning my pet shellfish," continued Bilberry. "It's method of attacking a destructive foe was extremely peculiar and even a lion has been slain by the daring methods of the fiery untamed. The whelk, when attacked and aroused in sudden fury, would quietly permit its enemy to swallow it—shell an' all. Then came the moment of most deadly peril to the foe. The maddened shellfish would escape from its shell which it would then contrive to send down the wrong way of the gullet. The infuriated creature thus secured a terrible revenge by choking its greater and more powerful enemy.

"This form of vengeance," went on the Chair, "has its drawback, however, and much resembles the case of the man who conceived and carried out the horrid plot—in pure grudge—of drowning himself in his neighbour's private water-butt. Of course, by doing so he succeeded in poisoning stone dead all those of the household who partook of the fearfully polluted liquid; but then, do ye see, he didn't live to exult over his great triumph, an' that, to my way of thinking, rather took the milk out of the cokernut of his revenge.

"But take up the tale of the whelk again," continued the unblushing narrator "In time I succeeded in completely subduing its extremely savage nature, and even taught the grateful creature to follow me about wherever I went, just as would a perfectly docile cat or dog. Up and down stairs the gifted thing would travel. And the pretty and vain little fellow took quite a pride in wearing a piece of coloured ribbon I always placed round its neck on a Sunday."

The two strangers—supposed travellers from foreign parts—shifted most uneasily in their seats. The reader will remember that these persons had very cleverly disguised themselves by darkening their skins with a juice-stain, and by other means. They were the innkeeper and his wife, well known to our readers and to Officer Bilberry.

"Ralph dear, pinch my arm—pinch it quite hard, or I shall have an awful fit o' laughter directly—I'm sure I shall!" Thus whispered Mrs. Drake.

"The daring old liar!" ejaculated Ralph Drake, sotto voce. "I feel like bursting with wrath! To think that the infernal old windbag hath the effrontery to dole out such wicked romances, an' that apparently sane men can calmly tolerate them—nay, they actually appear to believe this wild nonsense he is detailing. I shall be compelled to contradict the blatant old ass if I die for it!"

"Restrain thyself, Ralph!" pleaded Mrs. Drake, adding: "Remember, we are here to endeavour to learn if the blown-out old man-frog is at the bottom of the terrible charge brought against us—that of harbouring felons at our hostel. If he should discover our deception, it will make matters infinitely worse for us. Leave the old fool to me, Ralph; I'll warrant ye I'll confuse him, an' yet not betray our presence."

Although this converse had been but mumbled in this extremely low undertone, the Vice-Chair—Vice for short—had heard an indistinct buzzing at his back. The Vice saw his opportunity to proudly assert himself, and immediately sprang up—after the style of a Jack-in-the-box when the lid is opened.

"Gentlemen," he cried, in a tone of outraged dignity, "touching this tale of a shellfish—I must emphatically protest against interruptions on the part of Brother harmonics, and also against conversations being carried on while the ever venerated, illustrious, most exalted, rights noble, and worthy Chair is honouring us with the intensely interesting narrative of a pet animal, and—"

"Is a shellfish an animal, dear Vice?" demanded an unknown voice.

The glaring orbs of the Vice-Chair darted in all directions to discover the daring and unseemly interrupter, but in vain.

Officer Bilberry—or, rather, the Chair—rose to the occasion beamingly. The Vice instantly flopped into his seat, as in duty bound whenever the Chair resumed its pins.

"The great Fluffem, in his famous work on 'The Sea and its Denizens,'" commenced the Chair, in crushing pomposity, "distinctly describes the creature in question as an animal, and gives its Latin name, which is that of catchusancrackourshellus—hem!"

Thunders of applause greeted this great display of learning on the part of the bowing and beaming Chair. The Vice frantically hammered with his little wooden mallet at the oaken table-top, and only ceased when he succeeded in suddenly breaking the handle of his tool of trade—or, rather, pleasure.

The Pig and Pink Cushionites were so charmed and delighted by being informed of the Latin term for whelk that they rattled upon the long table between them with their strawyards—otherwise churchwardens—otherwise clay-pipes—until the bowls of many snapped off, and the further demands became necessary for fresh clays.

When the demonstrations of approval had at length subsided, the Chair resumed his story.

"Soon," commenced he, "I taught my little pupil the art of music, and to which it immediately became passionately attached. In time the gifted whelk learned to play a miniature violin—made expressly for its use—most divinely—"

"Ahem!" commenced that interrupter again. "Er—most revered and beloved Chair," he hesitatingly asked, "did—er—ther—er—fiery creature ever speak?"

"Man alive! no, sir!" thundered Bilberry, the gimlet eye at work again. "Neither did it ever interrupt, Sir—It knew its manners far too well for that!"

This was a scathing silencer, and the interrupter interrupted no more for the remainder of the meeting.

"Well, gentlemen," the Chair resumed, after a profound pause, "the latter end of my shellfish companion was extremely sad. Ye have all, no doubt, heard of whistling oysters? I was so fortunate as to possess one—nay, my bivalve[114] could whistle, sing, an' even dance a hornpipe to its own accompaniment. But, alas! the oyster and the whelk are of hostile tribes. A welcome, with a proper respect for its most ancient origin, looks down with supreme contempt upon an oyster. The two creatures, on their first meeting in my training-quarters, even after a most formal introduction, regarded each other with looks of the most deadly enmity. No word was uttered, but the bivalve commenced to sing, then whistle, and finally to set up a most graceful reel.

"The fiery and resentful whelk, in its envy appeared to lose its head. It sprang from its shell, balanced itself upon the tip of its spiral tail, and instantly set off, whirling around like a moth driven mad by the sight of a will-o'-the-wisp, or a tallow-candle. Between the two creatures, do ye see, gentlemen, so much ill-feeling rankled that each felt that the world could not go on in its usual well-greased state while both lived—"

"Rot! Infamous liar! Shameless fraud!"

This most startling interruption apparently came from the wide chimney opening above the brightly-flaming fire-logs.

Bilberry's face assumed all the tints of the rainbow, and even a few more.

"Gentlemen! Shame—shame on the villain who dares thus to outrage the feelings—" commenced the Vice, when another strange voice interrupted him with the words:

"That old idiot wrongly occupies the position of chairman!"

"Kick him out!" cried out a voice from still another quarter.

"Blood an' hounds!" yelled Bilberry, boiling over with rage. "This to me teeth! Man alive! Snake-bytes an' deadliest scorpions fastening upon me gullet! Spasms of gripe-poisons! The hind must perish instanter that dares to thus insult a Bilberry!"

---

[114] *Mollusks such as oysters, scallops, mussels and clams with an external hinged shell and a soft interior invertebrate.*

"An over-ripe Bilberry! A Bilberry rotten at heart!"

These added insults were uttered in still another totally unknown tone, and this time they apparently proceeded from under the table.

°Officer Bilberry, the champion yarn-spinner, holds forth. (*Continued from last week's number—no. 370.*)

The utterly confounded Bow Street runner sprang back—toppling his chair over in the act—and, with a great show of bravery, drew his hanger from the sheath still attached to his belt, and made a fierce lunge at some imaginary being lurking in the shadows under the table.

The most awful shrieks instantly followed; then the harrowing sound, as of dying moans.

Not for a moment had the ever-make-believe Bilberry supposed that his sword-blade would really pierce a human body. In his utter confusion and extreme funk he now imagined that he had actually slain some person crouching from observation under the table.

"Thunderclaps an' scathing lightning! The stain of murder upon the soul of a Bilberry! Then let chaos come!" he gasped, in unfeigned horror and alarm, falling into his chair, he imagined; but, having previously capsized that article, he fell, full weight, to the floor, shaking the inn to its very foundations.

The piercing shrieks of mortal agony reached the ears of the innkeeper and others in the bar-parlour. The latter threw open the door of the smoke-room.

"Heavens, we shall all hang! Who is killed and murdered?" frantically ejaculated the innkeeper.

"Officer Bilberry, the Bow Street runner," replied a voice, which appeared to come from under the very floor.

The runner glanced at his steel. It was perfectly stainless.

"Blood an' quick burials! I see it all! I'm bewitched!" yelled he, in utter dismay. "The coffin-visaged Ralph Drake's black arts! Ho! ha! But he'll swing, for I've lodged an information against him! Ho! ho! Harbouring Dandy Dick, the—"

"Who dares thus lightly use my name? What ho! make way there! Where is the insulter? I—Dandy Dick—will flay him alive!"

Several persons could be dimly seen in the outer and somewhat darkened passage. The latest unknown tones seemed to proceed from the group therein.

Bilberry sprang to his feet, and swiftly took his bearings. The in-window was low and wide. In an instant he had thrown it open and scrambled through, alighted on his feet, and bolted off for dear life.

"We have attained our objective, Ralph, let us now depart!" whispered Mrs. Drake in her husband's ear.

° Part 35. Vol. XIV.—No. 371. 12 December 1900.

MARK DANKLY, JONATHAN WILD'S AGENT—THE DESPERATE RESOLVE OF THE YOUTHFUL OUTLAW—JACK RANN DISAPPEARS IN THE QUAGMIRE.

It is now necessary that we take up one of the threads of our story somewhat long overlooked—namely, that connected with the captive highwayman, Jack Rann. Mark Dankly, a spy of Jonathan Wild's, and specially employed on the errand of seeking out one or more of the secret passes to the interior of the outlaw's stronghold at Finchley, as the reader may remember, succeeded in arresting the dashing young outlaw, Jack Rann. But, instead of taking the prisoner to Wild's house, or Newgate Gaol, Dankly had determined that his captive should lead himself (Dankly) and his party of police agents through one of the hidden pathways of the dangerous quagmires completely surrounding the Haunted Manor, Mark Dankly's main object being to learn of the secret means of reaching the Haunted Manor.

The winter night was moonless, and of pitch like blackness. The outlaw bands were all bound by the most terrible oaths to sacrifice their lives rather than betray to an enemy a means of reaching an entrance to their abode in the fastnesses of the Finchley Wilds.

Jack Rann had no thought of breaking his binding compact; but he now, mentally, most bitterly reproached himself for his neglect of not having made himself far more intimately acquainted with the intricacies of the deadly maze guarding the Haunted Manor, for his neglect of this now threatened to cost him his life.

The young outlaw had been gagged by means of his cravat, and his arms had also been pinioned behind. Mark Dankly held one end of the rope by which his victim was secured. The police agents held their fully-cocked firearms closely presented at the head of Jack Rann, and he had been sternly admonished that the merest suspicion of treachery on his part would instantly cost him his life.

"You have, I have heard, more than one hidden pathway through the morass?" asked Dankly of his prisoner.

Rann nodded his head. The former continued:

"Mr. Wild, when he could keep the matter secret no longer, informed us, his officers, that no less than three of your people and their horses most miserably perished in these very same hell-traps! The great chief of Newgate himself also most narrowly escaped falling a victim to your most infernal defensive bogs. You can therefore form a good notion of the desperate character of the men who willingly dare these dangers, and, depend upon it, in the event of treachery, the first victim to be swallowed up by your demon swamps must be yourself! Forward!" he sternly concluded.

Jack Rann cautiously advanced. A matter of twenty yards, and he had already stepped upon earth that, even in the severest time of winter, never became really hard, while the pitchlike shine of the quagmire had ever defied all the utmost efforts of King Frost.

Jack Rann continued to most bitterly curse his folly that he had not done as did all those who made the Haunted Manor their chief abiding place—namely, made himself perfectly familiar with all the secret paths through the morass. To reveal the one, deep underground declivity formed where the roundness of the earth permitted it, Rann well knew, might prove fatal, and rather than do so, he was resolved to face a most horrible end—even that of sacrificing his life in the awful depths of the morass. But existence is sweet to the youthful, and the brave young highwayman was resolved that he would not yield up his life without a severe struggle.

Before the gagging of their prisoner, the exchange of words had taken place:

"You number not more than two dozen in all, and will be indeed worse than mad if you attempt to face some hundreds of the fiercest of men!" Rann had said, with ill-concealed contempt.

Mark Dankly had replied:

"Our object is to find the track leading to the wall of the building. A combined attack, in overwhelming numbers, will then soon after be made in daylight. Once I find a safe path conducting me to your retreat, I shall not soon forget it. You must conduct us up to the very gates of your fortress, and from thence back by the same way to the spot."

"But your many links will betray your presence," answered Rann.

"We'll all carry them so near the earth that their flare will be pretty well concealed by the thickly-growing bushes, the many tree-stems, and tall, tangled briars. Then again, at the most, to save your brains, you can be compelled to give some signal that will allay any awakened suspicions on the part of your friends."

Thus was the young highwayman answered, after which he was immediately gagged.

Mark Dankly then addressed those at his command.

"My comrades," said he, "handsome reward and great honour will become ours. We shall succeed where even Mr. Wild himself has failed. Think of that, and let your eyesight be keen, and your foothold sure!"

Jack Rann had intended giving a signal to his fellow outlaws that would have resulted in the certain surprise and capture of the officers having him in custody; but the gagging had been effected to quickly, and he now felt convinced that all the prospect of saving his life was gone. But there yet remained to him the hope of inflicting a most terrible retribution upon the common foe.

The gag, which prevented the use of his tongue, did not affect his hearing.

Mark Dankly closely followed at the heels of Jack Rann, who happened to know some few of the twisting is of the path he was traversing, but was totally unable to follow it to its end—a former venture on his part having resulted in his being compelled to return, completely trapped, to the outer margin of the swamps.

On reaching a most desperately puzzling spot, the outlaw stopped, turned and faced Dankly, and then motioned that the gag should be removed. This was done.

"What do you mean, fellow?" savagely demanded Rann's captor.

"That we have now reached a most dangerous spot, and where the slightest false step means certain death!" answered the outlaw, adding: "I shall now need the free use of my tongue as well as eyes, and hands as well as feet, otherwise I cannot proceed."

In spite of the caution given to the contrary, Dankly raised his flaming link. It is strong, yellow glare played upon the fine features of Jack Rann.

"You may call out to your vile associates, and betray us," muttered the police agent. "We shall receive scant mercy at their hands," he added.

"As much mercy as I shall get from your brother tubes, even on mere suspicion of a desire on my part to lead you into a snare," Rann replied.

"What if I refuse to trust you?" sternly demanded Wild's emissary.

"In that event I will go no farther!" was the calmly resolute reply.

"I've half a mind to shatter your brains, villain! What shall now prevent me?"

Dankly threw forward his firearm, and lightly pressed the trigger. Jack Rann smiled defiantly. He knew that he was within an ace of death, yet not an atom of fear displayed itself.

"If you value not only your own life but also that of every one of your fellows, you will instantly lower your ugly and greedy-looking popgun!" sneeringly resumed the highwayman, "for the pressure of that trigger will mean the entire destruction of yourself and party if you kill me!"

"How so, varlet?" hissed Dankly.

"Without my guidance you cannot possibly proceed."

The smile upon the outlaw's face increased.

"Ha, ha! I will despatch you with as little compunction as I would a fly!" fiercely threatened the officer.

The burning brand, held in his left hand, increased the evil glitter of his eyes, and threw in stronger contrast the savage leer of his repulsive features.

"You will encompass your own doom and that of your men by the same act, for you will be unable to retrace your steps there, and must all perish here, in this dismal and deadly region!" was Rann's quite calm and taunting retort.

Seeing the slight value Rann based upon his own life, Mark Dankly lowered his tube. He now saw that everything depended on the way in which he conducted himself with the captured man.

"Go forward, disclose a path to your stronghold and back, and I swear then to let you depart. Your life and liberty depend on this! Refuse to obey, and, by all that's sacred, I'll slay you, even if we all perish as a consequence of my act!"

Daring and desperate as was the young outlaw, equally so was the man Mark Dankly. Jack Rann turned his back on the latter, and slowly picked his way, the lights held by those in his rear guiding him.

As he had feared, Rann had missed his bearings! The strange, mixed, leafless saplings, tall, tangled bush growths, and other masses of vegetation were so hindering in their resemblance to each other that the greatest skill and experience were required to enable one to safely traverse these extensive swamp tracts.

Jonathan Wild's myrmidons cautiously crept after Jack Rann. The earth was spongelike in places, in others a thin, glass-like film of ice floated over pools of mire, into which the feet sank deeply.

The highwayman now found his feet sinking deeper at every step. Death menaced him in its most hideous shape. To advance further meant certain destruction. To turn and confess his fatal error would be to invite the discharge of a dozen deliberately-levelled firearms.

Jack Rann cautiously and fearfully advanced. Before him, in the deep gloom, danced long, fantastic shadows, thrown by the low-carried, burning torches.

A hurried mental appeal to the Supreme was framed in the outlaw's frenzied brain. A terrific cry, or shriek, then pierced the night's deadly silence.

"Confusion! The wretch has betrayed us! He shall die! Fire, lads!" howled Mark Dankly.

A dozen tubes belched forth fire, lead, and smoke. The echoes shrieked out in startling clearness over the dreaded morass. But the police spies had fired at vacancy. Their prisoner had disappeared while uttering that dreadful cry quite as completely as if his form had evaporated into the atmosphere.

"Curses on my impetuosity!" thundered Dankly in despairing fury. "I have helped to bring about our complete destruction, for, if we escape this awful death-trap, we shall now surely fall into the hands of the vast hordes of robbers infesting the ruined building in the centre of this circular quagmire!"

"You are too harsh with the fellow, master!" grumbled one of Dankly's followers, adding: "That cry was not for the object of betraying us to any of his friends likely to be within its sound, so much as a yell of terror at having lost his footing!"

"The poor devil sank before we fired," remarked another of the party.

"The shout may have been the result of sudden terror, as you say," Smart replied, the leader of the spies. "But," he continued, "unless we can retrace our steps, all is up with us. Better death in conflict with the outlaw gangs than in these foul regions!"

"So say I," commented another spy. "There may be found a spark of mercy, even in their savage hearts; but in the foul, black bosom of these hungry pits there exists but the venom of all-consuming destruction!"

The dancing glow of the links was directed to the spot where the young outlaw had last stood. The solid earth here came to an abrupt end. The deep and extensive mire of the morass glittered like black polish, with bright and dancing streaks of yellow orange, reflected upon its surface from the glowing brands.

Mark Dankly's all-but-burnt-out torch fell from his hand, to instantly sink, with a hiss, into the soft liquid.

"Not the faintest hope of foothold there," he tremblingly remarked. "Turn back, men," he continued, "and use the utmost caution. Our only chance is to regain the margin of these yawning graves!"

The spies had followed the young outlaw along the narrow, twisting pathways in single file. The man forming the last of the line turned to now become leader. His link had now also burned itself so low that it could not safely be held.

"One of you set a fresh link ablaze!" he called out. Then he threw the end of the link into the bog.

"We have none but these now alight," answered several voices.

"Hasten, then, hasten!" cried Dankly, inwardly anathematising the folly that caused such a serious oversight.

His words were no sooner uttered than a cry of horror burst out, its intensity lifting its heroes' hair in overpowering fear. Then followed a sound as of one frantically battling for his life; then another horrible cry-half gurgle—then silence followed. One of Wild's spies had perished.

Another torch was now burned so low that it was impossible to hold it. The flaming pitch fell upon the holder's hand in small beads of fire. This link-end was cast away. Mark Dankly yelled at his men to put on their leathern gloves, but these articles proved of little avail one by one the flaming brans were perforce cast away, until at the darkness now added to the awful peril of their situation.

Curses, oaths, and bitterest regrets and reproaches now came from all Dankly's life would have paid the forfeit of his rashness in leading his men to almost certain destruction, but their firearms were un-primed, and to attack him with their cutlasses was next to an impossibility.

Suddenly hoarse yells of superstitious terror burst from every throat. The before ink like blackness of the morass regions had, as if by an electrical flash, become a flame with dazzling, glowworm-like meteors of fire, and the yet still more awe-inspiring sight of pale, white, and moving skeleton heads—devoid of body with these thrilling apparitions—their eyes of a brilliantly-glowing blood-red hue, and the phantom head darted about in all directions, even over the most deadly-dangerous spots of the extensive swamps.

The most piercing, blood-curdling shrieks now rose up, one after another. The party of spies were fatally sinking, one by one, their awful cries adding to the fear-paralysing terrors surrounding them. Mark Dankly thrust his fingers into his ears, closed his eyes, and, standing thus, momentarily expected to meet his doom in some weirdly awful form.

°THE INNKEEPER'S PEST—THE LADYKILLER—OFF WITH THE OLD LOVE ON WITH THE NEW—SWEET, SOFT NOTHINGS—OFFICER BILBERRY CONFIDES ONE LADY'S SECRET TO ANOTHER—THE OLD TOPER'S MIDNIGHT JOURNEY HOME, AND WHAT CAME OF IT.

Officer Bilberry had turned his back upon the Piebald Pig and Pink Cushionites for good (distinctly their good!). He had succeeded in running up a record-breaking score with mine host of the before-mentioned hostel. In those days it was the usual custom to "score up" or chalk on any bare, even space, the details of a patron's account owing. When a clear space was no longer to be found upon which to continue the score jottings, it was an understood thing that the debtor paid up. Then the delighted inn-proprietor would—with much gusto and graceful flourish—with a wet washleather, wipe out the chalk-marked indebtedness.

The eagle eye and retentive memory of the toper Bilberry were never at fault concerning the possibilities of continually adding to his score. When every available space of an inn of his patronage became conspicuously decorated with the crude white hieroglyphics, and the landlord, in a fit of desperation, would be either on the point of continuing the items of account upon the bare surface of his inn chimney pots, for want of further space, or firmly, and even rudely demanding immediate and full payment, then one of two or three things would happen. Bilberry would either utterly condemn the quality of the articles he had duly consumed; do the vanishing-trick forthwith; or suddenly accuse "mine host" of harbouring in his house highwaymen, and felons generally. Such-like tricks mostly succeeded, and the fearful old fraud would have enjoyed a long course of unlimited drinking free, gratis, and for nothing, and after which be free to take his patronage elsewhere.

In the case of the Pig and Pink Cushion Inn, Bilberry, having most completely "given the show away" by a cowardly and undignified bolt on the suspected advent of Dandy Dick, the old humbug had made a virtue of necessity, and never again returned to the Harmonic Brethren. "The most noble, gifted, learned, venerated, and is deemed Chair" had, at divers times, borrowed sums from each and every member of the Pig and Pink Cushionites; so that, with the unpaid score, he had netted a good round sum.

In his high-flying, flowery, flattering manner, the noble Chair had frequently well buttered and toasted the various members of the harmonic club, and he finally caused them each to pay somewhat dearly for that well-buttered toasts.

It had now become absolutely necessary that the famous old toper should seek "Fresh fields and pastures new," in the shape of an inn having for its

---

° Part 36 . Vol. XIV.—No. 372. 21 December 1900.

owners easily gullible personages, or an owner who should prove to be an easily gullible person. This object the old swashbuckler soon attained. A certain proprietress of an inn had long been in Bilberry's eye, her inn also had long been in his optic—a good-sized orb this, by the way—and the imaginary flavour of the inn's liquids had long been in his chronically parched lime-kiln of a face-opening—in his case most flatteringly termed a mouth.

The lady hostel-keeper's name was Martha Marman; the sign of her house that of the King and Punchbowl. Of course there was a story attached to the hostel, to the effect that one of England's Kings had one day it written up to the inn-door and called for a bowl of the inn's most famous blend of the goodly tipple, after the sampling of which his Kingship had called for further supplies for his courtiers. Finally the mixture had met with the full and unqualified approval of the Royal personage and his friends, and hence the supposedly origin of the inn's sign—this being a legend common to almost every inn of importance at the period of which we write.

One of the most remarkable features of old London thoroughfares and its populated outskirts, was its great number of signs. Every innkeeper, Mercer, and profession had his or its own particular sign. In nearly all cases the article bore some reference to the trade or profession of the house it decorated. The outdoor post, with a swinging-board at its top, was perhaps the most popular for all places of public resort. The ordinary tradesmen being content either to hang the emblem of his calling at right angles from his front-house, fix it over his door, or have it painted in any convenient and conspicuous space on his premises. The variety of designs were most remarkable, all the nations of the earth contributing to this object. To give the reader a slight notion of the far-fetched nature of these devices it is but necessary to mention a few examples.

"The Nun with the Bleeding Heart" is one, despairing reference to a legend of a nun of the Convent of Hatton. The lady in question being for ever subject to a state of the deepest melancholy, it is supposed.

"The King and Keys." This sign was originally that of a locksmith, and is still in use. The "Swan with two necks" —also still a trade sign—was once the "trade-mark" of a keeper of a popular hostelry in the city of London, the two necks being intended to imply that double the facility for drinking existed at that particular in—needless to add, a choice resort for Officer Bilberry in his day.

"The Jew's Heart and Blind Bat." This was once in vogue as an original sign-painting for a maker of string instruments of music. "Magpie and Stump." This did duty to imply that its owner trader as a timber-merchant. The illustration took the form of a black bird perched upon a tree-stem, the bird looking down at the sawn surface of the wood upon which he stood, with an expression on its face which seemed to imply the very reverse of approval of the quality of the goods.

Space forbids, or we could proceed with a description of this almost lost art ad infinitum.

The good old soaker Bilberry's method of procedure, when contemplating the besieging of a strange inn, partook somewhat of this form: He would make his first attack when armed with his last month's pay. The display of much golden bait would be pretty sure to tempt the inn-owner fish anxious for a nibble, or, in fact, considerable new blinks. The new patron would make it a point to cash up promptly for everything ordered; become "Hail, fellow, well met!" with every frequenter; and for a time make a very great display of liberality. Gradually the "sticking-up" process would commence. This would end only with the ultimate kicking-out of the debtor, or the ruin of the creditor; five out of every six times it would terminate in the latter case. In the sixth the Bow Street bully-boy would take the kicking and his future patronage together away with him.

We now catch Swashbuckler Bilberry red-handed in his latest feat of daring-do, in the form of preparing to obtain a term of wholesale swilling on the rush.

In this case the owner of the chosen inn is a "lone female," and therefore, as was his wont, Officer Bilberry commenced the siege by opening a running fire of most complimentary shots, and making protestations of love of a recklessly fervid kind.

"Aha, sweetest an' fairest, rarest an' dearest, o' thy sex, as the pretty ballad hath it! But, dear madam, thou art more captivating an' shapely than ever were fabled goddess. Venus herself need, abashed, shrink back into her shell an' blushingly direct its course to the deepest depths of her native home—the ocean's bed—an' remain in hiding there while such a peerless divinity as thyself condescends to grace the earth with thy most ravishing charms!" In this strain carried on the ogling Bilberry.

"Get along, you woefully headstrong, self-willed, passionately-disposed lady-killer!" replied to his latest charmer. "For thou art, in very truth, a comely gentleman and a fascinating!"

Officer Bilberry, it must be admitted, was coming out strongly in his Cupid frame of mind, and which, with him, was but three letters removed from a Cupidity-frame of mind also. The full force of his battery of flattery was this time directed against a sweetly-gushing young thing of not one day more than sixty-five years of age. And as Bilberry would insist in fondly terming her "A blushing, simple maiden coy," so, in grateful return, the guileless young widow of sixty-five summers, and the same number of winters—she had only buried a mere matter of six husbands—would continue playfully describing Bilberry as "a headstrong boy," although our well-known old living fraud had long ago looked upon the wrong side of seventy.

"Get along, thou young wildrake, how dare you say I am beautiful? He! he! he!" And the playful young person assumed her youngest and most fetching giggle.

"What!" cried Bilberry. "The concentrated essence of all the choicest dictionary terms, after being well boiled down, could not produce the proper term, sweet madam, wherewithall to adequately do justice to thy conglomeration of extra, double-distilled charms!" sighed he, adding: "Pray renew my measure with punch, angelic being!"

"With more than all the pleasure in the world, thou gayest of sparks, most impudent of young bloods, giddiest of butterflies, cruellest of flatterers, and most remorseless breaker of weak women's hearts!" These pretty terms were, so to speak, pelted at the head of Officer Bilberry, as would a skittish young maiden of thirteen pelt the dainties from a discharged bon-bon at the face of the little lad she one day meant to call her sweetheart.

"Well, my charmer," self-consciously remarked the Bow Street officer, "I must needs plead guilty to the soft impeachment, for the male Bilberrys ever were a daredevil, dashing, handsome set, although I say it, an'—Hang me!—ever remarkable for their fatal beauty!"

"Aha, thou sweet young villain, I dare believe thee!" shyly continued the sixth-time widow. "Come," she added, "dost thou wear the hearts thou hast broken at thy girdle, as Red Indians do the scalps they have taken?"

"Sweet madam, it is not for me to—ahem—speak of my many conquests of thy sex," remarked Bilberry, placing his sausage-like fingers upon his extensive breast, and turning the pupils of his goggle-eyes towards the back of his head. "There is, however," he continued, suddenly assuming a deeply-grieved vein, "an instance of a simple little occasional flirtation of mine that—to my everlasting regret—has been productive of some–ahem—wretched jealousy on the part of the husband of the once adorable creature I, for a time, was wont to entertain by whispering soft and sweet nothings in her dainty, seashell-like ear. Alas! I learn that her mind is—ahem—becoming deranged as the consequence of my refusing to patronise her place of resort, and her wretched, sour-cramped, morbid-minded, coffin-visaged, toadstool of a husband is continually threatening to commit self-destruction. Do you see, most charming of hostesses, I have a goodly following of the merriest of dogs in town."

"Quite so, good sir," replied the hostess; adding: "do pray inform me of the name of this, the last of thy victims, oh, wicked ogre of female-devouring capacity."

"Blood an' hounds! Gleaming blades o' steel! Poison-tipped daggers! Combats to the very death! Madam, give thy solemn pledge never to reveal the poor dear lady's secret!" demanded the ancient lady-killer, in a well-affected, serious strain of import.

"Oh, la, la, most certainly, good sir! I give thee my most sacred word that I will never, never divulge the awful matter—never. Oh, never, indeed, 'pon my soul!" was the giggling reply.

"Then the bright love-flame in question—since snuffed out—was none other than the notoriously-beautiful Mrs. Drake; the miserable, wet-Friday-afternoon-on-one-of-the-foggiest-days-in-November-faced ruffian, her husband, is the villain I told thee was dying of the green-eyed monster fever, and also contemplating suicide, through loss of profit, by my firmly refusing to visit his most inferior in, the Hole in the Wall."

In this manner the great Bilberry passed his evening, occasionally varying the entertainment with his highly-coloured and cruelly-distorted yarns of the highwaymen he had either captured or killed outright. Dandy Dick came in for his share of the bare-faced lies of mountainous heights, and seas of breadth.

The scanned company was amazed, as well it might be, and Bilberry, the human swipes-barrel, was filled to the over-flowing by closing-time, and, in this condition, he sought his home.

It was an ideal night for a soaker of the Bilberry brand. A beautiful fall of snow of some four or five inches thickness had taken place during the day. This white, snow-velvet pile carpet would be quite nice to fall on—no thaw, and yet not too much frost, so that the earth covering was like an enormousswandown quilt. Furthermore, there was a bright, full moon. So bright indeed was it, that its usual wintery farthing rushlight effect had given place to that equal in clearness and silver like brightness to one of our own electric-lighted street-lamps of to-day. Yes, the moon was distinctly looking up!

On making for his home after the closing of the inn, the filled-up officer found that he required each pavement, and the road centre at one and precisely the same moment. This pedestrian feat was somewhat difficult, so much so, that it necessitated his heavily falling against the shutters of closed-up business houses alternately on both sides of the street, when he would then most profoundly endeavour to think out the problem of how to walk in a considerable number of directions at one time—namely, forward, backward, to the right, and to the left, and, at the same time, to keep steadily on the right-hand pavement, and also on the left ditto, while occupying the centre of the roadway for the express purpose of stopping any traffic in the event of the same occurring in that unseemly hour.

Not succeeding in working out this difficult puzzle in every other conceivable attitude, the student of the impossible was finally compelled to flop down, face downwards and full length, in the clear, white snow. Bilberry having thus fallen into a brown—or should we say white?—study, finally came to the conclusion that the act of one man of walking, say, six ways at the same moment, was the simplest thing in the world—if he had but five other men to assist him!

Remarkable to relate, on attempting to rise, head first, the prone Bilberry found all the weight of his body centred in his upper portion. Again, on attempting to gain an erect posture, feet first, all the leverage rushed into his legs. In desperation he hit upon the plan of rolling sideways—tublike—from the road centre close up to the frontage of a closed-up business house.

Convenient iron bars here enabled the very much besoaked and belated Bilberry to scramble to the perpendicular.

A fresh difficulty now unexpectedly presented itself. The spotlessly-white snow roadway, sparkling in the moonlight, displayed a playful tendency to spring up and strike the Bow Street officer in the face. He succeeded in reaching the support of a signboard. Clinging to this, he extended one foot, and then, throwing all his weight into it, considerably steadied the roadway, and succeeded in keeping it in its place while his foot remained stationary. But there came other dangers, and to which the perils of those "that go down to the sea in ships" are as child's play.

The surrounding buildings suddenly became animated, and commenced to indulge in the most fantastic and frolicsome gambols. They joined hands, so to say, set up a right merry dance, and whirled themselves in a fearfully giddy circular waltz round and round the signpost clinging figure.

Then the support to which the rotund officer frantically held, also took it into its head to poke fun at the benighted man. It commenced to buck like a mustang bucking for a wager. Finally, it drew itself away from the fat-fingered clutch, kicked the startled Bilberry on the last button but two of his vermilion waistcoat, and sending him sprawling backwards full length into the snow. The roadway resented this liberty, turned itself up, sea-saw like, wrong end first, and through its helpless victim "legs overhead," as little boys term the trick.

But the acrobatic feat was not quite completed, and the very, very drunken lady-killer again found himself full length upon his back.

The surrounding housetops appeared to enjoy the scene hugely. The prostrate man now felt convinced that he could hear their shouts of laughter. The signpost now took the lead as a practical joker, bent its painted head downwards, and shrieked in madlike merriment in the deeply disgusted officer's face. Then the picture sign derided, and changed into two human faces. These faces yelled and yelled in utter-most glee.

"Ho, ho! He, he, he!" lovingly shouted one. "Hang me, if it isn't a confounded old runner! He isn't drunk, either—not in the slightest degree!"

"Oh, dear, no," said the other signboard face, also speaking in the ironical vein, "not over-drunk, perhaps, but I think one or two trifling hogs heads more might have made him just a leetle top-heavy! What ho, there!"—this to a crowd collected on the pavement some distance off—"Hi, there, young bloods! We've rare sport in view!"

"A Bow Street runner helplessly drunk! Ho, ho, ho!"

Officer Bilberry had fallen into the hands of the night terrors of London— the mohawks, or nightbirds—and the helpless old toper was now in for very rough usage at the hand of these aristocratic young ruffians.

°THE HIGHWAYMEN AND THE THAMES PIRATES—THE TERRORS OF THE THAMES STREAM MENACE WITH DEATH-- THE DEVOTED ADVENTURERS—DANDY DICK AND THE PIRATE LEADER—MOMENTS OF PERIL AND DEATH.

Dandy Dick saw opposing him a most remarkable-looking being, and a terrible foe to deal with, beyond a doubt. Extremely tall—considerably over six feet, in fact—with astounding width of chest, length of limb, and strength of muscle. The man's face was swathed-looking, his eyes cat-like in shape, with an expression of deep cunning and cruelty. A long, shaggy, black beard covered his bosom. His garb was half-sailor, half-robber, in appearance. The sailor hip petticoat of the period, and enormous thigh boots, and under pilot-jacket, and jumper, or blouse, with wide collar—these betokened the water-farer; while the three-cornered hat, long and wide-skirted open overcoat, double brace of pistols, and dagger-knife thrust in the black belt, which had a great, square, brass buckle, proclaimed the robber or freebooter.

We have attempted to describe a wretch who for many years reined as absolute king or ruler of the River Thames. The complete disregard—even contempt—for human life ever displayed by this monstrous being earned him the horrible name of the Red Rat, or Chief of the Red Rats; for he commanded an enormous following of creatures as villainous in their blood-thirsty natures as was himself. It was the boast of this daring, reckless, and completely-abandoned wretch that he held dominion over the one great river of which London alone could boast in those days.

The Thames robbers were a class most peculiar to themselves. The crimes were unique in fiendish nurse, and the broad bed of the old river very frequently refused to keep the secrets of these monsters. The finding of horribly-mutilated remains was so common as to call for but slight comment, except among horrified and grief-stricken relatives.

Smuggling, too, formed a branch of the evil transactions of the Thames Pirates.

There were those who openly declared that the Newgate thief-taker, Wild, was secretly in league with the pirate chief, and that the latter frequently tendered the great police-agent services of very great value in return for complete immunity from the law, so far as Wild himself could guarantee it. This may, or may not, have been the truth; but the fact remains that the great river was infested with these robbers to an almost incredible extent, and no perceptible diminution of these ruffians took place, even down to the commencement of the nineteenth century.

Dandy Dick confronted the chief of the pirates on reaching the bottom of the slime-covered and irregular stone steps, a few feet from which swiftly rushed on its course towards the river a black stream of great width and depth, on or

---

° Part 37. Vol. XV.—No. 373. 4 January 1901.

near the surface of which the young highwayman had expected to find the raft Fangs had mentioned as the outlaws' one hope of escape. Dandy Dick had, with madlike impetuosity, hurled himself forward, and singled out the enormous form of the pirate leader.

The Red Rats carried lanterns, in which candles burned. These and the torches of Dick and his comrades rendered the great tunnelling in which they were well illuminated.

The meeting of the outlaw foes was too precipitous to permit the general use of their firearms. The brawny pirate leader wielded a cutlass of most unusual length and weight. The rapier of Dandy Dick looked like a toy in contrast.

"Aha, those we seek!" yelled the great pirate. "The gallants of the Heath! The fine fellows of velvets of brilliant hues an' gold lace! The robbers the Court ladies rave about! It is good we meet, for the Court dames will now lose the pretty objects of their admiration!"

The voice of the freebooter leader was like the roaring of a bull. His cutlass leapt in the light like a thing of life, and curled round his massive head in a circle of reflected yellow and dazzling brightness.

"Despicable villain," fearlessly retorted Dandy Dick, his voice ringing out in clarion tones, "to rid the earth of such a human vulture as thyself would indeed make full atonement for all the faults of my past!"

"Dandy Dick, I have heard tell of thee and thine daring deeds!" defiantly replied the pirate leader. "We are rivals—the river robbers an' the highwaymen—outlaws of the roads, the Heath, an' footpads, cut-purses of the pleasure resorts. Ye reap rich spoils, and leave the Thames Pirates nothing to plunder!"

"Rivals!" thundered Dandy Dick, in supreme disgust. "We admit to no rivalry with such utterly degraded scum. If we are proscribed by the laws of our land, we avoid bloodshed, save in the defence of our own lives. Ye are remorseless butchers of men, women and children. We define our honour by contrast with the Thames Rats of Red!"

"Boasting gamecock, come on with thy child's blade, or I'll slice off thy insolent head with one stroke of my steel!"

The words were scarcely uttered before Dandy Dick had taken a bound, which instantly brought him within reach of the river pirate's steel.

Colonel Blood, Dick Turpin, and Will Wiffles had stood shoulder to shoulder with their captain, all three passive, but alert of eye, while the parley went on between the chiefs of outlaws. The followers of the pirate chief, so far as could be seen, vastly outnumbered the highwaymen; but the latter seldom paused in their purpose for such an obstacle.

The colonel, Turpin, and Wiffles exchanged significant glances. The pirate horde impatiently clutched their weapons, awaiting but a word or glance from the chief to commence the unequal battle.

No sooner was Dandy Dick within reach of the enormous blade than the pirate chief aimed a mighty blow at the head of his intended victim.

With the alertness of an antelope, Dick sprang aside, his blade on guard to catch the descending cutlass edge. A loudly-ringing, metallic sound instantly followed. Dandy Dick's fine Toledo steel had bent into a hoop, then snapped in two.

With a roar as of a lion the pirate leader leapt forward, and again threw back his fearful blade. This time he concentrated his utmost force to smite down the arm with most fatal intent.

Dandy Dick sprang aside, and snatched out a loaded fire-arm. His action would, however, have been too late. Colonel Blood, with the speed of thought, had aimed one of his heavy flintlocks with his utmost strength full at the head of the advancing pirate. A terrible thud followed. A gush of blood disfigured the fierce, revengeful visage; then the river marauder staggered back, bewildered, half fainting.

"A dash for liberty, lads!" exultantly yelled Colonel Blood. Dandy Dick drew a brace of pistols. They were primed, and their powder dry, thanks to the thoughtful care of the rat-tamer. Dandy Dick, Turpin and Wiffles combined gave a responsive cheer to the colonel's words. The highwaymen then threw themselves upon the foe. Not waiting for the command of their leader—who had now fallen, and relapsed into sensibility—the pirates met the enemy with a solid point of glistening steel.

A fearful conflict instantly took place. The condition of their leader helped to divert the attention of a few of the pirate gang. But the odds against the handful of adventurers was far too great to permit of anything but speedy defeat.

The stroke of the weighty sailor cutlass was far too formidable for the slender and quick-bending Court sword-blade.

"Give the beauties leaden cough-drops!" whispered Wiffles. "Our blades is too perlite an' gentle fer their strong beef-skewers!"

He suited the action to the word by discharging a brace of pistols full in the hideous faces of the piratical crew.

Two of the Red Rats fell forward, bathed in their life-blood, the face of one terribly shattered, the point of the colonel's steel seen for a moment coming out of the shoulder-blade of the other.

Dick Turpin had taken slow but sure aim, firing the flintlocks in swift succession. Sudden outbursts of anguish told the result. Two of the foe fell over their dying fellows. The colonel sprang aside, within an ace of having his head sliced in two from a ferocious-looking negro pirate. The naked, ebony breast of this man could be seen under his open shirt of red. Like a slender, silver serpent in the act of stinging, a rapier-point touched the black's bosom. Uttering a fearful groan, the pirate fell forward, the hilt of Colonel Blood's sword meeting the broad chest. In its death plunge, the negro's body tore the weapon from its owner's hand. A terrific thud next followed. The colonel, now in a state of demoniac fury, had shot out his left, catching an ordinary flow under the left jaw. At the same moment, with his right hand, the colonel seized the fellow's cutlass. The man went down, his sword remaining in the former's possession.

"Give 'em flint-lock snuff, pals!" yelled Wiffles, in utmost fury, firing full in the face of the nearest pirate, and laying him low. Then, all his pistols empty, the intrepid fellow used them as a club for each hand.

"Forward, comrades!" encouraged Turpin, making his blade dart like flashes of electricity. "Forward, lads! Death to the Thames vermin!"

"Yield, madmen! We are fifty to one!" shouted a pirate, who appeared next in command to the disabled leader.

"Yield to such human wolves? Never!" furiously retorted Dandy Dick, adding—"We'll tunnel our way through your solid bodies rather than surrender to such caitiffs!"

Each time the highwaymen, in matchless daring, threw themselves forward they were beaten back. Bristling points of steel menaced them at every turn. Shots sped past their temples and crumbled particles of stone from the wall of the sewer. The end was near. The compact belt of steel could not be turned or broken. Any moment the few adventurers could have been despatched—annihilated—but for the one fixed impression upon the minds of their enemies—namely that their chief had intended capturing the highwaymen alive, so that his patron, Jonathan Wild, might afterwards work his own will with them.

Forced back at each impetuous rush, the few devoted comrades were driven to the side wall of the wide and extensive main sewer in which they were. To the left of them were the stone steps reaching the smaller passageway through which they had come. Their foes thronged between them at the steps. To the left also of where the highwaymen stood at bay, some fifty yards away, could be heard the rushing and foaming torrent, near which they were bidden by Fangs, the rat-catcher, to seek the hidden raft. If they could but fight their way to these floating timbers chance of life yet remained to them.

During the brief pause, the pirates had held a hurried parlay. They now advanced resolutely to the attack. Death gleamed in their remorseless eyes.

"Yield yourselves up!" they thundered. "Throw down your arms and sue for mercy, or we will cut ye to pieces!"

WE RETURN TO THE FORTUNES OF JACK RANN—THE SUDDEN FALL INTO THE HORRIBLE MORASS—DESPERATION AND DESPAIR OF JONATHAN WILD'S SPIES—THE WEIRDLY TERRIBLE SPECTRAL VISITANTS OF THE BOGS—THE INTERIOR OF THE HAUNTED MANOR—THE CAPTIVES AND THEIR CAPTORS.

When Jack Rann gave out his thrilling note of despair, he had felt that his last moments in life were come. The handsome, youthful, and daring outlaw knew well that, the moment it became known that Mark Dankly, who followed closely in his tracks, that his enforced guide had missed his way, in his rageful spleen, the agent of Jonathan Wild would press the trigger of his loaded and already-presented firearm, and send the brains of his captive to bespatter the surrounding gloom-hidden bog-growths and scattered tree-trunks.

The jackboots of Rann had sunk in the soft, clinging ooze of the morass. He felt himself being irresistibly sucked down, and, in attempting to save himself, plunged forward, as he believed, to his inevitable and instant doom.

His ear-splitting cry drowned the sound of the parting bush-twigs into which he had fallen. To his extreme amazement, his extended hands came into contact with a firm support of some kind. Muttering a most fervent prayer of thankfulness to the Supreme Being for His mercy, Jack Rann remained perfectly motionless. His body was hidden and supported by the thick and tangled briars.

The outbusting explosions of the weapons of Wild's men had a very different object to that intended. Instead of slaying the outlaw, and sending his body to find a grave in the dreadful quagmire, the result was that of arousing the instant attention of the spies stationed in the near vicinity.

The alarming intelligence of the firing of a volley of bullets within the circle of their bog-belt was instantly made known to those within the Haunted Manor.

Quick as thought, the members of the criminal colony had seized and lighted their skeleton-head lanterns, and ignited the candles in the centres of many glass globes of various brilliant colours. The spectral-looking white skulls had ruby-red glass in their eye-sockets and cavities between the teeth. These lanterns and the small globes were next attached to the ends of long and thin black rods, which became invisible in the night gloom.

The feet of the outlaw scouts were covered with a soft material, which rendered them perfectly noiseless. The lantern-bearers were completely enveloped— their eyes excepted—by long coverings of loose black drapery, which, sack-like, covered the head, and descended even to the boots.

Most marvellous was the arrangement of secret artificial pathways, very narrow, and accompanied by invisible wire guards and traversing almost every direction of the bogs surrounding the stronghold.

Even on a bright-moonlight night, when the "Quagmire Guards," as they were termed, noiselessly glided about through the deadliest parts of the bog-tracts, nothing could be detected but the fear-inspiring heads, floating, as it seemed, in the night air, and dancing will-o'-the-wisp-like and brilliantly-dazzling little globes.

The exudations of foul gases, arising from some of the deepest parts of the swamps, gave out bright globular illuminations, which floated, danced fantasically, or gambolled like the phosphorescent fires of glow-worms in the great black void of night.

The frantic cry of Jack Rann had been heard. A skeleton head swiftly flew forward, and danced over the spot in which he lay hidden. The bright ruby rays from the eyes pierced the darkness, and threw two distinct blood-red streams of light into the concealing bush. There was a bright patch of vermillion, a yellow sparkling of gold lace. The red coat, with its gold-lace collar, revealed the ambush in which Rann lay concealed from his foes.

An invisible hand seized him. He was saved.

Mark Dankly shrieked aloud in utter extremity of mortal fear. The ghostly-white death-heads hovered above, darted forward, and at times almost touched him. The great glaring orbs of crimson, blood-red fire seemed to pierce him through and through—looked in the very depths of his soul, and read there that awful life-record of the blackest of black crimes.

Three of Dankly's men had already perished in the black depths of the morass. Those remaining were crouched upon their knees in line, and, like their chief, paralysed with dread, and afraid to move from their positions on soil that gradually permitted their limbs to sink lower and lower into its black, pitch-like substance.

Suddenly a blinding glare of light caused Dankly and his band to glance upwards. The terrifying ghostly visages had vanished, the will-o'-the-wisp-like fires also. In their place were apparently living men. They were armed, and held aloft lighted lanterns.

The thief-takers were rendered speechless with bewilderment.

Who were those beings who thus safely trod where no mortal man dared venture?

"Surrender quietly, and your lives may be spared from the horrible face now threatening ye! Hand over every weapon!"

A fierce voice thundered out these commands.

As men under the influence of some hideous nightmare, Jonathan Wild's emissarys mechanically drew their pistols, detached their hangers, and held them up. The articles were instantly taken by human hands.

Then the same stern voice was again heard, although its possessor could not be located:

"Arise, but take heed not to move a foot to the right or left until bidden!"

Mark Dankly and his companions instantly obeyed. Then a wide and strong plank touched Dankly's feet. He was bidden to step upon this and cautiously advance. Taking a few steps, in a moment Wild's agent felt his feet standing on firm ground. Those of his men remaining were next rescued one by one. Then each was blindfolded by his own cravat, held by a hand, and cautiously marched forward.

It was utterly impossible for them to judge of the route taken. Orders to halt were given from time to time, then to stoop low, sometimes to crawl for a distance upon hands and knees. Finally they were commanded to halt, and the bandages were removed.

The sudden brilliant light that met their view rendered them for a time semi-blind. By degrees the surroundings grew plainer. The utmost fear then seized upon Mark Dankly and his men. They found themselves in an enormous vault-like chamber. This was crowded with silent spectators—outlaws beyond a doubt everyone—criminals of every type—fierce, resolute, hardy men—resolute, remorseless, and bloodthirsty where their own lives were concerned.

Mark Dankly—hatless, bloodshot of eye, ghostly visage, and mire bespattered—stood at bay, as one who well knew the turn of a hair might decide his doom.

No sooner were the cravats taken from the eyes of his underlings then they exhibited signs of most craven fear.

"Curse ye!" furiously hissed their leader, between his gleaming teeth. "Poltroons! caitiffs! We have already faced a far worse death than that which now confronts us! Bullet, poison, steel, or rope—any of these before that pit of hell we've just escaped!"

"Beware!" cried a voice, apparently at his side, and close to the ear of Dankly. "Refuse to answer all our questions quietly and truthfully, and the horrid depths of the morass shall yet entomb thee!"

In quaking fear, Mark Dankly turned round, and glared in the direction of the awful tones; but he saw nothing but the stone masonry of the vault-like chamber.

An awe-inspiring personage came from a recess behind the black folds of falling drapery—a tall, stern, and majestic-looking man, with long, jet-black hair and beard, eyes piercingly bright, and lit up with unearthly fires. He was garbed in a long sable robe, as a magician, wore a conical-shaped hat, and this and his sable robe were covered with cabalistic characters. Coiled round his waist, as a living girdle, were the brilliantly marked and brightly glittering and sinuous folds of a great snake, of the terrible cobra-di-capello species.

The captives glared in open-mouthed apprehension as the startling figure advanced towards them. The reptile slowly moved its coils, and presently its hideous heart appeared. The greatly expanding jaws opened, its blood-red and forked tongue protruded, darting like a flame of fire. The round, protruding eyes sparkled like vermilion beads, tipped with sparks of gore.

The captives shrank back, and crouched against the stone wall in fear-laden wonderment—mortal terror.

The tones that now came to the captured spies thrilled them as would the full, rich tones of a grand organ, tuned to a dirge of some solemn tragedy.

"The vilest wretch moving in the ranks of created beings is Jonathan Wild, the Newgate carrion-bird—human vulture—vampire—a thing so base as to cause men who value manhood to blush a human nature! When a created being can sink so low 'tis no boon nor boast to count as one of the living! And thou, base wretches, art the mercenaries of this monster!"

"We have fallen into thy hands; we ask mercy, good sir!" humbly muttered Mark Dankly.

The enormous gathering of outlaws, as by one impulse, gave utterance to a fiercely-exultant yell. Their firearms were drawn, swords rattled from their sheaths.

"Death to Jonathan Wild!" they mutually cried. "Death to the thief-taker's cunning, cringing, cowardly spies!"

Their rage-trembling shouts were deafening. They moved forward, arms flashing, eyes pitiless, brows contracted, teeth clenched.

The necromancer held up an arm.

"My brothers," he cried, "check thy righteous wrath. Our leader, Dandy Dick, is in peril. Mayhap these meaner ruffians—creatures of a greater villain—can be compelled to disclose to us the mysterious cause of the non-appearance of our missing chief, and certain of our comrades."

The necromancer turned his gaze upon Mark Dankly, and his most abjectly terrified men.

"Listen!" he cried. "Dandy Dick and certain of his friends have been missing since making an attack upon the house of your master one night back. Inform us of the cause of this—it will be well known to you if our leader is in Wild's power or dead. In return for this information I will undertake that all your lives shall be spared."

"Good sir," meekly and earnestly answered Dankly, "myself and fellows have been in this neighbourhood for some weeks past—have had no communication whatever with Mr. Wild or any one of those in his service. How, therefore, can we know of a circumstance of so a recent date as that you mention?"

The necromancer made a sign to the crowds of onlooking outlaws. They gathered in a closer ring. Their looks and savage gestures fully told of their vengeful purpose. Gently muttering some curious terms, and caressingly passing his hand over the reptile's folds, the necromancer pointed the head of the snake until its fire-filled orbs took in the visage of the leader of the spies. In a flash the venomous thing had reached the stone flags forming the floor of the vault-like robbers' cavern. The cobra-de-capello gracefully yet quickly glided over the intervening space between its master and the spell-bound Dankly. No sooner had it reached within a yard of its intended victim than the creature formed into its three fatal coils. Next it raised up its head and some three feet lengths of body, distended its jaws, threw out its forked tongue, and commenced the forward and backward movements, the third of which denotes the moment of its vicious bite, and infliction of death.

"Mercy! mercy! Spare my life!" frantically pleaded the captive Dankly, wildly attempting to flee; but a circle of countless pistol-tubes held him in agonised indecision. At the merest fraction of time before the fatal attack the necromancer emitted a low, droning sound. The reptile instantly ceased its movements. Its owner's intention had been but to terrify Mark Dankly into a statement, and, seeing this to be useless, he caused the reptile to cease its purpose.

At this supreme moment a firearm exploded with most startling effect. The leader of Wild's party swiftly swirled round, threw up his hands to his heart, upon which a patch of blood had appeared. A despairing groan followed, then the man crashed down, face forward, to the flags.

A second shot had instantly followed the first. A ball sped past the head of the necromancer, to lodge in the brain of the young outlaw immediately behind him. Without a sound this second victim fell—a corpse before reaching the stone flooring.

"Treachery!" yelled the assembled officers, in shouts of rage that filled the vast chambers with a sound as of the sudden roaring of many lions.

Two more shots replied. Again the outlaw magician most narrowly escaped, but the pellets found their fatal course to the hearts of two of the crowd of robbers. With awful groanings each sank back, and instantly expired in the arms of a fellow outlaw.

The clinging wreaths of smoke curled upwards. Three of the captive spies were now seen, each standing at bay, holding a pistol from which a ribbon of smoke issued. The perilous mystery was fathomed. These treacherous ruffians had succeeded in retaining their loaded firearms. The chief had received the death intended for another.

No sooner was the incident grasped by the enraged outlaws than a terrific volley burst forth. The powder cloud moved upwards, disclosing three riddled and stretched-out forms where a moment before the treacherous spies had stood.

"No mercy—no quarter to the gallows crows! Exterminate the whole gang of cowardly assassins! treacherous crows! degraded vermin!"

Uttering these and other cries of madlike fury, the proscribed gang impetuously threw themselves upon their prisoners.

The four adventurers again face death—Charmed lives—The voice from the iron Tube—Fangs' fearful army—The raft—Escaped—The German innkeeper.

Surely the four adventurers bore charmed lives! Their countless and crowding foes were now making human targets of the fearless little band. The pelting of the leaden hailstorm created showers of particles of stone dust from the sewer tunnel wall, against which Dandy Dick, Colonel Blood, Dick Turpin, and Will Wiffles stood.

The flaring lanterns carried by the Thames Pirates threw great fantastic and black shadows of the highwaymen's forms against the slime-wetted the stone wall.

Dandy Dick had whispered the word for all torches to be cast away. He held his own flaming brand straight into the fierce and hideous face of a red-bearded ruffian, who had a moment before all but succeeded in blowing out the brains of the former. The torch set the beard ablaze, and almost blinded the fellow, who yelled, cursed, and danced in pain and fury.

Sheathing their slender rapiers—they were next to useless against the strong, weighty sea cutlass—highwaymen each levelled a brace of flintlocks, desperately determined to return the fire, even if they perished the moment after. It was more than marvellous that neither Dandy Dick, Colonel Blood, Dick Turpin, or Wiffles, had as yet been hit. But their eyes were keen, their movements agile, their courage matchless.

The pirates had hastily removed their wounded leader held a brief consultation, and evidently, by their deadly glances and preparations, determined to bring the unequal battle to a swift conclusion. Seeing this, the highwaymen, as one, threw up their pistols—eight tubes of unerring aim—and fired. Eight yells, followed by the same number of forward-crashing forms; these writhing out their last moments in exquisite torments then expiring.

This truly awful incident not only told of the nature of the men encompassed by a flashing bolt of rage-distorted visages, firearms, and flashing steel, but furthermore held in check, in temporary stupor the attacking hordes. Then came a something, striking all with awe and inexplicable wonderment.

"Ho, there, my good Masters! Those whom feed my little people with my chosen food are for ever after the friends of my trained warriors! Fangs, the rat-trainer, can hear all, and sends his army to the rescue of his guests!"

Every eye sought for palpable explanation—every ear eagerly strained for further sound. The four deserted comrades, with their backs to the reeking and foul-smelling stones, were alone able to judge from whence the startling, speaking-trumpet-like sounds came. An iron pipe, rusty and green with age and damp, with distended, bell-shapen mouth, protruded from the wall above. Evidently the rat-trainer was using this tube—which might extend even to his secret dwelling-place—both for hearing and speaking. There was little time for speculation now. The alarming words were still singing in deep, clarion-like notes, when a curious sound followed. It was like the swift pattering of heavy rain drops, or onrushing of a surging whirlwind. A living black cloud swept its course down the upper passage, through which the fugitives had come, down the slimy stone-steps like a fell, destructive torrent.

The Thames pirates saw their imminent peril. Fangs, their sworn exterminator, had let loose his myriads of highly-trained rodents. They were flying onward—the fierce, frenzied, venomous creatures, who eagerly courted death in their lust of hatred of those they had for years been taught to fly at, bite, rend, torment, kill!

Curses loud and deep, yells of horrified alarm, mingled with other confusing sounds of sudden panic and general stampede! The living, leaping, resistless flood spread itself in every direction. Its throbbing, darting, horrid blackness covered everything as with a pall. The creatures heeded the four silent, hand-clasped comrades, but flew past them as if they were but images of stone. Not so the Red Pirates! In their precipitate fight most of them escaped; but several of the last to flee were overborne, torn to the earth by sheer weight of numbers by the rat army. Once down, the shocking, sickening, unequal contest was over in but seconds. The rodents had been taught to attack the throat. Their victim's death was no sooner assured than the black cloud of terror flew on again. The battle had commenced. Some four human creatures had been sacrificed to the fury of the terrible pests, yet in a few seconds they had gone.

The four friends were alone. "The raft! the raft!" shrieked the tones from the tube. Instantly the words were obeyed.

Dandy Dick now again to his steel, and lead on in the direction previously given by Fangs. To their right a wide cutting faced them. The sounds of the rushing of a powerful torrent came to their ears. Many lanterns had been left behind by the pirates. Two of these were still alight. This piece of good-fortune was taken advantage of. A run of a few moments through a circular sewer-way, a foot deep in water, brought the adventurers to the side of a vast tunnel, running at right angles, of lower depth, and a course-way for a deep, broad, black stream, of a frightful velocity, madly hissing, leaping, and spray flying on its way to the distant river.

It was here the raft was found, thrown aside high and dry, yet firmly secured by ropes to an iron ring in the stone wall in case the flood should rise at any time, and drift it away. With the utmost despatch the raft was cast upon the torrent. The four adventurers then threw themselves upon it, and found firm loops in the lashings by which they could cling. They had one lighted lamp with them. A long pole, with an iron hook, was lashed to the planks. This being unfastened, the moorings within severed, and the raft instantly sped on its way. The colonel held himself firmly by the cord lashings with one hand, and with the other held the pole, and kept watchful guard against projecting portions of the stone passages through which they darted, carried by the onrushing stream with alarming velocity.

Dame Fortune ever favours her bravest sons. The distance the raft had travelled must have been no mean one, but in a few minutes it had emerged from a final underground boring, and swirled into the great Thames stream, which, at this point, was over three hundred yards in width near its one and only bridge.

To the no small astonishment of the four friends, it was broad daylight. Frost was in the air. They were famished, chilled to the bone, wet, and mud-covered. Their crude support was drifting past a landing-stage when the colonel threw out his pole, and, with its hook, caught hold of one of the timber uprights of the landing-steps. The river was covered with a grey mist; no moving craft was observed. They landed, and let the raft drift with the tide. The outlaws now greatly regretted being without their long cloaks. Their extremely fine, if soiled, costumes were calculated to create suspicion. Their pistols were placed out of sight. The colonel, it transpired, had got an ugly gash on the back of his right hand. He had twisted a 'kerchief round it, and then drawn one of his leathern gauntlets on. Dick Turpin, with a grim smile lifted his hat, and displayed a serious-looking flesh-wound on the head, which, however, had bled but little. He laughingly explained that "his hat had originally cost him many a crown, but had now finally saved him one!"

"We have taken human life, comrades," sadly remarked Dandy Dick. "The evil was done in the preservation of our own, which alone can justify it. Yet, for all that, my conscience reproves me for the shedding of a fellow-creature's blood!"

"I approve of those sentiments, Dick," said the colonel; "but," he continued, "we provoked no attack, and, had we remained passive, I shudder to think of what would have happened to us all!"

"I've already got a choice sample on my upper storey of the forbearance intended to be shown to us," chimed in Turpin, "and the number of escapes we had were enough to last us a lifetime!"

"I'm mortal sorry as we was compell'd ter give them red 'errings—I mean Red Rats—their qui-eat-us, but I'd now be mortaler sorrier still if they'd book'd us fer a free passage ter kingdom come, an' ne'r a chance ter return any change!" reflectively put in Will Wiffles.

"That outstanding character the rat-catcher has given us most ample proof of his trustworthiness. Our wounded friend will surely be safe in his keeping—of that I feel convinced," thoughtfully remarked Colonel Blood.

"That cheerful cuss is a most terrible creatyer when 'e's gets 'is fins tied up in a knot—'e is, as ther dewour'd stickleback remark'd ter 'isself arter unnin' unawares inter ther pike's too much countinounce!" put in Wiffles.

"Ough!" shudderingly ejaculated the colonel. "I shall not forget in a hurry the hideous giant Fangs, and his ruthless, hideous, pygmy army!"

"Which, a-beggin' yer parding, Colon-iel," corrected Wiffles, "pig-me ain't quite ther too corriot vord, vich I sey sho'ld more properlee be rat-me!—an' thereby 'angs a tail, as ther passing cat sed when ther mantrap 'ad snapp'd 'ers off!"

"You are quite in order, Will, old comrade!" quaintly returned the colonel, adding, "to answer you in your own style, 'I stand corrected, sir,' as the little boy observed to his schoolmaster, while receiving a caning!"

"Vich 'e wo'ldn't stand, but most likely lay acrost a knee, but if 'e didn't stand 'e'd pretty sartenlee understand, which is a distinction without no difference!" readily added Wiffles.

"Confound Jonathan Wild, Thames Pirates, and rats, red and black, an' their highly pungent kingdom! Give me terra firma!" remarked Dick Turpin, in extreme disgust.

"Don't know about terrer firmer," speculated Wiffles. "I never hopes to meet a firmer terror then all ther choice creatyres as yer've numerat'd 'u'd make if they was bottl'd an' cork'd up together, an' 'ad a good shakin'!"

The adventurous spirits had by this sprang up the old, rotten wooden steps of what afterwards proved to be the Arundell Stairs.[115] Few persons were yet astir. There was a well-known inn near by—within a few yards of bluff King Hal's palace; in fact, refine building in question then being occasionally in the use of King George of Hanover and his family.

The highwaymen would run a fearful risk by entering in broad daylight a public resort. Each a notoriously proscribed outlaw, descriptions of their personal appearances, with rich rewards offered for their capture, stuck up in every available space. A wanted felon could then boast of being better advertised than even royalty itself, and royal folk were never backward in the art of puffing in any period of the world's history.

Extreme hunger will dare all things. The inn was found already open, for many of its frequenters were of the water side, and favoured early rising.

Mine host proved to be a German of enormous dimensions, and whose constant pipe was the size of a pint pot. The suet-pudding complexion of the inn-keeper waxed even more suet-and-puddingly as he took stock of his remarkably suspicious-looking patrons.

Dandy Dick boldly strode forward, and landed a smack upon one of the broad, flat shoulders that caused the recipient to shake like a huge jelly.

"We require entertainment, and of the very best your house affords!" cried Dandy Dick, exhibiting a crape purse, through the holes of which a plentiful stock of gold could be seen.

---

[115] Near Victoria Embankment.

°THE RAFT—ESCAPED—THE GERMAN INNKEEPER—

(Continued from last week's issue –No. 373).

"I'm von oniest inn-keeper, mine friendts, ant my name is Von Squintch," replied the man.

"Von squint, two squints, three squints! that all ther same ter us! Keep on squintin' till you're black an' blue in ther face, if it pleases yer. But bear in mind as yer've got ter act straight, as ther brandy-legged bow man w'isper'd ter 'is wery crooked bow!" cried Wiffles, adding—"as they say in Yorkshire, ve vants zummut ter yeat, an' zummut ter sup!"

"Vell, mine goot friendts, dot ish a gonsideration. Emph!" grunted the innkeeper, heartily drawing his pipe, which politely sent up a guttural response to him through its long, choked-up, bronchial tube-like stem.

"We can pay you well, non heer," chimed in the colonel.

"V-e-ll, mine goot friendt, dot ish the gonsideration!"

Mine host did not speak his words. He preferred to sing them, and in a more or less high falsetto tone.

Dandy Dick smiled, and placed a few spade guineas into the broad, flat, not too clean, and quickly extended palm.

"Garnish your board with goody, tempting viands, and nectar in plenty, and such as would tempt the gods, good fellow. If there's more to pay at the finish, ye have but to name it."

"Py der soul oft me bore tead mudder! dem ish der gonsiderations vot governs der whole vorld!" earnestly commented the extensive host, contemplating the sparkling pieces greedily, and with dilating eyes. Then he looked up and proceeded, throwing in several hoodwinks: "Beoples gome der my blace of resort—goot beoples, pad beoples, straight beoples, gruiked beoples—all der sames, der gonsideration ish der gonsideration! Dem vot bays der pill straight ish der goot beoples! Dem vot don't bay nodings, dem's der pad peoples!"

Another wink or two, and a vigourous draw at the choked-up bronchial tube, then mine host solemnly beckoned to the highwaymen to follow him. To their intense delight and surprise, he conducted them into a most inviting cosy-looking back retreat, furnished extremely well, and with a fire of logs that crackled, hissed, spluttered, and exploded out a hearty welcome in the frost-pierced and utterly famished four.

*

Again the door was most gently opened. This time a lady entered. She was unmistakably of the Teutonic brand, and of even more elephantine proportions than her inferior half. The innkeeper followed. Each bore a tray with something thereon that filled the little chamber with clouds of the most appetising odour.

° Part 38. Vol. XV.—No. 374. 15 January 1901.

"Mine goot vrow here haf got oxdale proath, mit galves' brains," commenced Mynheer, when Turpin muttered, sotto voce:

"Dear! Dear! Oxstale proth—a deadly disease! Calves' brains is a common enough complaint, though. I very frequently meet with many thus afflicted."

"I haf got a peautiful Cherman dish, vitch I prew mit mine own hands, too!" continued the host proudly, and smiling most greasily.

"We like the use of hands in preference to feet in the making of soup generally," quietly remarked the colonel.

Delightfully clean, shining, hot dishes were next brought, and spread over a tablecloth of snow whiteness. No sooner was Wiffles served with a dish of busily-steaming oxtail than he fell to, armed with a great ladle in each hand.

The innkeeper and his better—two stone better—half continued to enter, each time their smiles broader and greasy, each time with something extremely good and sometimes rare.

Wiffles suddenly looked up, after disposing of a trifling matter of seven or eight dishes of most excellent oxtail.

"Sayt, Mynheer Von German Sausage," he gravely commenced, "don't yer think as this 'ere ox-stale 'ud been better ox-new?"

"Vot ish der gonsideration, mine ferry goot frindt?" asked the model host, with most commendable anxiety.

"This 'ere poor beast of an ox 'ad a deal o' trouble afore 'e died, Mynheer Sausage," went of Wiffles, looking as solemn as a judge passing a sentence of death—"a 'eep o' grief I'm a-thinkin'."

"Vhy for dot?" asked Mynheer.

"Ther poor thing must a-fretted all ther flesh off 'is tail—every partercul, in fact; an' as fer their licker itself, it's that thin that a fly 'ud drop ter bottom ov it like a stone!"

"Pay no heed to that rattle-brained fellow, mine host; you have done extremely well. We are gratified," said Dandy Dick presently.

"You are great fools—thanks, thanks, my vorthy friendts!" proudly replied the innkeeper, himself and his wife bowing repeatedly.

"That is indeed so," put in the colonel. "Pay no regard to our ever-jocular comrade; he will die joking. Ha! ha!"

"Aha, our friend ish shockuler! And he will die choking! Haw! haw! haw!" The innkeeper was vastly tickled. "Vell, vell!" he cried. "May der goot chentleman lif fer effer, and aftervords die joking! Haw! haw! haw! Die choking ish der broper gonsideration! Haw! haw! haw!"

"Cho King, Joe King, Tal King, Val King, Run King, Fork King! Jist as yer likes, pals. If I'm a-goin' ter fare well fer ever, 'Then fare thee well fer ever!' as ther song sez. 'For there's nothing like a jolly good bust out,' as ther greedy little boy observed, "ceptin' a rattlin' good tuck-in and,' continued ther same little 'un, 'there's nothink in ther world can beat a good tuck-in, 'ceptin' another an' a better tuck-in!' But a-talking serious-like about a-dyin', a-chokin'. If it's a-bein' choked be ther kisses o' a pretty wench, then I'd choke this 'ere werry minit!"

A great buzz of words and angry commotion suddenly put a stop to the jestings of the witty Wiffles. The host and hostess turned pale and exhibited great fear.

"Look ye, host, no treachery!" thundered Dandy Dick, springing to his feet. "If you have betrayed us, by heavens your life shall pay instant forfeit!" Thus saying, he presented a firearm at the innkeeper's head.

A FELON FATHER AND A FELON SON—DRINK LEADS TO CRIME—BNLUESKIN'S FOLLY—THE DARING ROBBERY—DETECTION—THE WATCH—A FIGHT FOR LIBERTY—THE ROUND HOUSE OF ST. GILES—THE BOAST.

We left Jack Sheppard and his ever-faithful companion Joe Blueskin within a short distance of St. Giles's. The elder outlaw, having a proper regard to the undue notice and even danger they might incur as the consequence of their unusually fine garments, had suggested the advisability of delaying their visiting the Rookery or Blackbirds' Nest—the latter being the term most applied to their retreat by its denizens—until after dark; and even then not without each wearing a mask and long cloak, and being extremely well-armed.

The two horsemen drew up at the Crown. This inn had gained considerable notoriety in consequence of its being at this period one of the halting-places of the hangman's cart when on its way to Tyburn. A bowl of ale was brought forth and handed to the condemned culprit, in which to drink his farewell to all earthly ties.

Tom Sheppard, burglar and footpad, and father of Jack Sheppard, had received the "fatal bowl" at this very house.

The outlaw son had no recollection of his father; the child was born either a few months before or after the degrading death of his sire. All the same, the son's reflections on entering the inn were like red-hot irons thrust into both brain and heart. The wayward, reckless lad of unlicensed passions mentally speculated upon the time of his taking the farewell cup—for that he was ultimately doomed to perish upon Tyburn Tree he never entertained the slightest doubt.

In spite of the depressing associations connected with the place, Jack Sheppard soon completely cast of his gloom. His companion had a secret motive for his visit to this inn, as will presently be seen; and he shamelessly applied the lad with drink to such an extent that the felon father was soon forgotten, and his fate; and the place resounded with most hearty laughter as the result of the extremely diverting sayings and antics of the youthful robber.

Suddenly Jack Sheppard sprang from his seat, picked up his pistols from a side-table where he had previously ostentatiously place them, thrust them into his pockets, and then expressed his determination to sally forth from the inn.

It was barely dusk. Blueskin well knew the obstinate nature he had to deal with. He pulled a long face, shook his head, and then sought the keeper of the inn. The latter pulled a still longer face than Blueskin on hearing the intention of the youthful outlaw.

"This quarter is always crowded with dabsmen, me fly covey," remarked the landlord. "You see, the Blackbirds of the Rookery require their wings clipped pretty often. There's the Giles's Roundhouse just near, and expressly kept for the purpose of taking some of the flyness out of the highfliers. It's a pity you gave the lad so freely of the drink, me knowing covey."

"I now see my folly, and deeply regret it," replied Jolly Nose, adding: "We are old pals. You know you can trust me. Give me the secret password to the sanctuary for to-night. If we should be pounced upon by a nobbler gang we might seek protection in the Rookery."

"That's sound sense, me flash power. If ye get into any mess, fly with the younker[116] to the nearest barrier of the Blackbirds' Nest, and shout out these words: 'Llirb Gnik.' The flash lads there'll then defend you with their lives."

"Llirb Gnik?" echoed Joe Blueskin. "Is that slang?"

"It is," was the whispered reply, "King Brill, and he's the chief ruler of the boys of the colony; and be careful how you approach him, for he is both thick and tough."

Blueskin had obtained the great secret password. Jack Sheppard, with the magnificent air of an Eastern potentate,[117] had paid the score, and already strolled from the hostelry.

The mad-brained lad did not go near the stables, and for this his watchful companion felt thankful, for they were less likely to attract attention on foot.

"To the Oxford Road, and thence to Tyburnia!" (afterwards termed Tyburn) gaily sang out Sheppard, pointing out the way with a beautiful golden-topped cane.

Blueskin was aghast. Two seconds before Sheppard was without a cane. Looking back the elder outlaw saw a shop they had passed but an instant before. The rack of walking-sticks, unbrellas, and fancy canes, standing at the door explained the theft.

A quaint, old-fashioned watchmaker and jeweller's shop next attracted the lad's attention. His companion stood at his elbow.

A very beautiful pair of diamond bracelets took the fancy of the recklessly daring boy.

---

[116] Youngster.
[117] Monarch or autocratic ruler.

"Pruttier than the steel darbies,[118] and much nicer to wear, too, you see, they can be taken off whenever you wish, and quite without the assistance of the gaoler. 'Umph! I think I'll make a present of them to the adorable one of my heart. Keep a sharp look-out, Blue-parchment Chops. "I'll—"

"No, you won't!" Blueskin held the boy firmly by the coat-sleeve. "Jack—Jack lad, I came with you to seek your poor, heartbroken mother, not to stand by while you plunge deeper into the vortex of utter ruin! You will go to your mother with clean hands."

"Spoken like a book!" sneered the lad, an evil light coming into his fine eyes, a look of stony determination fixing itself on his pale face.

"What do you mean, Jack lad?" anxiously asked Blueskin, releasing his hold.

"Will you stop me?" demanded the lad.

"From going to your mother redhot in crime? Yes," quietly retorted Blueskin.

In a flash Jack Sheppard had produced a pistol, cocked it, and levelled it at the head of his dearest friend.

"Fire, Jack lad. I've made you drunk. You know not what you do. If you kill me, I deserve it!"

"I'll blow your brains out, Sky Mug, if you dare to interfere in my business! If you don't care to stand in, go away! Ta! ta!"

The coolness and effrontery of Jack Sheppard took away the breath of his companion. He stood glaring at the boy, speechless and motionless. The next moment the lad had uncorked his weapon, thrust it into his pocket, and entered the shop.

Jack Sheppard had a good supply of genuine gold coins with him. The superior garments and consummate acting of the stranger took the jeweller off his guard. The purchase of an expensive ring looked like genuine business.

Next the lad asked the price of a pair of gold bracelets set with diamonds. Those that had first aroused his admiration were placed before him with several others.

They did not quite please his fancy, he lightly remarked, and then directed the attention of the shop man to some watchs hanging in a case behind him.

The instant the man turned, Jack Sheppard adroitly slipped the diamond bracelets into a pocket of his wide-skirted coat.

The daring theft was observed. A man had kept his eyes fixed upon the young robber from the first moment of his entering. There was a small, dimly-lighted room at the far end of the counter. In this stood the unsuspected spectator of the robbery.

A loud shout was instantly set up for the police.

"Watch! watch!" yelled the man, dancing from the inner room, or office.

"Help! Robbery!" shrieked the person behind the counter.

---

[118] Handcuffs, named after Father Derby, a sixteenth-century money lender and extortionist.

Before the lad could make good his escape he was seized by both the jeweller and his assistant.

Sheppard attempted to draw a firearm, but succeeded only in tumbling the stolen articles from his pocket to the floor.

Blueskin had rushed to the assistance of Jack on hearing the first note of alarm. A terrific struggle instantly ensued. The burly outlaw snatched his short, heavy cudgel from the button and loop to which it was ever secured—when not in use—inside his roomy outer coat skirt. With this murderous weapon he floored the first jeweller and then his man.

The Fates were against the robbers. A large number of the watch had just left the St. Giles's Roundhouse to take their turn at night duty. These quickly surrounded the scene of robbery. Springing their rattles and yelling at the topmost pitch of their voices, the Charlies added to the clamour already raised by those of the shop.

The attack was so unexpected, and the number of the attackers so overwhelming, that in moments the struggle was over. The two outlaws had each received a fearful cudgelling. They were disarmed, securely bound, and hurriedly dragged off to the Roundhouse. The captives were heavily ironed, and then together thrust in a cell shaped like the quarters of a circle. Their gaolers refused them the permission of a lighted lantern, and laughed at their discomfiture.

"Curse you all!" cried Jack, examining his handcuffs. "The prison is not yet built that can hold me!"

"No, indeed, Jack lad!" chimed in his companion. "we'll get out of this as easily as kicking off an old boot!"

"Faix an' we'll see all about that, me foine daandy gunpowthur sparrks!" grinned a tall and red-haired Irishman. "If yer can git out ive the St. Goiles's Roundhouse you'd escaape from Newgate itself, begorra!"

"And that also I may do before I die!" defiantly retorted Jack Sheppard.

"Haark at him now!" cried the amazed Paddy. "Sure it's not loike a trrue human being he talks, at all, at all! Foreby it's faar more afther ther meanner av ould Satan himself!"

OFFICER BILBERRY IN THE POWER OF THE TERRORS OF OLD LONDON—THE AROUSED INNKEEPER—A CRUEL PRACTICAL JOKE AND ITS CONSEQUENCES—A VICTIM OF DRINK MANIA—THE STARTLING APPARITION AND THE MOHAWKS.

"The gay old cock is filled to the bung! To the pump with him! We must water his grog for him! To the pump, lads!"

The Mohawks were abroad, making night hideous with their untutored, savage-like mingled noises, and striking terror into the breast of any belated wayfarer who happened to be within the vicinity of their operations. These creatures were the sons of either members of the aristocracy or the wealthy classes. Their supposed object was that of innocent practical joking, and it was a point of honour (?) with them to pay liberally for all the damages resulting from their excesses.[119]

So far as the practical joking was concerned, this really constituted the only bright spot in an otherwise extremely black and shocking picture.

Raymond Raithwood, the blue-blooded libertine, was one of the heads, or ringleaders, of these roaming night roisterers, but was still suffering from a rapier-thrust given him by his cousin Dandy Dick, the captain of the outlaw lads of Old London.

The fearful old toper Officer Bilberry had been found by a "skylarking" band of the Mohawks lying full length upon his back in the snow-covered roadway, arms extended, and gazing reproachfully at the moon, as if he fully expected that celestial body to come down and help him to his feet.

"P-h-e-w!" gasped one of the gay marauders, who happened to bend over the head of the prostrate man. "P-h-e-w! The old hog's breath is strong enough to create an earthquake, or breed a second plague of London! Put a light to the punch-gas and the fellow will go up like a fire-balloon, and when he reaches a certain altitude burst into brilliant shooting-stars of fire. 'Twill be a most glorious sight!"

"Ah!" cried another Mohawk, "an' then the witches, their brooms in the clouds, would claim the gas-burning carcass to cut up into little fire goblins to put into the deadly marshes to inveigle[120] the benighted traveller to his death that they—the sky ogresses —might seize his soul for an offering to Satan, their master!"

"'Twere a pity, gentlemen, to spoil good grog by setting it a fire an' sending it up to the witches, or placing this fine round, living barrel under a pump—"

"What a deadly insult to the pump!" interrupted another voice.

"What we do with this condensed distillery, say, friends?"

"Blood an' hounds!—hic!" gasped Bilberry, getting a dim perception of what was going on—"blood—hic!—an'—hic!—hounds! Stan'—hic!—off, in the—name of the—hic!—King!"

A chorus of derisive yells—mad like, mocking laughter—greeted these remarks.

"Behold, gallants," cried a Mohawk, "the dead-drunk speaketh!"

"Stand off in the name of the King, forsooth!" lovingly mimicked a former joker. "If the King were here he'd stand off nothing short of a mile! Stand off in the name of King Tipple, for of a surety he can blast thee with a breath!"

---

[119] The has echoes of the earliest historical reports of Spring-Heeled Jack. In January 1838, the Lord Mayor of London received a letter detail Jack's exploits from the 'Resident of Peckham' in which the author complained that it was "a certain band of aristocrats" who were the perpetrators of the so-called "pranks". Likewise, the riotous actions of the Marquis of Waterford and his companions resonates of Mohawk-like behaviour.

[120] Deceive, or, more usually persuade someone to do something they do not wish to do.

The Mohawks finally decided that their helpless victim should be compelled to take still more drink as a fitting punishment for having already taken far too much. There was, perhaps, something of an Irishman's logic in this decision. The fact of its being long past closing time for all properly conducted inns weighed little with the young bloods, if indeed it did not actually add to the zest of their practical joke.

With the wildest demonstrations of savage song the rioters seized the unfortunate officer by the shoulders, arms, and legs, lifted him from the road-centre, and, in hurried rough-and-tumble style, bore him along in the direction of the nearest hostelry.

"Concentrated essence of—hic!—scorpion's venom!" muttered Bilberry, his head bobbing backwards and forwards like that of the toy-donkey rejoicing in the possession of a nicely dislocated spine, and to be seen in full working order in the Lowther Arcade of to-day.[121]

A few minutes' joltings sufficed to enable his tormentors to land the incoherently muttering Bow Street runner at the closed door of a wayside house of public resort.

A perfect tornado of more or less costly sticks and canes showered against the door and shutters, the noise being more than enough to instantly arouse the whole household, with a conviction that either the end of the world had arrived, or the Mohawks had collected at the door. The female members thus disturbed from their slumbers would by far have preferred the former to the latter calamity. Not so perhaps the male, for, if the young bloods could be but humoured in their whims, money would sometimes flow from their purses like a golden torrent.

A night capped head appearing at one of the upper windows was the signal for a volley from most exquisitely-made firearms. To their justice, be it recorded, in all cases the shots were purposefully aimed very wide of the mark.

Impatient at the delay, the Mohawks had again seized the growling and endless-oath-producing drunken officer, and were using his enormous bulk as a battering-ram—that is to say, held by shoulders and legs, he was repeatedly hurled against the door with—to him—most painful force.

There is no knowing what would have been the final result to the human battering-ram had not the landlord speedily opened the door.

Hearing the unfastening of the chains, the lusty wielders of the officer paused until the drawing of the final bolt. Then, putting all their strength into the effort, they sent Bilberry at the yielding door and let him go.

Like a great, soft indiarubber ball the helpless creature shot into the broad passage-way, and instantly made a complete "floorer" of the innkeeper and

---

[121] Demolished in 1902, this arcade ran from The Strand to Adelaide Street; however, the author presumably did not know it was built in 1830 and therefore constructed considerably later than when this story is set.

three or four of his male servants. There was to be seen what appeared but a great knotted mass of heads, arms, and legs, and a lighted lantern or two, with Officer Bilberry, in the centre, clutching the scared landlord's wig—which had fallen off in the scramble—and incoherently calling upon the article to "Surrender in the King's name!"

This, it goes without saying, the wig could not do, and it therefore maintained a most discreet and dignified silence.

In a trice the innkeeper had extricated himself. As he rose to his feet, bruised, shaken, and greatly indignant, several well-filled purses were thrown at his head. This golden shower decided him to put up with the rough usage, and to make a strong endeavour to please the wealthy rioters.

Like magic the inn was lighted up, fires blazing, and liquor of every brand the house could supply forthcoming. Officer Bilberry, now in, if possible, a still more helpless condition—for fermenting liquors, if well shaken, ferment still more—had been fixed into a great armchair in the inn's public parlour.

"Ho, there, landlord!" imperiously cried one of the Mohawks. "We must do honours to this, our guest. We are about to create him a brother Mohawk. Bring paint and brush—red, blue, yellow, green, black. Gadzooks! this is a blood of many virtues; and for each virtue he possesses a colour shall be given him!"

Fearful of refusal, the host sought and found pots of paint, with which he occasionally re-adorned the exterior of his house. These he brought, with their respective brushes.

No Red Indian, in his maddest moments of warrior zeal, ever depicted himself as did the practical jokers bedaub the full, round, over-fleshy face of the dimly-conscious Bilberry, who, really under the impression that he was being beautified, assumed a broad smile of an extremely imbecile nature.

The shouts of laughter made the rafters of the old in echo and re-echo. The straight-up, short hair of the Bow Street officer was plastered with a thick and a flaring vermilion. His hands were painted blue, and his visage in streaks of every colour available. Meanwhile, bottles, measures, and glasses of drink, had been poured down the ever-willing throat of the matchless rooker.[122]

The liquid at last flowed from the corners of the great, coarse, thick-lipped mouth as though indeed the drinker could not possibly retain one drop more.

This shameful and cruel prank soon resulted in its victim displaying the extreme symptoms of drink mania, whereat the ruffians, who deemed themselves the cream of society, forsooth, shrieked with such merriment as only a pandemonium of evil spirits in revelry could match.

Firstly, the terribly-besotted man imagined he saw, in the person of one of those surrounding him, the beautiful lineaments of Mrs. Drake. He made the most grotesquely-funny attempts at love-speeches and amorous demonstrations ever heard or seen.

---

[122] Cheat or swindler.

Next he saw, in a grandly-arrayed tormentor, the person of Dandy Dick. The length and extravagant nature of his oaths and threats set his auditors into fits of uncontrollable shrieks of merriment.

Finally, Bilberry's surroundings became alarmingly mixed—a bewilderment of confusion and mad-like whirl of motion.

Those overcrowding around him commenced to perform the most astounding feats and antics—serious, solemn, grave, tragic, quaint, comic, wildly fantastic and screamingly funny.

The host came into the room bearing a steaming bowl of punch upon his feet, while he gravely walked on his hands. The bowl shot upwards without assistance, careered gracefully towards Bilberry, and then poured the whole of its boiling content down his eagerly-opened throat, after which it inverted itself, and flopped over the officer's head.

Next one of the Mohawks playfully walked up the wall, and then about the ceiling head downwards, with as much safety and ease as a fly.

More wonderful and bewildering still, those about him, shrieking like fiends let loose from Hades, commenced to take off their heads, and even arms and legs. The heads commenced to wildly chase each other round and round the room then the limbs joined in the impish game. Some of the heads grew tired, but returned to the wrong bodies. A leg or an arm would fix itself in the place where a head should be; then the heads had nothing for it but to fix themselves where arms and legs were rightly intended. After this the misplaced heads grew reckless of their proper resting-places, and, utterly ignoring their respective bodies, independently started a game of ninepins on their own.

"Poor old wretch! he's got a fearful attack of delirium tremens safe enough! We'll rouse him in a water-butt, if this inn boasts of one. A pond would be better. Hurl his fat carcase upon the ice and it would easily give way!"

The voice had a dim, far-away sound in the ears of the drink-besotted wretch; then he knew no more.

The remorseless rioters were preparing to carry their threat into execution, when a strange and most startling apparition appeared in their very midst. Whether it rose up from the solid floor, descended from the ceiling, or shaped itself out of the very atmosphere itself, none could tell. Its aspect was so terrible that its observers were stricken dumb and motionless. Their hair tingled at its roots, tongues clove to the roofs of their mouths, limbs and bodies became as if turned to stone![123]

---

[123] At the end of this section there is a note: "This successful story will come to a conclusion in one or two weeks; time, and an entirely new and original Comic School Serial will then commence, entitled "Birchem's Boarding-School." Look out for opening chapters. It seems unusual that the editor cannot precisely note there are four issues remaining until the end of this story, and at this stage it seems like there are a significant number of plot strands that need to be resolved.

°THE DUTCH[124] INNKEEPER IN A BLUE FUNK—FOUR TUBES PROMISE DEATH IN THE EVENT OF TREACHERY—THE SECRET PANEL—WILL WIFFLES IS HIMSELF AGAIN—DANDY DICK'S DOUBLE.

"Shentlemens," cried the Dutchman host in most abject terror, "you shall plow mine head all ovder mine vickedt oldt prains ive I've blayedt draiter mit you! Dem isn't Pow Streedt drunners oudtzide! Mine Got, if I'm vound oudt I'm disgovered! Mit highwaymans in mine house I shall pe hangdt tead as vot you gall de nail-door!"

"Moonheer von Dutch Cheese, who told ye ve vas 'ighvaymen?" demanded Will Wiffles,

"Aha, the cat's out of the bag, you rascally, bold-headed old baboon!" snarled Dick Turpin. "You took us for unlawful toll-collectors, did you? And you have invited in the scarlet-chested gentry, now, haven't you?"

Up went the third deadly tube. Three flint-locks now threatened the life of the tragically-scared innkeeper. His wife had already silently slunk down senseless with fright into a great armchair, where she remained a shapeless heap—as if, indeed, the family washing had just been brought home and thus deposited.

"Sirrah, if you have blayedt de draitor mit us," sneeringly hissed Colonel Blood, cleverly mimicking the Dutchman's bad English, "you won't pe hangedt, mine friendt, you will be shot—and shot dead as any number of doornails!"

The colonel now added his own levelled pistol to the other three menacing weapons.

The great commotion in the front bar-room of the inn that, in the first place, had alarmed the four outlaws, still continued. It increased in vigour, but there appeared to be a person or persons endeavouring to keep a strong body of men from advancing towards the back parlour, or snuggery, in which the highwaymen had but scarcely terminated their long-wanted meal.

"Daddy Dutcher," muttered Wiffles, re-electing to speak, and still keeping his weapon poised, "you will show us a vay out o' this 'ere fix, if yer walues yer life, otherwise ve'll make a riddle o' yer carcase, through which cabbiages can be strained; or ve'll turn yer inter a gridiron ter grill a chop or steak on; an' very quick's ther vord, too—as ther man sed—vat vas a-being choked wive a small 'ot tater— ter ther doctor's as vanted ter take a veek's consultation afore they operated."

The extremity of the innkeeper's fear became most pathetic; there was, too, an expression upon his face that spoke so eloquently of his honesty that of one accord the highwaymen all lowered their arms.

° Part 39 Vol. XV.—No. 375. 15 January 1901.

124 Previously he was "German", but some of the words he used such as 'Mynheer were distinctively Dutch.

At this the Dutchman brightened up. He silently drew the bolts of the door, then made grotesque frantic notions towards a patch of hanging drapery in a far corner of the room.

Colonel Blood darted to the spot indicated, and drew aside the material. A partly-opened sliding-panel was then revealed.

"Gid town der stebts! Schredt sbring to der bannel! Hidt mine friendts in der undergroundt valdt dill der Pow Street drunners co away. Shisst! Gid town, mine friendts—gid town." Thus the innkeeper, in a low whisper, frantically entreated his secret guests to depart by the panel-opening.

The four adventurers instantly acted on an impulse, and crept through the opening one after another. A terrific banging now came to the bolted door.

The panel closed with a click. The innkeeper nervously held the hangings to steady their motion. Next he cast a quick glance around in search of any telltale evidence of the lawless nature of his hidden guests; but they had taken all their belongings with them, neither weapon, hat, nor mask remained to throw any suspicion upon their owners.

The outlaws, on passing beyond the panel—which they closed with a spring after them—found themselves in a short and narrow passage, which terminated at the head of a flight of wooden stairs. On descending the stairs, a storage-cellar was reached. A cheerful fire blazed here in, and a lighted lantern hung from a chain attached to one of the great beams forming the roof.

This underground chamber was not only warm and cheerful, but was also provided with table and seats, as if the place were used for living purposes.

Dandy Dick and the colonel, after hastily examining the place, noiselessly crept up the steps, their firearms held in readiness for any emergency—and strained their ears with a view to catch any conversation likely to be carried on in the room they had just vacated.

The mingled sounds of many voices could be plainly heard. The high-pitched tones of the host above all. He was frantically declaring that the gallants recently occupying that apartment were of the highest repute. His wife's voice joined his own (she must have recovered from her swoon in a suspiciously quick manner) and was loud in its praise of the unquestionable honour and standing of their recent patrons, and which she and her spouse earnestly protested had left the hostel by a back-door.

Quietude soon followed. Soon after, the secret panel opened, then the now extremely jovial-looking person of the Dutchman descended the steps, the equally stout hostess following. Each bore a tray containing more relays of steaming eatables and drinkables.

"By all that's good and commendable, this worthy couple take us for turkeys that require stuffing into condition for the Christmas table!" whispered Colonel Blood, with a merry smile.

"If I eat a mouthful more I shall find myself in the condition of a Lord Mayor after his first banquet—wedged so tightly in his chair that he is unable to be extricated without the aid of a saw. 'Tis said this is but deemed a necessary proof that his worship has had enough."

Dick Turpin ventured this remark, whereat Will Wiffles added one of his characteristic clinchers:

"'Yer carn't 'ave too much ov a good thing,' as ther cat remarked when it fell inter the pail o' milk."

In the turbulent times of which we write, innkeepers frequently found their most liberal patrons among those of the lawless order. It was to the ultimate profit of a host to be known as a person to be trusted by a fugitive from justice, and this may explain the loyalty of the Dutch host to his highwaymen patrons. The latter forthwith rewarded him handsomely and arranged to remain feasting and making merry in their snug quarters until the darkness of night should set in. Then the four adventurers had determined to make for their many comrades awaiting them in their stronghold—the Haunted Manor of the Finchley Wilds.

*

It was a glorious winter night. The moon rode majestically through the heavens, a dazzling sight—queen of space, gracing the earth with her radiant smile.

A party of four horsemen, cloaked and masked, slowly careered over the frost-hardened road towards the neighbourhood of Highbury. The landscape presented a beautiful aspect—white, hoarfrosted trees against a black-grey sky, the moon's rays touching every object with their brightly sparkling silver sheen.

The sudden clatter of swiftly-approaching steed-hooves arrested the attention of the four horsemen. They noiselessly directed their steeds towards the spot enveloped in the deep shadows thrown by the ruins of a disused old barn and thickly-clustered tall trees. Silent as statues remained the party. The on-galloping hooves were coming to this very spot, and were evidently those of two animals.

"Friends, methinks those sounds indicate the suspicious circumstance of one rider chasing another." This voice was that of Colonel Blood, and whose companions were no others than Dandy Dick, Dick Turpin, and Will Wiffles.

"Stay!" cautioned Dandy Dick; adding: "Jonathan Wild possesses all the cunning of his Satanic Majesty in addition to his own. We cannot be too wary of his wiles. This may be another of his deep-lain traps."

"Keep silent and alert, your primed pistols in readiness, lads," recommended the colonel, setting the example by withdrawing a firearm from its holster at the saddle-bow.

"Shall we challenge these fellows?" whisperingly asked Turpin.

"No; it is of first importance that we learn the meaning of this strange manœuvre," cautioned Dandy Dick; well remembering not a few of the extremely clever snares prepared for him by the great thief-taker.

A moment more, and the first fleeing rider's animal madly clattered along the road, then shot past the shadowy lurking-place in which the highwaymen were. Dandy Dick had leaned well forward over his steed's neck, the better to observe the horsemen. Had a pistol exploded full in his face the young highwayman would not have given a more sudden start of incredulous amazement.

The fleeing vision he had seen was that of—himself, or, at least, so marvellously a counterfeit presentment, that the likeness quite took away his breath.

The rider had won neither mask nor cloak, and the apparel so plainly to be noted in consequence, was of the same superb, dandyish cut and most costly style generally affected by Dandy Dick himself. As to the handsome and distinguished-looking face, natural, long, flowing locks, and tall, graceful, and lithe figure, these were also amazingly like that each of Dandy Dick's friends were as equally startled and impressed as was the prototype of the strange horsemen.

Before the concealed outlaws could recover from their state of helpless amazement two more mounted men dashed at break-neck speed past them.

"Ho! stop there!" fiercely yelled one of the latter two. "Surrender, Dandy Dick, highwayman and footpad, and with a price upon thy head! Yield thyself up!" The explosion of two firearms immediately followed this summons. The first horsemen had been aimed at but missed.

"Never!" was the reply, expressed in full, clear, fearless tones.

Then another weapon burst out its complement of fire, lead, and smoke. One of the two pursuing horsemen uttered a piteous groan, attempted to keep his position in the saddle and rein in his animal, but in the effort, he shot over the beast's head, fell full length in the moonlit road, and lay there motionless.

Scarcely had this happened before the second pursuer was fatally shot. He dropped forward and crashed to the frost-hardened earth.

"Just Heaven!" gasped Dandy Dick, at length recovering from the extreme stupor into which he had been thrown by the preceding mystifying events, "what can this black jugglery mean? What foul fiend's work is this?"

A wild, thrilling, sardonic laugh came to him, borne upon the frost-laden night air. The exultant sound appeared to his startled ears to be so fully charged with vindictive glee as to be almost inhuman.

Colonel Blood, Turpin, and Wiffles suddenly shook off the strangely-powerful lethargy that had held them in its clutches, speechless and motionless.

"Police-officers or not, we must first see to the injured men," humanely cried the colonel, springing from his horse, and making towards the prostrate forms. But a moment's examination shocked him with the appalling fact that both were dead.

Dandy Dick greeted this news with a fiercely-muttered oath. In a trice his fleet steed was flying after his mysterious double. A few seconds only, then two explosions almost simultaneously burst upon the still night air. The bright moonlight outlined the form of Dandy Dick and his steed, with its lines of flashing silver. The young highwayman was distinctly seen to throw up his arms, as if in an involuntary spasm of agony, reel in his saddle, then fall.

A LONDON PLAGUE SPOT IN THE OLDEN TIME—BLIND HOPPY—A CUNNING PLOT INTO WHICH A CUNNING PLOTTER FALLS—THE SUPPOSED SPY AND HIS ASSAILANTS— A RUTHLESS FIEND—TRAPPED IN THE DEADLY DENS OF THE ROOKERY OF ST. GILES'S—AT BAY.

We must now take the reader into the very heart of the vice-reeking colony then variously known by the terms of St. Giles's Rookery, the Blackbirds' Nest, and the St. Giles's Sanctuary.

The inhabitants of the Rookery were of the vilest and most degraded class possible to imagine. They had constructed strong gates and barricades at every entrance and exit to their colony, and no person was permitted either to enter or leave without first giving a prearranged secret password. The Bow Street police, Jonathan Wild's own guards, or janissaries, and even the King's troops had the lawless classes repeatedly set at defiance, and beaten off from the gates of their domain. They usually armed themselves with any and every conceivable kind of weapon, swarmed upon their housetops, and hurled stones, articles of furniture, flaming pitch, and even molten lead, down upon the forms of their foes, who were compelled to crowd in the narrowest and most torturous of alleys, courts, and dark passageways before they could reach the entrance to the Rookery itself.

A well-known inhabitant of the place in question was a supposed impostor known as Blind Hoppy, a beggar and most daring thief, and whose eyesight was of the best. He, however, invariably wore a great green shade over his eyes.

Hoppy ambled upon a wooden leg, the limb it supported being always slaved in bands of dirty rags, but was really as sound as his eyesight. A slouched hat, face and head hidden in bandages, eyes covered with the usual great green shade, a fearfully patched and ragged cloak, a great thick staff, and a pedlar's pack hanging from a tangled mess of things around the neck—this was the well-known part beggar, part thief, wholly impostor, familiarly known as Blind Hoppy.

The darkness of night had set in; the man supposed to be Blind Hoppy had passed all the guards by giving the secret signs. In spite of the boisterous greetings and coarse jests of the crowds, he passed unheeding on his way, and kept his head lowered and back arched as he hobbled along, occasionally growling out some incoherent reply in a deep and guttural tone. On he went through dark, devious ways and crooked alleys, and passed indescribably revolting signs of debauchery and riot.

It was evident that this personage was extremely well acquainted with all the many and most intricate turnings, for he never once paused, but hobbled along, with a sort of hop-and-skip motion, nor looking to right or left.

The man had at length plunged into a narrow space of pitch-like darkness. There were many narrow passages leading to and from this garbage-filled slum square. A drink-bloated and most horrible-looking female had sprung from an open doorway and seized the arm of the cripple.

"Come, Hoppy dear, you sha'n't pass my door before you pay for a dram of gin. Come inside, dear, an' take a share of the soothing balm with me!"

Blind Hoppy jerked out a fierce oath of disgust, and attempted to wrench his arm free.

"Leave go, you cursed old hag!" he savagely snarled.

"Oh, you're in Blind Hoppy's toggery, my flash cove, but you're not the man for all that! Ho, there, boys of the Rookery! A spy! a spy!" the woman shouted at the topmost pitch of her voice.

"Confusion! Cease that infernal clamour, you foul-looking old fury!" desperately muttered the man.

Before the creature could regain her temporary lost breath he had seized her by the full, fleshy throat. His cruel fingers were throttling her. His victim was of powerful frame, and instantly bravely struggled for life. Seeing a flat, open cellar-way in the pavement, with a dim light coming therefrom, the sturdily-built ruffian swiftly caught up the form of the woman in his arms, and deliberately threw her into the broad-opening. A loud crash and piercing shriek of pain and fright followed.

Blind Hoppy, or his imitation, flew from the spot, and darted into one of the black-looking, narrow exits, but an indistinct form at once blocked his further progress.

"Ugly style of love-making that!" growled a rough voice. "Blest if I don't think Moll Flinders was right! You are not Hoppy at all, but a cursed spy!"

Briskly stepping back, the other snatched a something from his right-hand coat skirt pocket—a short metal cudgel. A mighty swishing of this object through the gloomy atmosphere followed. Then came a sharp ejaculation of mingled pain, rage, and amazement. Two further swift swirlings, two more bursts of pain, rage, and amazement, and then a weighty substance slid down by an unseen wall, silent, limp, and apparently lifeless.

The murderer-fugitive flew on and on, up one black alley, down another still blacker, turned, doubled, and finally, his teeth giving out a most peculiarly-horrible, grating sound, he pantingly halted before a tumbledown-looking building situated at the end of a cul-de-sac. Glaring lights flared from the windows, coarse yells of shuddering ribaldry, snatches of low songs, and blasphemous oaths, came from this den as from the jaws of the very pit of Hades. The door stood wide open. The man with the wooden leg ambled up the filth-laden, broken, and creaking stairs.

Room-doors were opened, heads protruded. A jest or curse of contemptuous greeting would follow imaginary recognition of the well-known figure of the bent old cripple as he slowly mounted upwards. Here and there a lighted lantern, hanging from the time-discoloured walls, guiding him on his way. The topmost garret reached, a door faced him, through the chinks of which a light came.

"Come in, Hoppy dearie—come in an' take a seat, poor man—take a seat!" croaked the voice of an apparently extremely aged woman, in response to the rap of the old man's cudgel.

The supposed blind cripple entered the room. It was indeed a fearful den. Smoke-blackened rafters formed the ceiling, with the inside of the bare roof-tiles seen between them. The plaster had in places fallen from the walls in great fantastically-shaped gaps. Where the plaster had remained sound, curious prints of the period were stuck upon the walls. These were mostly portraits of highwaymen, footpads, and notorious cut-purses.

A scene from the "Beggars' Opera" occupied a most conspicuous place over the mantelpiece. Gay, the poet, had but just recently written and produced his brilliant work, and it was then the talk of London.[125] Captain Macheath is seen in this gaudily-coloured daub—the highwayman is heavily ironed—seated in the condemned cell of Newgate, pledging a bumper to his two mistresses, each of whom it stands lovingly by his side. A rickety deal table occupies the centre of the attic; a heap of littered straw occupies one end of the room; a fire blazes on the hearth, and doubled over it is an age-bent form dressed in shabby black, with silver white hair falling from under a cloak-head, and half concealing a much grimed and haggard face.

"Mother Mouldy!" hailed the man on entering, first cautiously closing the door, and then removing the green shade, and displaying a most evil pair of eyes, after which he seated himself near the door.

"That's me, Hoppy dearie. He! he! he!" croaked the old dame. "I'm called Mother Mouldy because of me age an' time-whitened locks. He! he! Well, I suppose youth must have its joke; but it's not in the best of taste for green youth to joke at hoary age, is it, Blind Hoppy dearie? He! he! he!"

"And it's not in strictly good form for age to jest at a moment when most serious matters are to be discussed. You know, dame, that I am not the person you mention. You sent that most notorious impostor to me with a proposal. I gave a large sum to the old scoundrel for the loan of this fearful rig-out, and the knowledge of the secret passwords to this your choice abode, and for full details of how to reach you. Mother Mouldy, for a sum of ten guineas, is prepared to divulge to me the precise details of a secret meeting-place

---

[125] *The Beggars' Opera*, written by John Gay, was first performed in January 1728. It is set around Newgate prison and some of the content concerns a theif-taker's daughter marryi9ng a highwayman.

hereabouts of certain proscribed persons—to wit, Dandy Dick, Colonel Blood, and many others, especially Jack Sheppard!"

"He! he! he! Softly, dearie; softly dearie!" croaked the old dame, with a mysterious chuckle that somewhat perplexed her visitor. "You're quite right, dearie," she went on; "but the money first, the information after, dearie. He! he!"

"Dare to attempt to play me false, you hag, and I'll dash out your addled brains!" growled the man, placing ten golden pieces on the table.

The woman stretched out her arm, and eagerly snatched up the golden coins.

"Play you false, dearie?" she cried, in a louder voice than she had before used, adding: "who would dare play fast an' loose with the terrible Jonathan Wild, eh, dearie? Jonathan Wild—"

"Confusion! Cease, you babbling old idiot!" the man hissed, springing erect, and menacing the woman with his staff. "Should it but be known that I have ventured into this deadly region my life would not weigh against that of a fly!"

"True, dearie, I had forgot," whined the old crone, in a quieter tone. Then she continued: "Now to business, dearie. You hanged Tom Sheppard, I believe, dearie?"

"I did," replied the visitor, with a gleam of fiendish triumph, "though, curse me, if I can tell what that has to do with you!"

"Ah, but it has, dearie!" the woman continued "and you have solemnly taken oath to hang Tom Sheppard's son, too, dearie!"

"I have, woman!" hissed the man, with a terrible oath. "And you'll help me to keep my vow!"

He had unstrapped the wooden leg while speaking, for the limb it supported was becoming cramped.

"Help you to keep your vow? Ah, indeed, when I've ten thousand times sworn to prevent you!"

The woman's voice had now risen to a perfect shriek. She started up. Her visitor leapt to his feet at the same instant.

The black-robed female now stood boldly erect. She threw the hood from her head; next the white locks were drawn aside. The half-crazed, once-beautiful Mrs. Sheppard stood before Jonathan Wild.

"Trapped, Jonathan Wild—trapped!" The words rang out in a startling cry. "Blind Hoppy owed ye many's the grudge! Hoppy fell into our views. The boys of St. Giles's Sanctuary are now waiting to give ye a warm welcome! A few yards of rope, a scalding tar-barrel, and then a short shrift at the further end of a tall signpost! Ha! ha! Jona—"

The thief-taker a aimed a furious blow at Mrs. Sheppard, but with unsuspected agility she darted aside, and by doing so undoubtedly saved her life. The great bludgeon slipped from Wild's grasp. He leapt after it. There followed a danting gleam of reflected fire glow, and the point of a steel blade struck Wild full in the breast. The power of the blow caused him to stagger back, with a sudden gasp of terror. For the moment he believed himself fatally pierced. The next he remembered his coat of mail, and knew he was unhurt.

A torrent of rage-laden expletives streamed from his ashen lips; his teeth gave out their horrible, gnashing sound; he felt that his position was indeed most critical, and that it was of most vital importance to silence the half-demented woman into whose snare he had so blindly walked. He snatched out a pistol, then as hastily replaced it, fearing the result of his explosion.

Before he was aware of her intention, Wild found himself again attacked by Mrs. Sheppard. She had sprung upon him like a wild-cat. A great gash now marked its crimson course along the left side of his evil and white looking visage. The blood trickled down upon his cravat, spots fell upon his hand.

With a quick movement, he caught the wrist of his assailant as the knife again swooped down. A desperate struggle followed, in which he gained possession of the knife. Mrs. Sheppard then seized his left hand between her teeth, and held it there until the teeth met. Wild gave no cry, but, when the lacerated member was again free, caught the frenzied woman by her now flowing hair; then, exerting to the utmost his enormous strength, he succeeded in forcing his victim's head backwards, then bared her neck with the right hand, in which he now held the knife. Another instant, and he would have severed her thin, white throat!

The room-door, with a terrific crash, tottered from its rusty hinges.

A burly, bleary-eyed ruffian stood in the doorway. A cudgel had flown from his hand, and caught the thief-taker a crushing blow behind the right ear as he stood with his back to the man. Stunned for the moment, the thief-taker released Mrs. Sheppard, who fell in a dead swoon to the floor. Wild then fiercely turned to face his later assailant, but reeled back some paces before he could recover himself. He had thus reached the centre of littered straw. Seeing that caution was no longer of avail, he snatched out a brace of firearms, and stood on the defensive.

"Come up, me covies!" yelled the new-comer. "Old Mother Mouldycrust an' the cheerful Hoppy have worked the lay, smart! They've done the fake glorious! Put the salt on the pretty chief robin's tail at last!" frantically shouted the new-comer, evidently calling to associates below.

A storm of exultant yells and the thundering of many heavy feet instantly followed.

A furious crowd came surging up the stairs. Jonathan Wild saw that his life now depended on mere moments. Savage as a famished tiger, brave as a lion at bay, he mentally determined to spare no human being while he had the power and means of inflicting death in defence of his own life.

°Jack Sheppard and Joe Blueskin in the lock-up cage of St. Giles's—The two robbers make merry under grave circumstances—The plan of escape—The piece of tin and the timber beam—Surrounded by peril—The magic password.

"It's all your fault, Bluechops. If you hadn't insisted on coming with me on my journey to see my poor mother, I shouldn't have been tempted to try the nimbleness of my wit, fingers, and feet. As the result, here I am again fixed in roadhouse limbo—toad-in-the-hole-pie like!" growled Jack Sheppard sulkily.

"May I be hanged for a most lovable and patient monster—honest thief that I am—if every calamity under the sun isn't of my doing—nay, if the sky itself fell, it would be Joe Blueskin's doings!" expostulated his companion.

"Of course it would; for no one else on earth would dream of putting his blasphemous shoulders to such a work, since that strong chap Atlas dropped it!" sarcastically sneered the lad.

"Dropped it? I'm not well up in the classics, Jack lad," remarked Blueskin, adding, "but I remember somewhere reading of the fellow you mentioned. He did every other man's dags by carrying the world upon his shoulders, but I never before heard that he dropped it. I suppose, then, that he wanted better pay, or perhaps to stroll round the corner to get a tankard of ale; but even then he might have propped the globe up somehow—balanced it on a clothes-line, a street-post, or—"

"Shut up, old Blue-gizzard! You're always getting your poor sheep's-brains muddled and entangled. If you had lived in the time of Atlas, and he had asked you to take a turn in holding up the world, he'd no sooner have turned his back then you would have sneaked his burden—the whole universe—if you had known a Jew fence that would have taken it off your hands at a price!"

"Aha!" Joe Blueskin sighed. "Jack, lad, the annexing of the whole world in one lump—smuggling it away in your coat-pocket on a dark night when no watchful Charlies were about—would be too ambitious an undertaking for a poor obscure footpad like me. It would be far more in the line of such a high-handed robber as Alexander the Great; and, now I come to think of it, he really had some such notion in his head, an' wasn't so far off completely carrying it out."

"Alexander the Great was more like you than you are aware of, Blue-tinted frontispiece," said Jack Sheppard.

Jolly Nose drew himself up proudly, blushed, and replied, in a well-pleased tones:

"It may have been so, Jack lad. I've always heard that he was a very handsome fellow."

"I didn't mean in that way," dryly put in the caustic young outlaw; adding: "I meant in respect to his great love of—ahem!—excessive drinking."

"Oh, ah!" Blueskin coughed to hide his secret discomfort. "I protest," he said, "both on behalf of my alleged prototype and myself. It is a gross injustice to say that Alexander or Joe Blueskin ever drank too much."

"You evidently know little of your country's history," contemptuously continued Jack, "or you would be acquainted with the manner of the great conqueror's death. Shall I tell you?"

"Pray proceed, most profoundly learned historian," ironically answered the elder robber; "but," continued he, "don't make too cocksure of my ignorance of this world's history."

Jack Sheppard cleared his voice, and assumed quite the air of importance of a person telling for the first time that which was really a very musty and cobwebby piece of historical lore.

"Alexander the Great," commenced he, "had spent one whole night feasting and drinking. On the second night he entertained twenty illustrious guests, pledged them all in a bumper of wine, and then insisted on doing them a like honour severally. He afterwards called for a favourite golden goblet, which he had named 'the Hercules Cup.' This vessel held six bottles of wine. The terror of the world next insisted on drinking to a Macedonian general present named Proteas. Alexander coiffed the whole contents of the Hercules cup and then ordered it to be refilled. A second time he drained the cup to the dregs in honour of the same Proteas. Immediately after the hero of countless conquests fell to the floor. Soon after, this warrior-prince died, as the result of drinking. He had all but conquered the world by his valour and resistless energy, but was himself at last conquered by his besotted weakness for wine."[126]

"Thanks, Jack lad, for the flattering comparison you make between the first Alexander and myself," remarked Jolly Nose. "It is strange," he continued, "how shallow persons mostly contrive to express the very opposite of what they contend. Your story does not prove that the great general the world greatest general the world ever knew died because he drank too much. The contrary seems most likely the case—namely, that he couldn't drink enough; for if his guzzling capacity had been greater he would not have had enough, and consequently could have consumed more."

"Really, now," caustically sneered the lad, "what profound reasoning is thine! If a man taketh too much liquor, it is a proof that he hath not had enough. Such reasoning is on a level with that of the idiotic scientist who once gravely stated that a man couldn't live a moment after he expired unless he possessed an unusually robust constitution, in which case he might possibly exist some half-hour or so after."

---

[126] It is traditionally believed that Alexander fell ill and died (or was poisoned).

"Jack, my crony," impatiently muttered Blueskin, "let us not waste our time in vain and foolish bickerings. We're in durance."[127]

"That's so, Cerulean visage," dolefully agreed the younger captive; "and, what's more," he continued punningly, "I can't in-dure this in durance. It's too cribbed, cabined, and confined. Why, a couple of mice wouldn't have room enough to dance a reel in this place."

"We are slightly larger and bulkier than mine, Jack, and therefore I suggest that we execute a reel out of this space. And there must be no sham about that reel, either. Humph! that's as good an attempt as your wretched pun on the words in durance."

Jack Sheppard laughed softly. A sign his companion understood. The lad of many words was becoming more himself again—his own reckless, careless and utterly fearless itself.

When the two outlaws had first been thrust into the St. Giles's Roundhouse the first care had been to make an examination of the surroundings. They were in perfect darkness, and therefore their investigations were perforce made by means of their hands. The lock-up was divided into four compartments, each of which terminated in a central acute angle. Three of these divisions, the two robbers judged, were used as cells, the fourth as an apartment for those in charge of the circular building.

From a few moments after their being imprisoned, Sheppard and Blueskin, from the fact of the deep silence reining, concluded that they were the only occupants of the little gaol. In searching the floor the lad's hand had come into contact with a piece of tin some few inches long, and shaped somewhat like a knife-blade. With this he had cleared away a space in the plaster of the dividing wall. The material consisting of mere lath and plaster, Jack Sheppard suggested that they should work their way through into the next compartment, with which they had already discovered to be that used by the keepers of the roundhouse.

Their weapons had all been taken from them. Blueskin was seriously concerned over this. On elevating his hand, the tall, sturdy robber felt a beam. This crust from one partition to the other. He threw his full weight upon it, but without effect. Then the lad clutched his companion round the waist, adding his own weight. A few sudden jerks brought the timber length down, a shower of particles of plaster and dust coming with it. The weight of this article was sufficient to fell an ox with ease.

The prisoners were about to use the beam-end to batter a hole in the lath and plaster when their ears caught the sound of heavy footsteps. The roundhouse guard were returning.

Blueskin and Sheppard muttered furious imprecations upon their bad luck. The former threw himself down upon the rough timber form—the only furniture in their dormitory—and commenced to think out a fresh plan of escape.

---

[127] In prison.

Presently was heard the sound of a key entering a lock. Jack Sheppard had fixed his eye to the slight opening he had made with his piece of tin. He hastily whispered into his companion's ear the information that one guard alone had returned.

The door was flung open. A man holding aloft a lighted lantern stood peering into the interior. His voice was then heard, but before he could articulate a word the weight of the beam crashed down with cruel force upon his head. The man, thus rendered utterly senseless, was falling backwards, when Blueskin seized his swaying body, swung it round, and then cast its limp weight into the corner of the triangular-shaped cell.

"What's that, Banks?" cried a voice. The sound of the falling body had alarmed another of the keepers who happened to be at the outer door of the cage.

He came quickly forward. Blueskin and Sheppard silently held back within the shadows. Suspecting something wrong, the new-comer drew a pistol from his coat-pocket, carefully examined flint, steel, and wad, cocked the trigger, and then boldly advanced.

The terrible Blueskin, without compunction, let fall the full weight of his new-found weapon upon the head of the second comer. The unfortunate man was instantly rendered senseless, and fell to the floor, silent and inert.

The prone men had each a brace of loaded pistols and a sidearm. The two robbers seized these. The lad snatched up a bunch of keys from beside the first victim.

"Quick, Jack lad!" gleefully cried Blueskin. "The cage door is invitingly open; the birds may now merrily hop the twig, tra-la-la!

> "So gay an' free,
> From tree to tree,
> With a pip-pip-pip!
>   An' a chip-chip-chip!
> For the world they care not a fig,
> While merrily hopping the twig—tra-la-la!"

The reckless robber's merriment was ill-timed. A firearm exploded within a yard of his face, and a bullet tore a scarlet groove along his cheek. The sensation was like the contact of a red-hot rod.

"Aha, knave!" the great outlaw thundered, "you want to add a deeper tint of gunpowder-blue to my already damaged complexion, do ye?" A third police-agent had confronted Blueskin. The man swiftly drew a second pistol, carefully levelled it, his finger about to press the trigger. Down swooped the timber-beam with murderous force. Its victim fell with a smashed skull.

"This is a sickening business, Jack lad!" gasped his companion. "But they would have taken our lives first an' inquired into the justice of the thing after. 'Kiss me, an' I will kiss in return; kick me, an' I'll kick, too!'—That's my motto."

The two had leapt over the motionless bodies, and sprang through the open outer door. The explosion of the flint-lock had, however, brought a great crowd to the spot. Several of the watch could be detected by their red waistcoats, lanterns, official cudgels, and night-rattles.

A frightful yelling and confusion of voices greeted the appearance of the two escaped prisoners. Their fine garments caused them to be mistaken for members of the Mohawk gangs; these were universally execrated by the rabble. Crowds rushed forward. They were armed with all kinds of rude weapons. Blueskin threw himself into a posture of defence.

The aspect looked black enough for the two escaped felons.

"Secure them! Down with the wretches! They must have murdered the guards of the roundhouse, otherwise they could not have slipped them!"

At this moment the man first brought down by Blueskin's timber weapon had revived. His face, bathed in blood, appeared at the roundhouse door. This spectacle greatly enraged the majority of the mob. Pistols were fired, clubs and great stones sent whirling through the air, and narrowly escaping the heads of the two outlaws. Blueskin was already in despair of escape, when he suddenly thought of the password known to the lads of the Rookery of St. Giles's. With the lungs of an ox he roared out the strange word in thieves' lingo.

"They're birds of the right feather, after all, Rookery lads!" cried many voices in union. "All blackbirds that come to roost in the Rookery of gay St. Giles's are welcome! The fine covies seeking asylum in our sanctuary are never turned away! Rescue, lads—rescue!" shrieked many hoarse and savage throats. In a few moments all factions opposed to Blueskin and Sheppard were either routed or disabled. The exterior of the lock-up presented the appearance of a small battlefield.

The escaped captives were borne upon the shoulder of their rescuers into the gates of the felons' colony.

"Where are ye bound, lads?" asked many voices of Jack Sheppard and Blueskin.

"I am seeking Mrs. Sheppard!" answered the criminal son.

"Ah, Mrs. Sheppard, the mother of the lad prison-breaker lives with old Mother Mouldy. You'll need to be nimble," excitedly continued the same speaker, "if you wish to find either of 'em alive, for the flash ken they live in is in flames!"

THE STARTLING APPARITION AT THE INN—THE SUPERNATURAL TERROR OF THE MOHAWKS—THE UNNAMEABLE SPECTRE—THE COMING TO OF OFFICER BILBERRY—MRS. BILBERRY SHOWS UP—THE AMIABLE SPOUSE AND THE HEEL OF A BOOT.

The presence of the frightful apparition in their midst had rendered the Mohawks incapable of either thought or action. With the exception of the full knowledge of the startling presence before them, all its beholders it seemed utterly incapable of comprehending anything further, or even able to protect themselves, or make an effort at flight.

The apparently supernatural being towered above the tallest of his beholders. A long, black cloak had at first covered the form, but the hood and voluminous folds of this had been thrown back so that the figure now stood in clearly-defined outline. The face was most horrible to behold. It recalled the semblance of the Prince of Evil himself, or the ideal characteristics usually associated with the fallen angel.

A great, tangled mass of blood-red hair descended from the hideous head, upon which great horns protruded. These, the great mass of hair, and also the face, were all of the same vivid, sanguinary hue, and gave out a luminous red glow, as if indeed the figure was formed of some brilliant molten material or solid fire.

The aristocratic young bloods were transfixed in extreme terror; the roots of their hair tingled as with contact with electrical heat. Their visages, in parts, actually resembled those in death, but with touches here and there that reflected the blood-red radiance emitted by the unnameable presence.

"Sin-steeped villains, aristocratic rabble, creatures boasting of high breeding, pure birth, yet ever proving thyselves, by thy actions, lowest of ruffians, meanest of mongrels, cursed miscreants, I am sorely tempted to strike ye all pulseless as ye stand, and speechless and helpless with overwhelming convictions of thine own iniquities!"

The words thus emanating from the dread visitant were uttered in deep, unearthly, and fear-thrilling tones that froze the very blood of its heroes in extremest horror.

The apparition that had stricken the Mohawks temporarily motionless, by added terrors restored to them the full possession of their faculties. The midnight marauding gallants dimly became conscious of the fact that the floor upon which they stood had gradually become heated. Then followed an inexplicable and incredible thing. Tiny flames darted about their feet as if endowed with life. The jets were of dazzling brightness, and swiftly reached the limbs of the Mohawks. The majority of these wore silk stockings of various hues and adorned with clocks (strange designs).

The bodies of fire first leapt about the feet and lower limbs, then flitted upwards. Before either a limb could be moved, or voice raised in protest, the crowd of dismayed, splendidly-garbed ruffians were literally covered with tiny jets of red fire. Like the sting of an adder, these tortured and blistered wherever they touched. There was a strange absence of actual burning, yet the smarting agony of contact of the little imp-like fire-flames rendered those attacked frenzied with suffering. Suddenly endowed with full life and activity, their yells became ear-splitting; their efforts to escape the startling stings, blistering, agonising smarts, were mad like and deadly.

In a few moments from the first appearance of the unexplainable phenomenon the Mohawks had fled. Not one of them had remained in the vicinity of the inn.

°THE COMING TO OF OFFICER BILBERRY—MRS. BILBERRY SHOWS UP—THE AMIABLE SPOUSE AND THE HEEL OF A BOOT.

The infamous deeds enacted, in their so-called "nocturnal pranks," by the well-to-do gallants that flooded the streets of Old London in the hours of midnight and early morning, had rendered the very name of "Mohawk" a term of shuddering terror to all claiming a title to respectability and virtue. Thus the innkeeper bethought him of his wife and daughters. His attendants had followed him to the loft, to which he had previously sent his womenfolk.

One result of this was that the blood-curdling visitant had appeared and departed without either the inn-proprietor or any of his household having seen or even heard it.

The utterly drink-besotted Officer Bilberry had fallen to the floor, and remained there completely oblivious to everything. On his return to the lower floor the host found the inn deserted, with the one solitary exception of the helplessly-drunken Bow Street runner. The young bloods had not paid their score, but the various articles they had left behind in their precipitous flight represented a very fine booty to the finder.

Bilberry might have slept an hour or a year; he had not the faintest conception of anything that had transpired, excepting that he had fallen asleep. An inn once visited by the terror-inspiring Mohawk was apt to lose its repute as a properly-conducted establishment. The owner kept his own counsel, and, as Bilberry's memory for all past circumstances appeared to have gone off with his condition of inebriation, he remained in total darkness of all that had transpired. One thing vastly soothed him. This was that the host never uttered even the faintest whisper of the word "pay." Not but what the wily old toper and "bilker" was fully prepared with a fairy-tale excuse or "get out." But, all the same, it was in far nicer form to be spared the necessity of measuring out yards and yards of barefaced lies.

When at length the gallant mip-mopper was upon the point of rising from the very comfortable bed into which the host had considerately had him placed, to his (the former's) no small astonishment Mistress Bilberry entered the room. Now, this person was most remarkably like her very choice spouse. This is often the case with man and wife. "Like likes like!" is a good old truism, if not an over-elegant one. Had not Mrs. Bilberry been of the softer sex, she might well have passed for a twin-brother of the redoubtable officer.

"Eustis, Adolphus, Edmund, Timothy, my sweet Bilberry, I have at last found thee!" shrieked Mrs. B. hysterically.

Then the amiable creature threw her arms about the extensive and raw-red neck of her husband, and hugged him so closely that he commenced to turn

---

° Part 41. Vol. XV.—No. 377. 26 January 1901.

purple in the face, and vainly endeavoured to articulate words of protest. When at length she released her gasping victim, the lady sat herself upon the foot of the bed, and burst into a wild flood of tears for no particular reason whatever.

In the midst of this most touching distress, one of the tear-jerking orbs suddenly lighted upon the ample nether garments worn by her husband. The article hung over the back of a chair in the company of the officer's vermilion waistcoat, and outer coat, with facings of the same colour.

Like an eagle swooping upon its prey, the tender wife sprang forward, seized the garments, and, with electrical quickness, turned out every pocket. Each one was as empty as the fatal cupboard owned by the Mrs. Hubbard of story-book fame.

Oh, the glare of those eyes that the fond Bilberry had so oft admired! The concentrated contempt expressed in the drawn-down corners of those lips that the doting B. had so many thousands of times kissed! And, alas! the intense rage—nay, deadly anger—expressed in those now so firmly-clenched hands that a gallant husband had so oft pressed and fondled!

"You hoary-headed old creature! Every penny of your money gone!"

Here was a change indeed. From tear-melting tenderness to mercenary grimness. From the woman of love to the woman of mammon.[128] But the end of this domestic drama was not yet reached. The ample Mrs. B. became a perfect startler in the way of energy and activity. The amazon-like creature had pounced upon one of the heavy Jack-boots worn by the runner still in bed. Considerately holding this in such a manner that its intended recipient should receive the full force of the heel, the lady seized the open-mouthed but speechless Bilberry by a tuft of his brushlike hair with her left hand, and commenced to belabour him with the right, containing the pedal covering, the sharp edge of the heel of which commenced to inflict a series of deep indentations in the top of his skull.

The excited and powerful Mrs. B. accompanied her unique performance with such threats and terms the reverse of endearing that, thinking the Mohawks had again paid him a visit, the host flew into the room.

The arms of the lady were seized. Finding her efforts thus checked, Bilberry's (in many ways much) better-half then most gracefully flopped to the floor, and commenced to afford her audience of two a very clever imitation of a faint of a supposed hysterical order.

Mrs. B. could not be induced to recover from her most alarming condition until the perspiring Bilberry, still in his night raiment only, most emphatically assured her that he had concealed two spade guineas of his month's pay in one of his stockings.

The sight of the golden coins produced a most electrical effect. The fit of hysteria and anger instantly passed away, and the strangulation embraces were

---

128 Mammon was a Biblical demon representing greed. Used here it represents money.

again resumed. Finally the host gently hinted at the desirability of their speedy departure. The two Bilberrys took the hint and levanted.[129]

When at length their abode was reached—like the dutiful wife she ever was— it suddenly occurred to Mrs. Bilberry that her erratic mate had not received quite enough boot-heel to make the domestic lesson a lasting one. She therefore sought and found another leg ornament of much stouter heel.

Officer Bilberry, although such an extreme terror to little boys and very old persons of abnormally nervous temperaments, was quite a beating lamb in the presence of his redoubtable second half. The valiant officer, however, contrived to beat a retreat by crawling into his fowlhouse at the rear of his dwelling.

Unable to reach her intended prey, in consequence of her much superior proportions, Mrs. B. changed her mind. She would go to the nearest pool, she declared, and their end her domestic affections by "making a hole"—it would require to be a large one—"in the water."

But, as his spouse had regularly threatened to do this desperate deed, every time a domestic tiff arose, for the last thirty-odd years, Bilberry was not ever alarmed, and continued to remain in the fowlhouse until the enemy finally and unmistakably simmered down her anger.

*

Jonathan Wild had been trapped by consummate cunning. The half demented are known at times to display amazing craftiness. This had proved to be the case with Mrs. Sheppard. Herself and misguided son had endured most persistent and cruel persecution from the great thief-taker, and in her continual broodings for revenge the woman had at length schemed out a snare into which her impeccable enemy had now deliberately walked with wide-open eyes.

It was well known that the chief criminal-tracker of Newgate had been in the habit of daringly venturing into the Rockery, or outlaws' colony of St. Giles's, when it suited his purpose. Threats against his life was so common that Jonathan Wild had ceased to notice them, except by a malevolent gleam of eye or contemptuous curl of lip. He was, however, face-to-face with the danger now. His life hung in the balance, and the weight of a hair would turn the scale against him.

"The snarling, evil old rat is cornered at last, lads! Our greatest enemy, the pitiless destroyer of the pick of our bonny flash boys, is now at our mercy!" shrieked the Rookery dwellers in a breath, as they pushed their way into the garret where Mrs. Sheppard had so cleverly impersonated the part of old Mother Mouldy.

The unfortunate woman had already been removed from the room, but she still remained in the deep swoon consequent upon the brutal handling she had received from her (for years) most persistent persecutor Jonathan Wild.

In stepping back to the furthest wall facing the door, Jonathan Wild had moved into the centre of the heaped-up straw, which had long done duty for

---

[129] To run away leaving unpaid debts.

the two women inhabiting this most wretched den—a garret in the heart of one of the, then, worst plague spots in all London.

"You'd better let me depart; I'm well armed. I knew the risks I ran in coming into your murder shambles, and I will not scruple to sacrifice any person that impedes my progress from here!" thundered Wild, producing two of his loaded firearms.

"Ho! ho! We got you tight enough now—you who have never halted at the shedding of innocent blood! Ha! ha! You've had your music, Jonathan; but the piper demands his payment now!"

One of the foremost of the outlaws, with an exultant yell, levelled a pistol; but before he could press the trigger Wild had sped a bullet through the man's brain. The death of one of their number inflamed the Rookery denizens into a condition of utmost fury. Firearms were exploded full at the thief-taker, but he escaped as if by magic. A flaming torch struck him full in the face, then fell into the thickly-littered straw. There was a sudden flare of light, and the thief-taker stood in the very centre of a circle of leaping tongues of fire!"

In an instant the room was filled with blinding, crackling, leaping flames. The crowd fell back from the door, heat and smoke forcing them to retreat. Some of the most daring continued to fire their pistols into the room, determined, if possible, that their prey should not escape them alive.

A fiendish yell of laughter came apparently from the very centre of the mass of seething, roaring fire. Nothing human surely could live for a moment in that compact space of the destroying element. Yet that exultant shriek evidently came from the throat of Jonathan Wild.

CONCERNING JONATHAN WILD AND HIS VILLAINIES—JACK SHEPPARD'S MEETING WITH HIS HALF-CRAZED MOTHER—JONATHAN WILD IN SUPREME PERIL—HIS WORD OF HONOUR AND HOW HE KEPT IT.

The mere presence of Jonathan Wild to those who knew him was of itself a terror. The yell of extreme exultation heard emanating from him at the very moment when he was supposed to be enveloped in flames, and either already dead, or beyond hope of escape, filled all who heard it with a supernatural fear too extreme to be described. Each and all concluded that the Prince of Evil had evolved from the centre of his own favourite element, seized upon the soul of that crime-steeped thief-taker, and borne it to eternal torments.

The explanation of Wild's sardonic yell was simple enough, as his enemies soon after found to their deep mortification.

When the mass of loose straw caught fire upon which the Newgate official stood at bay, confronting a murderously inclined crowd of the lads of the St. Giles's Rookery, his first act was to spring back against the back wall of the garret. The flames spread from the loose, dry straw to the next nearest objects—an old table, one chair, and an inverted basket. As the heavy body of the flame-surrounding man struck against the wall of the room, the trembling of this instantly proved to him that it was really no wall actually, but simply a wooden partition, placed there originally for the purpose of dividing one large chamber into two.

This boarding had been concealed by a stout covering of paper. There was in its centre a door, which had long been in disuse as the result of the divided chamber being tenanted by different persons. The slight recess was at once seen, and by dashing the full weight of his body against it the door instantly yielded. It was at this moment that the loudly-mocking laughter came from the chief of Newgate. The next moment he had sprang into a darkened room, and dashed to the door, as the leaping flames sprang into it.

Jonathan Wild found himself in perfect darkness. But before he either had time to think or move, a strong hand had seized him by the cravat. Then he felt the icy-cold nozzle of a pistol pressed against his forehead.

"You are a cunning, clever rogue, Jonathan! You have escaped the fire raging in the little sky-parlour there, but you won't escape the fire awaiting you in this iron tube within an inch of your desperately-wicked brain!"

"Who are you? Loosen your grip, fellow!" gasped the half-strangled Wild.

"I'm Tim Flinn, a St. Giles's lad, and I well know you, Jonathan, and you well know me, for I've been in your clutches more than once, and got out of 'em again. But you won't escape my grip now—not with your life, you black-hearted villain!"

The threatening voice was harshly grating and remorseless in tone. Jonathan Wild had discharged all his firearms, and then hurled them at the oncoming rubble an instant before the straw upon which he stood had ignited. To attempt to draw either his bludgeon or cutlass would be to invite the death with which he was now threatened.

"Tim Flinn," commenced Wild, speaking with great difficulty, for his capturer now twisted his knuckles so firmly in the other's neck-covering, that the pain of the pressure on his windpipe was unbearable, "you are again wanted for more than one crime. I offer you one hundred guineas and my written undertaking that you shall never more be molested by me or my assistants, my sole condition being that you help me to get clear of this devils' nest."

"Where is the loose?"[130] demanded the other, not releasing his hold, or removing his weapon.

"S'death! I'm not a living mint! You can have my note-of-at hand, and get the money before I can reach my house, if you wish it that way, or I will meet and accompany you personally to my bank to-morrow morning," protested the thief-taker.

---

[130] Money.

Tim Flinn cogitated for a few moments.

"Your word, oath, written bond, or sworn vow are not binding with you," he said at length. "Anyhow, I can gain nothing by turning you over to my pals," he added, "so hand over what pretty little metal plates you now have about you."

The captive drew out a well-filled purse and passed it to the other. "There is a trap in the roof of this attic, walk a yard or two to your right, and you will knock your ugly nose against the steps leading to the tiles. My own crib is the garret in the house next to this. If I can smuggle you into that, you may escape getting your throat slit by our boys. Wouldn't they delight over the job! Ho! ho! ho!"

Tim Flinn laughed under his breath at the very thought of the result of Jonathan Wild's capture by the desperadoes of St. Giles's.

The lawless rabble had fled in utmost horror from the burning garret as the flames spread, and the demoniacal laughter burst from the supposed fire-consumed man. The roaring sounds coming to their ears, and the suffocating sense of heat, warned those in the as yet untouched room that they had little time to tarry.

Wild had found and clambered up the steps leading to the roof. The trapdoor was already open. Flinn had heard the alarming shouts occasioned by the rabble, and had entered by this same means. Creeping over the roof, under cover of the darkness, another trap-entrance was soon reached. The abode of Tim Flinn was thus entered.

Jonathan Wild was disguised in the great coal scuttle-shaped bonnet of the period, a woman's white skirt, and a black cloak and hood. Stooping until almost double, and hobbling along with a stick, the thief-taker, in company of Flinn, cleverly escaped undue notice, and reached beyond the sentinels and barriers of the lawless colony.

Flinn had finally been completely beguiled into the belief that Jonathan Wild would keep faith with him. Next day the former duly presented himself at the latter's banking-house. A number of janissaries sprang from a place of concealment and arrested the duped felon. Within a month Tim Flinn took the fatal journey to Tyburn. He had been proved guilty of horse-stealing and other crimes, and was condemned to be hanged on one of the gibbets standing at the cross-roads near the Tyburn woods. Thus the thief-catcher had paid his debt of gratitude.

Jack Sheppard and Joe Blueskin were taken by their guide into the very heart of the criminal haunt, in which the felon-lad expected to find his half-crazed mother.

The two outlaws would have been attacked, robbed, and stripped of their finery, and even left naked, but for the magic power of the password given to Blueskin by his friend, the keeper of the Crown Inn.

"Rare fine high-toby (highway) boys! Wizzen slitters of the fust water, then!" proudly explained the guide whenever the mob interrupted their progress.

The flames finally located the exact spot sought. When it became known that the gaily-dressed strangers were none other than Jack Sheppard, the daring prison-breaker, and his friend Joe Blueskin, alias Jolly Nose, the welcome ovation given the notorious outlaws baffles all thoughts of description.

°Jack Sheppard broke through the throng surrounding him, and attempted to make his way into the now fiercely-fire-raging building in which his mother had made her home. Men and women excitedly pulled the despairing lad away. His mother had been taken into the next habitation, he was informed. Into this, then, he dashed, only to find Mrs. Sheppard almost at the point of death. Deep and long-continued privations, extreme mental suffering, and, lastly, cruel usage sustained at the hands of Wild, and the shock occasioned by seeing her room ablaze, all these combined had brought the poor woman to the condition in which her unhappy son found her. A most heartrending scene followed, Jack Sheppard fiercely upbraiding himself for his heartless wrong-doing and cruel and unnatural neglect of his lonely and defenceless parent.

Most piteously the woman besought her son to turn from his vicious ways. Her prayers and entreaties were pathetic in the extreme. His father, she hysterically reminded him, had ended his career upon the scaffold;[131] and now, alas! she was doomed to meet her fastly-approaching end with the despairing conviction that her only child was fast drifting to the same deeply-degrading fate that had claimed her husband, even in the prime of his manhood.

The then truly penitent lad most solemnly promised his mother that he would henceforth renounce all his evil companions, and follow an honest, honourable course. But once more was he permitted to see that ever fondly-loving mother before she finally entered the long, long sleep. Within a twelve month from the most painful interview now described, the boy prison-breaker had amazed the world by his series of extraordinary feats included in his task of breaking out of Newgate Gaol.

He was, however, soon again captured. It has been recorded that Jonathan Wild had made a vow that he would firstly lure into paths of vice Mrs. Sheppard's only child, and finally encompass his doom upon the s"caffold. The cause for this atrocious resolve having been the rejection of his addresses by the widow of Tom Sheppard, whose end at Tyburn Wild is also said to have chiefly brought about.

Within a few months after the public execution of the boy-felon Jack Sheppard, Jonathan Wild himself paid the penalty of his many crimes upon the very same scaffold to which he had so fiendishly consigned the poor, friendless, and deeply persecuted—if wayward and obstinate—only son of a woman previously half-crazed as the result of deep affliction.

° Part 42. Vol. XV.—No. 378. 7 February 1901

[131] According to Daniel Defoe, Tom Sheppard was a carpenter and "an honest inductrious man" who died when Jack Sheppard was young, p. 4.

DANDY DICK BROUGHT TO GRIEF BY HIS DOUBLE—THE MEETING OF THE OUTLAWS OF THE HAUNTED MANOR AT FINCHLEY—RAYMOND RAITHWOOD'S DOOM—THE WRONGED RIGHTED—THEIR CONCLUSION.

To return to the further adventures of Dandy Dick and his comrades, the outlaw lads of Old London.

On reaching the spot—brightly revealed by the moonlight on the frost-covered roadway—the highwaymen found the deeply-cherished comrade and leader lying in an insensible condition, as the result of a wound in his left temple. Colonel Blood displayed deepest grief and rage combined. In a few seconds, however, his knowledge of such matters soon proved to him that Dandy Dick was but stunned. The bullet had happily glanced off the frontal bone of his skull sideways, and thus, by the merest accident, was spared a youthful life. The mounted police agents, unhorsed, and lying prone in the road, were discovered to be both dead.

It was decided that men should be sent from the stronghold to give interment to the victims of the most mysterious wretch impersonating Dandy Dick. Not one of the highwaymen doubted for a single moment that this deception was due to the restless cunning of Jonathan Wild, whose evil energies never slept when an enemy was to be removed from his path.

A rustic gate was found unhinged, and lying by the roadside. The highwaymen spread their cloaks upon this article, laid the still insensible body of Dandy Dick thereon, and thus proceeded to carry their comrade to the Haunted Manor, but a short distance away.

Colonel Blood and Dick Turpin bore the burden between them. Wiffles had secured all the steeds—including those possessed by the slain police-agents— lashed them head to head, and, thus leading the animals, followed his companions.

To prevent surprise, or suspicion of the advent of strangers, the party gave out secret signal cries. In a few moments they were surrounded by outlaw spies. Great indeed was the joy resultant from the return of the leader and his companions.

This happiness was only manifested, however, after the recovery of Dandy Dick.

For some days his devoted companions unanimously insisted on Dandy Dick keeping to his bed. In a week he was himself again, if his ugly wound had not quite healed.

Following close upon these events, spies brought in the intelligence of the capture of a highwayman long passing himself off as the famous Dandy Dick, and who had committed many fearful crimes in the former's name.

Astounding disclosures followed, Jonathan Wild being deeply implicated. This infamous plot, intended for the purpose of utterly ruining all the hopes of Sir

Edgar Mortiemor in the obtaining of a free pardon from King George for his outlawed nephew, resulted in greatly favouring the designs of Dandy Dick's noble-minded relative.

Dandy Dick's double duly expiated his many evil offences upon the fatal Tyburn Tree.

The day was close at hand when Dandy Dick, with the lovely, accomplished, and high-born Maude Mortiemor as his smiling bride, would again hold up his head with the proudest in the land, for it was contended by many of those powerful at Court that, by the act of preserving the life of his King from the Jacobite conspirators and assassins, the young nobleman outlaw had fully established his right to a free and unconditional pardon.

On the eve of this fortunate event a great—if perfectly secret—banquet was held in the vaults of the Haunted Manor at Finchley. Tom King had returned, Fangs, the rat-trainer, having faithfully kept his vow, and received a very handsome reward in return for his fidelity.

Dandy Dick, more gorgeously dressed than ever, presided at the head of the festive board. Colonel Blood, Tom King, Dick Turpin, Will Wiffles, the mysterious necromancer Daddy Delph, Nat Flint, Jack Rann, Sixteen-String Jack, and hosts of others, formed the guests. This was destined to be the last of Dandy Dick's enacting the part of an outlaw.

The beautiful Mrs Drake, filled with dread of discovery of her occasional masqueradings in the character of Dandy Dick, had, with her husband, fled the country.

Officer Bilberry was finally kicked out, neck-and-crop, from the employment of Bow Street runner, and gradually dwindled down to the low state of an inn-loafer, who amused inn-frequenters by the reciting of his shameless fairy tales.

Will Wiffles had whispered to Miss Dolly Tripitt his firm determination of tying himself up for life with a Tripitt, and the young lady in question is not recorded to have expressed any objection beyond that the happy event should take place at the marriage of Richard Raithwood, otherwise Dandy Dick. The latter, as the final act of his life of outlawry, gave unconditional liberty to the prisoners captured by his band in the quagmires surrounding the Haunted Manor.

Raymond Raithwood had slowly recovered from the serious wounds he had received from the rapier-blade of Dandy Dick on the eventful night when the two young men—of the same kin, yet as unlike in dispositions as to human beings could possibly be—faced each other in a duel intended to be to the death. This was on the night of their meeting together under the roof of their uncle, the fine old English aristocrat, Sir Edgar Mortiemor.

No sooner was the sinister Raymond Raithwood restored to health and his usual youthful vigour than he determined to celebrate the occasion by a midnight debauch of an even more than usual reckless and vicious nature. To this end he caused an enormous number of the midnight revellers, known as the Mohawks, or young-bloods, to assemble at a certain hostelry at their usual hour, that being when most respectable and orderly citizens had retired to rest.

The wrenching off of door-knockers, assaults upon members of the watch, or "old Charlies," as they were more commonly termed, practical jokes played upon signboards of commercial and other premises, and suchlike wanton pranks, far exceeded in number any similar night's work these well-to-do and educated ruffians had ever before perpetrated.

In the early hours of the morning, and when the leader of these marauding bands was in a most wine-inflamed condition, a band of roaming gipsy-robbers chanced to fall foul of the mad like roysterers.

The provincial footpads were first attacked. They offered a most stubborn resistance. Several of the latter were slain, others most cruelly wounded.

The leader of the gipsy-thieves, with amazing daring, fought his way to the spot where Raymond Raithwood savagely contended against two copper-coloured desperadoes.

"Leave that coxcomb to me, lads!" cried the chief of the roaming Romanys. "I recognise in him the abductor of my lost beautiful Rebecca," he furiously added, "and I have sworn that my blade shall drink his life's blood!"

A most terrible conflict instantly commenced. The gypsy using his long-bladed knife or dagger alone against the rapier of almost double length.

The Mohawks, in their drunken imbecility, shrieked with supreme delight at the exciting novelty of the horrible spectacle. The Romany chief, in a few passes, was mortally pierced by the steel of the black-hearted Raymond Raithwood. In his death-throes the robber clung to the hilt of the sword, which quite touched his blood-streaming bosom, and, with his final effort in life, plunged his blade deeply into the heart of his slayer. Then, with a quivering moan, in which the beloved name of his wronged Rebecca mingled, the ill-fated footpad fell lifeless to the earth.

Raithwood fell back bathed in blood, and was caught in the arms of one of his less drunken companions. Sternly admonishing others of the still jesting crew, the supported induced a few to assist him in bearing the rapidly-expiring Mohawk leader to an inn nearby. The innkeeper was aroused from his bed. Raymond Raithwood was placed upon a couch, and a leech (doctor) instantly sent for.

In the so-called "good old times," cupping, or blood-letting, was the remedy for every ailment to which model could possibly become liable. The hairdresser, or barber, usually combined the business of leech, or blood-letter, with his other calling. The man actually dying primarily from loss of blood was duly bled of what little of the life-blood still remained to him.

Finding himself sinking fast, Raymond Raithwood entreated his companions to bring the host and an independent witness to his bedside. It so happened that a justice of the peace had put up at the inn for the night. Seeing the gravity of affairs, the innkeeper aroused the guest, and brought him to the bedside of the dying man.

Completely overwhelmed by a conviction of the enormity of his evil deeds, the dying man made a full confession of all his crimes, many of which were far too terrible for human pardon, if indeed for the extension of mercy in the Judgement hereafter to come.

The full details of the forging of Sir Edgar Mortiemor's name to documents for enormous sums were related, every particular also being given as to the deeply cunning scheme by which Raithwood had contrived to make it appear, in the near and certain event of detection, that the guilt alone rested upon the shoulders of Richard Raithwood, his own cousin, and nephew and actual heir to Sir Edgar Mortiemor's great wealth and vast estates.

We have hitherto only known the deeply-wronged victim of Raymond Raithwood by a name—that of Dandy Dick—given him in merry jest by his fellow-adventurers.

This name, however, was destined afterwards to become one of universal interest and even terror, and worthy of historical record.

The confession of the deeply repentant Raithwood was duly written down, and signed by the law's representative and proper witnesses.

Sir Edgar Mortiemor, Lady Mortiemor, and their it exquisitely lovely daughter Maude had long enjoyed the privilege of visiting Court. King George the Second held the handsome old baronet in high esteem.

When at length Sir Edgar had fully recovered the all but fatal effects of a bullet-wound received in the temple—but which, by the merest chance in the world, had missed penetrating the brain—his first visit was made to the King's palace in St. James's.

It so happened that the King was of somewhat of a superstitious nature, and ever endeavouring to find a seer, or prophet, able to forecast the Royal destiny. Those about the Royal person, eager to curry favour with the monarch, were consequently ever most anxious to gratify the regal whim whenever possible.

An aged dame had been found by a certain courtier. This woman, attired in a quaintly-designed Egyptian costume, was brought before King George at the same hour that Sir Edgar, Lady Mortiemor, and their daughter entered the King's presence.

It was a startling and weirdly romantic sight—that of an extremely aged, bent, and deeply wrinkled crone, with long, silvery tresses hanging about her shoulders and down her back, a strange glitter of triumphal hatred burning in her sunken orbs, and her lean right arm and bony fingers extending upwards, as she, in a highly-pitched key of excitement, poured out in a swift torrent her supposed words of prophecy.

"Woe, woe, woe to England's great monarch," she was crying, "if his greatest foe is permitted to still flourish! Woe, woe, woe to this fair and prosperous land if its ruler's bitterest enemy—the blackest traitor to the poorest and most unfortunate of the King's subjects—is allowed to continue his infamous course of crime disguised by the name of justice! Woe, woe, woe!"

"What can the strange old creature mean? We care not for the subtle riddles she puts to us. Tell the prophetess—if indeed she be a prophetess—that her King wishes her to speak plainly. Accuse whom she may of treason to our throne or person, she shall come to no harm. That is our Royal promise and her warrant."

Thus encouraged by her sovereign ruler, the old creature grew far bolder, and her words became less invested with mystery.

"The Jacobites plotted to kill England's great King," the dame proceeded. "The chief instrument in their pay was a treacherous wretch employed by his Majesty's own Government, and who would have succeeded in his most infamous design but for certain proscribed men hiding in ambush in St. James's Park. These hunted fugitives saw their King's deadly peril, and most gallantly flew to his rescue!"

"By my Royal sceptre, but the prophetess speaks words of truth!" declared the King, starting from his regal seat in his extreme excitement. "Let her but reveal to us the names of the arch- traitor and those of our deliverers, and she shall claim her own reward. As for the dastard-traitor, the horrible doom for treason felony shall be his; and, if my deliverers were proscribed by our Parliament ten thousand times over, the Royal prerogative shall procure them free pardon!"

There could be no mistaking the sincerity of the King. Without hesitation the words were uttered.

The chief agent employed by the Jacobite plotters was described as no other than Jonathan Wild, the English Government's chief police-agent.

When the prophetess pronounced the identity of the rescuers of the King, the greatest astonishment was displayed by every person in the Royal presence, but by the latter amazement greater still.

The most notorious highwaymen of the times with the rescuers of the King's person from the intentions of would-be assassins!

On the mention of Dandy Dick as one of these, Sir Edgar Mortiemor related to the King and his surrounding courtiers the details of the grandly heroic conduct of his young kinsman, Colonel Blood, Dick Turpin, Tom King, and one Will Wiffles, during the fire at his mansion at Holloway. To the lion-hearted friends mentioned were due the saving of his wife, daughter, and himself, including a tirewoman, he declared. The baronet did not omit a graphic account of the doings of the fiend-like incendiaries on the night in question.

The King appeared willing enough to grant free pardons to all the outlaws mention; but certain of his admirers were strongly against such an act of Royal clemency, one mentioning, as a most sanguinary proof of the depravity of Dandy Dick, the cold-blooded murder of Squire Brancome, on Finchley Common, on the night of 15 of November of that same year.

The reputed prophetess again raised her shrill and thrillingly-excited tones. The old soothsayer declared that she herself witnessed the enacting of that awful deed, that the murderer was Jonathan Wild, and that he would have also taken her life had she not fled from his bullets.

King George was far more delighted than he cared to admit to find that he really owed his life to outlaws; for the fact gave a most distinct spice of the romantic to the affair, and most glowing accounts of the incident would in consequence find their way all over the habitable globe.

When Sir Edgar Mortiemor left the monarch, the former secretly carried away with him the free pardon of all those engaged in the timely succour of their liege-lord and sovereign.

It should be mentioned here that the King never after regretted his clemency. Even in after years, when the man of such unparalleled daring, Colonel Blood, actually stole the Crown Jewels from the Tower of London, succeeding in all but getting clear off with them, the King would not permit his chief Minister, Walpole,[132] to order any kind of punishment to be inflicted, and this in spite of the persistent clamouring is of his rageful and indignant subjects.

In after years the handsome and gallant Sir Richard Raithwood Mortiemor, wedded to one of the sweetest and yet most stately of all the Court dames—the only daughter of Sir Edgar Mortiemor—became not only a most popular and steadily-advancing courtier, but actually the bosom-friend of his grateful King.

King's jesters had already died out; but it was a whim of the wealthy Sir Richard Raithwood Mortiemor—he had inherited the whole of the wealth of his late uncle—to reinstitute the custom.

Will Wiffles in due course became an educated man, and won for himself quite a reputation as a wit of his time. But perhaps he never quite got over his love for his original wheezes. When he had finished up the telling of one of his never-to-be-exhausted stock of humorous stories, he would generally remark, in his irresistibly droll manner:

"'One cannot, you know, continue spinning the same yarn for ever,' as the unfortunate spider tearfully observed, after seeing no less than fifteen of his completed extra special strong webs blown by the cruel winds into nothingness!"

Perhaps, with these appropriately philosophical words, we may aptly include those of our sad farewell to our ever kindly indulgent readers of the MARVEL. Thus the authors tearfully and tremblingly take up their finishing dips of ink to subscribe that inevitable final word—their pen is weeping, too—its tears are black!—

THE END.

---

[132] Robert Walpole (1676–1745), MP for King's Lynn and generally accepted to be Britain's first Prime Minister.

**Advert from the issue preceeding the beginning of the
Dandy Dick serial**

Read the exciting, truthful and unparalleled history of Colonel
Blood, the man who actually stole from the Tower of London
the Crown Jewels of England.

Read the whimsical and side-splitting wheezes of Wiffles
the Witty Outlaw.

Read about the most comical character Bilberry the Bow
Street Runner—human windbag! bully, fairy-tale relater, and
most contemptible coward.

You cannot fail to be completely enthralled by the perusal
of the most sensational deeds, hairbreath escapes from the
officers of Justice, &c., and acts of the greatest gallantry as
performed by the youthful highwayman Dandy Dick, the man
who, having a price upon his head, yet saved the King's life at
the nost deadly risk to his own.

Read the astounding, yet true historical details of the career
of the infamous Jonathan Wild, thief-maker, thief-taker,
crime-factor, crime-repressor, and the greatest ruffian and
renegade the world ever knew.

Never before published: the authetic records f the Spectral
Horseman, the Mystery of the Heath, the True Life of Dick
Turpin and his famous mare Black Bess.

Watch and wait for the incredible revelations concerning
captivating Dandy Dick, fashionable gallant, favourite at
Court—both of King and high-born dame—and yet midnight
robber of the heath and starlit glen; outlaw with a price on his
head, and King George's friend in one.

www.ingramcontent.com/pod-product-compliance
Lightning Source LLC
Chambersburg PA
CBHW070815190726
48292CB00006B/2021